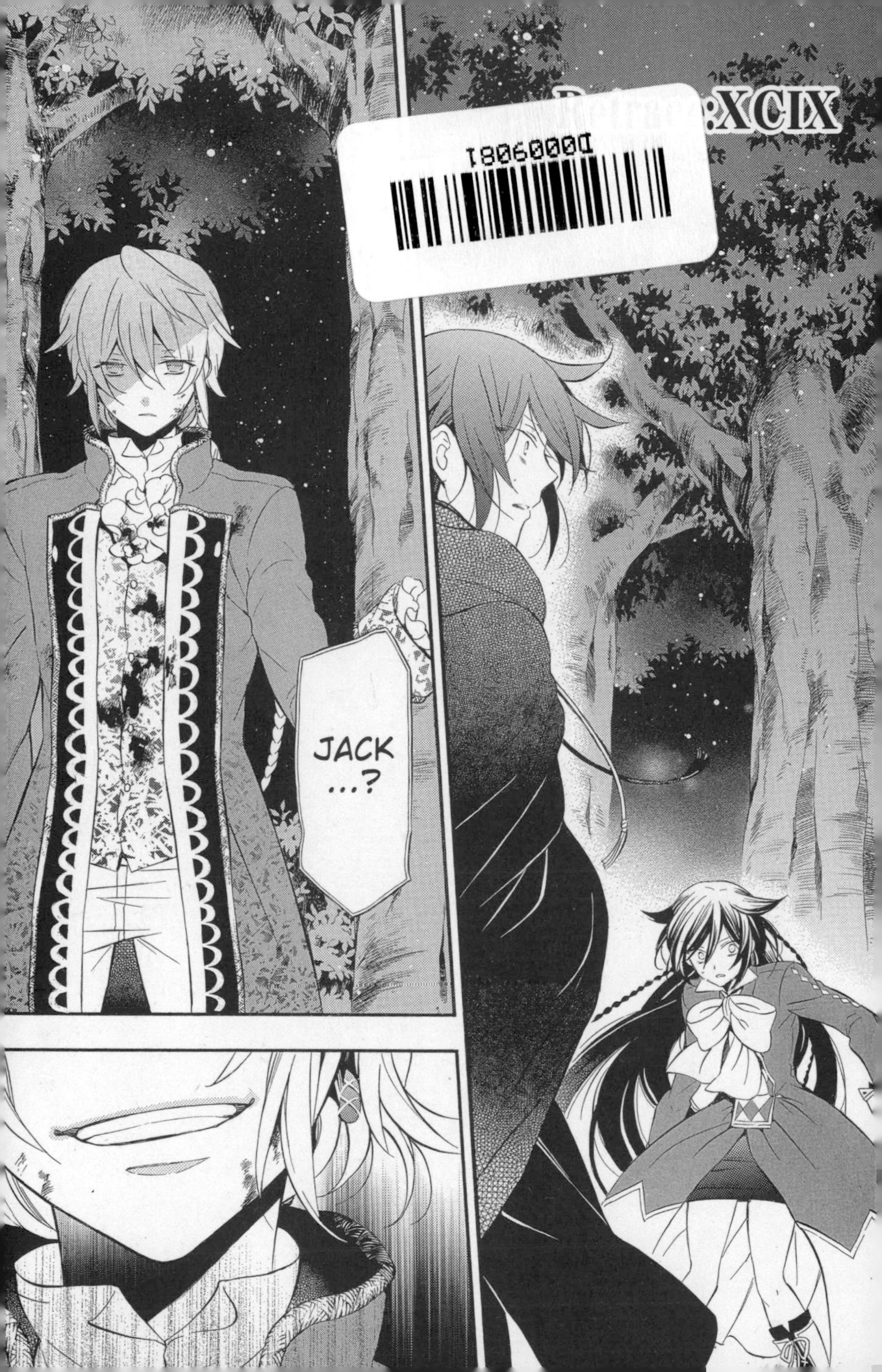
:XCIX
JACK ...?

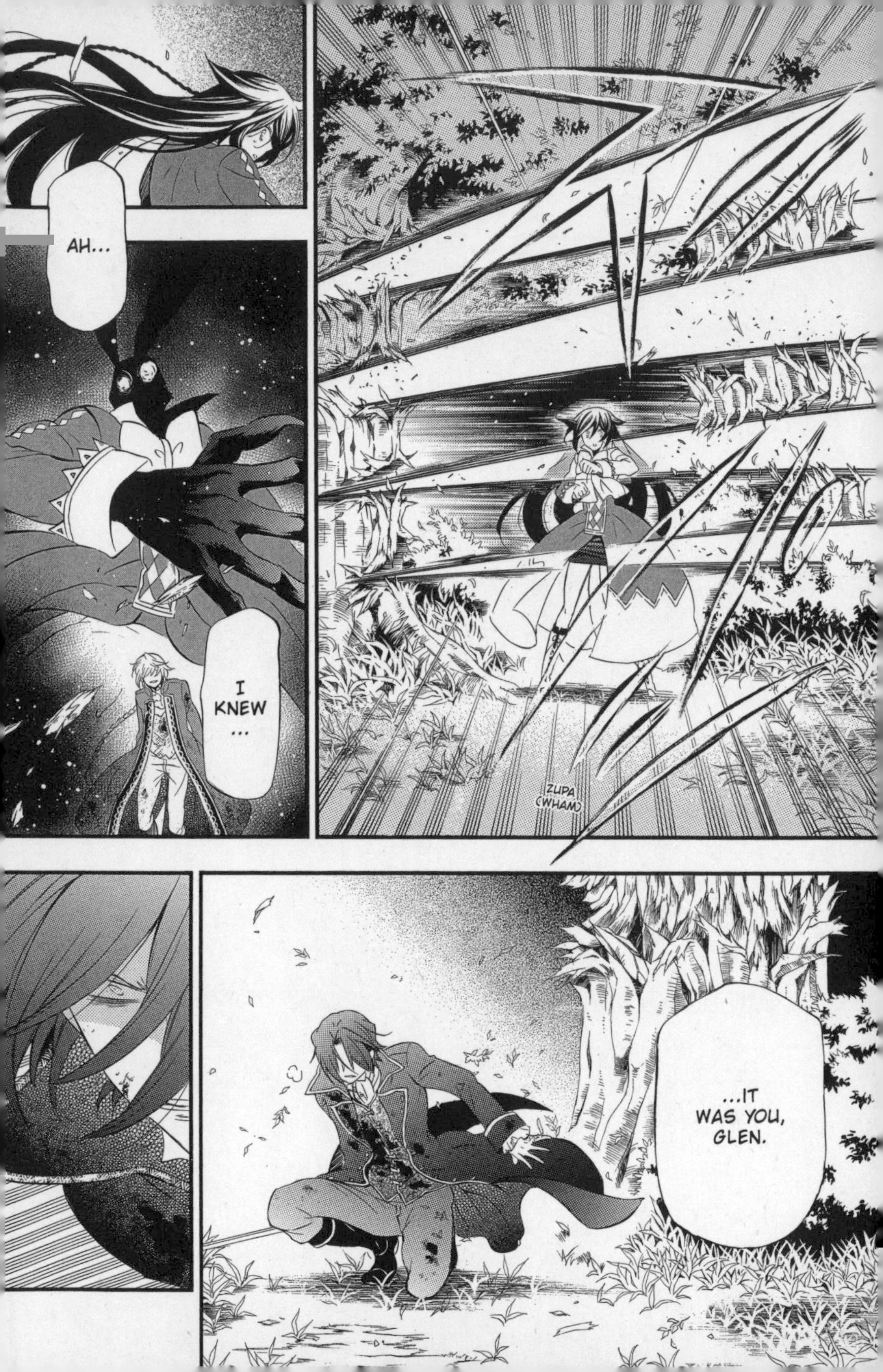
ZUPA (WHAM)
AH...
I KNEW ...
...IT WAS YOU, GLEN.

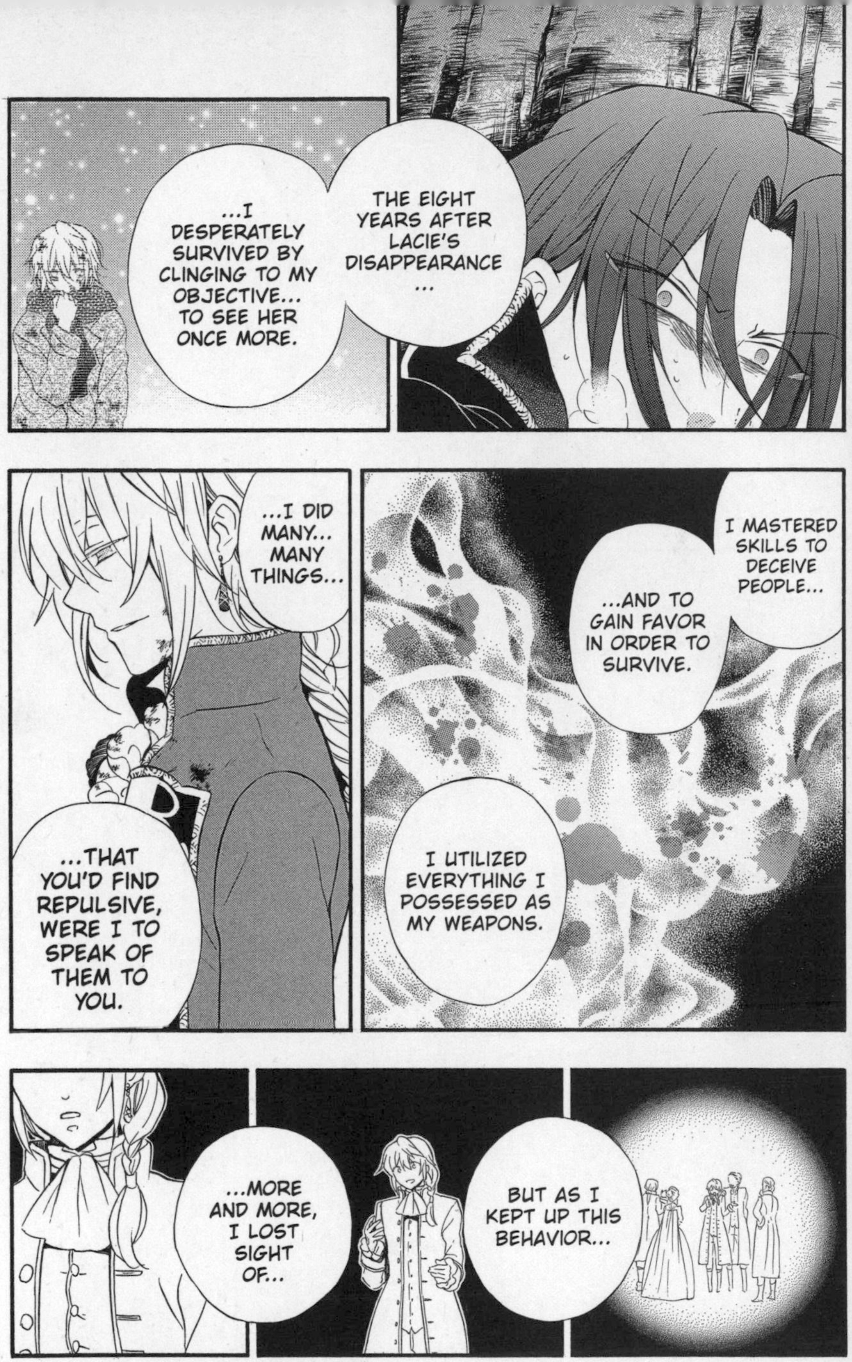
THE EIGHT YEARS AFTER LACIE'S DISAPPEARANCE ...
...I DESPERATELY SURVIVED BY CLINGING TO MY OBJECTIVE... TO SEE HER ONCE MORE.
I MASTERED SKILLS TO DECEIVE PEOPLE...
...AND TO GAIN FAVOR IN ORDER TO SURVIVE.
I UTILIZED EVERYTHING I POSSESSED AS MY WEAPONS.
...I DID MANY... MANY THINGS...
...THAT YOU'D FIND REPULSIVE, WERE I TO SPEAK OF THEM TO YOU.
BUT AS I KEPT UP THIS BEHAVIOR...
...MORE AND MORE, I LOST SIGHT OF...

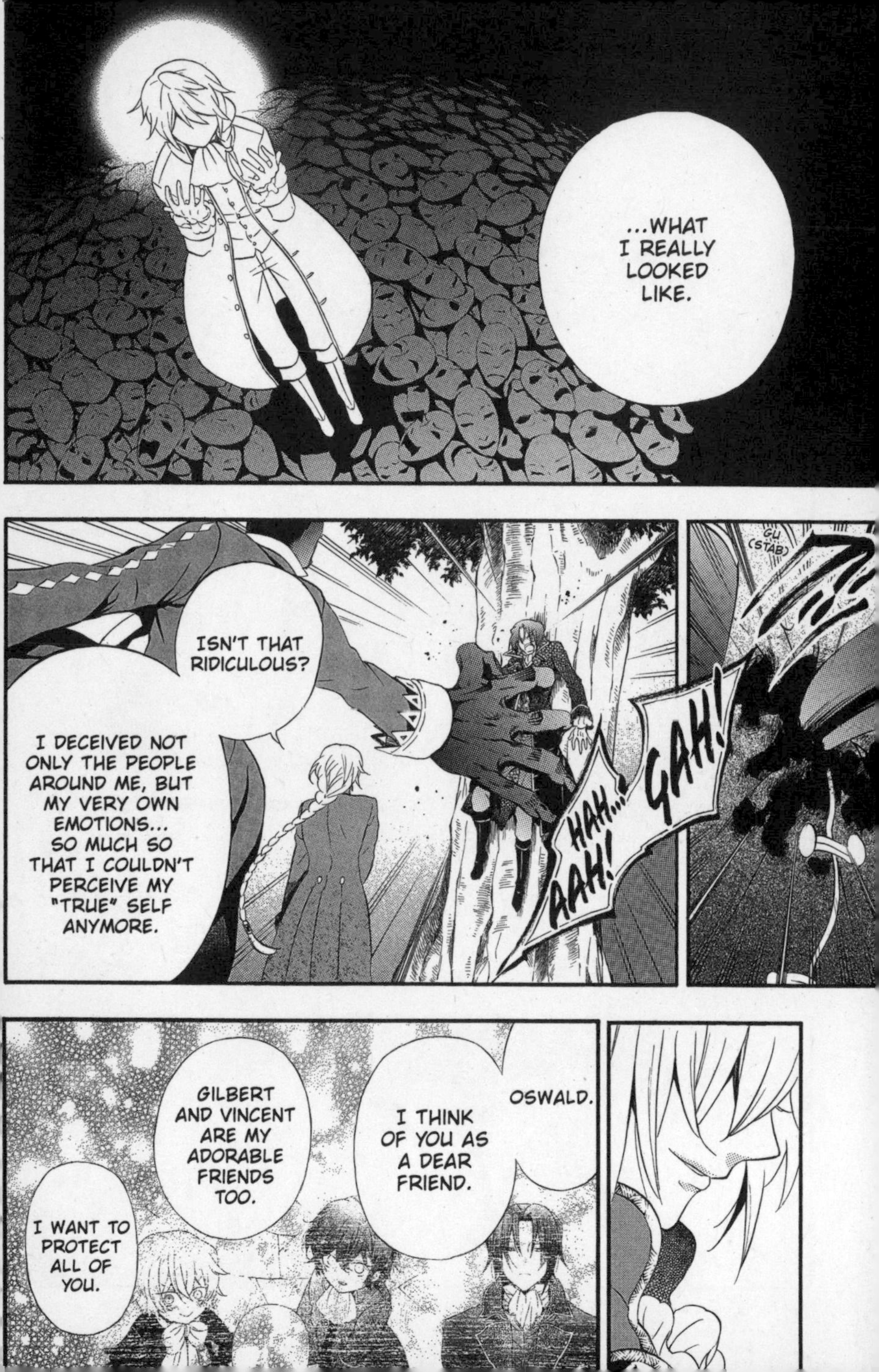
...WHAT I REALLY LOOKED LIKE.
GU (STAB)
GAH!
HAH... AAH!
ISN'T THAT RIDICULOUS?
I DECEIVED NOT ONLY THE PEOPLE AROUND ME, BUT MY VERY OWN EMOTIONS... SO MUCH SO THAT I COULDN'T PERCEIVE MY "TRUE" SELF ANYMORE.
OSWALD.
I THINK OF YOU AS A DEAR FRIEND.
GILBERT AND VINCENT ARE MY ADORABLE FRIENDS TOO.
I WANT TO PROTECT ALL OF YOU.

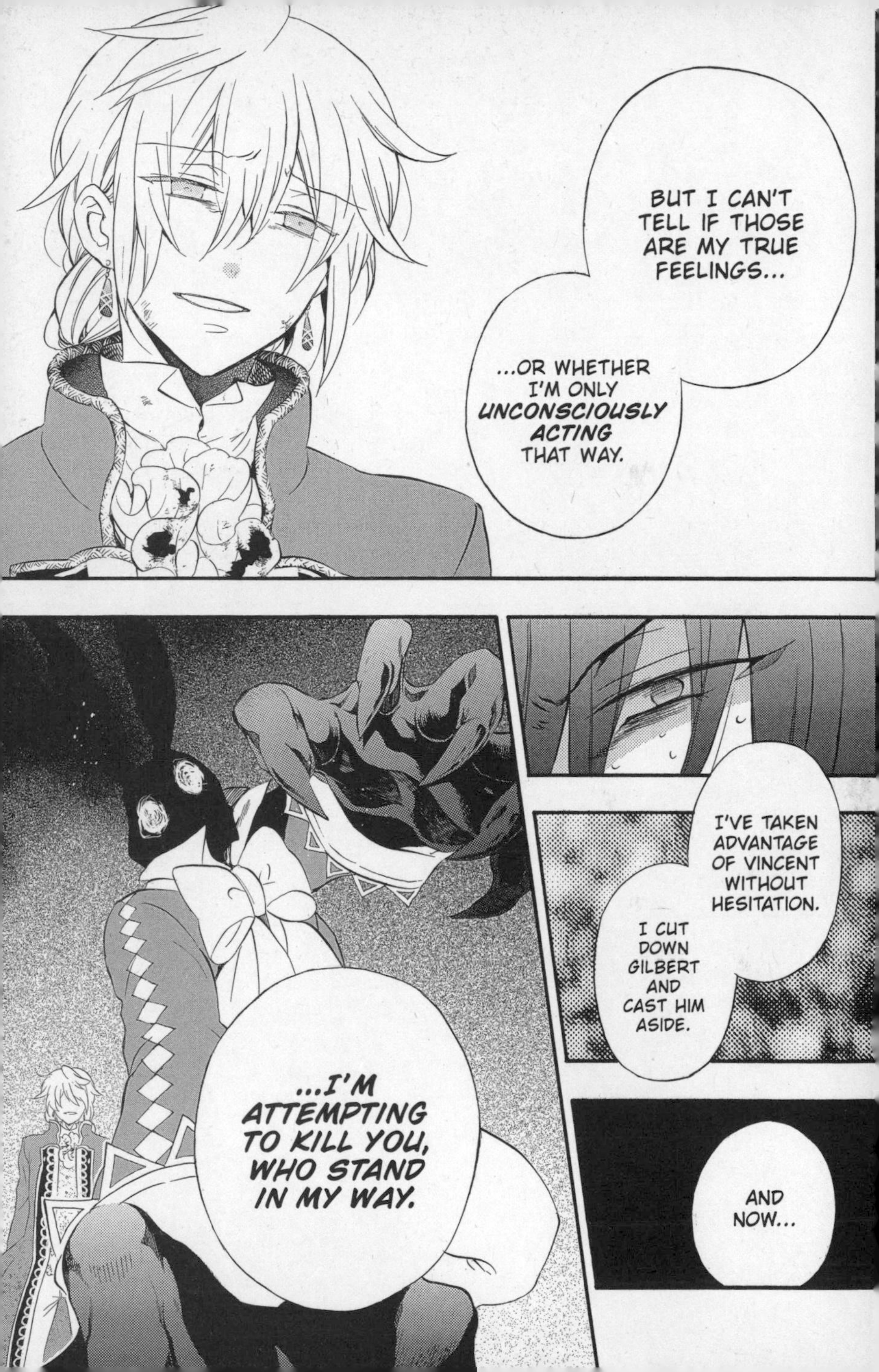
BUT I CAN'T TELL IF THOSE ARE MY TRUE FEELINGS...
...OR WHETHER I'M ONLY *UNCONSCIOUSLY ACTING* THAT WAY.
I'VE TAKEN ADVANTAGE OF VINCENT WITHOUT HESITATION.
I CUT DOWN GILBERT AND CAST HIM ASIDE.
AND NOW...
...I'M ATTEMPTING TO KILL YOU, WHO STAND IN MY WAY.

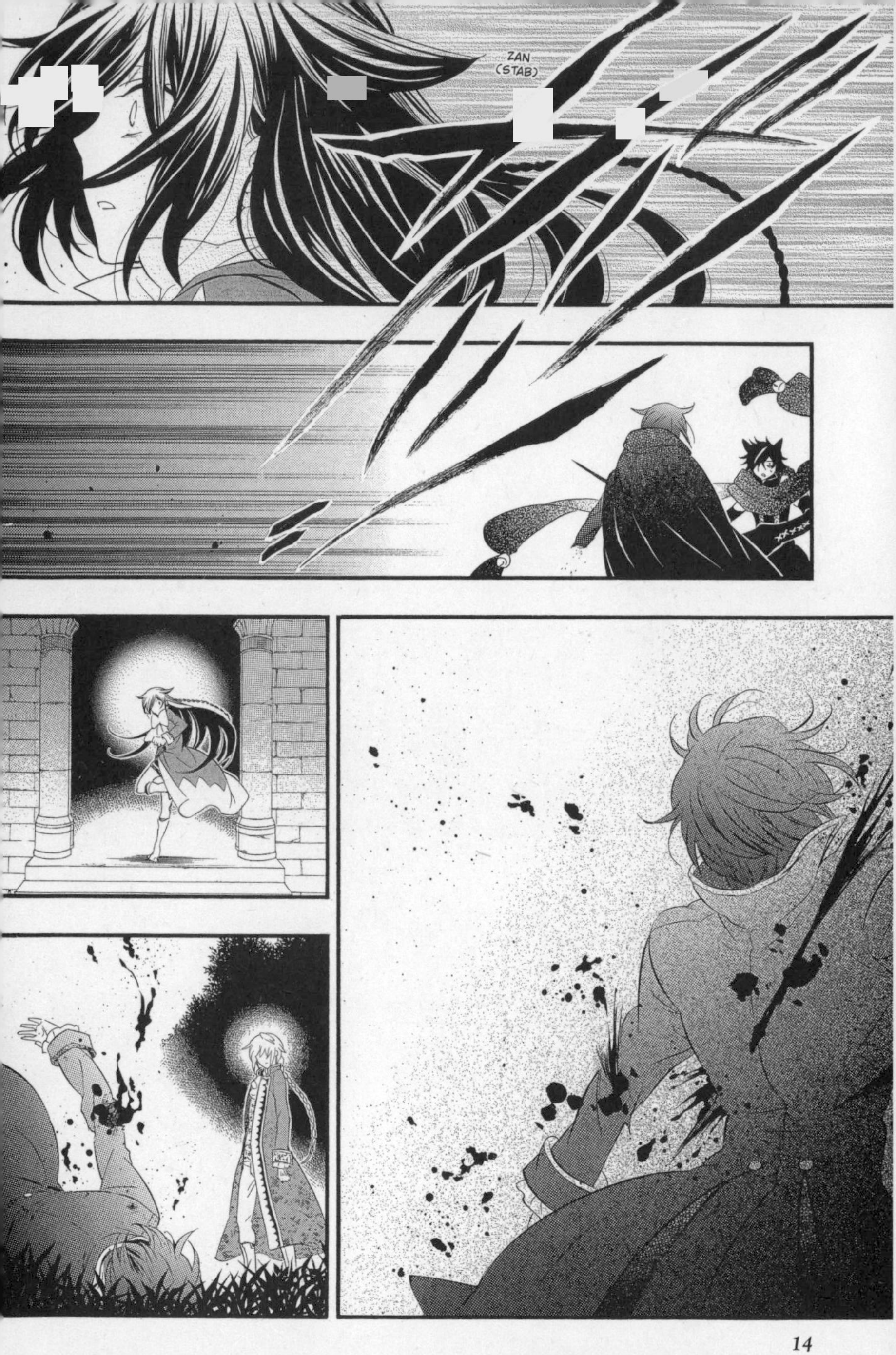
ZAN
(STAB)

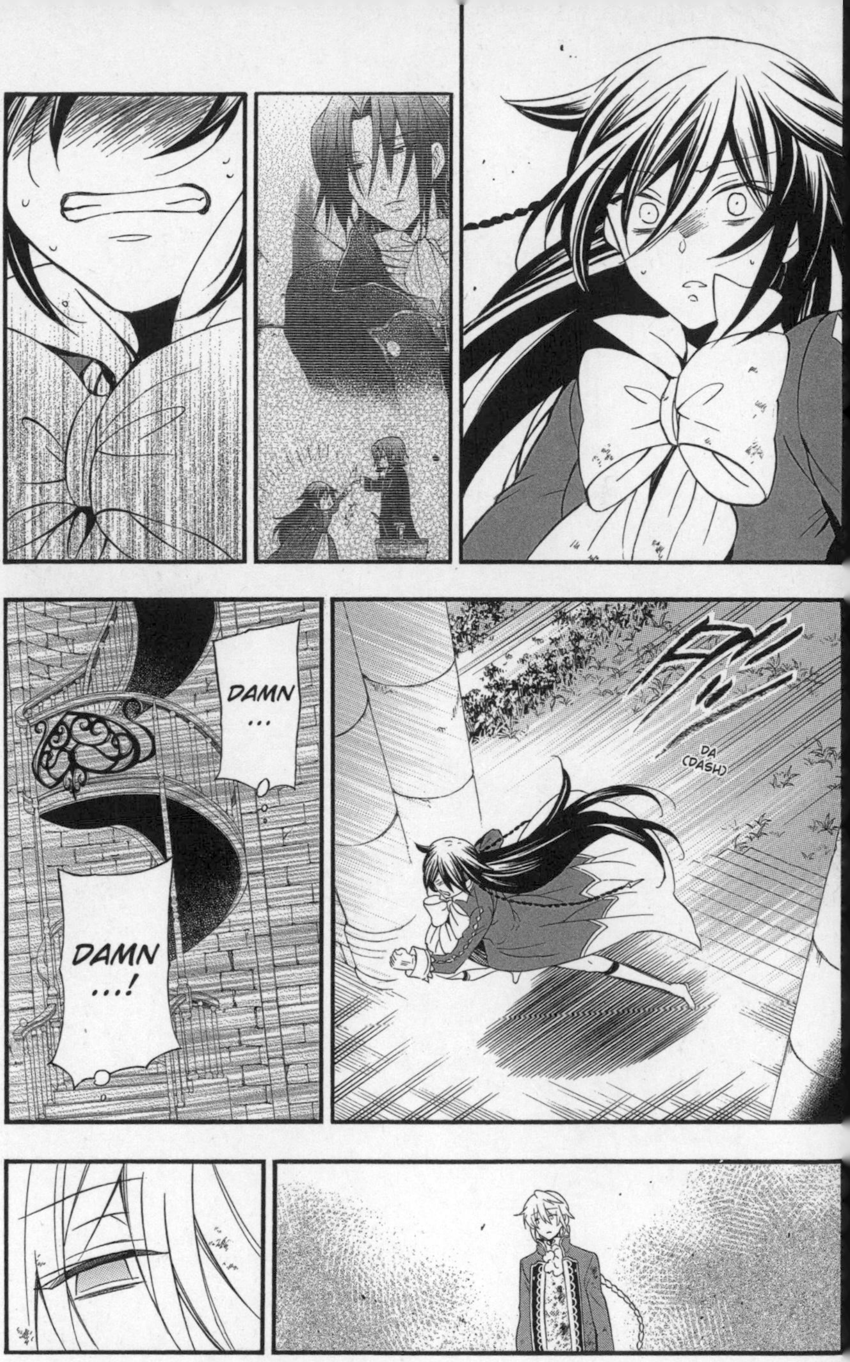
DA (DASH)
DAMN ...
DAMN ...!

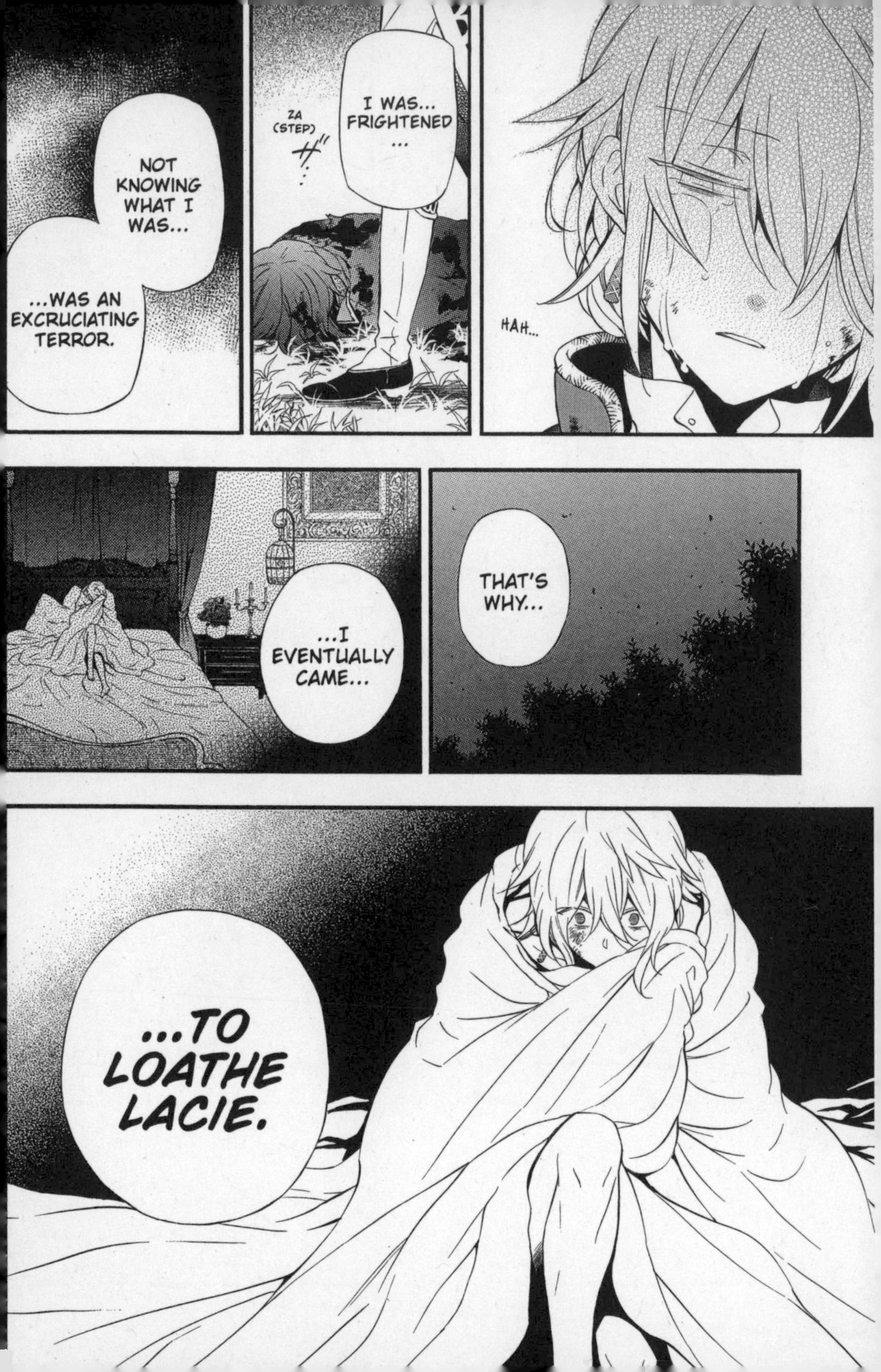
HAH...
I WAS... FRIGHTENED...
ZA (STEP)
NOT KNOWING WHAT I WAS...
...WAS AN EXCRUCIATING TERROR.
THAT'S WHY...
...I EVENTUALLY CAME...
...TO LOATHE LACIE.

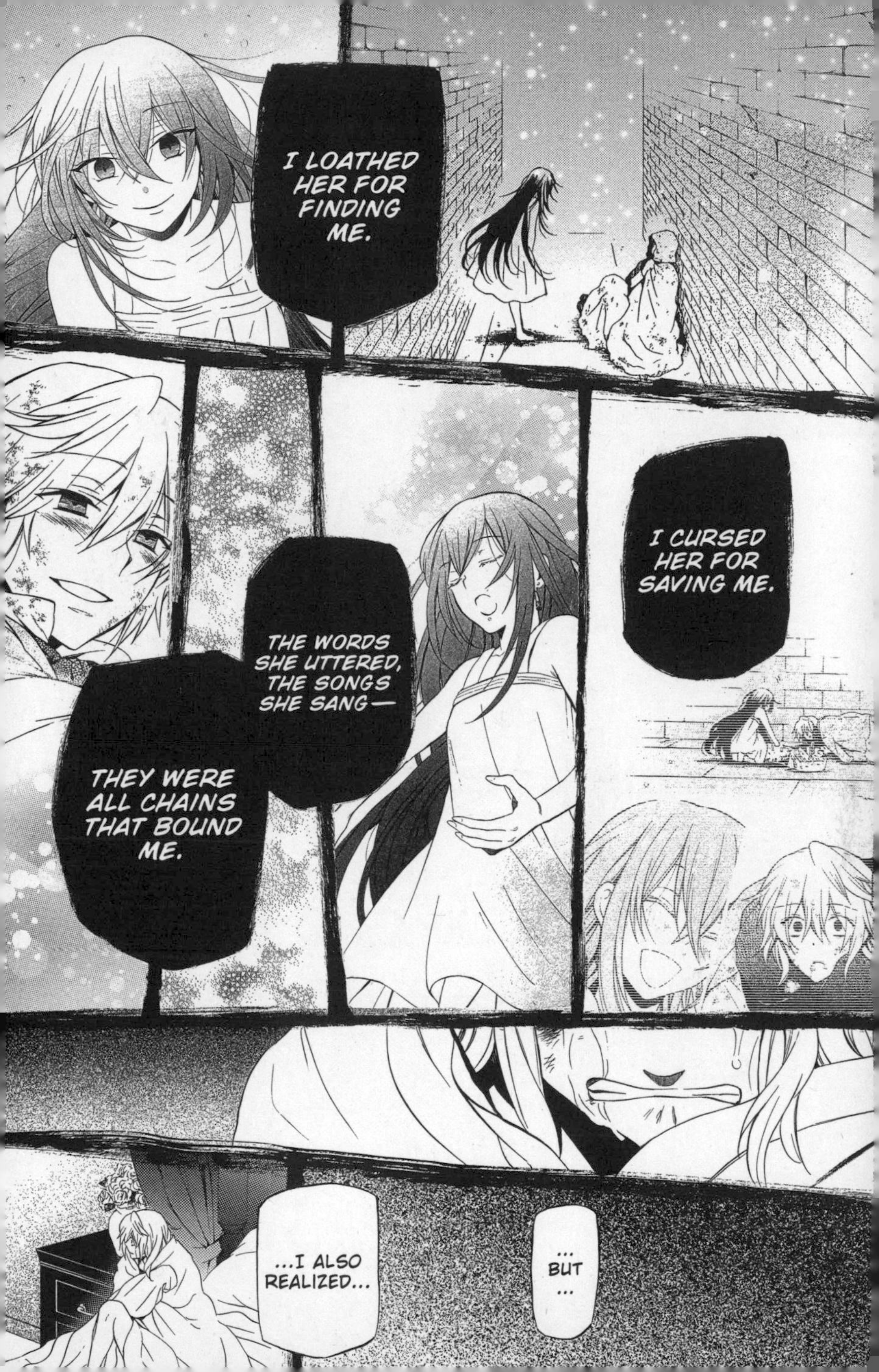
I LOATHED HER FOR FINDING ME.
I CURSED HER FOR SAVING ME.
THE WORDS SHE UTTERED, THE SONGS SHE SANG—
THEY WERE ALL CHAINS THAT BOUND ME.
...BUT...
...I ALSO REALIZED...

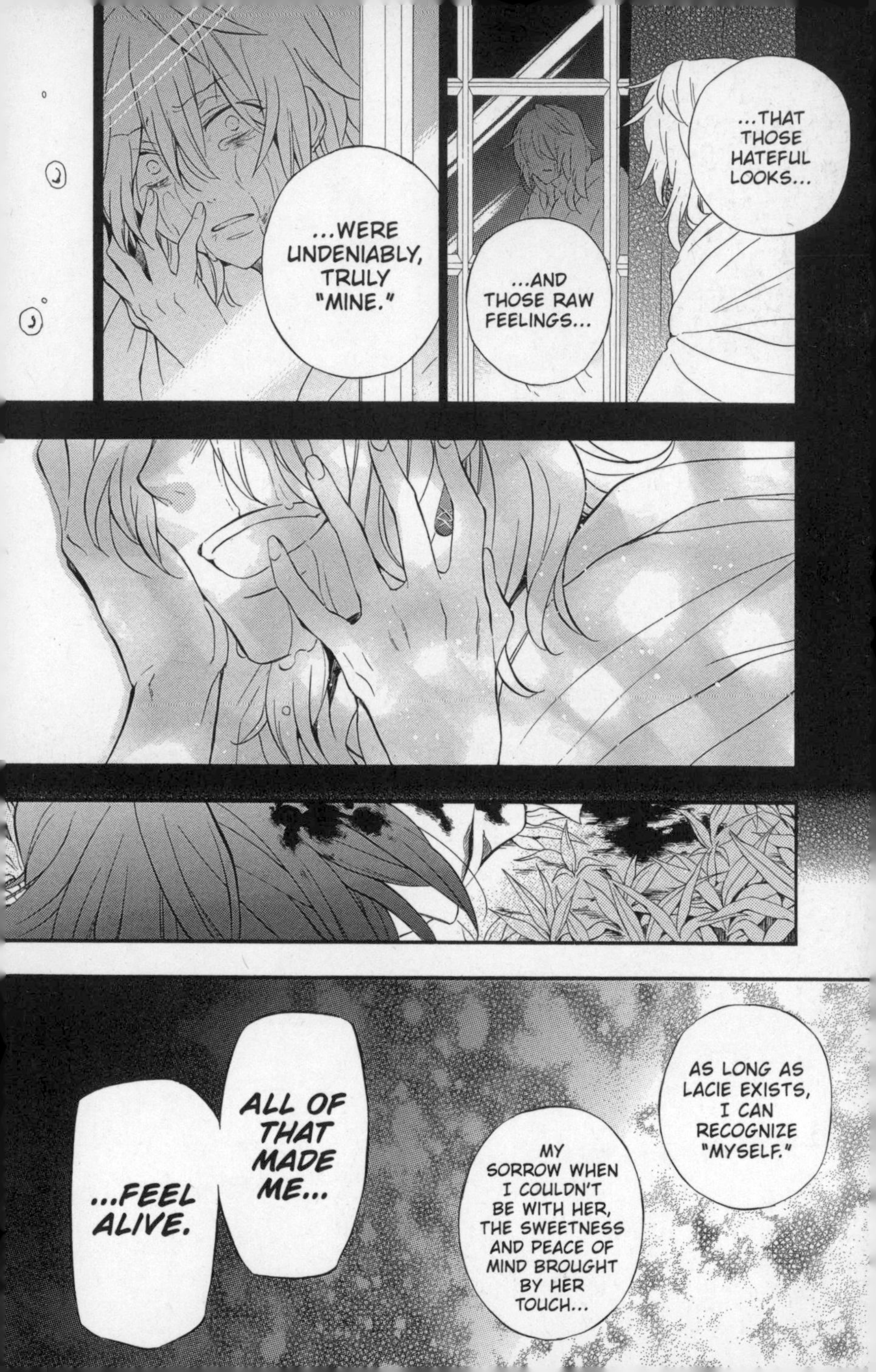
...THAT THOSE HATEFUL LOOKS...
...AND THOSE RAW FEELINGS...
...WERE UNDENIABLY, TRULY "MINE."
AS LONG AS LACIE EXISTS, I CAN RECOGNIZE "MYSELF."
MY SORROW WHEN I COULDN'T BE WITH HER, THE SWEETNESS AND PEACE OF MIND BROUGHT BY HER TOUCH...
ALL OF THAT MADE ME...
...FEEL ALIVE.

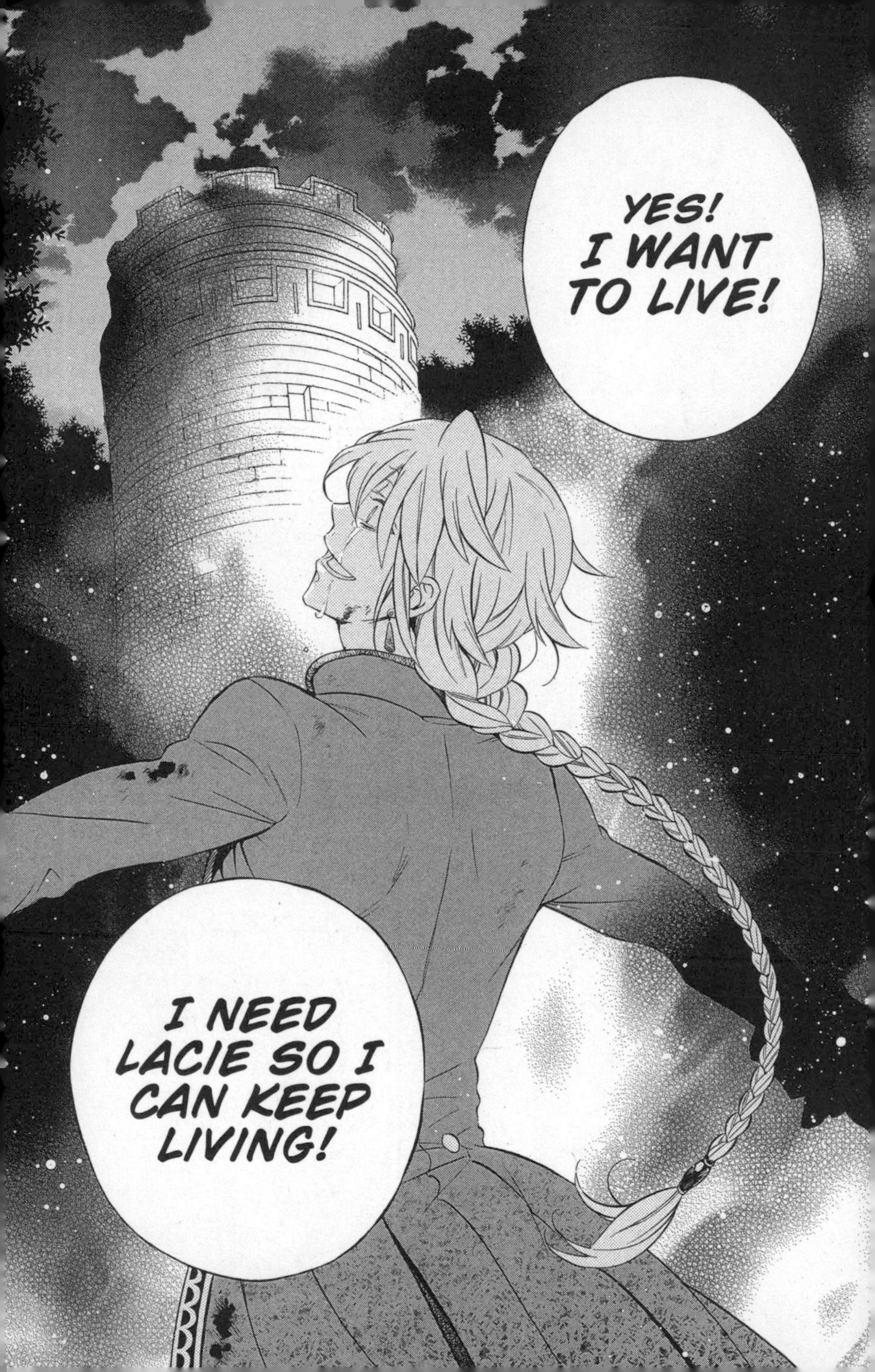
YES! I WANT TO LIVE!
I NEED LACIE SO I CAN KEEP LIVING!

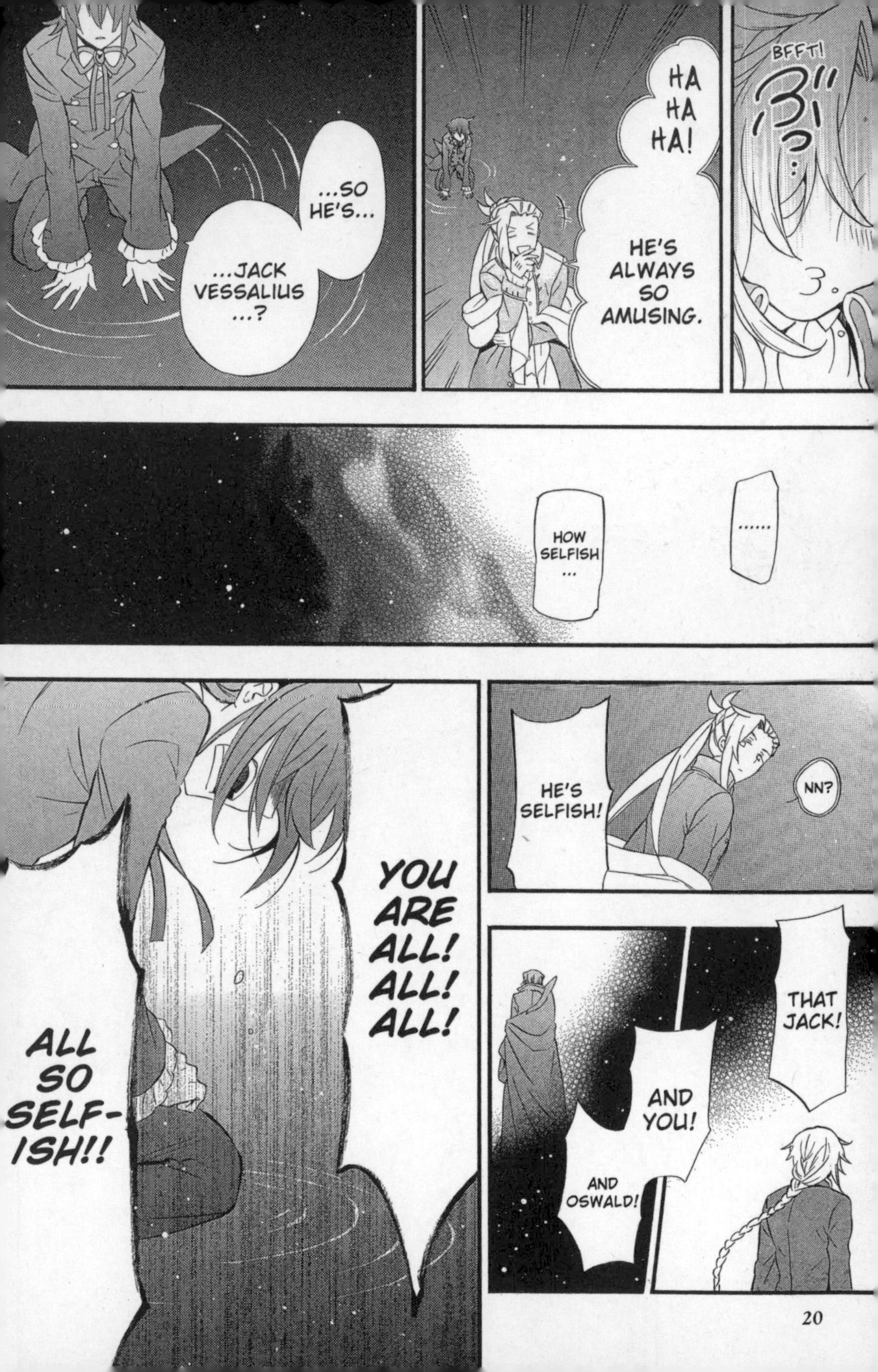
BFFT!
HA HA HA!
HE'S ALWAYS SO AMUSING.
...SO HE'S...
...JACK VESSALIUS ...?
......
HOW SELFISH ...
NN?
HE'S SELFISH!
THAT JACK!
AND YOU!
AND OSWALD!
YOU ARE ALL! ALL! ALL!
ALL SO SELF-ISH!!

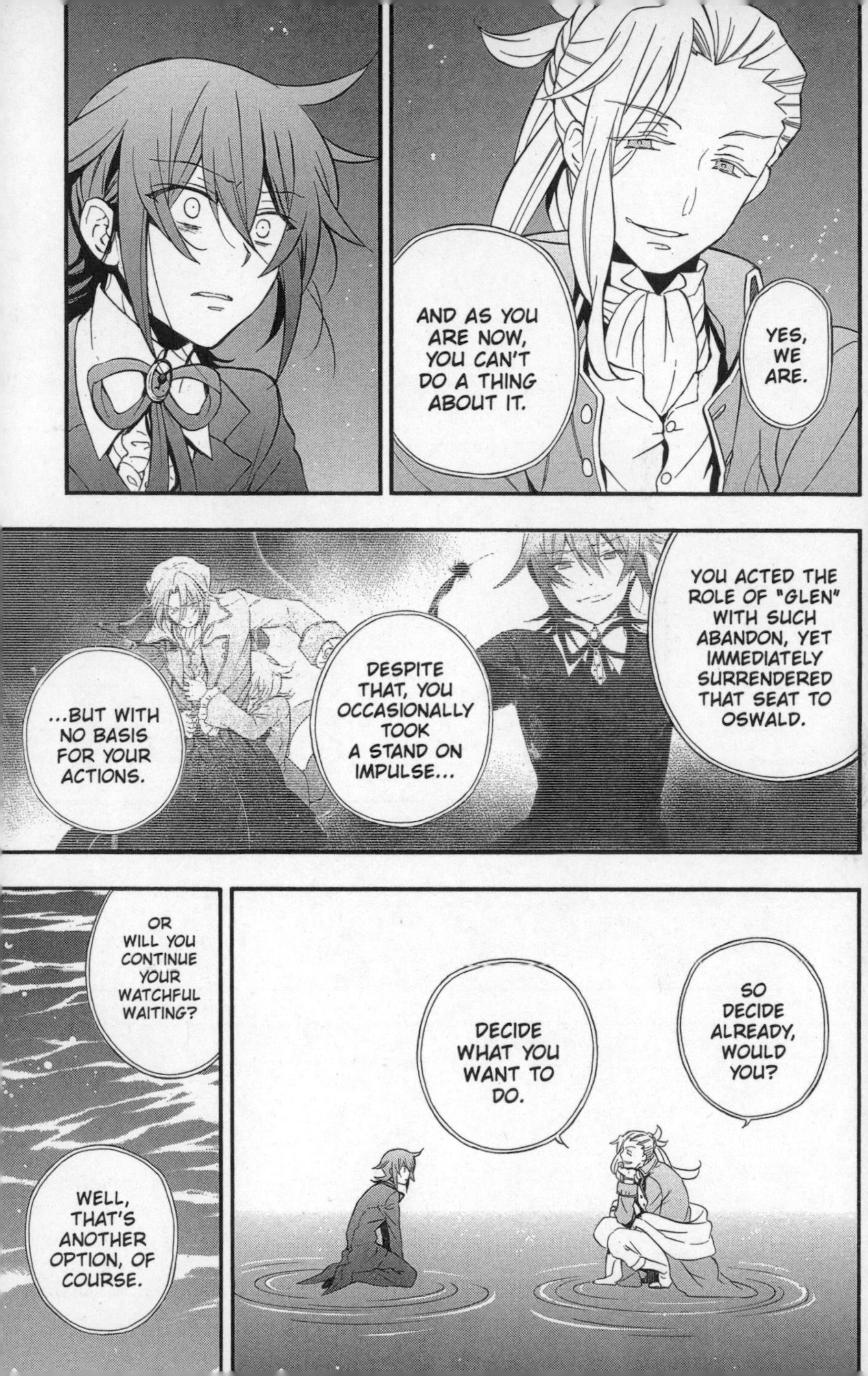
YES, WE ARE.
AND AS YOU ARE NOW, YOU CAN'T DO A THING ABOUT IT.
YOU ACTED THE ROLE OF "GLEN" WITH SUCH ABANDON, YET IMMEDIATELY SURRENDERED THAT SEAT TO OSWALD.
DESPITE THAT, YOU OCCASIONALLY TOOK A STAND ON IMPULSE...
...BUT WITH NO BASIS FOR YOUR ACTIONS.
SO DECIDE ALREADY, WOULD YOU?
DECIDE WHAT YOU WANT TO DO.
OR WILL YOU CONTINUE YOUR WATCHFUL WAITING?
WELL, THAT'S ANOTHER OPTION, OF COURSE.

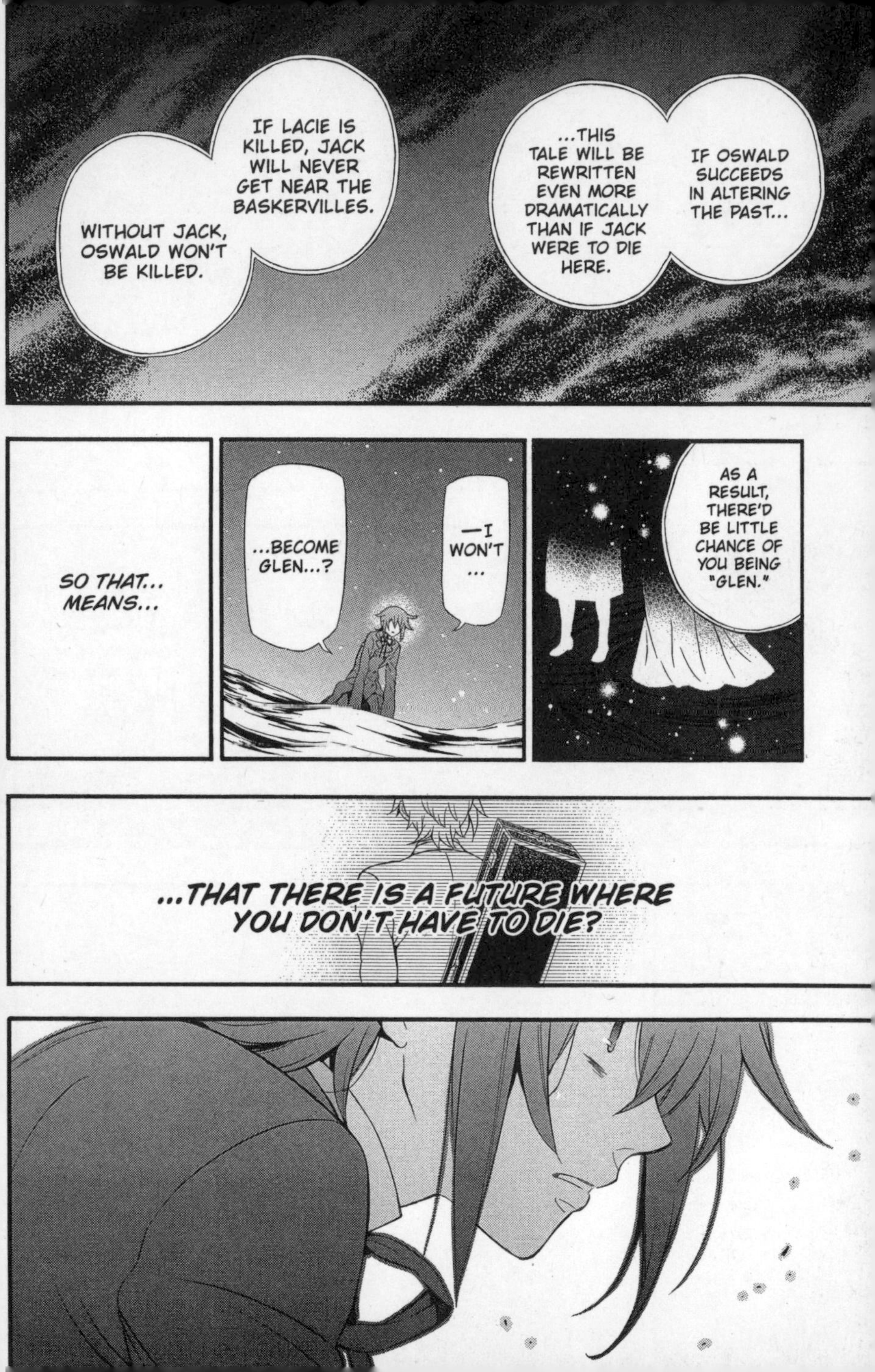
IF OSWALD SUCCEEDS IN ALTERING THE PAST...
...THIS TALE WILL BE REWRITTEN EVEN MORE DRAMATICALLY THAN IF JACK WERE TO DIE HERE.
IF LACIE IS KILLED, JACK WILL NEVER GET NEAR THE BASKERVILLES.
WITHOUT JACK, OSWALD WON'T BE KILLED.
AS A RESULT, THERE'D BE LITTLE CHANCE OF YOU BEING "GLEN."
—I WON'T ...
...BECOME GLEN...?
SO THAT... MEANS...
...THAT THERE IS A FUTURE WHERE YOU DON'T HAVE TO DIE?

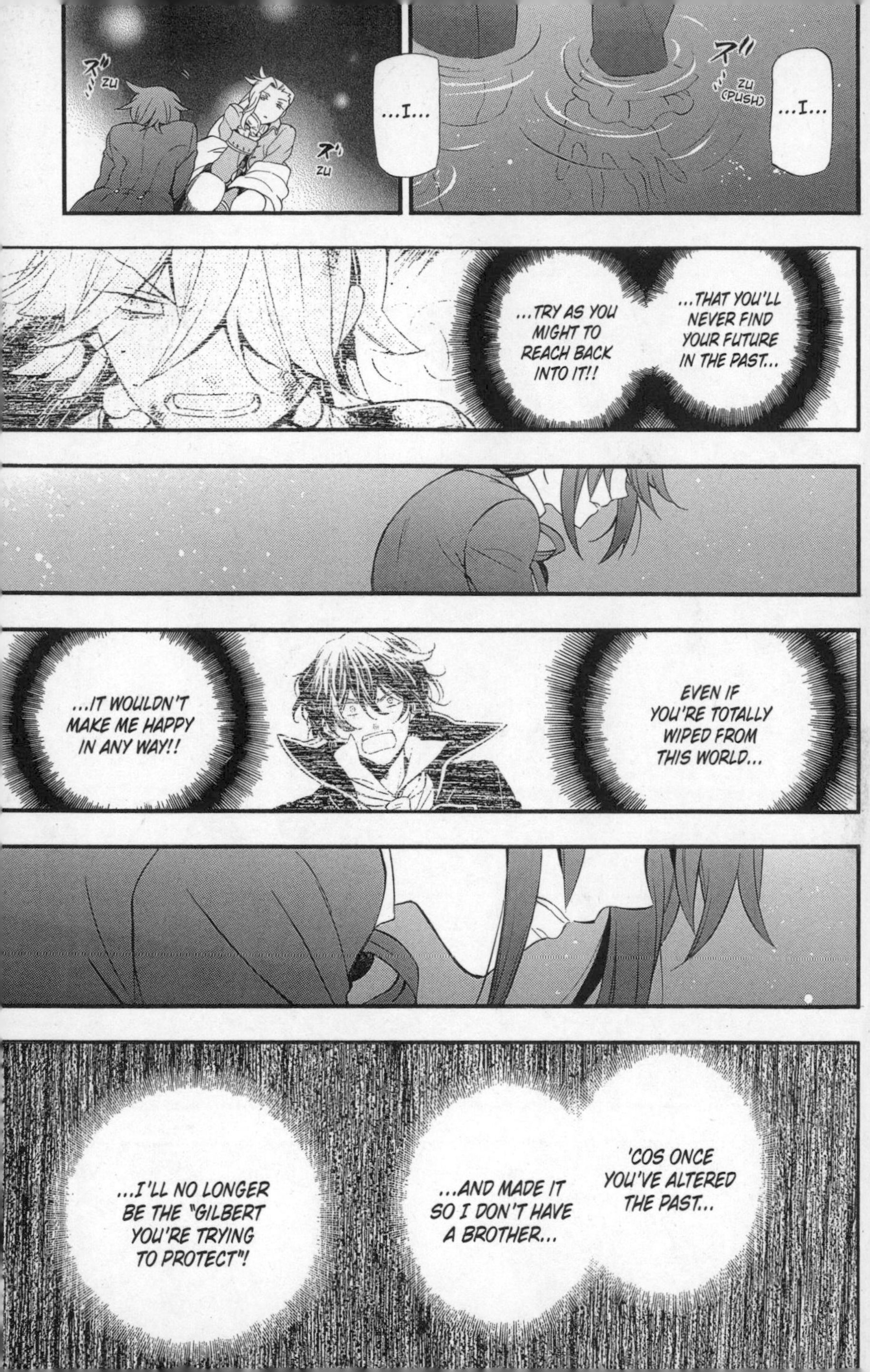
...I...
ズ
ZU (PUSH)
...I...
ズ
ZU
ズ
ZU
...THAT YOU'LL NEVER FIND YOUR FUTURE IN THE PAST...
...TRY AS YOU MIGHT TO REACH BACK INTO IT!!
EVEN IF YOU'RE TOTALLY WIPED FROM THIS WORLD...
...IT WOULDN'T MAKE ME HAPPY IN ANY WAY!!
'COS ONCE YOU'VE ALTERED THE PAST...
...AND MADE IT SO I DON'T HAVE A BROTHER...
...I'LL NO LONGER BE THE "GILBERT YOU'RE TRYING TO PROTECT"!

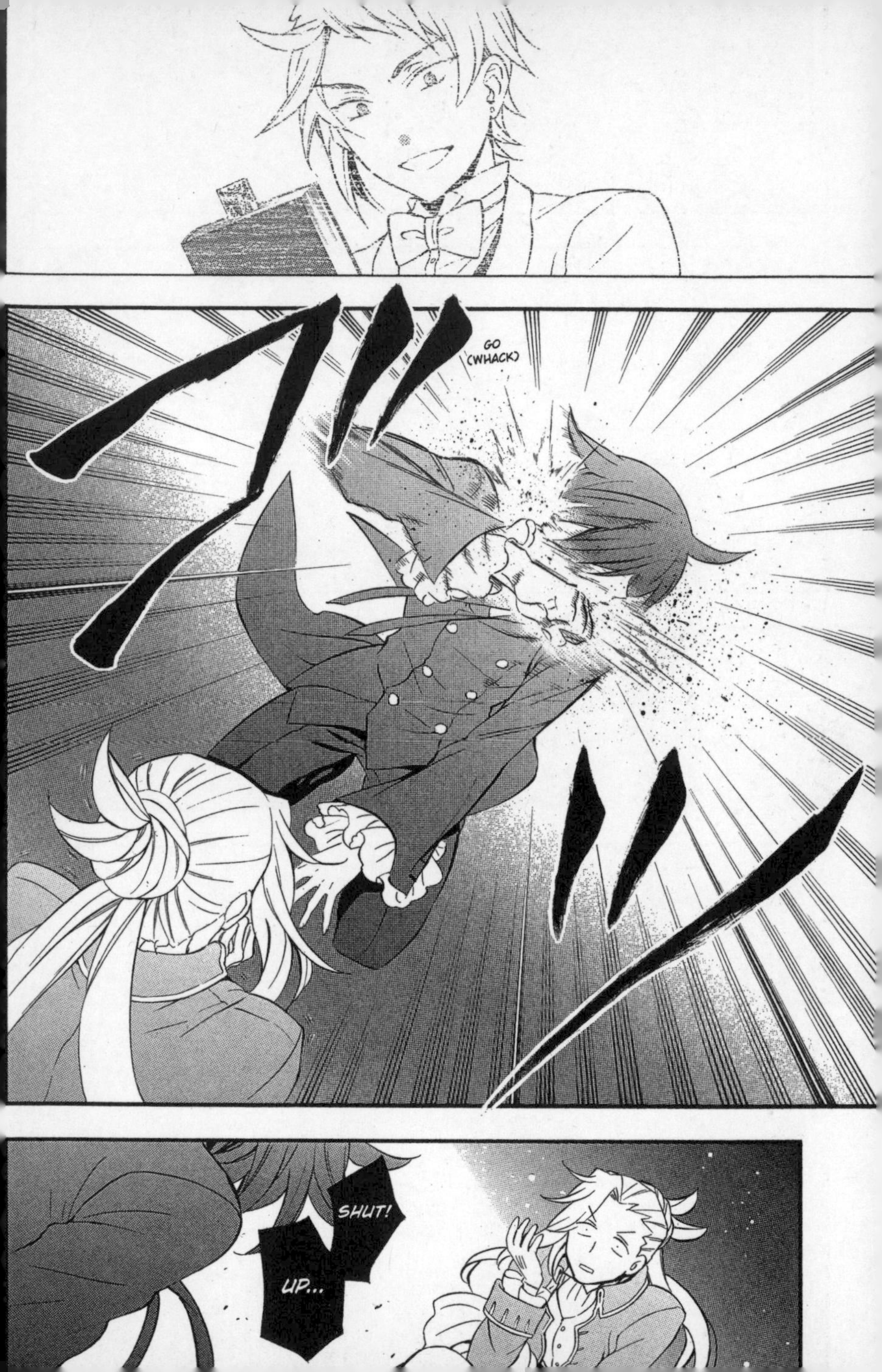
GO
(WHACK)
SHUT!
UP...

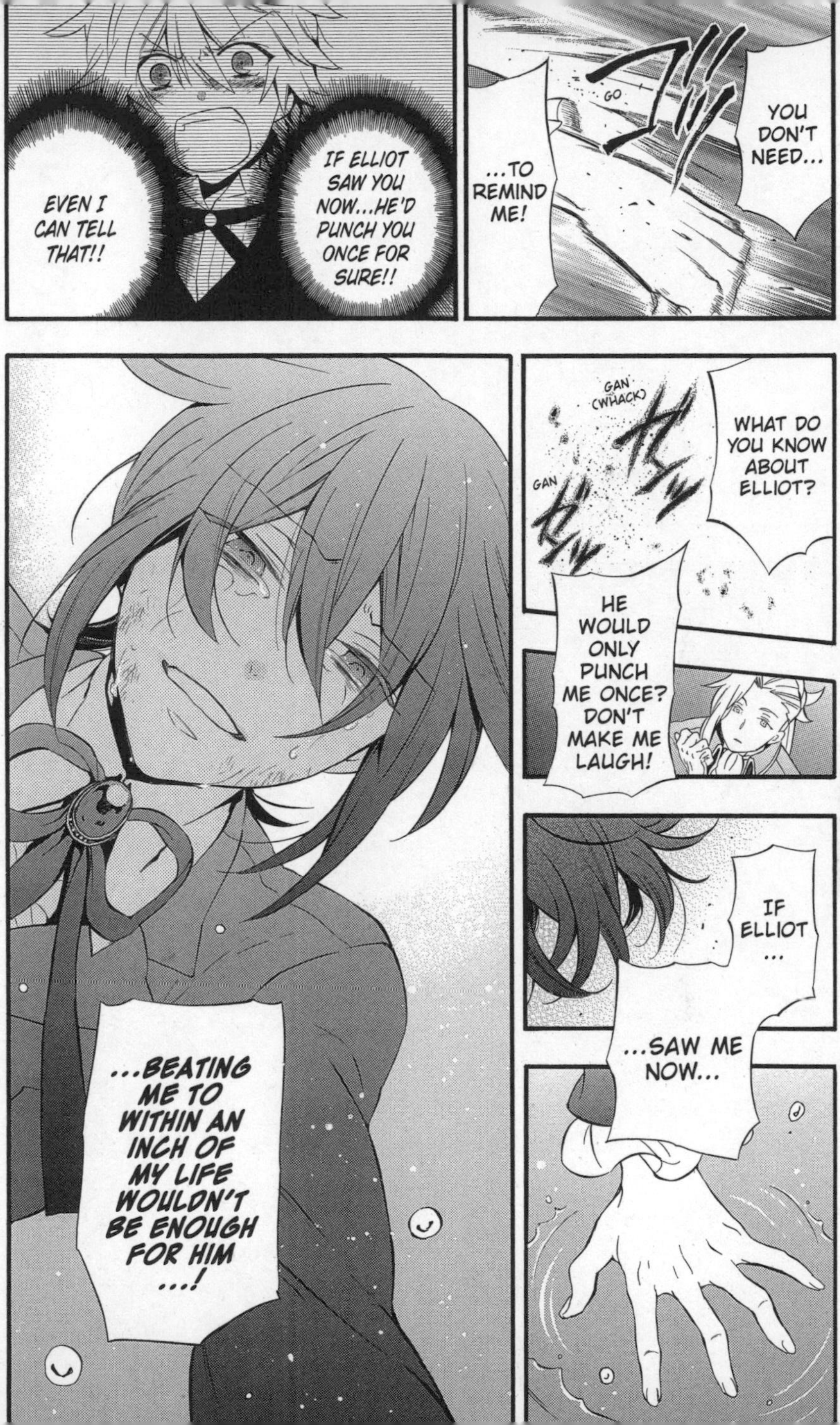
YOU DON'T NEED...
GO
...TO REMIND ME!
IF ELLIOT SAW YOU NOW...HE'D PUNCH YOU ONCE FOR SURE!!
EVEN I CAN TELL THAT!!
GAN (WHACK)
GAN
WHAT DO YOU KNOW ABOUT ELLIOT?
HE WOULD ONLY PUNCH ME ONCE? DON'T MAKE ME LAUGH!
IF ELLIOT ...
...SAW ME NOW...
...BEATING ME TO WITHIN AN INCH OF MY LIFE WOULDN'T BE ENOUGH FOR HIM ...!

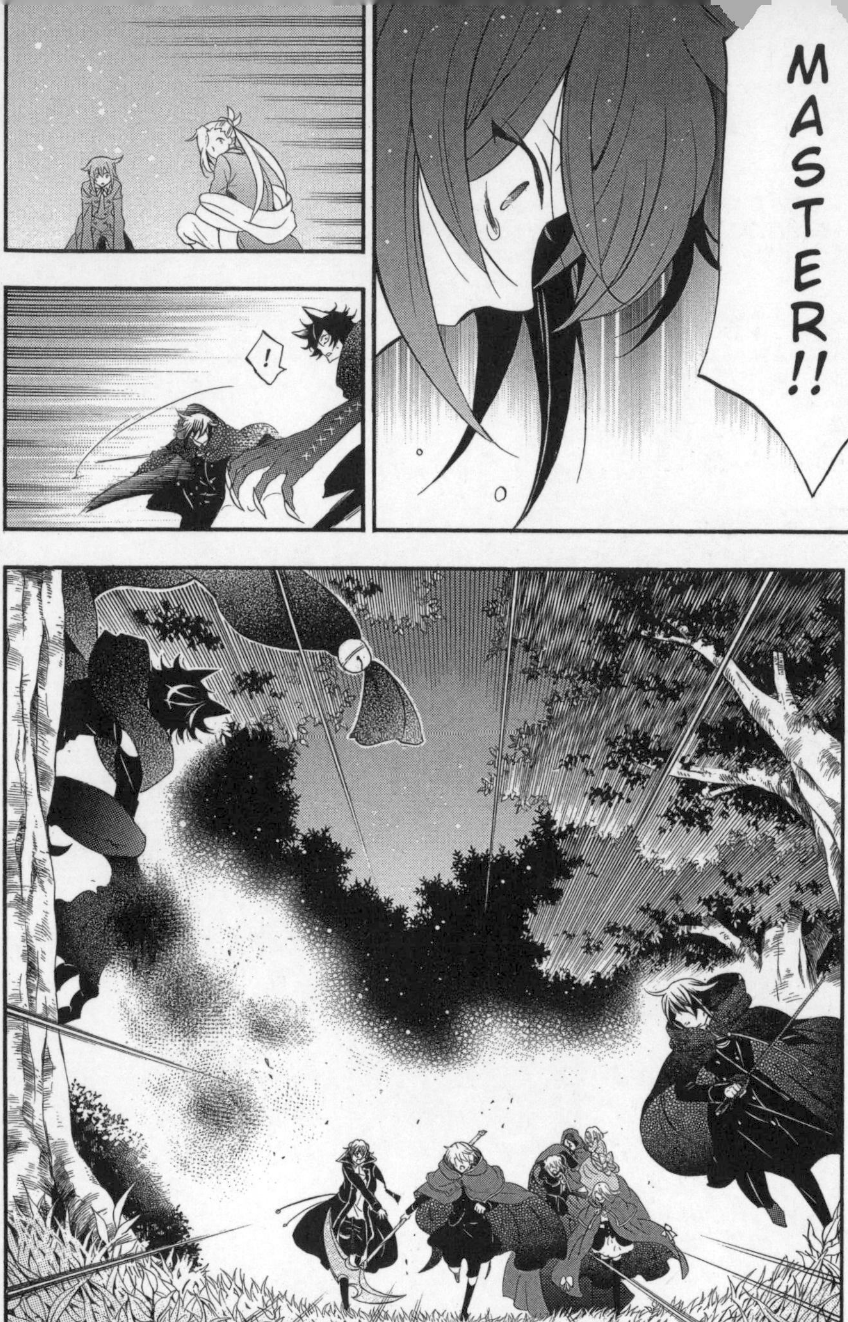
MASTER!!
!

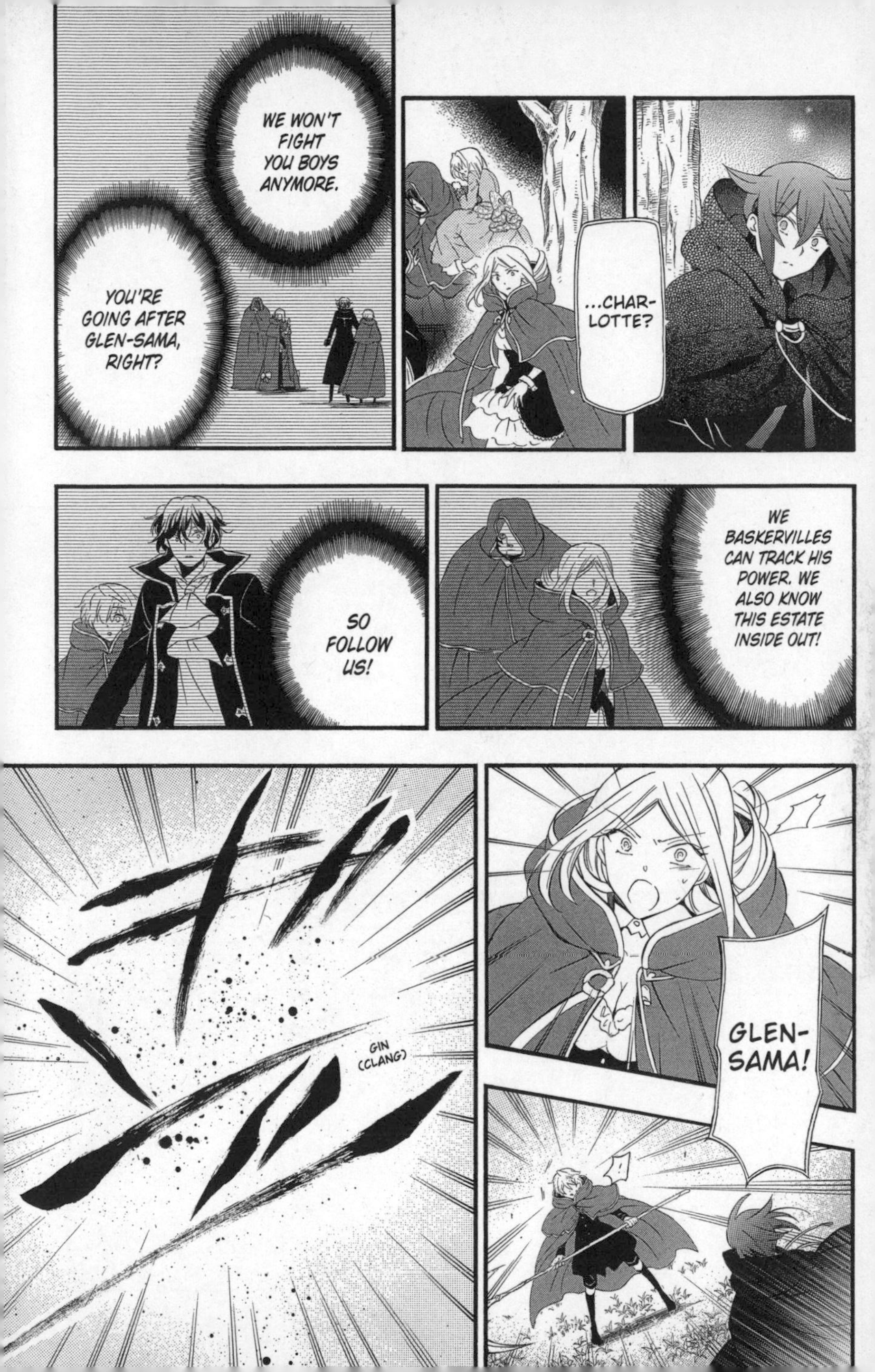
...CHAR-LOTTE?
WE WON'T FIGHT YOU BOYS ANYMORE.
YOU'RE GOING AFTER GLEN-SAMA, RIGHT?
WE BASKERVILLES CAN TRACK HIS POWER. WE ALSO KNOW THIS ESTATE INSIDE OUT!
SO FOLLOW US!
GLEN-SAMA!
!
GIN (CLANG)

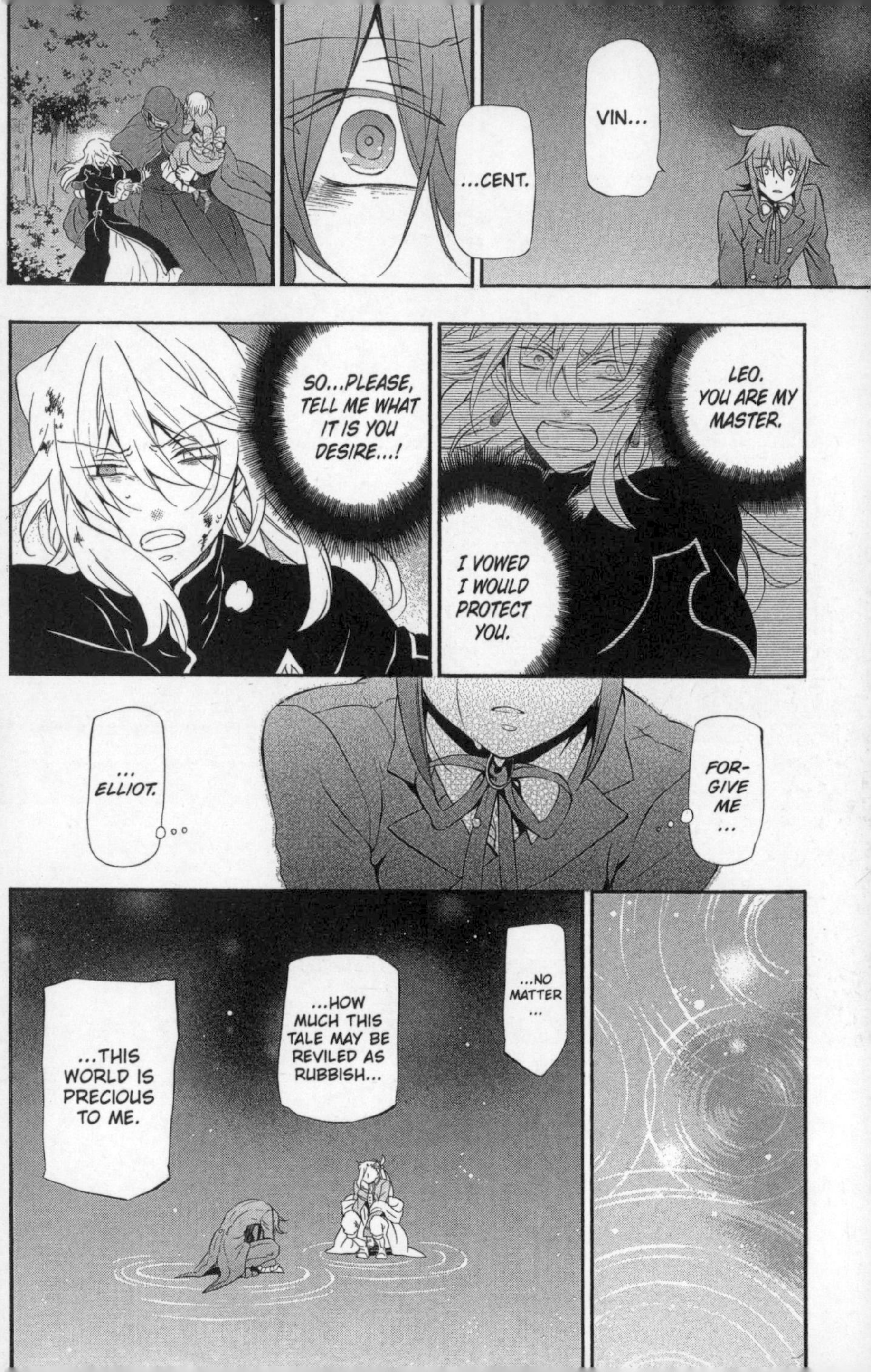
VIN...
...CENT.
LEO. YOU ARE MY MASTER.
I VOWED I WOULD PROTECT YOU.
SO...PLEASE, TELL ME WHAT IT IS YOU DESIRE...!
FOR-GIVE ME ...
... ELLIOT.
...NO MATTER ...
...HOW MUCH THIS TALE MAY BE REVILED AS RUBBISH...
...THIS WORLD IS PRECIOUS TO ME.

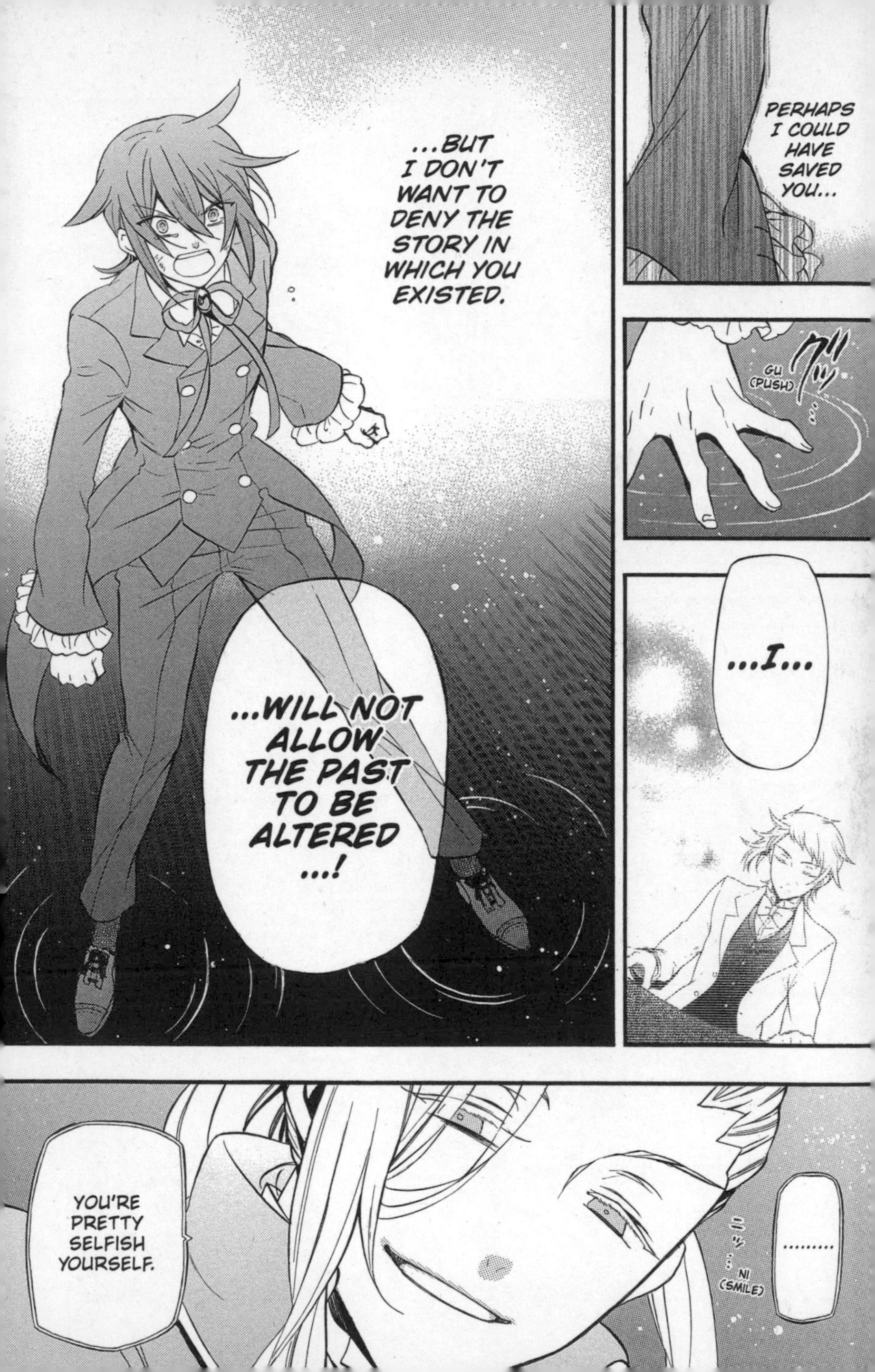
PERHAPS I COULD HAVE SAVED YOU...
GU (PUSH)
...I...
...BUT I DON'T WANT TO DENY THE STORY IN WHICH YOU EXISTED.
...WILL NOT ALLOW THE PAST TO BE ALTERED ...!
....
NI (SMILE)
YOU'RE PRETTY SELFISH YOURSELF.

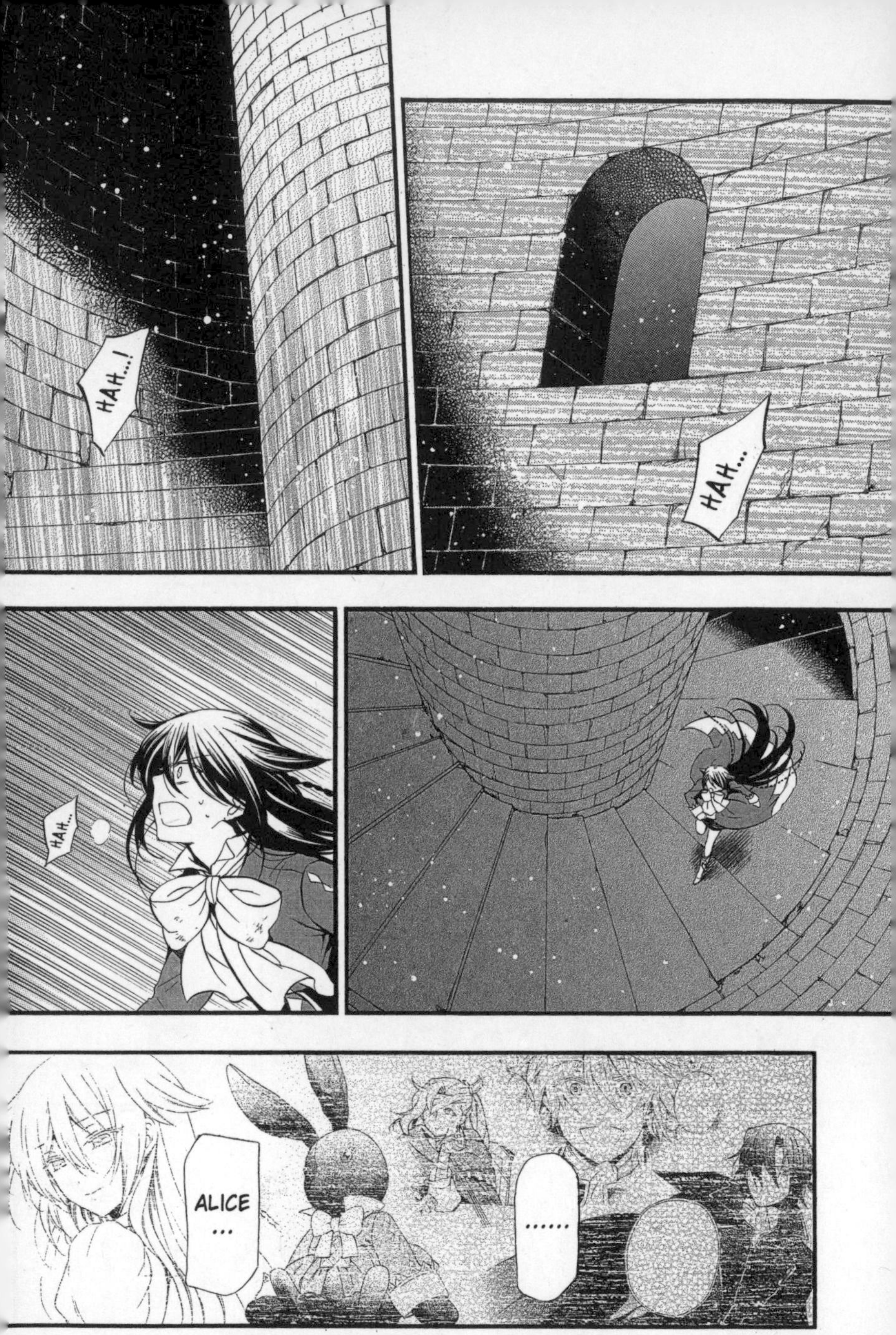
HAH...
HAH...!
HAH...
......
ALICE ...

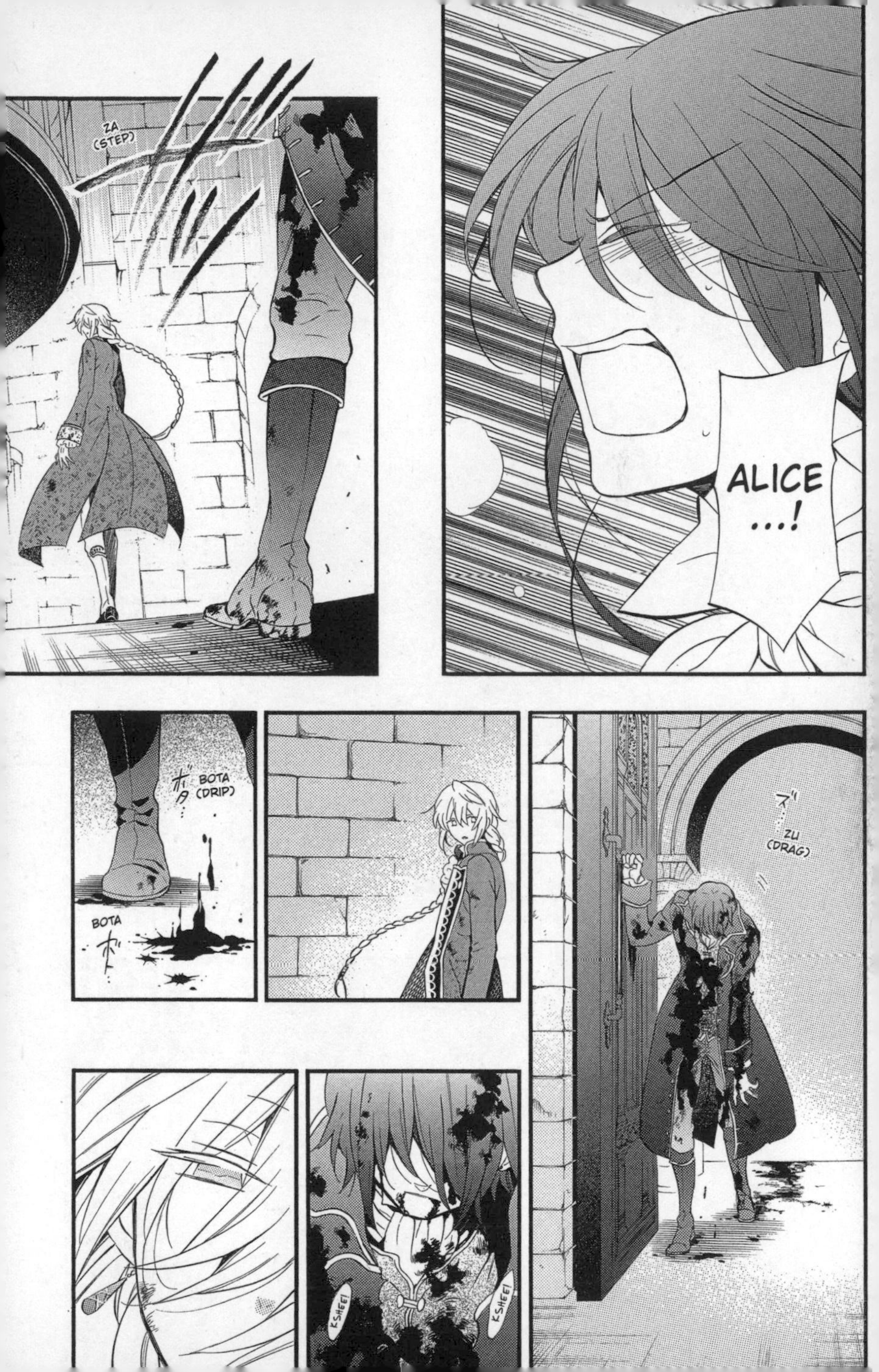
ALICE ...!
ZA (STEP)
ズ ZU (DRAG)
ボタ BOTA (DRIP)
ボ BOTA
KSHEE!
KSHEE!

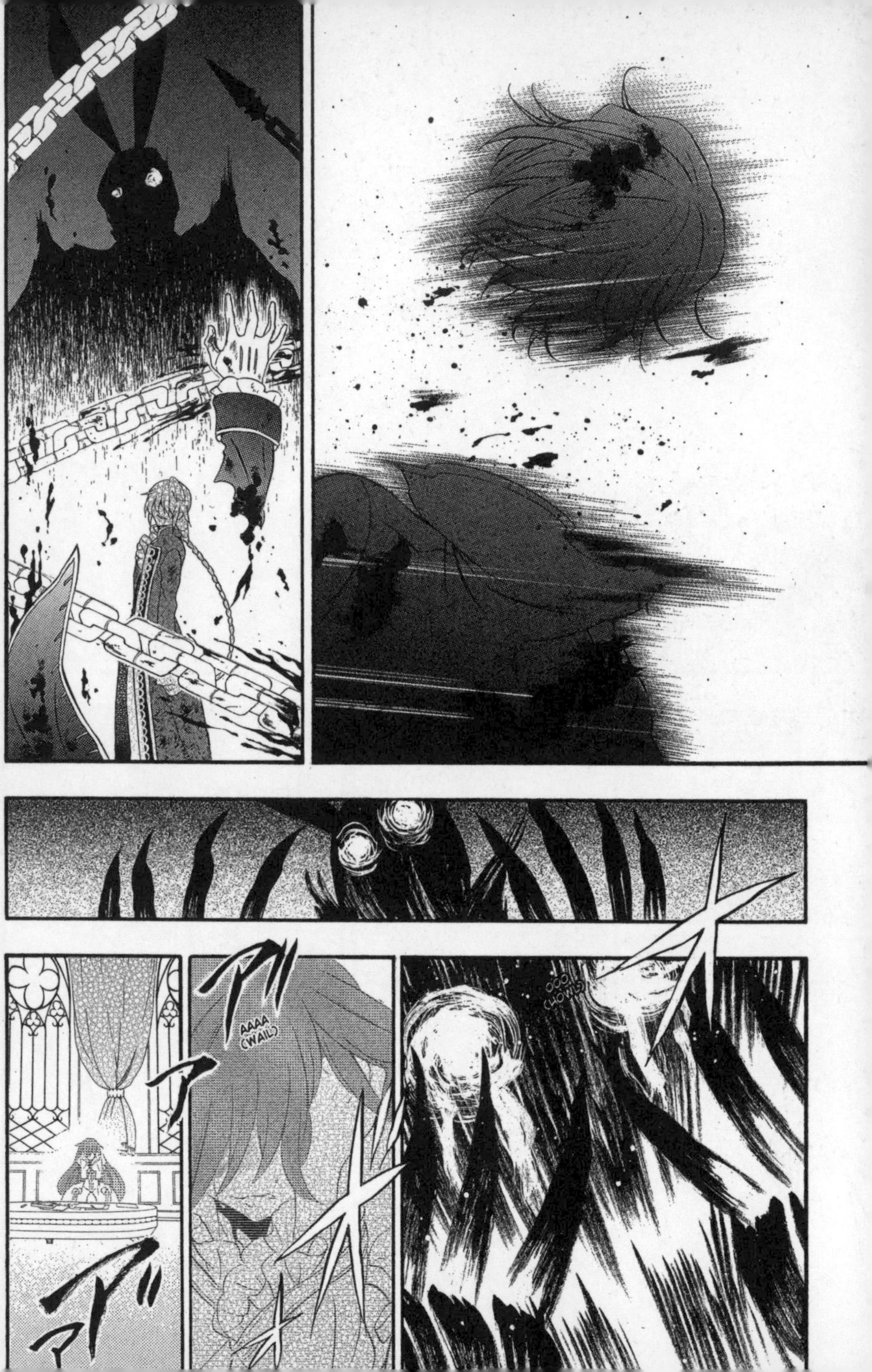
OOO
(HOWL)
AAAA
(WAIL)

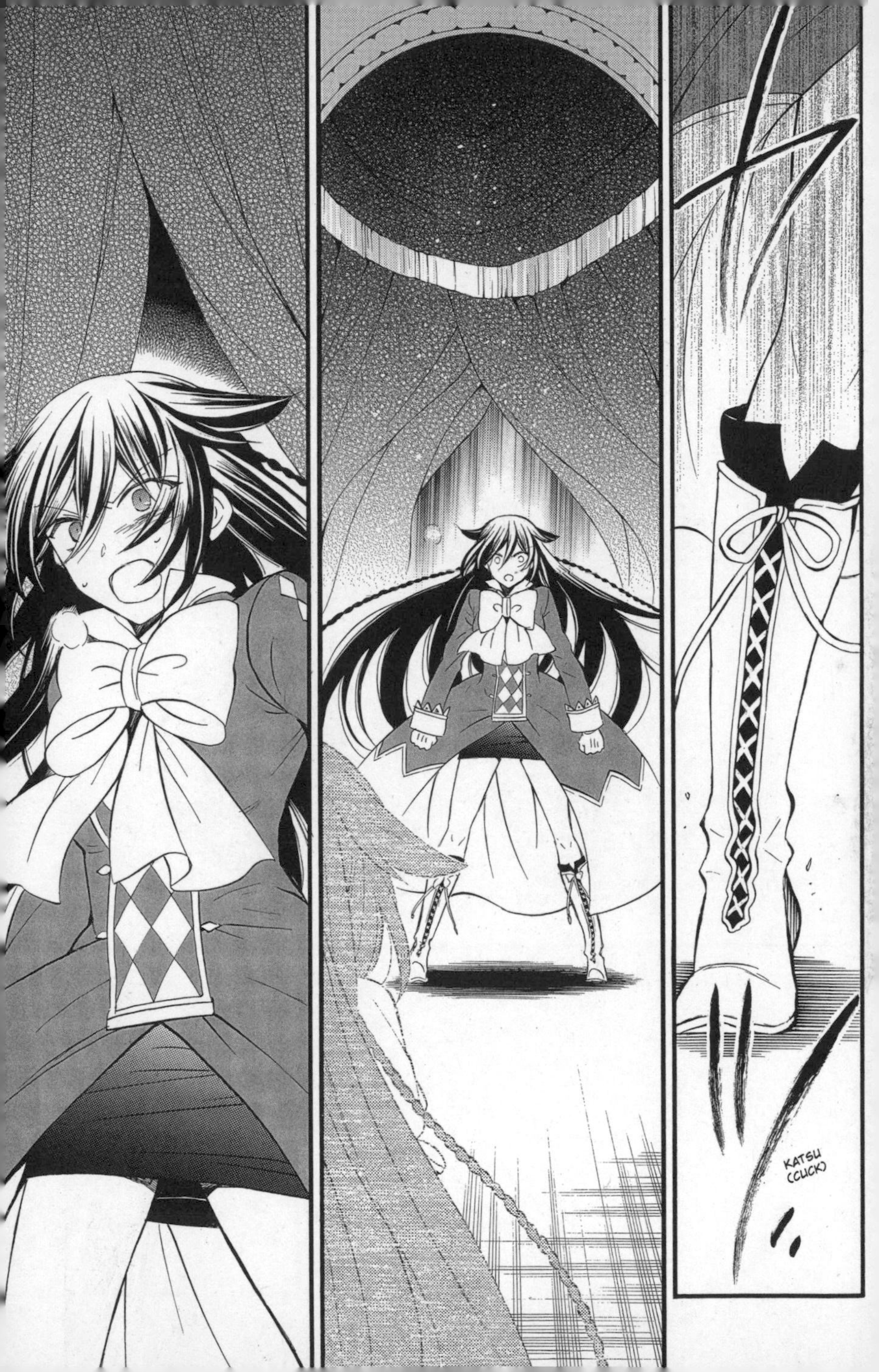
KATSU (CLICK)

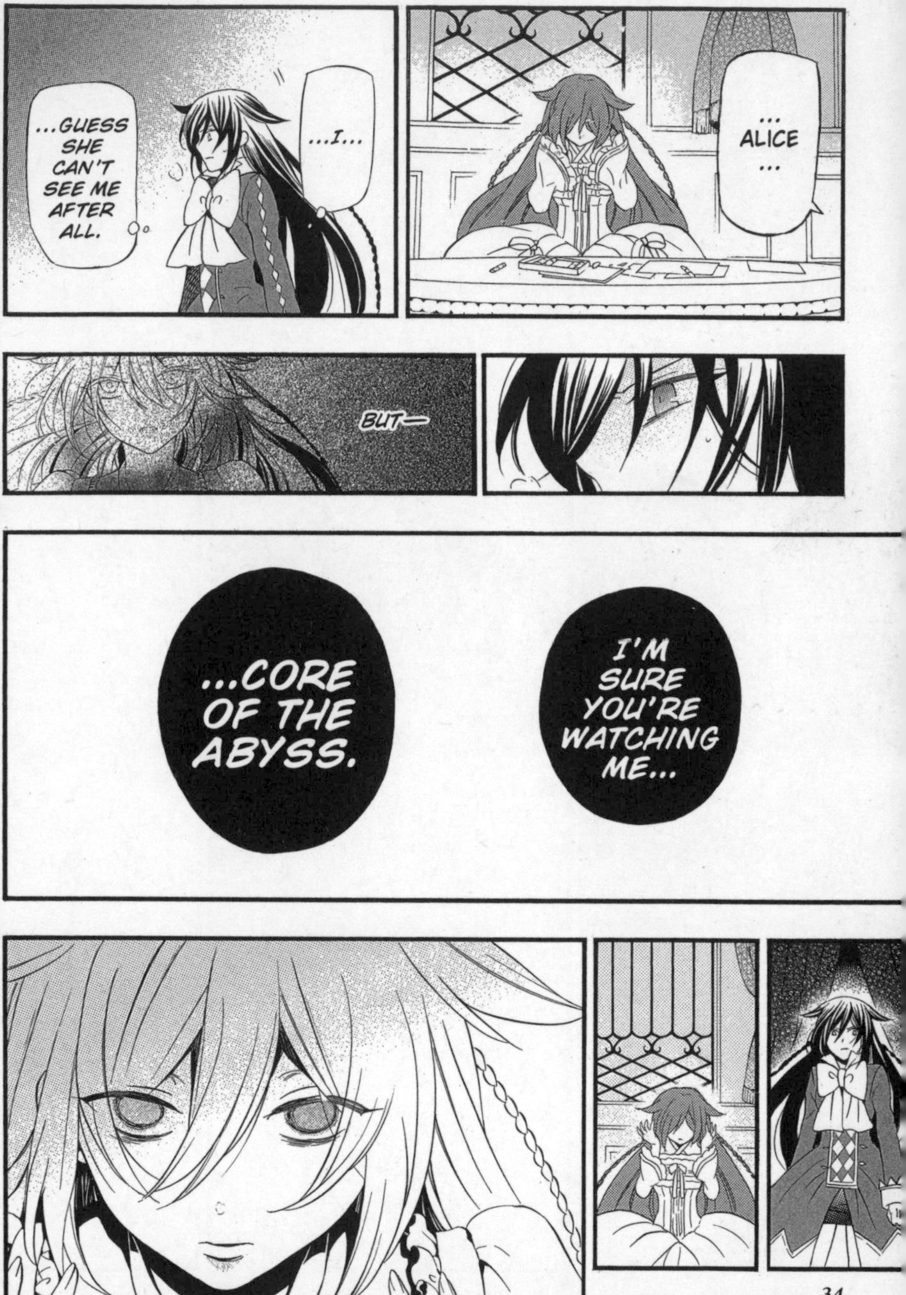
... ALICE ...
...I...
...GUESS SHE CAN'T SEE ME AFTER ALL.
BUT—
I'M SURE YOU'RE WATCHING ME...
...CORE OF THE ABYSS.

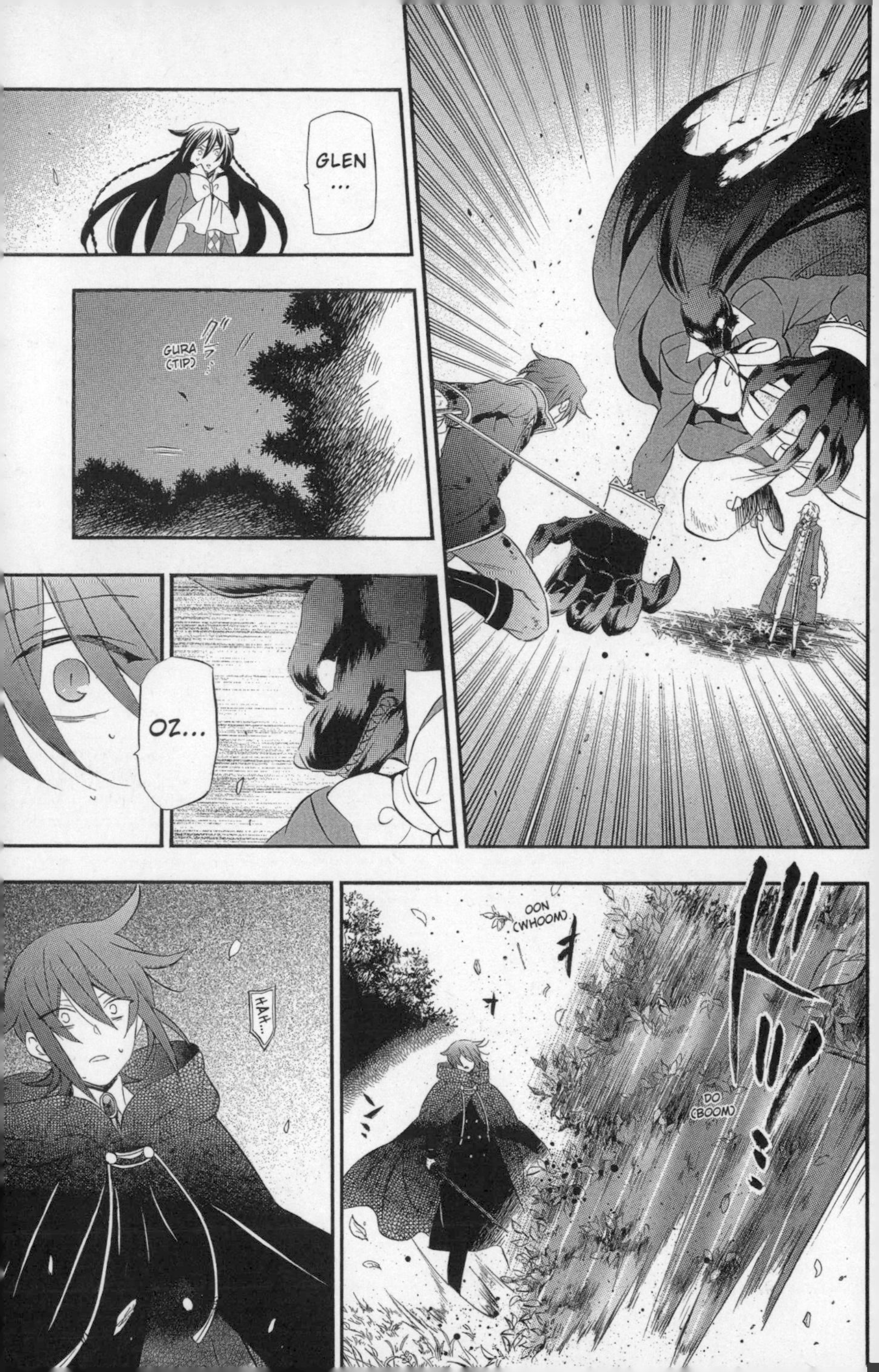
GLEN ...
GURA (TIP)
OZ...
OON (WHOOM)
DO (BOOM)
HAH...

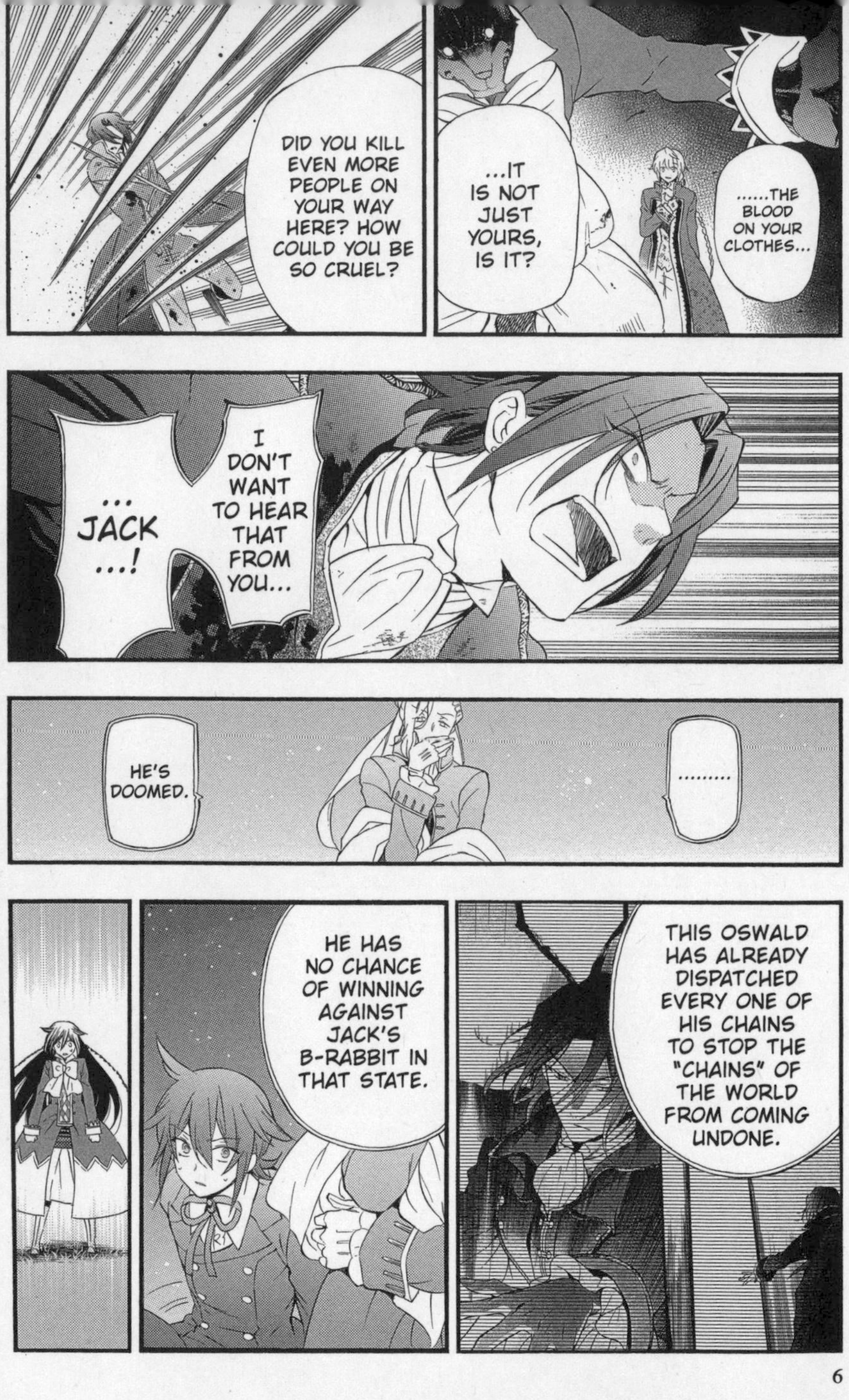
......THE BLOOD ON YOUR CLOTHES...
...IT IS NOT JUST YOURS, IS IT?
DID YOU KILL EVEN MORE PEOPLE ON YOUR WAY HERE? HOW COULD YOU BE SO CRUEL?
I DON'T WANT TO HEAR THAT FROM YOU...
...JACK...!
....
HE'S DOOMED.
THIS OSWALD HAS ALREADY DISPATCHED EVERY ONE OF HIS CHAINS TO STOP THE "CHAINS" OF THE WORLD FROM COMING UNDONE.
HE HAS NO CHANCE OF WINNING AGAINST JACK'S B-RABBIT IN THAT STATE.

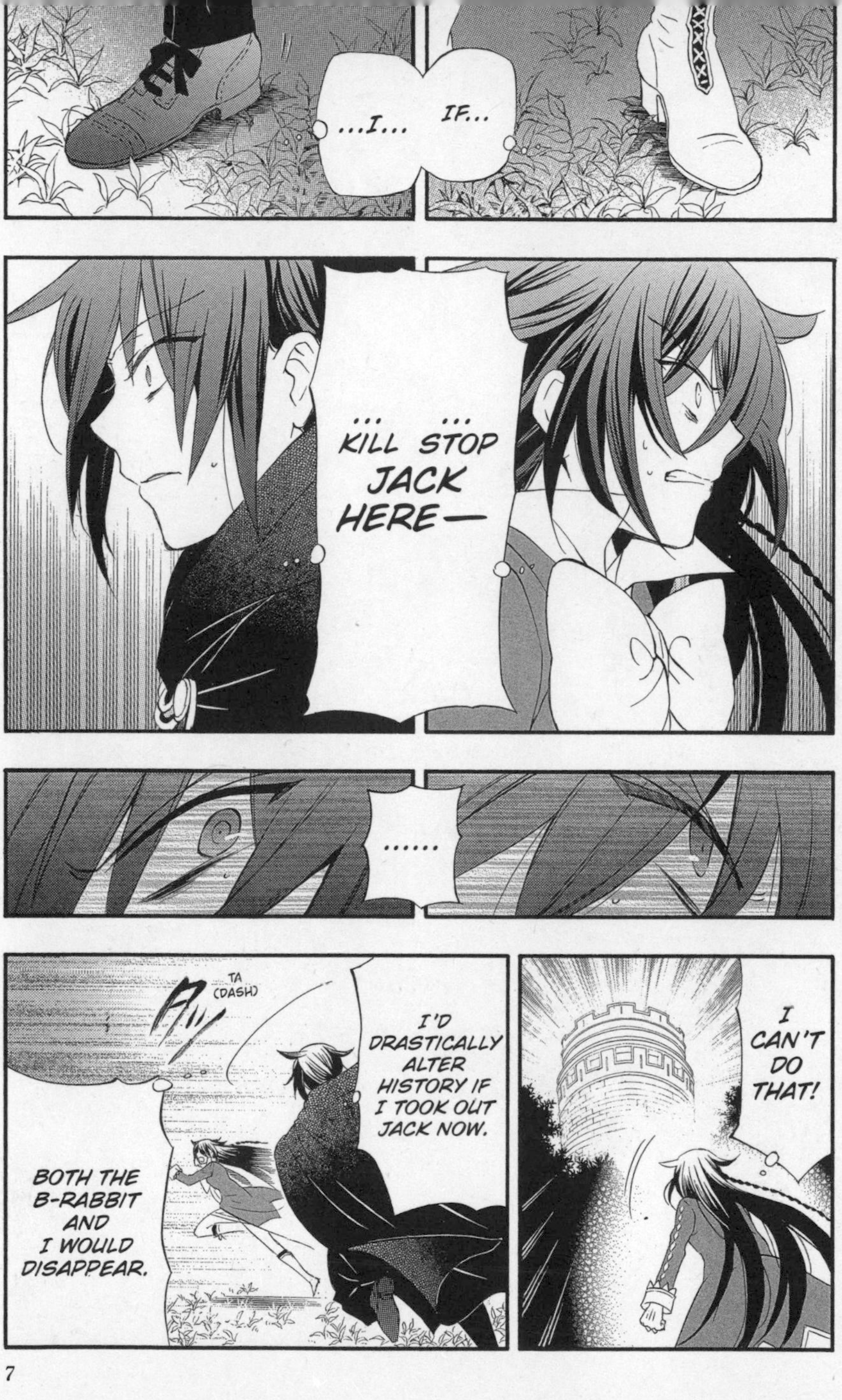
IF...
...I...
... ... KILL STOP JACK HERE—
......
I CAN'T DO THAT!
I'D DRASTICALLY ALTER HISTORY IF I TOOK OUT JACK NOW.
TA (DASH)
BOTH THE B-RABBIT AND I WOULD DISAPPEAR.

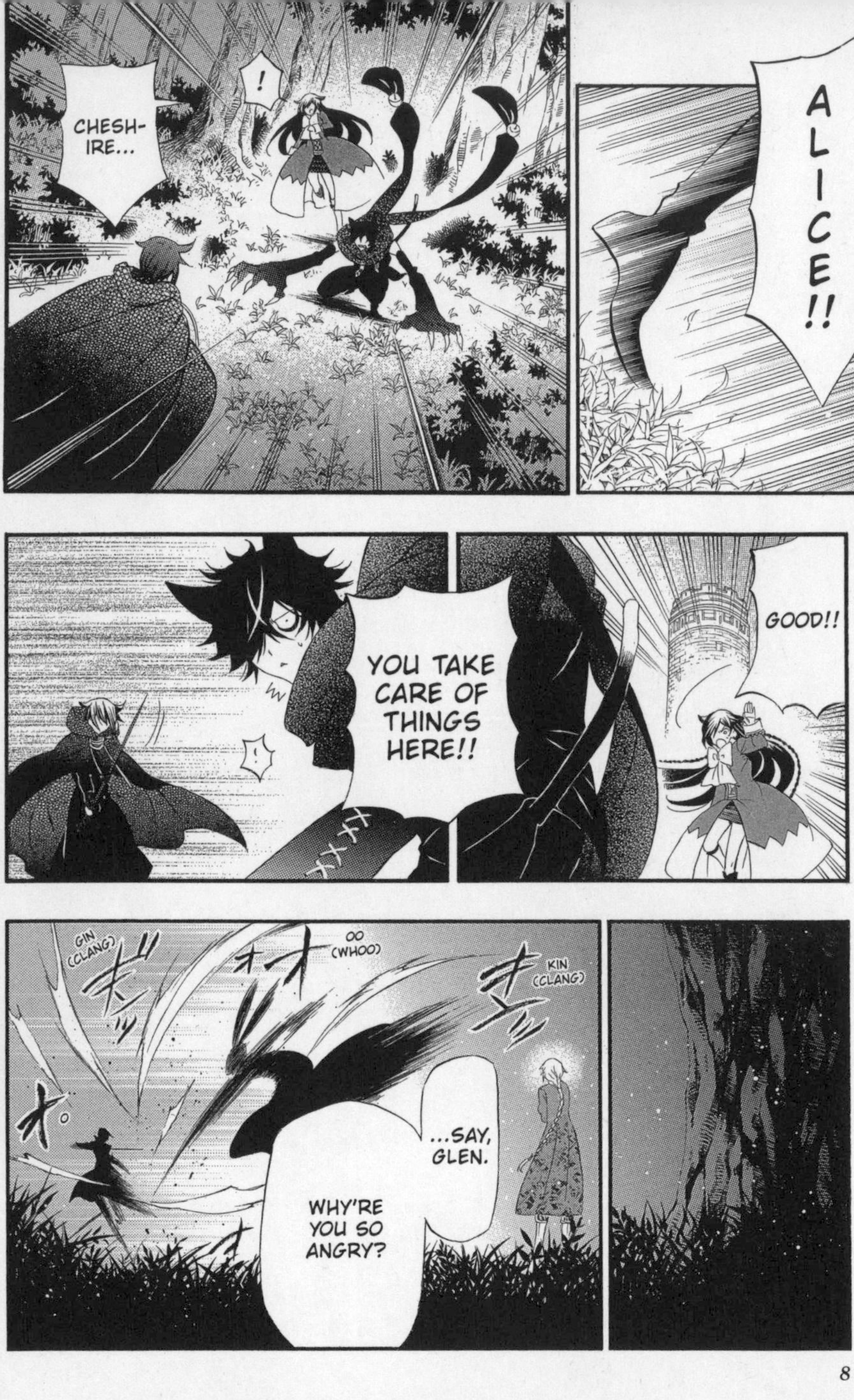
ALICE!!
CHESH-IRE...
!
GOOD!!
YOU TAKE CARE OF THINGS HERE!!
!
KIN (CLANG)
OO (WHOO)
GIN (CLANG)
...SAY, GLEN.
WHY'RE YOU SO ANGRY?

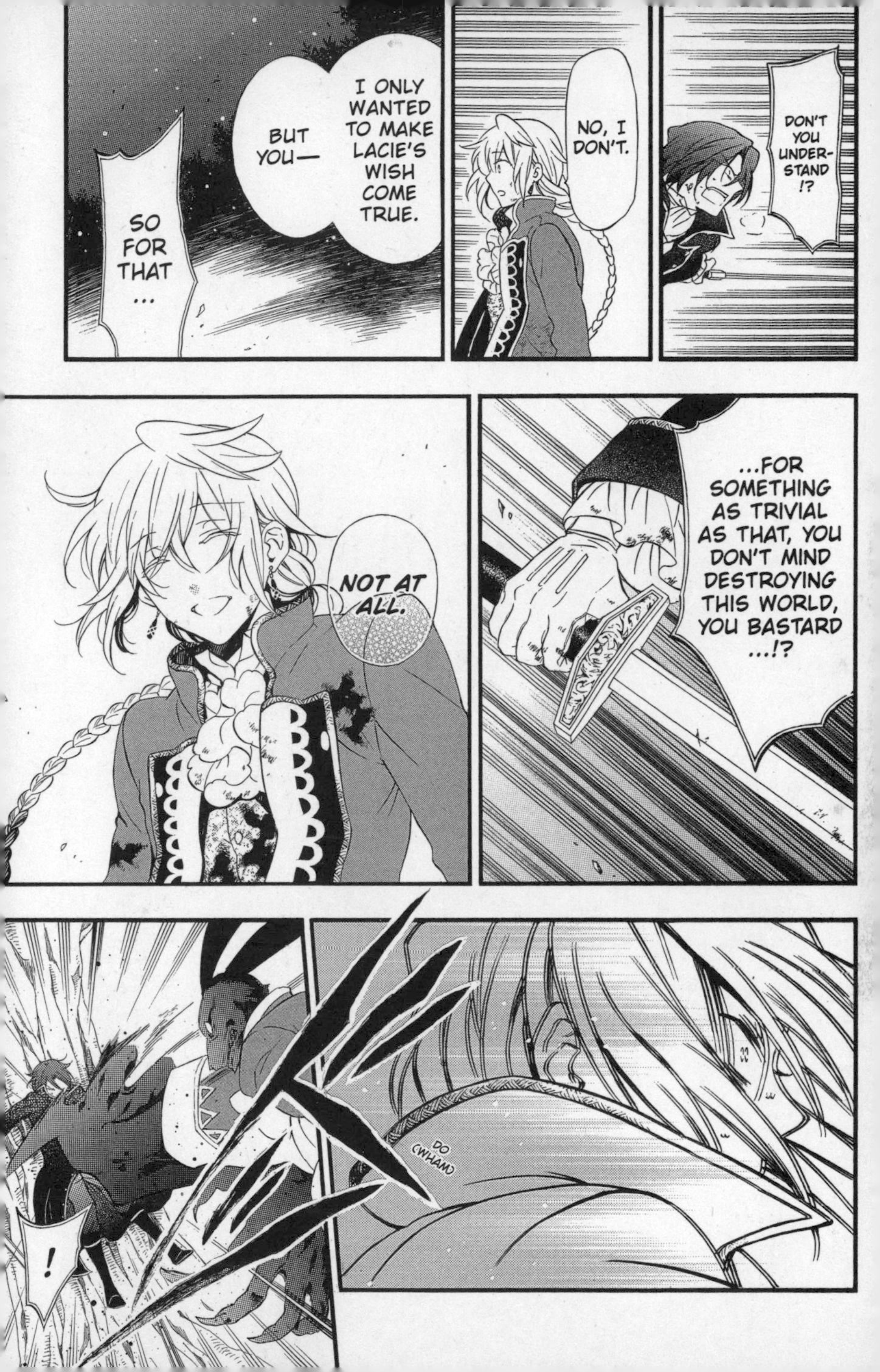
DON'T YOU UNDER-STAND!?
NO, I DON'T.
I ONLY WANTED TO MAKE LACIE'S WISH COME TRUE.
BUT YOU—
SO FOR THAT...
...FOR SOMETHING AS TRIVIAL AS THAT, YOU DON'T MIND DESTROYING THIS WORLD, YOU BASTARD...!?
NOT AT ALL.
DO (WHAM)
!

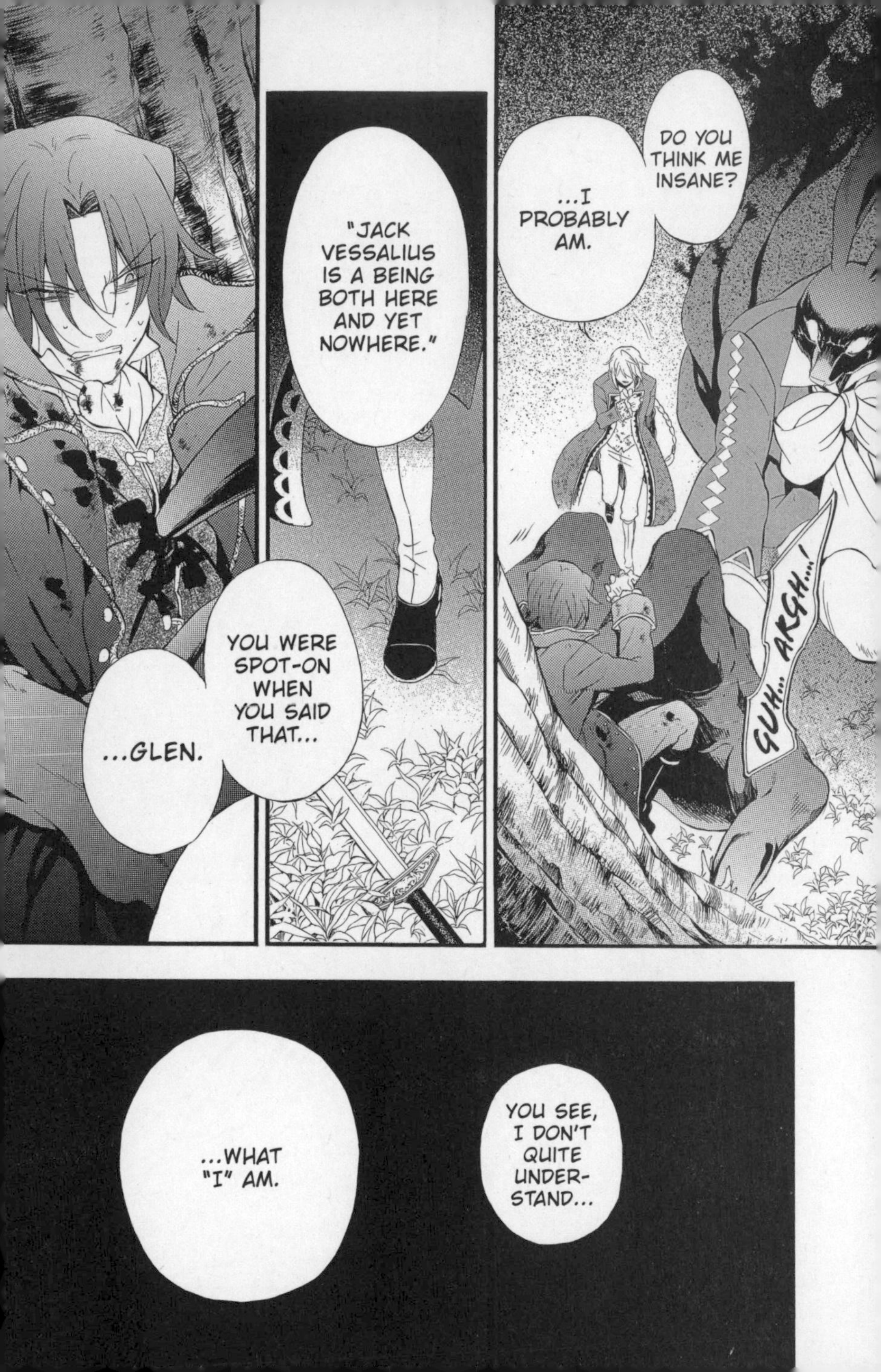
DO YOU THINK ME INSANE?
...I PROBABLY AM.
GUH... ARGH...!
"JACK VESSALIUS IS A BEING BOTH HERE AND YET NOWHERE."
YOU WERE SPOT-ON WHEN YOU SAID THAT...
...GLEN.
YOU SEE, I DON'T QUITE UNDER-STAND...
...WHAT "I" AM.

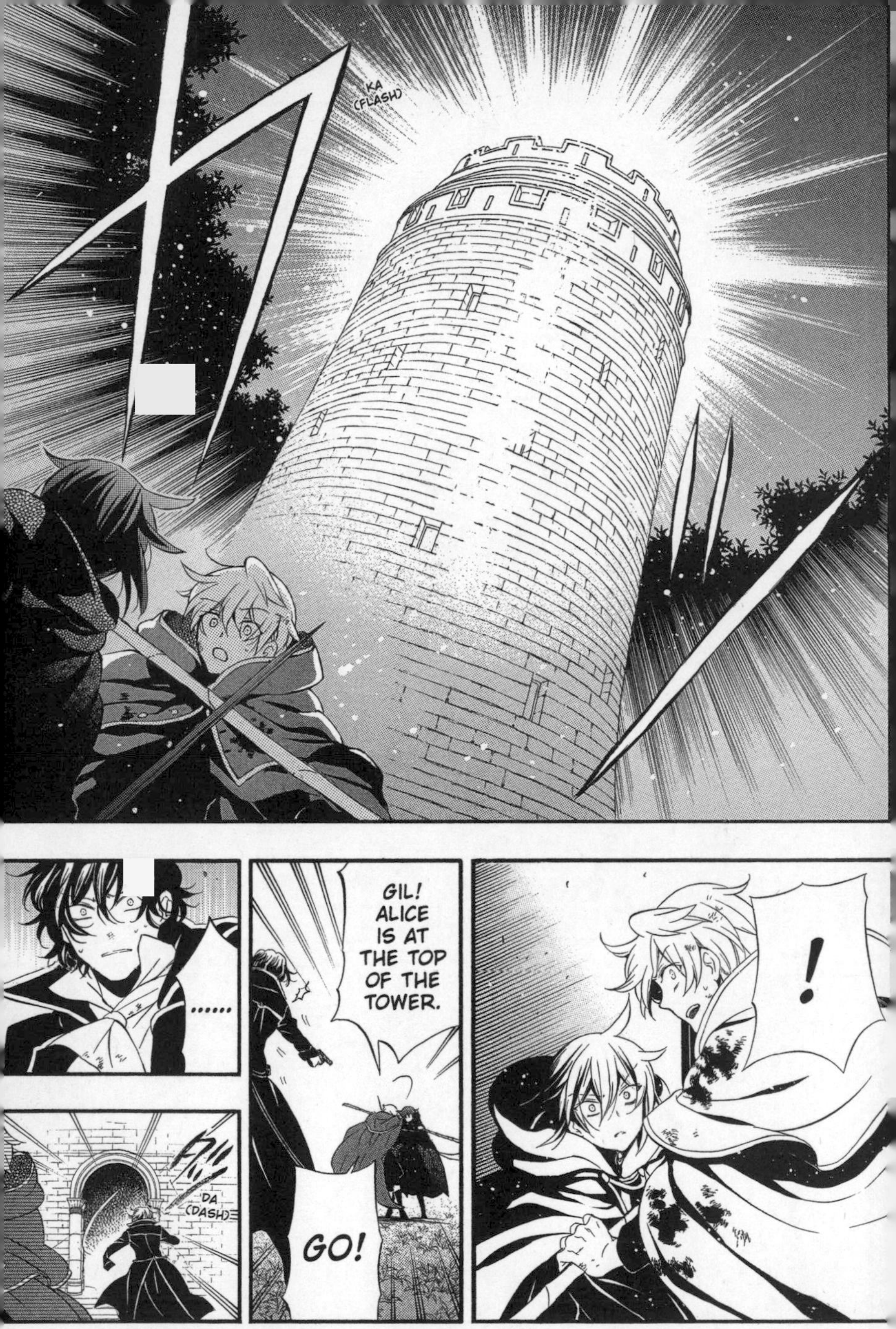
KA
(FLASH)
!
GIL! ALICE IS AT THE TOP OF THE TOWER.
GO!
......
DA
(DASH)

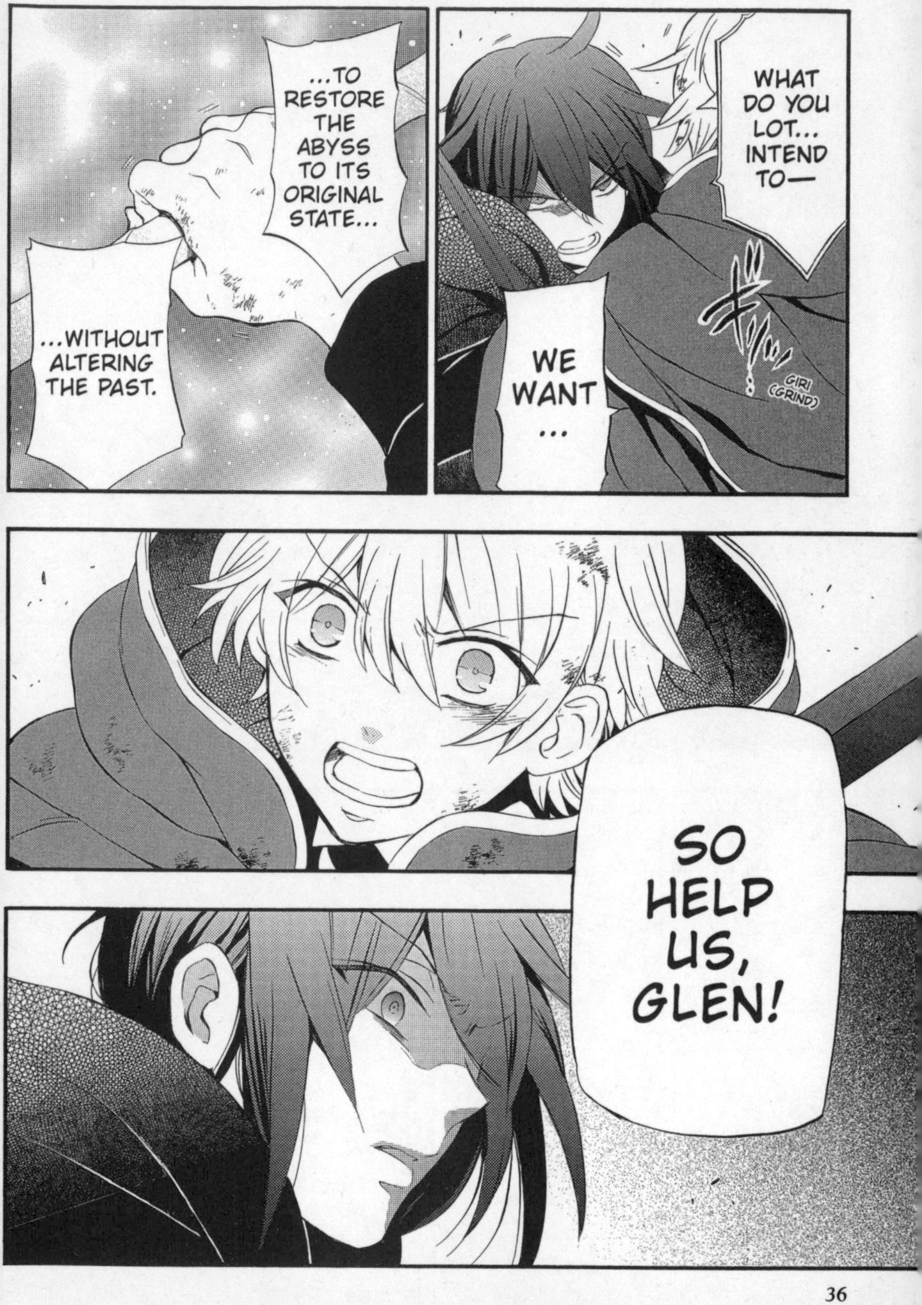
WHAT DO YOU LOT... INTEND TO—
GIRI (GRIND)
WE WANT ...
...TO RESTORE THE ABYSS TO ITS ORIGINAL STATE...
...WITHOUT ALTERING THE PAST.
SO HELP US, GLEN!

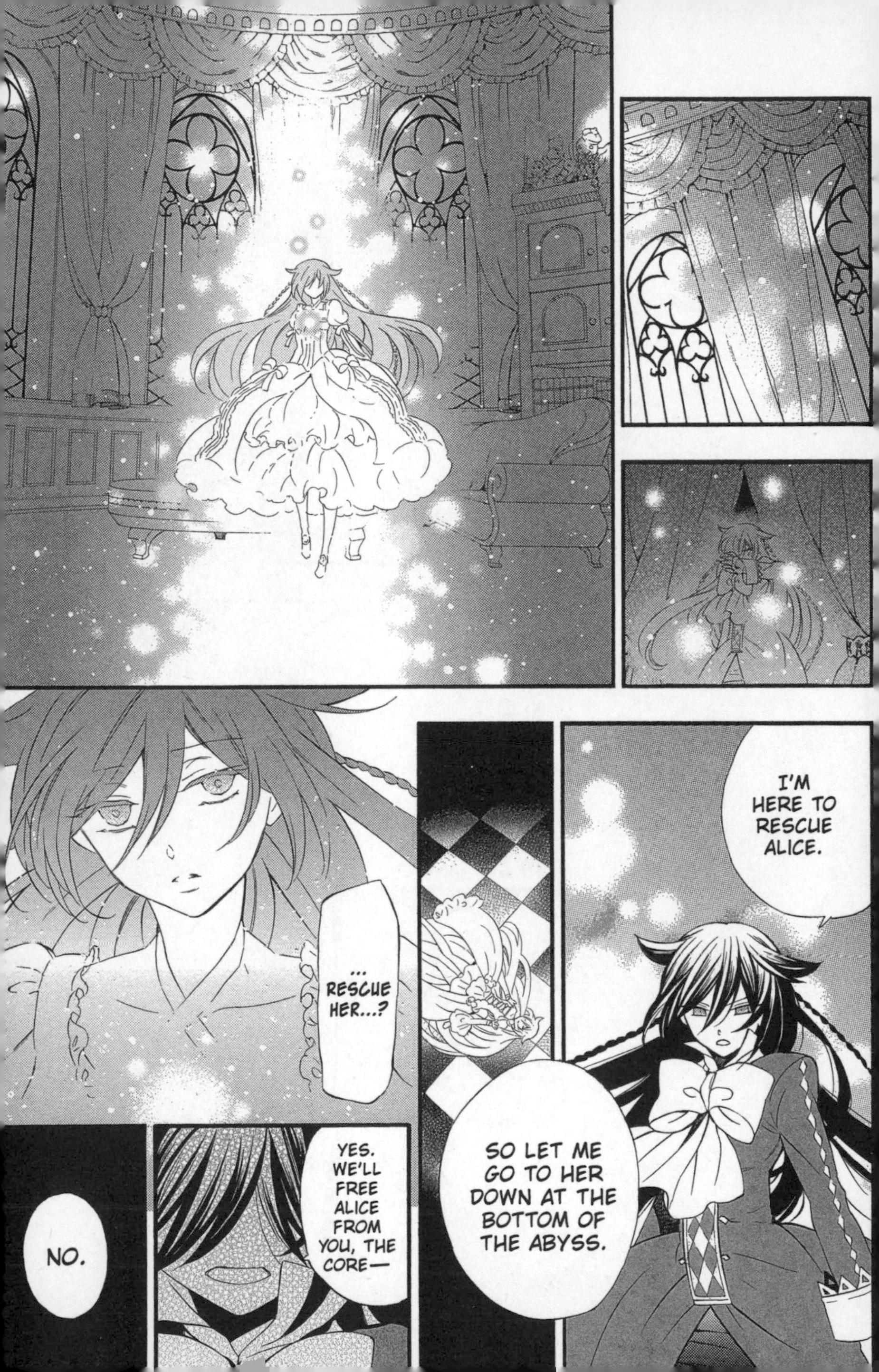
I'M HERE TO RESCUE ALICE.
SO LET ME GO TO HER DOWN AT THE BOTTOM OF THE ABYSS.
...RESCUE HER...?
YES. WE'LL FREE ALICE FROM YOU, THE CORE—
NO.

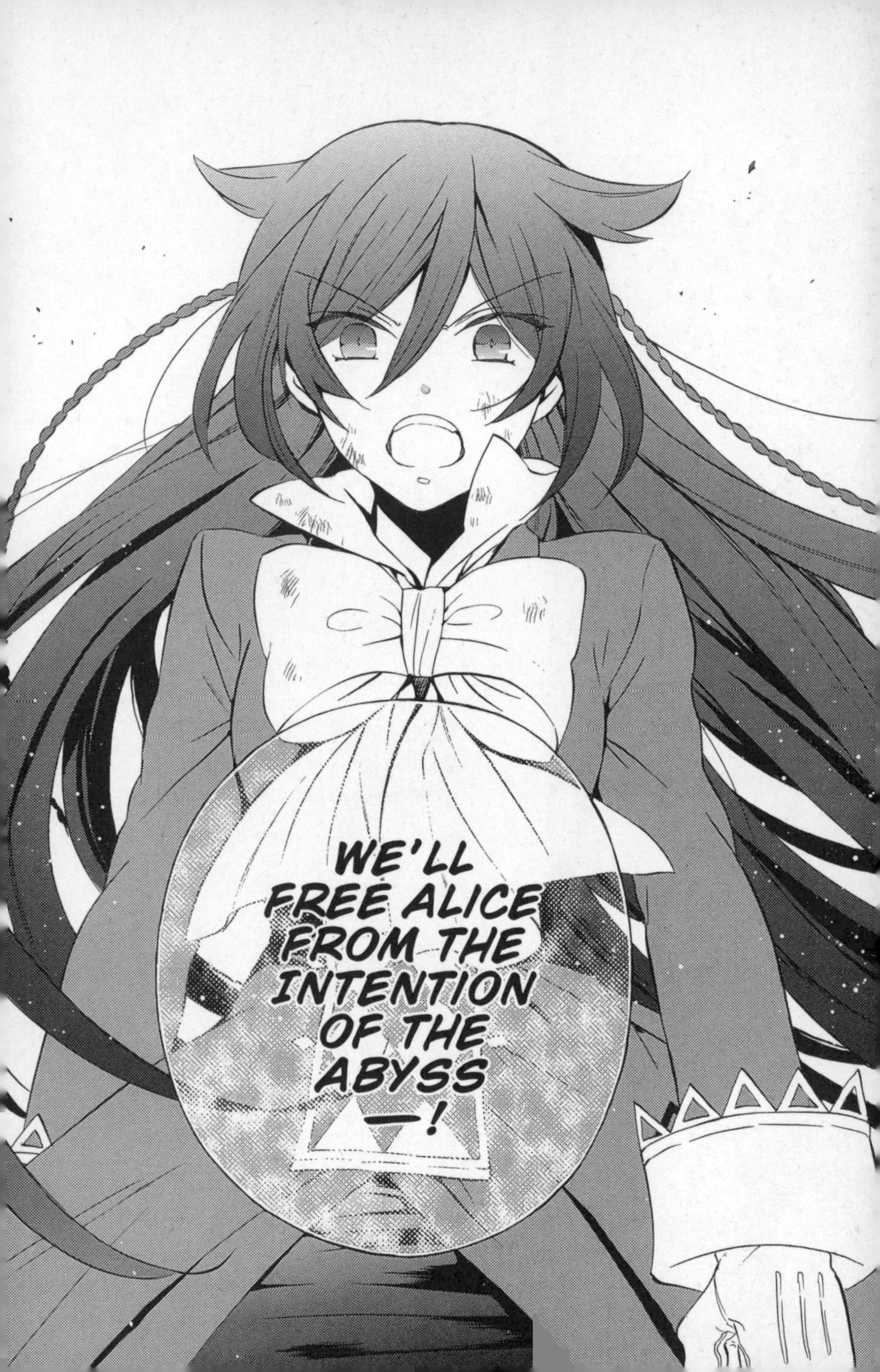
WE'LL FREE ALICE FROM THE INTENTION OF THE ABYSS—!

Retrace:XCIX Shade

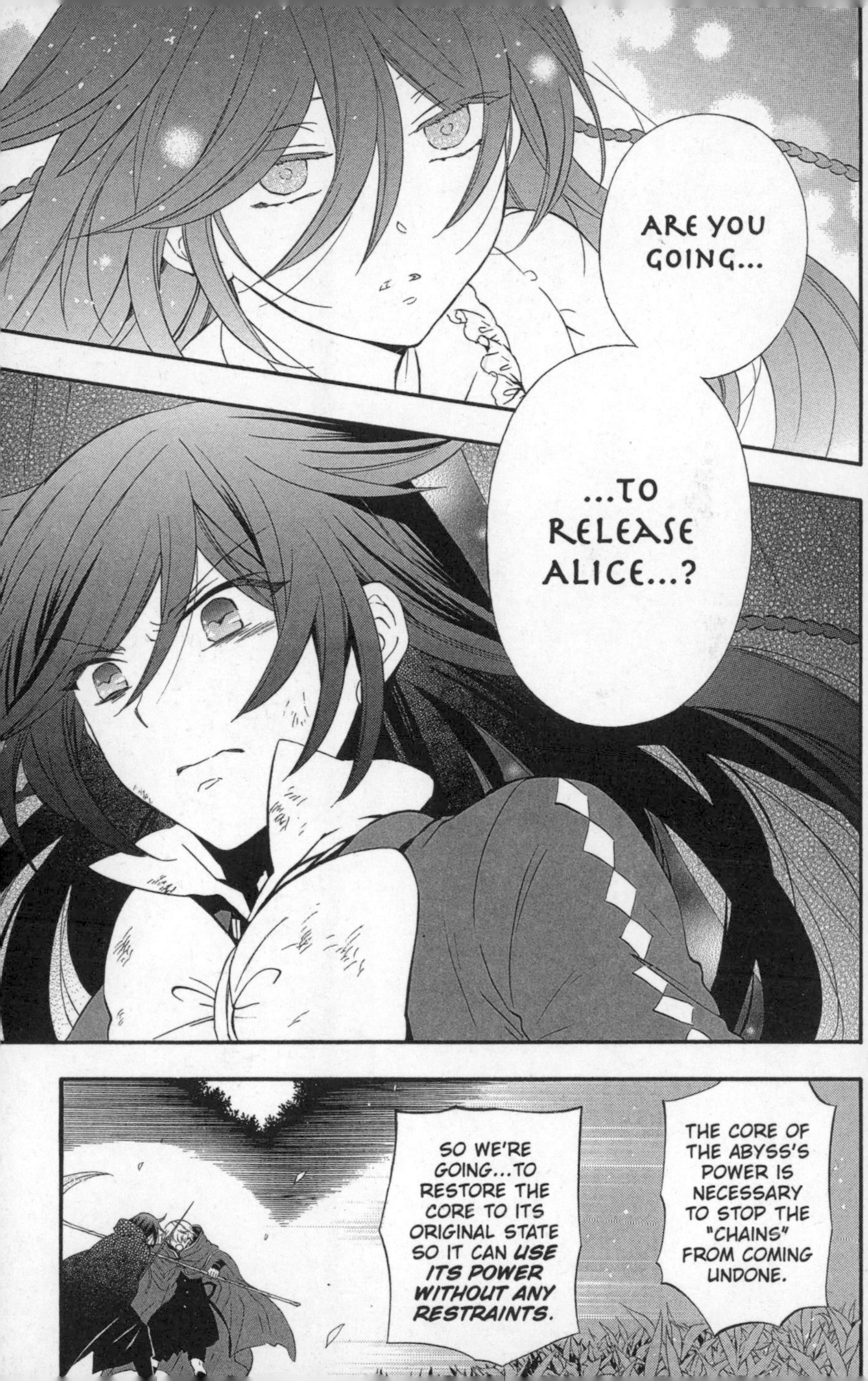
ARE YOU GOING...
...TO RELEASE ALICE...?
THE CORE OF THE ABYSS'S POWER IS NECESSARY TO STOP THE "CHAINS" FROM COMING UNDONE.
SO WE'RE GOING...TO RESTORE THE CORE TO ITS ORIGINAL STATE SO IT CAN *USE ITS POWER WITHOUT ANY RESTRAINTS*.

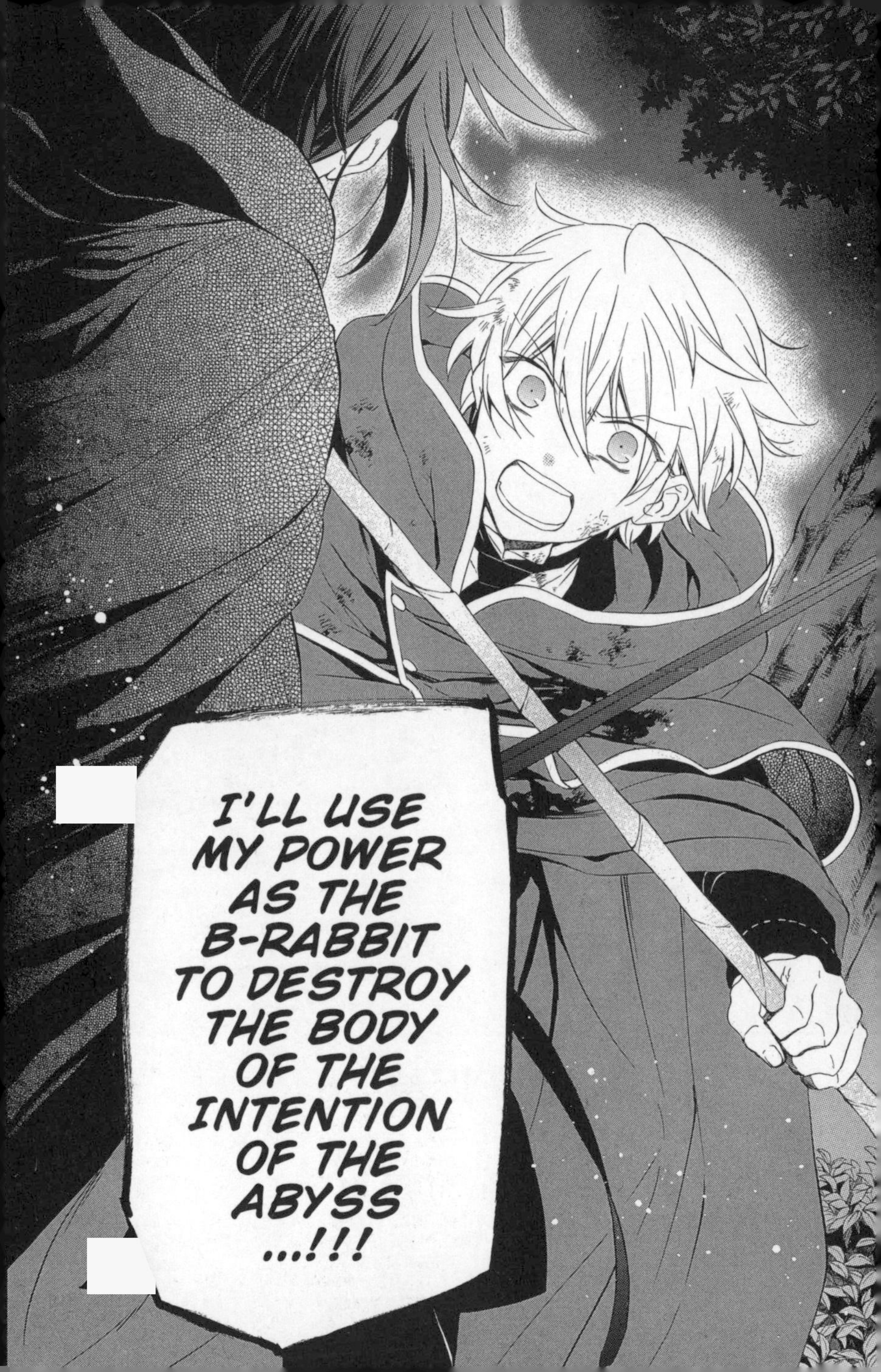
I'LL USE MY POWER AS THE B-RABBIT TO DESTROY THE BODY OF THE INTENTION OF THE ABYSS ...!!!

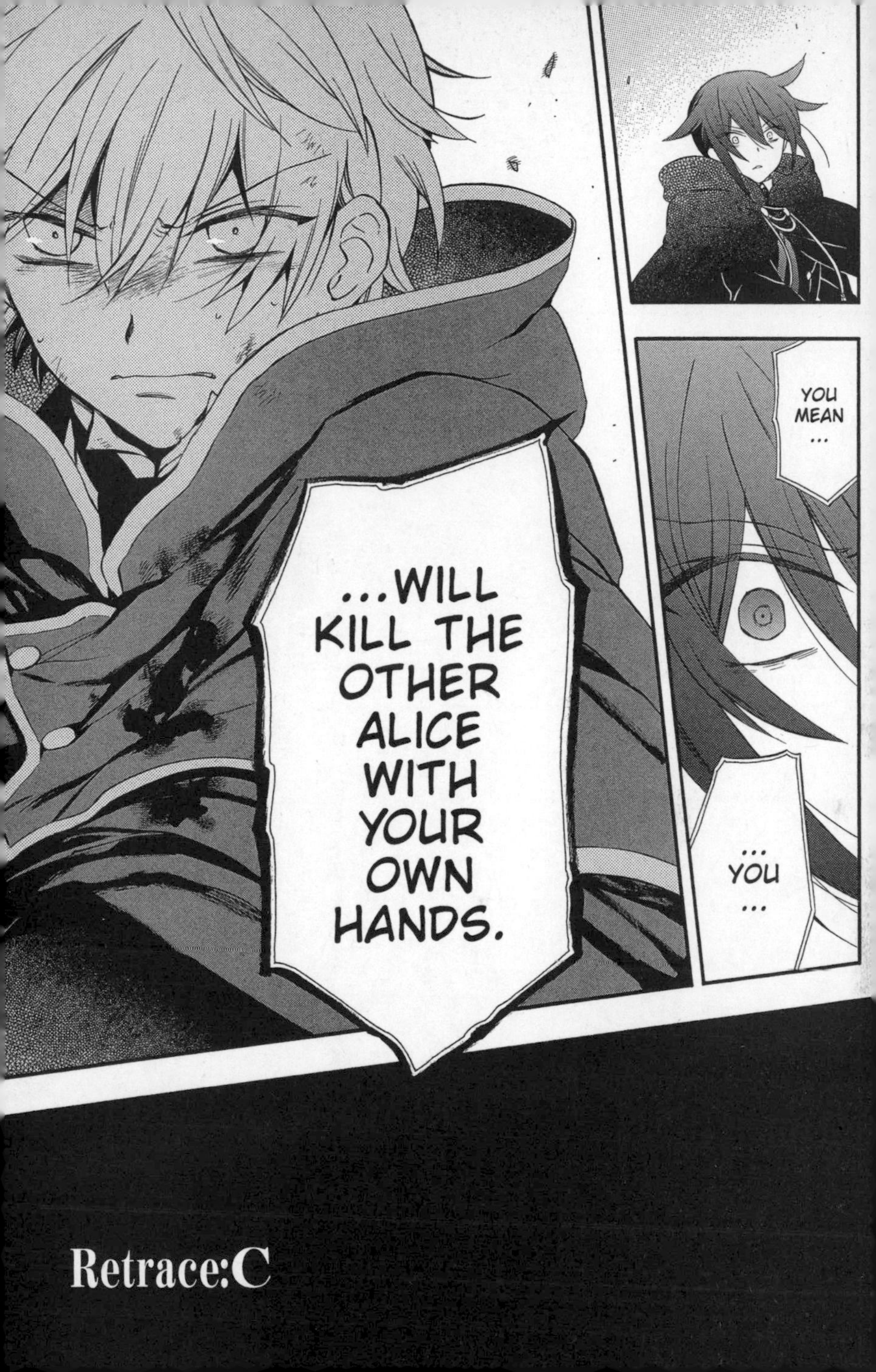
YOU MEAN ...
... YOU ...
...WILL KILL THE OTHER ALICE WITH YOUR OWN HANDS.

Retrace:C

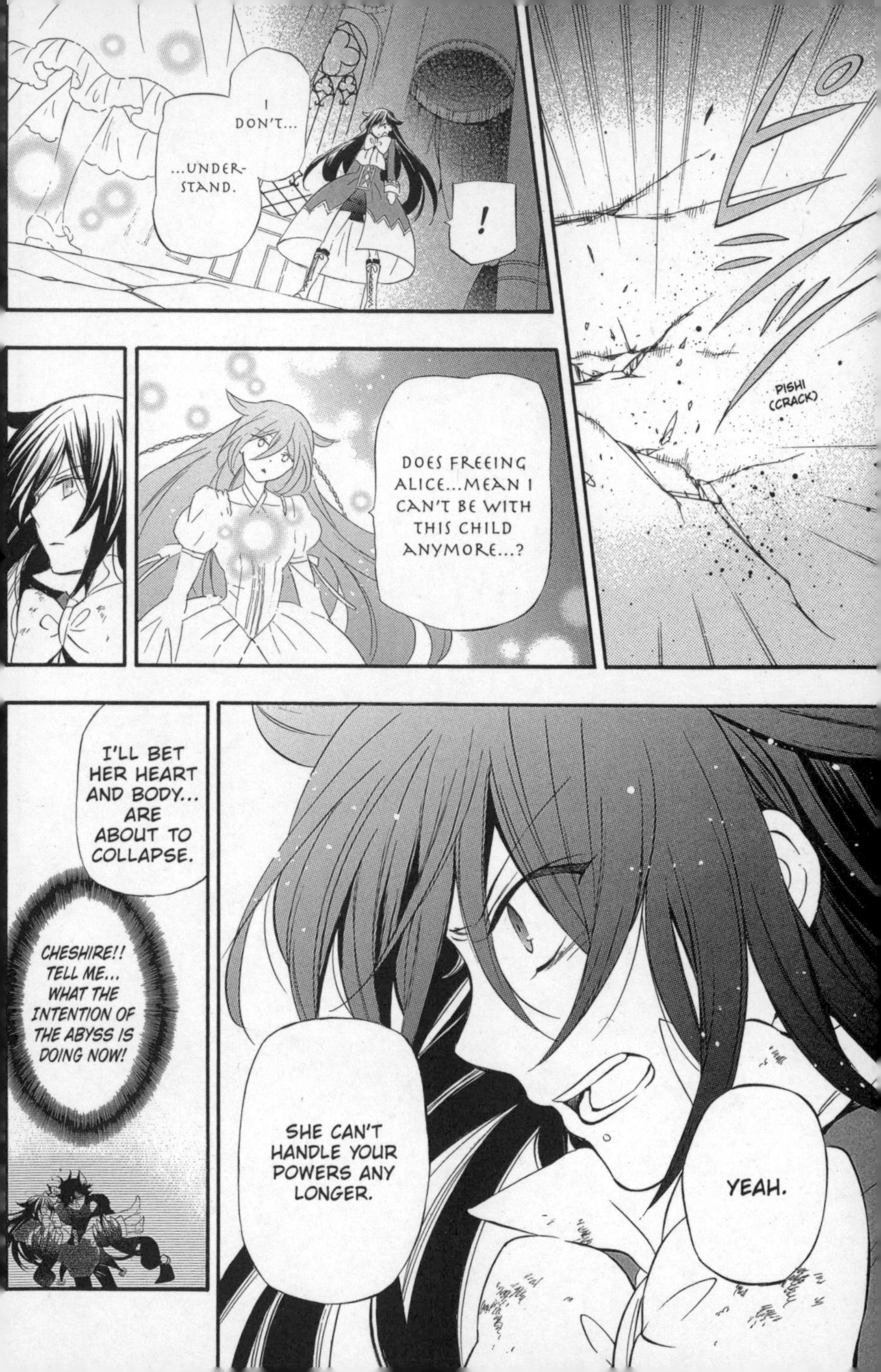
PISHI (CRACK)
I DON'T... ...UNDER-STAND.
!
DOES FREEING ALICE...MEAN I CAN'T BE WITH THIS CHILD ANYMORE...?
YEAH.
SHE CAN'T HANDLE YOUR POWERS ANY LONGER.
I'LL BET HER HEART AND BODY... ARE ABOUT TO COLLAPSE.
CHESHIRE!! TELL ME... WHAT THE INTENTION OF THE ABYSS IS DOING NOW!

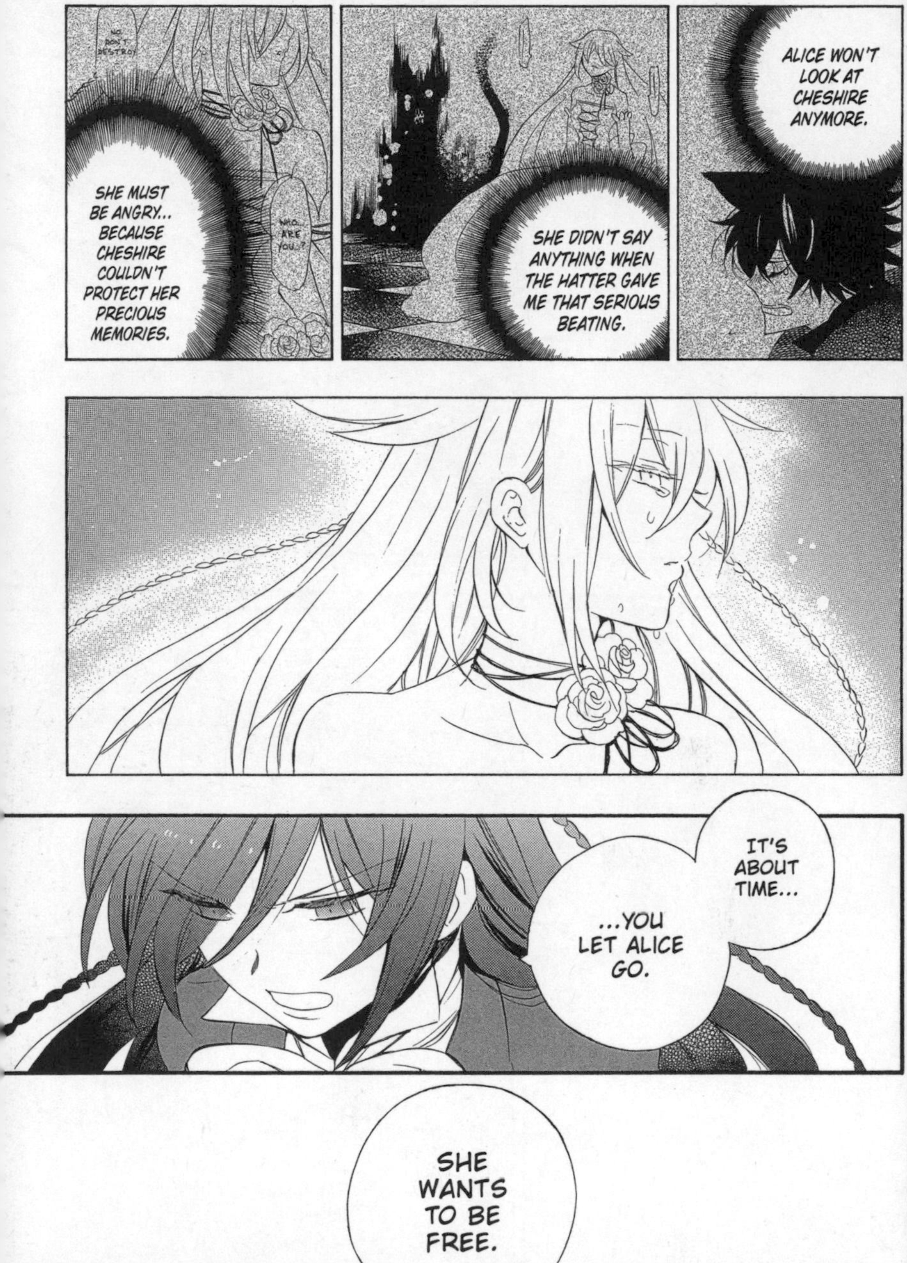
ALICE WON'T LOOK AT CHESHIRE ANYMORE.
SHE DIDN'T SAY ANYTHING WHEN THE HATTER GAVE ME THAT SERIOUS BEATING.
NO DON'T DESTROY
SHE MUST BE ANGRY... BECAUSE CHESHIRE COULDN'T PROTECT HER PRECIOUS MEMORIES.
WHO ARE YOU...?
IT'S ABOUT TIME...
...YOU LET ALICE GO.
SHE WANTS TO BE FREE.

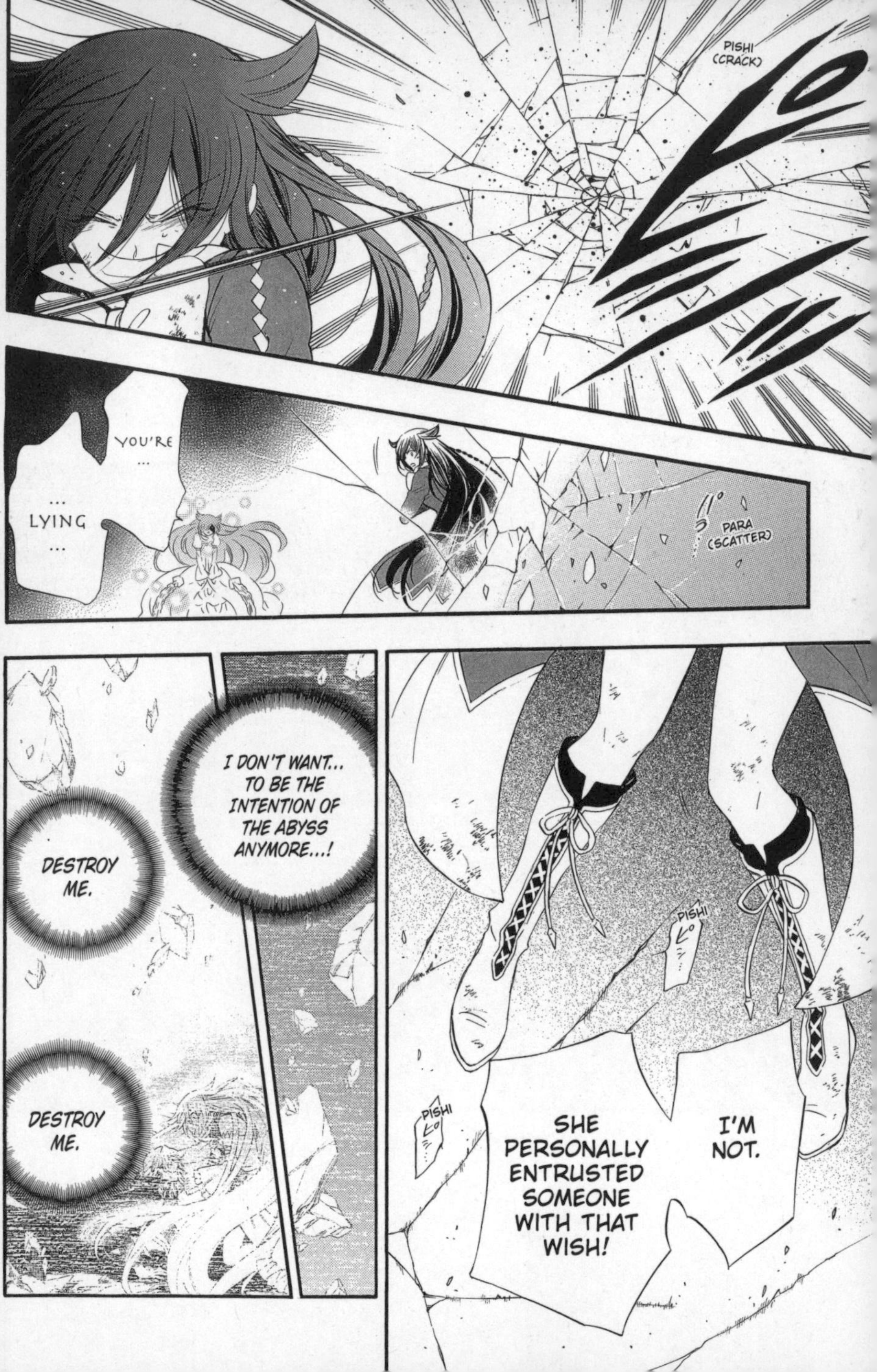
PISHI (CRACK)
PARA (SCATTER)
YOU'RE ...
... LYING ...
PISHI
I'M NOT.
SHE PERSONALLY ENTRUSTED SOMEONE WITH THAT WISH!
PISHI
I DON'T WANT... TO BE THE INTENTION OF THE ABYSS ANYMORE...!
DESTROY ME.
DESTROY ME.

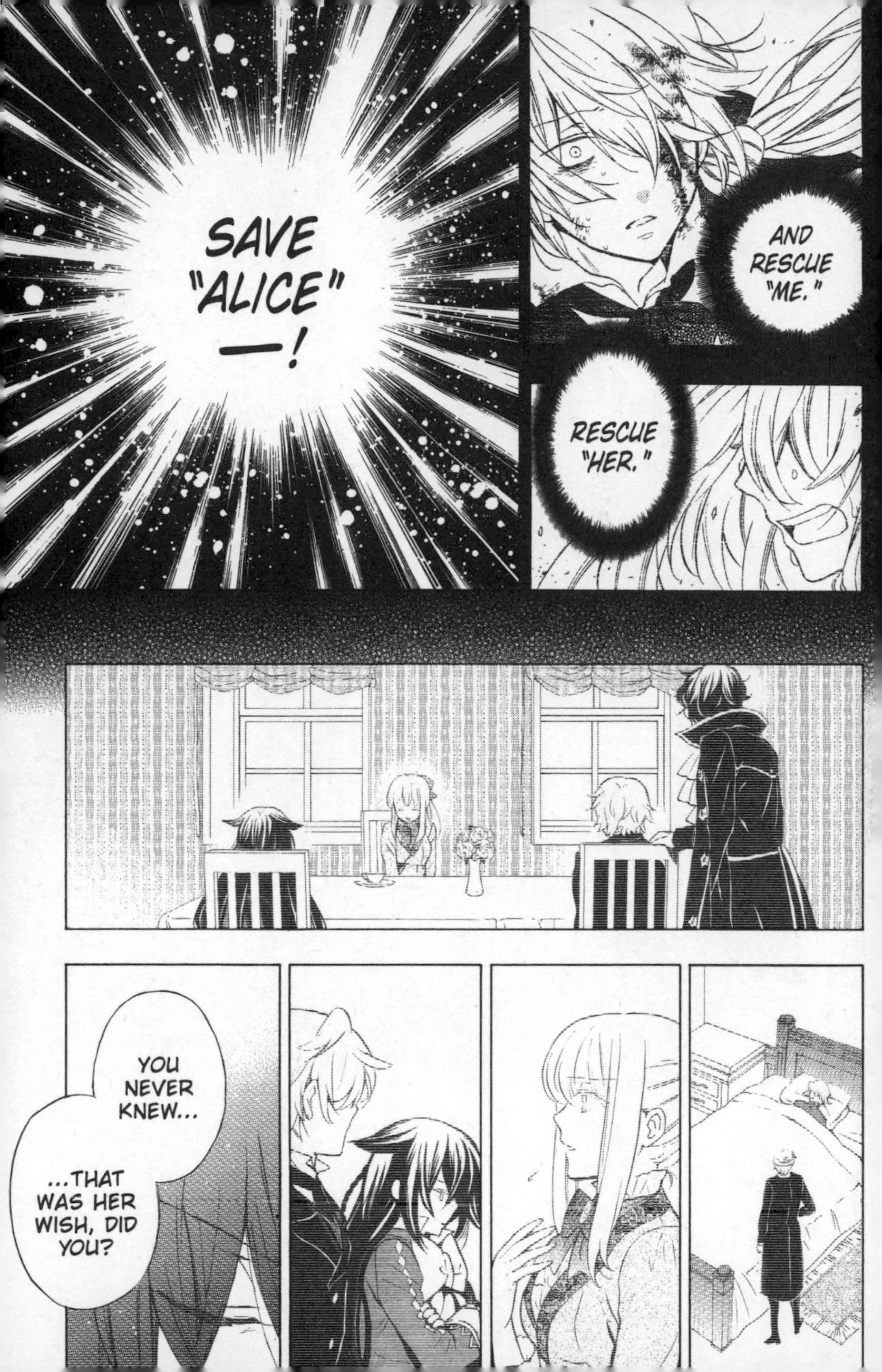
AND RESCUE "ME."
RESCUE "HER."
SAVE "ALICE" —!
YOU NEVER KNEW...
...THAT WAS HER WISH, DID YOU?

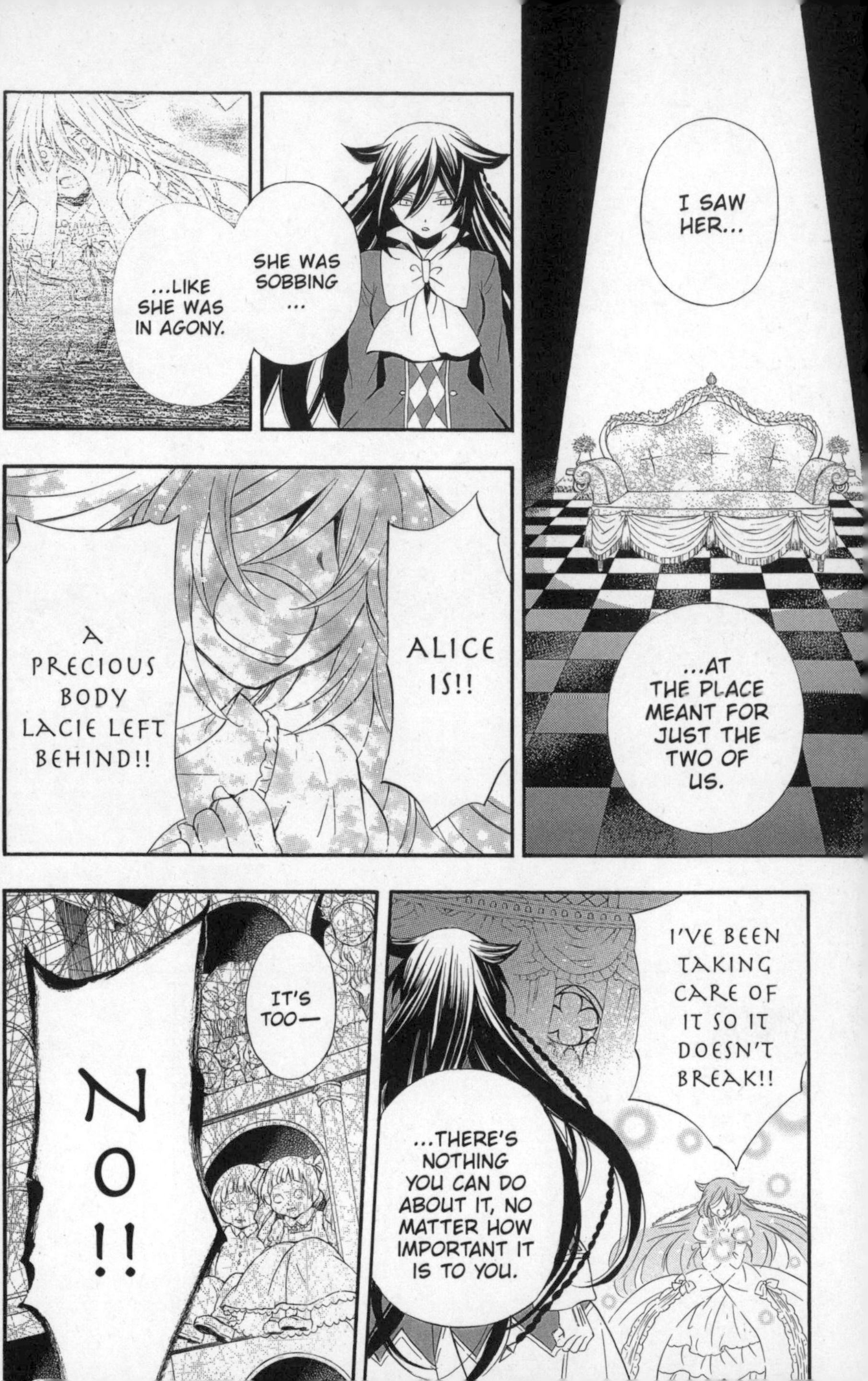
I SAW HER...
...AT THE PLACE MEANT FOR JUST THE TWO OF US.
SHE WAS SOBBING ...
...LIKE SHE WAS IN AGONY.
ALICE IS!!
A PRECIOUS BODY LACIE LEFT BEHIND!!
I'VE BEEN TAKING CARE OF IT SO IT DOESN'T BREAK!!
...THERE'S NOTHING YOU CAN DO ABOUT IT, NO MATTER HOW IMPORTANT IT IS TO YOU.
IT'S TOO—
NO!!

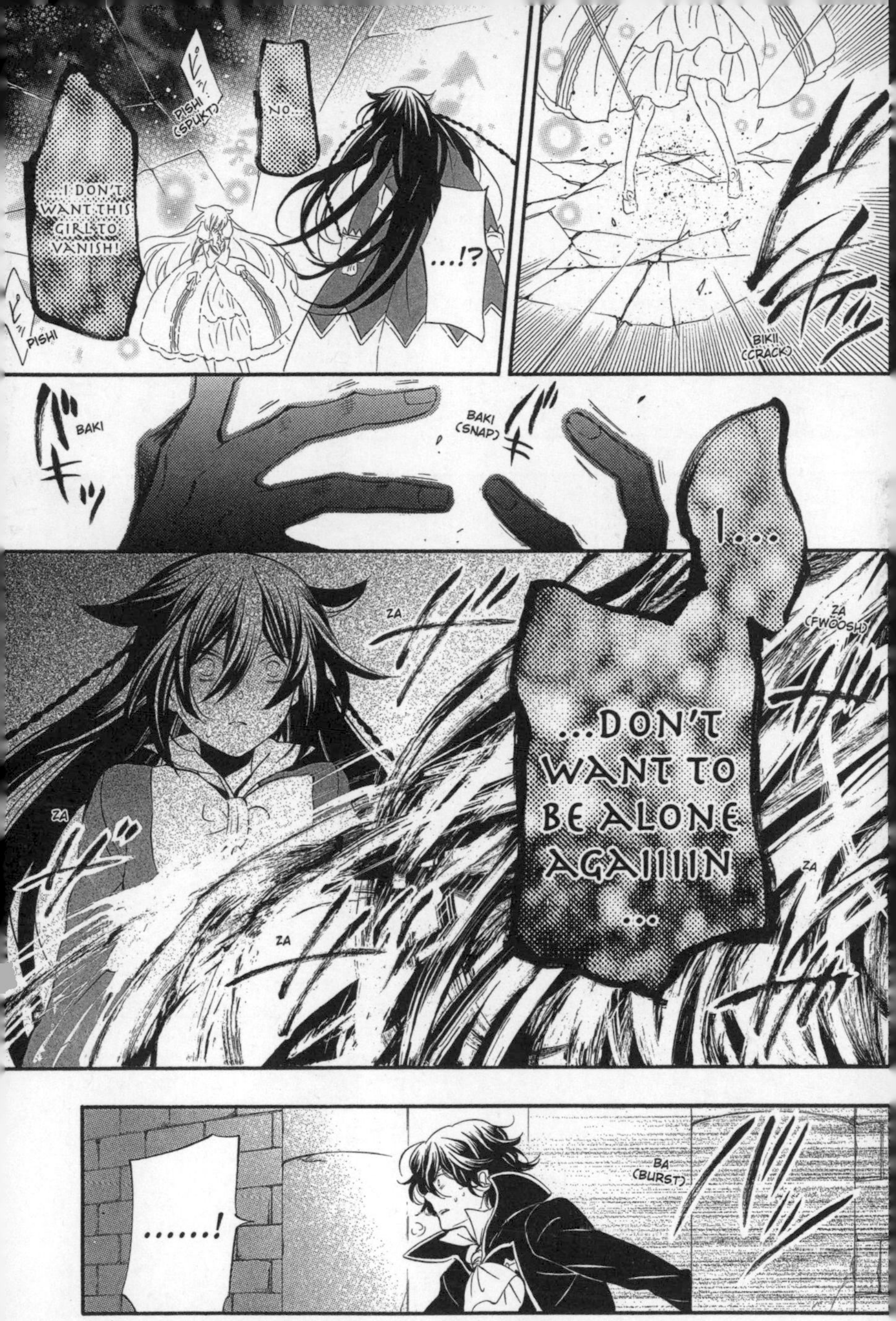
BIKII (CRACK)
No...
PISHI (SPUKT)
...I DON'T WANT THIS GIRL TO VANISH!
...!?
PISHI
BAKI (SNAP)
BAKI
I...
...DON'T WANT TO BE ALONE AGAIIIIN...
ZA (FWOOSH)
ZA
ZA
ZA
ZA
BA (BURST)
......!

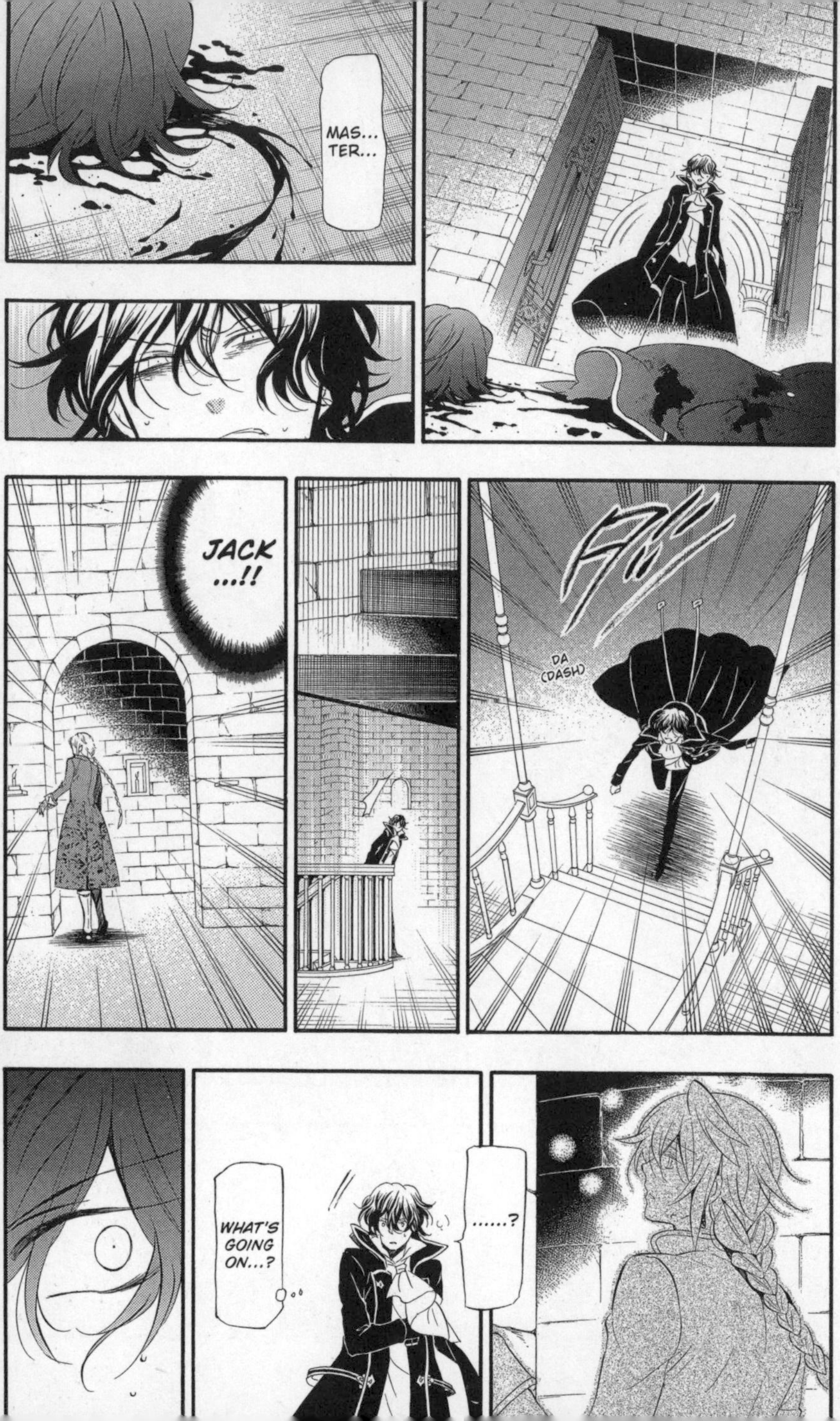

MAS... TER...
DA (DASH)
JACK ...!!
......?
WHAT'S GOING ON...?

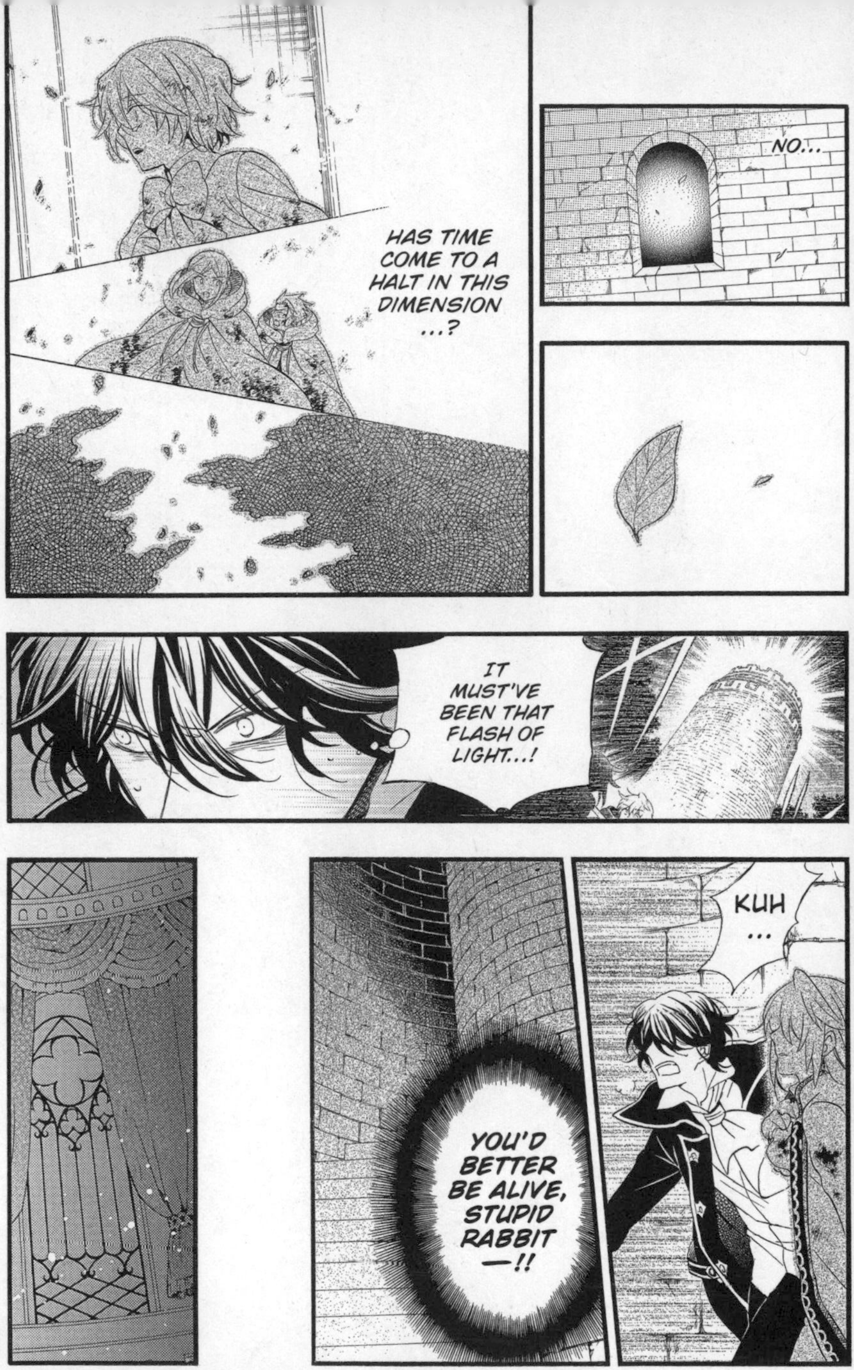
NO...
HAS TIME COME TO A HALT IN THIS DIMENSION ...?
IT MUST'VE BEEN THAT FLASH OF LIGHT...!
KUH ...
YOU'D BETTER BE ALIVE, STUPID RABBIT —!!

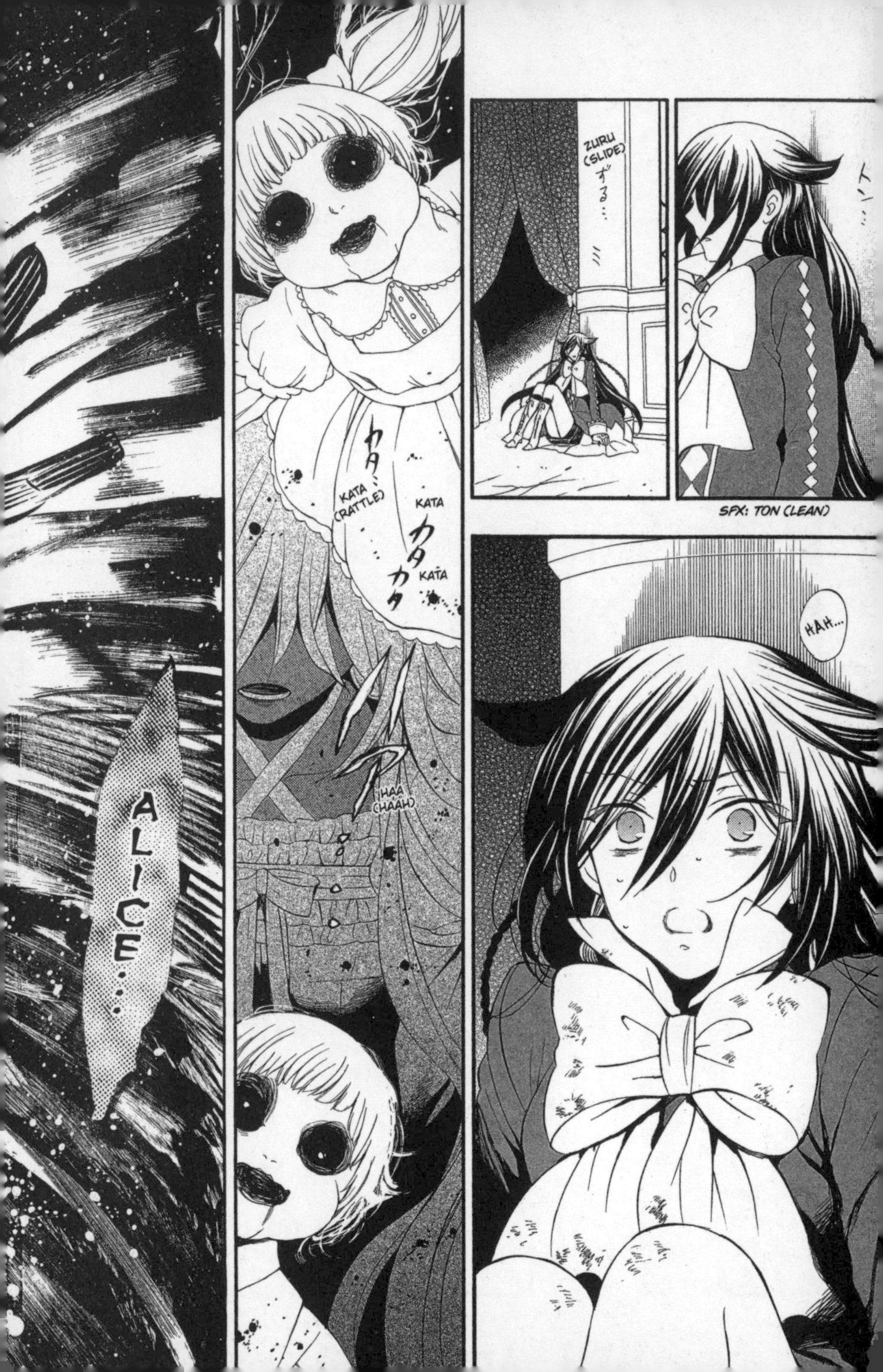
トン…
SFX: TON (LEAN)
ZURU (SLIDE)
ずる…
HAH…
カタ
KATA (RATTLE)
カタ
KATA
カタ
KATA
HAA (HAAH)
ALICE…

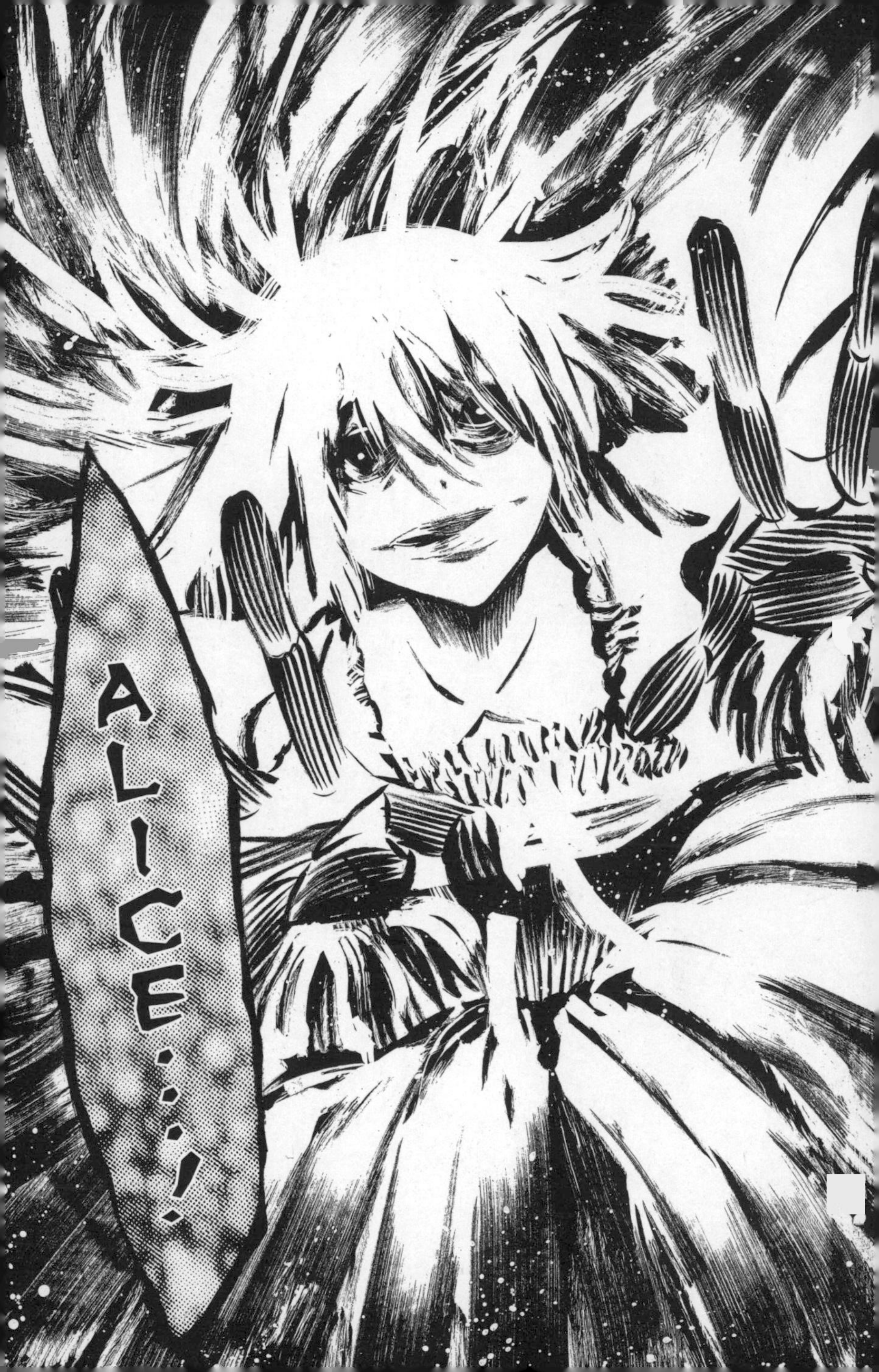
ALICE...!

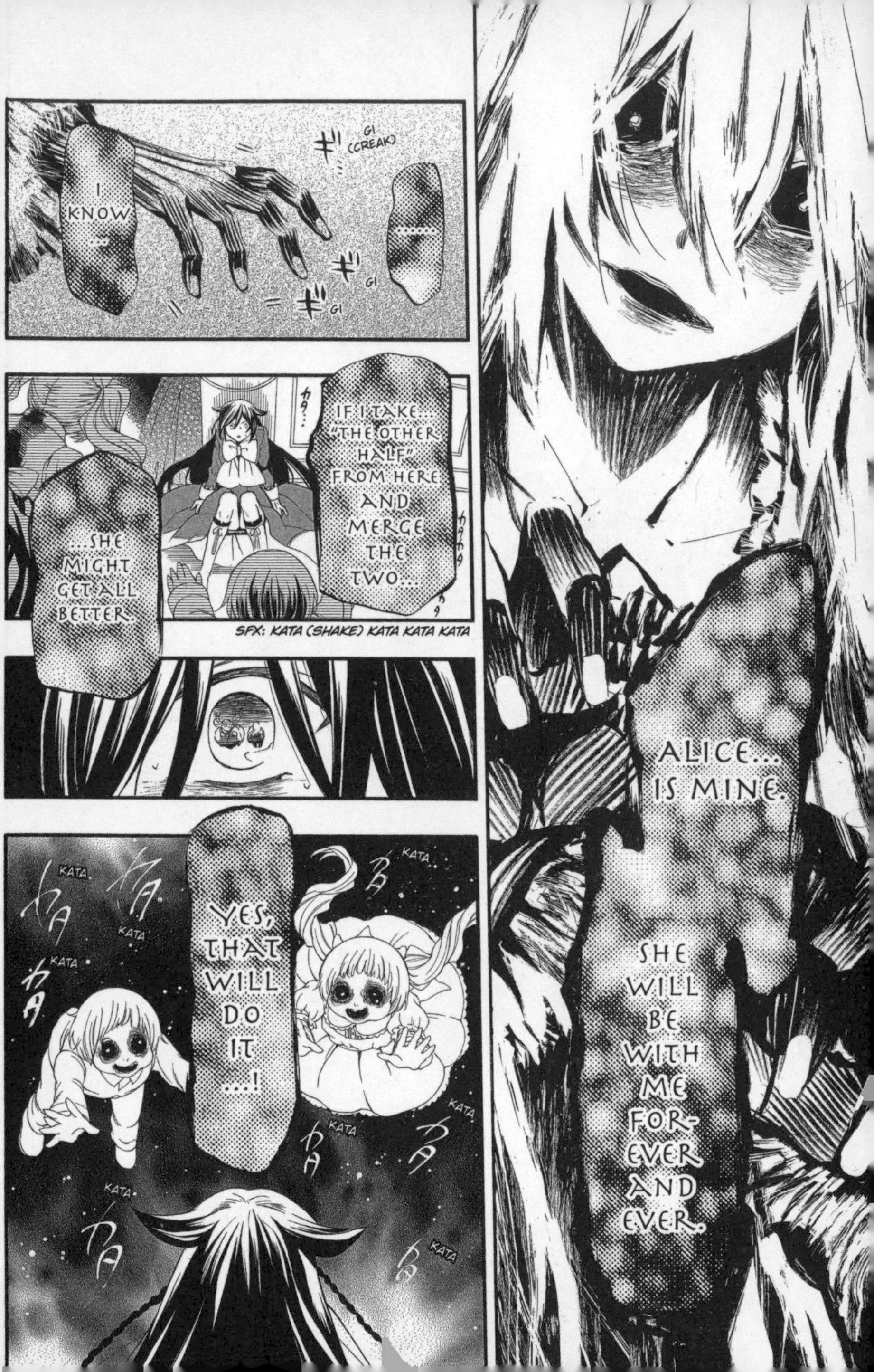
ALICE... IS MINE.
SHE WILL BE WITH ME FOR-EVER AND EVER.
GI (CREAK)
......
GI
GI
I KNOW...
IF I TAKE... "THE OTHER HALF" FROM HERE AND MERGE THE TWO...
...SHE MIGHT GET ALL BETTER.
SFX: KATA (SHAKE) KATA KATA KATA
KATA
YES, THAT WILL DO IT...!
KATA
KATA
KATA
KATA
KATA
KATA
KATA

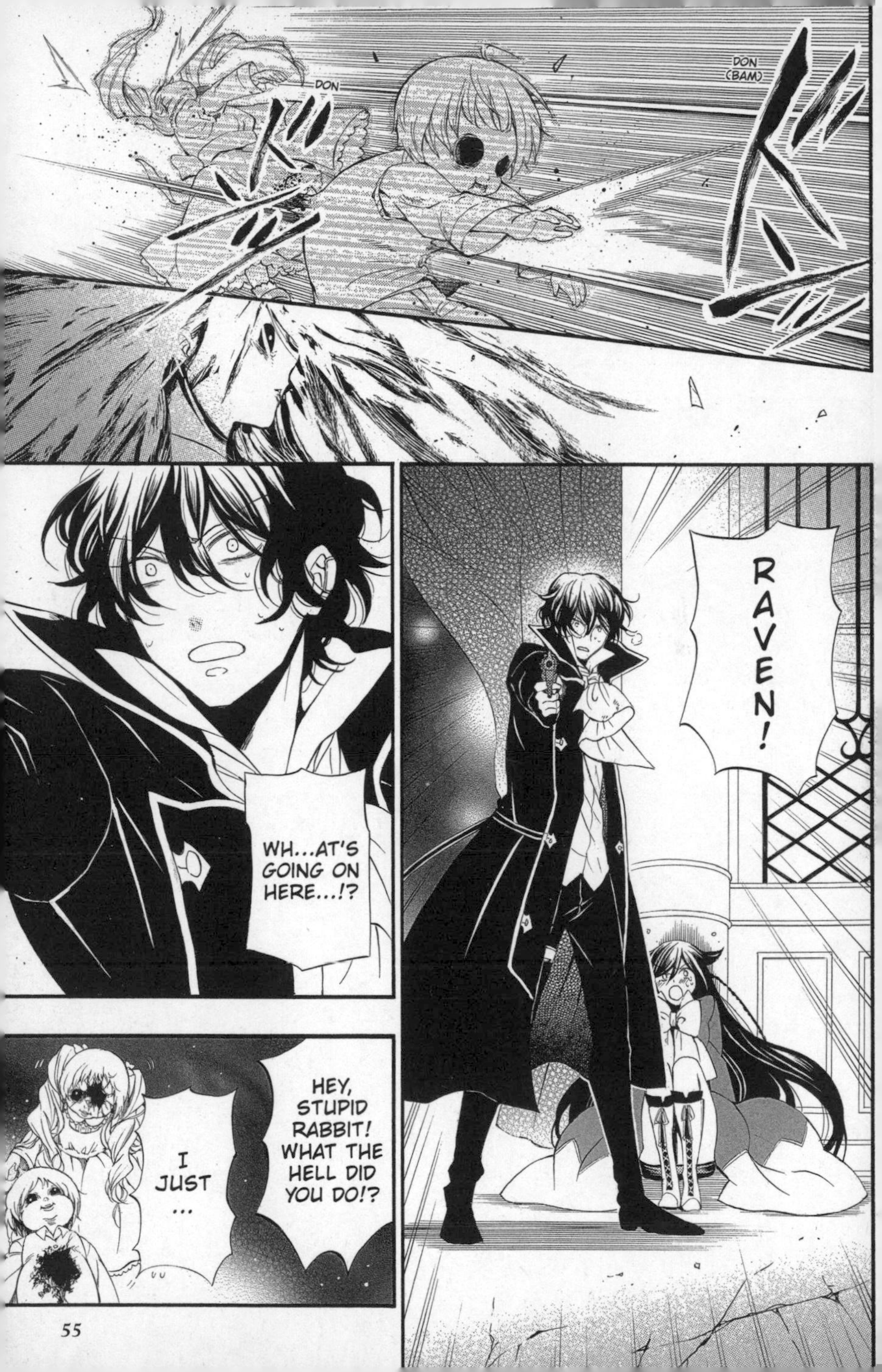
DON (BAM)
DON
RAVEN!
WH...AT'S GOING ON HERE...!?
HEY, STUPID RABBIT! WHAT THE HELL DID YOU DO!?
I JUST ...

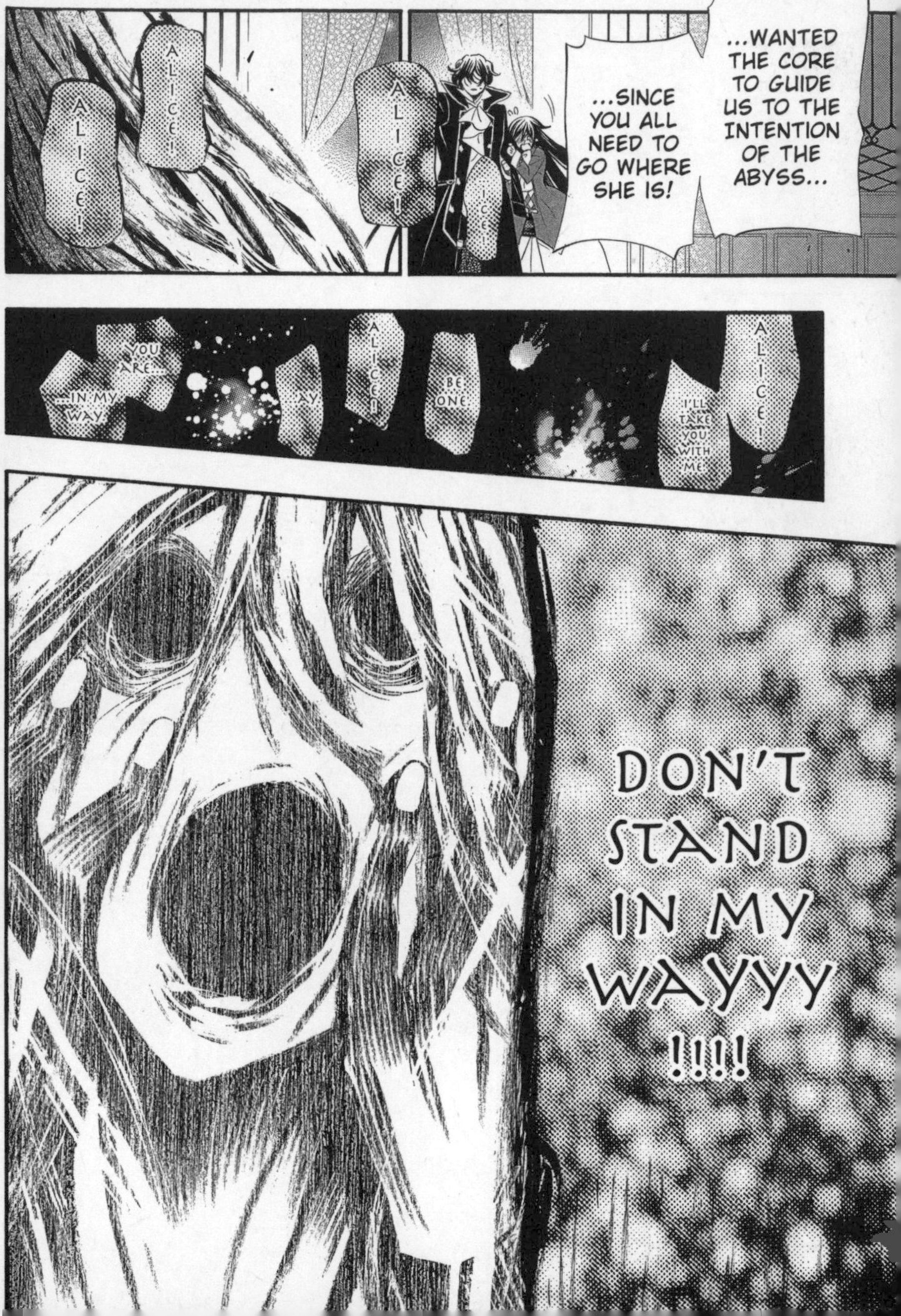
...WANTED THE CORE TO GUIDE US TO THE INTENTION OF THE ABYSS...
...SINCE YOU ALL NEED TO GO WHERE SHE IS!
ALICE!
ICE!
ALICE!
ALICE!
ALICE!
I'LL TAKE YOU WITH ME
BE ONE
ALICE!
AY
YOU ARE...
...IN MY WAY
DON'T STAND IN MY WAYYY!!!!

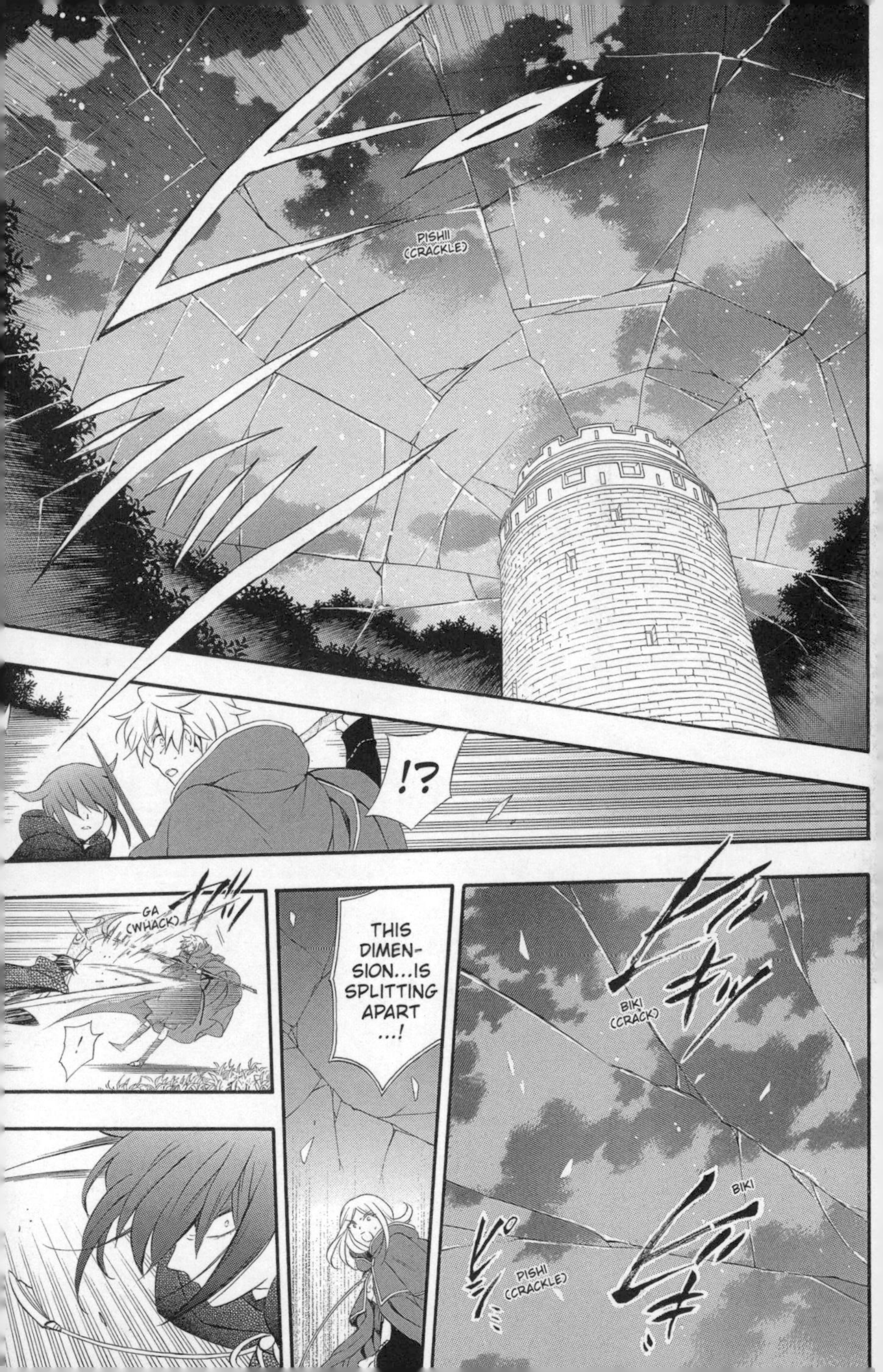
PISHII (CRACKLE)
!?
BIKI (CRACK)
BIKI
PISHI (CRACKLE)
THIS DIMENSION...IS SPLITTING APART...!
GA (WHACK)
!

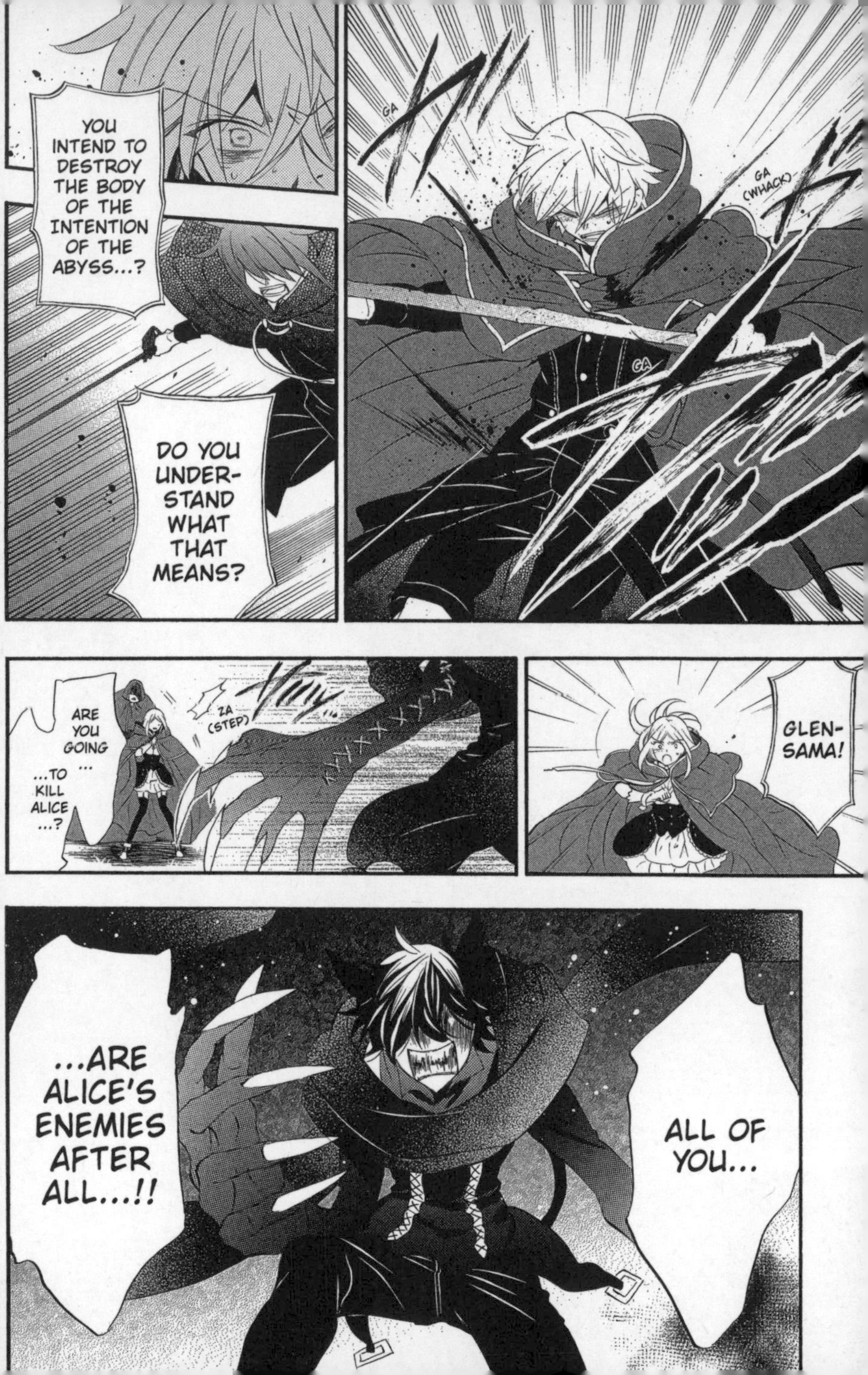
GA
GA (WHACK)
GA
YOU INTEND TO DESTROY THE BODY OF THE INTENTION OF THE ABYSS...?
DO YOU UNDER-STAND WHAT THAT MEANS?
GLEN-SAMA!
ZA (STEP)
ARE YOU GOING...
...TO KILL ALICE...?
ALL OF YOU...
...ARE ALICE'S ENEMIES AFTER ALL...!!

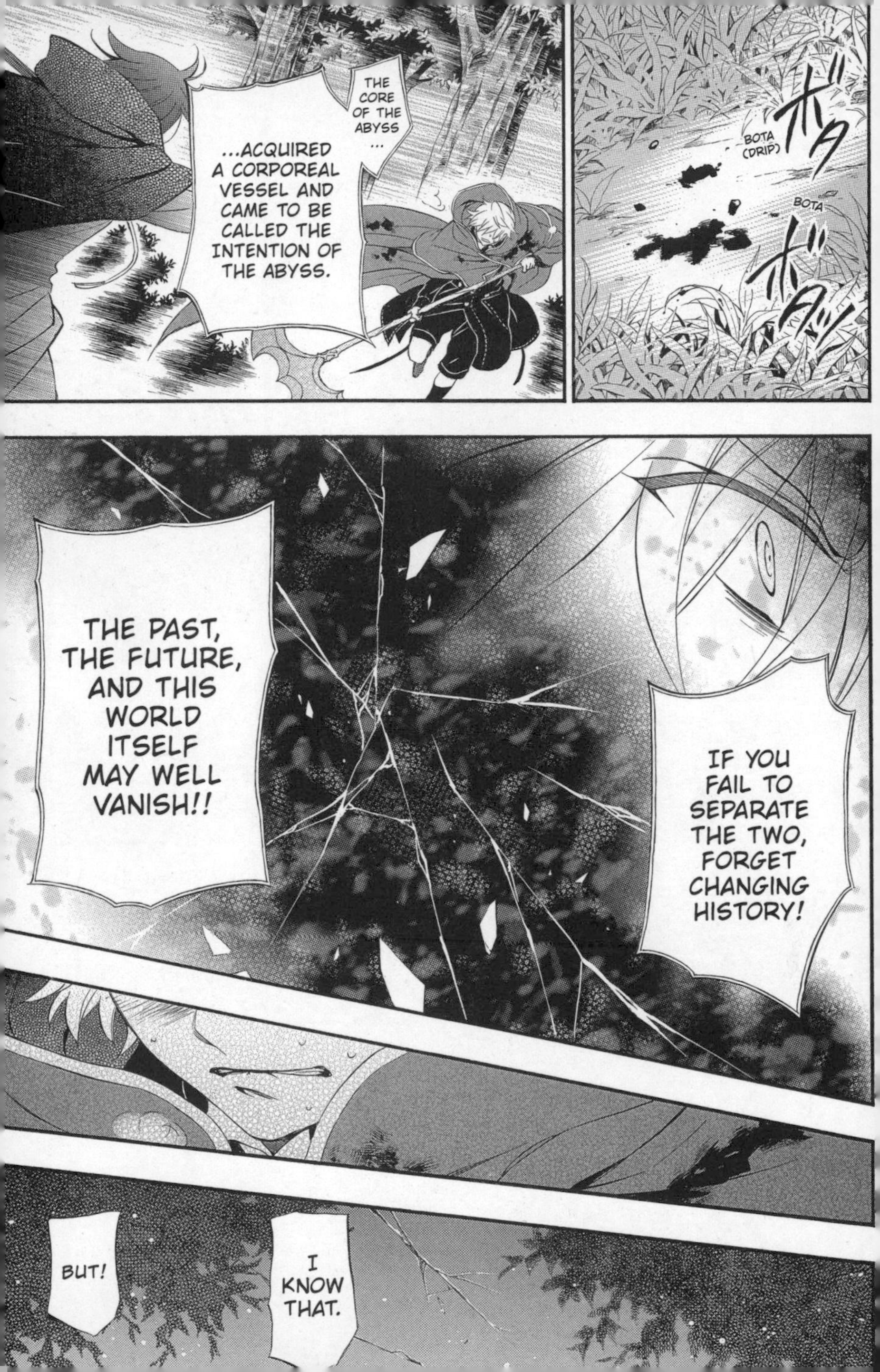
ボタ
BOTA (DRIP)
BOTA
ボタッ
THE CORE OF THE ABYSS ...
...ACQUIRED A CORPOREAL VESSEL AND CAME TO BE CALLED THE INTENTION OF THE ABYSS.
IF YOU FAIL TO SEPARATE THE TWO, FORGET CHANGING HISTORY!
THE PAST, THE FUTURE, AND THIS WORLD ITSELF MAY WELL VANISH!!
I KNOW THAT.
BUT!

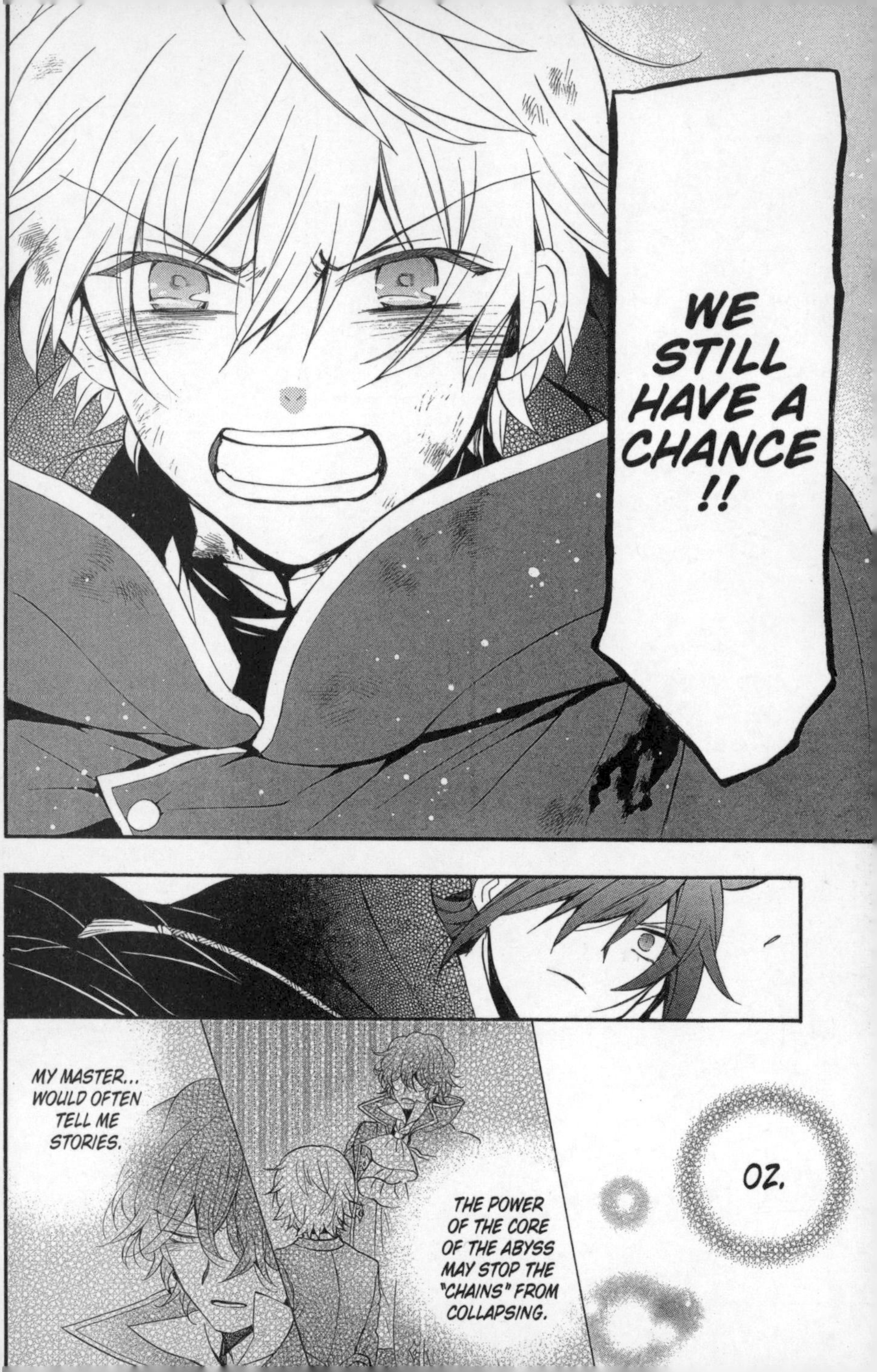
WE STILL HAVE A CHANCE !!
OZ.
THE POWER OF THE CORE OF THE ABYSS MAY STOP THE "CHAINS" FROM COLLAPSING.
MY MASTER... WOULD OFTEN TELL ME STORIES.

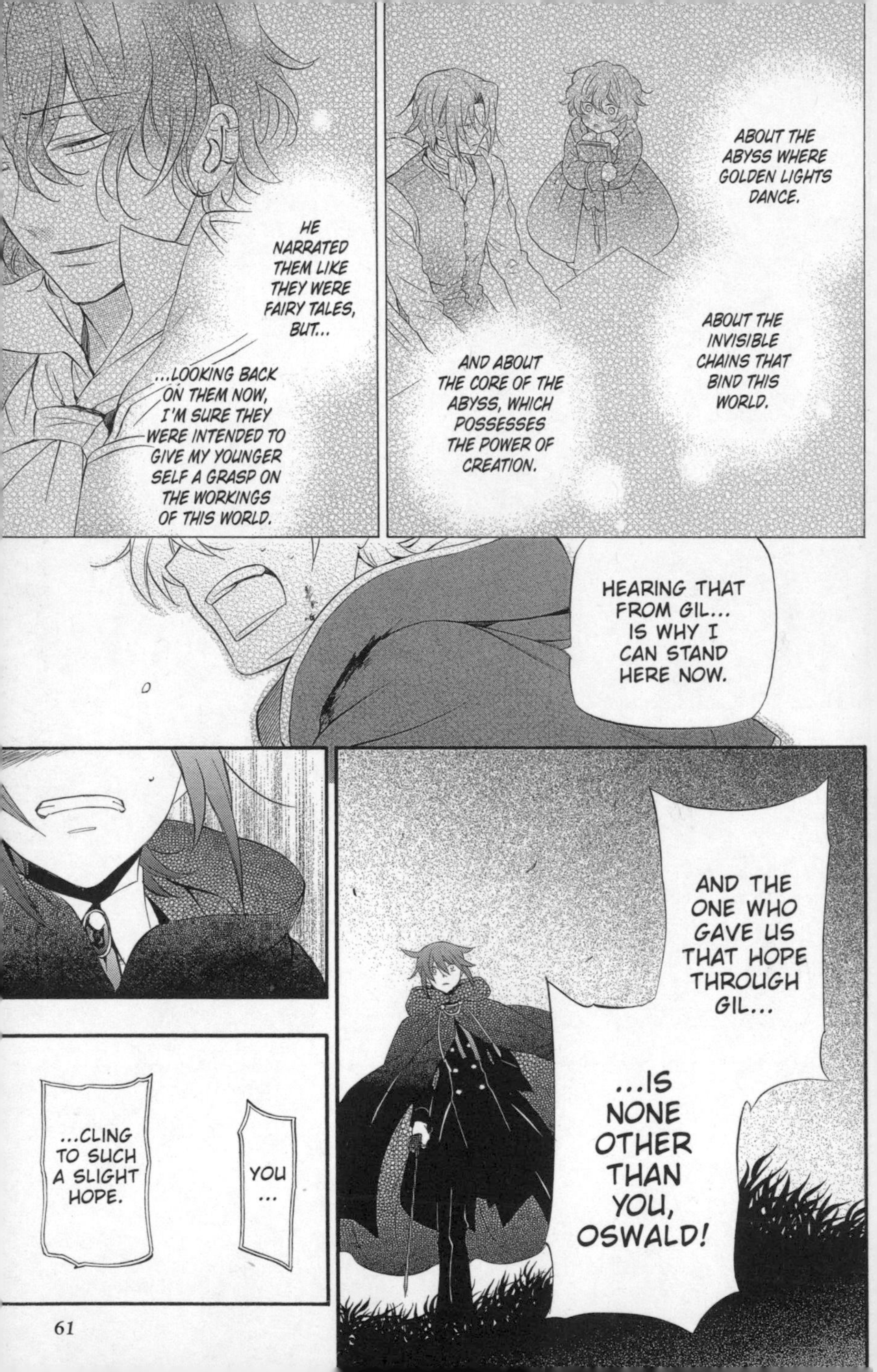
ABOUT THE ABYSS WHERE GOLDEN LIGHTS DANCE.
ABOUT THE INVISIBLE CHAINS THAT BIND THIS WORLD.
AND ABOUT THE CORE OF THE ABYSS, WHICH POSSESSES THE POWER OF CREATION.
HE NARRATED THEM LIKE THEY WERE FAIRY TALES, BUT...
...LOOKING BACK ON THEM NOW, I'M SURE THEY WERE INTENDED TO GIVE MY YOUNGER SELF A GRASP ON THE WORKINGS OF THIS WORLD.
HEARING THAT FROM GIL... IS WHY I CAN STAND HERE NOW.
AND THE ONE WHO GAVE US THAT HOPE THROUGH GIL...
...IS NONE OTHER THAN YOU, OSWALD!
YOU...
...CLING TO SUCH A SLIGHT HOPE.

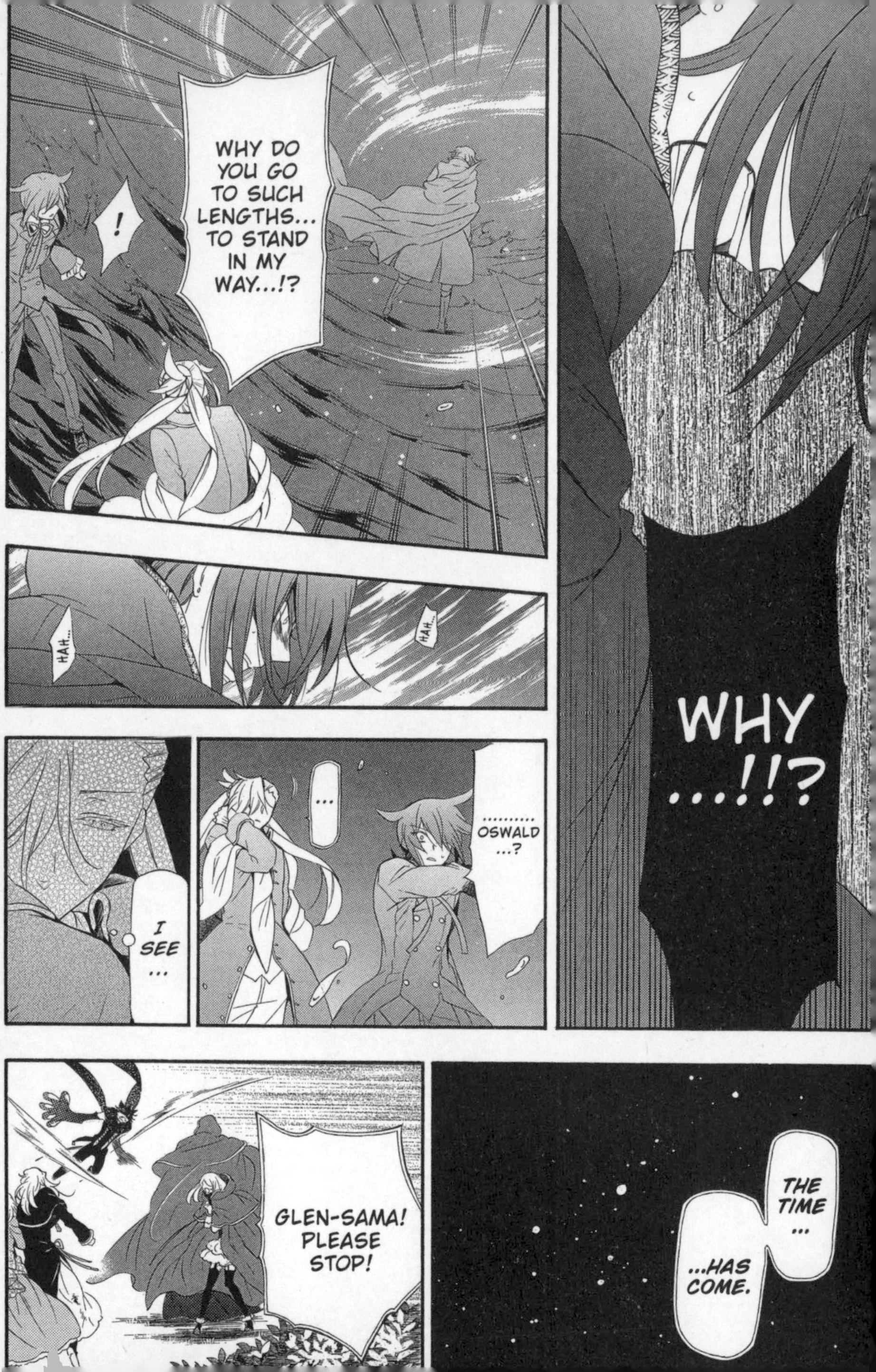
WHY ...!!?
WHY DO YOU GO TO SUCH LENGTHS... TO STAND IN MY WAY...!?
!
HAH...
HAH...
.........OSWALD...?
...
I SEE...
THE TIME...
...HAS COME.
GLEN-SAMA! PLEASE STOP!

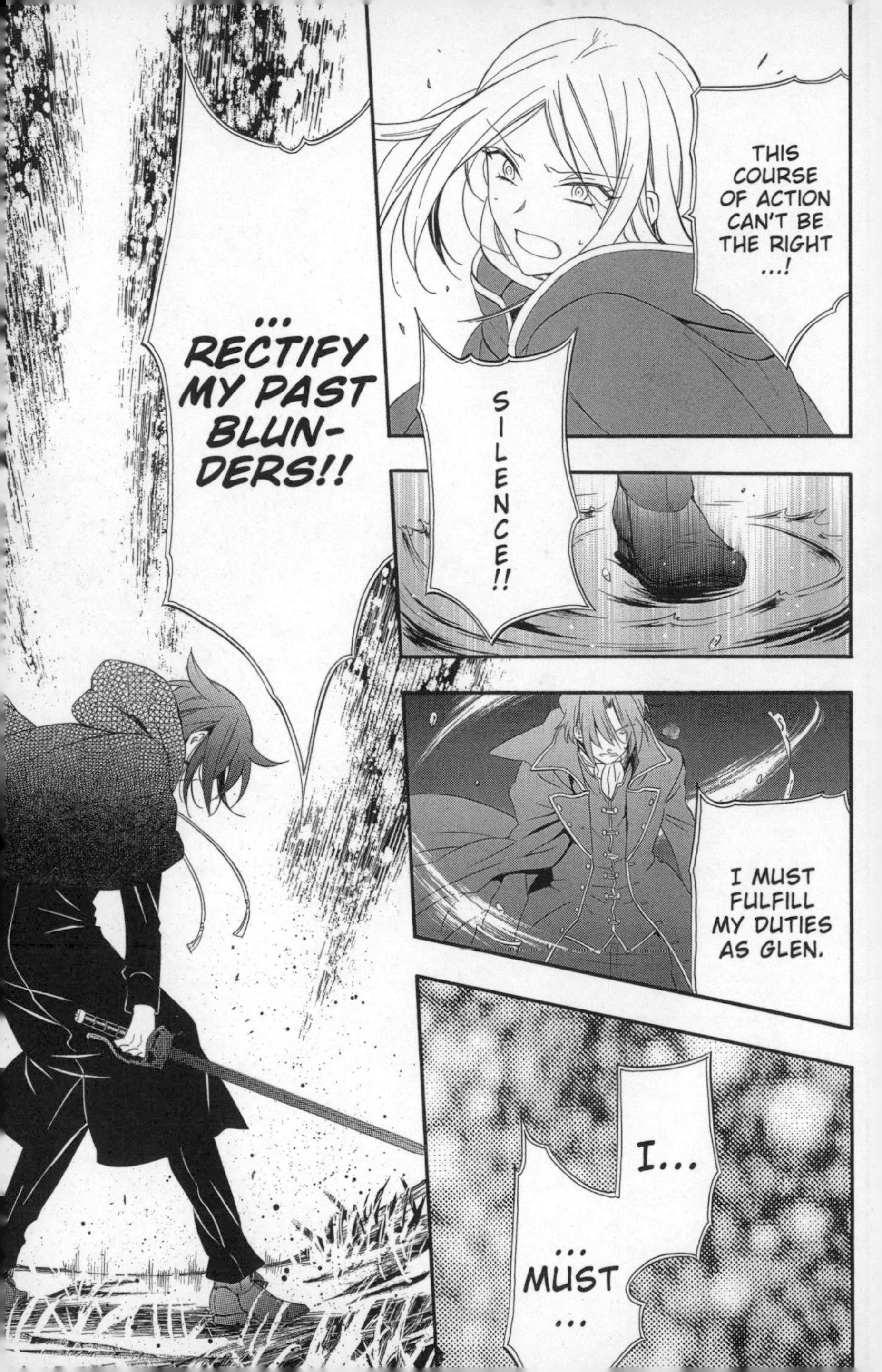
THIS COURSE OF ACTION CAN'T BE THE RIGHT ...!
SILENCE!!
I MUST FULFILL MY DUTIES AS GLEN.
I...
...MUST...
...RECTIFY MY PAST BLUN-DERS!!

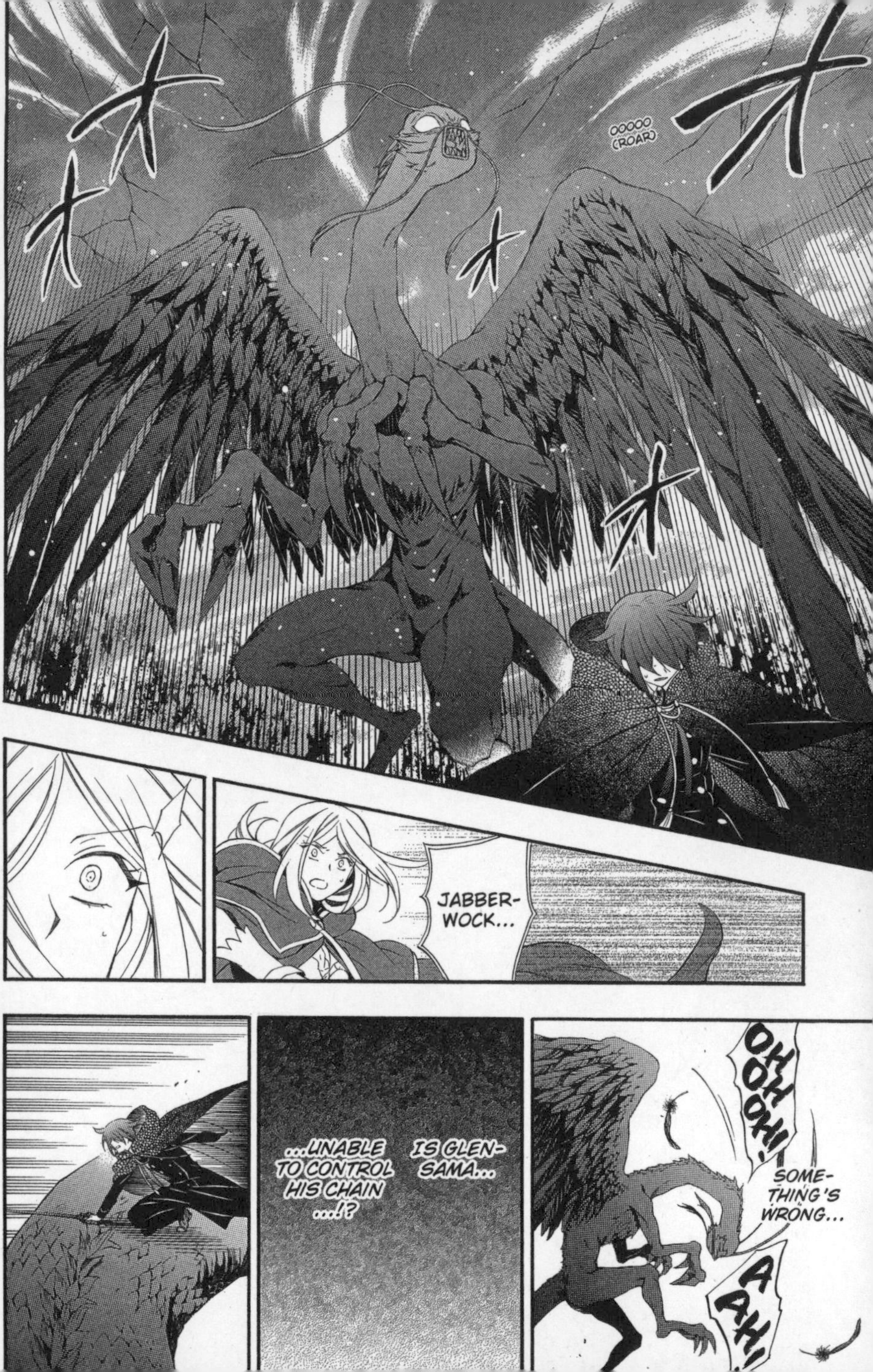
OOOOO
(ROAR)
JABBER-WOCK...
OH OH OH!
SOME-THING'S WRONG...
A AH!
IS GLEN-SAMA...
...UNABLE TO CONTROL HIS CHAIN ...!?

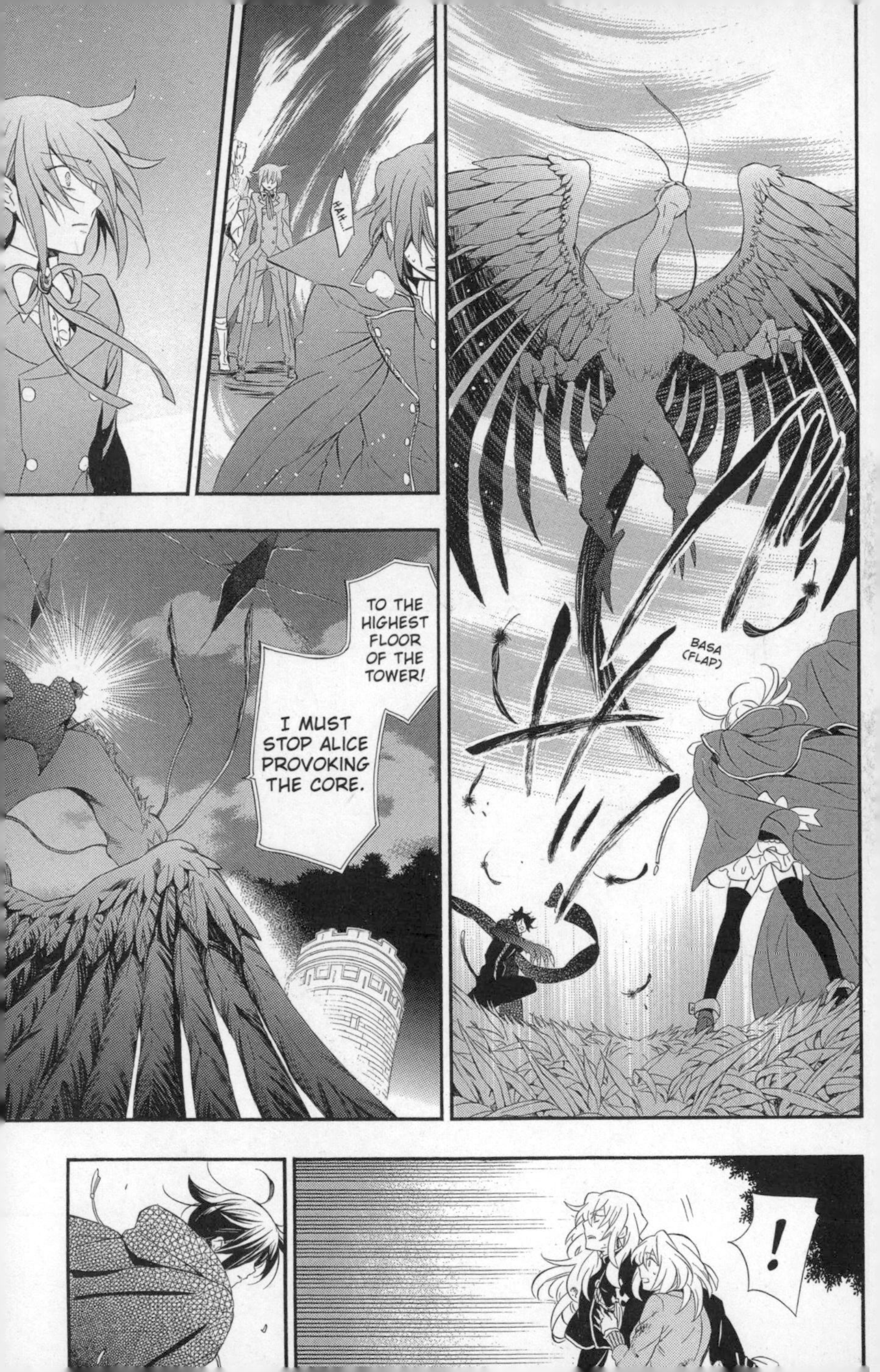
BASA (FLAP)
HAH...
TO THE HIGHEST FLOOR OF THE TOWER!
I MUST STOP ALICE PROVOKING THE CORE.
!

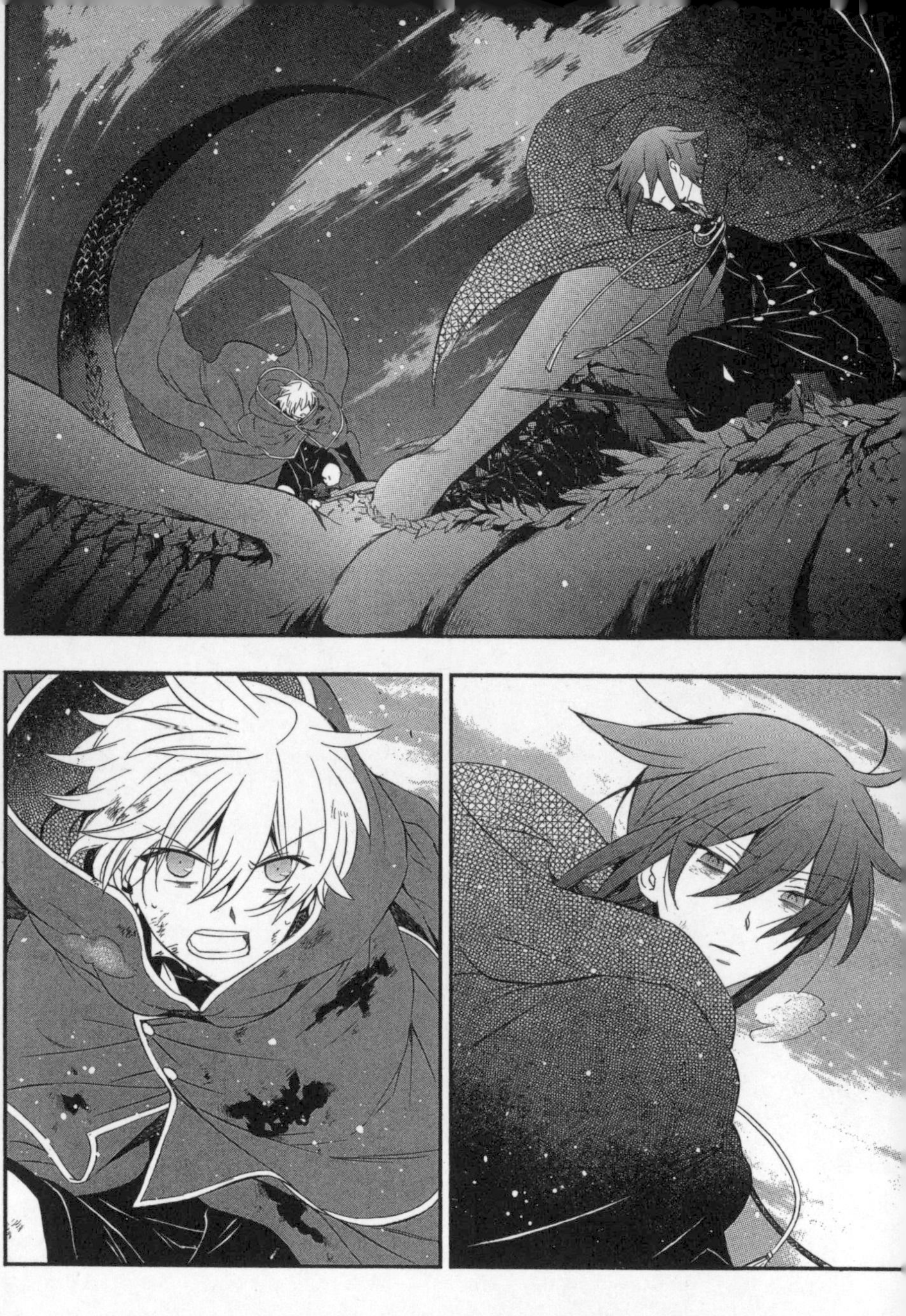

I PROBABLY WOULDN'T HAVE BEEN ABLE TO DO MUCH ALONE.

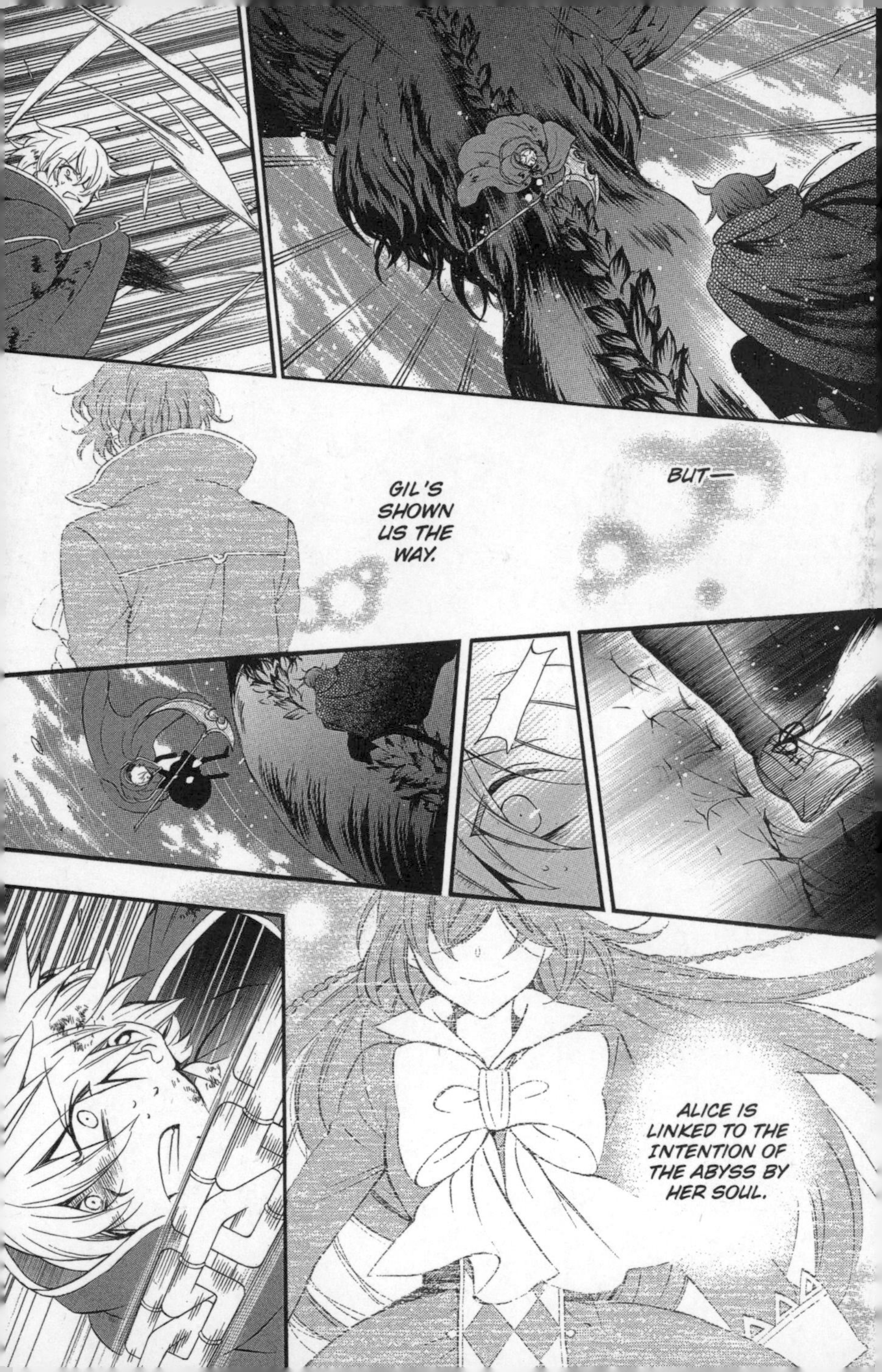
BUT—
GIL'S SHOWN US THE WAY.
ALICE IS LINKED TO THE INTENTION OF THE ABYSS BY HER SOUL.

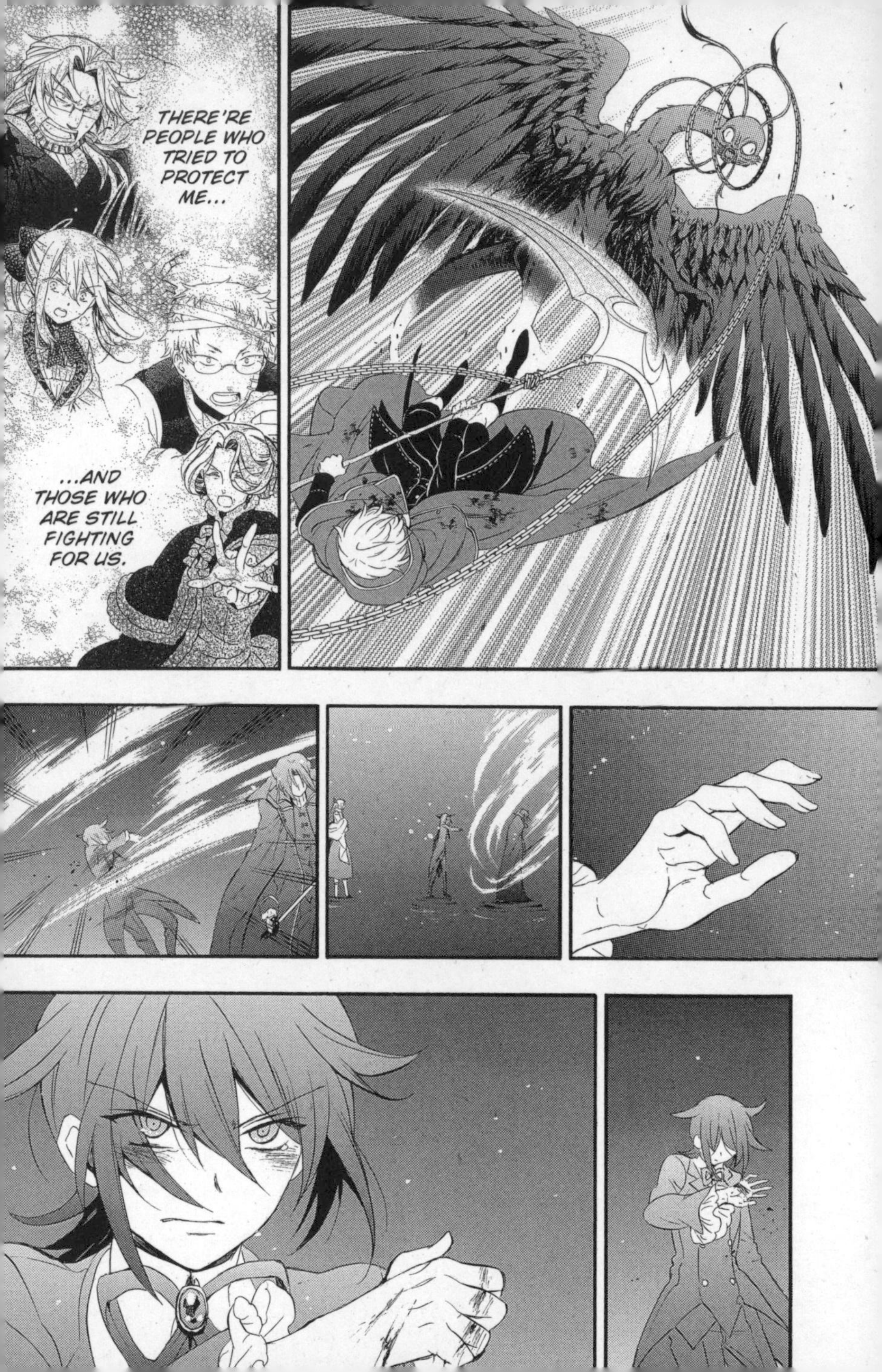
THERE'RE PEOPLE WHO TRIED TO PROTECT ME...
...AND THOSE WHO ARE STILL FIGHTING FOR US.

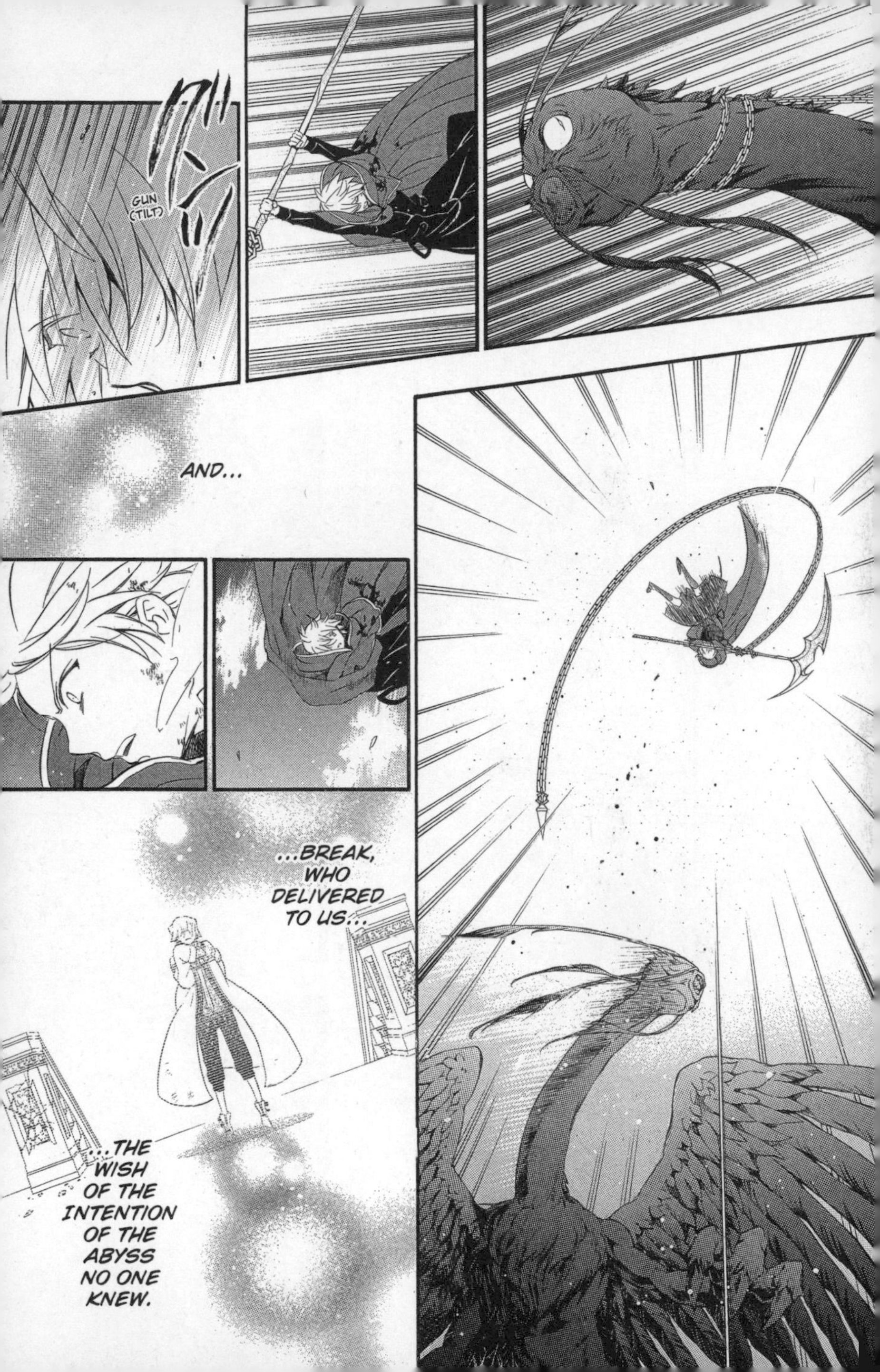
GUN (TILT)
AND...
...BREAK, WHO DELIVERED TO US...
...THE WISH OF THE INTENTION OF THE ABYSS NO ONE KNEW.

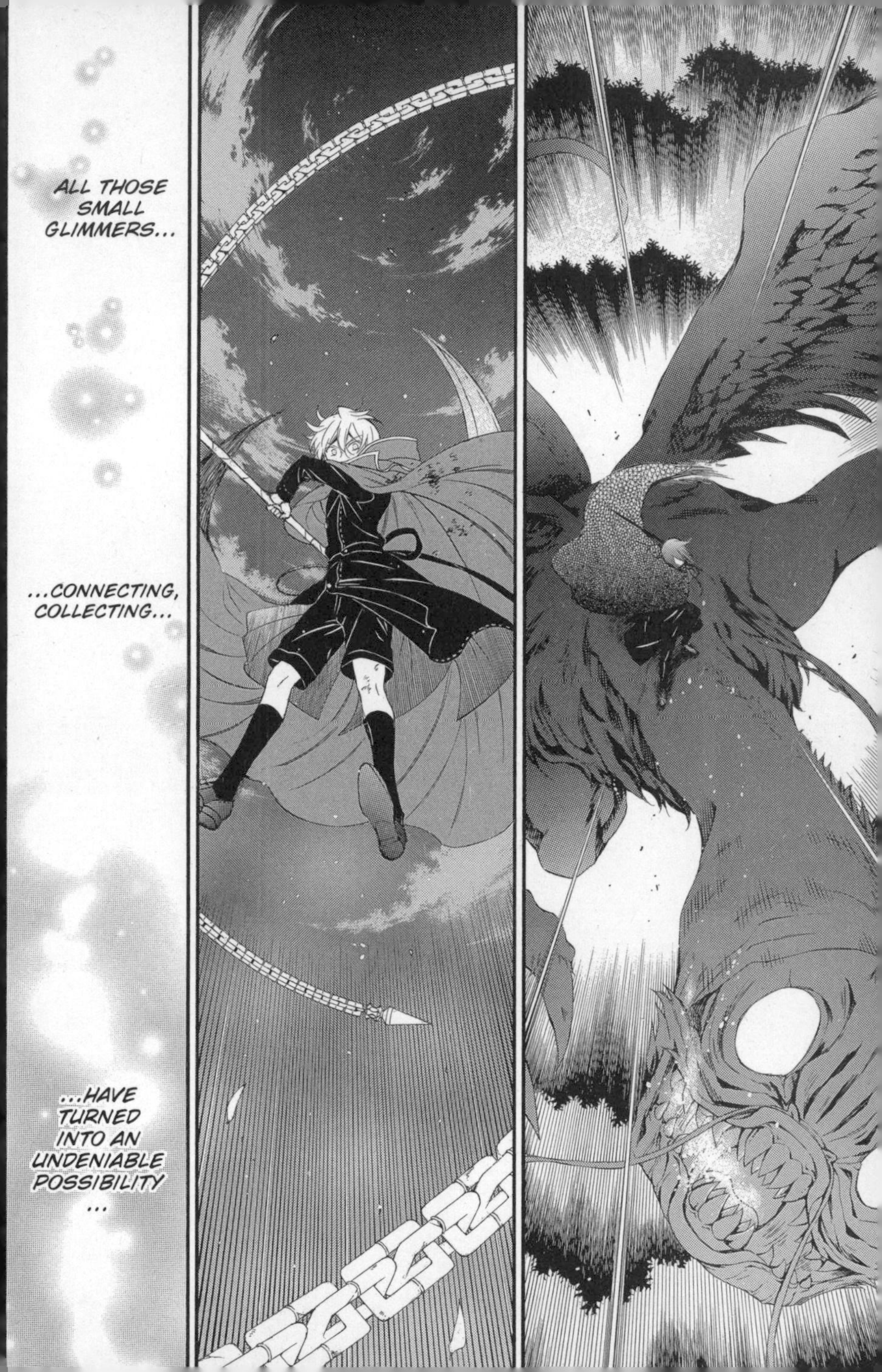
ALL THOSE SMALL GLIMMERS...
...CONNECTING, COLLECTING...
...HAVE TURNED INTO AN UNDENIABLE POSSIBILITY ...

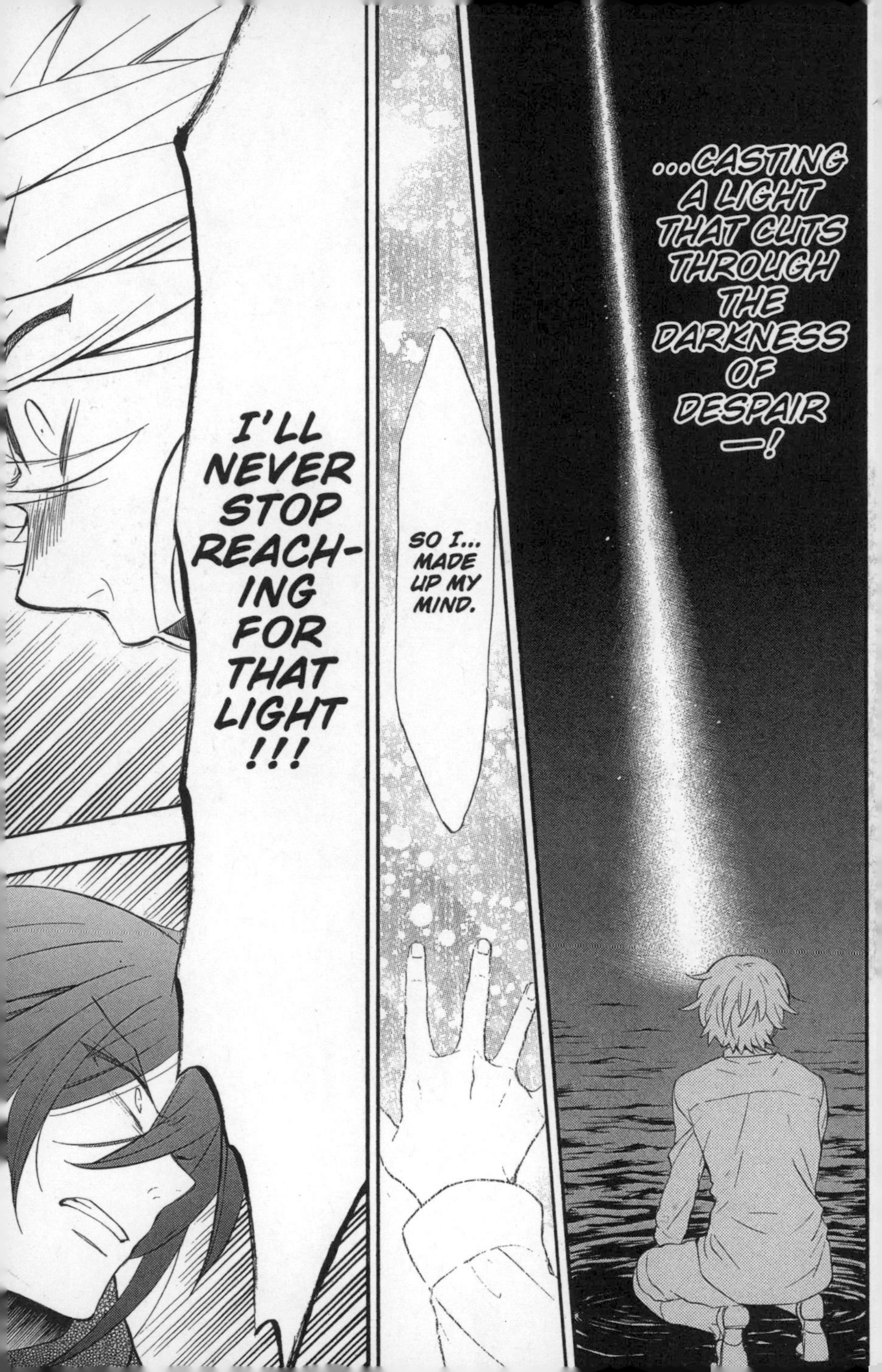
...CASTING A LIGHT THAT CUTS THROUGH THE DARKNESS OF DESPAIR—!
SO I... MADE UP MY MIND.
I'LL NEVER STOP REACHING FOR THAT LIGHT!!!

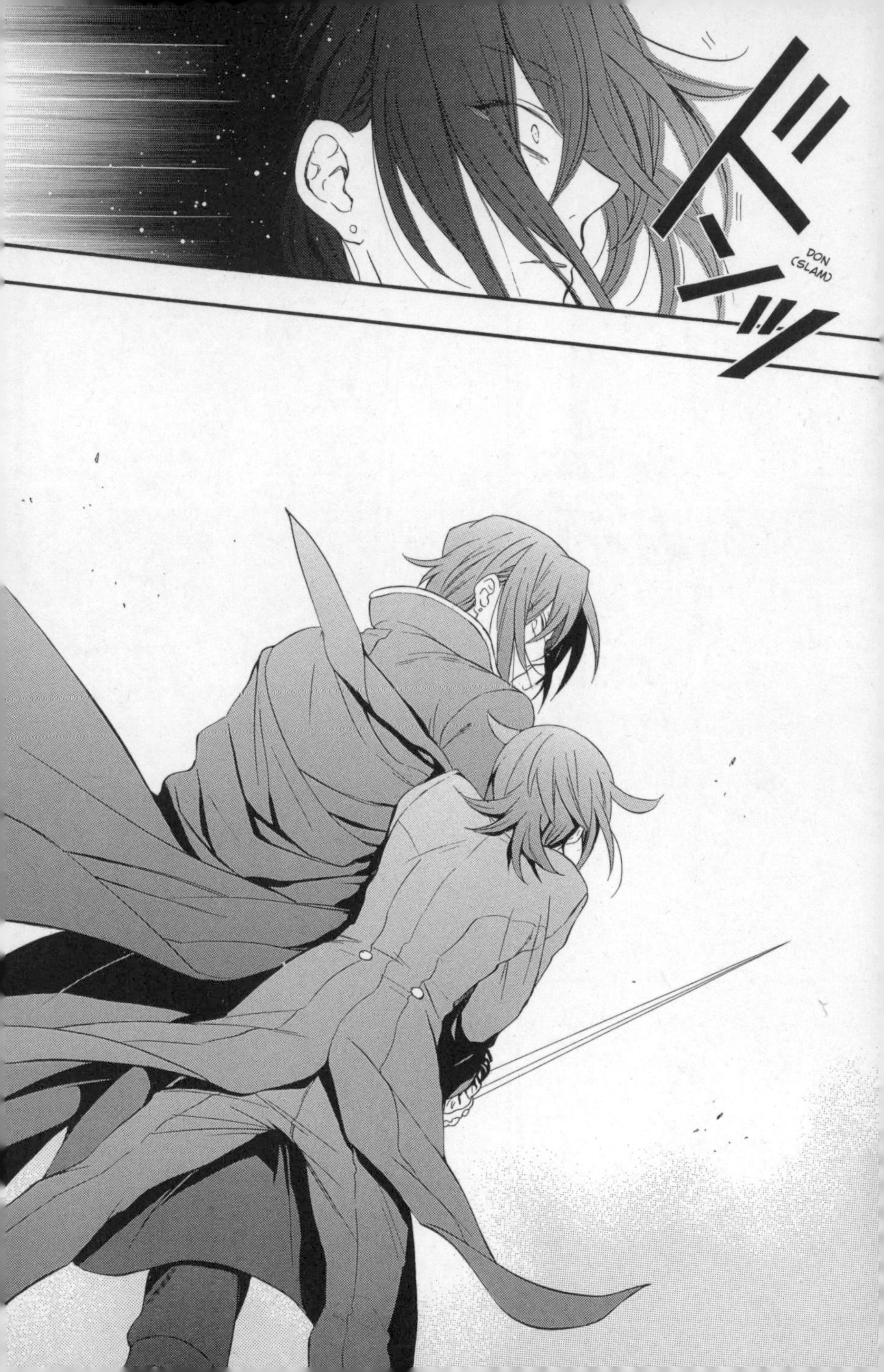
DON
(SLAM)

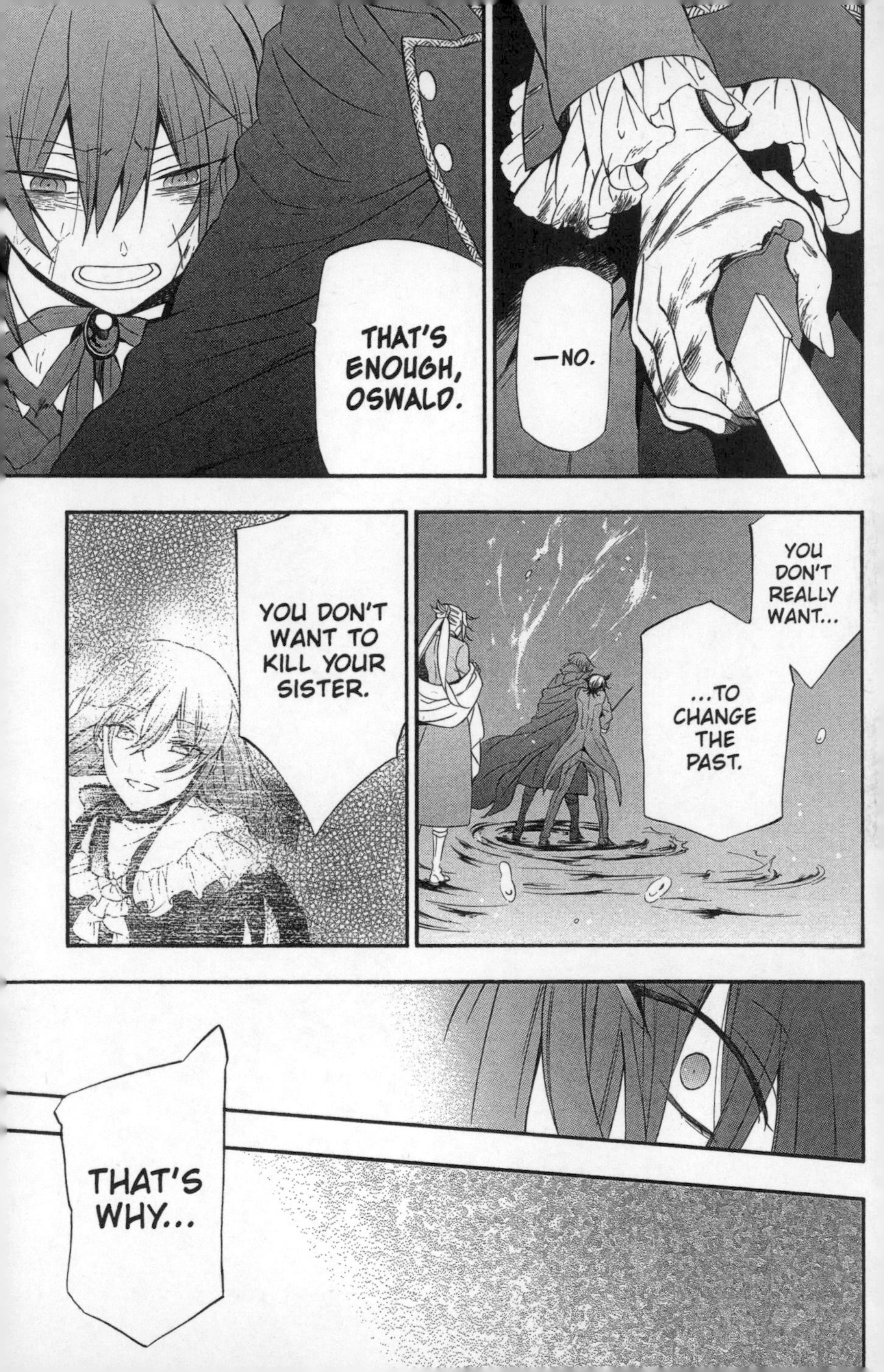
—NO.
THAT'S ENOUGH, OSWALD.
YOU DON'T REALLY WANT...
...TO CHANGE THE PAST.
YOU DON'T WANT TO KILL YOUR SISTER.
THAT'S WHY...

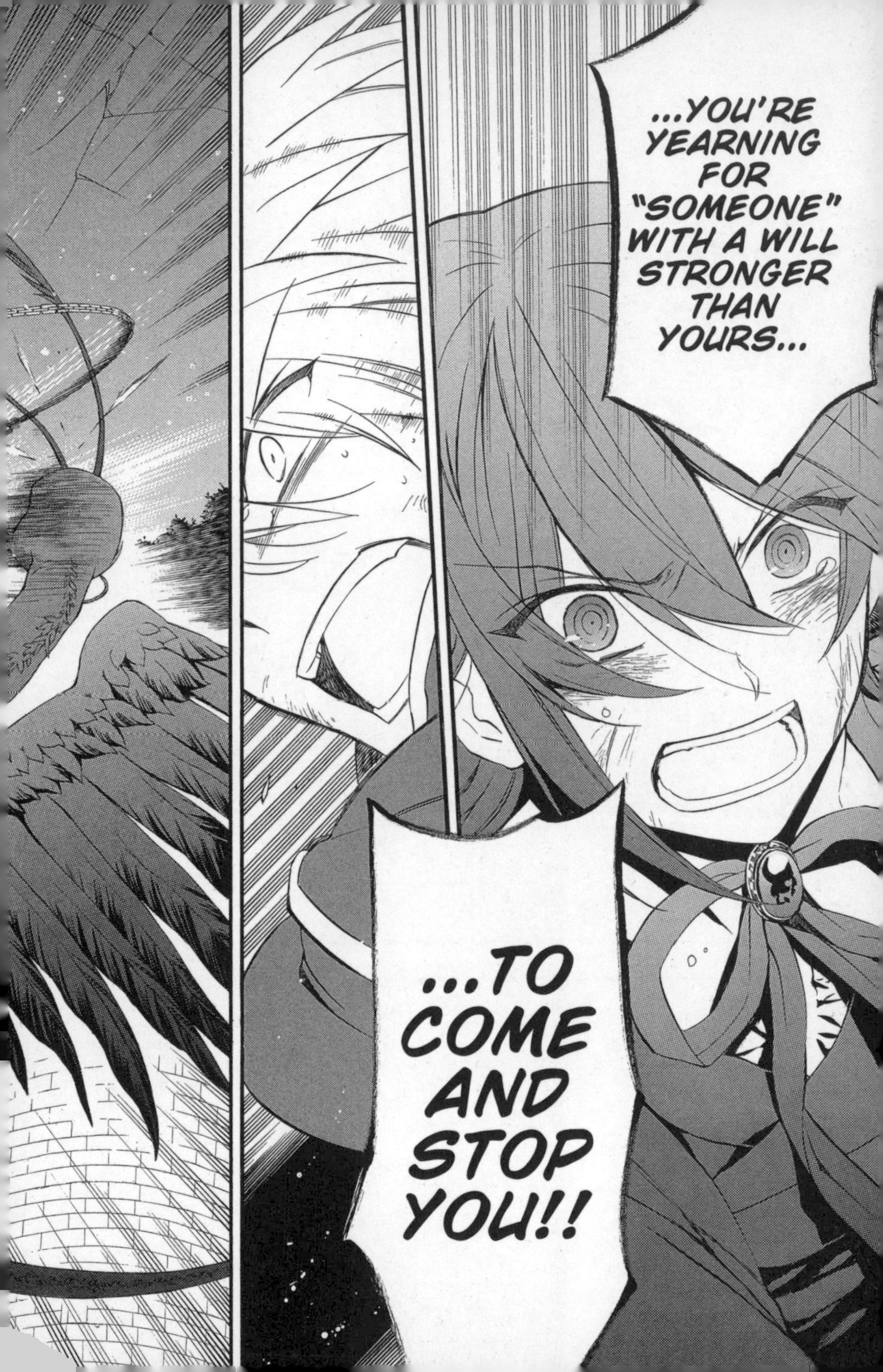
...YOU'RE YEARNING FOR "SOMEONE" WITH A WILL STRONGER THAN YOURS...
...TO COME AND STOP YOU!!

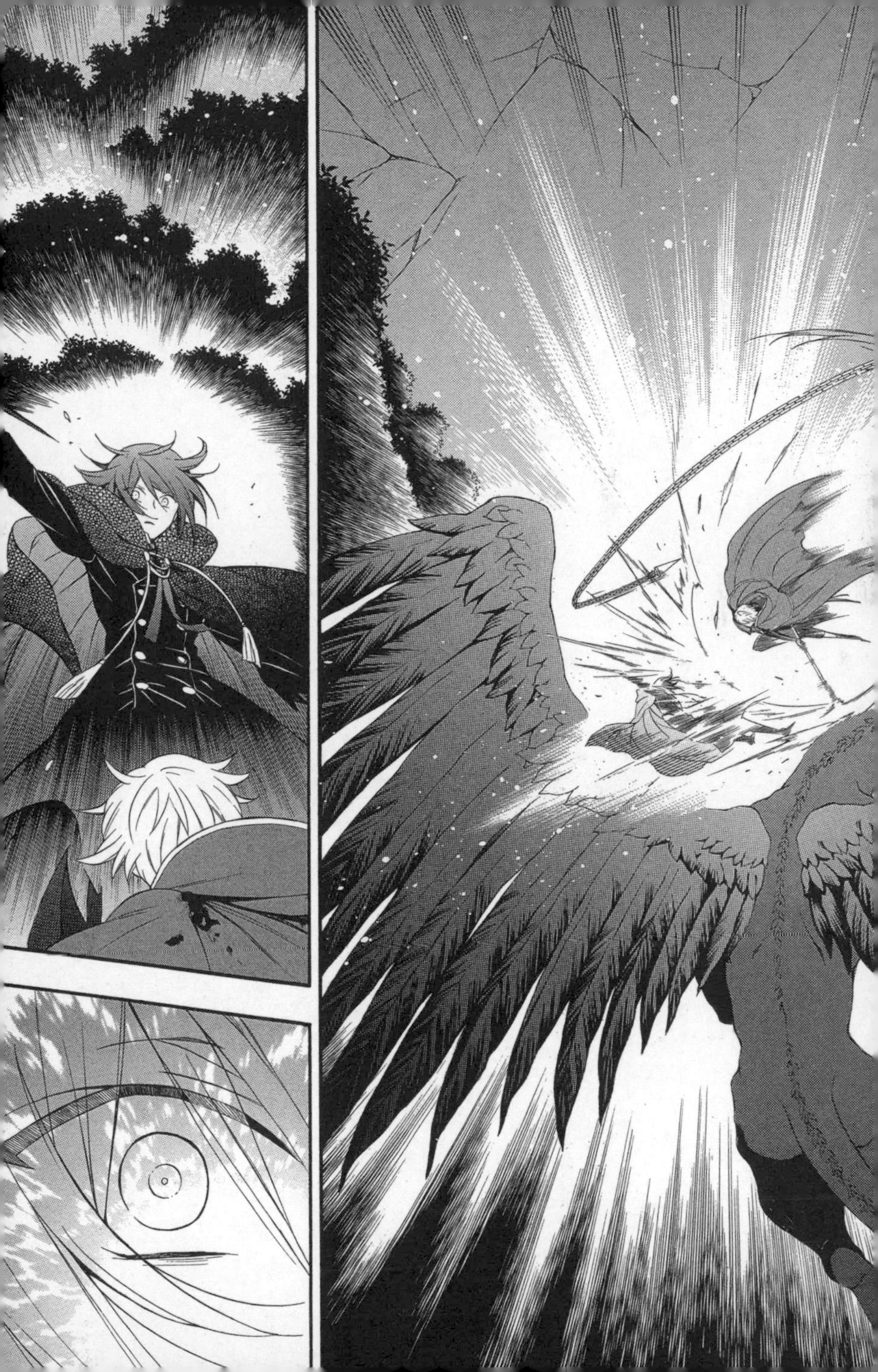

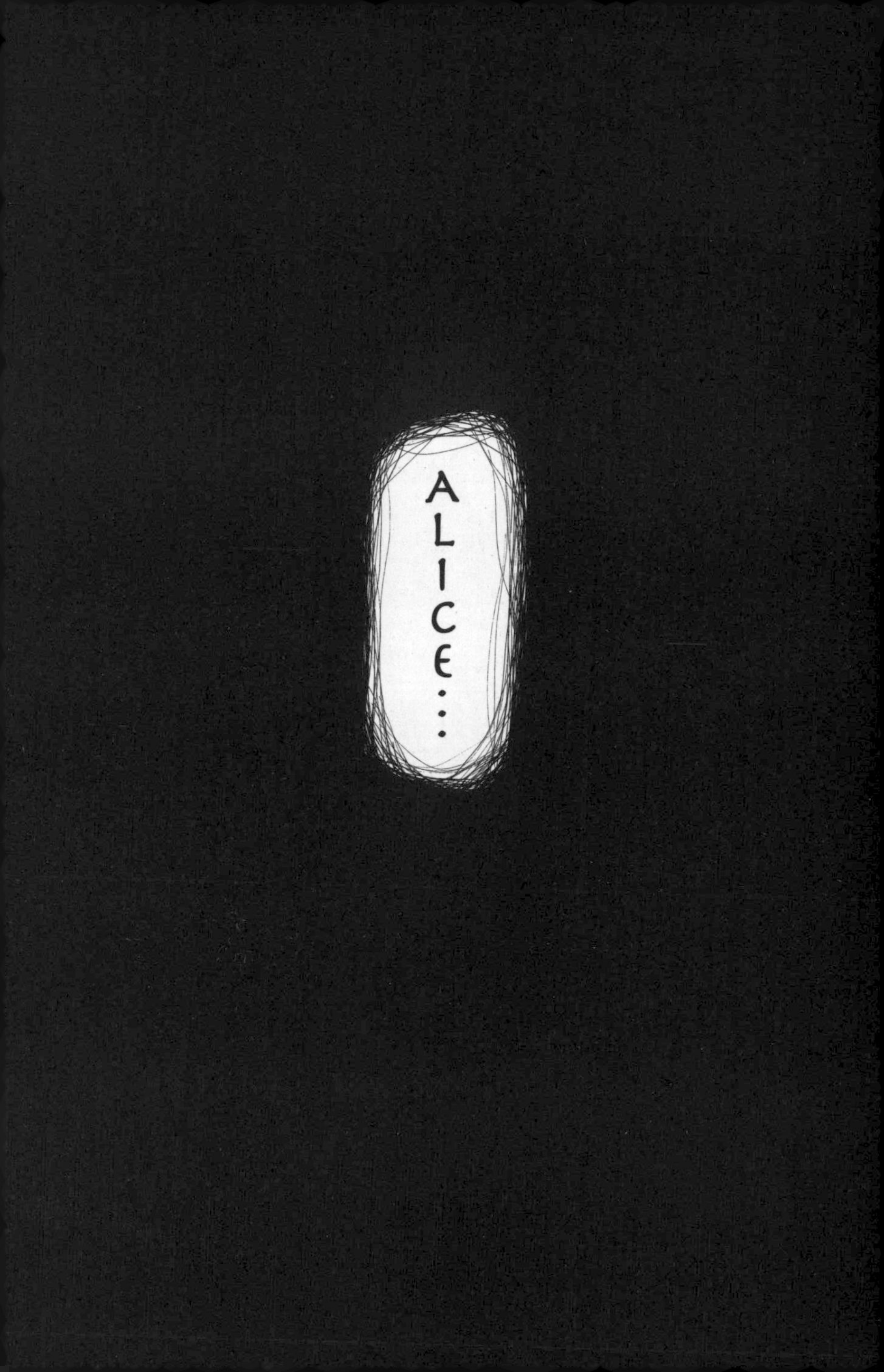
ALICE...

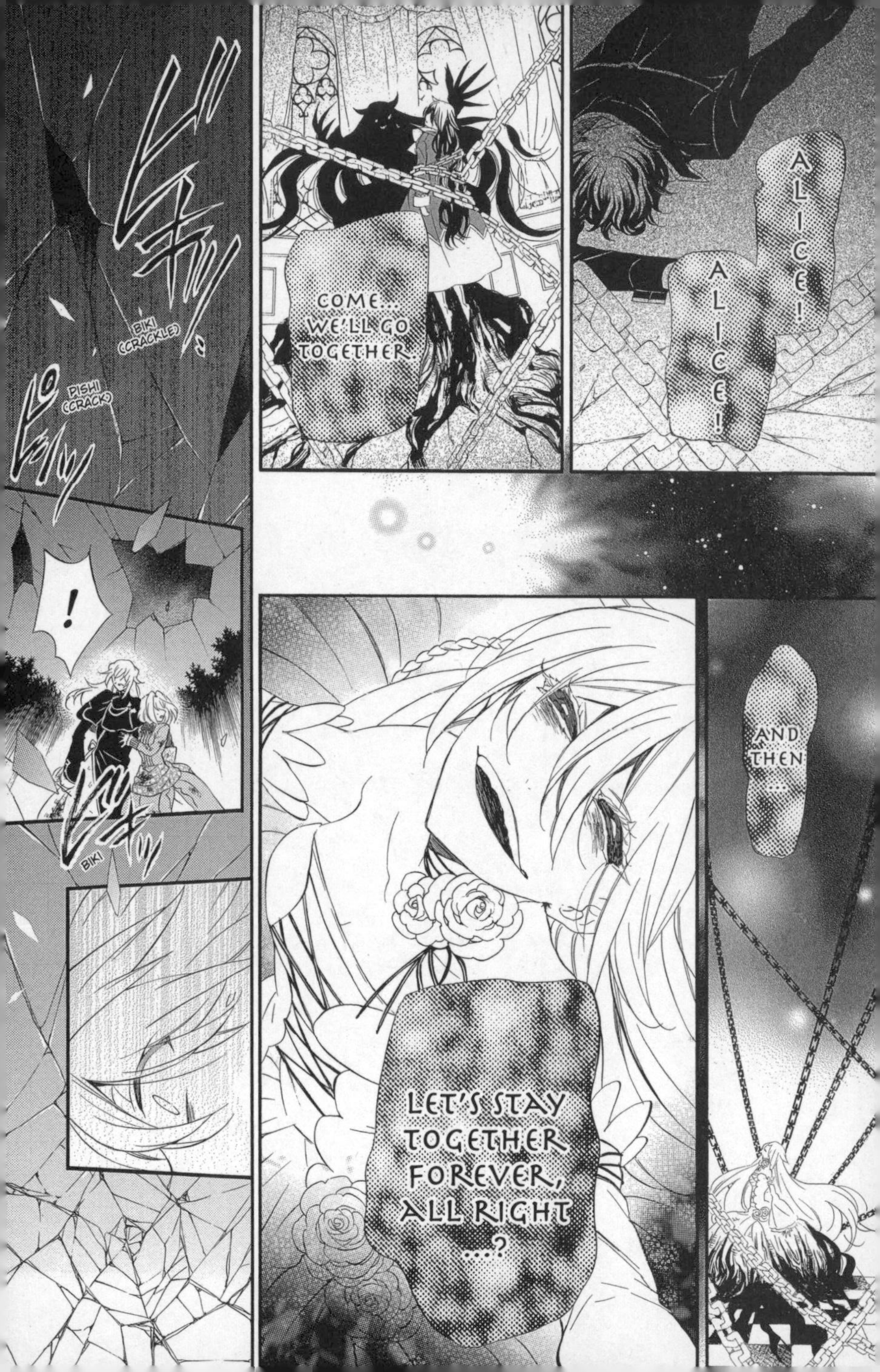
ALICE!
ALICE!
COME... WE'LL GO TOGETHER.
AND THEN ...
LET'S STAY TOGETHER FOREVER, ALL RIGHT ...?
BIKI (CRACKLE)
PISHI (CRACK)
!
BIKI

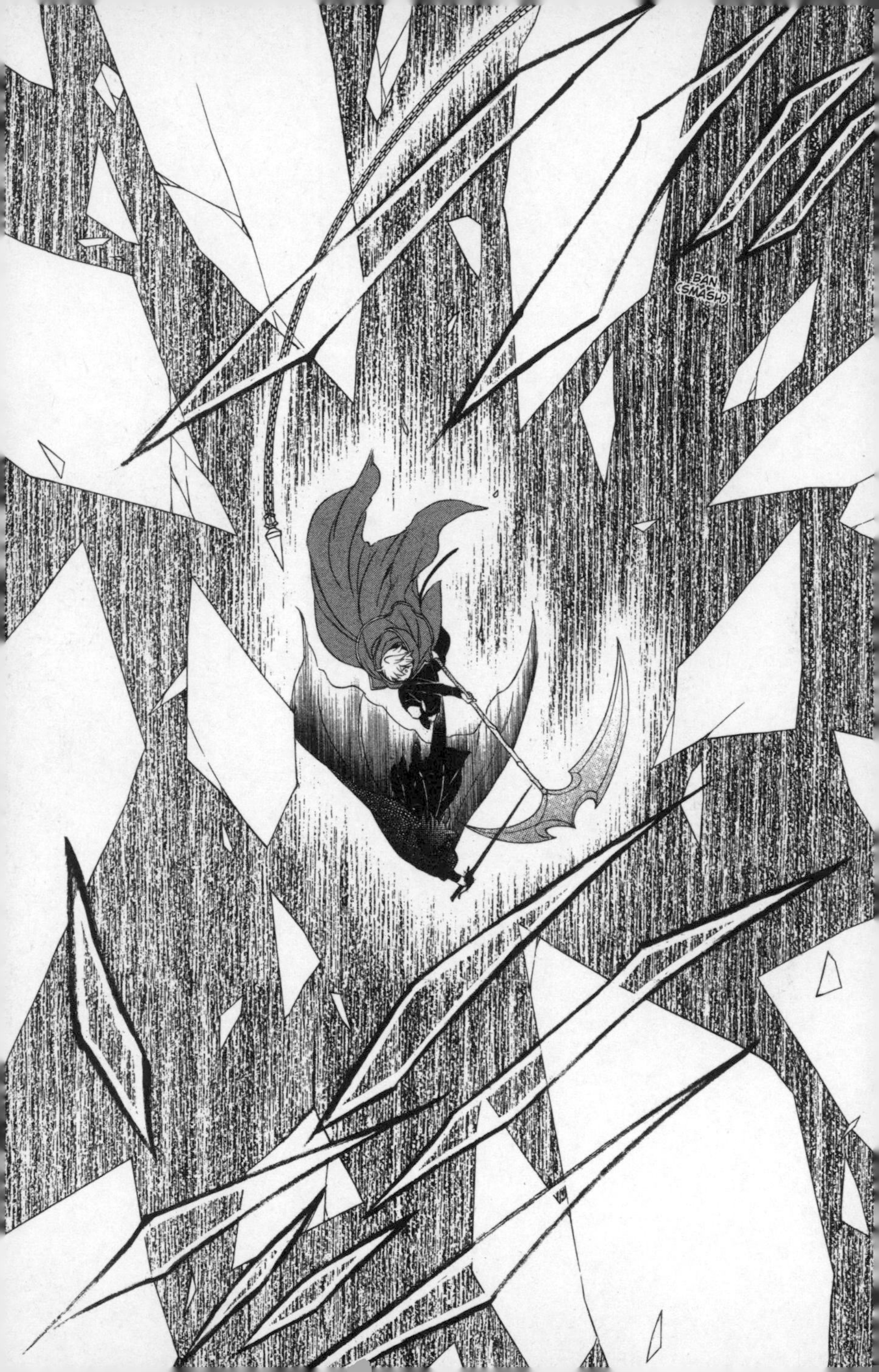
BAN
(SMASH)

Retrace:C Ossia

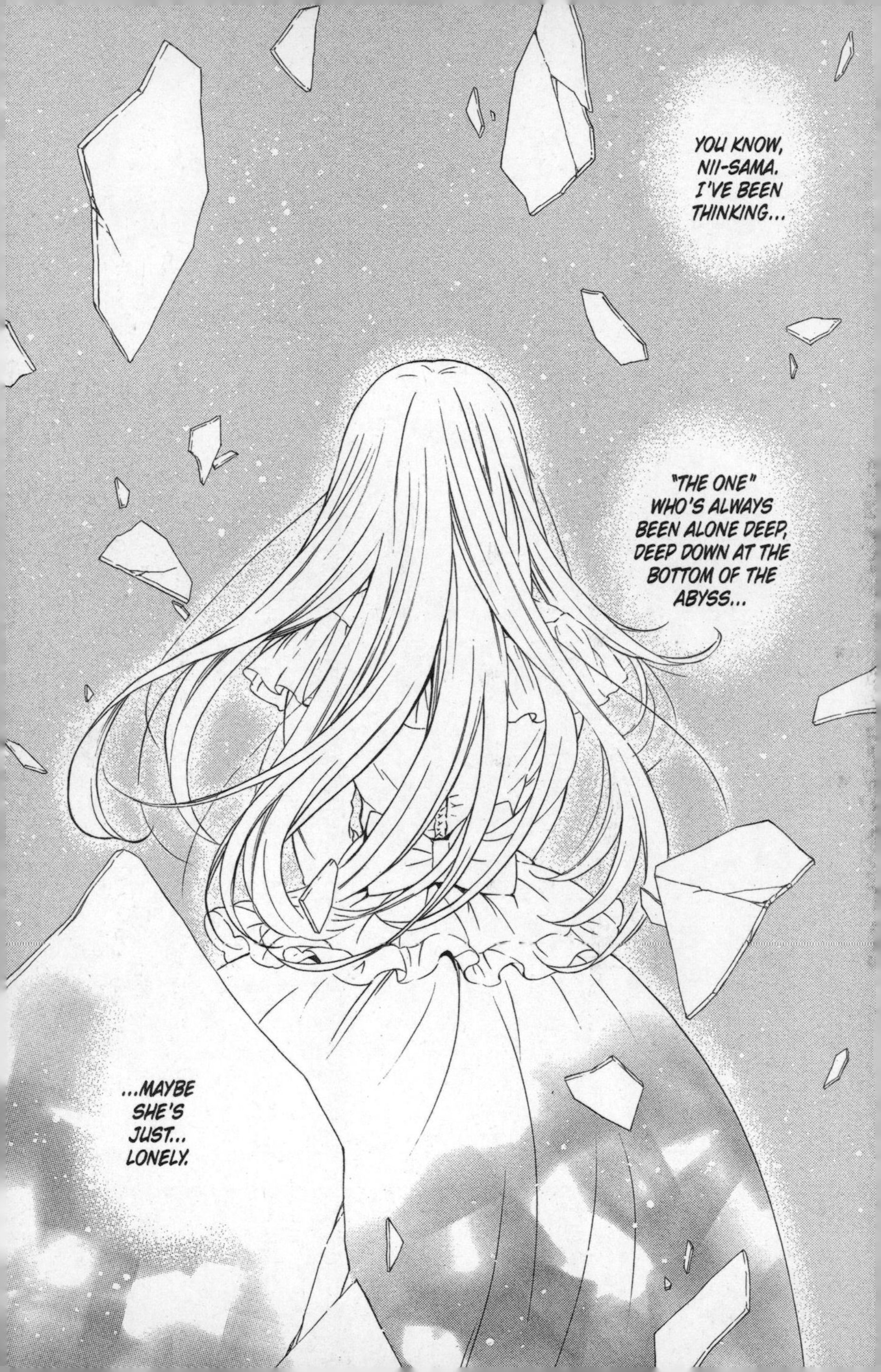
YOU KNOW, NII-SAMA. I'VE BEEN THINKING...
"THE ONE" WHO'S ALWAYS BEEN ALONE DEEP, DEEP DOWN AT THE BOTTOM OF THE ABYSS...
...MAYBE SHE'S JUST... LONELY.

Retrace:CI

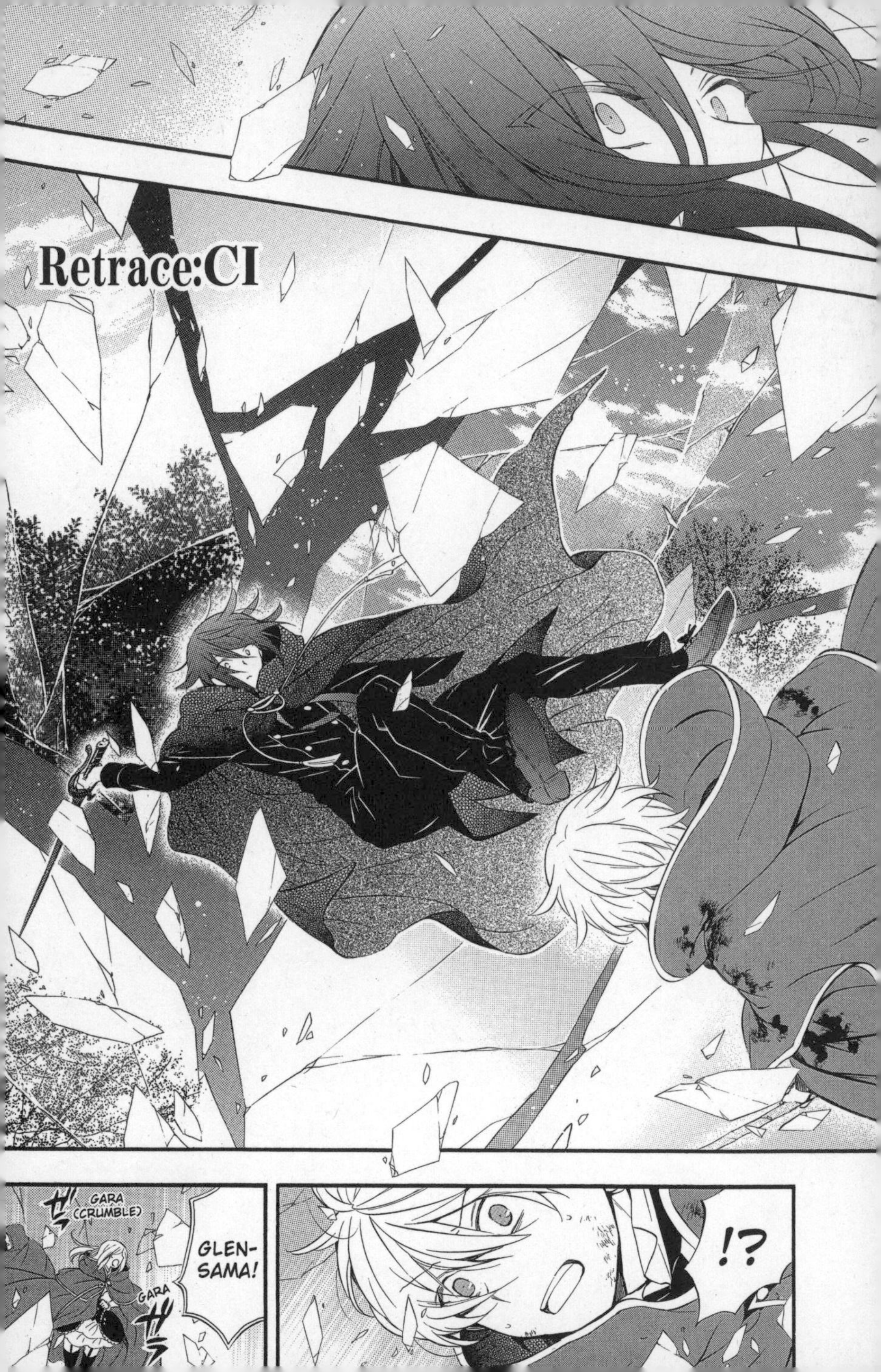
!?
GARA (CRUMBLE)
GLEN-SAMA!
GARA

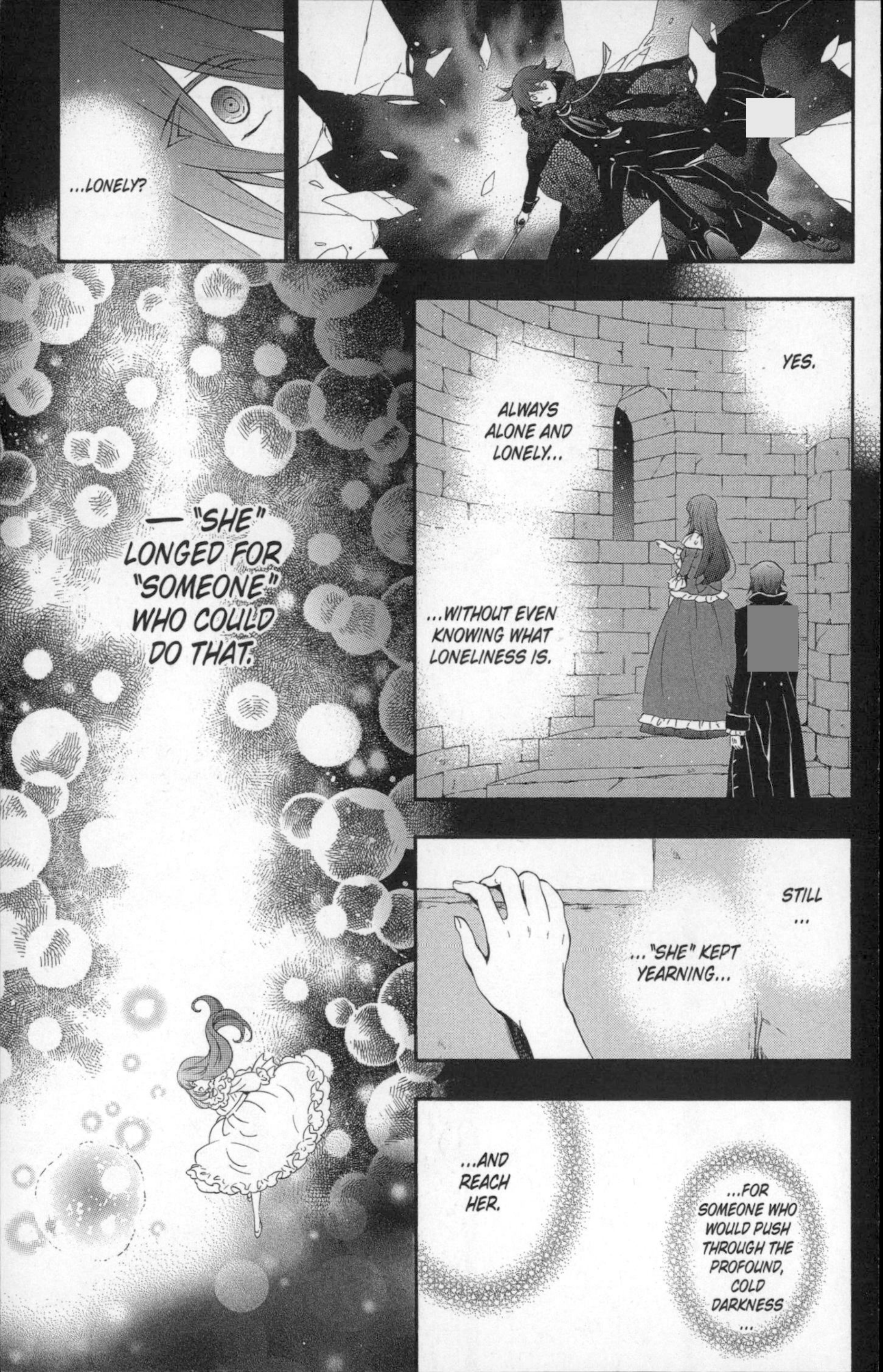
...LONELY?
YES.
ALWAYS ALONE AND LONELY...
...WITHOUT EVEN KNOWING WHAT LONELINESS IS.
STILL...
..."SHE" KEPT YEARNING...
...FOR SOMEONE WHO WOULD PUSH THROUGH THE PROFOUND, COLD DARKNESS...
...AND REACH HER.
—"SHE" LONGED FOR "SOMEONE" WHO COULD DO THAT.

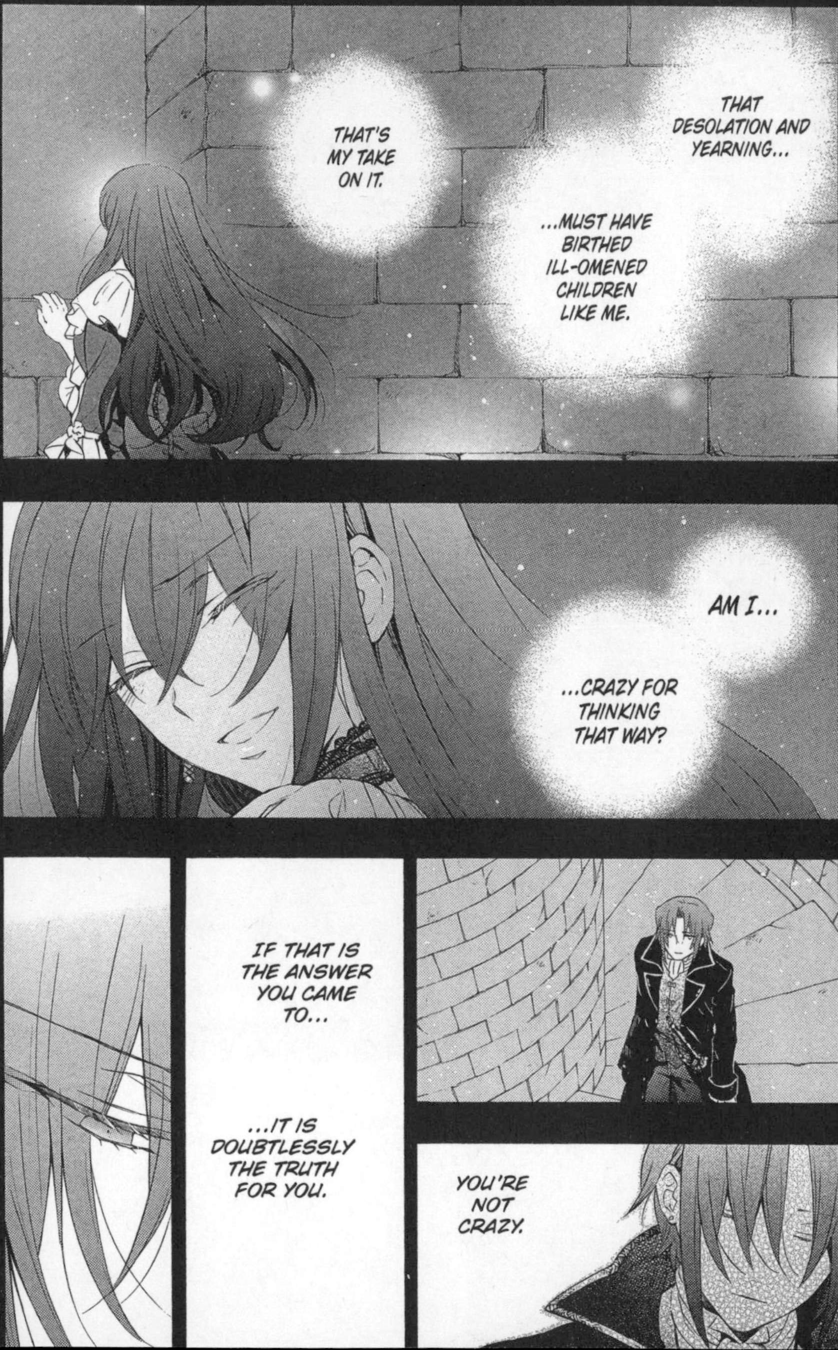
THAT DESOLATION AND YEARNING...
...MUST HAVE BIRTHED ILL-OMENED CHILDREN LIKE ME.
THAT'S MY TAKE ON IT.
AM I...
...CRAZY FOR THINKING THAT WAY?
YOU'RE NOT CRAZY.
IF THAT IS THE ANSWER YOU CAME TO...
...IT IS DOUBTLESSLY THE TRUTH FOR YOU.

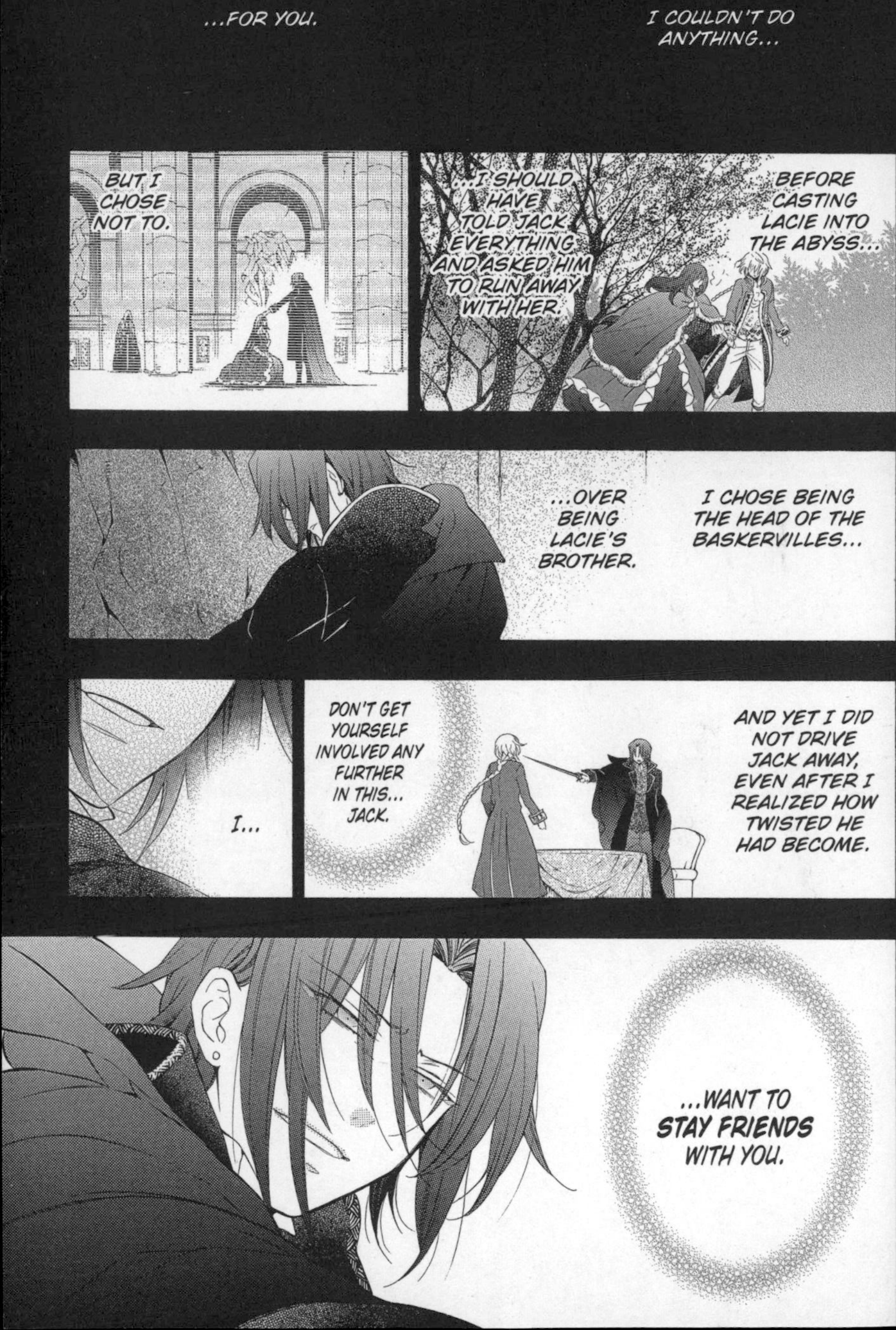
I COULDN'T DO ANYTHING...
...FOR YOU.
BEFORE CASTING LACIE INTO THE ABYSS...
...I SHOULD HAVE TOLD JACK EVERYTHING AND ASKED HIM TO RUN AWAY WITH HER.
BUT I CHOSE NOT TO.
I CHOSE BEING THE HEAD OF THE BASKERVILLES...
...OVER BEING LACIE'S BROTHER.
AND YET I DID NOT DRIVE JACK AWAY, EVEN AFTER I REALIZED HOW TWISTED HE HAD BECOME.
DON'T GET YOURSELF INVOLVED ANY FURTHER IN THIS... JACK.
I...
...WANT TO STAY FRIENDS WITH YOU.

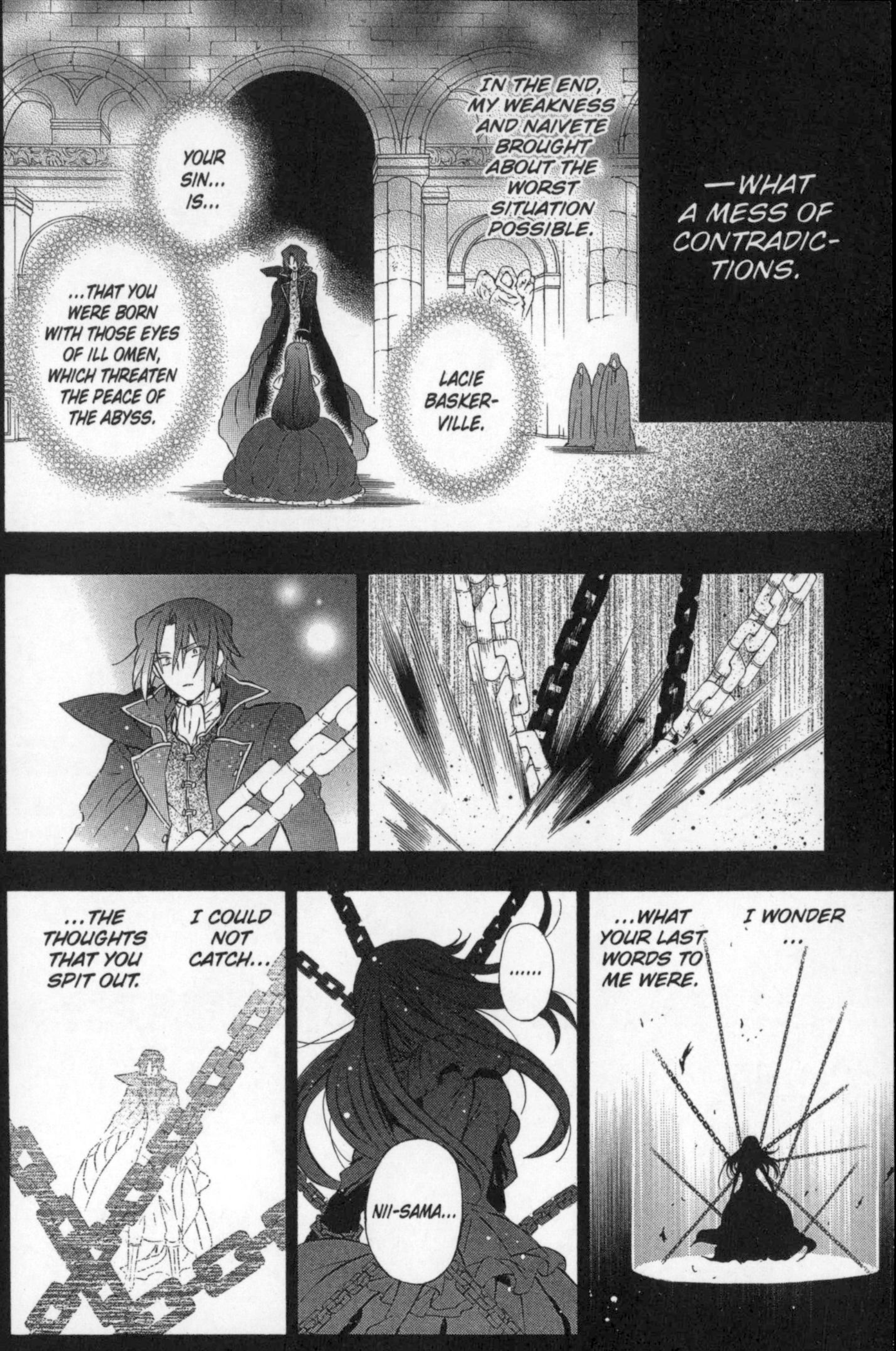
—WHAT A MESS OF CONTRADIC- TIONS.
IN THE END, MY WEAKNESS AND NAIVETE BROUGHT ABOUT THE WORST SITUATION POSSIBLE.
YOUR SIN... IS...
...THAT YOU WERE BORN WITH THOSE EYES OF ILL OMEN, WHICH THREATEN THE PEACE OF THE ABYSS.
LACIE BASKER- VILLE.
I WONDER ...
...WHAT YOUR LAST WORDS TO ME WERE.
......
NII-SAMA...
I COULD NOT CATCH...
...THE THOUGHTS THAT YOU SPIT OUT.

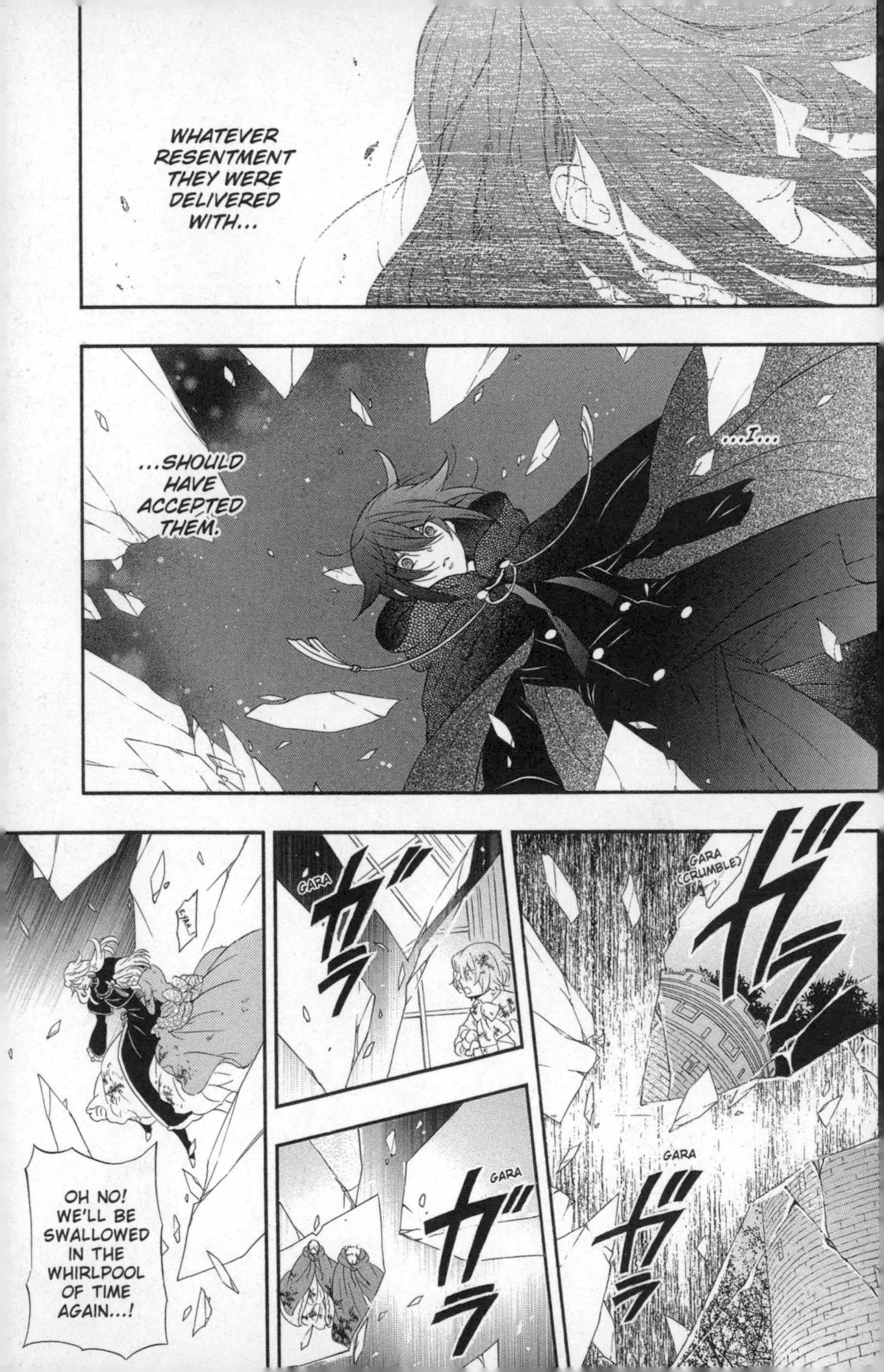
WHATEVER RESENTMENT THEY WERE DELIVERED WITH...
...I...
...SHOULD HAVE ACCEPTED THEM.
GARA (CRUMBLE)
GARA
GARA
GARA
EYAH...!
OH NO! WE'LL BE SWALLOWED IN THE WHIRLPOOL OF TIME AGAIN...!

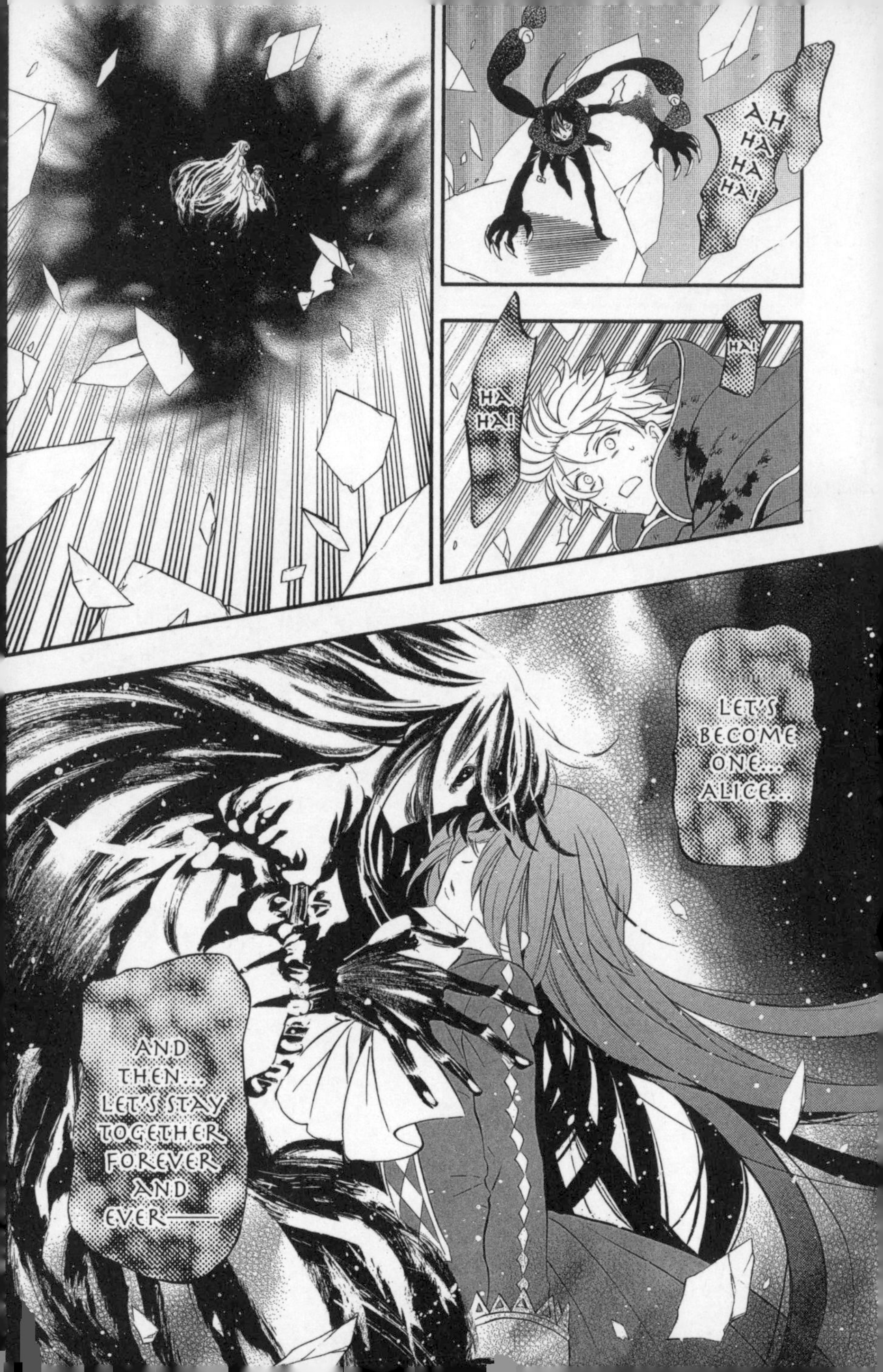
AH HA HA HA!
HA!
HA HA!
...LET'S BECOME ONE... ALICE...
AND THEN... LET'S STAY TOGETHER FOREVER AND EVER——

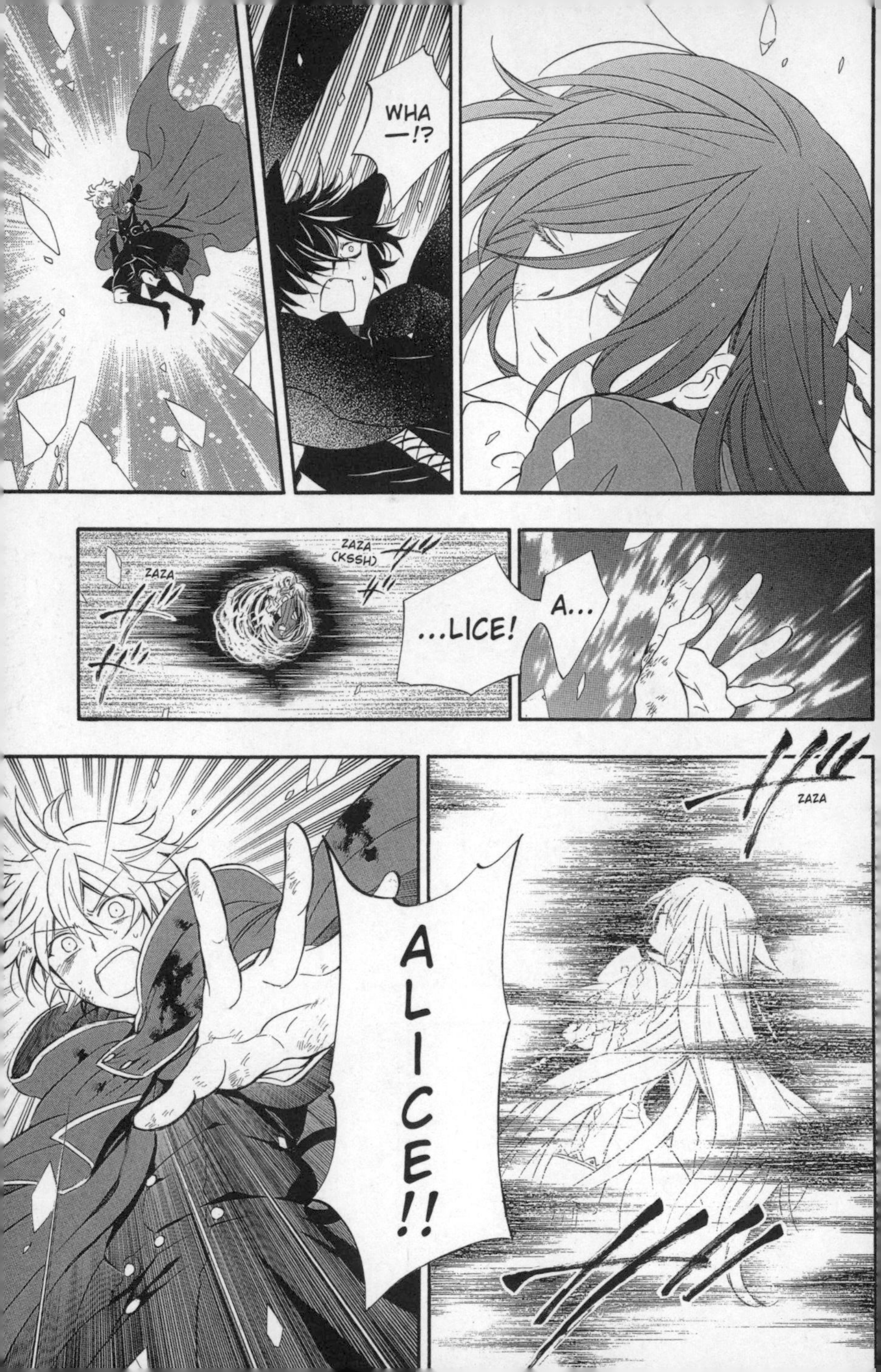
WHA—!?
A...
...LICE!
ZAZA (KSSH)
ZAZA
ZAZA
ALICE!!

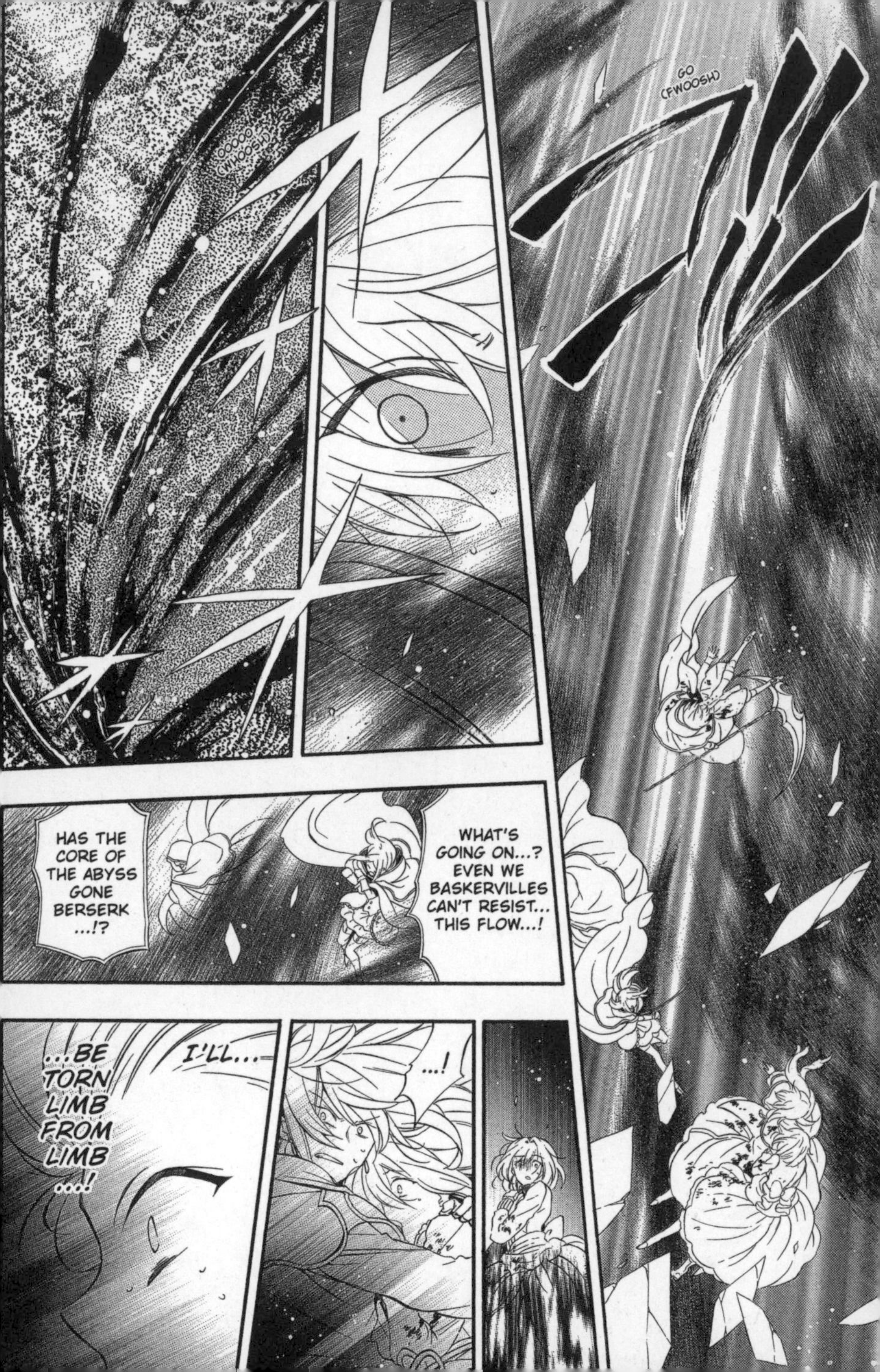
GO
(FWOOSH)
OOOOO
(WHOOSH)
WHAT'S GOING ON...? EVEN WE BASKERVILLES CAN'T RESIST... THIS FLOW...!
HAS THE CORE OF THE ABYSS GONE BERSERK ...!?
...!
I'LL...
...BE TORN LIMB FROM LIMB ...!

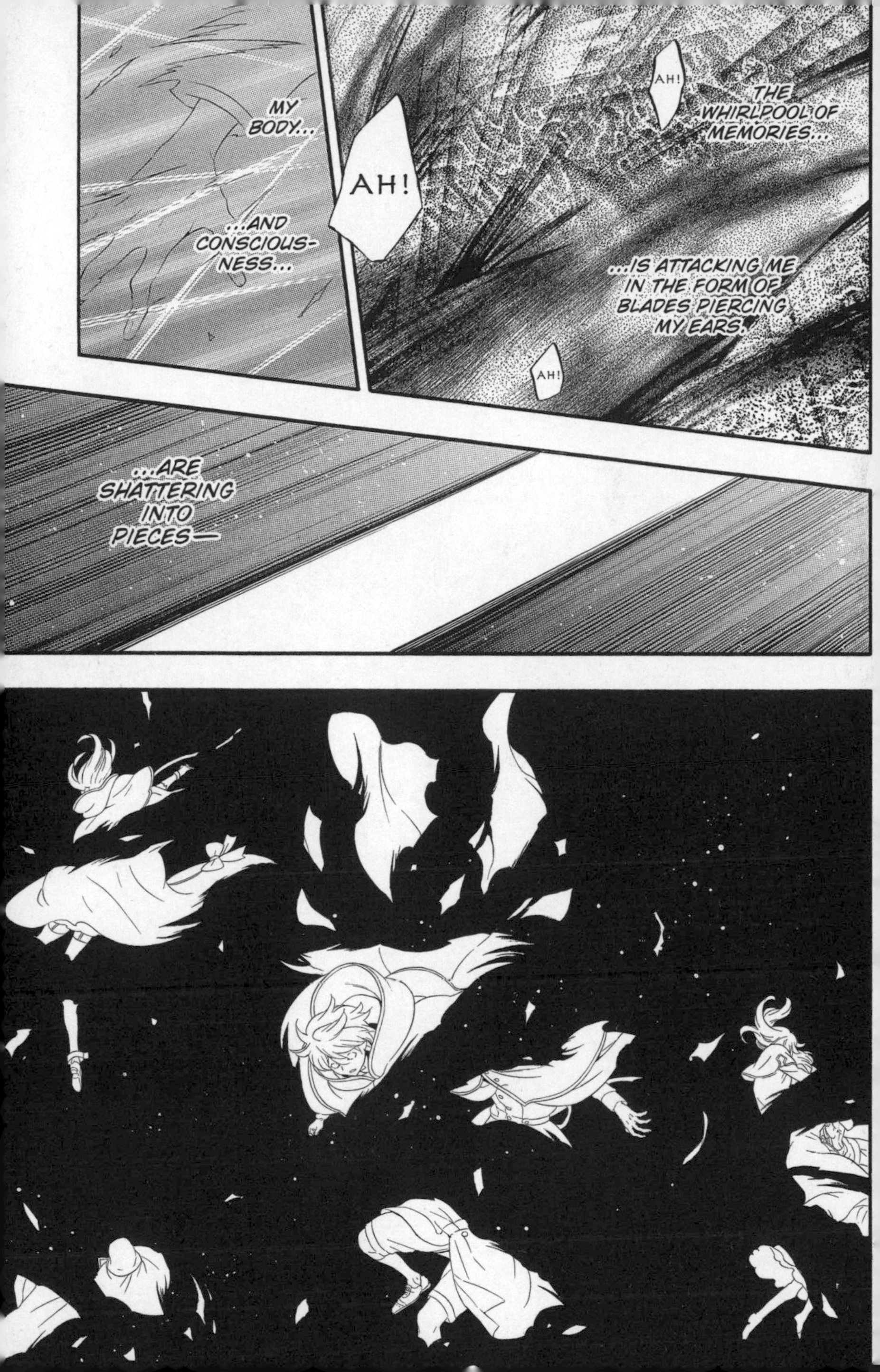
THE WHIRLPOOL OF MEMORIES...
AH!
AH!
...IS ATTACKING ME IN THE FORM OF BLADES PIERCING MY EARS.
AH!
MY BODY...
...AND CONSCIOUS-NESS...
...ARE SHATTERING INTO PIECES—

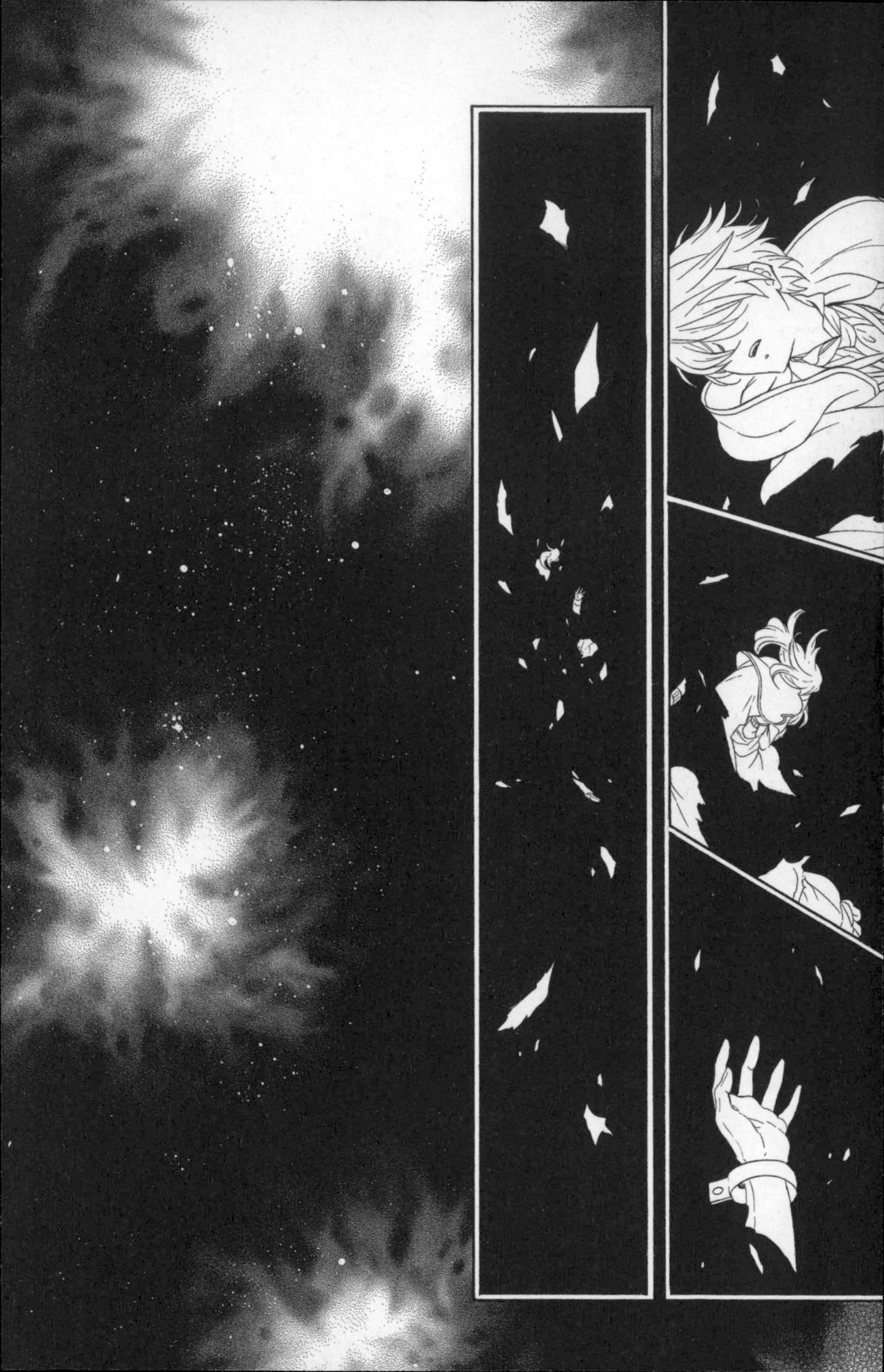

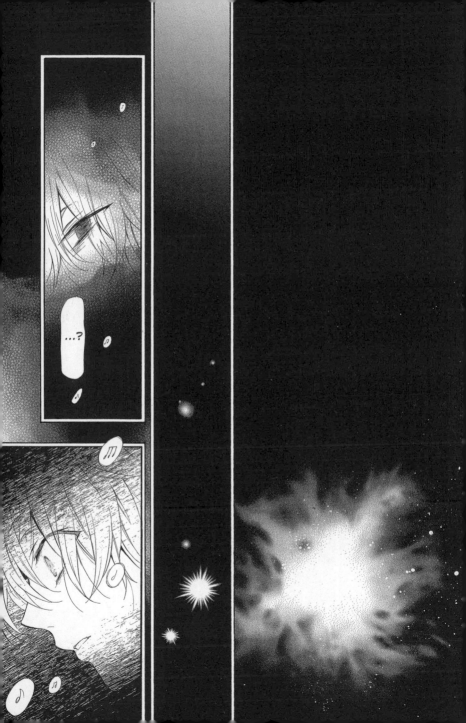

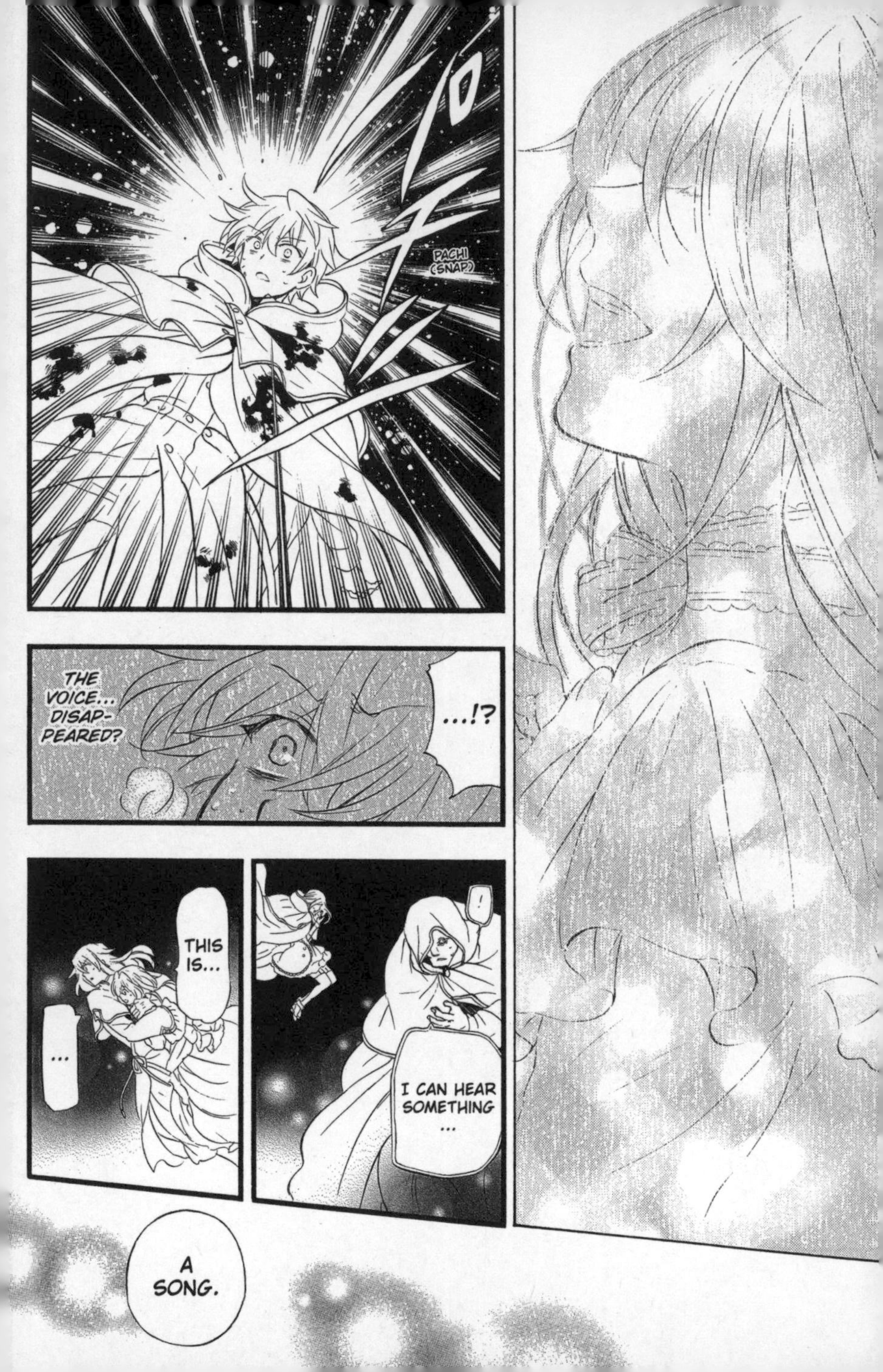
PACHI (SNAP)
...!?
THE VOICE... DISAPPEARED?
!
I CAN HEAR SOMETHING ...
THIS IS...
...
A SONG.

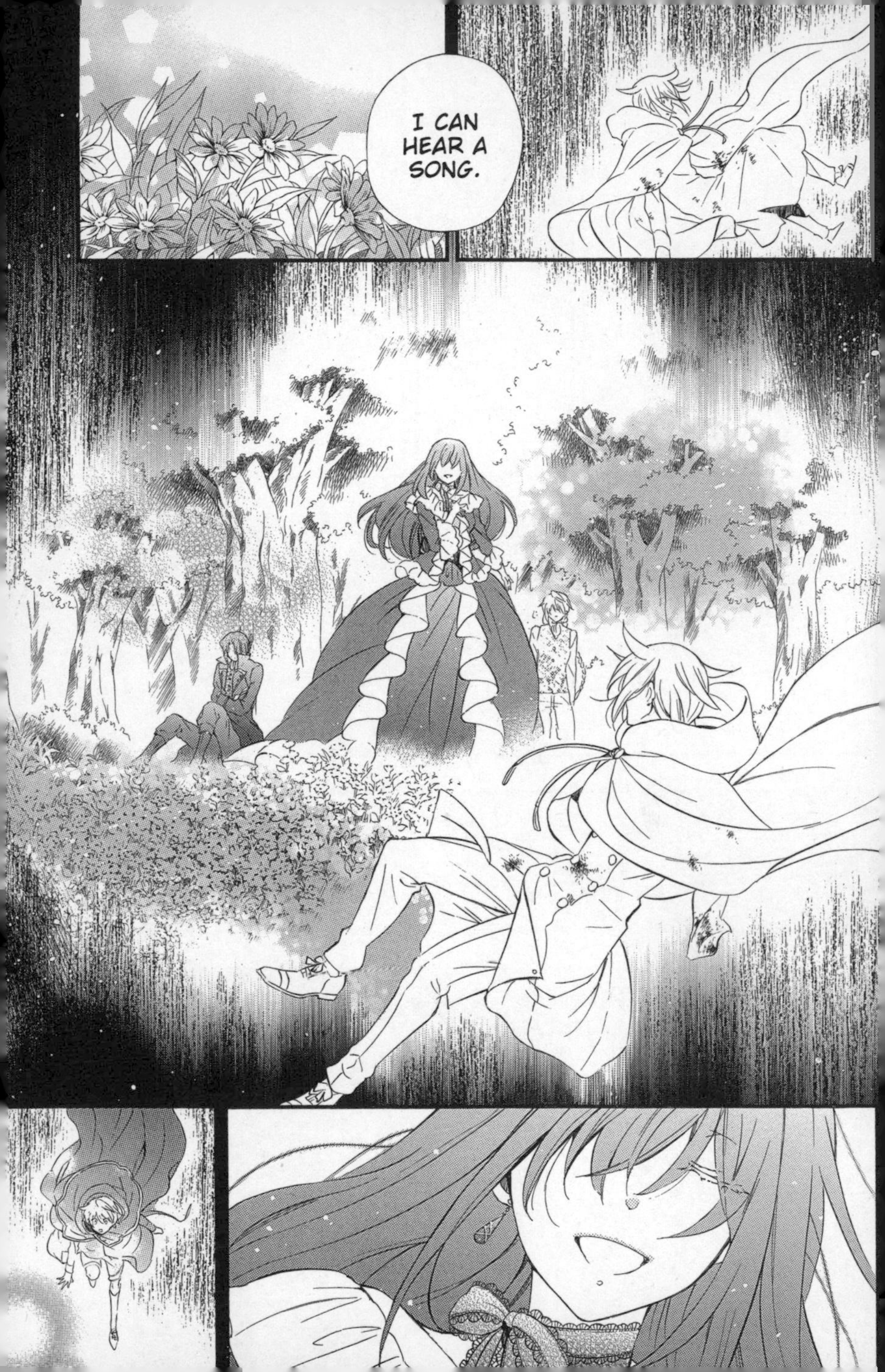
I CAN HEAR A SONG.

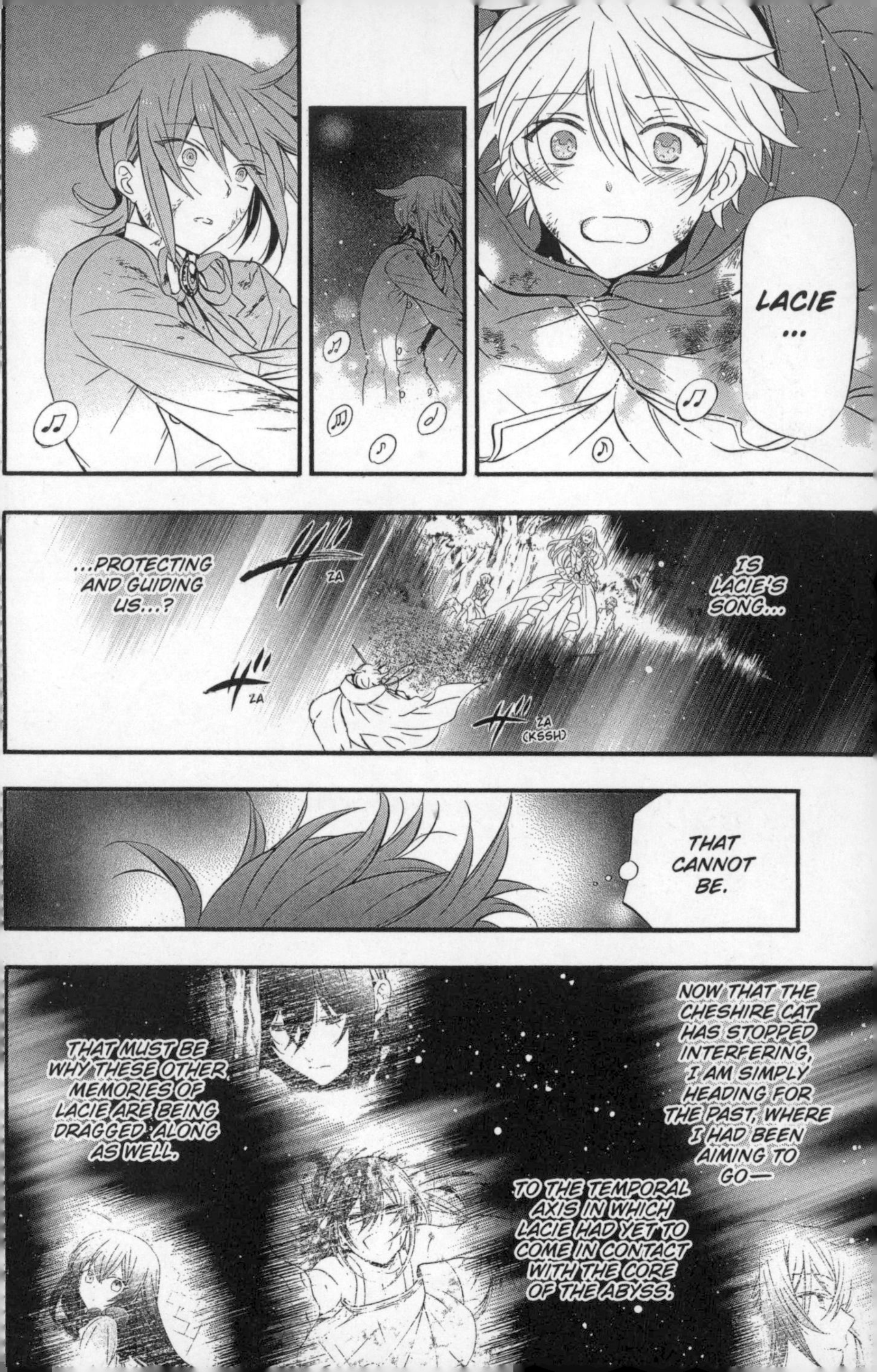
LACIE ...
IS LACIE'S SONG...
...PROTECTING AND GUIDING US...?
ZA
ZA (KSSH)
ZA
THAT CANNOT BE.
NOW THAT THE CHESHIRE CAT HAS STOPPED INTERFERING, I AM SIMPLY HEADING FOR THE PAST, WHERE I HAD BEEN AIMING TO GO—
TO THE TEMPORAL AXIS IN WHICH LACIE HAD YET TO COME IN CONTACT WITH THE CORE OF THE ABYSS.
THAT MUST BE WHY THESE OTHER MEMORIES OF LACIE ARE BEING DRAGGED ALONG AS WELL.

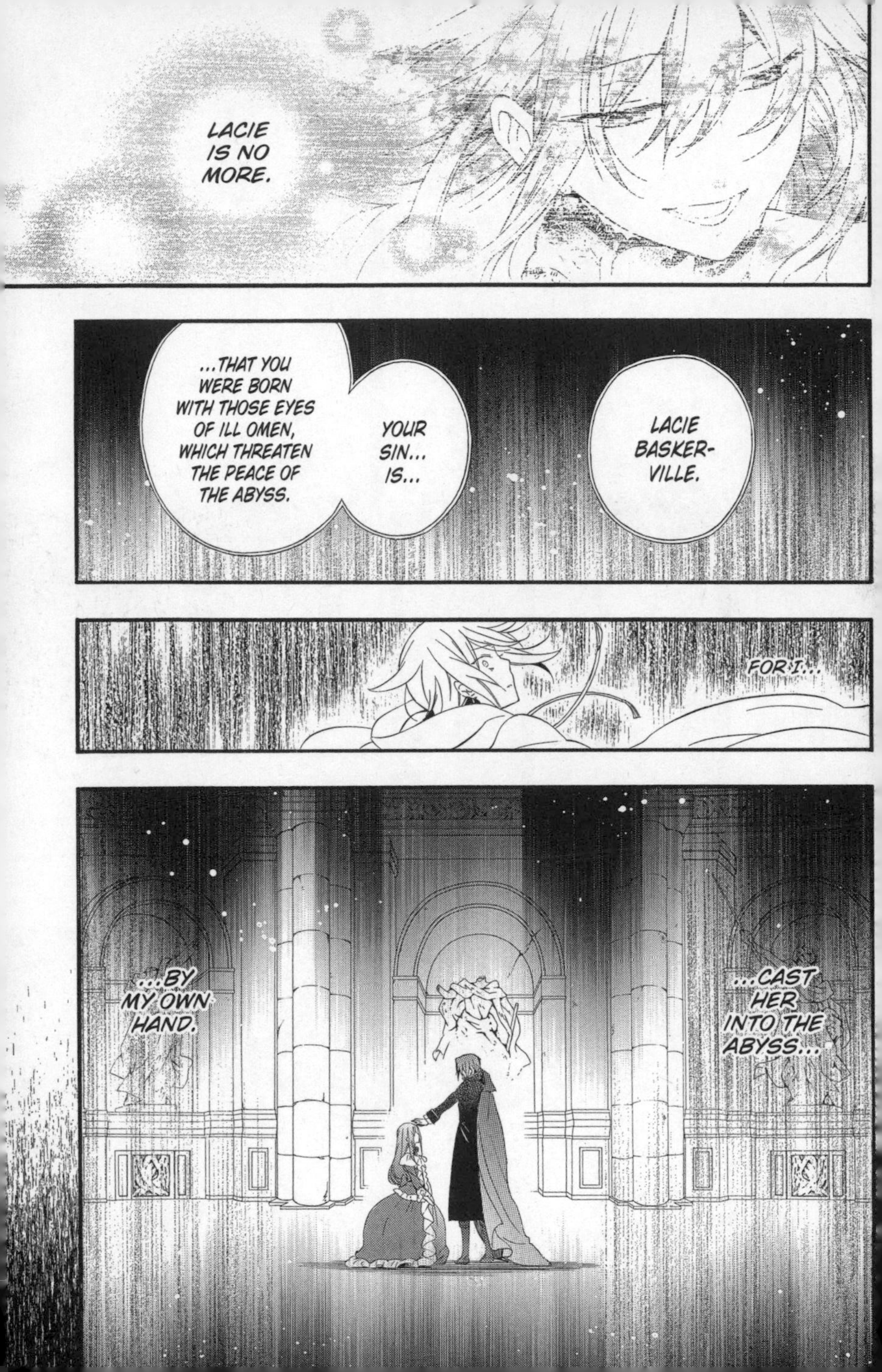
LACIE IS NO MORE.
LACIE BASKERVILLE.
YOUR SIN... IS...
...THAT YOU WERE BORN WITH THOSE EYES OF ILL OMEN, WHICH THREATEN THE PEACE OF THE ABYSS.
FOR I...
...CAST HER INTO THE ABYSS...
...BY MY OWN HAND.

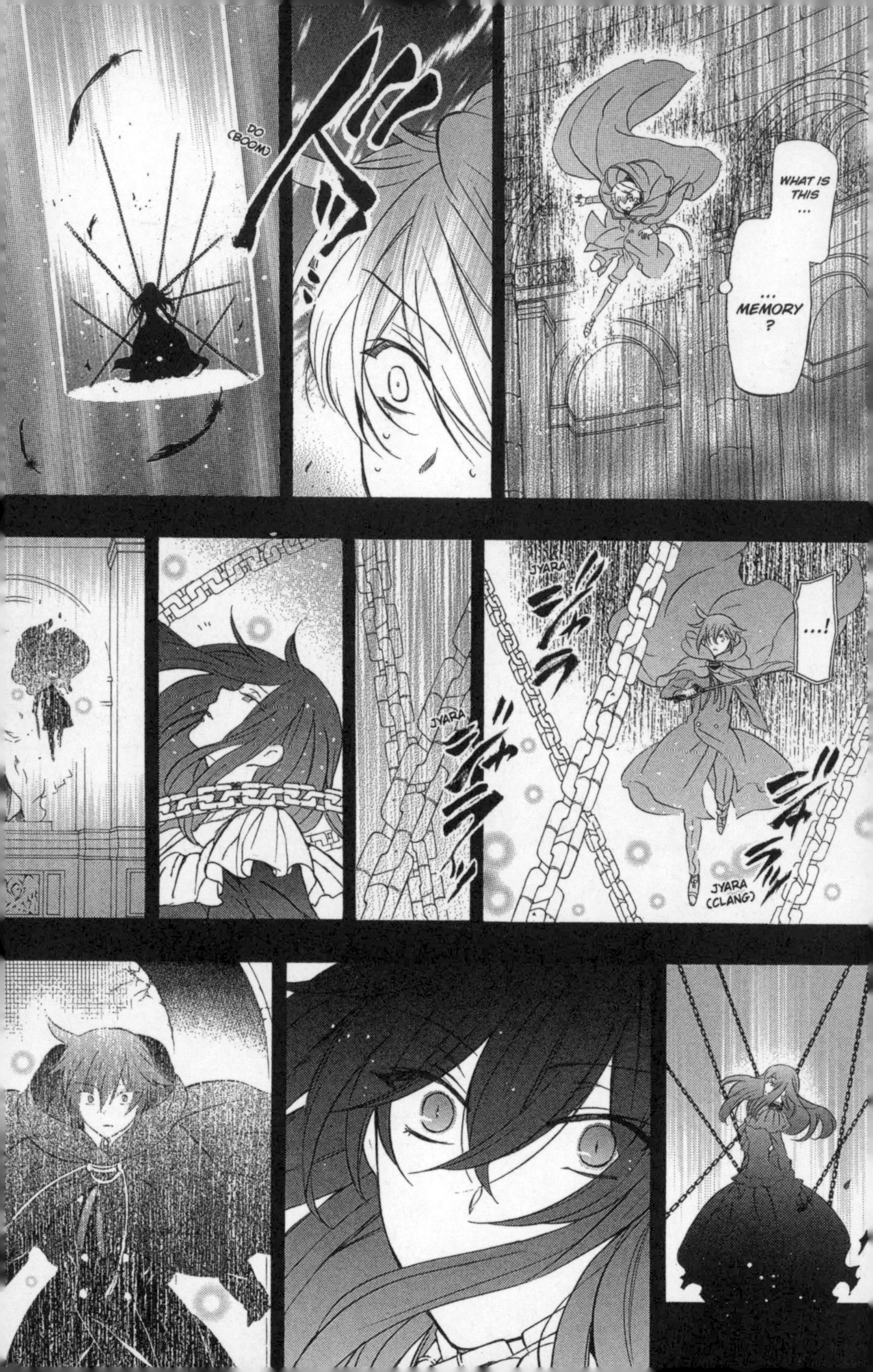
WHAT IS THIS ...
... MEMORY ?
DO (BOOM)
...!
JYARA
JYARA (CLANG)
JYARA

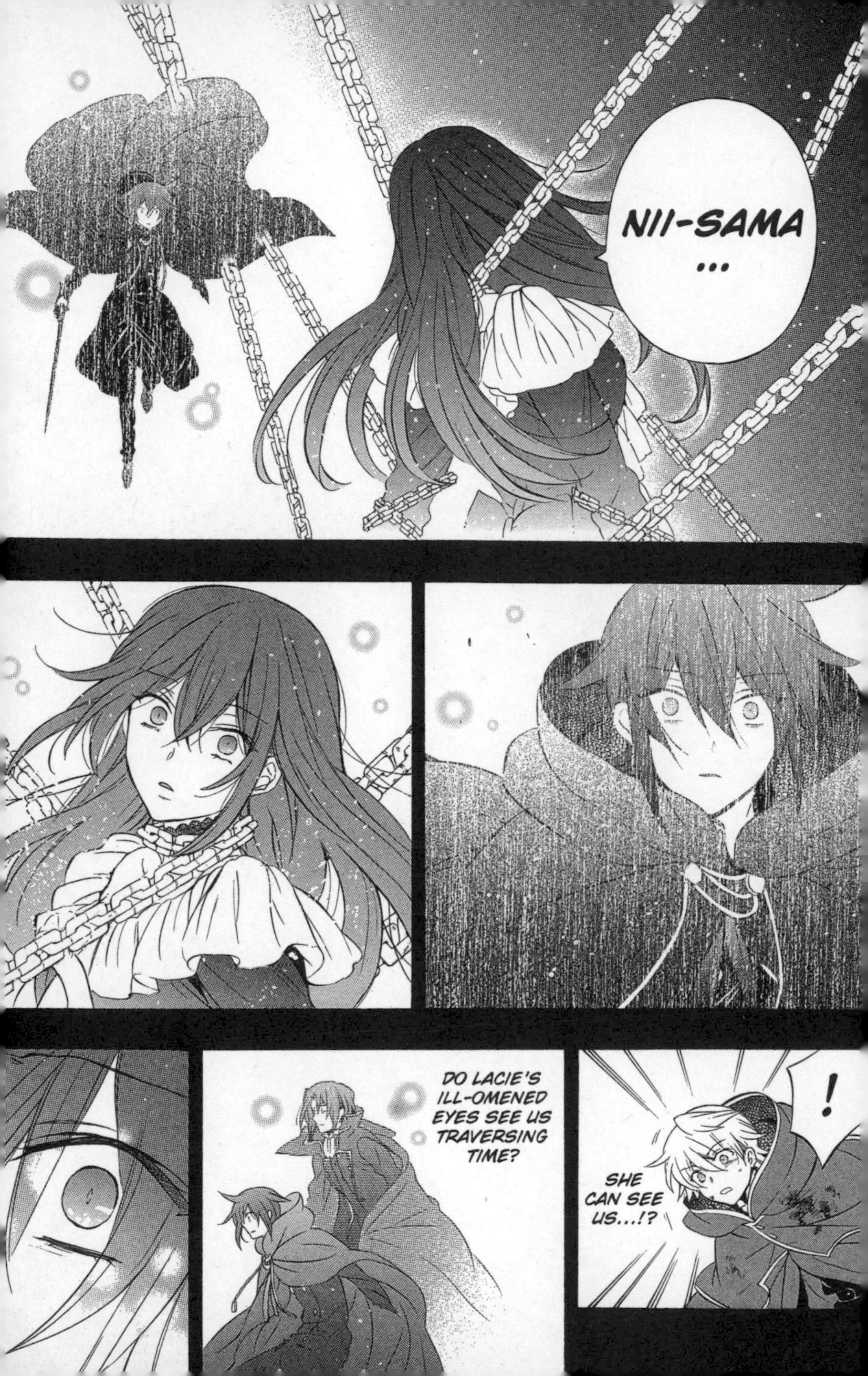
NII-SAMA ...
!
SHE CAN SEE US...!?
DO LACIE'S ILL-OMENED EYES SEE US TRAVERSING TIME?

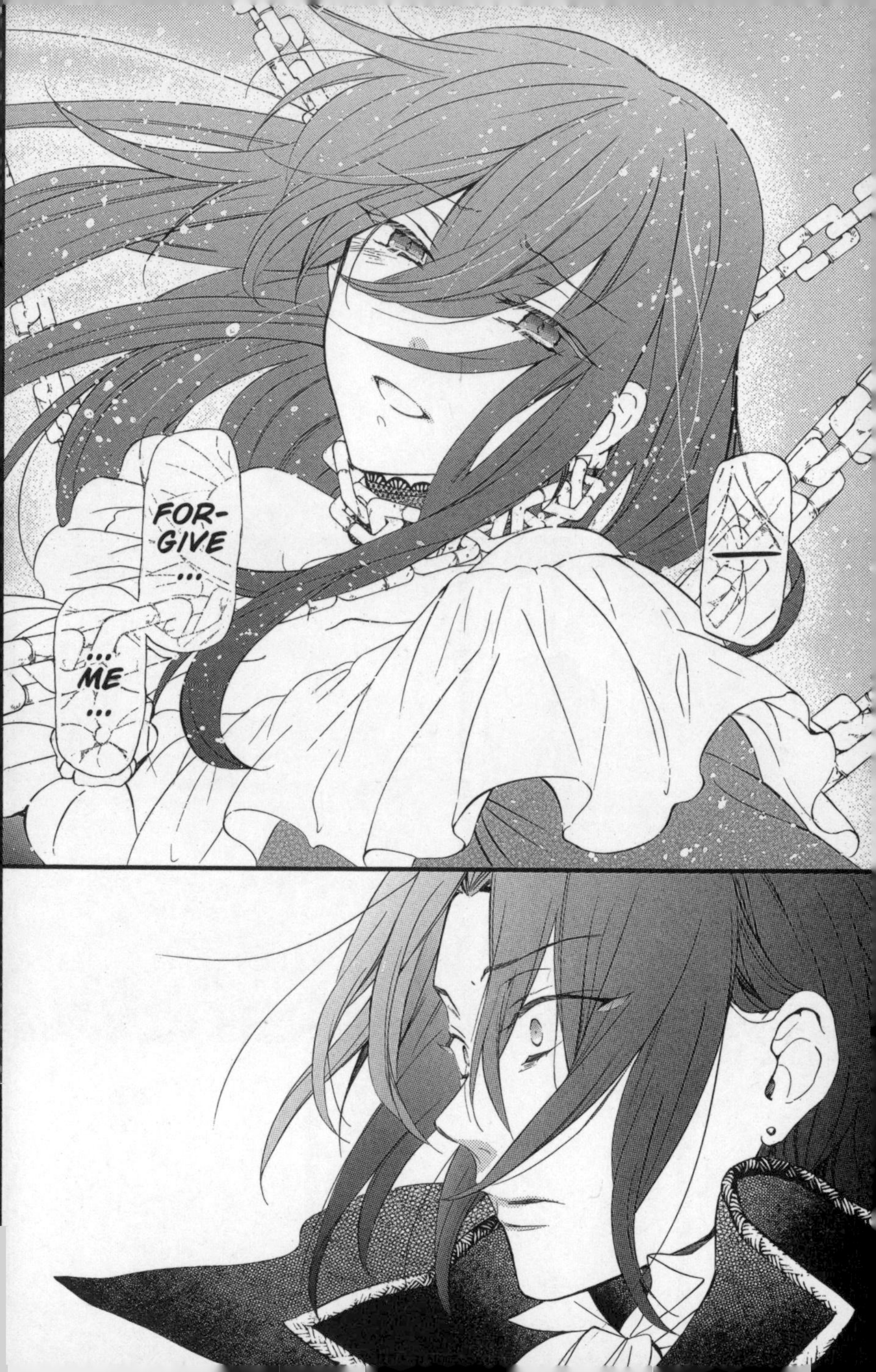
FOR-GIVE ...
... ME ...

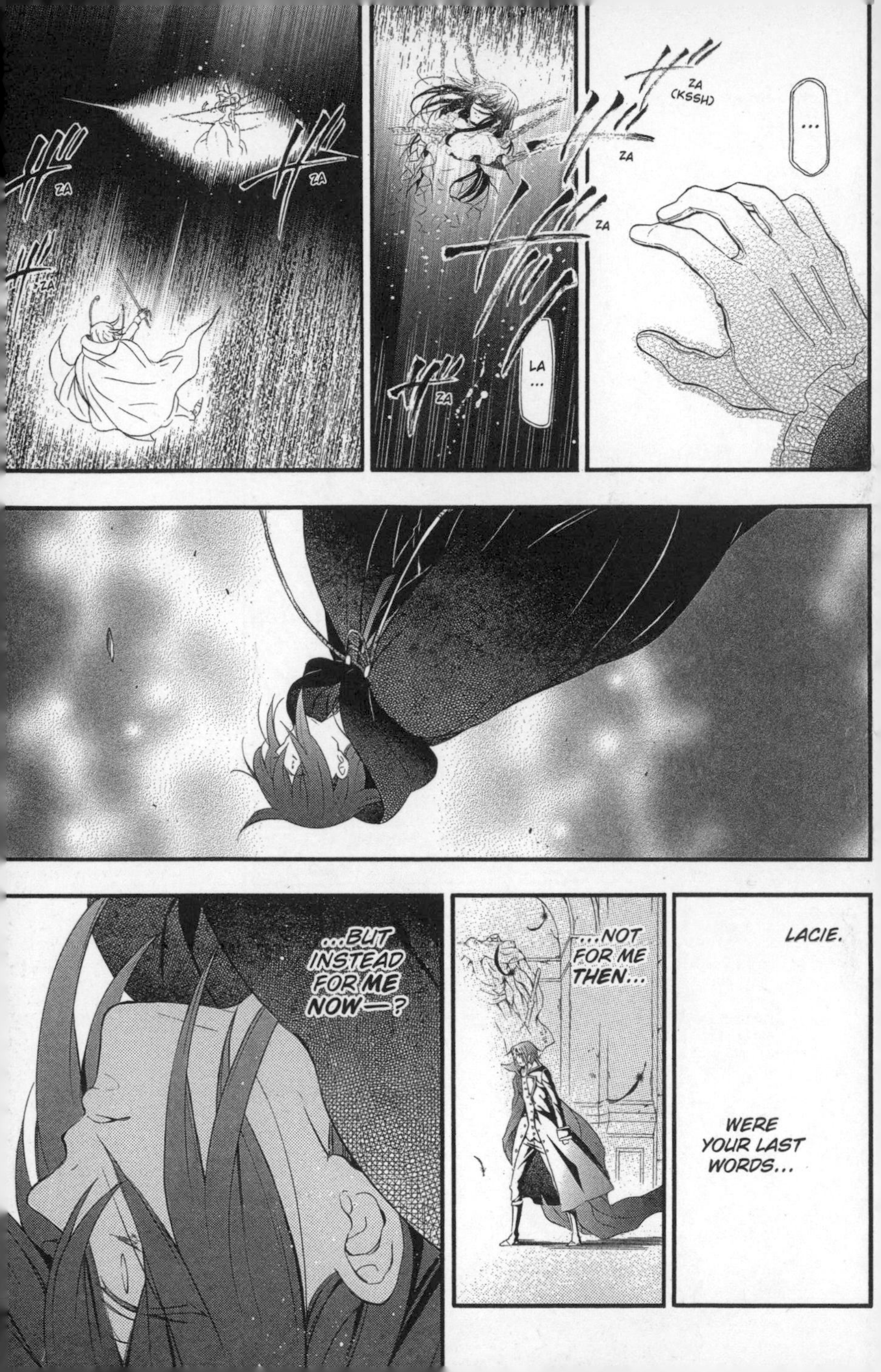
...
ZA (KSSH)
ZA
ZA
LA ...
ZA
ZA
ZA
ZA
LACIE.
WERE YOUR LAST WORDS...
...NOT FOR ME THEN...
...BUT INSTEAD FOR ME NOW—?

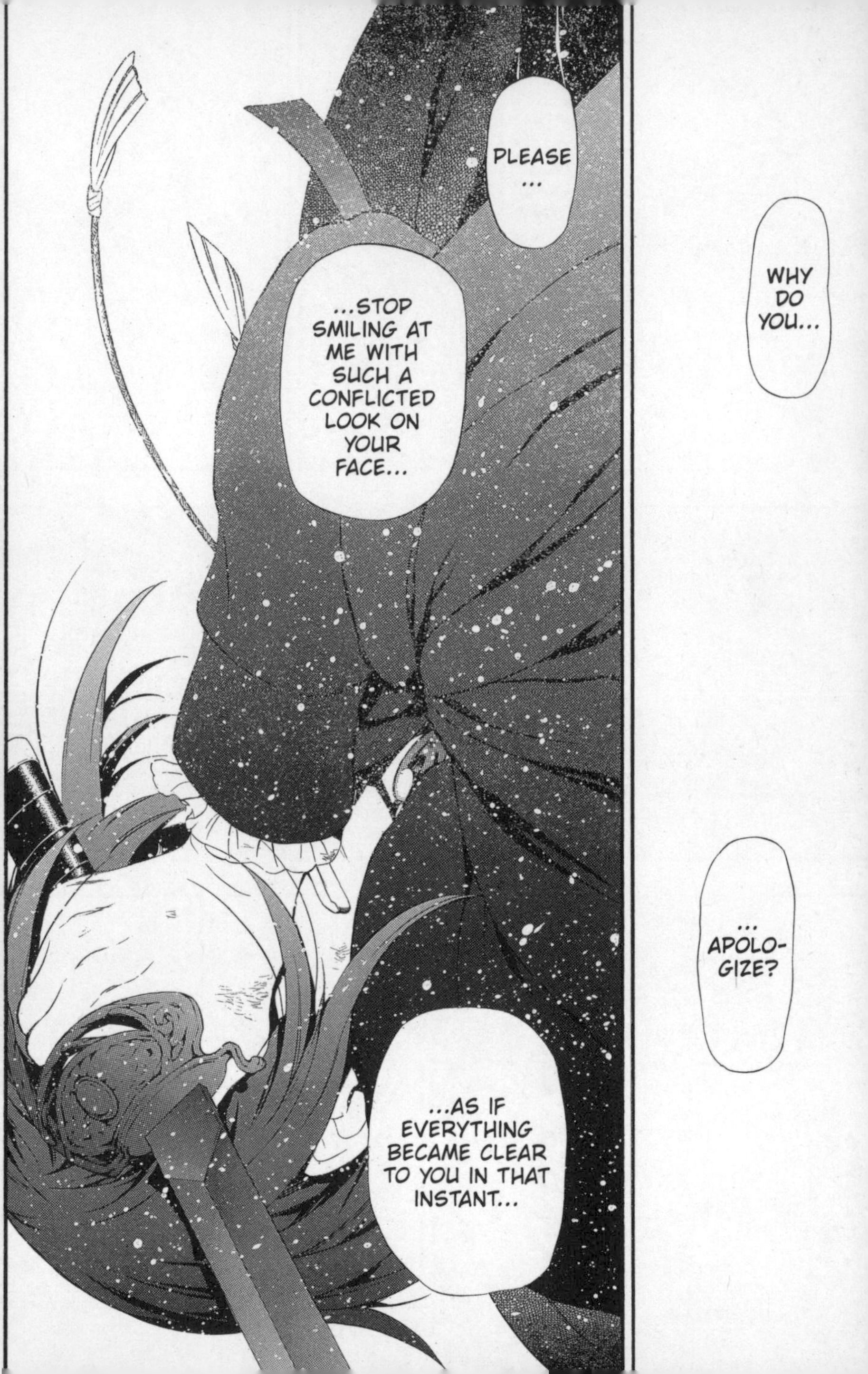
WHY DO YOU...
...APOLOGIZE?
PLEASE...
...STOP SMILING AT ME WITH SUCH A CONFLICTED LOOK ON YOUR FACE...
...AS IF EVERYTHING BECAME CLEAR TO YOU IN THAT INSTANT...

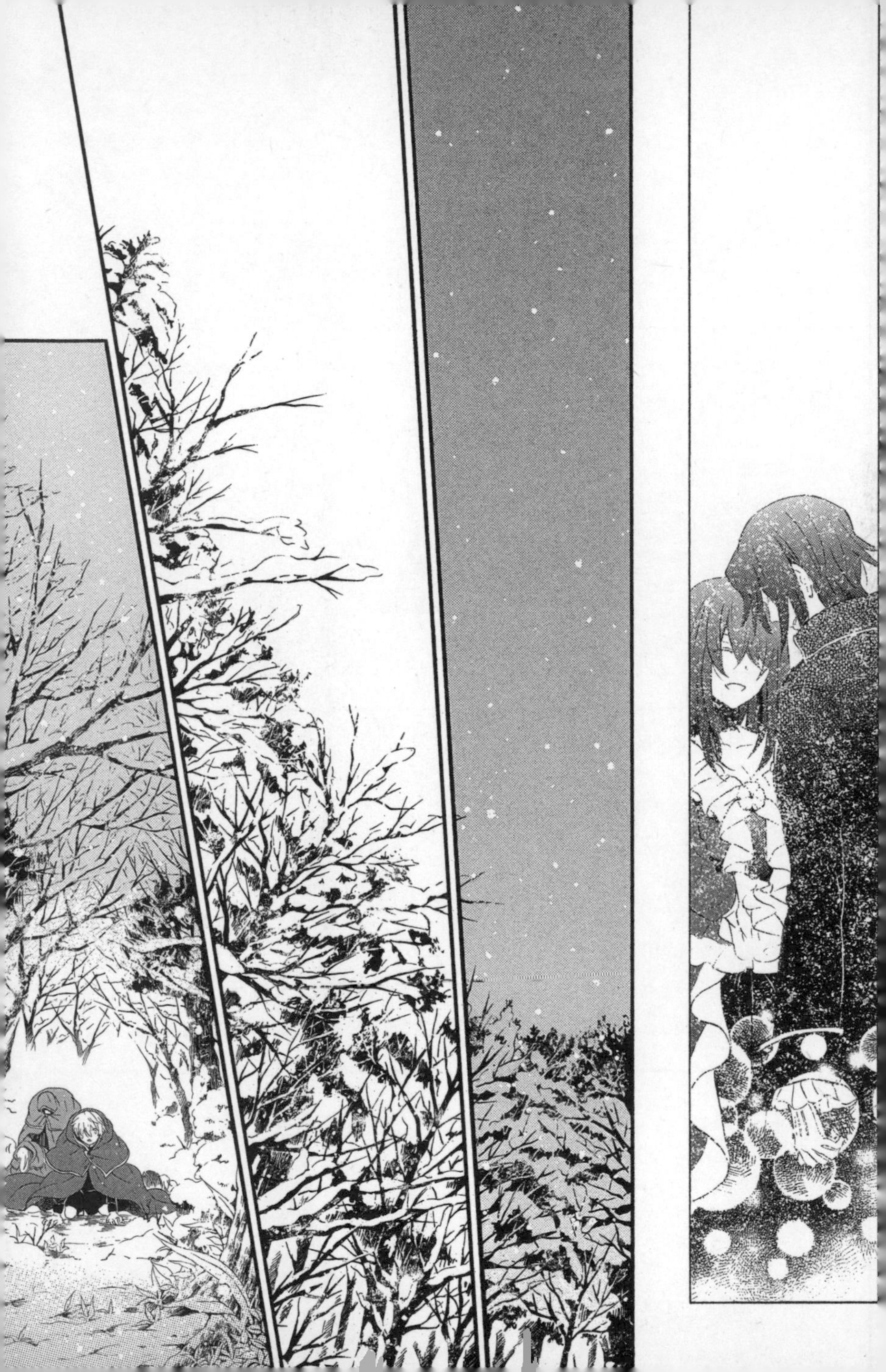

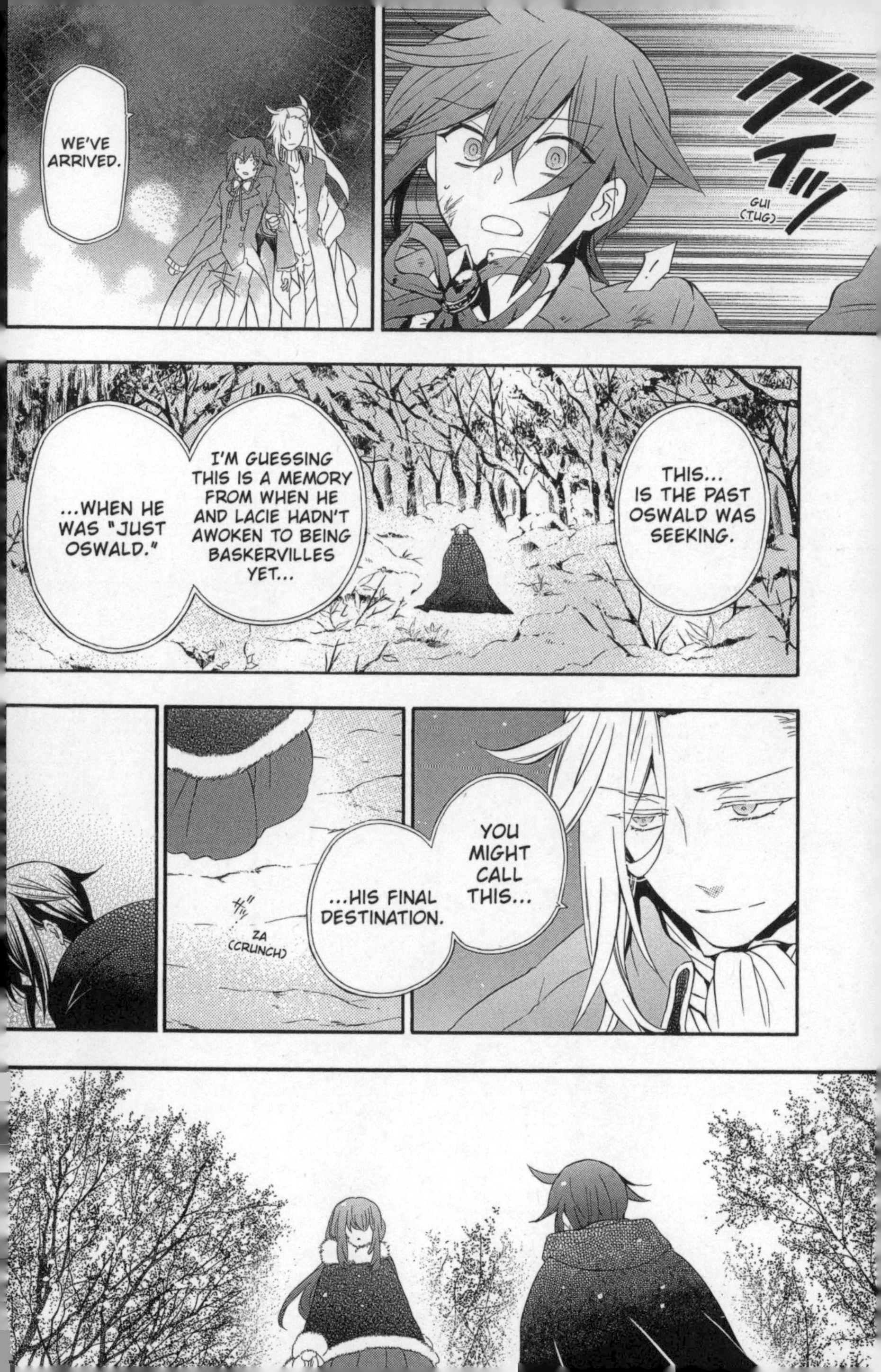
GUI (TUG)
WE'VE ARRIVED.
THIS... IS THE PAST OSWALD WAS SEEKING.
I'M GUESSING THIS IS A MEMORY FROM WHEN HE AND LACIE HADN'T AWOKEN TO BEING BASKERVILLES YET...
...WHEN HE WAS "JUST OSWALD."
YOU MIGHT CALL THIS...
...HIS FINAL DESTINATION.
ZA (CRUNCH)

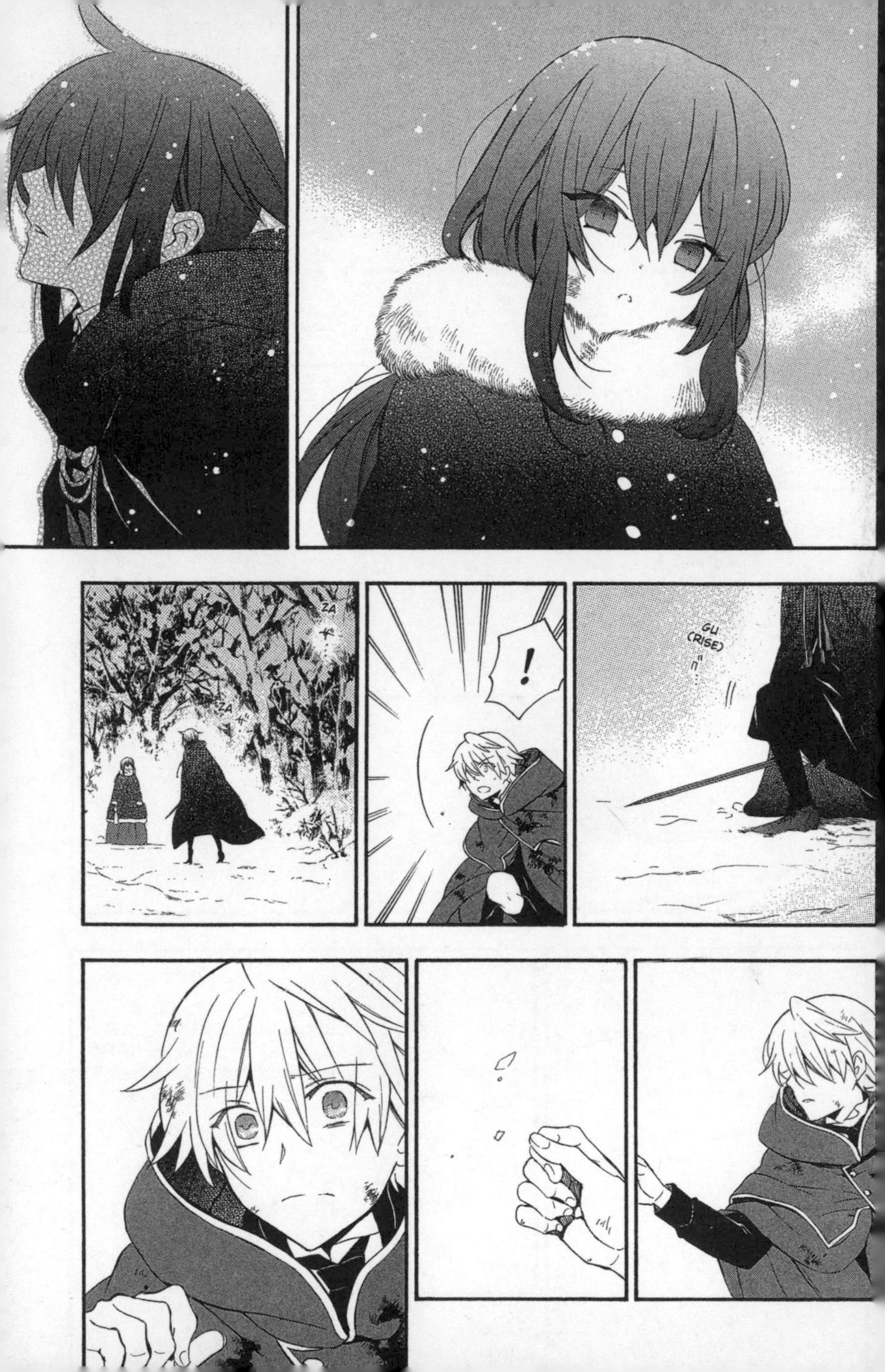
GU
(RISE)
!
ZA
ZA

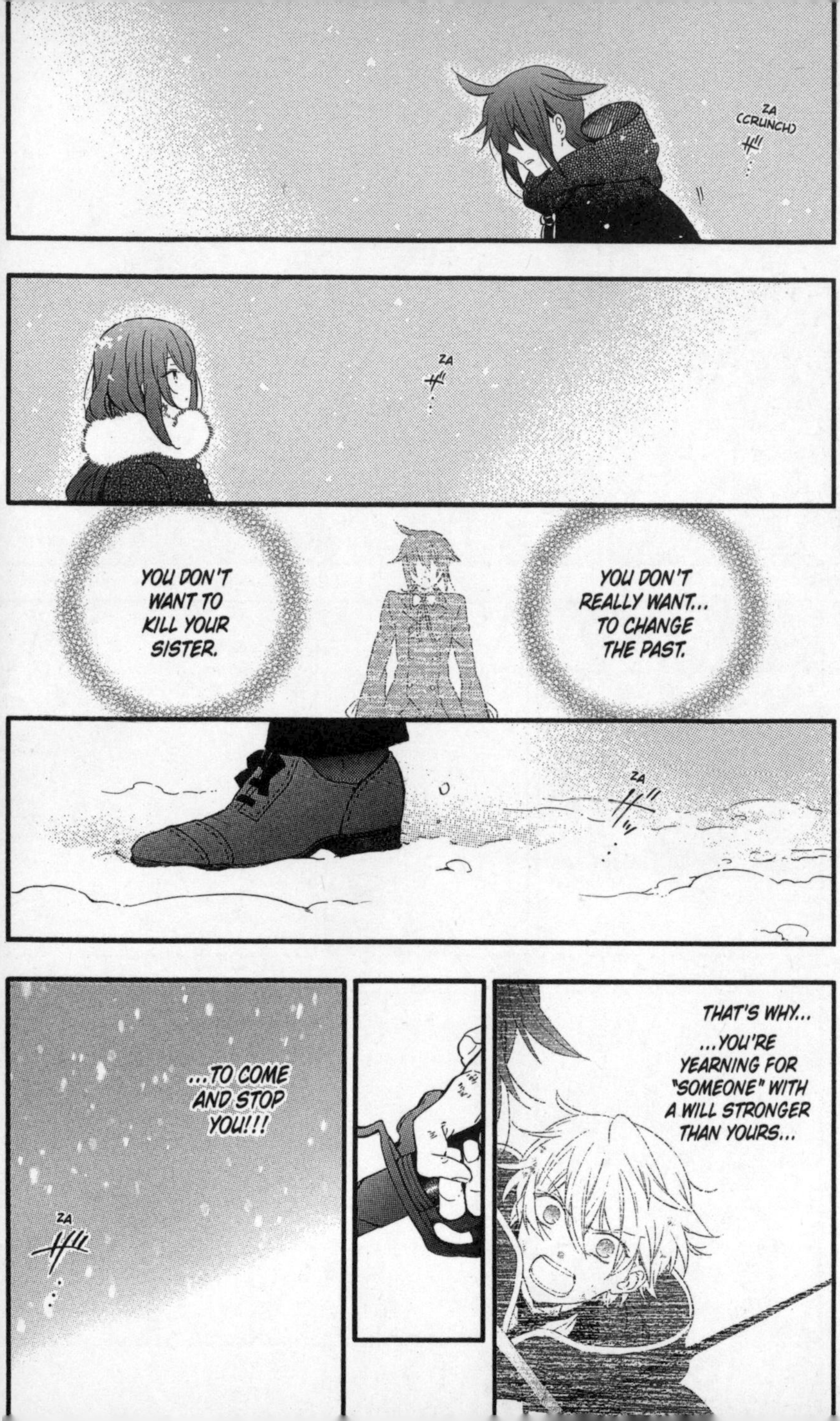
ZA
(CRUNCH)
ZA
YOU DON'T REALLY WANT... TO CHANGE THE PAST.
YOU DON'T WANT TO KILL YOUR SISTER.
ZA
THAT'S WHY...
...YOU'RE YEARNING FOR "SOMEONE" WITH A WILL STRONGER THAN YOURS...
...TO COME AND STOP YOU!!!
ZA

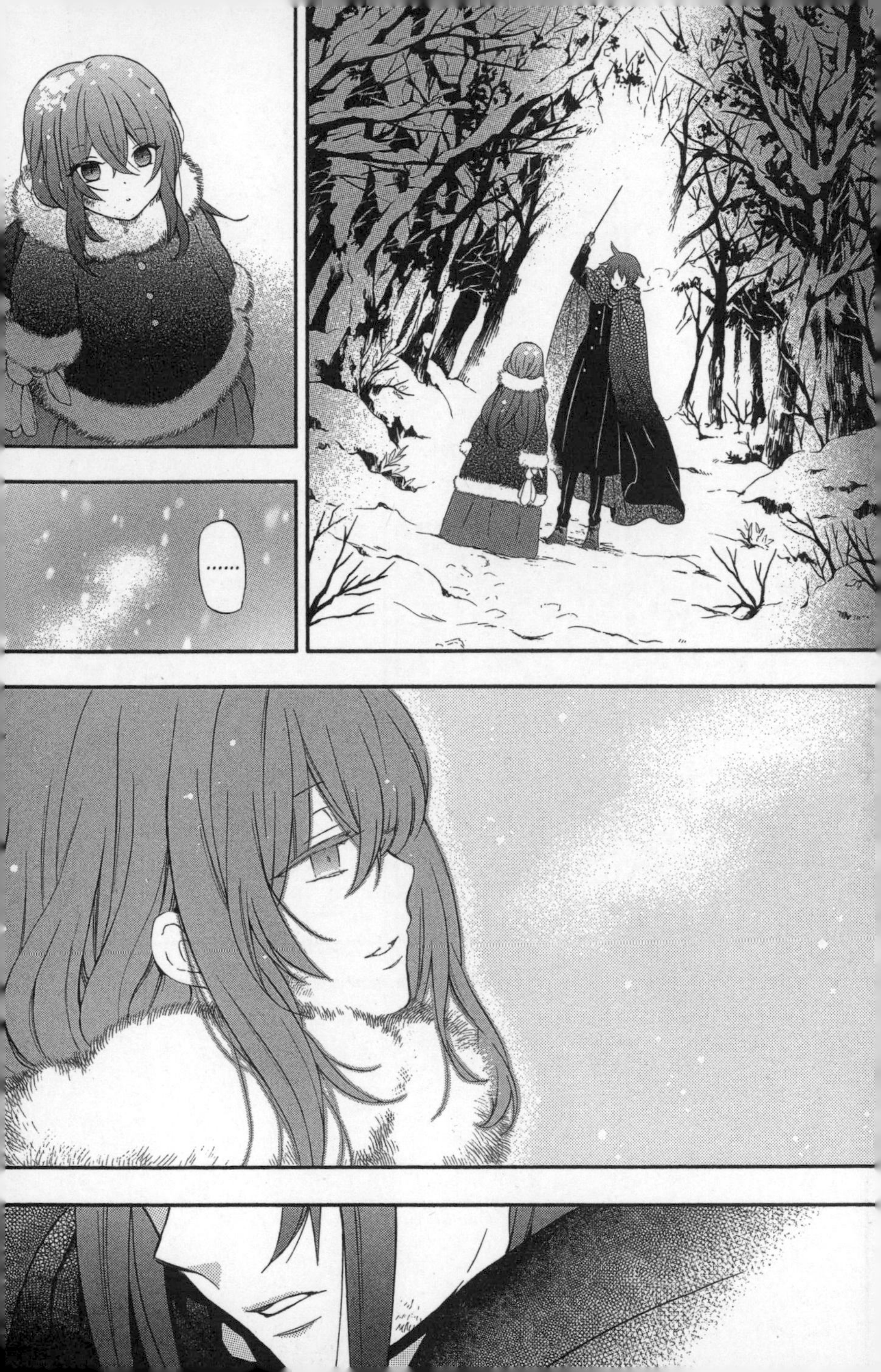
......

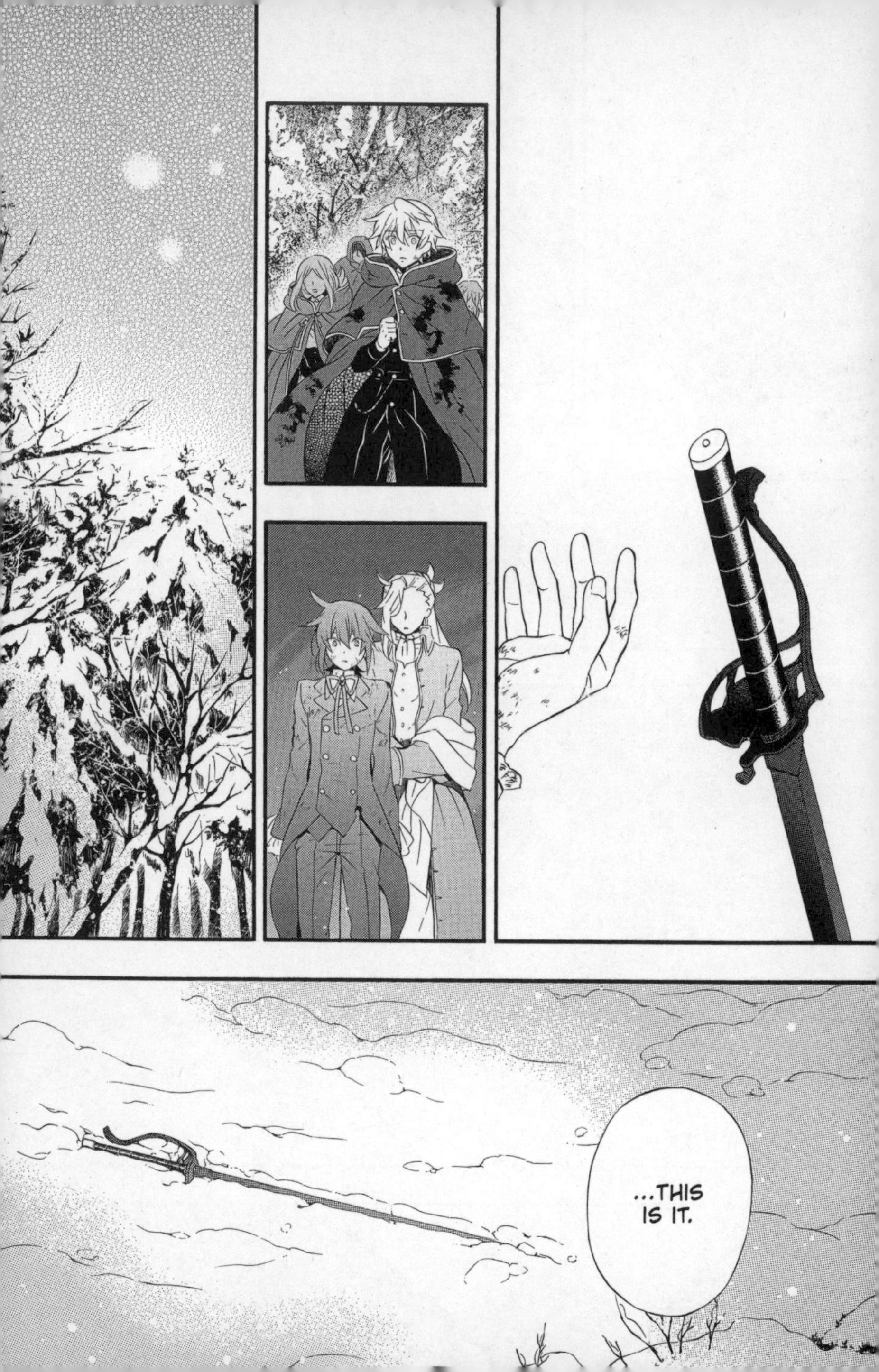
...THIS IS IT.

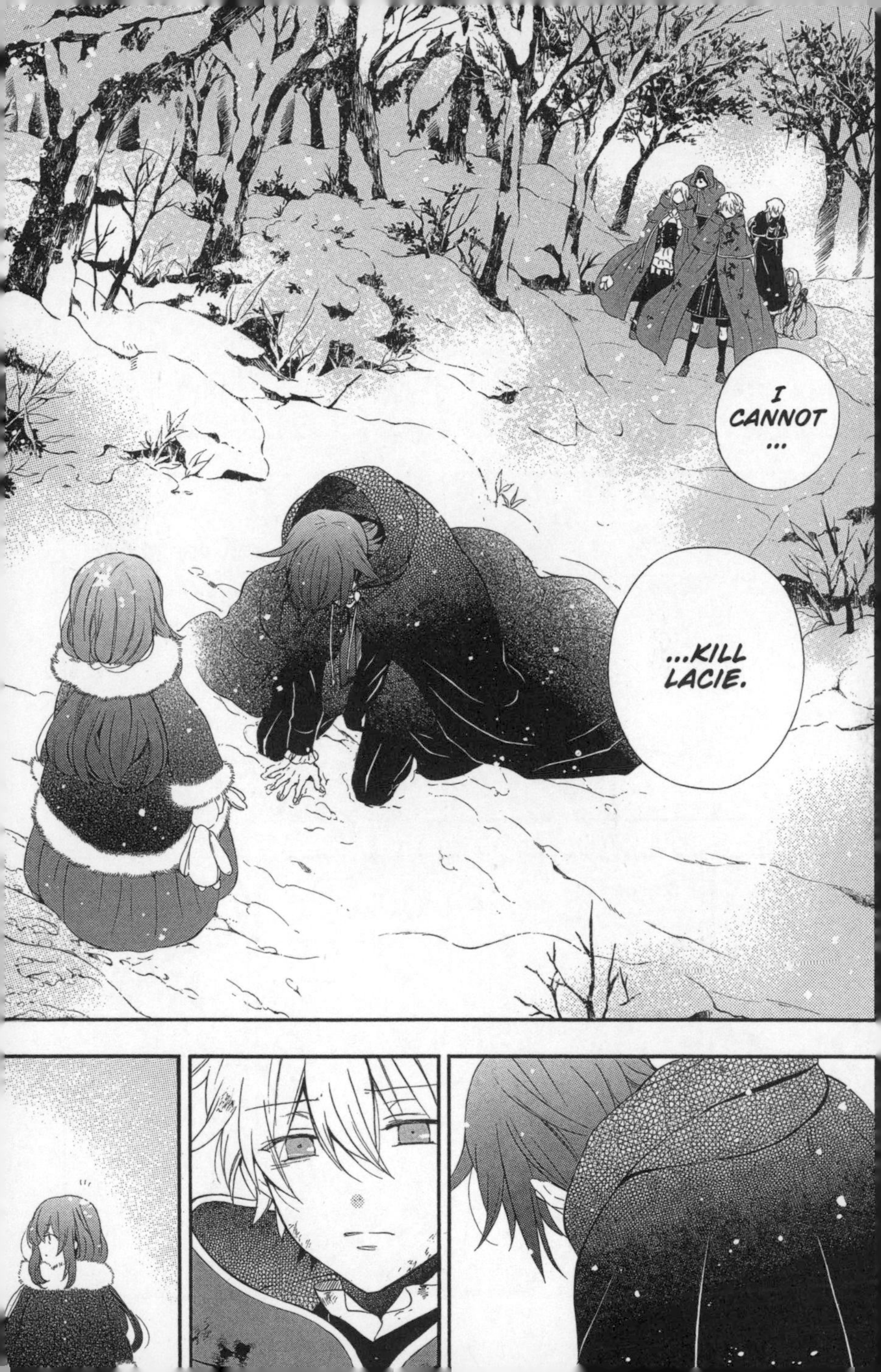
I CANNOT ...
...KILL LACIE.

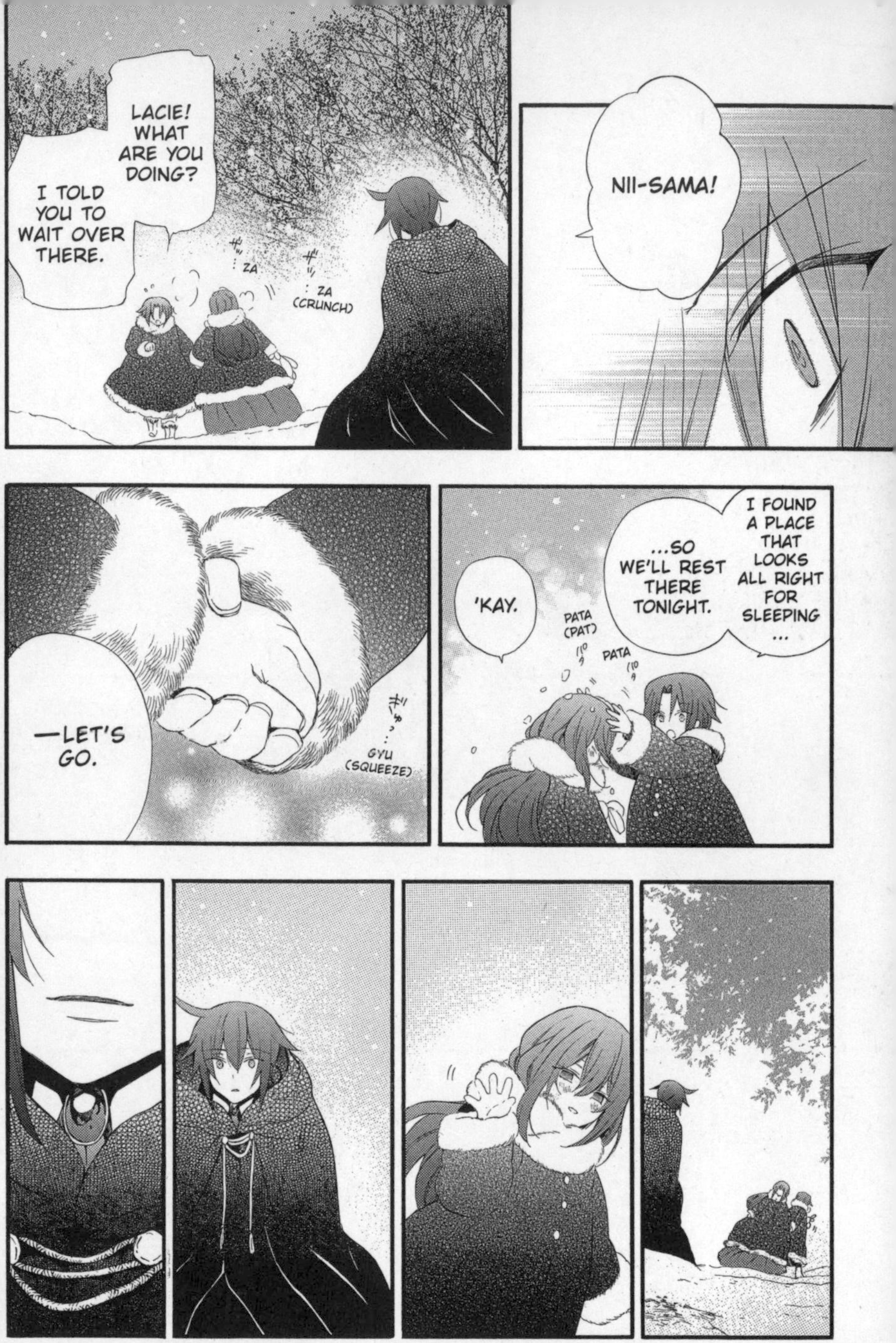
NII-SAMA!
LACIE! WHAT ARE YOU DOING?
I TOLD YOU TO WAIT OVER THERE.
ZA
ZA (CRUNCH)
I FOUND A PLACE THAT LOOKS ALL RIGHT FOR SLEEPING...
...SO WE'LL REST THERE TONIGHT.
PATA (PAT)
PATA
'KAY.
GYU (SQUEEZE)
—LET'S GO.

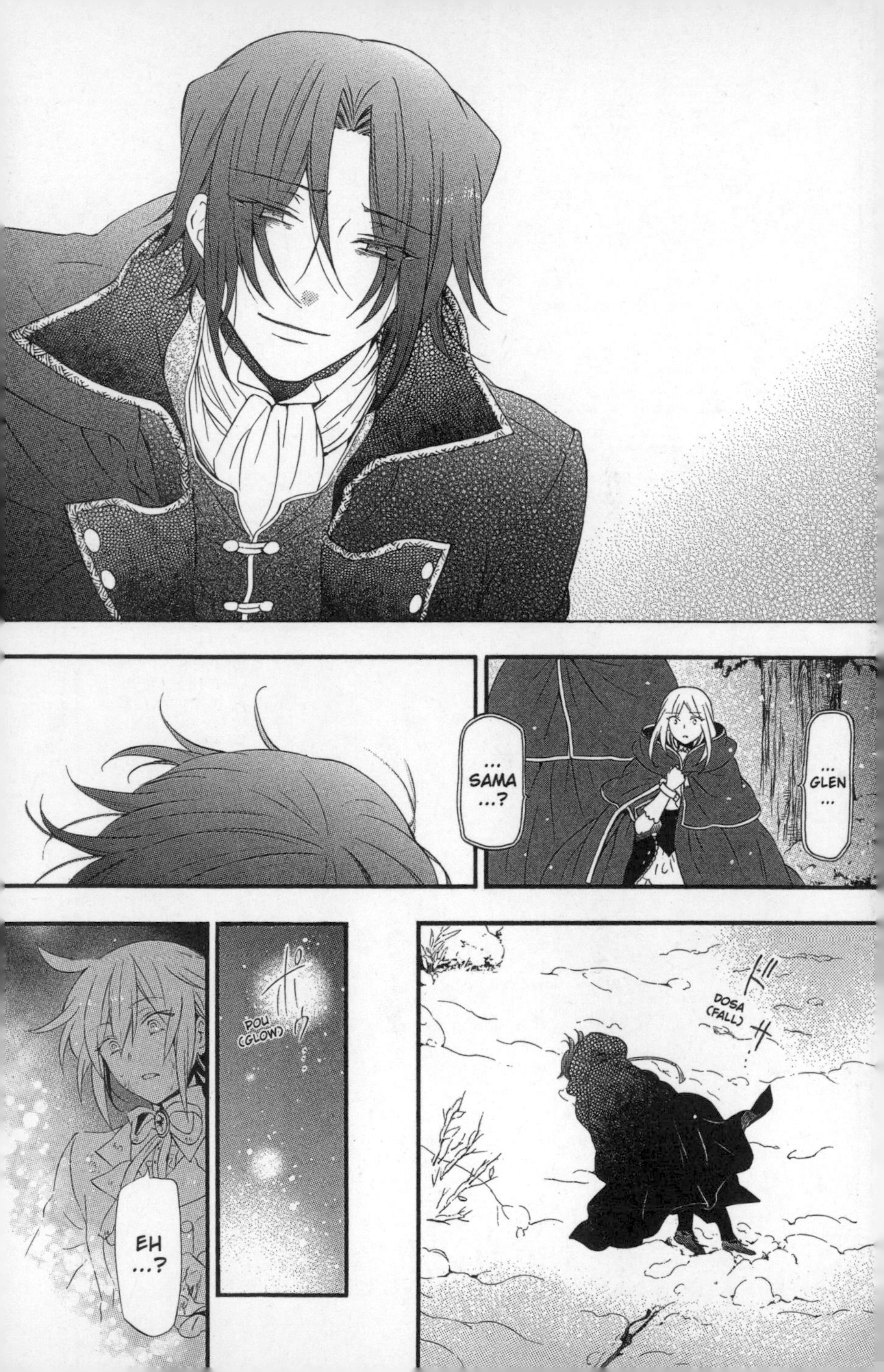
...GLEN...
...SAMA...?
DOSA (FALL)
POU (GLOW)
EH...?

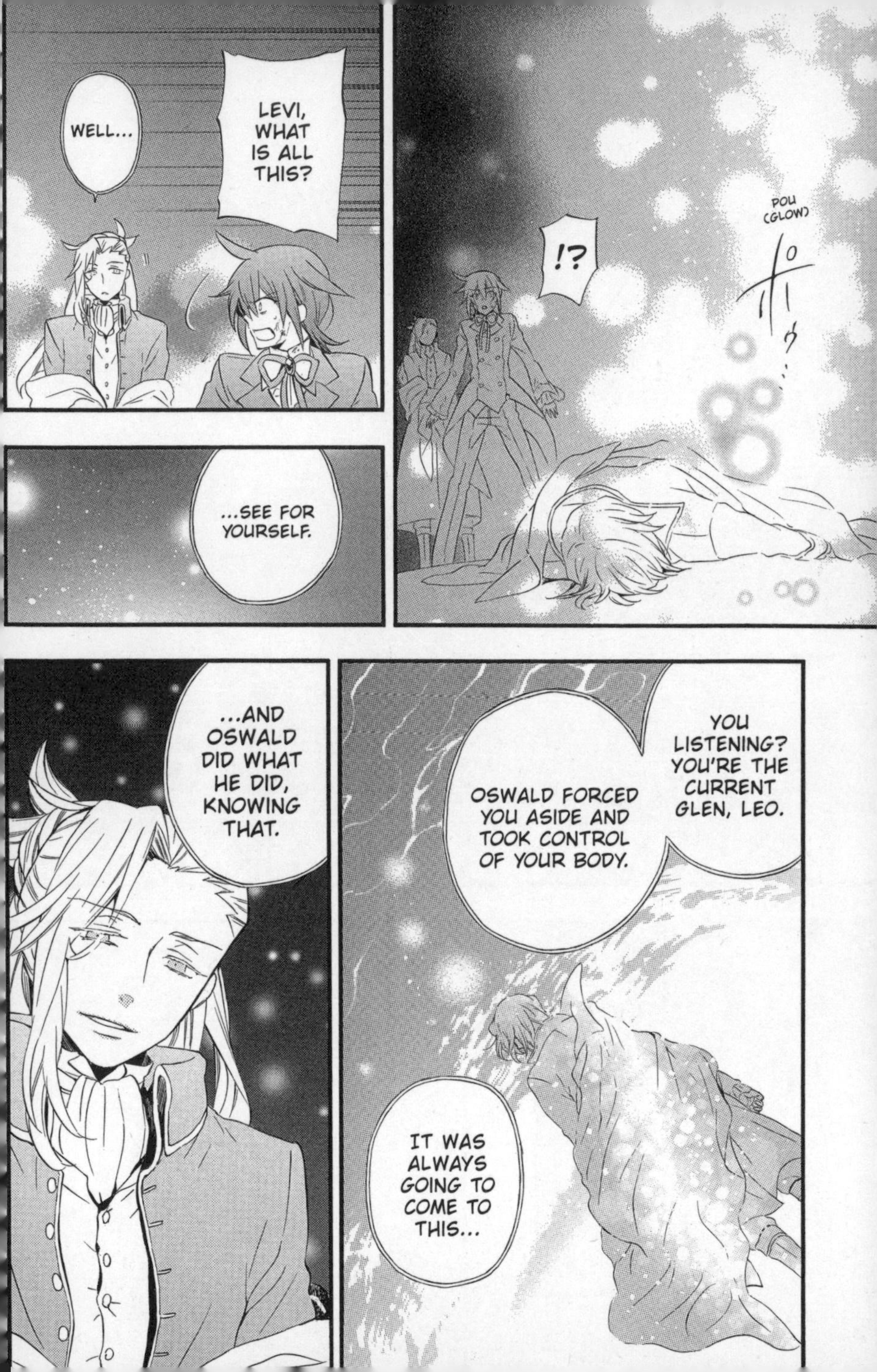
POU (GLOW)
!?
LEVI, WHAT IS ALL THIS?
WELL...
...SEE FOR YOURSELF.
YOU LISTENING? YOU'RE THE CURRENT GLEN, LEO.
OSWALD FORCED YOU ASIDE AND TOOK CONTROL OF YOUR BODY.
IT WAS ALWAYS GOING TO COME TO THIS...
...AND OSWALD DID WHAT HE DID, KNOWING THAT.

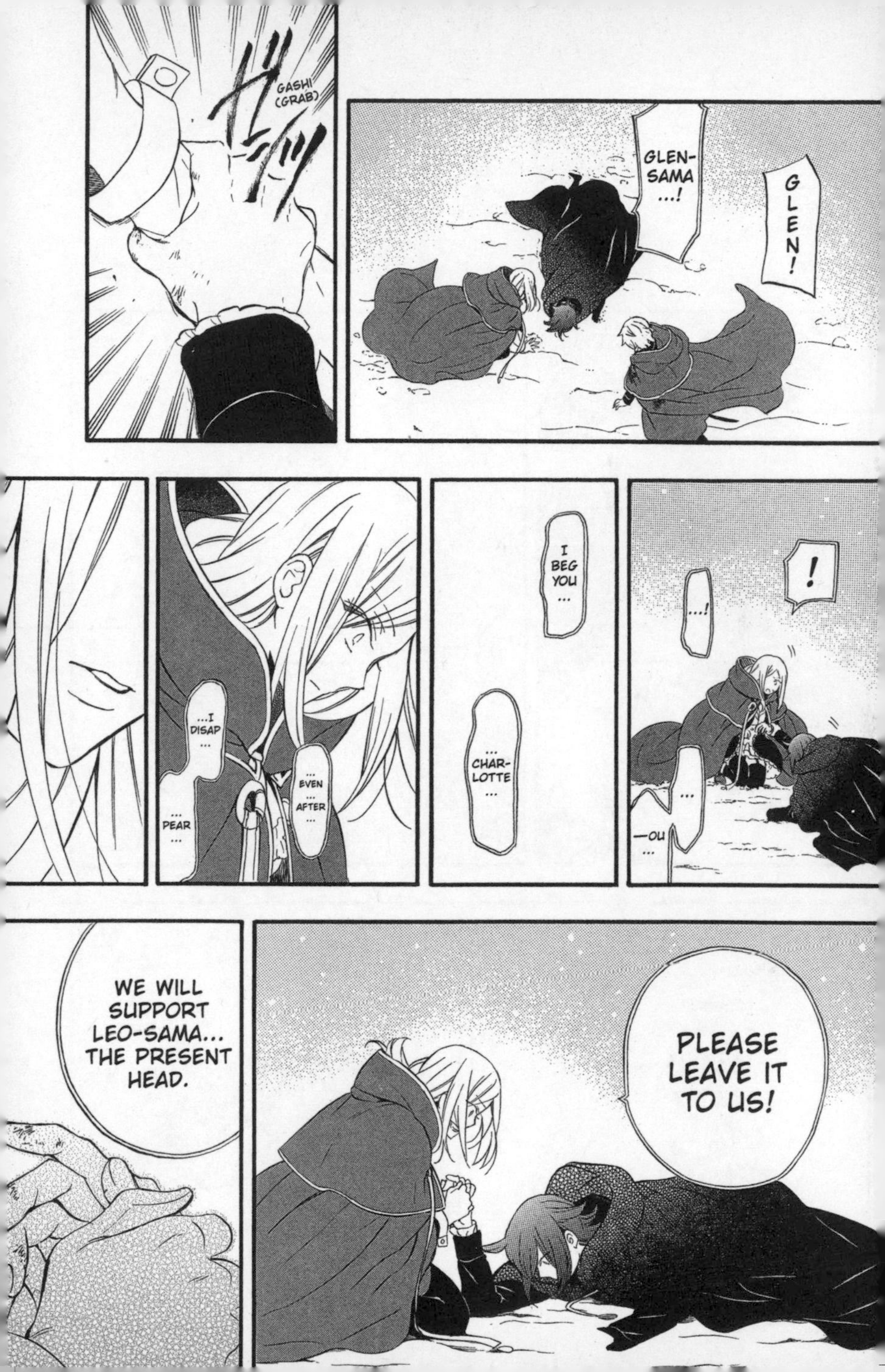
GLEN!
GLEN-SAMA ...!
GASHI (GRAB)
!
...!
... —OU ...
I BEG YOU ...
... CHARLOTTE ...
... EVEN ... AFTER ...
...I DISAP ... ... PEAR ...
PLEASE LEAVE IT TO US!
WE WILL SUPPORT LEO-SAMA... THE PRESENT HEAD.

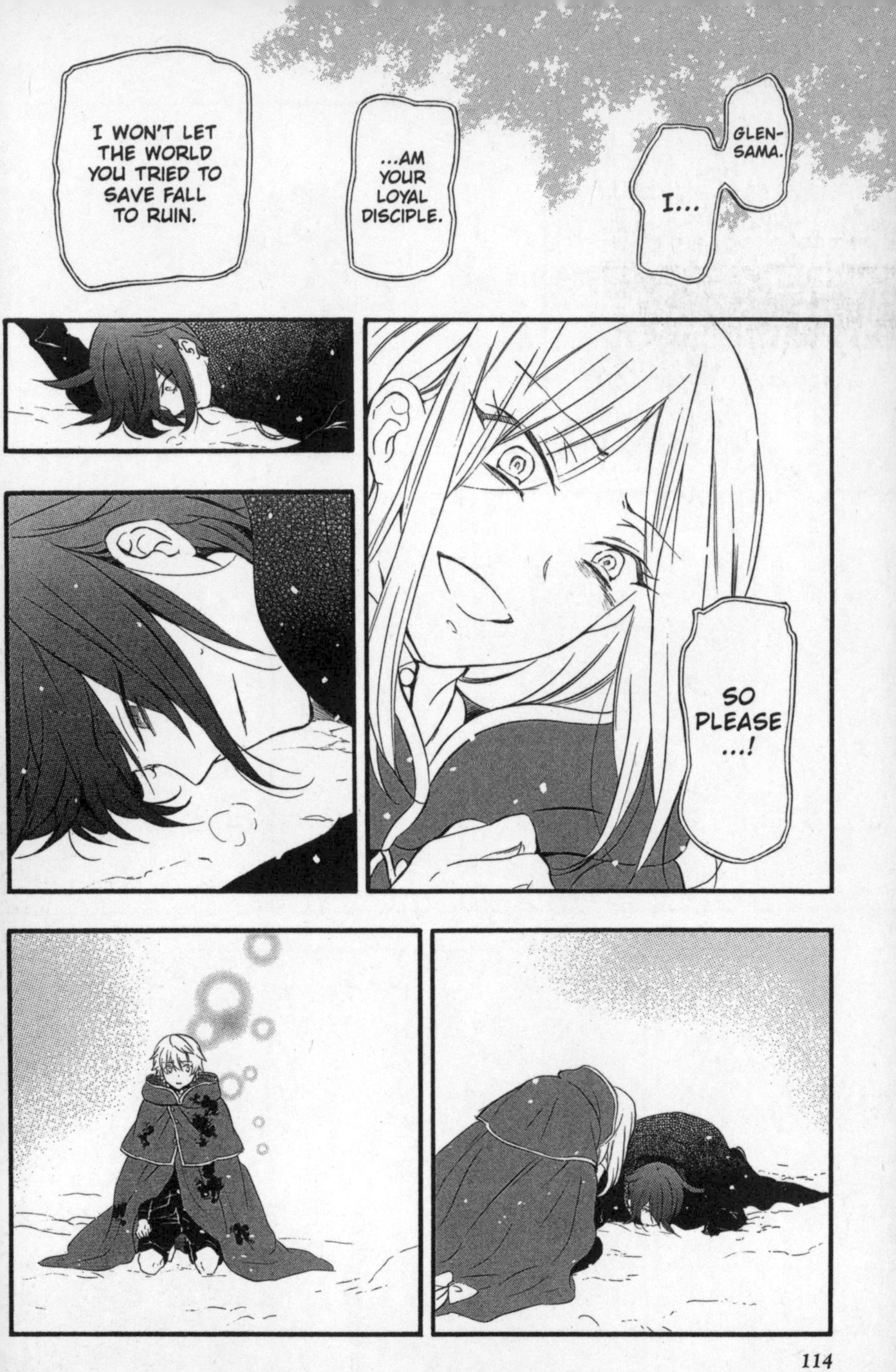
GLEN-SAMA.
I...
...AM YOUR LOYAL DISCIPLE.
I WON'T LET THE WORLD YOU TRIED TO SAVE FALL TO RUIN.
SO PLEASE ...!

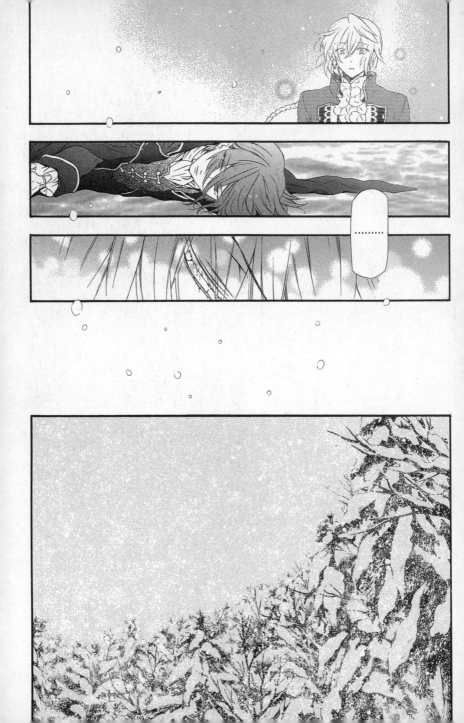

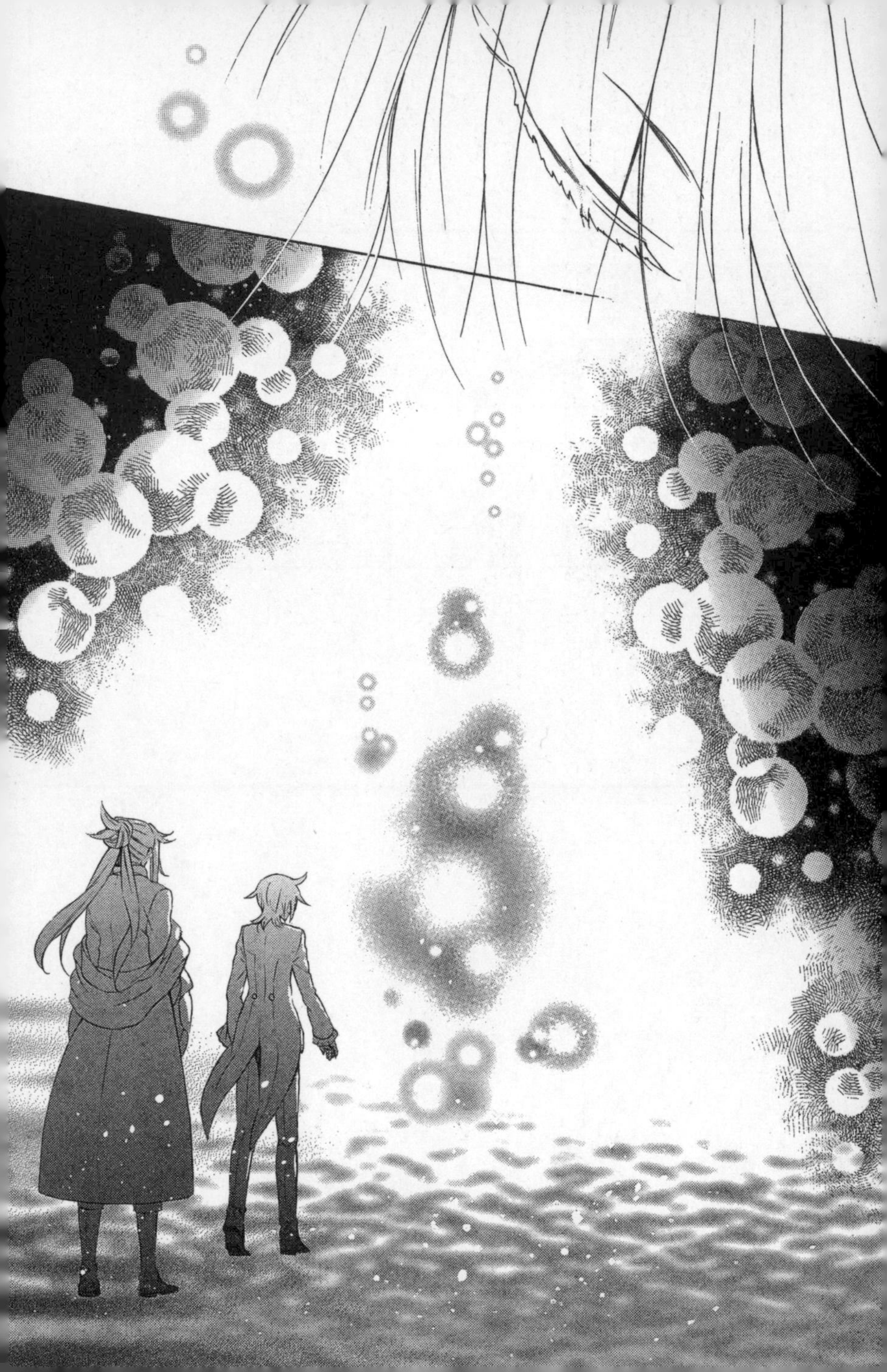

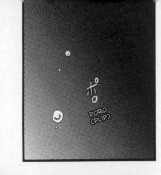

PORO
(PLIP)

...ARE
YOU
SAD?

...NOT
SURE.

I'M...

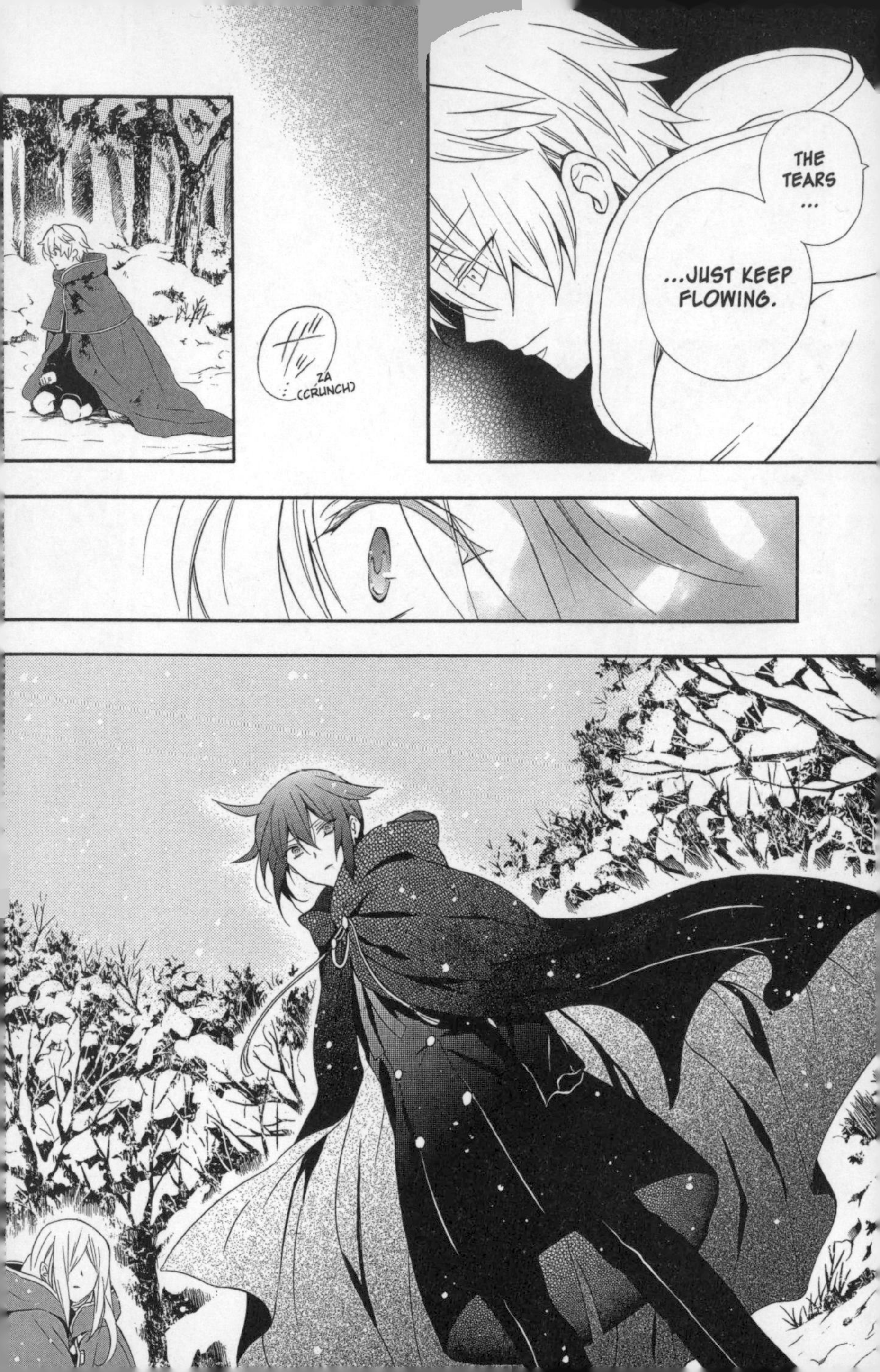
THE TEARS ...
...JUST KEEP FLOWING.
ZA (CRUNCH)

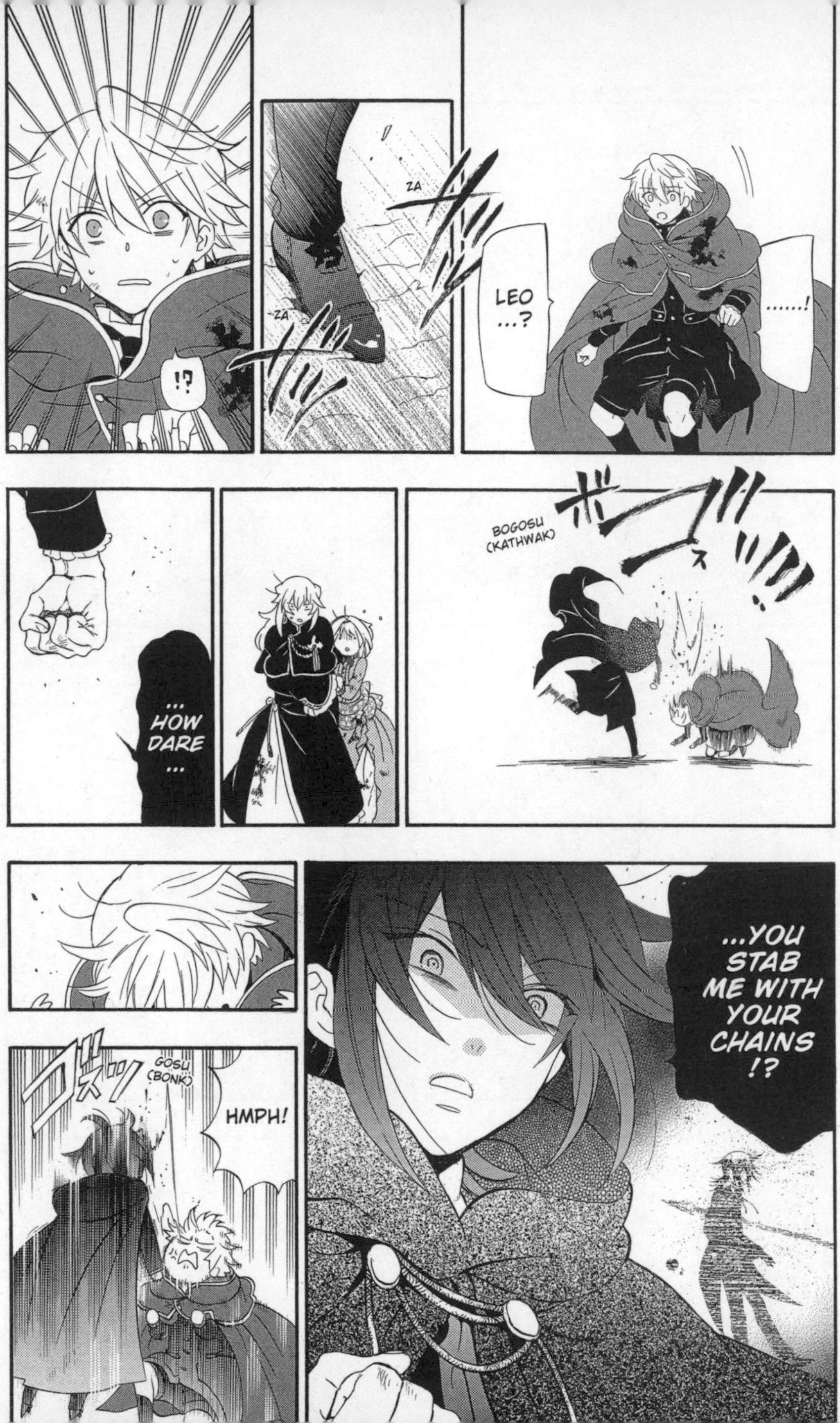
......!
LEO ...?
ZA
ZA
!?
BOGOSU (KATHWAK)
... HOW DARE ...
...YOU STAB ME WITH YOUR CHAINS !?
GOSU (BONK)
HMPH!

SFX: BOGA (WHACK) / POKA (WHAP)

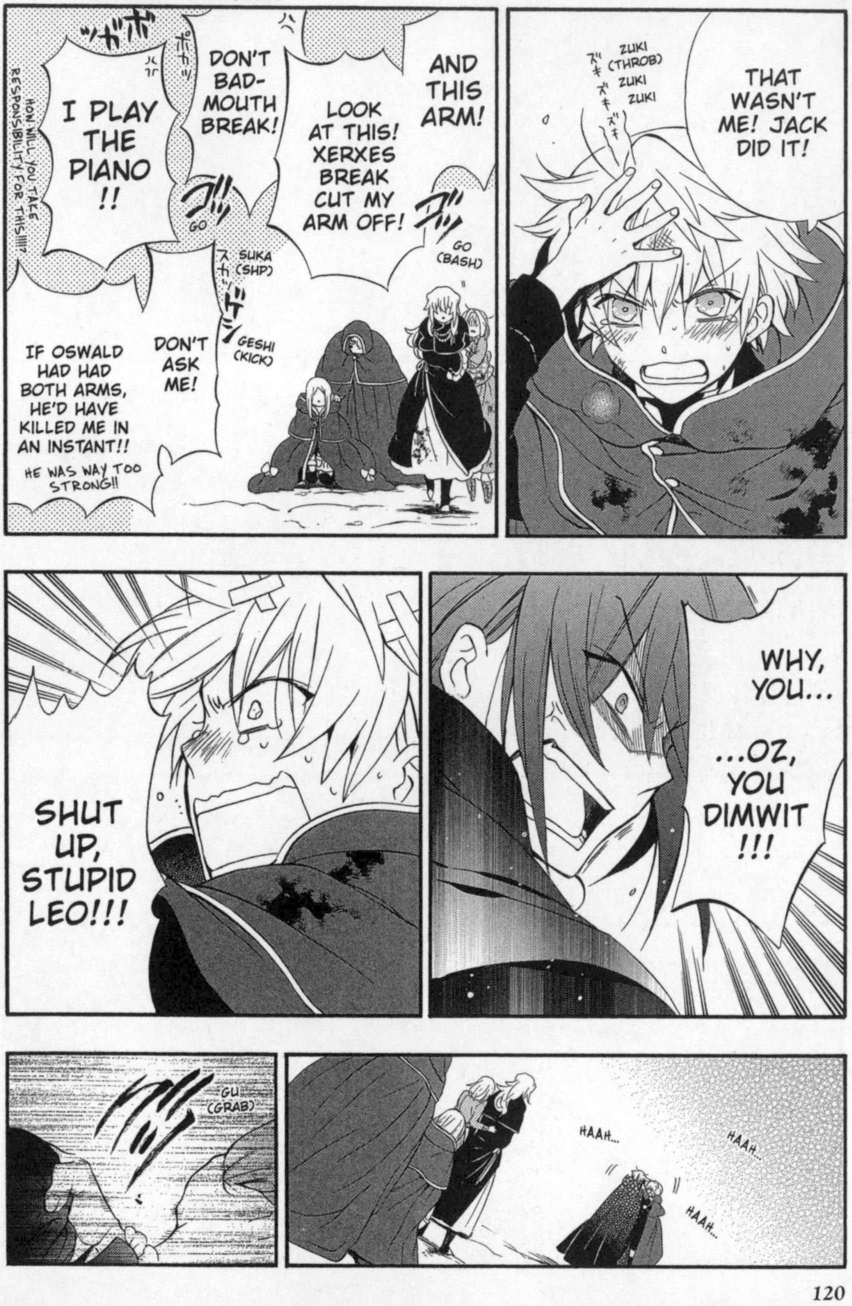
ZUKI (THROB) ZUKI ZUKI
THAT WASN'T ME! JACK DID IT!
AND THIS ARM!
LOOK AT THIS! XERXES BREAK CUT MY ARM OFF!
DON'T BAD-MOUTH BREAK!
I PLAY THE PIANO!!
HOW WILL YOU TAKE RESPONSIBILITY FOR THIS!!!!?
GO (BASH)
GO
SUKA (SHP)
GESHI (KICK)
DON'T ASK ME!
IF OSWALD HAD HAD BOTH ARMS, HE'D HAVE KILLED ME IN AN INSTANT!!
HE WAS WAY TOO STRONG!!
WHY, YOU...
...OZ, YOU DIMWIT!!!
SHUT UP, STUPID LEO!!!
HAAH...
HAAH...
HAAH...
GU (GRAB)

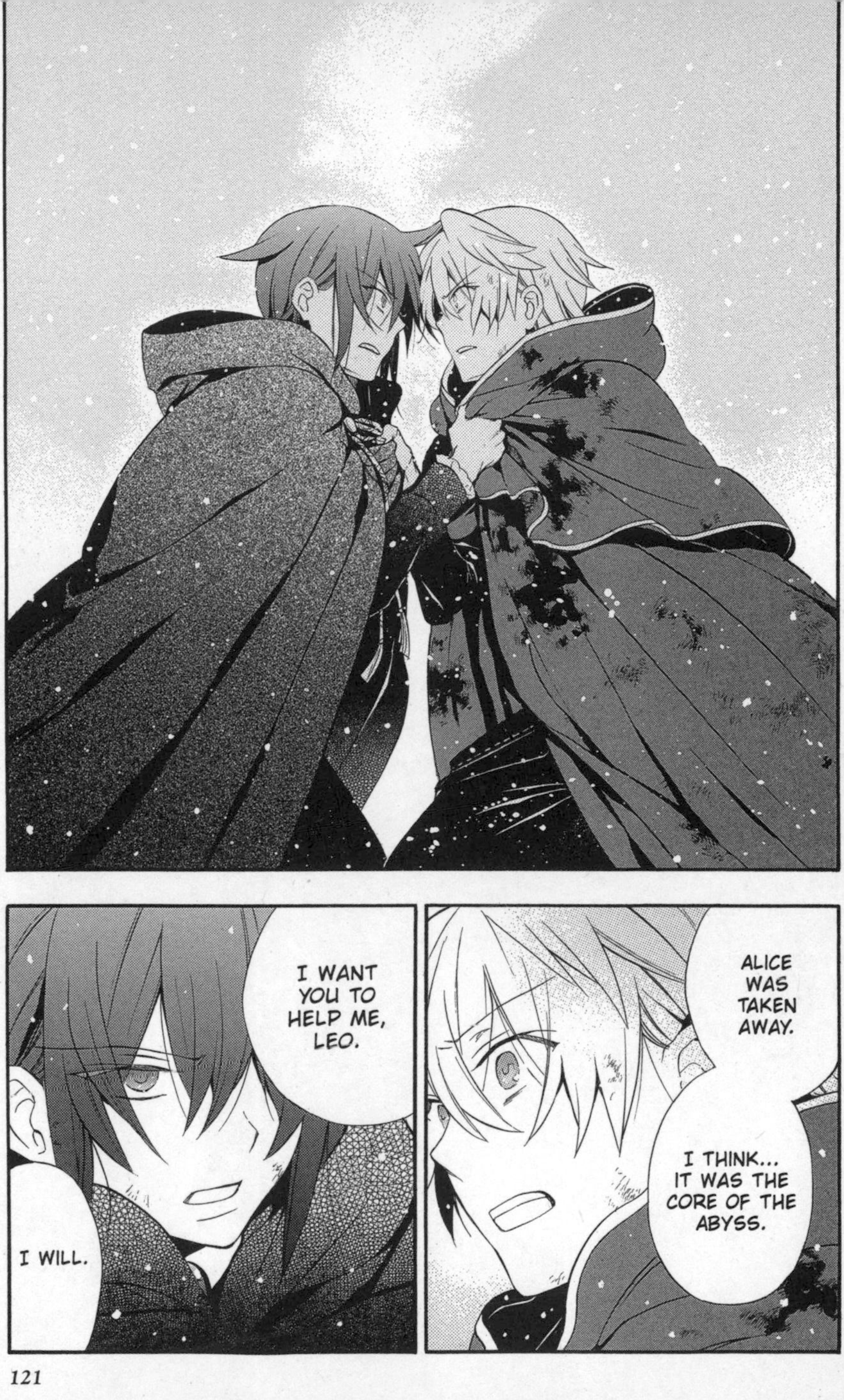
ALICE WAS TAKEN AWAY.
I THINK... IT WAS THE CORE OF THE ABYSS.
I WANT YOU TO HELP ME, LEO.
I WILL.

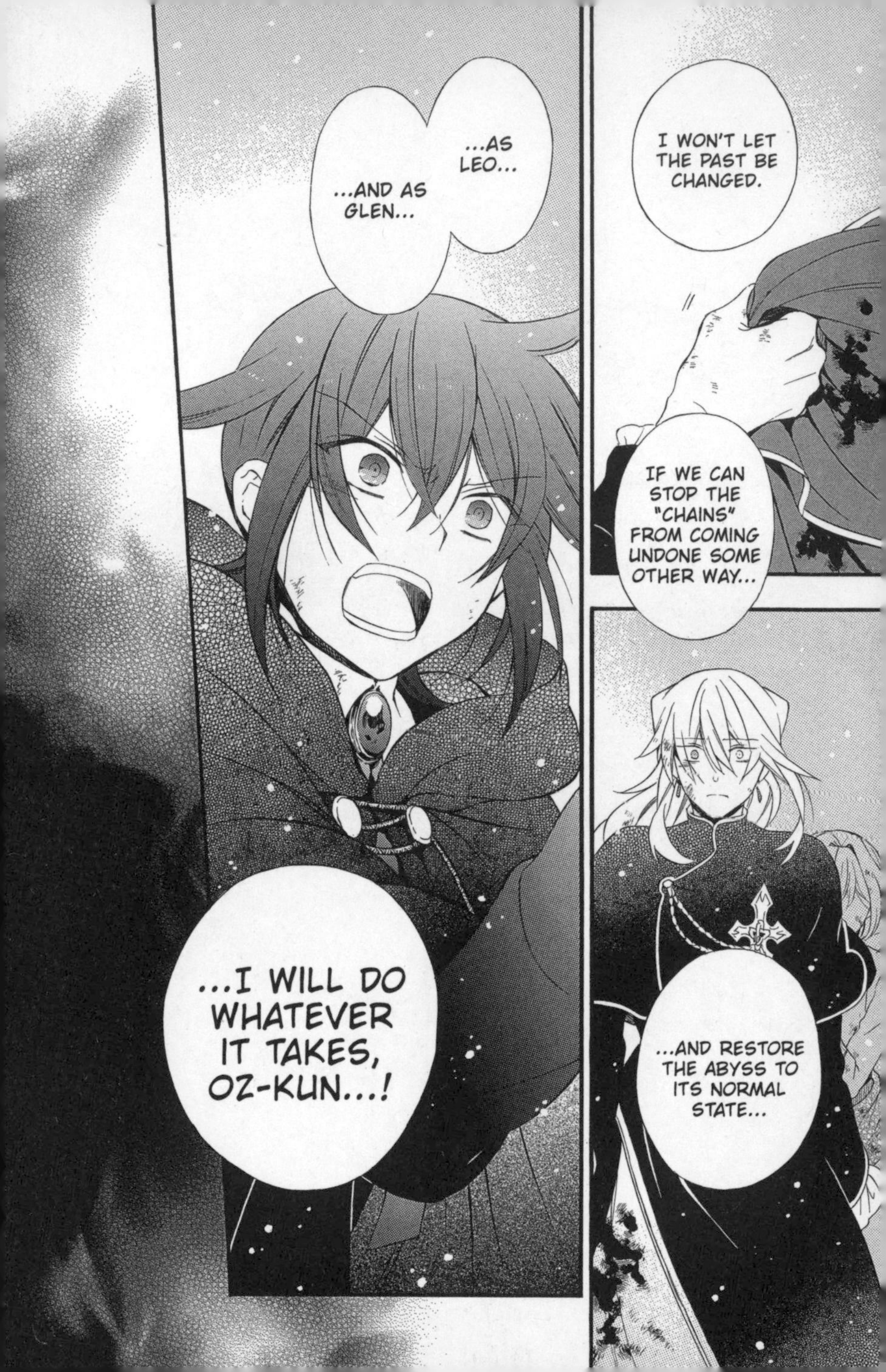
I WON'T LET THE PAST BE CHANGED.
IF WE CAN STOP THE "CHAINS" FROM COMING UNDONE SOME OTHER WAY...
...AND RESTORE THE ABYSS TO ITS NORMAL STATE...
...AS LEO...
...AND AS GLEN...
...I WILL DO WHATEVER IT TAKES, OZ-KUN...!

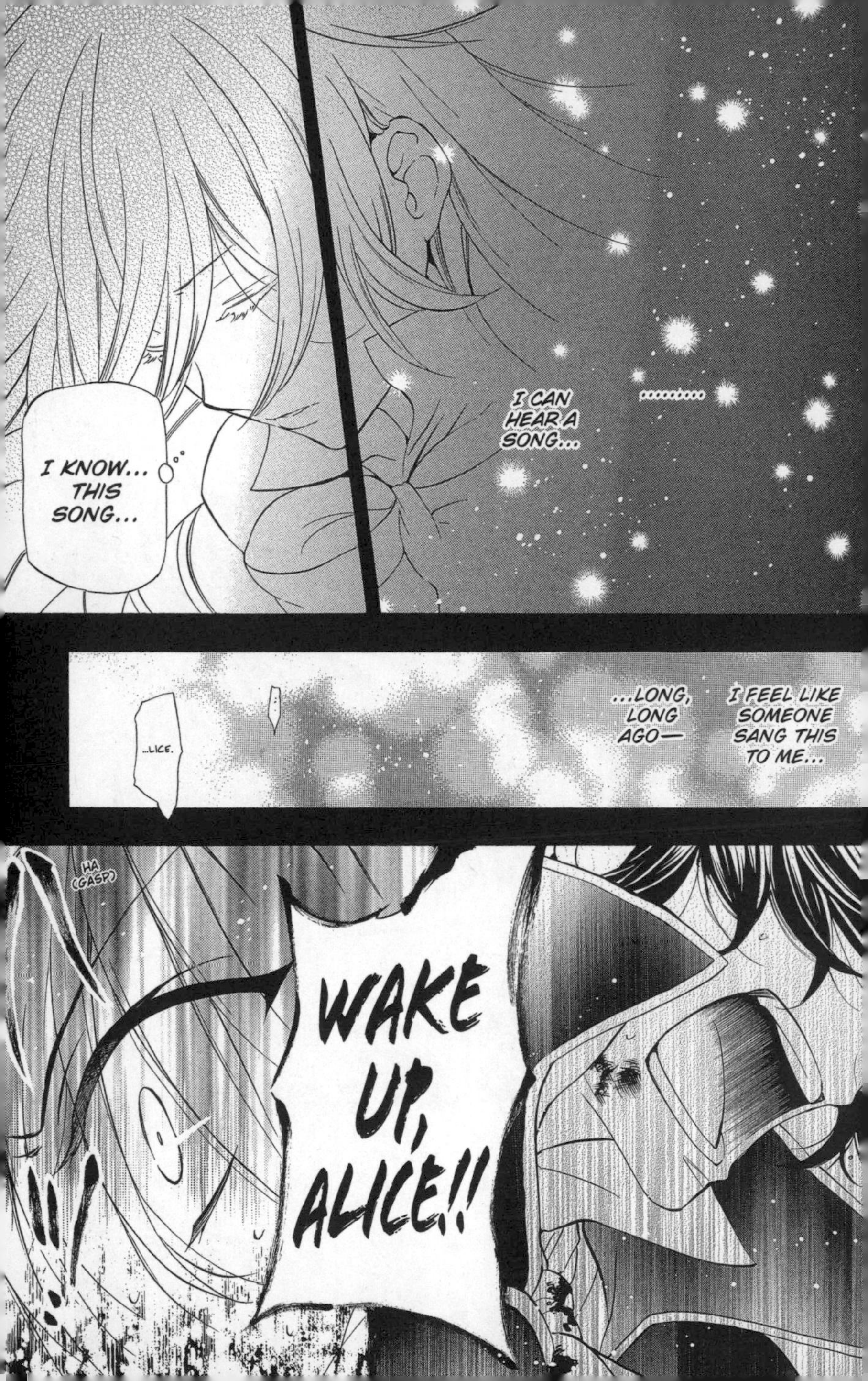
....
I CAN HEAR A SONG...
I KNOW... THIS SONG...
I FEEL LIKE SOMEONE SANG THIS TO ME...
...LONG, LONG AGO—
...
...LICE.
WAKE UP, ALICE!!
HA (GASP)

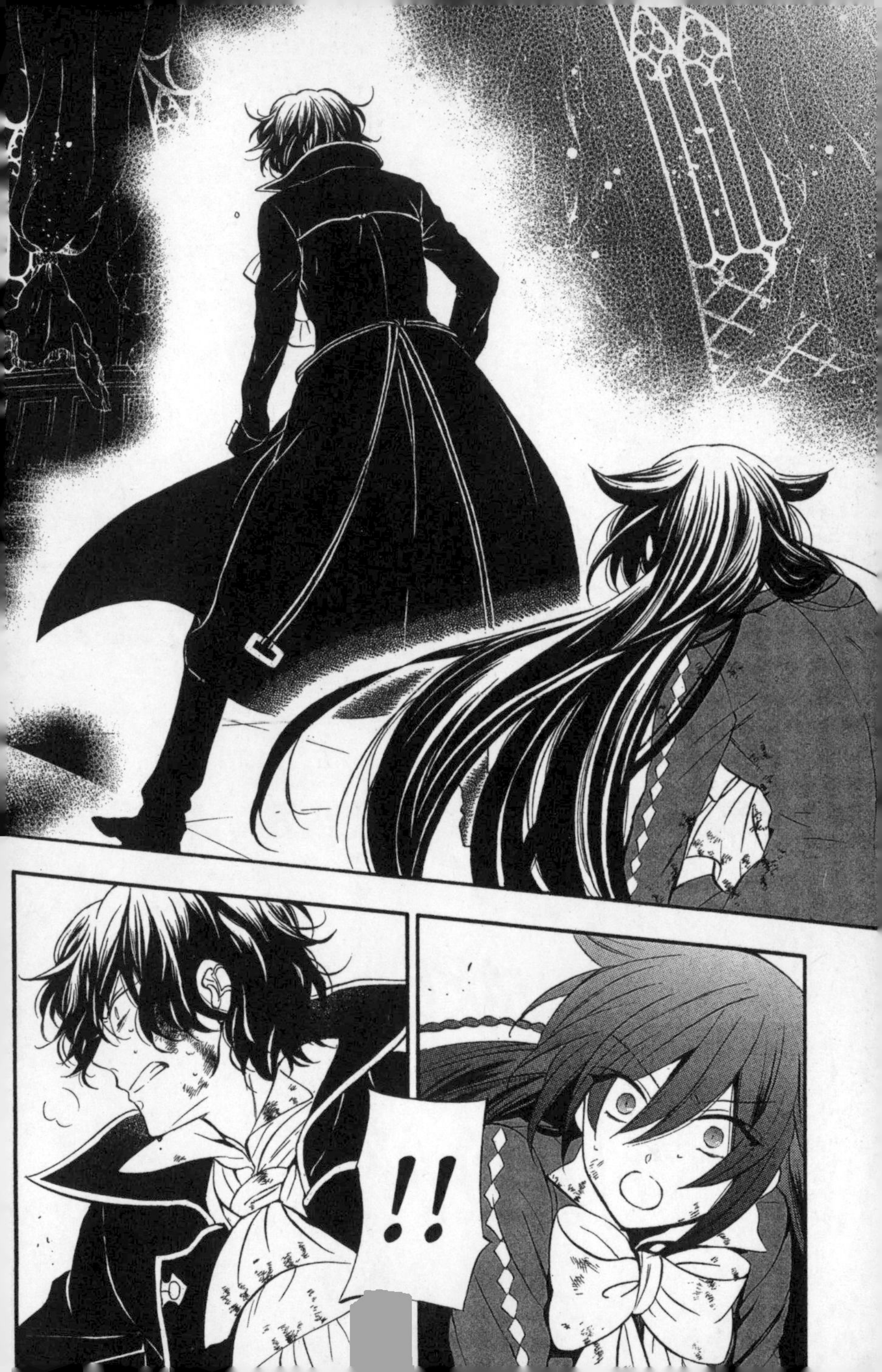
!!

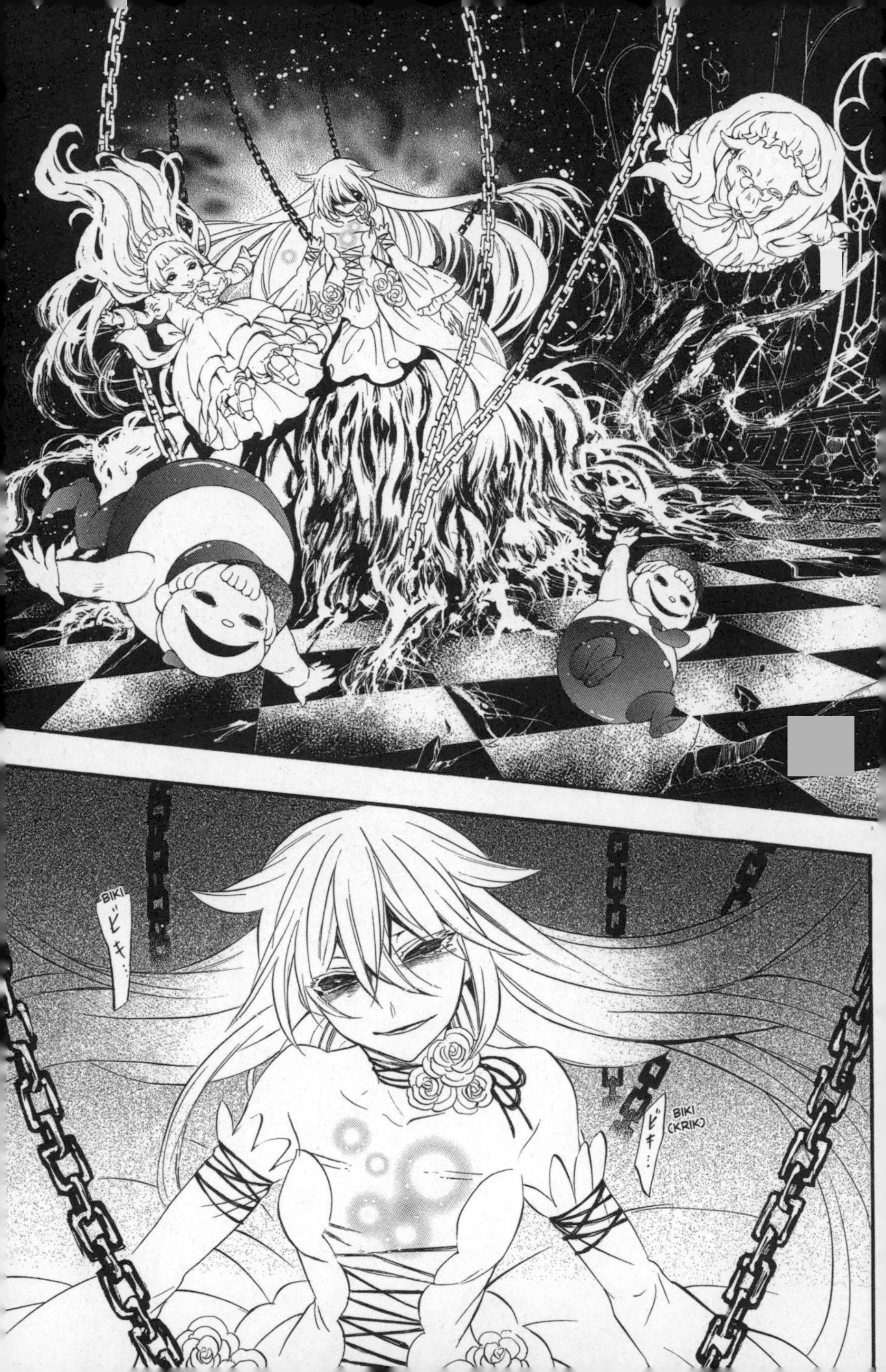
ビキ…
BIKI (KRIK)
ビキ…
BIKI

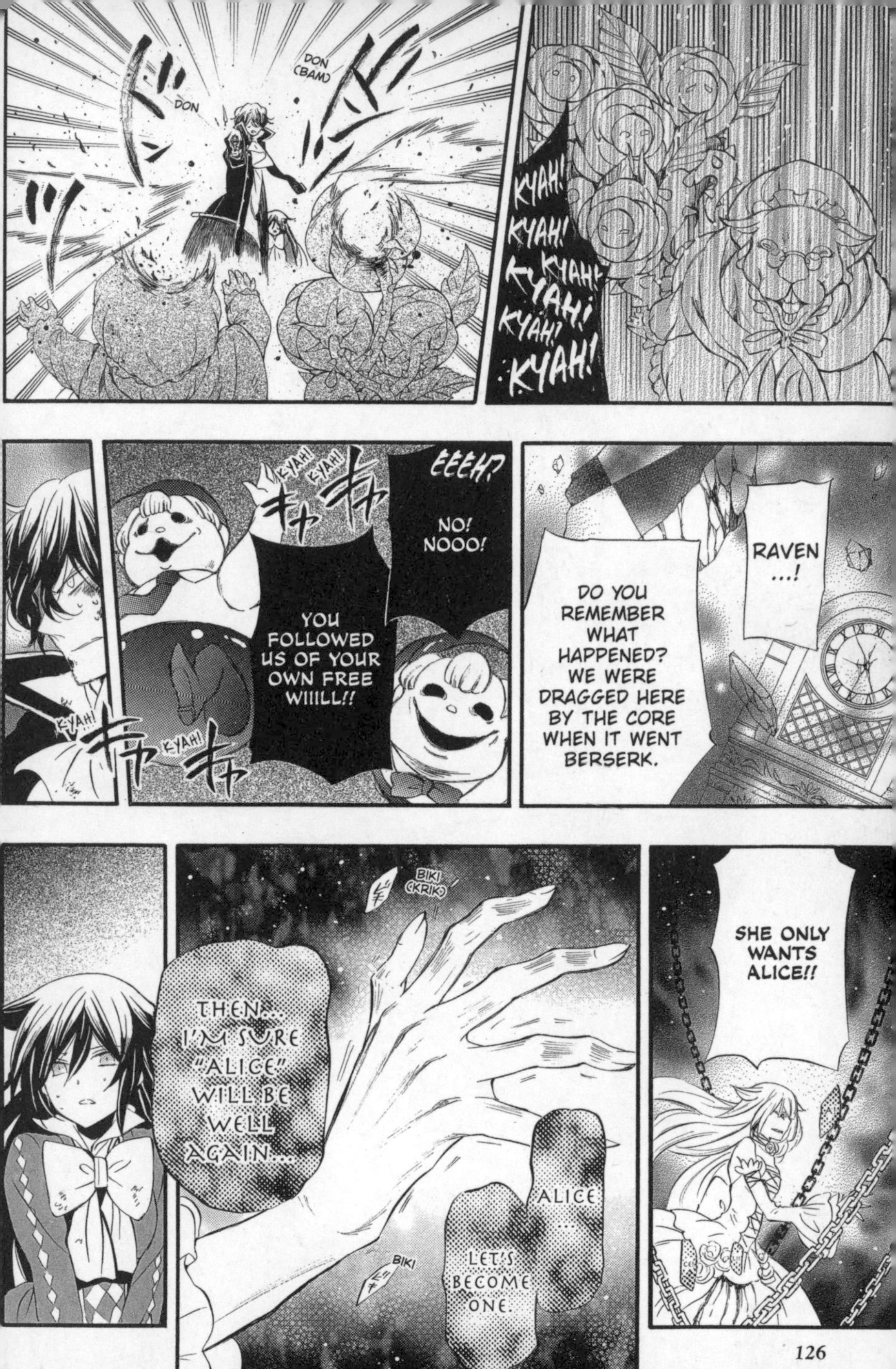
KYAH! KYAH! KYAH! KYAH! KYAH! KYAH!
DON (BAM)
DON
RAVEN ...!
DO YOU REMEMBER WHAT HAPPENED? WE WERE DRAGGED HERE BY THE CORE WHEN IT WENT BERSERK.
EEEH?
NO! NOOO!
KYAH! KYAH!
YOU FOLLOWED US OF YOUR OWN FREE WIIILL!!
KYAH! KYAH!
SHE ONLY WANTS ALICE!!
BIKI (KRIK)
THEN... I'M SURE "ALICE" WILL BE WELL AGAIN...
ALICE...
LET'S BECOME ONE.
BIKI

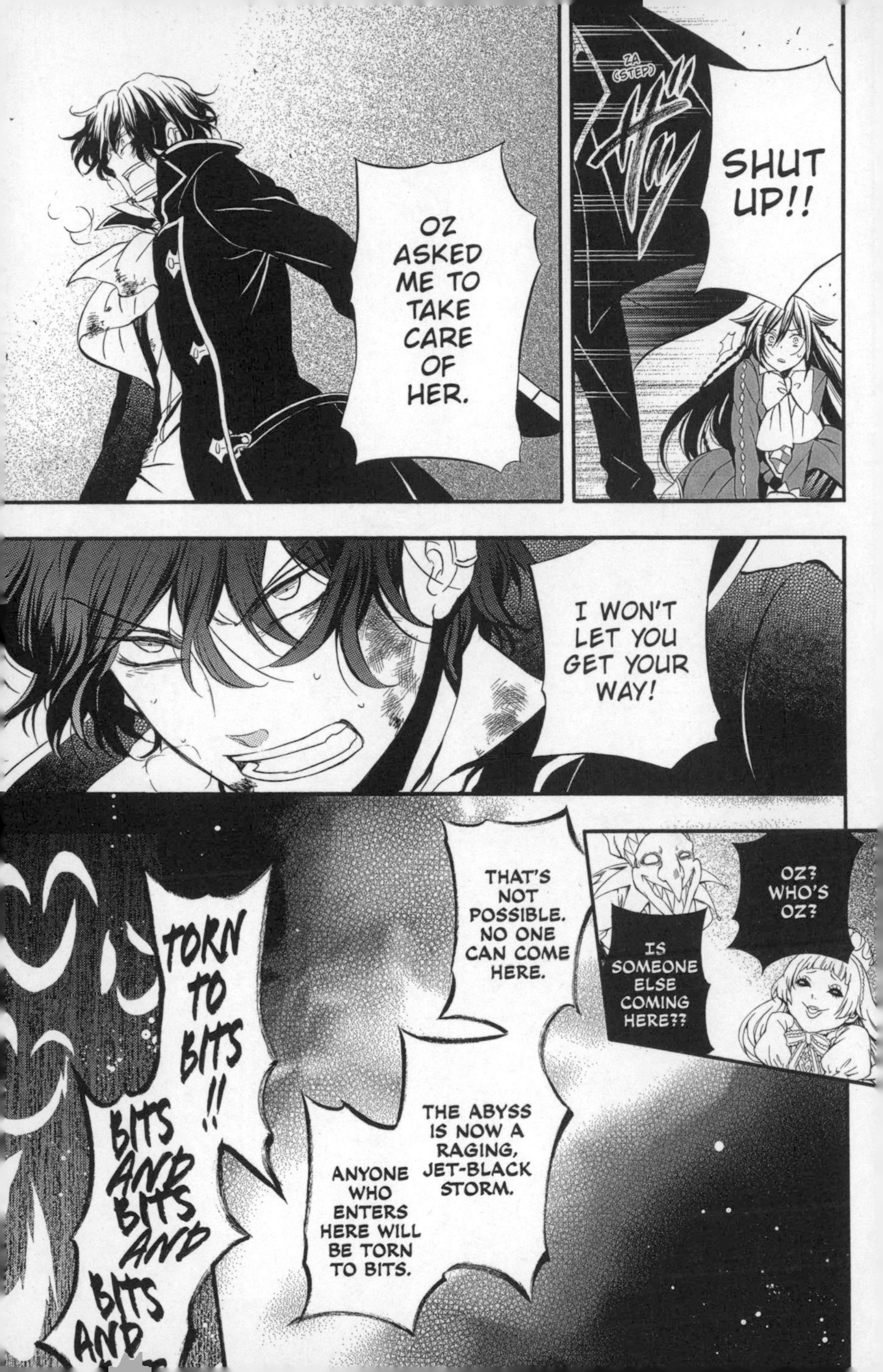
ZA (STEP)
SHUT UP!!
OZ ASKED ME TO TAKE CARE OF HER.
I WON'T LET YOU GET YOUR WAY!
OZ? WHO'S OZ?
IS SOMEONE ELSE COMING HERE??
THAT'S NOT POSSIBLE. NO ONE CAN COME HERE.
THE ABYSS IS NOW A RAGING, JET-BLACK STORM.
ANYONE WHO ENTERS HERE WILL BE TORN TO BITS.
TORN TO BITS!!
BITS AND BITS AND BITS AND

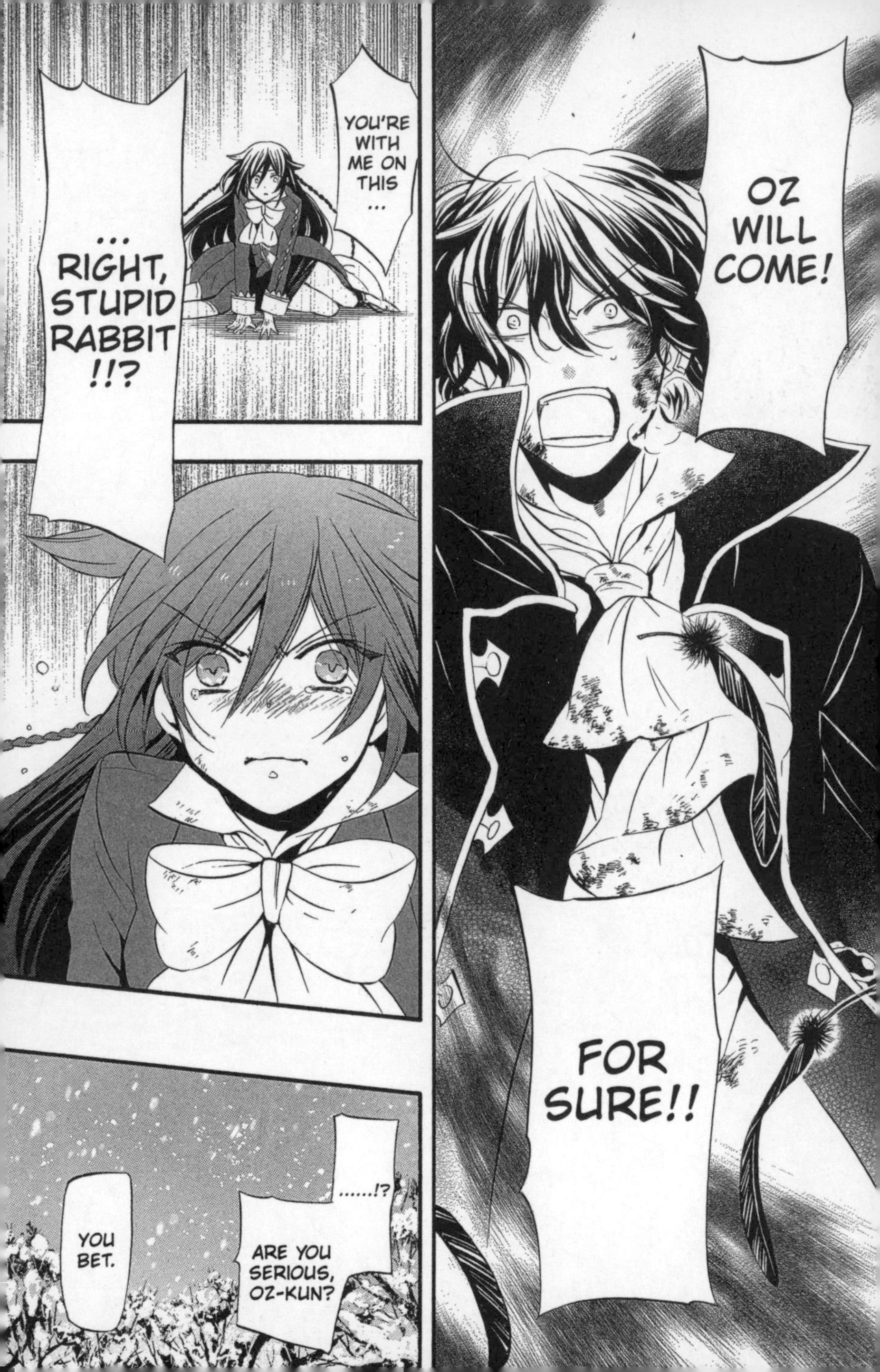
OZ WILL COME!
FOR SURE!!
YOU'RE WITH ME ON THIS ...
... RIGHT, STUPID RABBIT !!?
......!?
ARE YOU SERIOUS, OZ-KUN?
YOU BET.

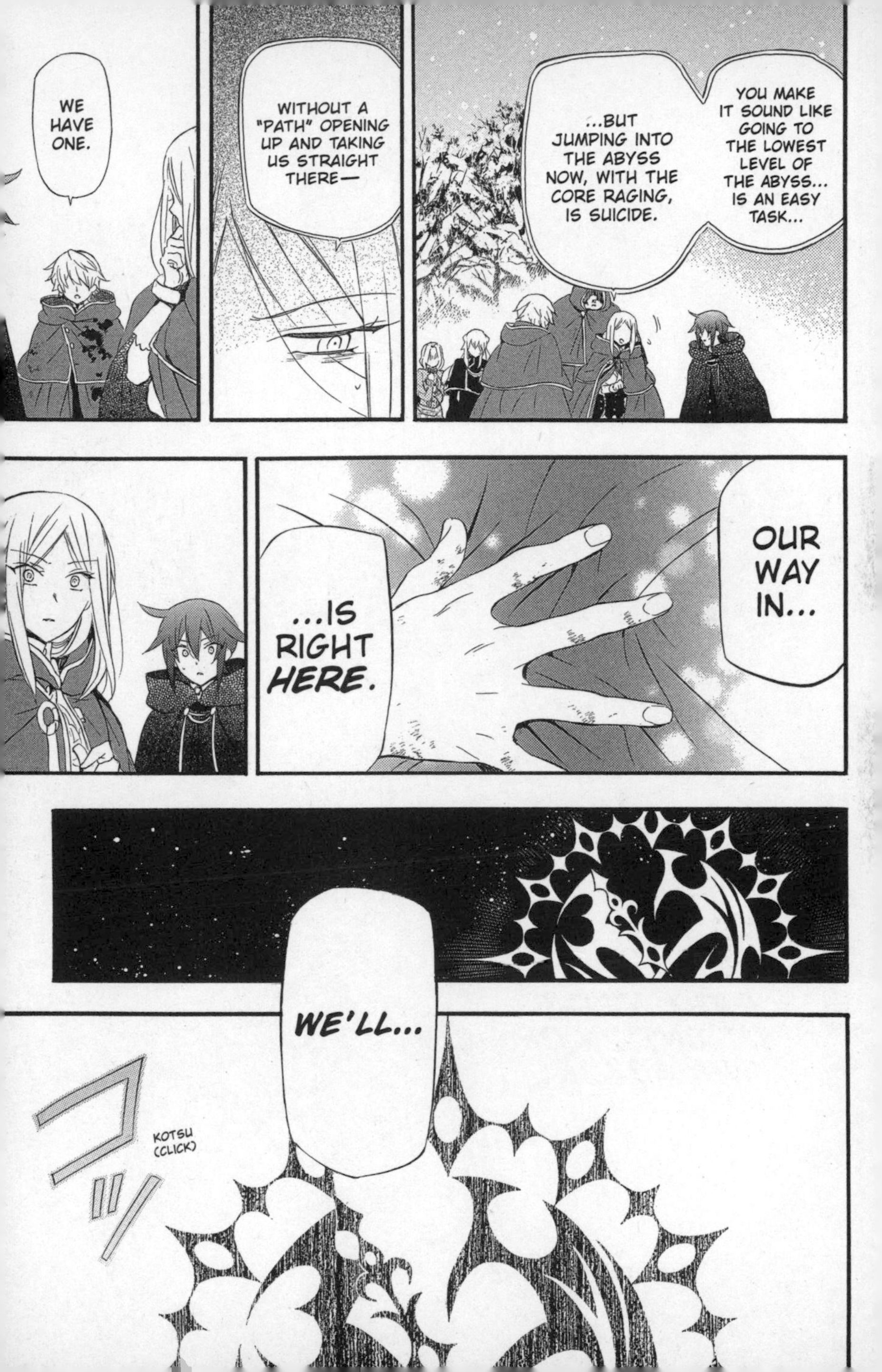
YOU MAKE IT SOUND LIKE GOING TO THE LOWEST LEVEL OF THE ABYSS... IS AN EASY TASK...
...BUT JUMPING INTO THE ABYSS NOW, WITH THE CORE RAGING, IS SUICIDE.
WITHOUT A "PATH" OPENING UP AND TAKING US STRAIGHT THERE—
WE HAVE ONE.
OUR WAY IN...
...IS RIGHT *HERE*.
WE'LL...
KOTSU (CLICK)

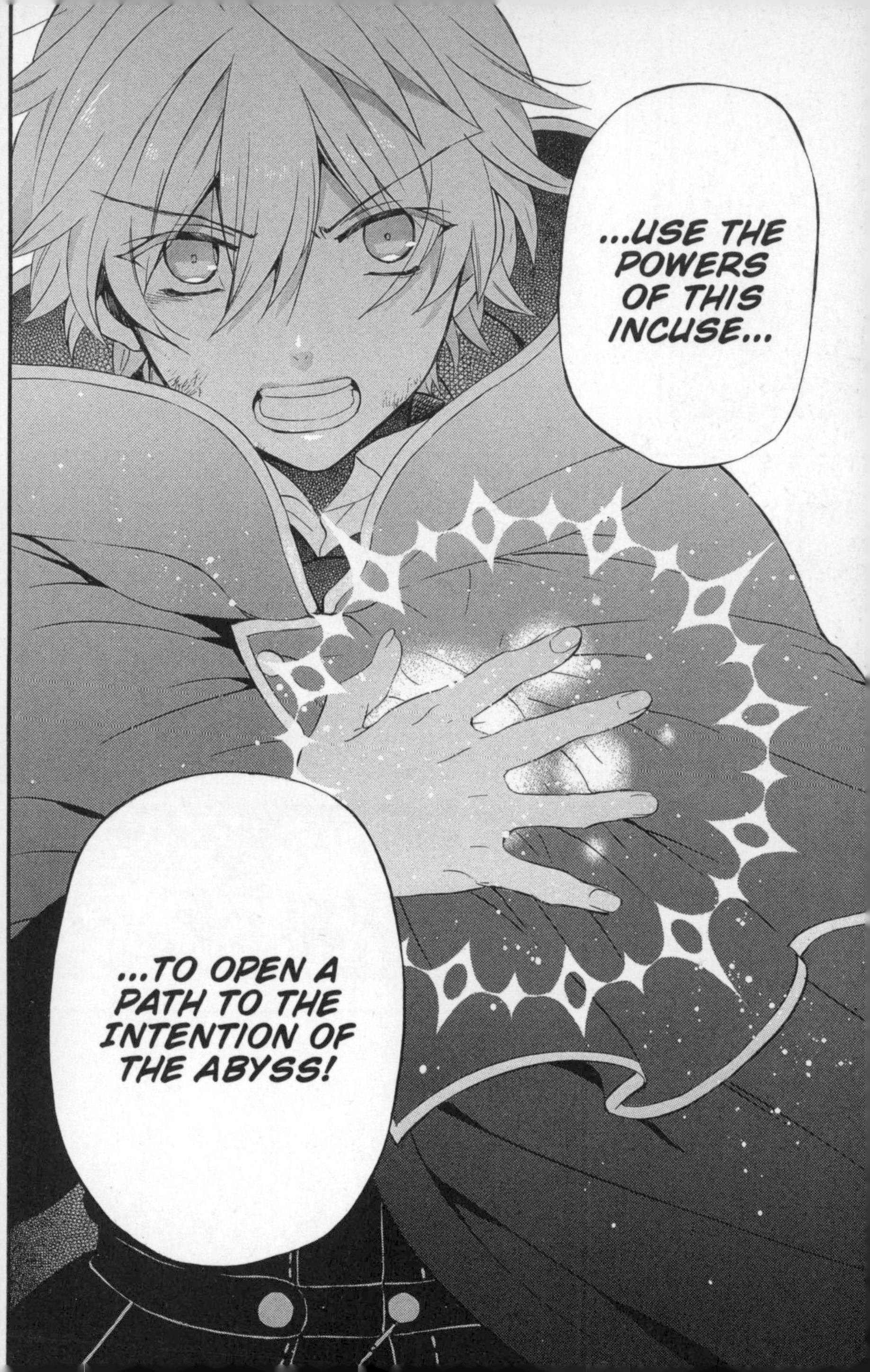
...USE THE POWERS OF THIS INCUSE...
...TO OPEN A PATH TO THE INTENTION OF THE ABYSS!

Retrace:CI Oswald

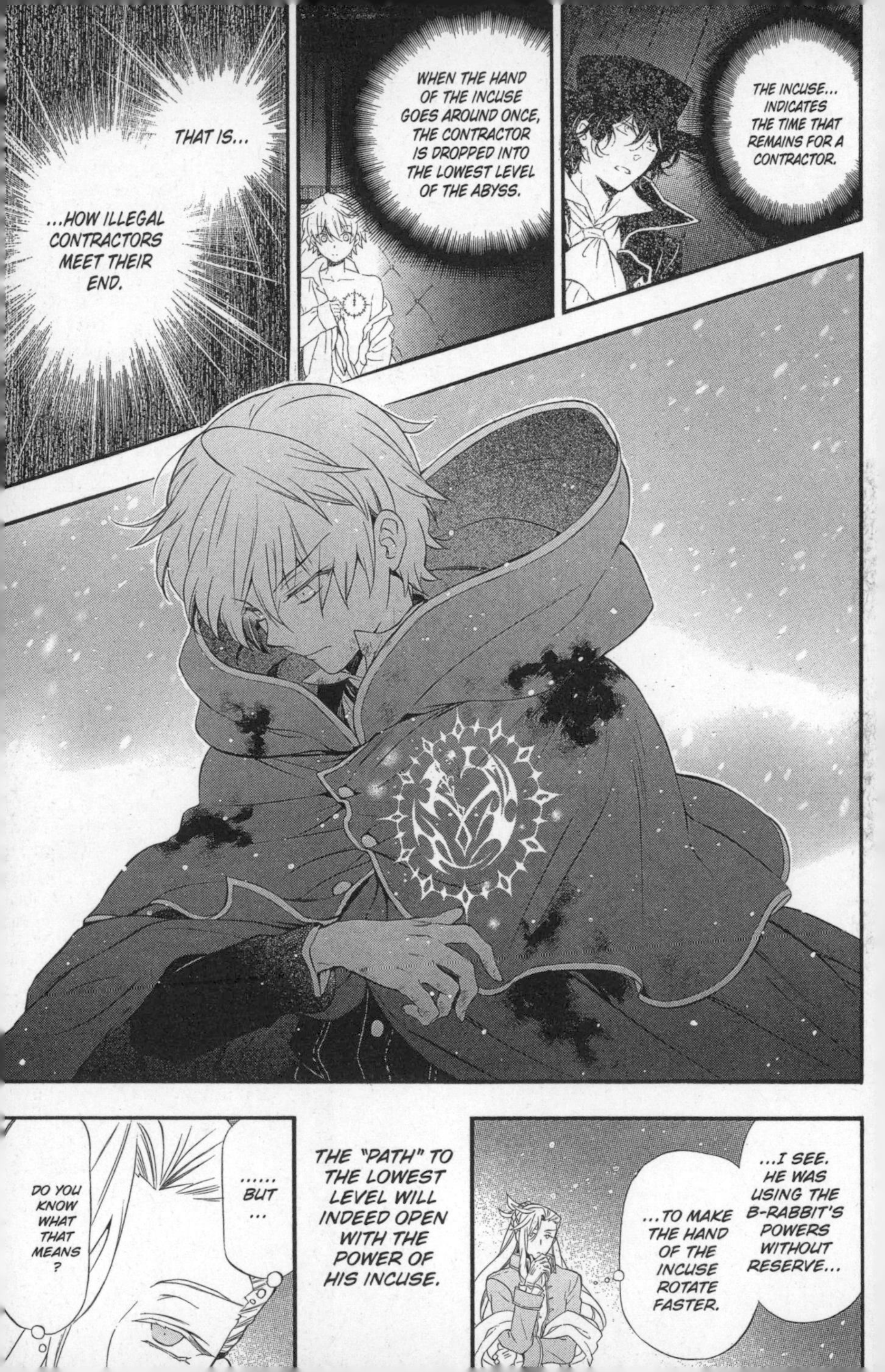
THE INCUSE... INDICATES THE TIME THAT REMAINS FOR A CONTRACTOR.
WHEN THE HAND OF THE INCUSE GOES AROUND ONCE, THE CONTRACTOR IS DROPPED INTO THE LOWEST LEVEL OF THE ABYSS.
THAT IS...
...HOW ILLEGAL CONTRACTORS MEET THEIR END.
...I SEE. HE WAS USING THE B-RABBIT'S POWERS WITHOUT RESERVE...
...TO MAKE THE HAND OF THE INCUSE ROTATE FASTER.
THE "PATH" TO THE LOWEST LEVEL WILL INDEED OPEN WITH THE POWER OF HIS INCUSE.
......BUT...
DO YOU KNOW WHAT THAT MEANS?

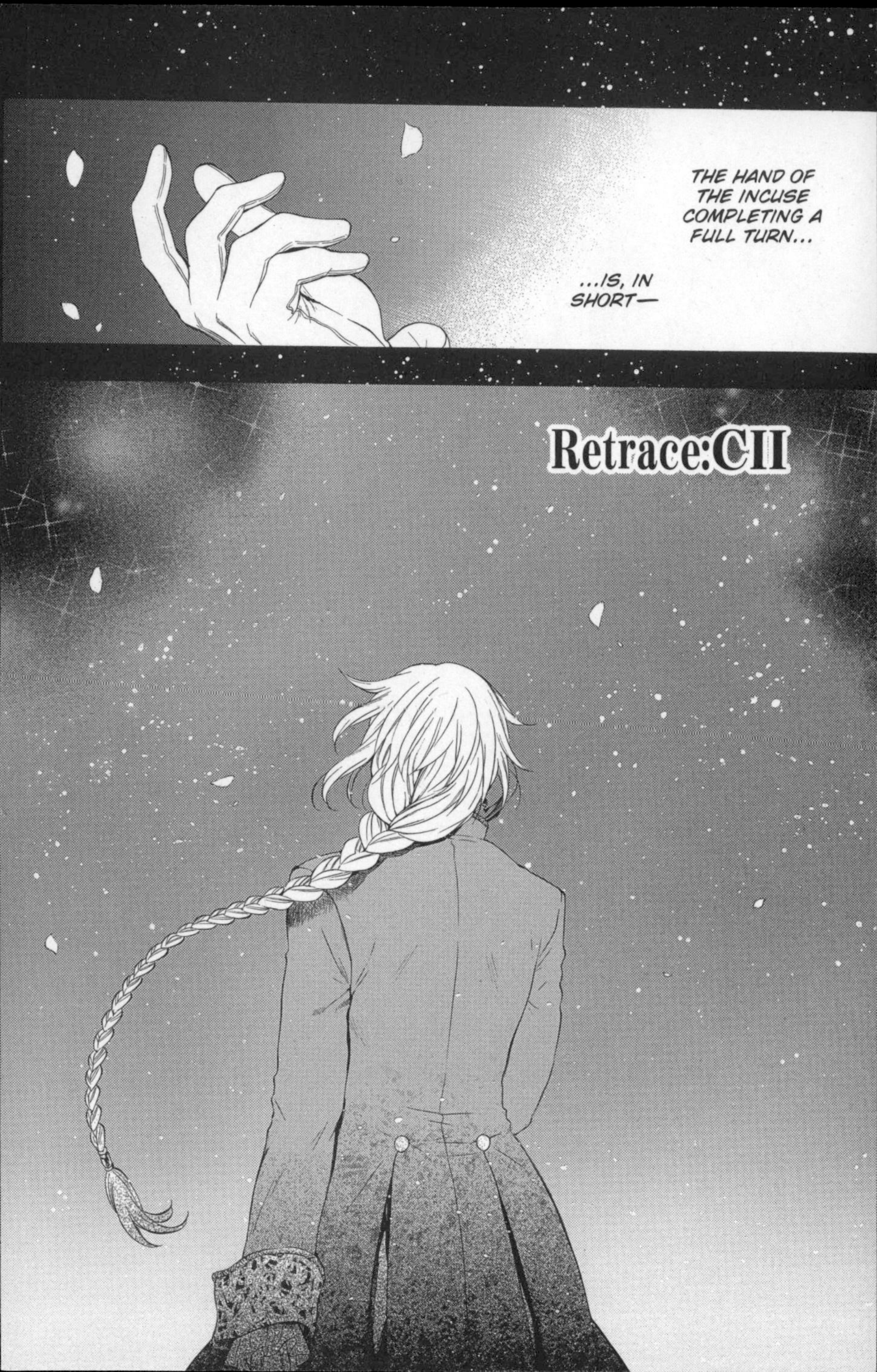
THE HAND OF THE INCUSE COMPLETING A FULL TURN...
...IS, IN SHORT—
Retrace:CII

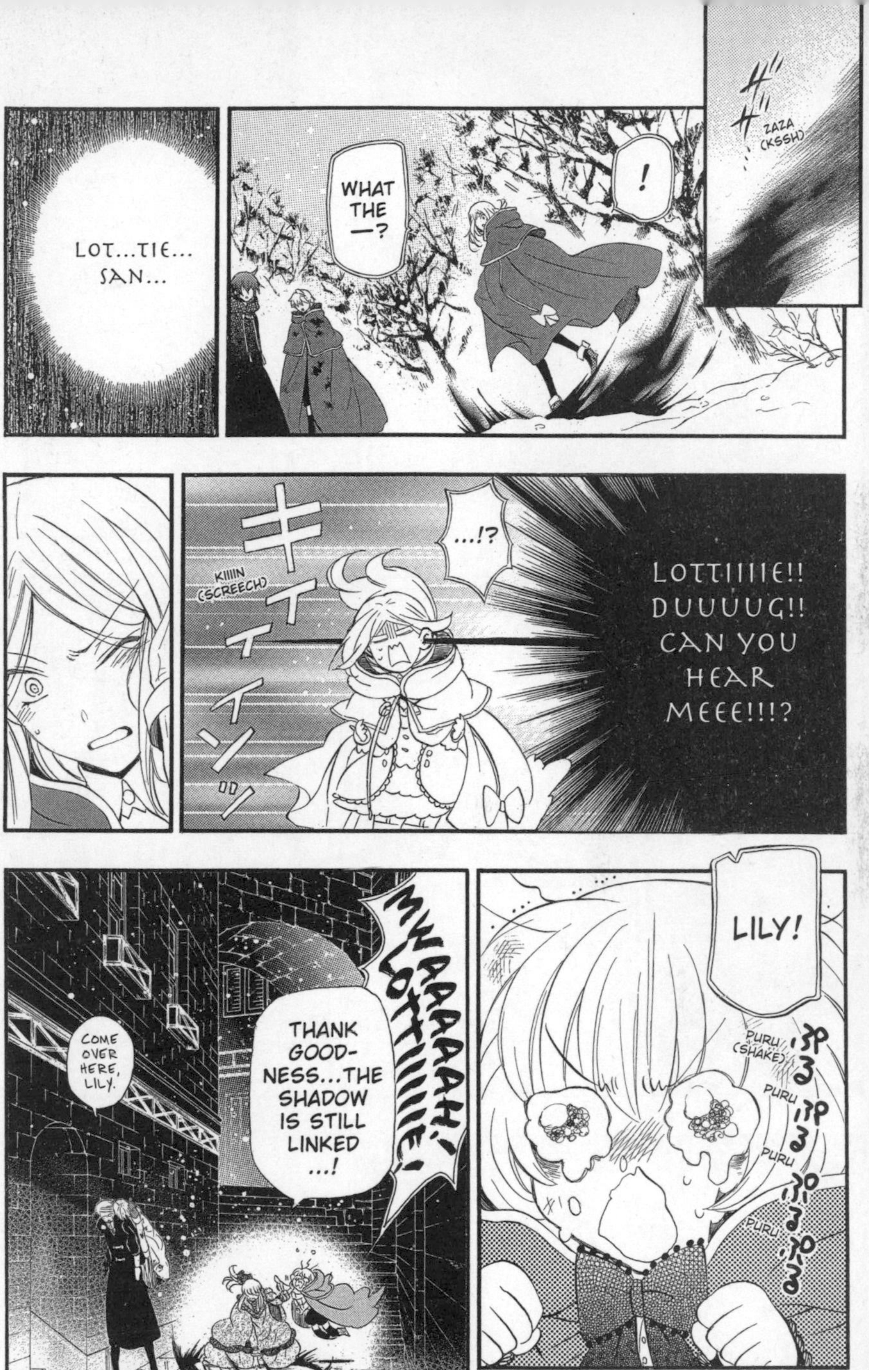
ZAZA (KSSH)
!
WHAT THE—?
LOT...TIE... SAN...
...!?
LOTTIIIIE!! DUUUUG!! CAN YOU HEAR MEEE!!!?
キイイイン
KIIIIN (SCREECH)
LILY!
ぷるぷるぷるぷる
PURU (SHAKE) PURU PURU PURU
MWAAAAAH! LOTTIIIIIE!
THANK GOOD-NESS...THE SHADOW IS STILL LINKED ...!
COME OVER HERE, LILY.

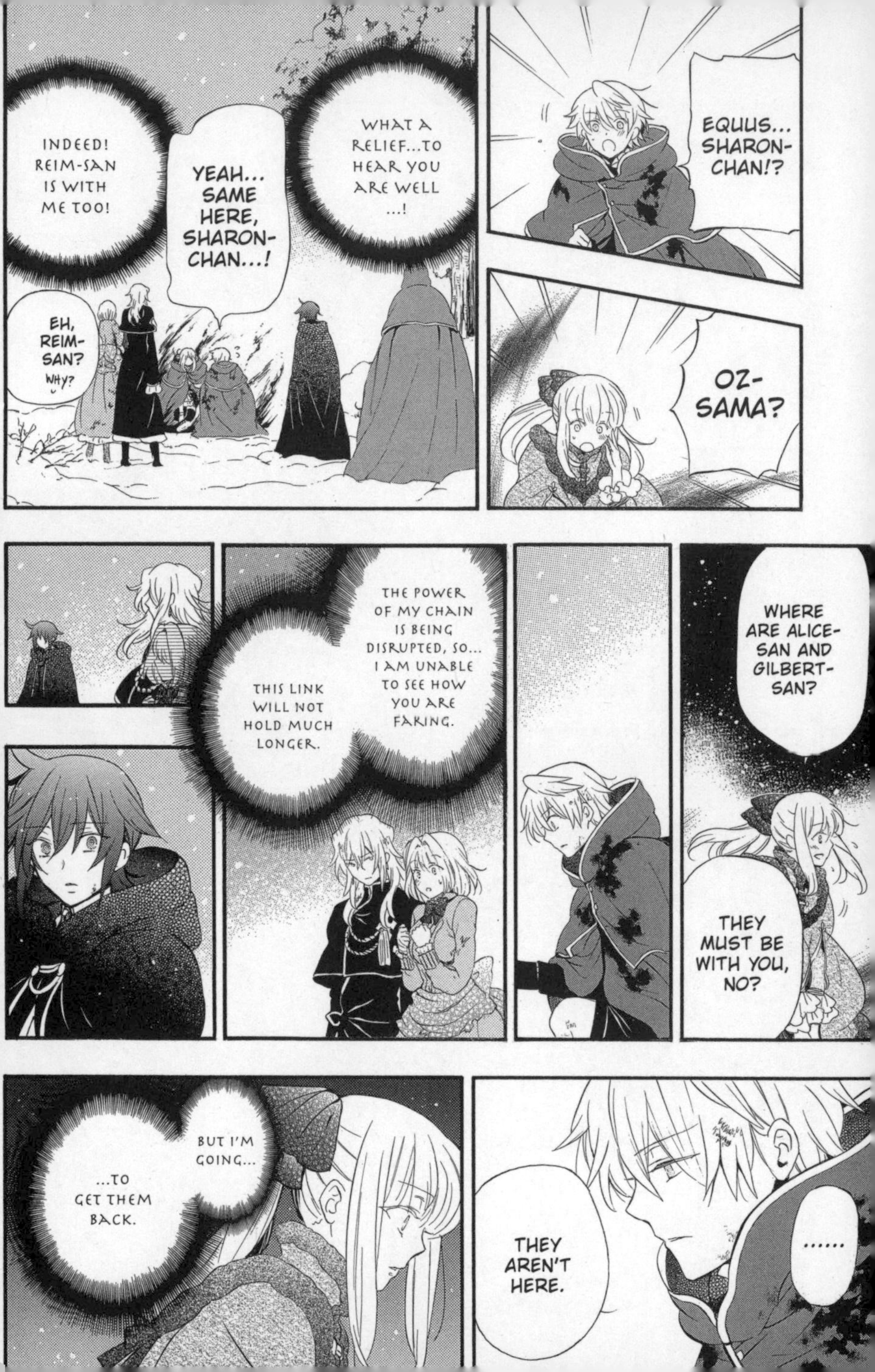
EQUUS... SHARON-CHAN!?
OZ-SAMA?
WHAT A RELIEF...TO HEAR YOU ARE WELL ...!
YEAH... SAME HERE, SHARON-CHAN...!
INDEED! REIM-SAN IS WITH ME TOO!
EH, REIM-SAN? WHY?
WHERE ARE ALICE-SAN AND GILBERT-SAN?
THEY MUST BE WITH YOU, NO?
THE POWER OF MY CHAIN IS BEING DISRUPTED, SO... I AM UNABLE TO SEE HOW YOU ARE FARING.
THIS LINK WILL NOT HOLD MUCH LONGER.
......
THEY AREN'T HERE.
BUT I'M GOING...
...TO GET THEM BACK.

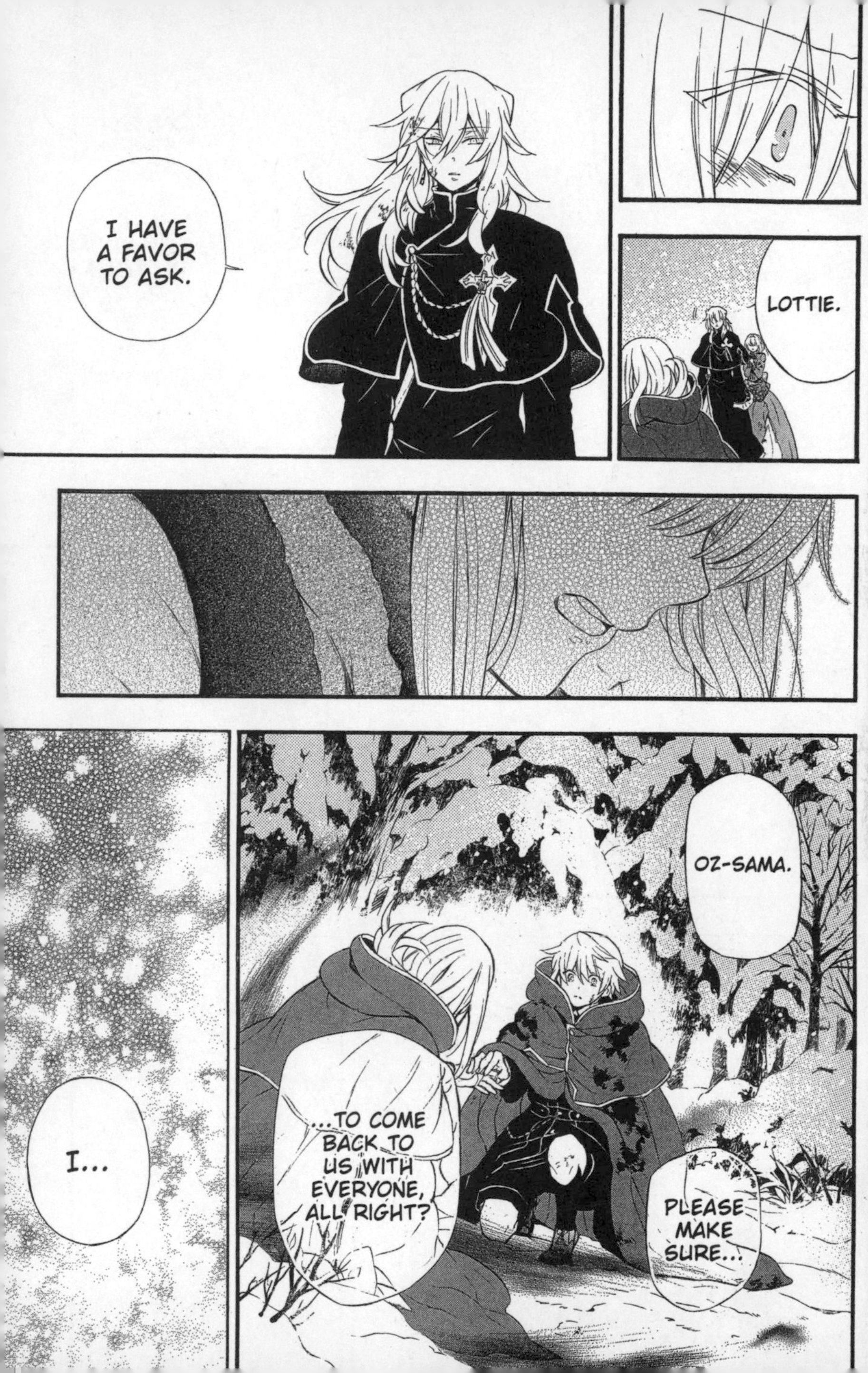
LOTTIE.
I HAVE A FAVOR TO ASK.
OZ-SAMA.
PLEASE MAKE SURE...
...TO COME BACK TO US WITH EVERYONE, ALL RIGHT?
I...

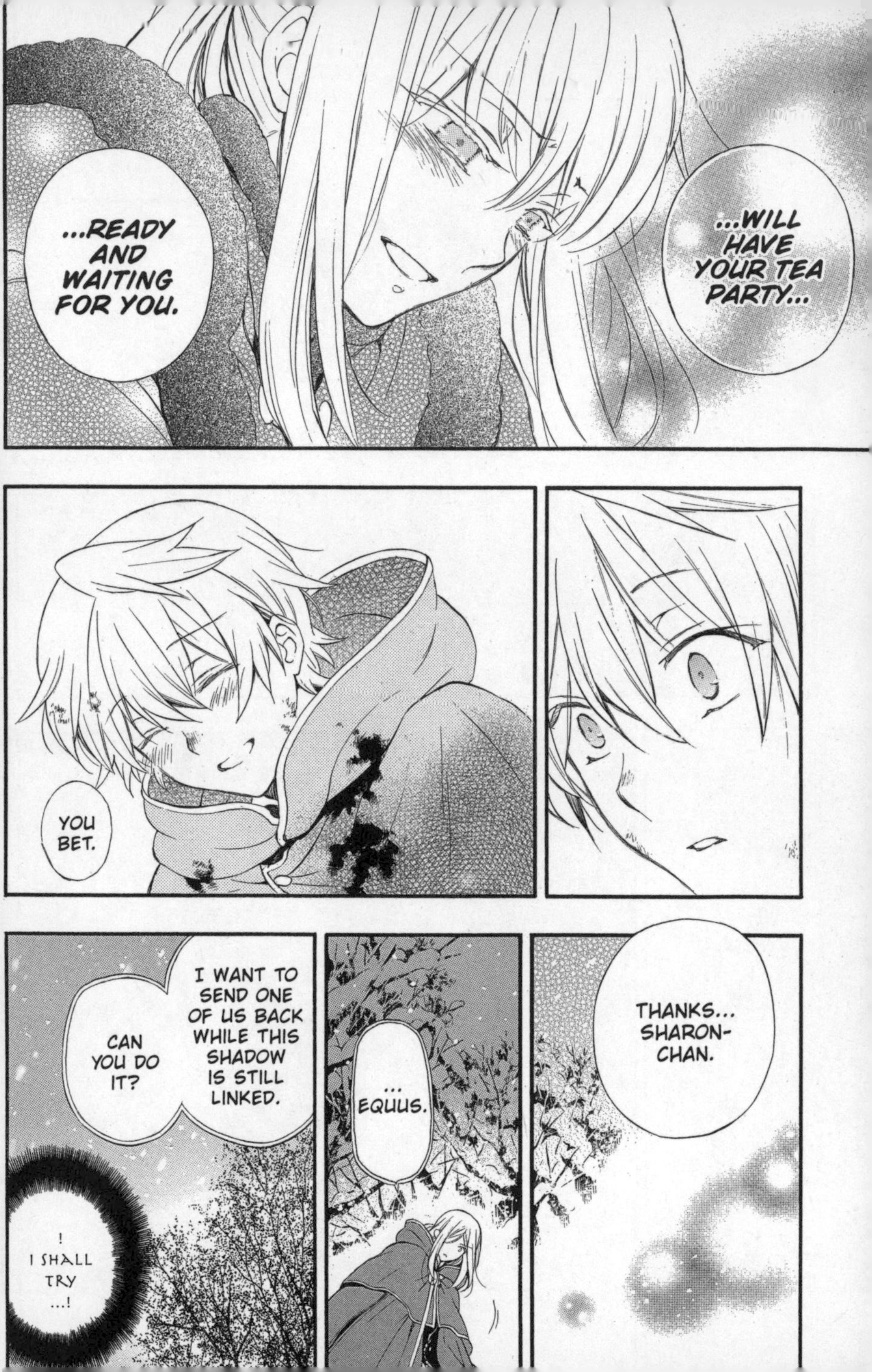
...WILL HAVE YOUR TEA PARTY...
...READY AND WAITING FOR YOU.
YOU BET.
THANKS... SHARON-CHAN.
... EQUUS.
I WANT TO SEND ONE OF US BACK WHILE THIS SHADOW IS STILL LINKED.
CAN YOU DO IT?
! I SHALL TRY ...!

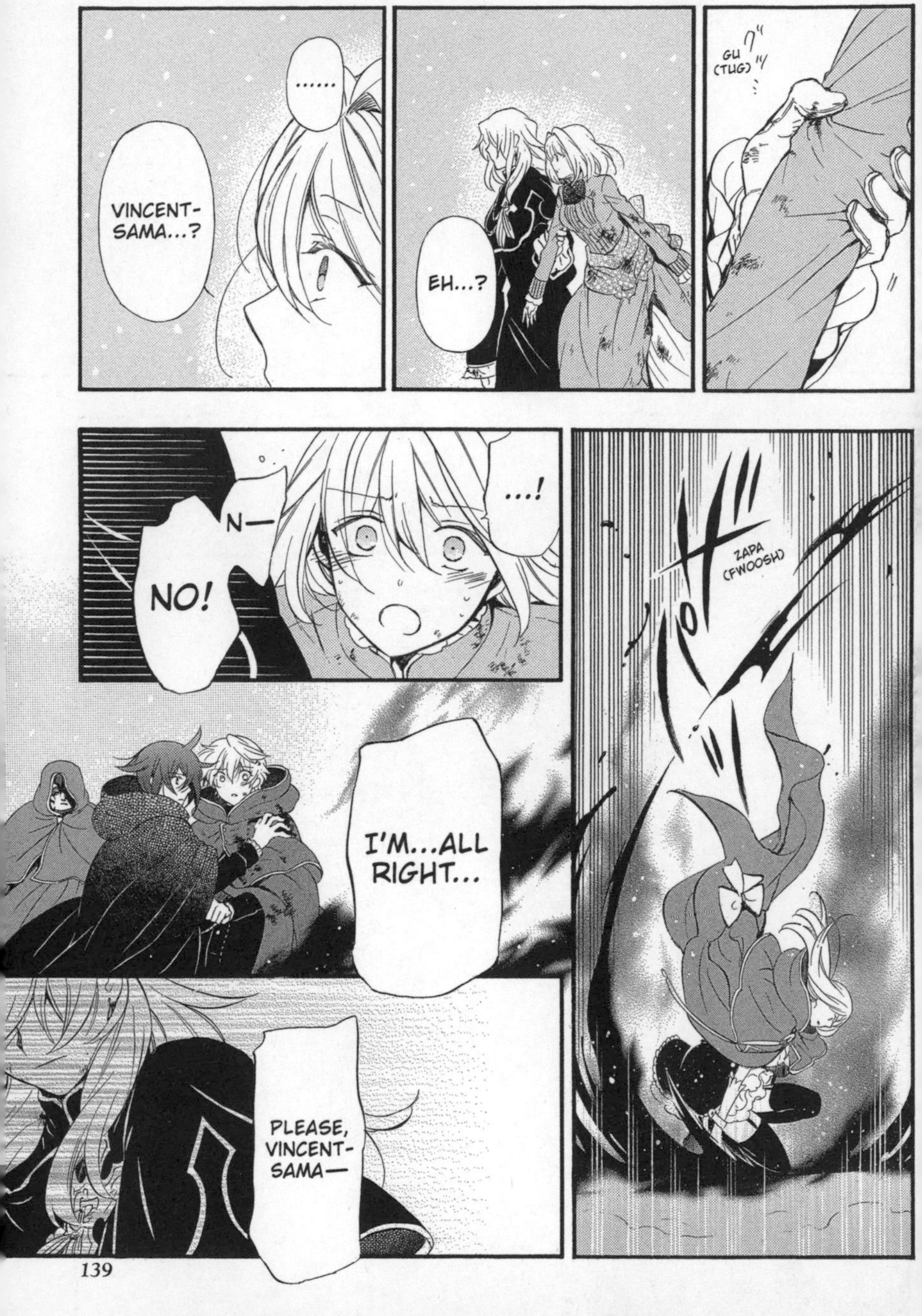

GU (TUG)
EH...?
......
VINCENT-SAMA...?
ZAPA (FWOOSH)
...!
N— NO!
I'M...ALL RIGHT...
PLEASE, VINCENT-SAMA—

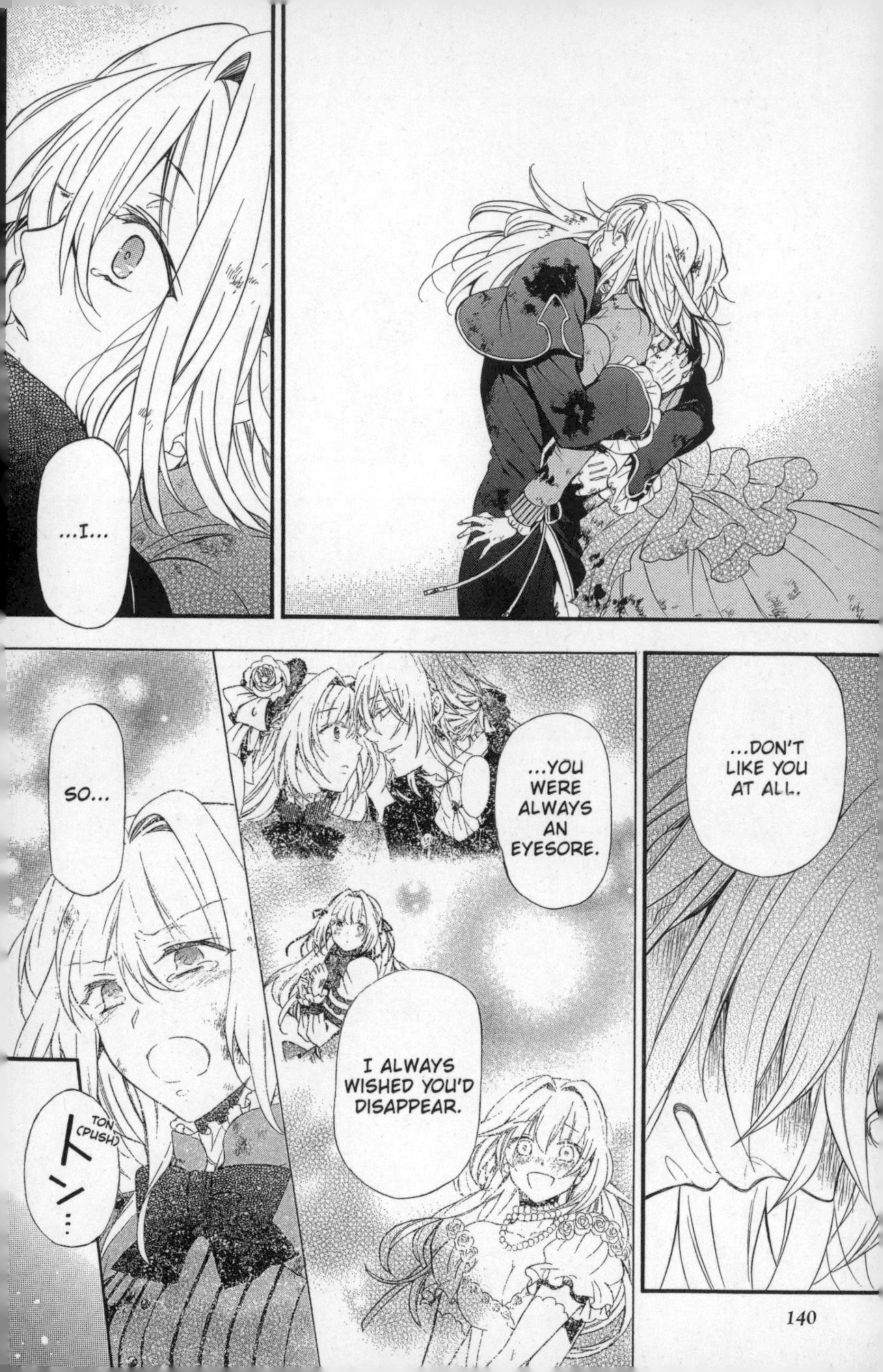
...I...
...DON'T LIKE YOU AT ALL.
...YOU WERE ALWAYS AN EYESORE.
I ALWAYS WISHED YOU'D DISAPPEAR.
SO...
TON (PUSH)
トン…

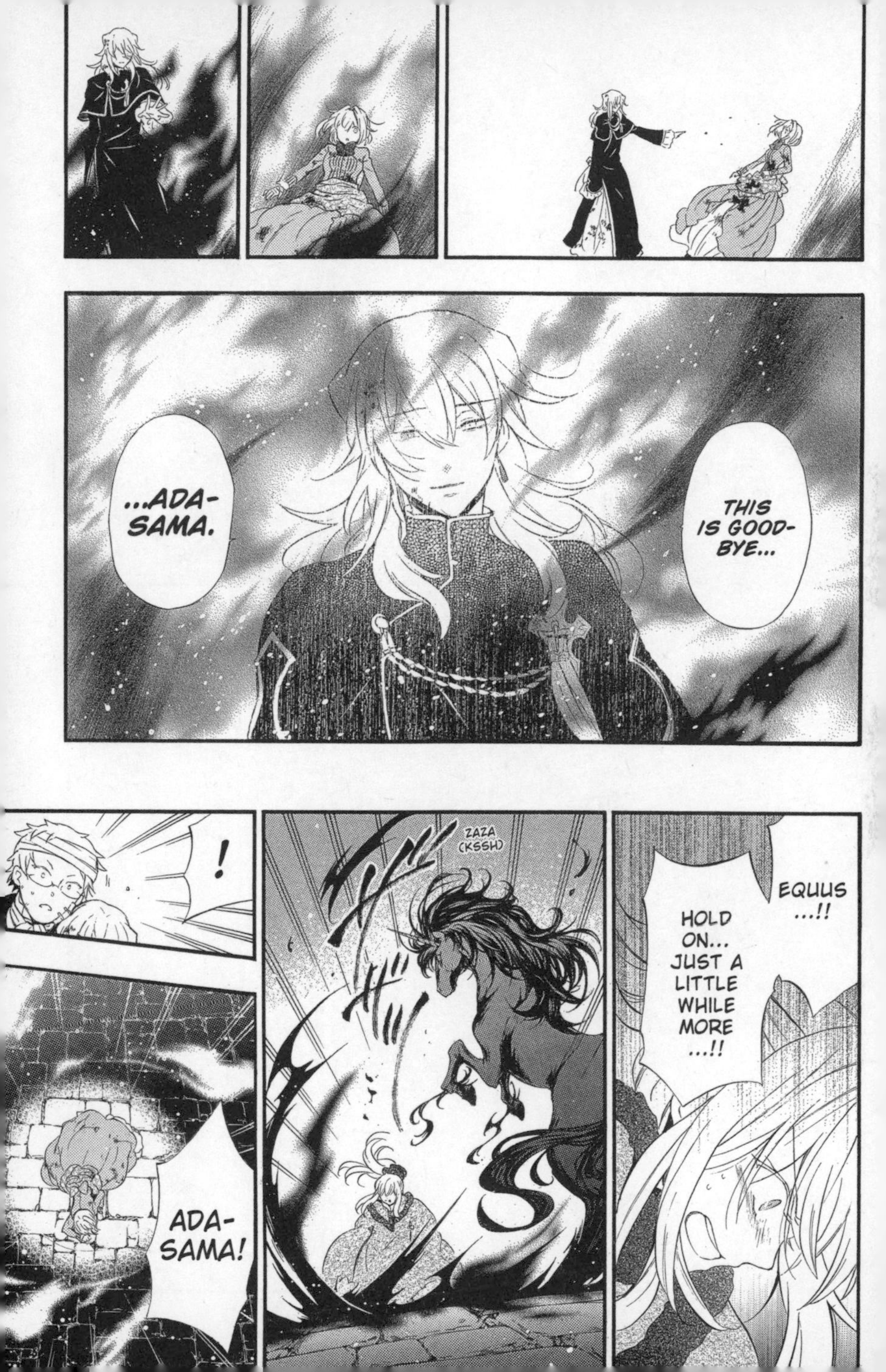
THIS IS GOOD-BYE...
...ADA-SAMA.
EQUUS ...!!
HOLD ON... JUST A LITTLE WHILE MORE ...!!
ZAZA (KSSH)
!
ADA-SAMA!

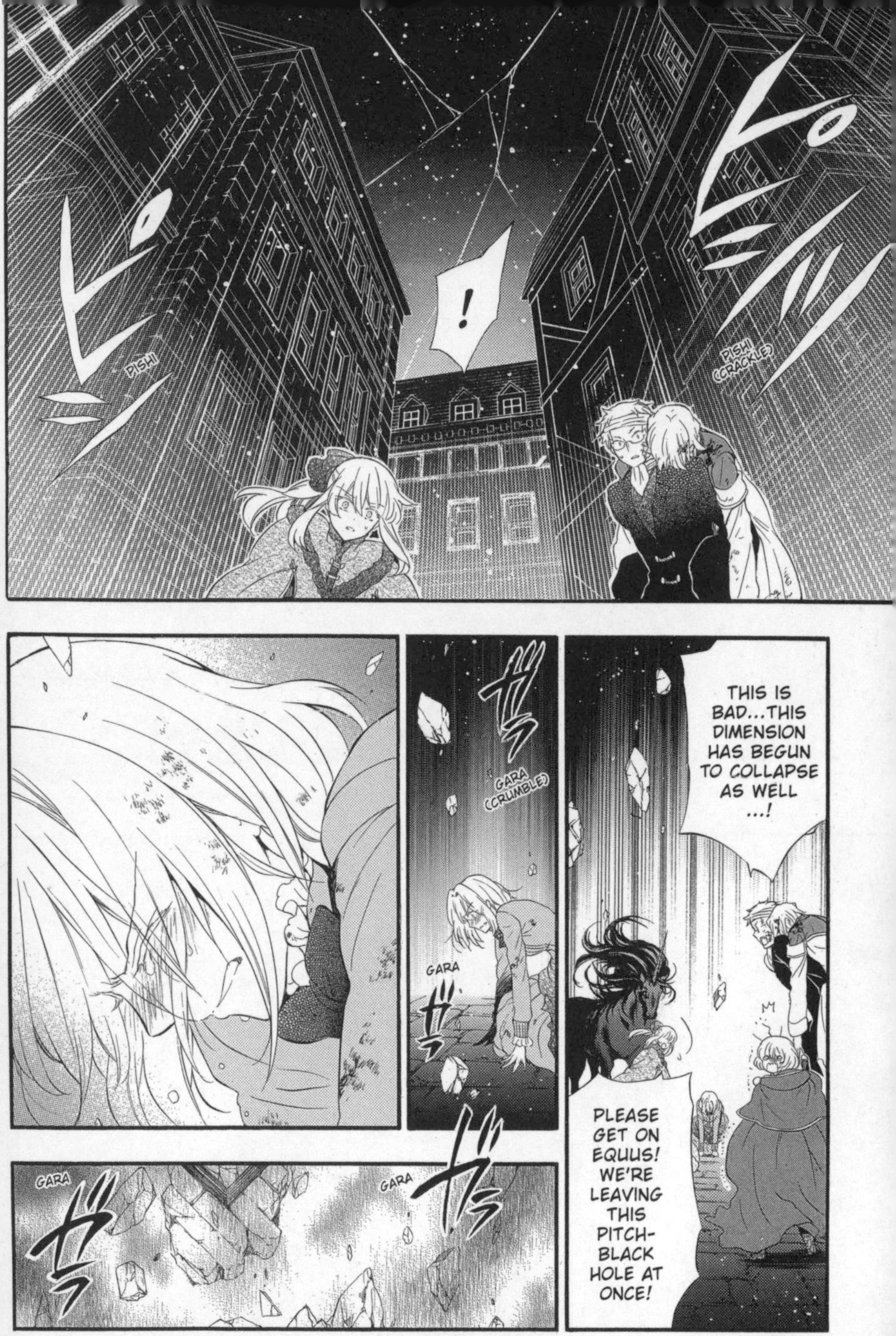
PISHI (CRACKLE)
!
PISHI
THIS IS BAD...THIS DIMENSION HAS BEGUN TO COLLAPSE AS WELL ...!
PLEASE GET ON EQUUS! WE'RE LEAVING THIS PITCH-BLACK HOLE AT ONCE!
GARA (CRUMBLE)
GARA
GARA
GARA

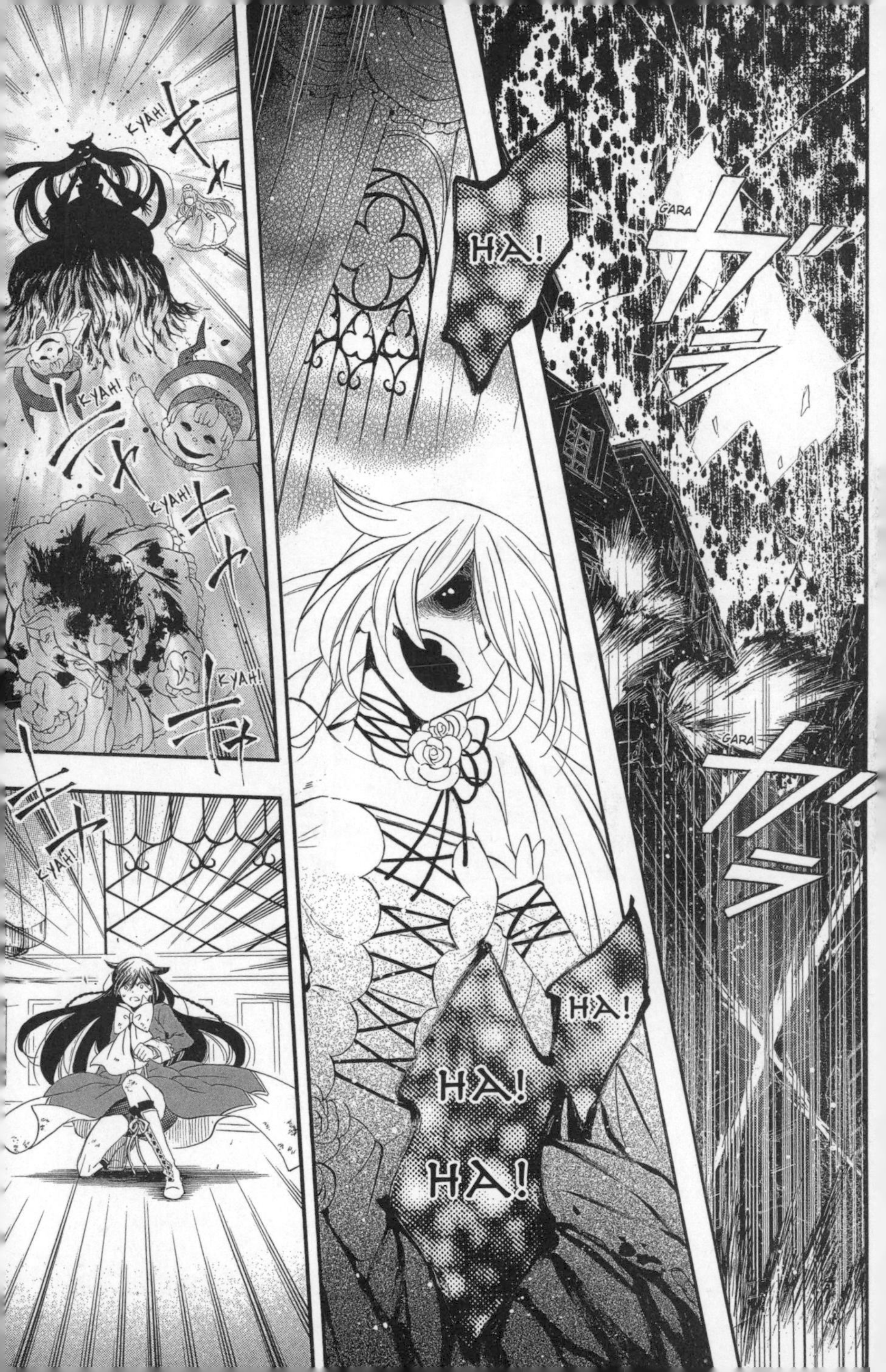
GARA
GARA
HA!
HA!
HA!
HA!
KYAH!
KYAH!
KYAH!
KYAH!
KYAH!

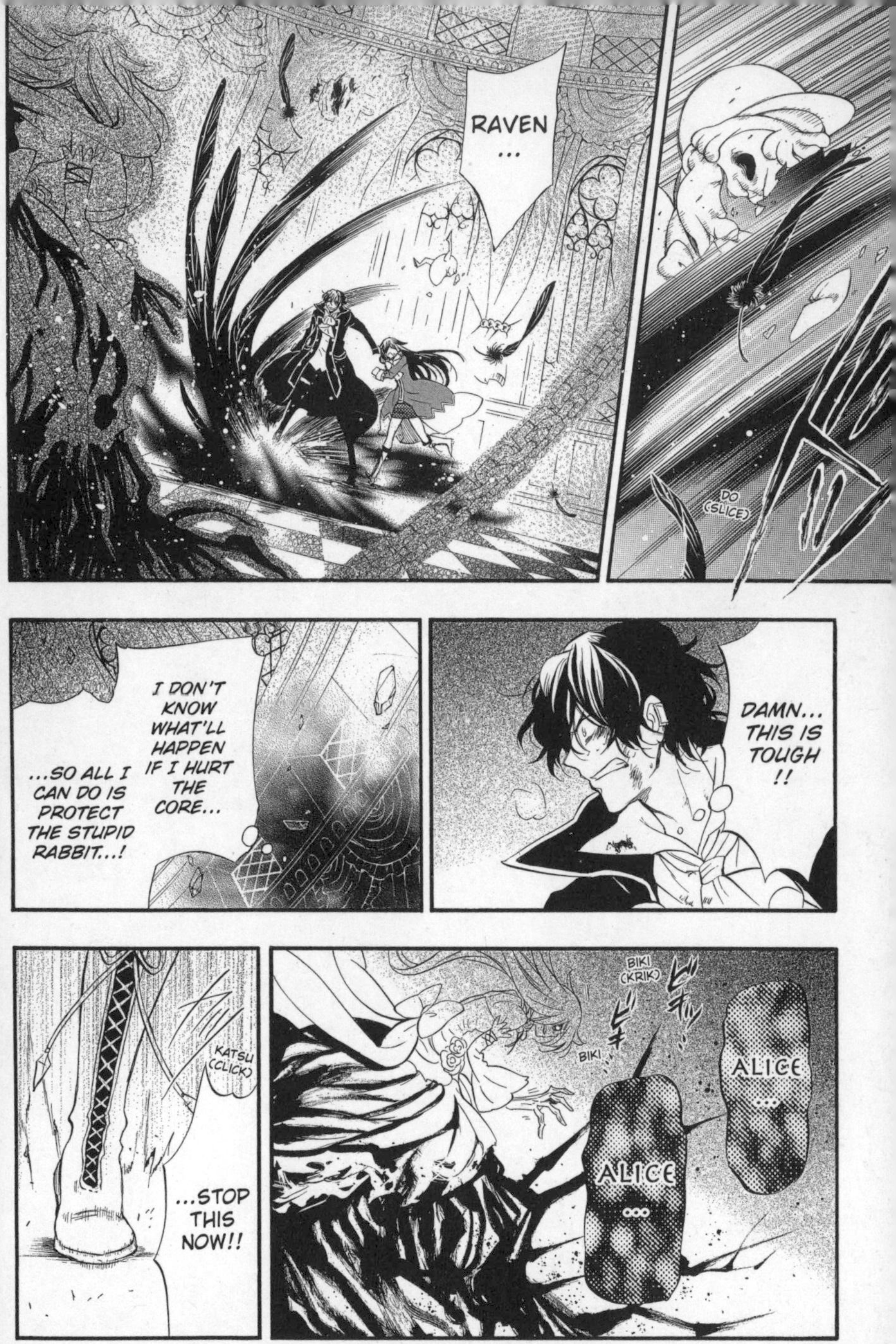
DO
(SLICE)
RAVEN
...
DAMN... THIS IS TOUGH !!
I DON'T KNOW WHAT'LL HAPPEN IF I HURT THE CORE...
...SO ALL I CAN DO IS PROTECT THE STUPID RABBIT...!
BIKI
(KRIK)
BIKI
ALICE
...
ALICE
...
KATSU
(CLICK)
...STOP THIS NOW!!

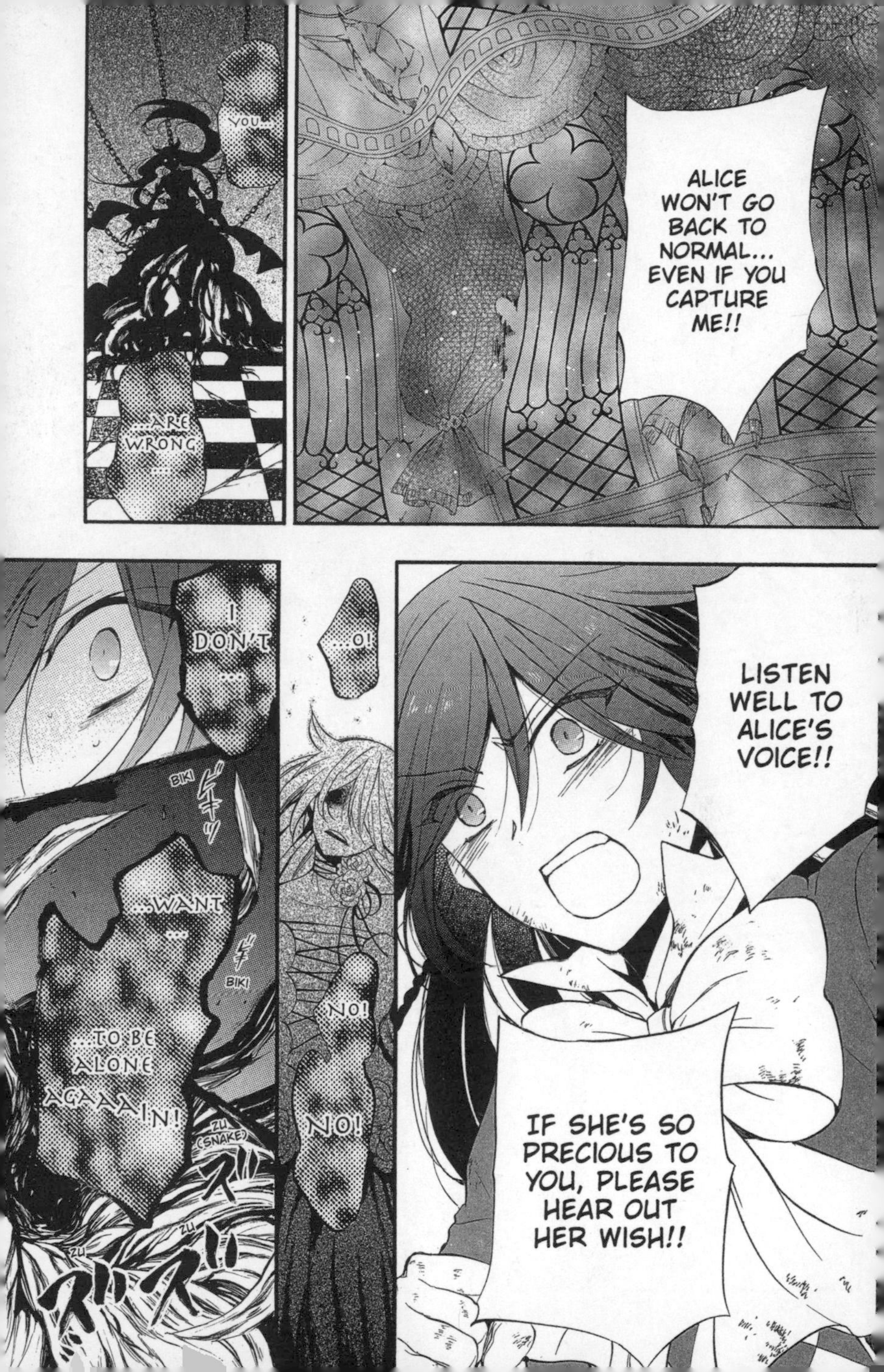
ALICE WON'T GO BACK TO NORMAL... EVEN IF YOU CAPTURE ME!!
YOU...
...ARE WRONG...
LISTEN WELL TO ALICE'S VOICE!!
IF SHE'S SO PRECIOUS TO YOU, PLEASE HEAR OUT HER WISH!!
...O!
NO!
NO!
I DON'T...
BIKI
...WANT...
BIKI
...TO BE ALONE AGAAAIN!
ZU (SNAKE)
ZU
ZU

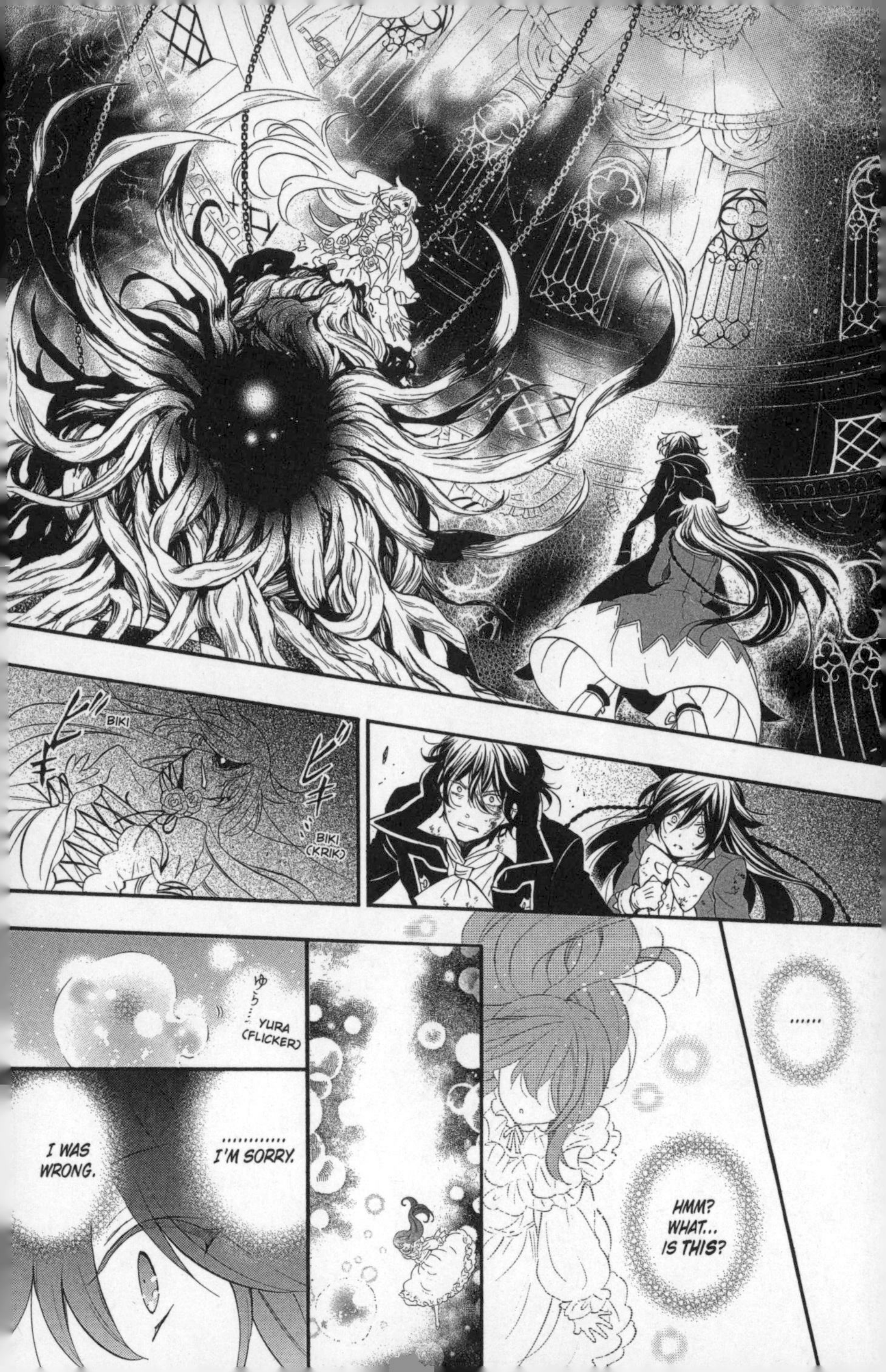

!
ビキ…
BIKI (KRIK)
ビキ
BIKI
……
HMM? WHAT... IS THIS?
ゆら…
YURA (FLICKER)
.... I'M SORRY.
I WAS WRONG.

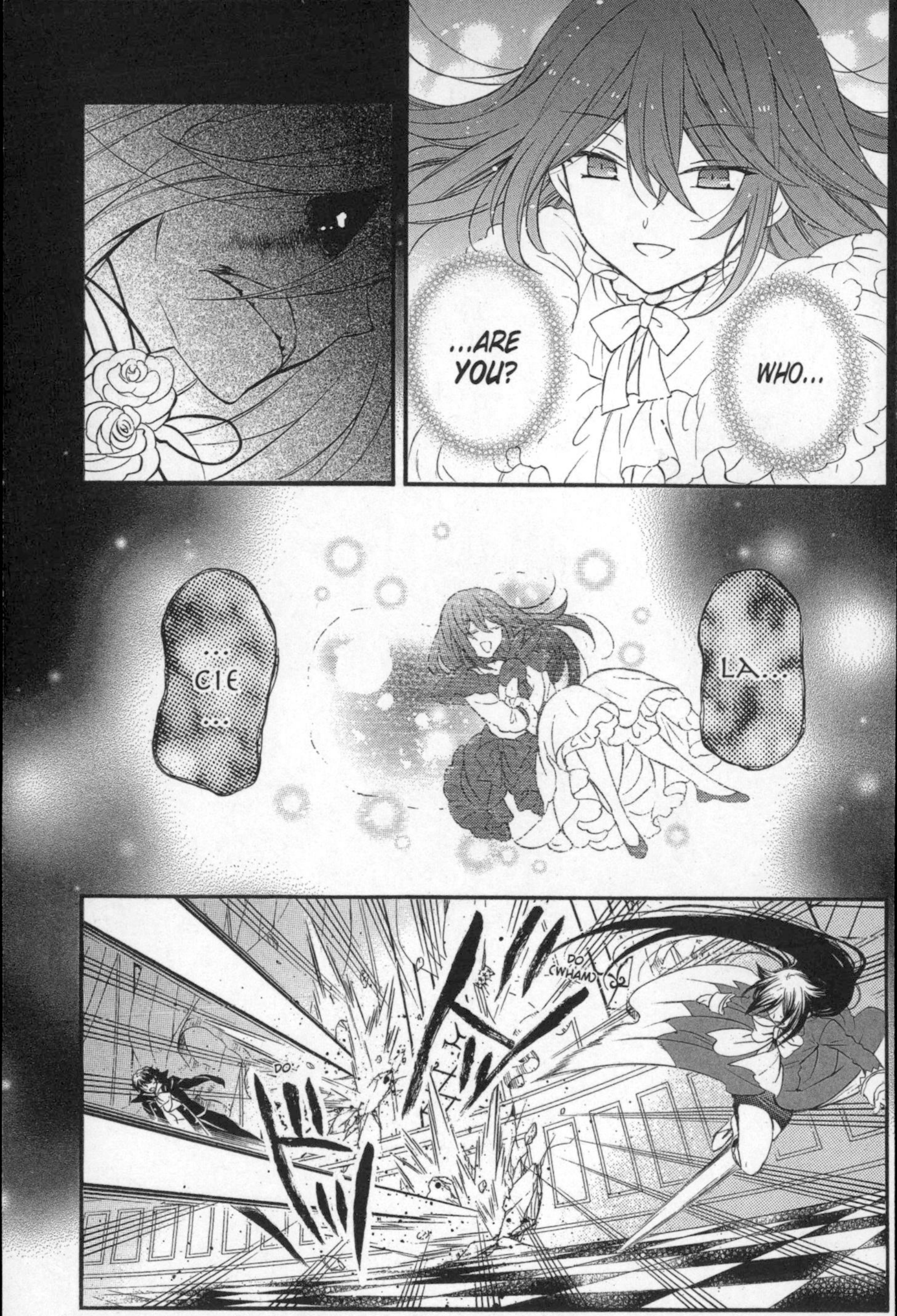
WHO...
...ARE YOU?
LA...
...CIE...
DO (WHAM)
DO

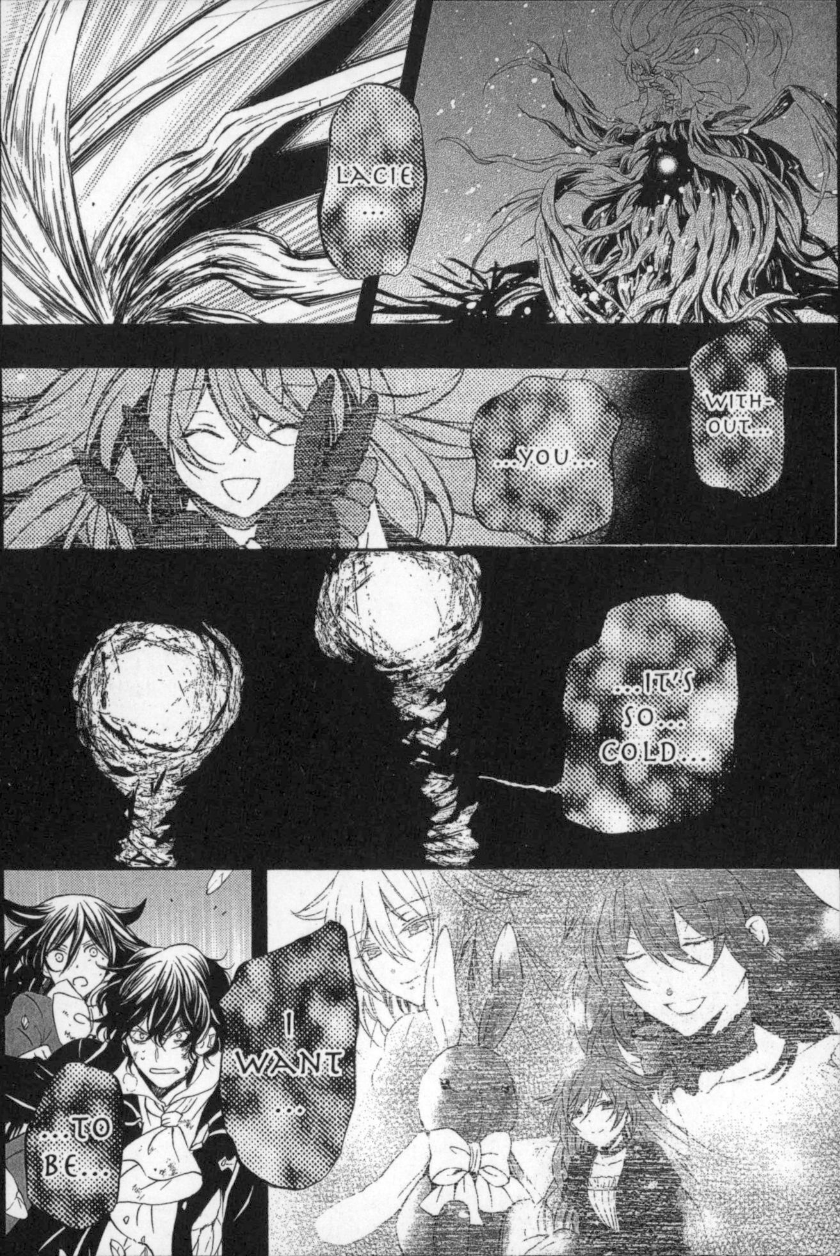
LACIE ...
WITH-OUT...
...YOU...
...IT'S SO... COLD...
I WANT ...
...TO BE...

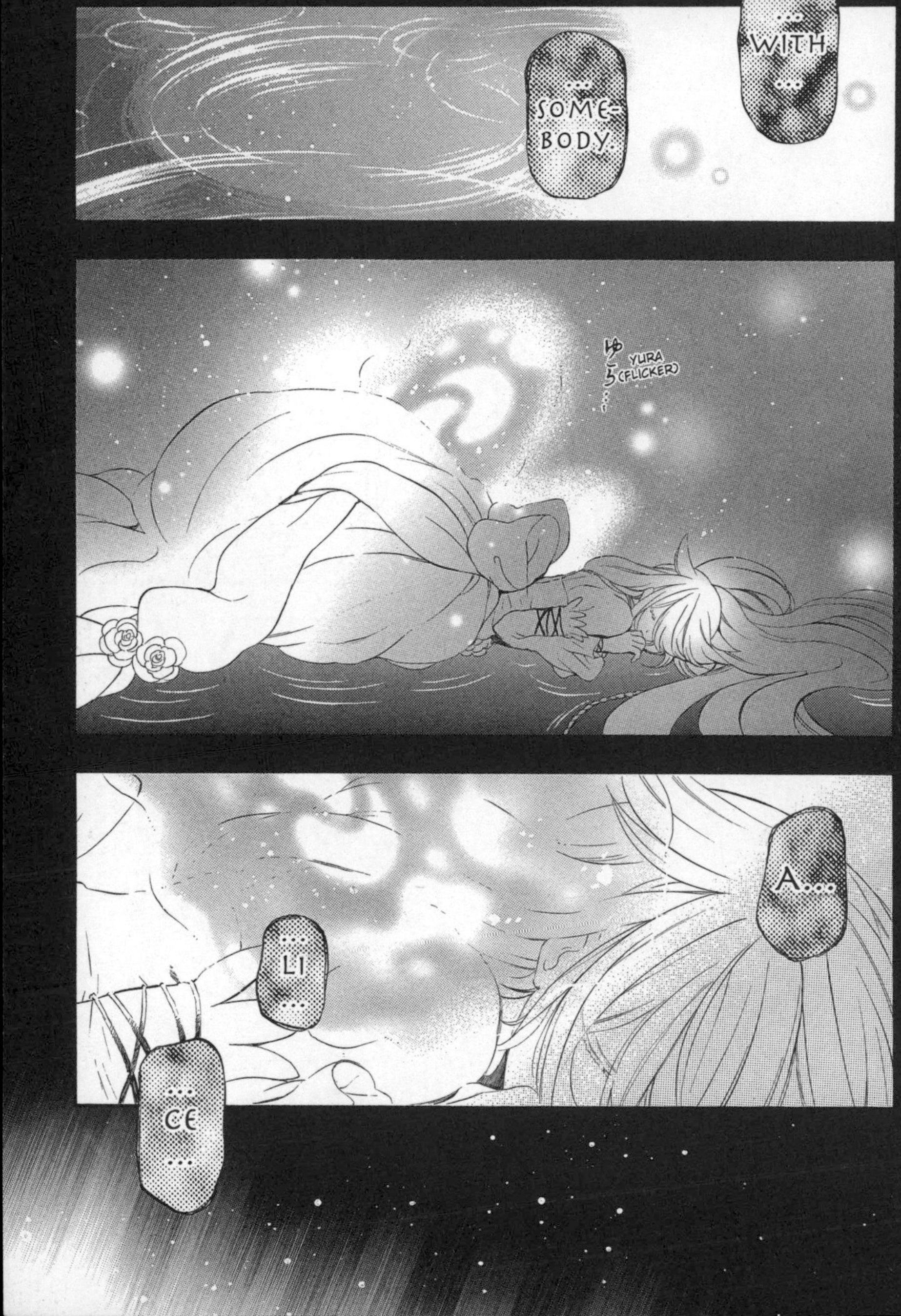
...WITH...
...SOME-BODY.
ゆら…
YURA (FLICKER)
A...
...LI...
...CE...

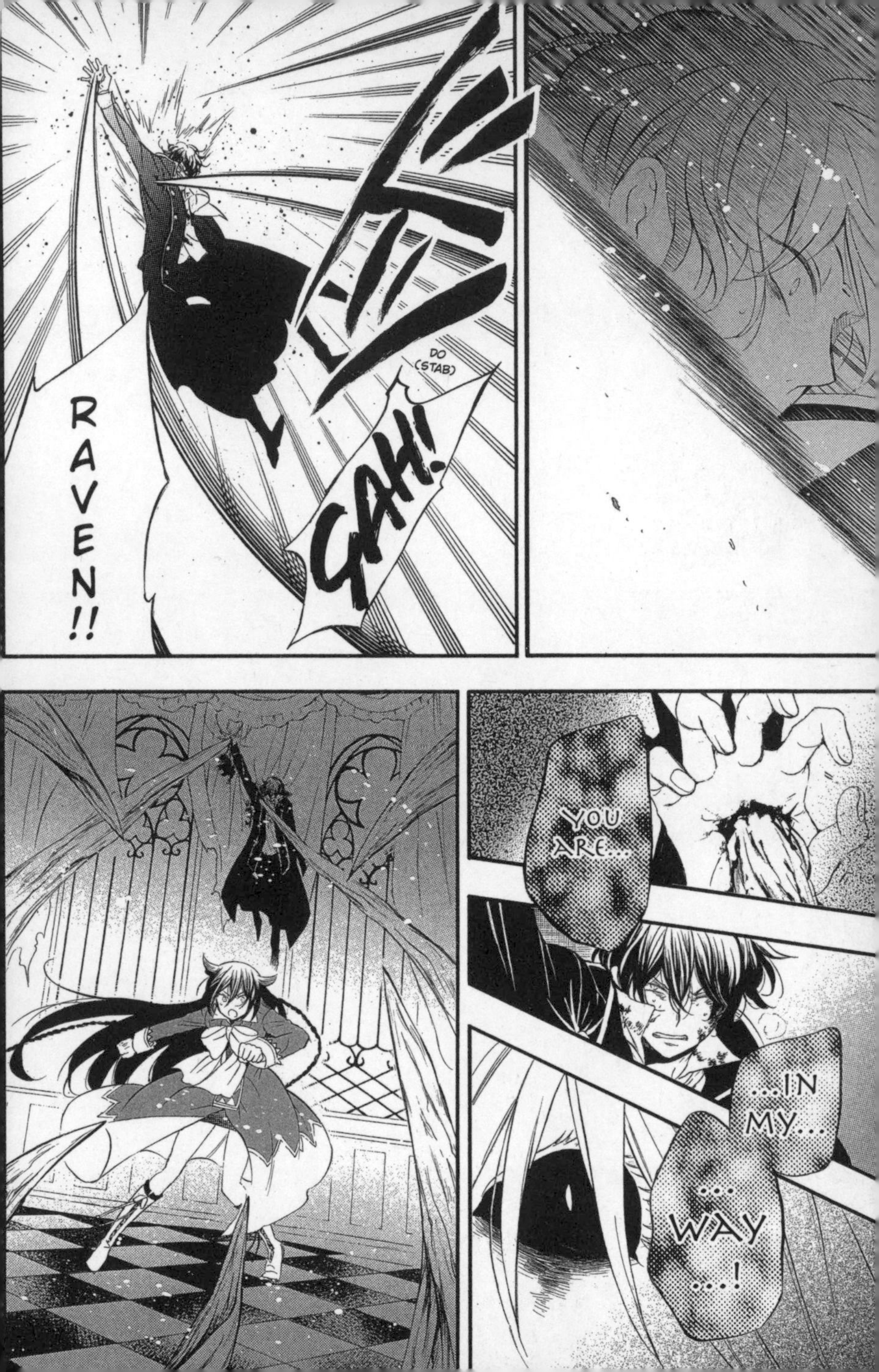
DO (STAB)
GAH!
RAVEN!!
YOU ARE...
...IN MY...
...WAY...!

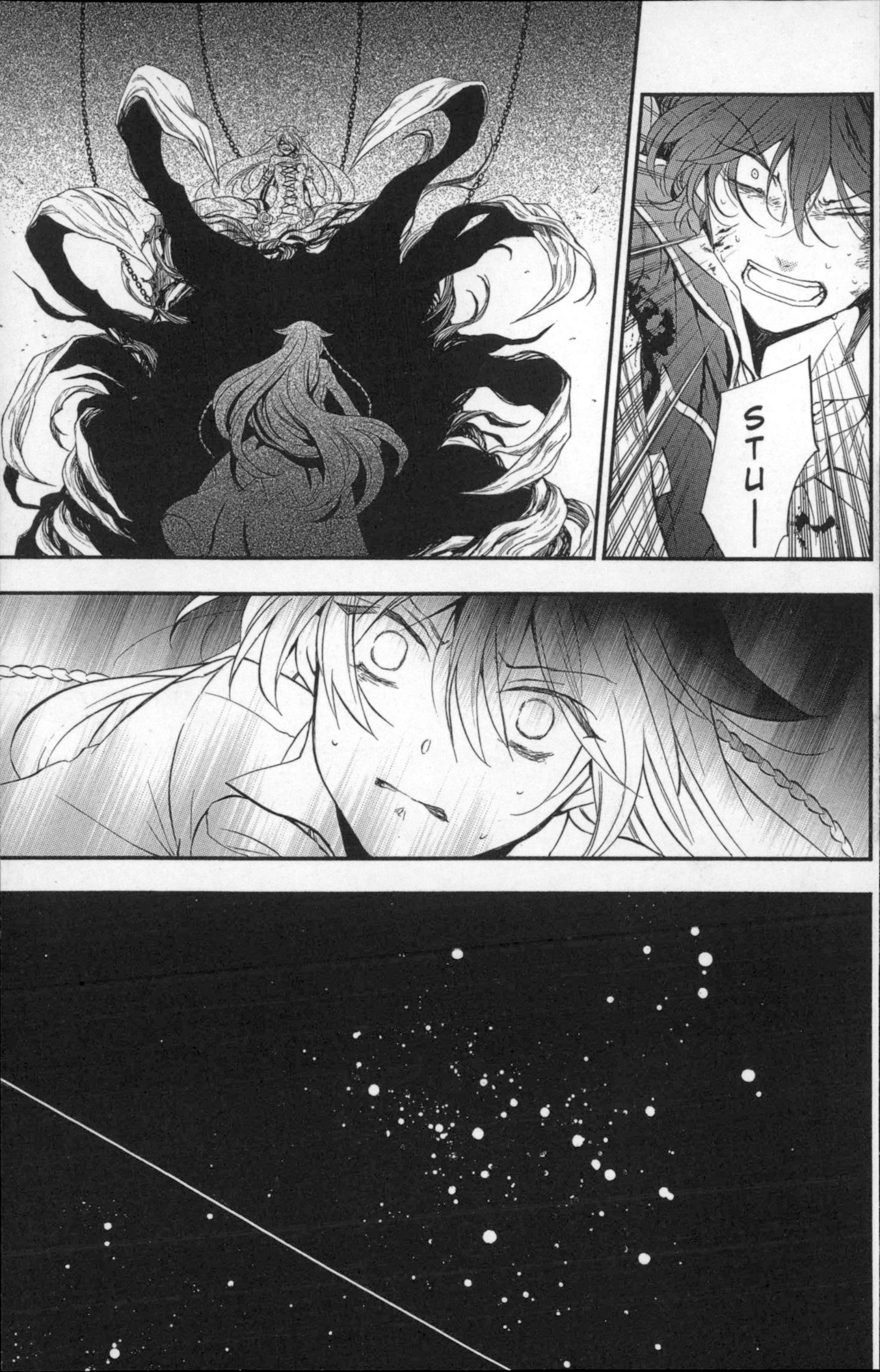
STU—

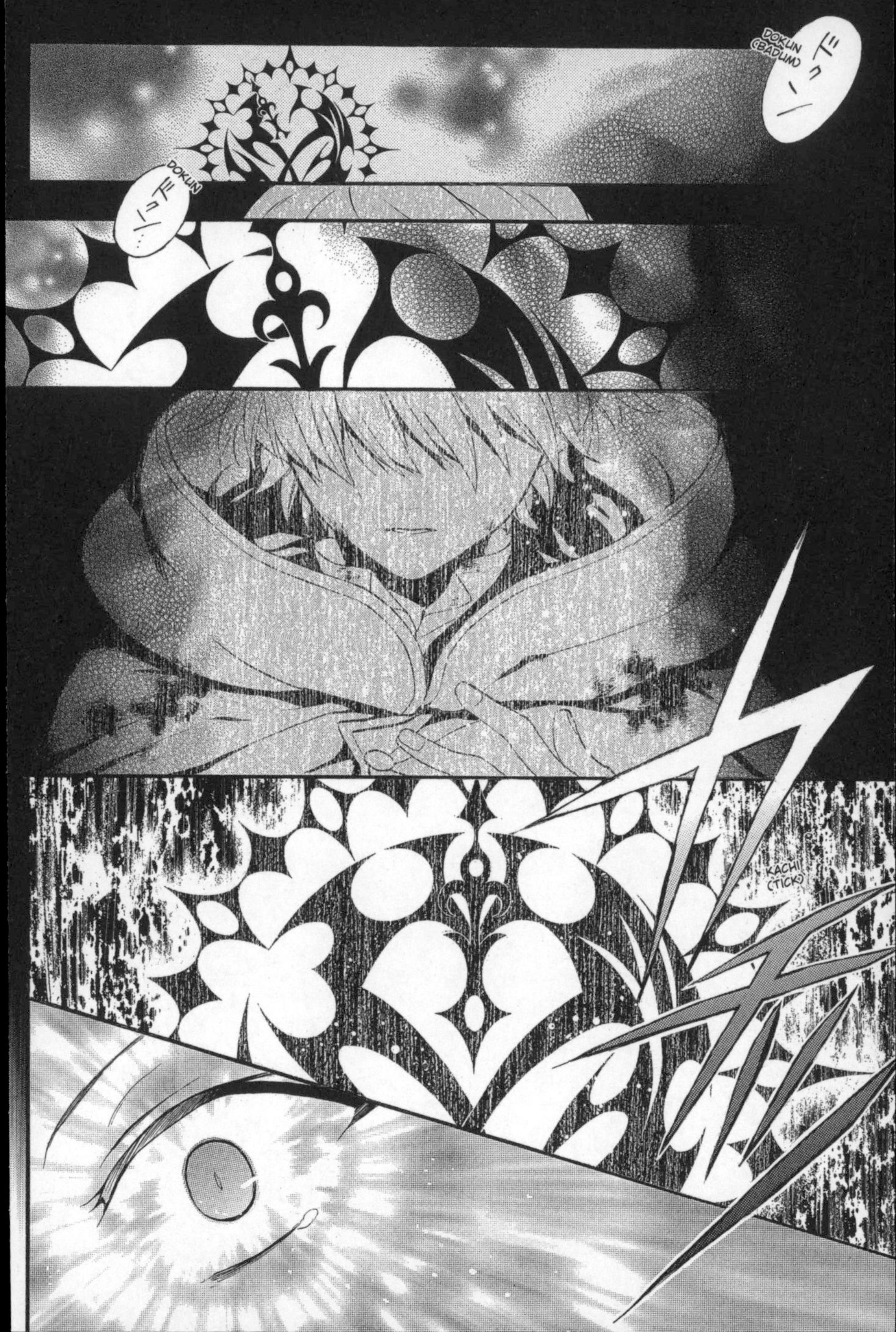
DOKUN (BADUM)
DOKUN
KACHI (TICK)

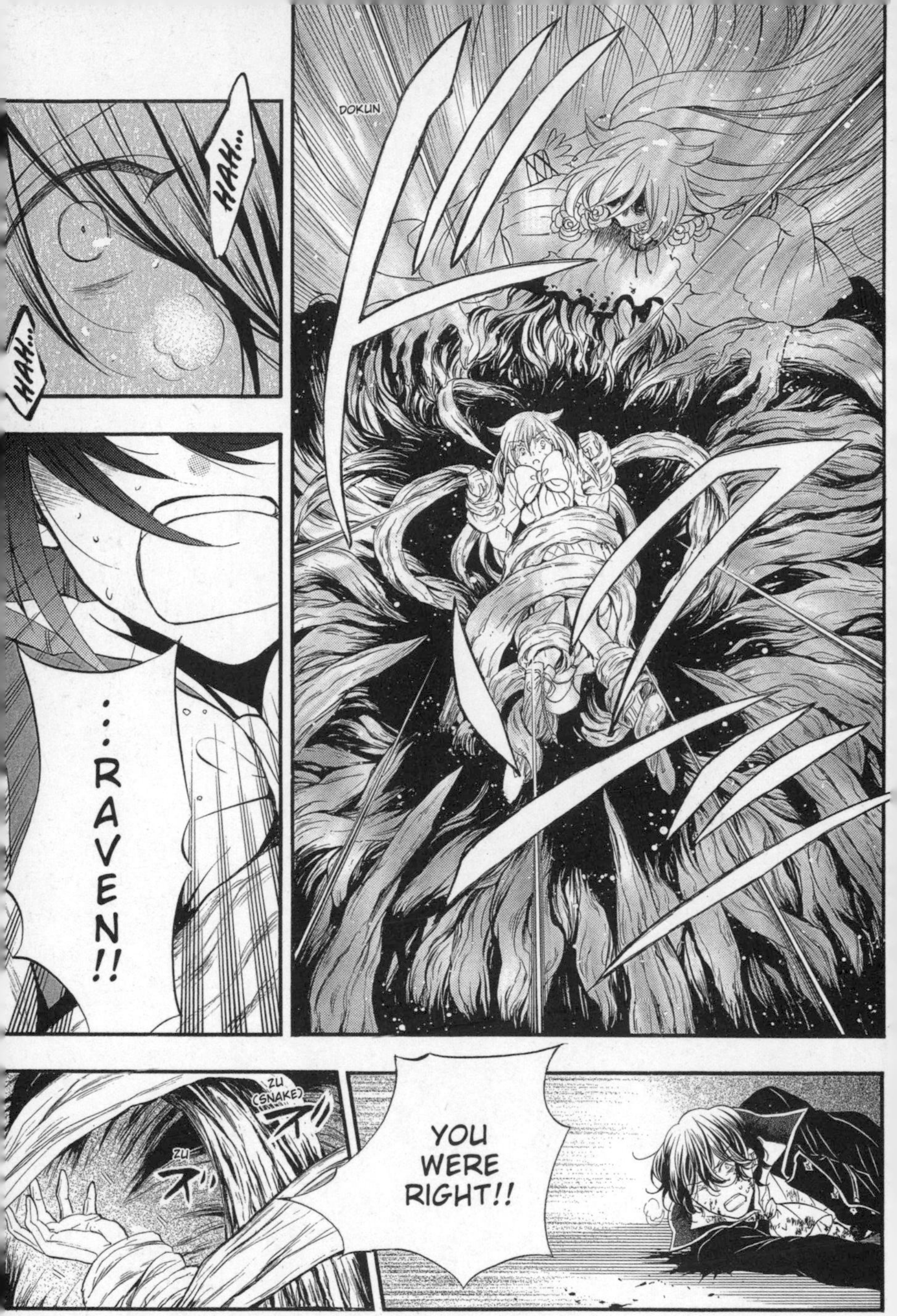
DOKUN
HAH...
HAH...
...RAVEN!!
YOU WERE RIGHT!!
ZU (SNAKE)
ZU

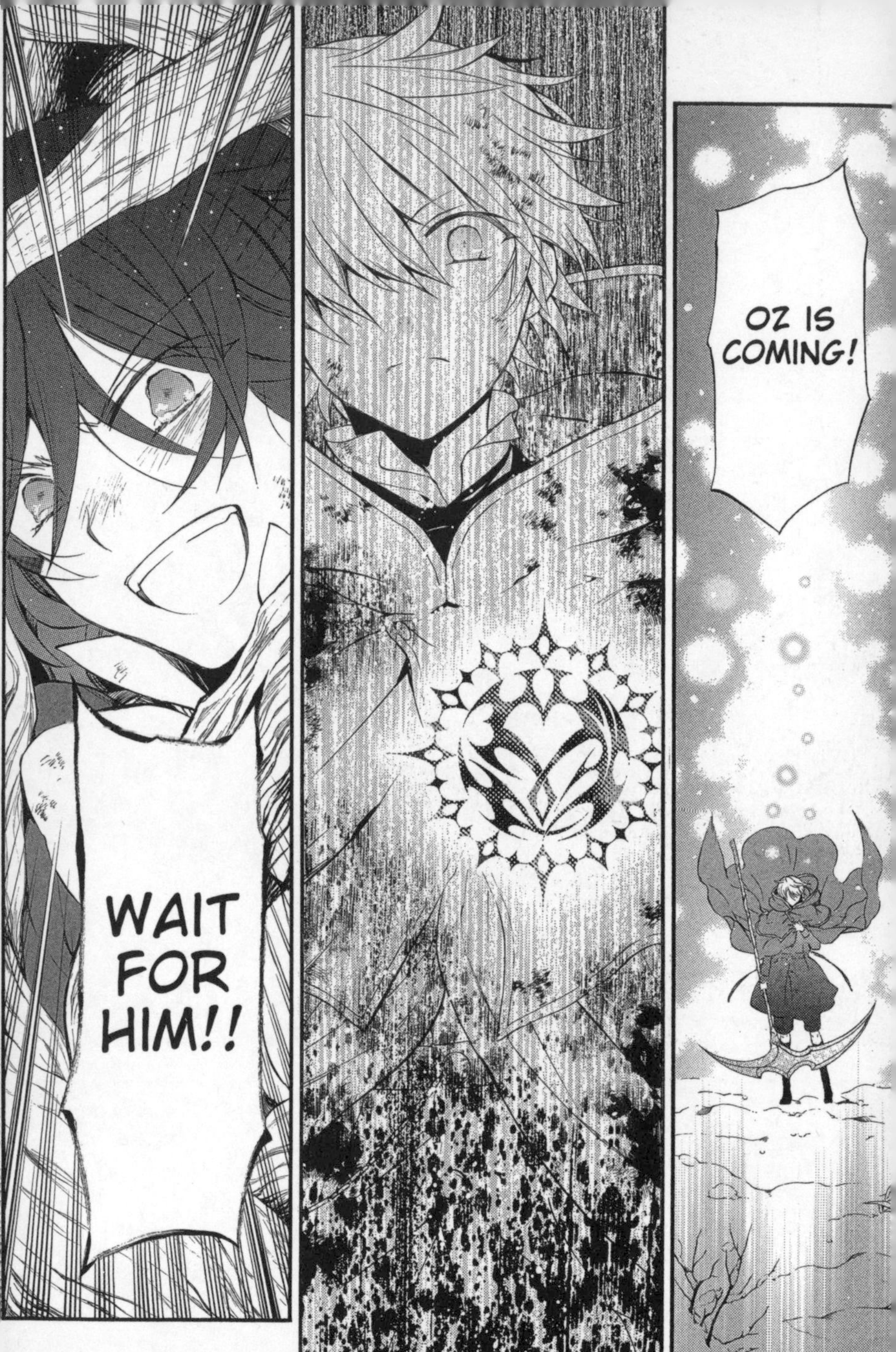
OZ IS COMING!
WAIT FOR HIM!!

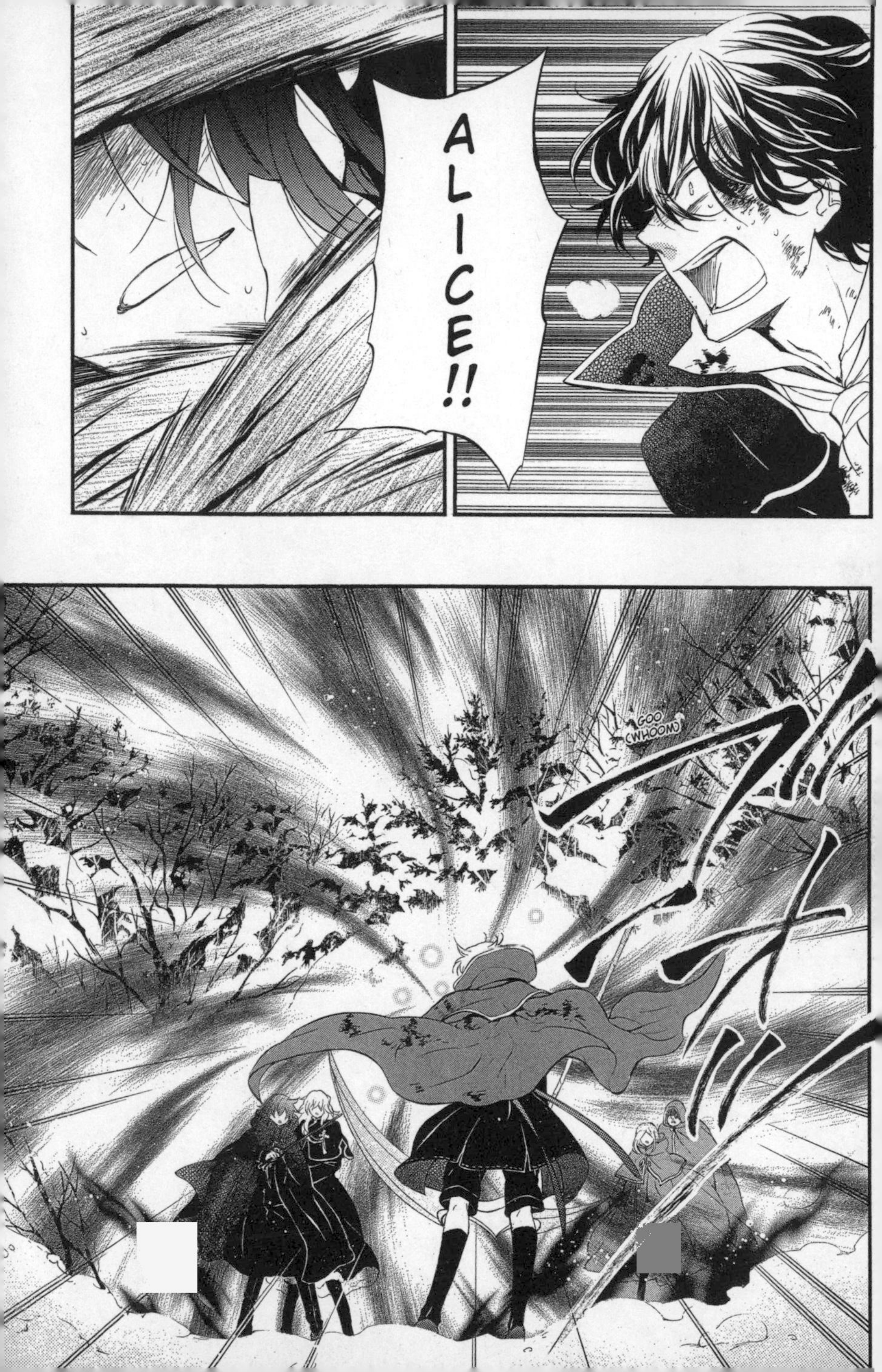
ALICE!!
GOO (WHOOM)

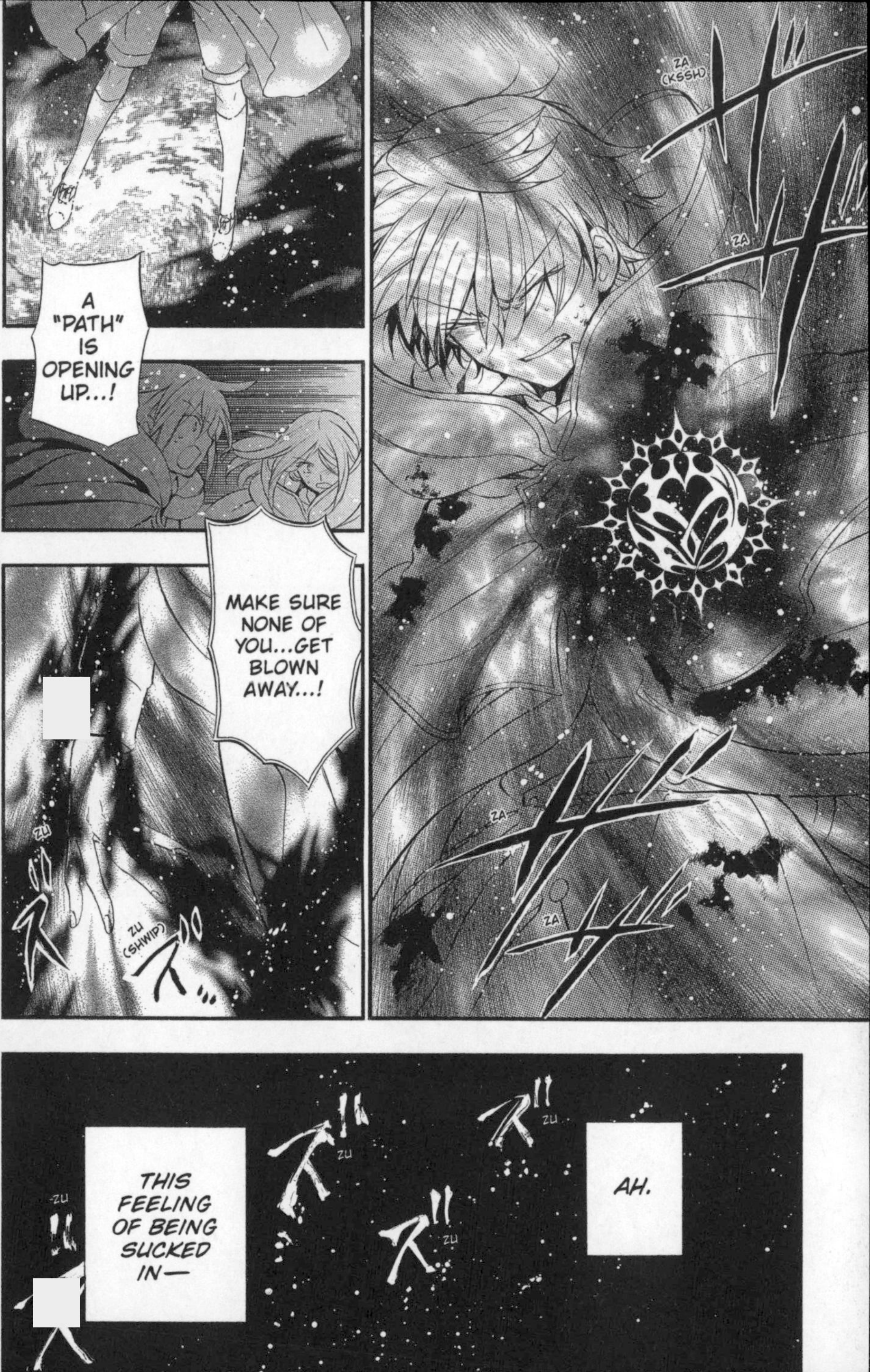

ZA (KSSH)
ZA
ZA
ZA
A "PATH" IS OPENING UP...!
MAKE SURE NONE OF YOU...GET BLOWN AWAY...!
ZU (SHWIP)
ZU
AH.
ZU
ZU
ZU
THIS FEELING OF BEING SUCKED IN—
ZU

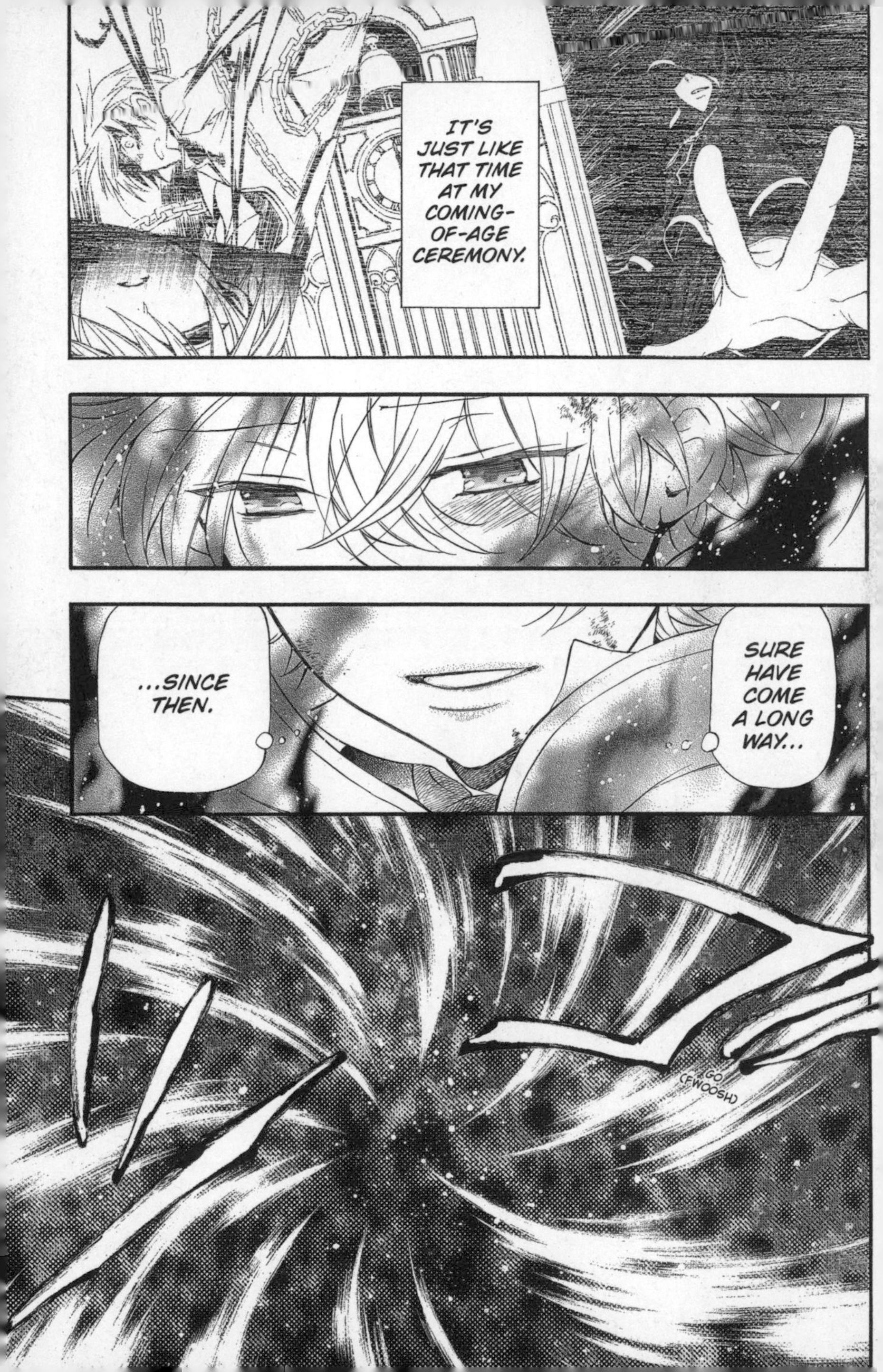
IT'S JUST LIKE THAT TIME AT MY COMING-OF-AGE CEREMONY.
SURE HAVE COME A LONG WAY...
...SINCE THEN.
GO (FWOOSH)

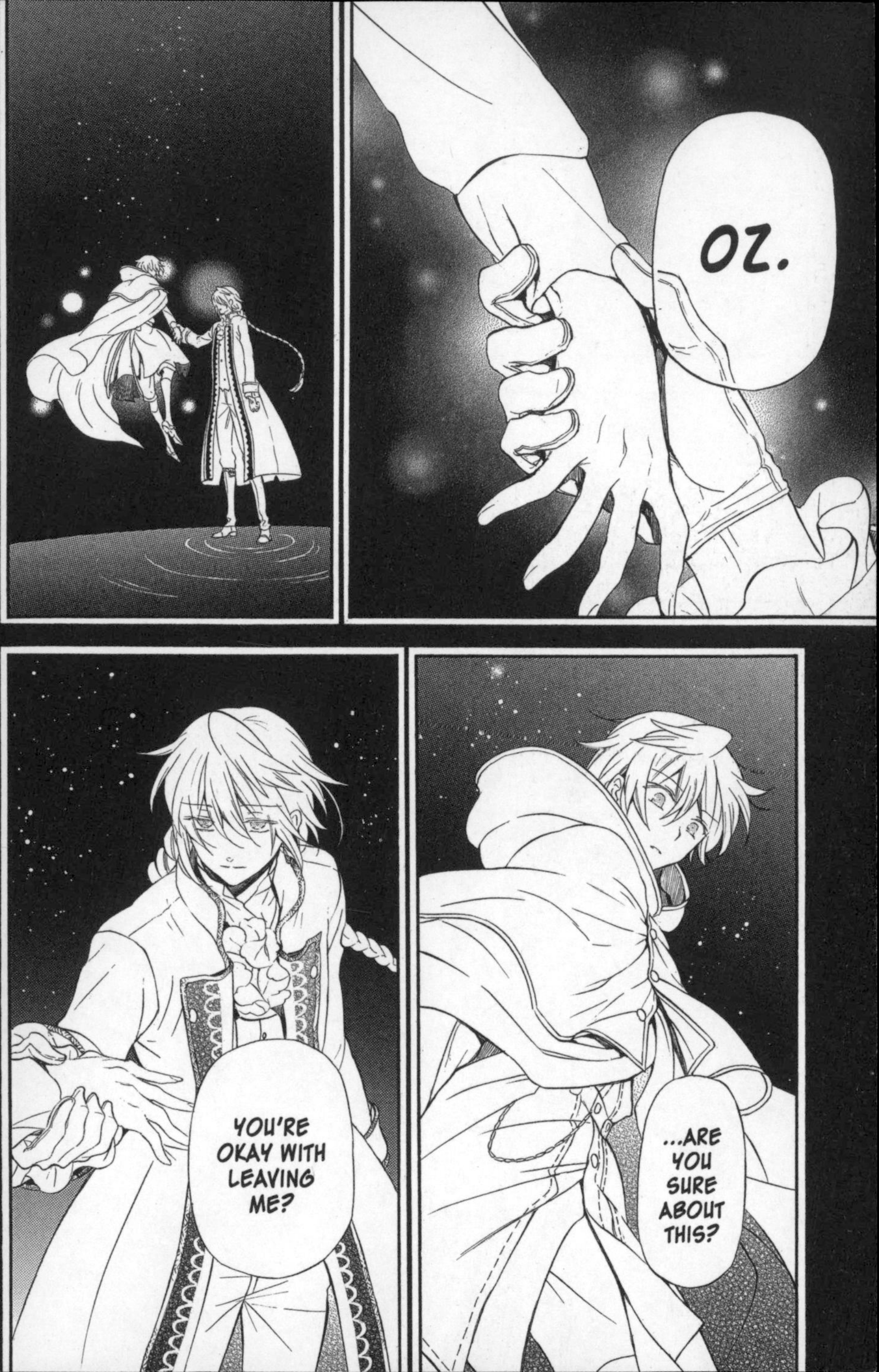
OZ.
...ARE YOU SURE ABOUT THIS?
YOU'RE OKAY WITH LEAVING ME?

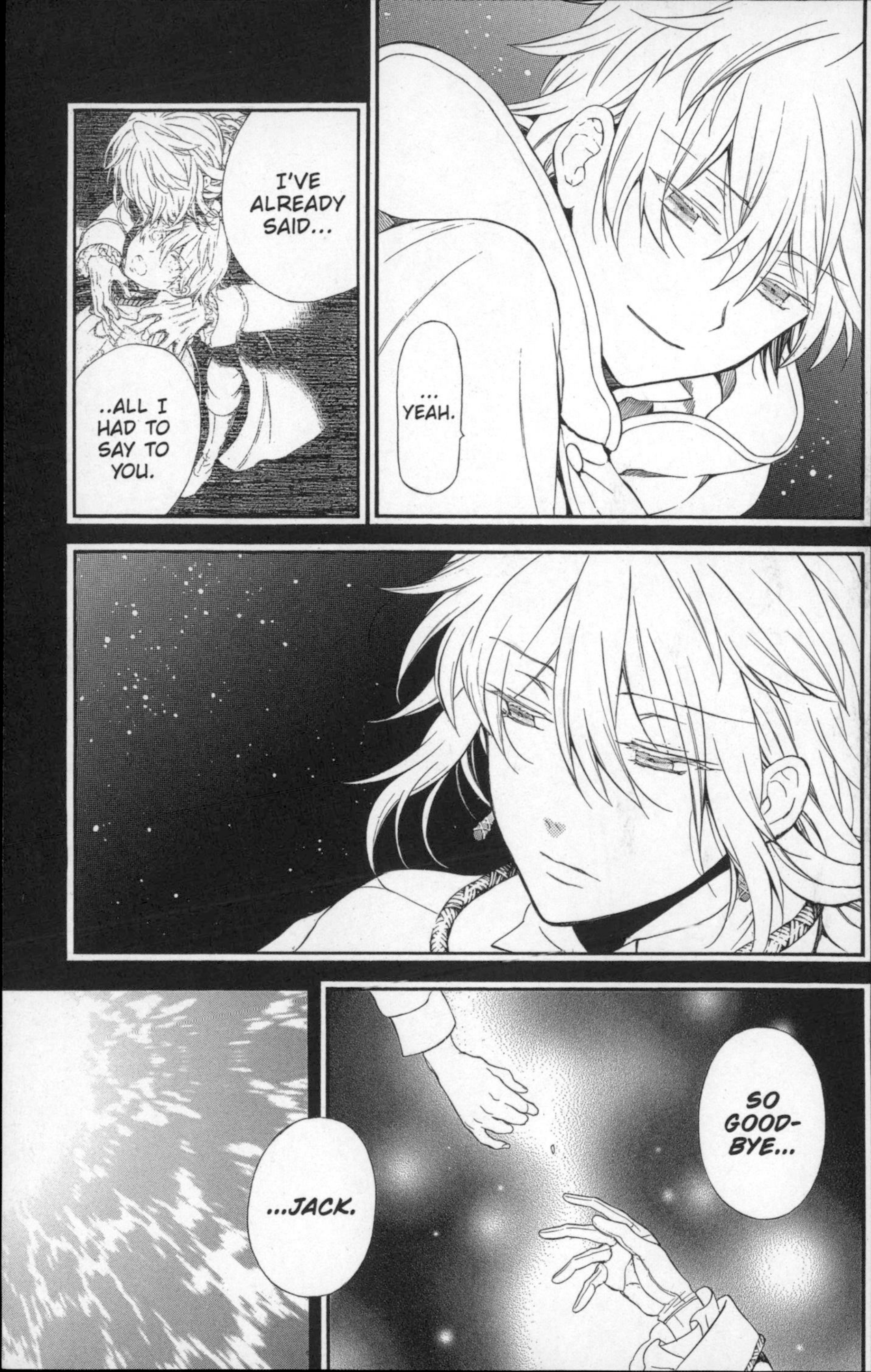
... YEAH.
I'VE ALREADY SAID...
..ALL I HAD TO SAY TO YOU.
SO GOOD-BYE...
...JACK.

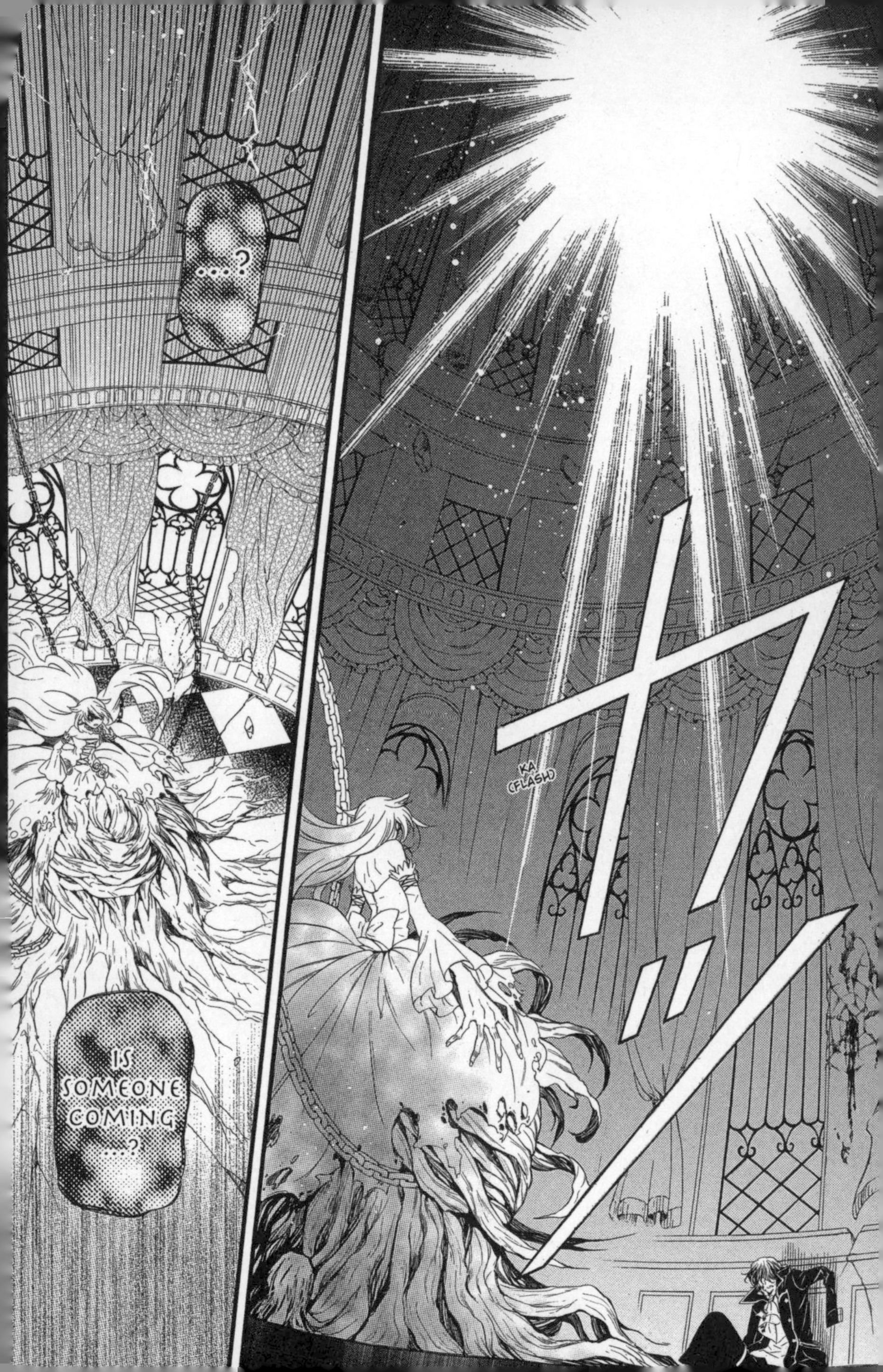
KA (FLASH)
...?
IS SOMEONE COMING ...?

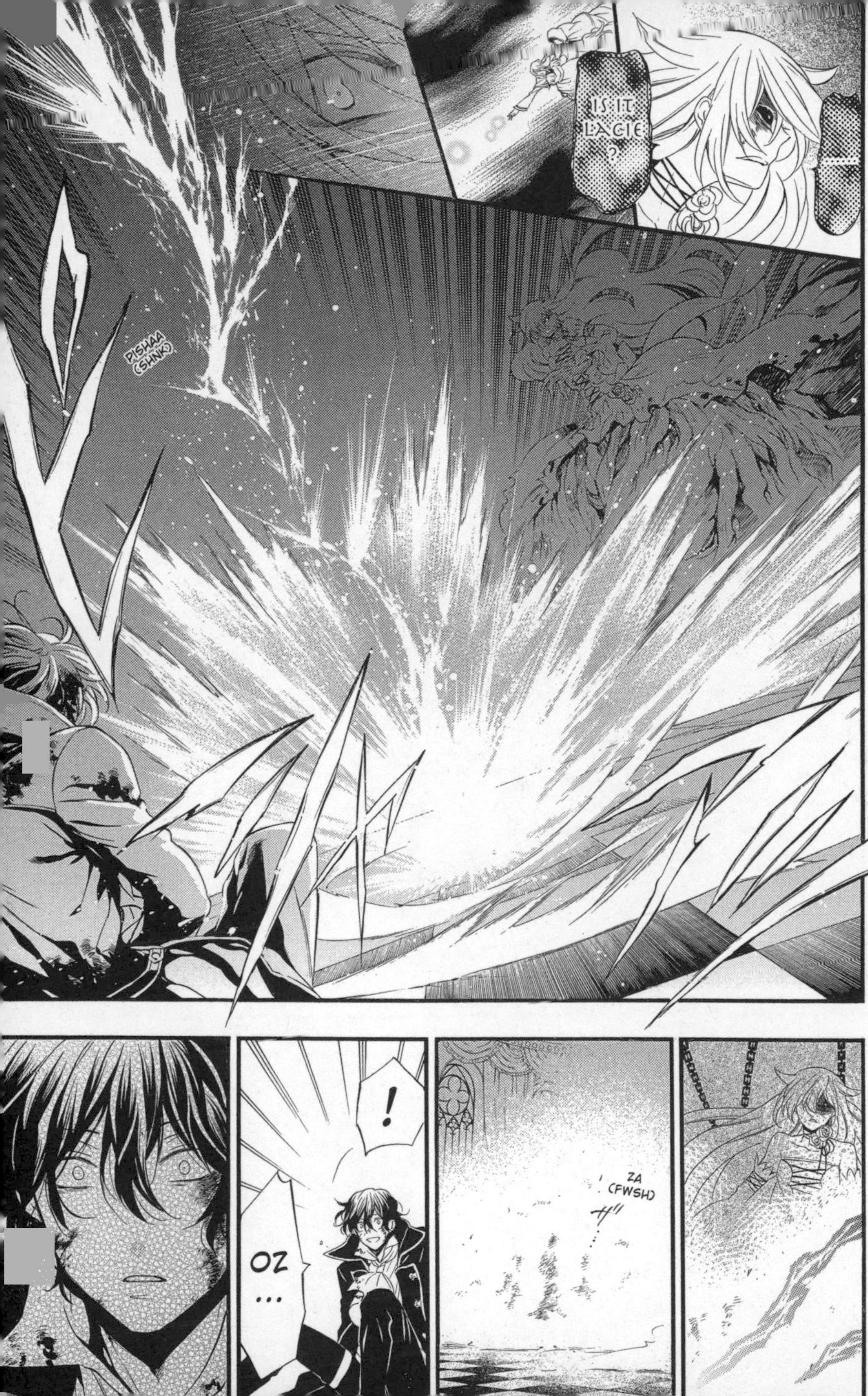
IS IT LACIE ?
PISHAA (SHNK)
ZA (FWSH)
!
OZ ...

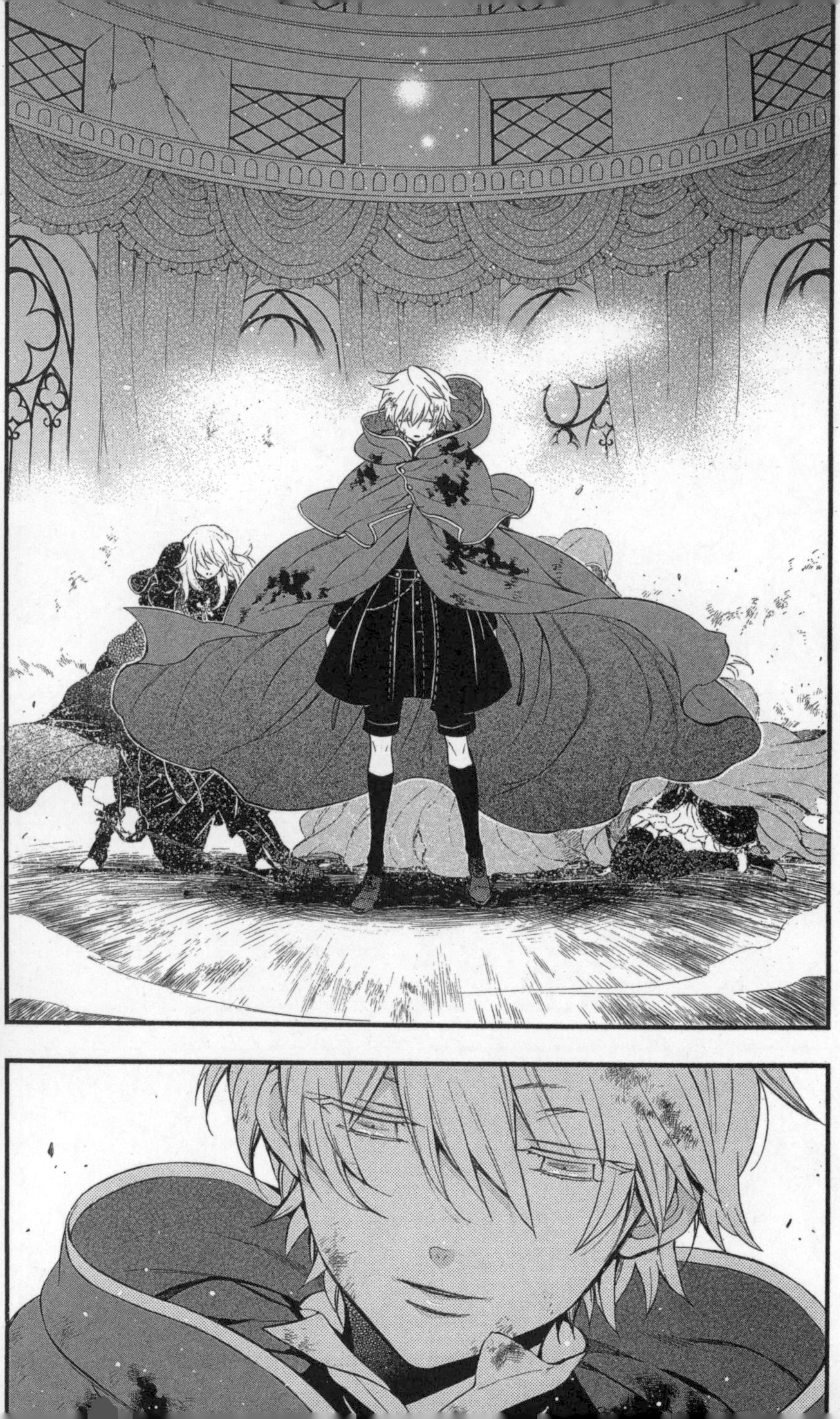

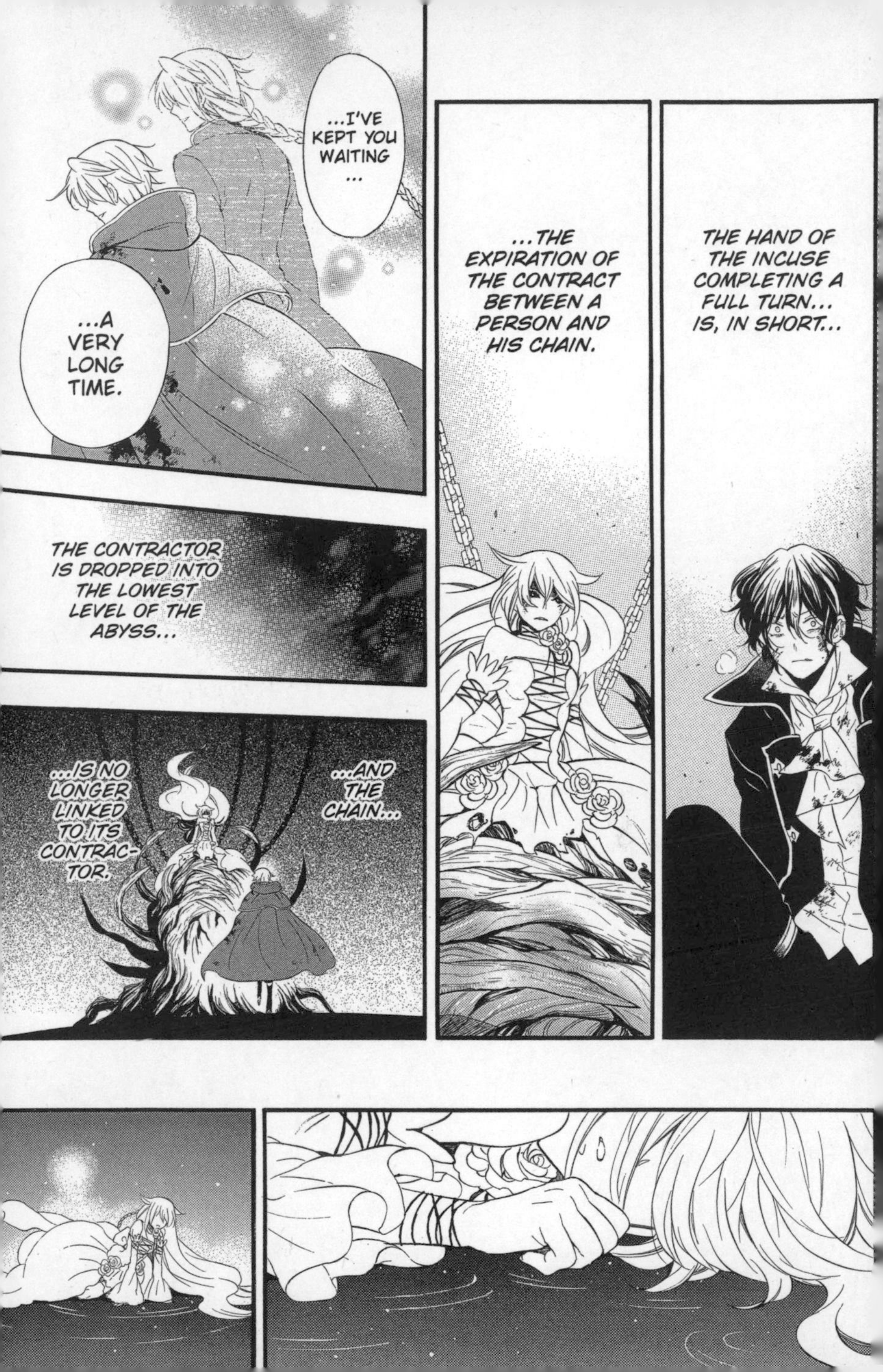
THE HAND OF THE INCUSE COMPLETING A FULL TURN... IS, IN SHORT...
...THE EXPIRATION OF THE CONTRACT BETWEEN A PERSON AND HIS CHAIN.
...I'VE KEPT YOU WAITING ...
...A VERY LONG TIME.
THE CONTRACTOR IS DROPPED INTO THE LOWEST LEVEL OF THE ABYSS...
...AND THE CHAIN...
...IS NO LONGER LINKED TO ITS CONTRAC-TOR.

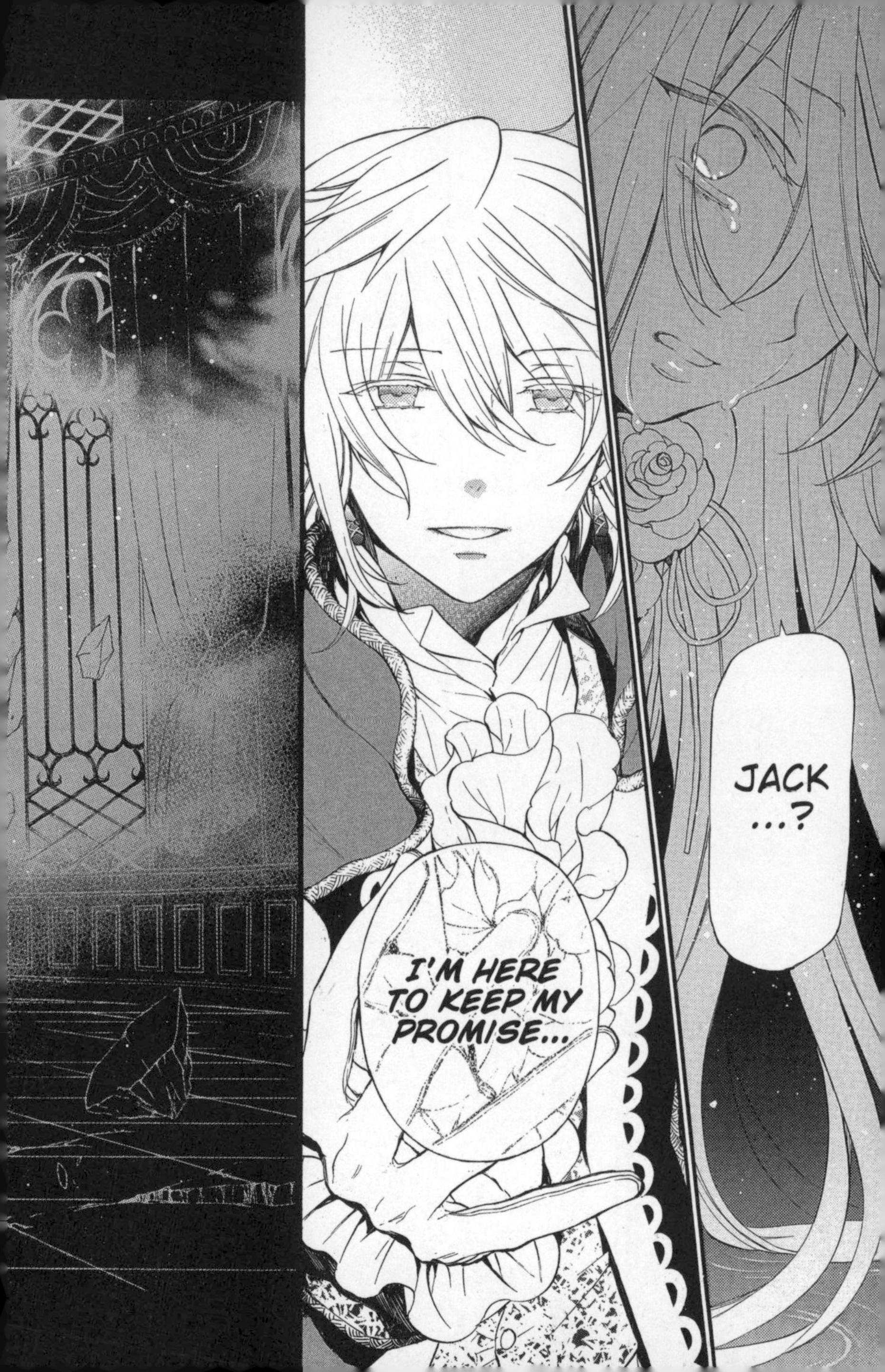
JACK ...?
I'M HERE TO KEEP MY PROMISE...

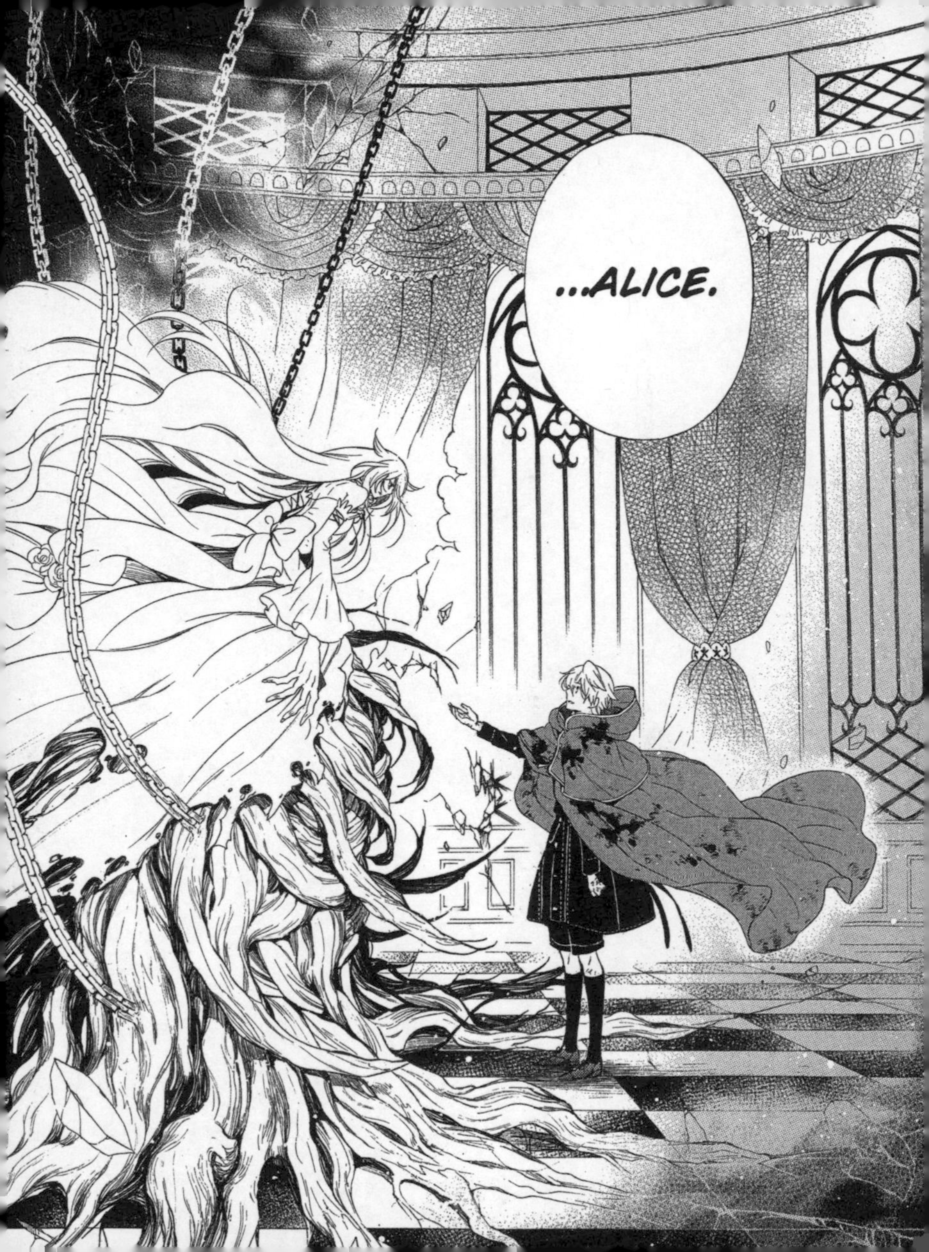
...ALICE.

Retrace:CII   The Nursery

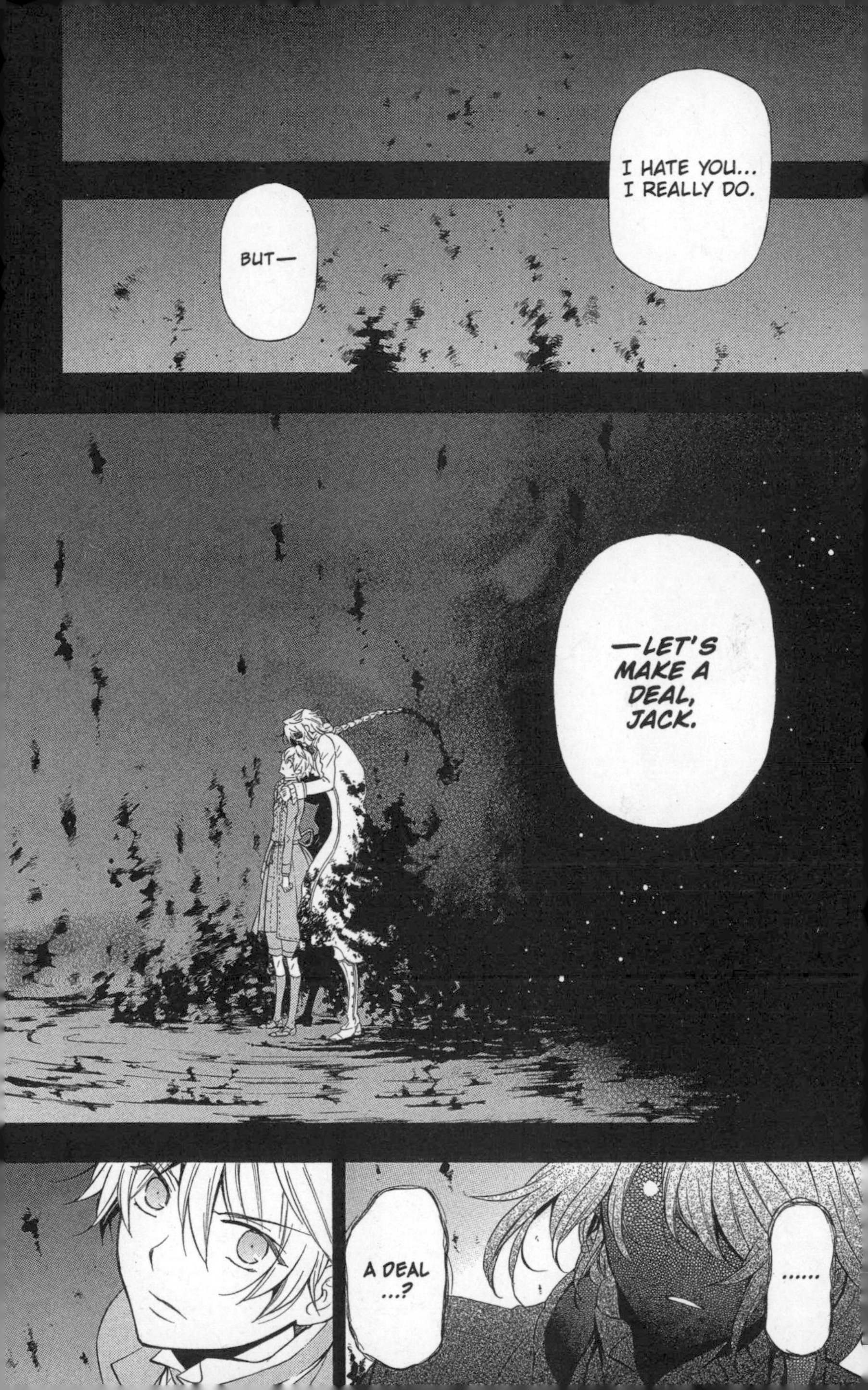
I HATE YOU... I REALLY DO.
BUT—
—LET'S MAKE A DEAL, JACK.
......
A DEAL ...?

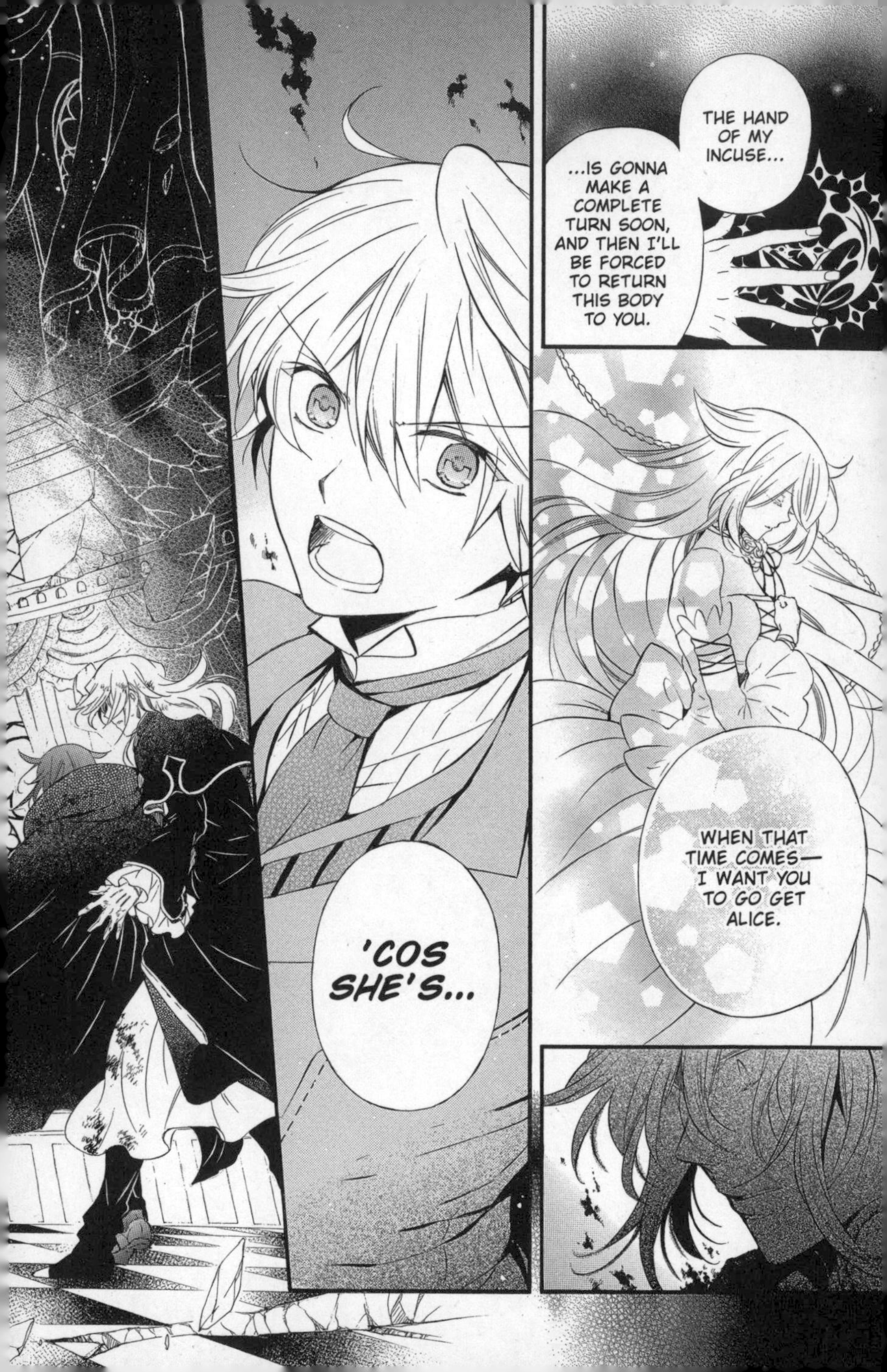
THE HAND OF MY INCUSE...
...IS GONNA MAKE A COMPLETE TURN SOON, AND THEN I'LL BE FORCED TO RETURN THIS BODY TO YOU.
WHEN THAT TIME COMES— I WANT YOU TO GO GET ALICE.
'COS SHE'S...

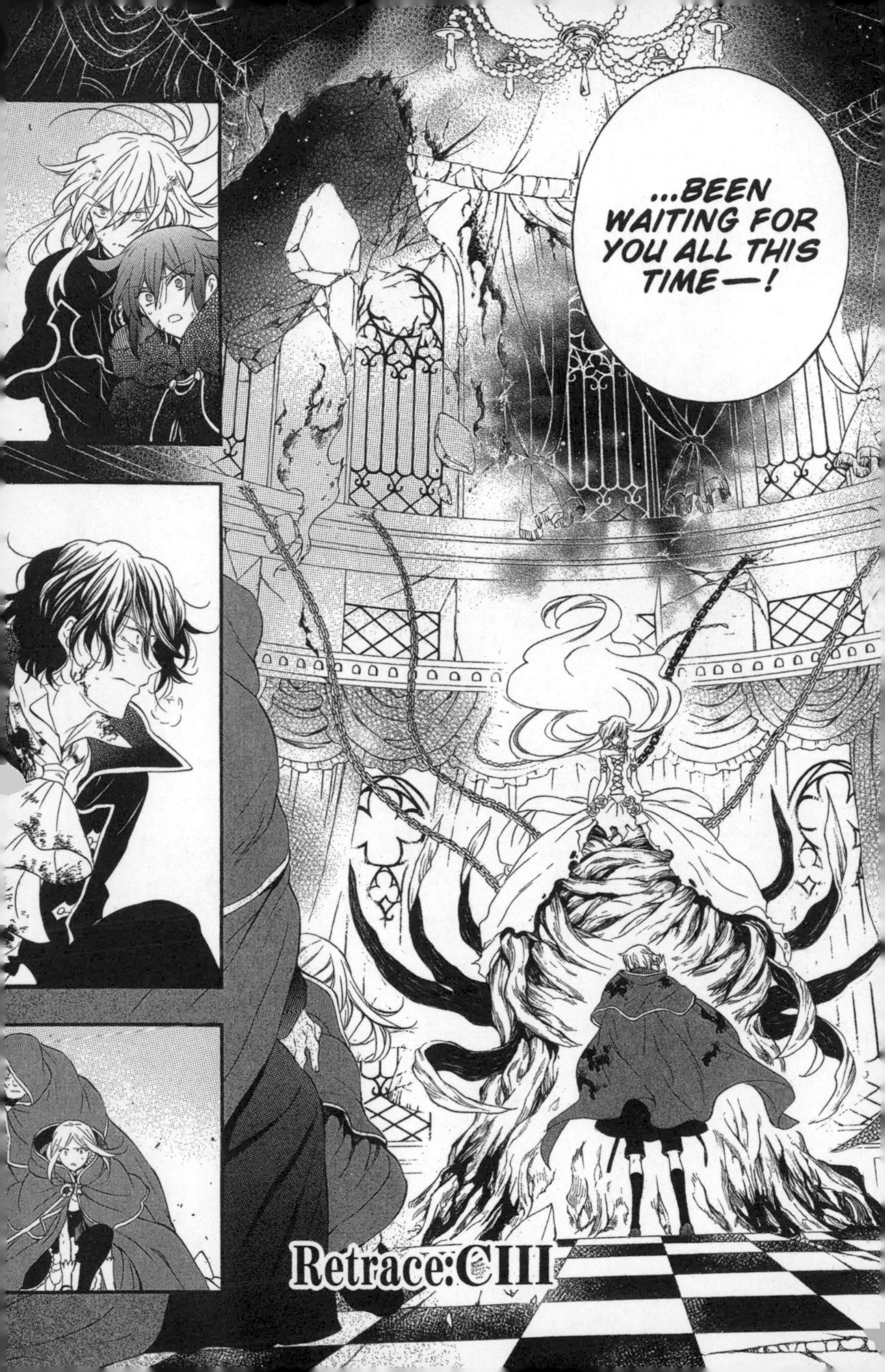
...BEEN WAITING FOR YOU ALL THIS TIME—!
Retrace:CIII

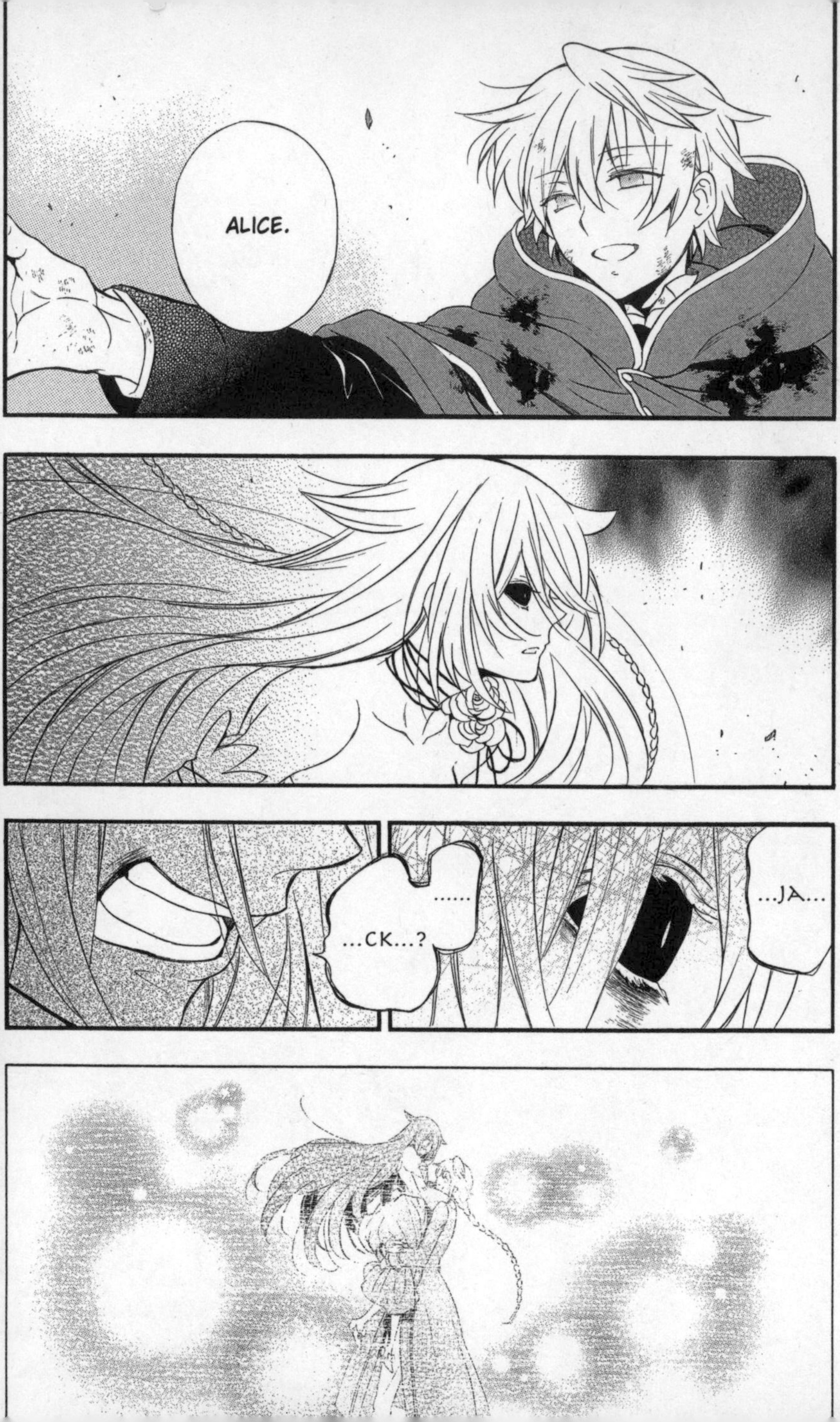
ALICE.
...JA...
......
...CK...?

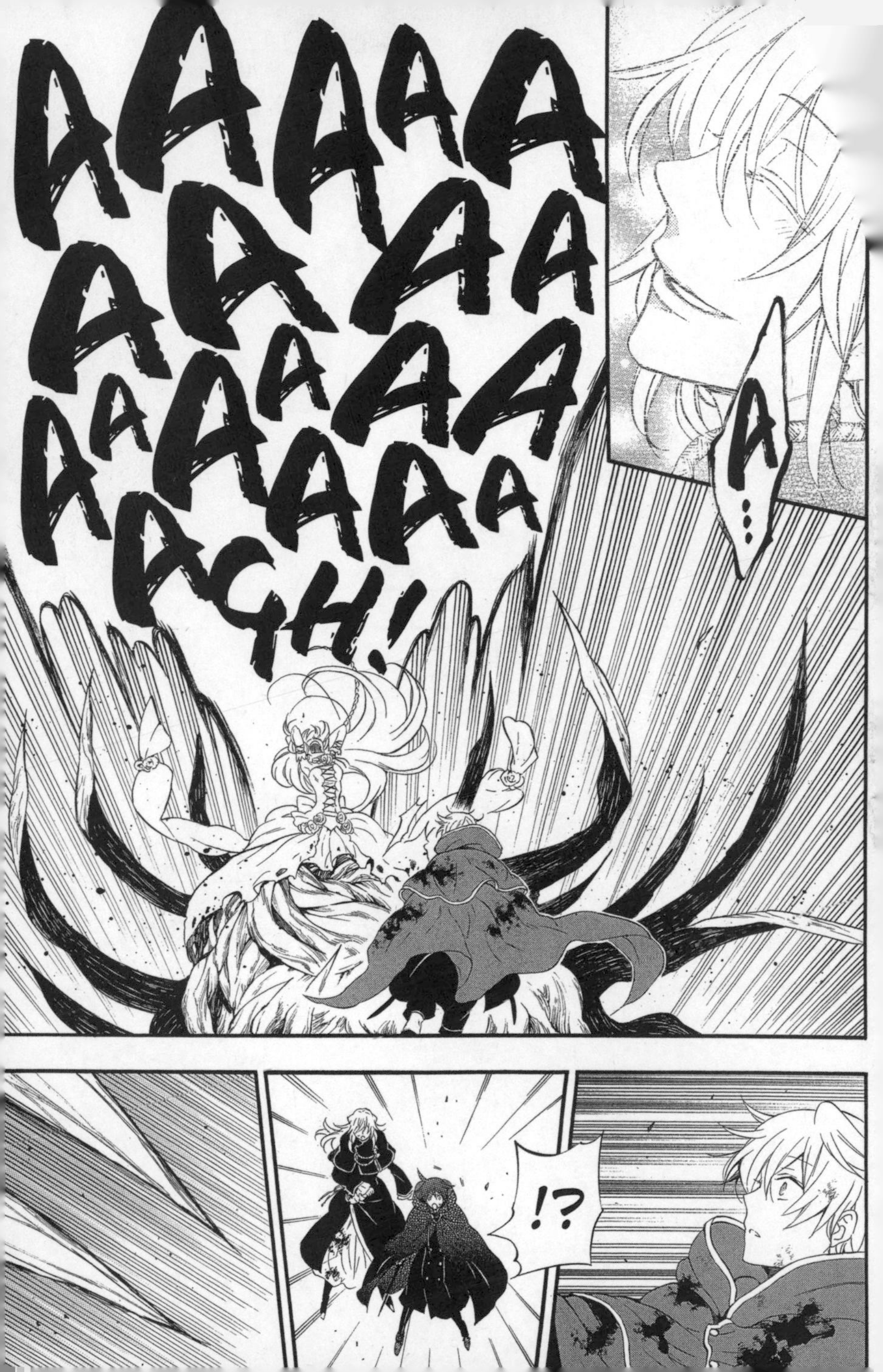

A...
AAAAAAAAAAAAAAAAAAAAAAAAGH!
!?

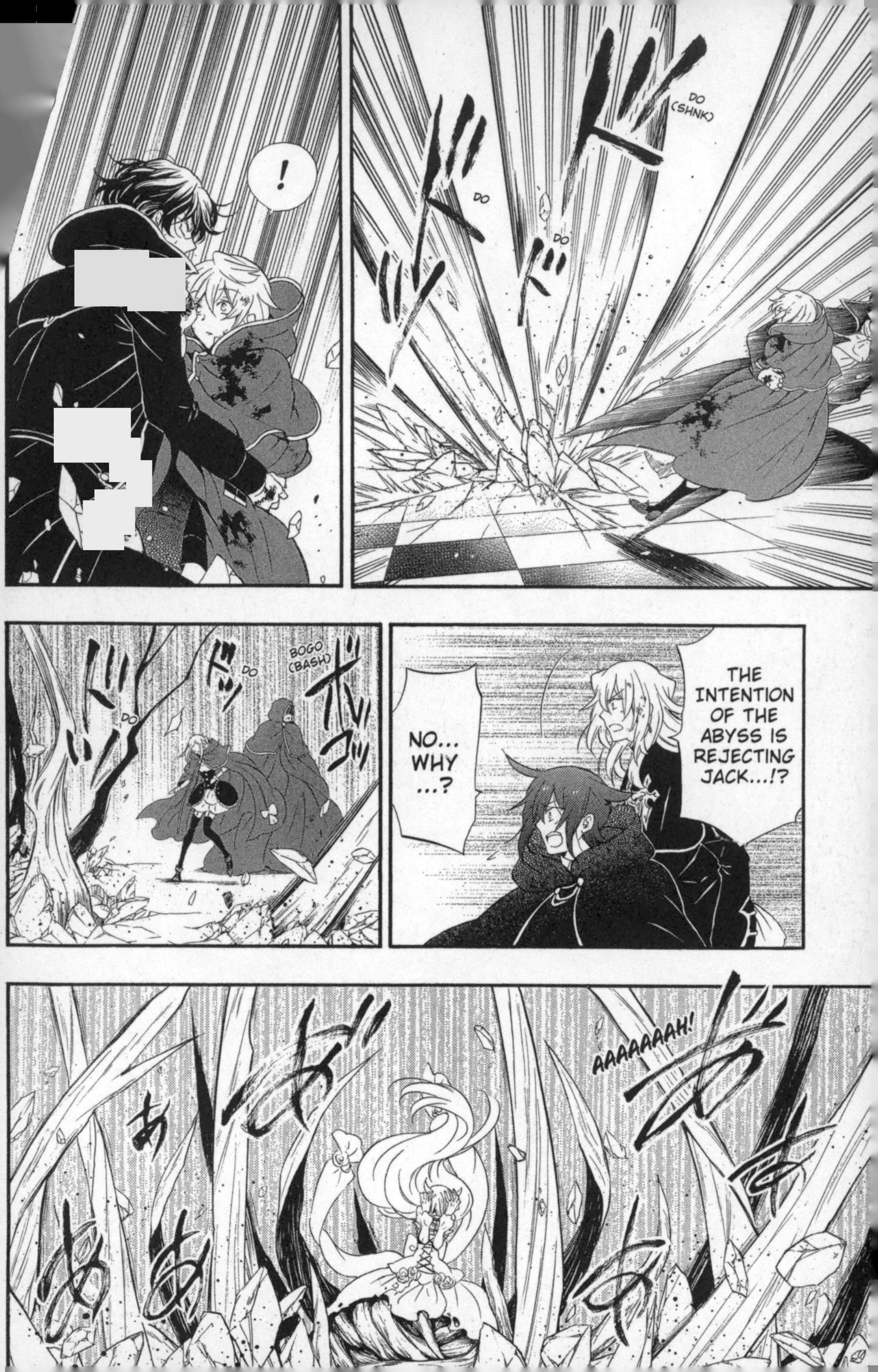
DO
(SHNK)
DO
DO
!
THE INTENTION OF THE ABYSS IS REJECTING JACK...!?
NO... WHY ...?
BOGO
(BASH)
DO
DO
AAAAAAAH!

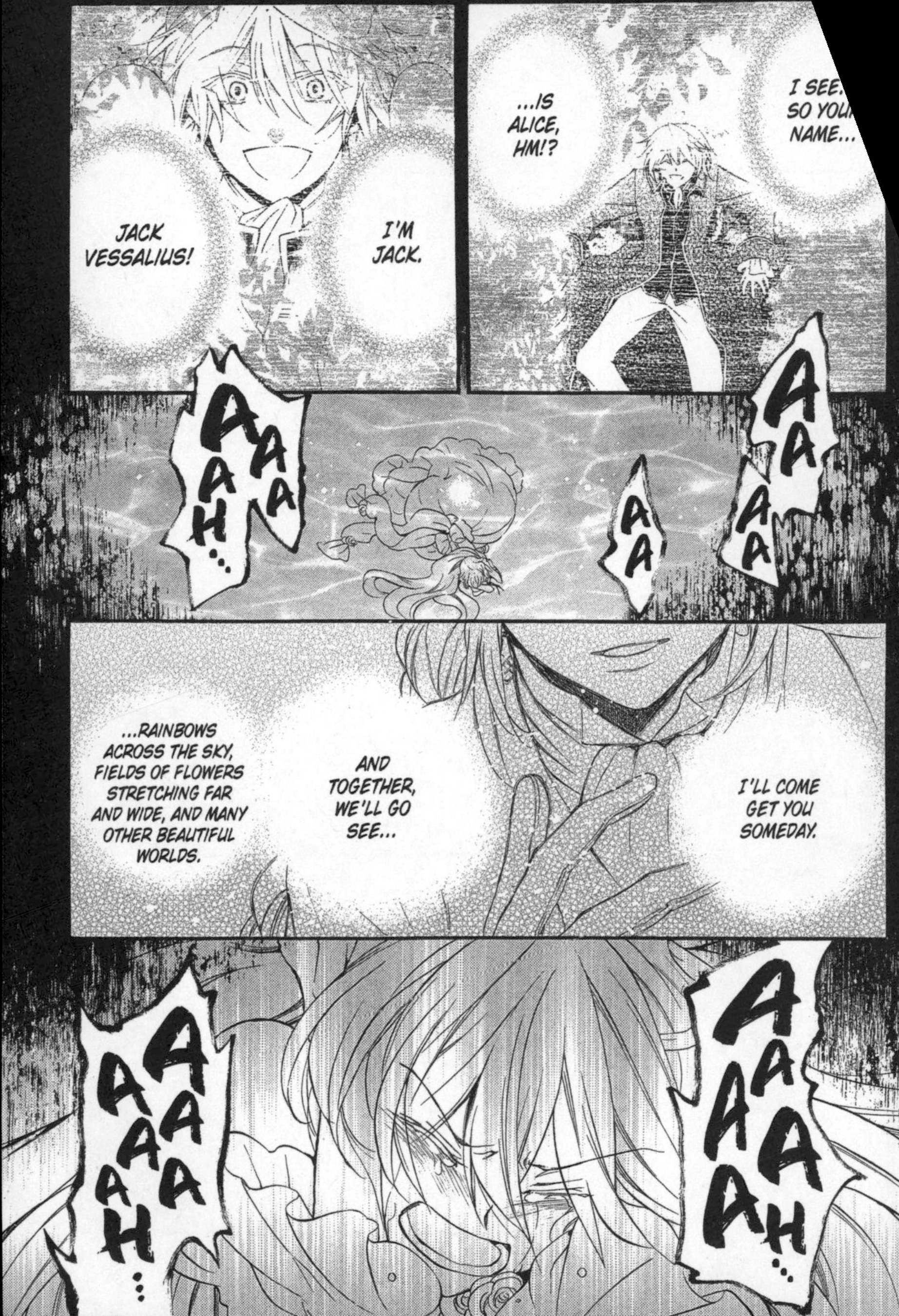
I SEE. SO YOUR NAME...
...IS ALICE, HM!?
I'M JACK.
JACK VESSALIUS!
AAAA
AA
AAAAH...
I'LL COME GET YOU SOMEDAY.
AND TOGETHER, WE'LL GO SEE...
...RAINBOWS ACROSS THE SKY, FIELDS OF FLOWERS STRETCHING FAR AND WIDE, AND MANY OTHER BEAUTIFUL WORLDS.
AAAAAAH...
AAAAAAAAH...

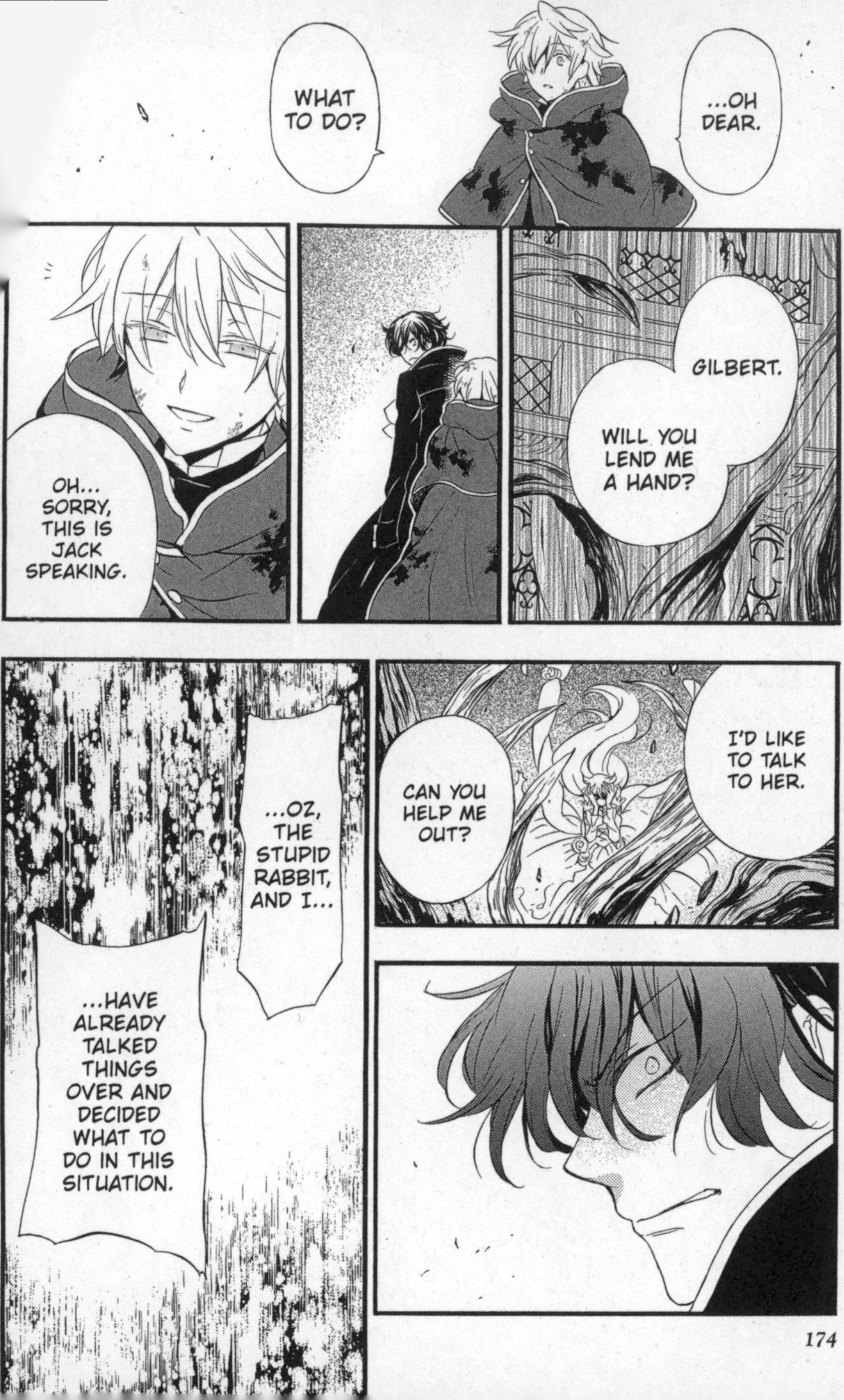
...OH DEAR.
WHAT TO DO?
GILBERT.
WILL YOU LEND ME A HAND?
OH... SORRY, THIS IS JACK SPEAKING.
I'D LIKE TO TALK TO HER.
CAN YOU HELP ME OUT?
...OZ, THE STUPID RABBIT, AND I...
...HAVE ALREADY TALKED THINGS OVER AND DECIDED WHAT TO DO IN THIS SITUATION.

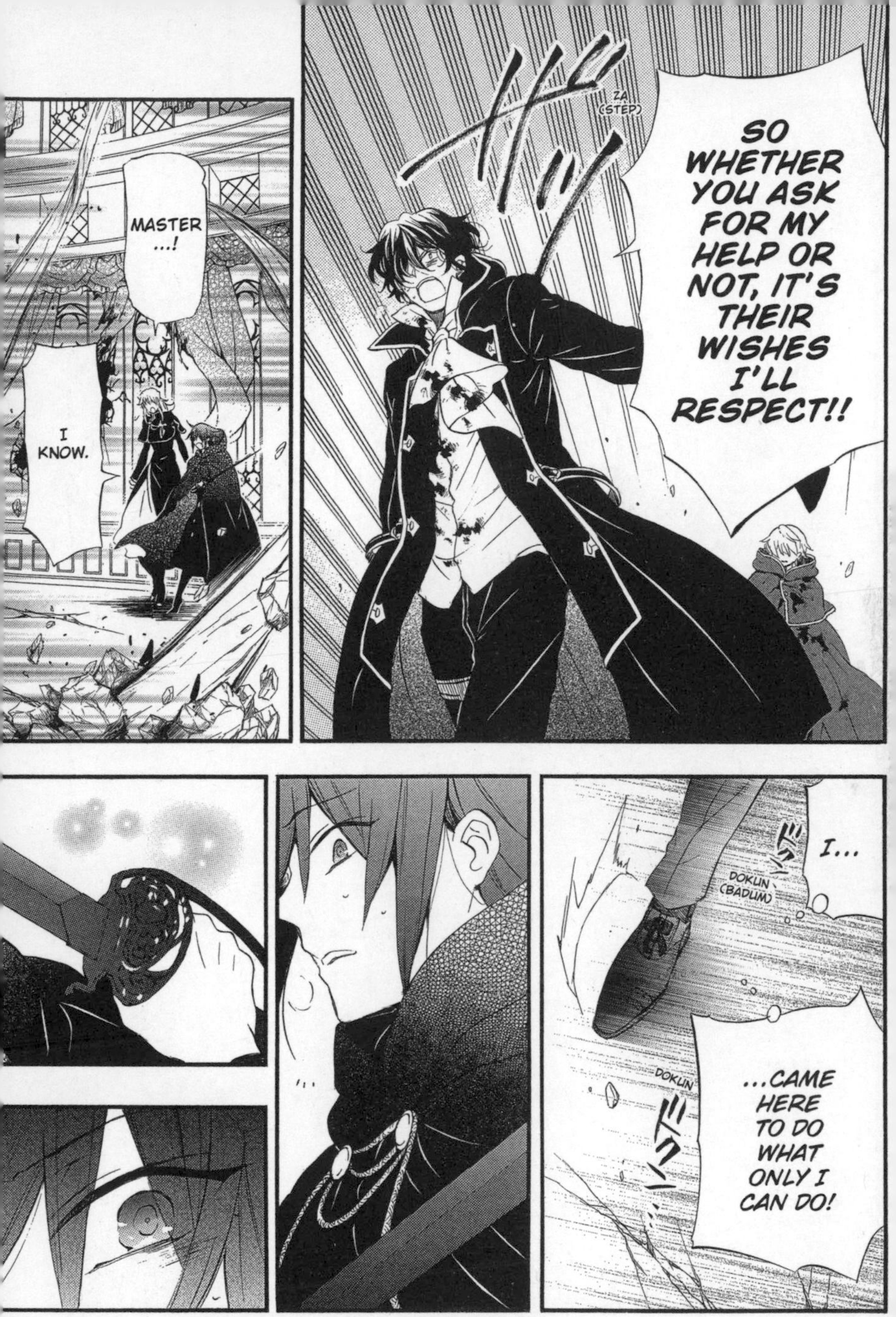
SO WHETHER YOU ASK FOR MY HELP OR NOT, IT'S THEIR WISHES I'LL RESPECT!!
ZA (STEP)
MASTER ...!
I KNOW.
I...
DOKUN (BADUM)
...CAME HERE TO DO WHAT ONLY I CAN DO!
DOKUN

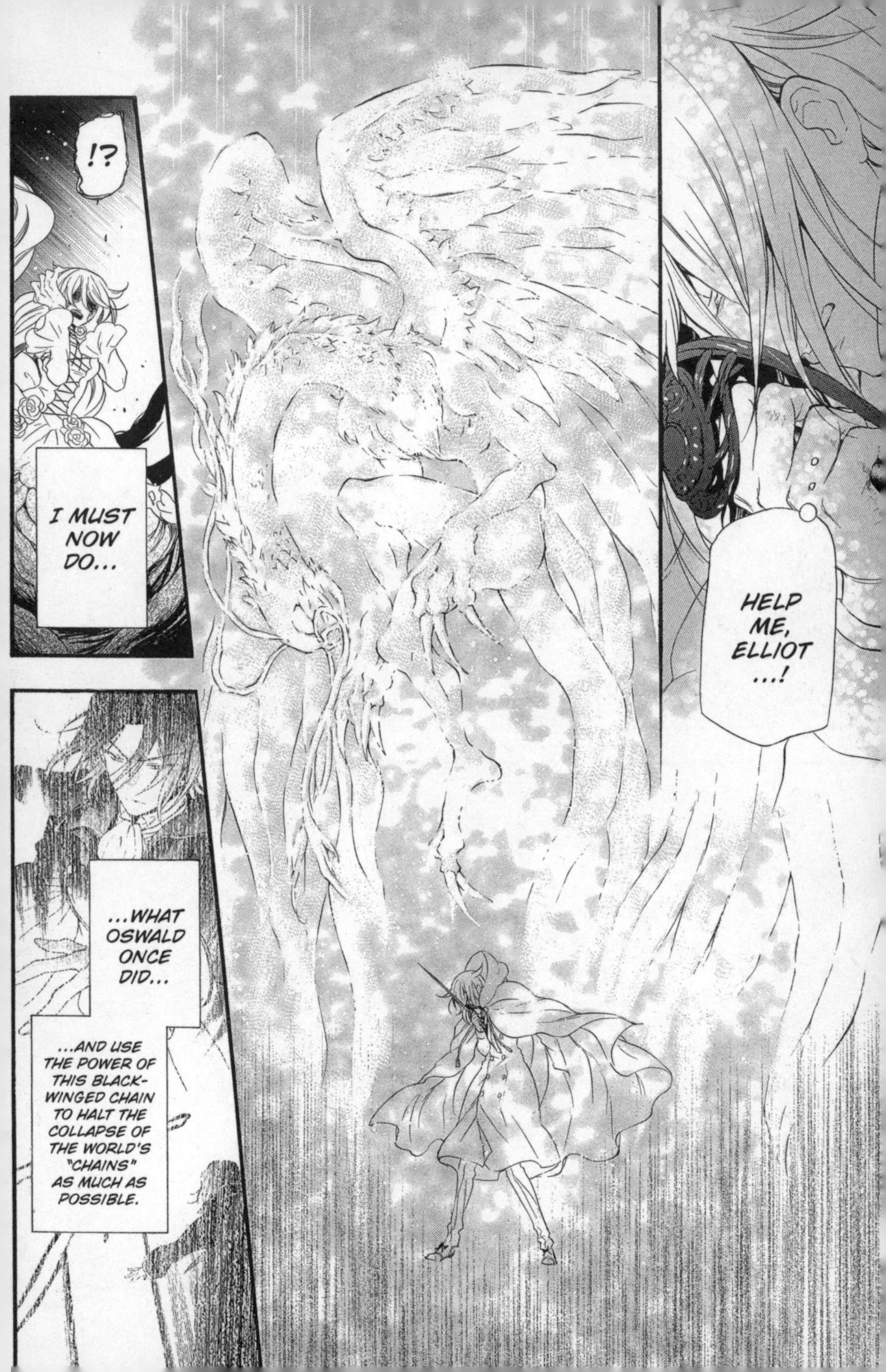
HELP ME, ELLIOT ...!
!?
I MUST NOW DO...
...WHAT OSWALD ONCE DID...
...AND USE THE POWER OF THIS BLACK-WINGED CHAIN TO HALT THE COLLAPSE OF THE WORLD'S "CHAINS" AS MUCH AS POSSIBLE.

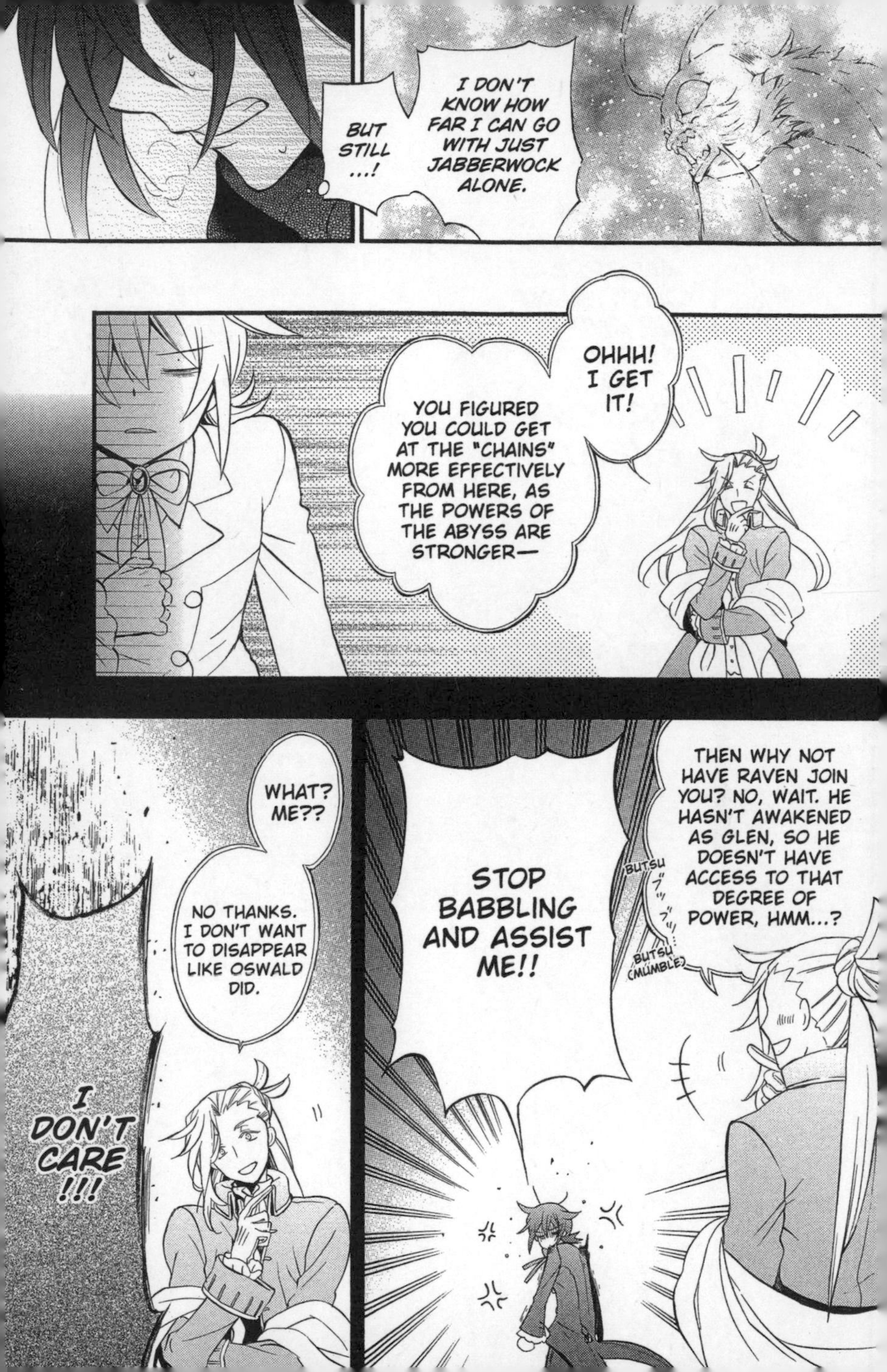

I DON'T KNOW HOW FAR I CAN GO WITH JUST JABBERWOCK ALONE.
BUT STILL ...!
OHHH! I GET IT!
YOU FIGURED YOU COULD GET AT THE "CHAINS" MORE EFFECTIVELY FROM HERE, AS THE POWERS OF THE ABYSS ARE STRONGER—
THEN WHY NOT HAVE RAVEN JOIN YOU? NO, WAIT. HE HASN'T AWAKENED AS GLEN, SO HE DOESN'T HAVE ACCESS TO THAT DEGREE OF POWER, HMM...?
BUTSU BUTSU (MUMBLE)
STOP BABBLING AND ASSIST ME!!
WHAT? ME??
NO THANKS. I DON'T WANT TO DISAPPEAR LIKE OSWALD DID.
I DON'T CARE!!!

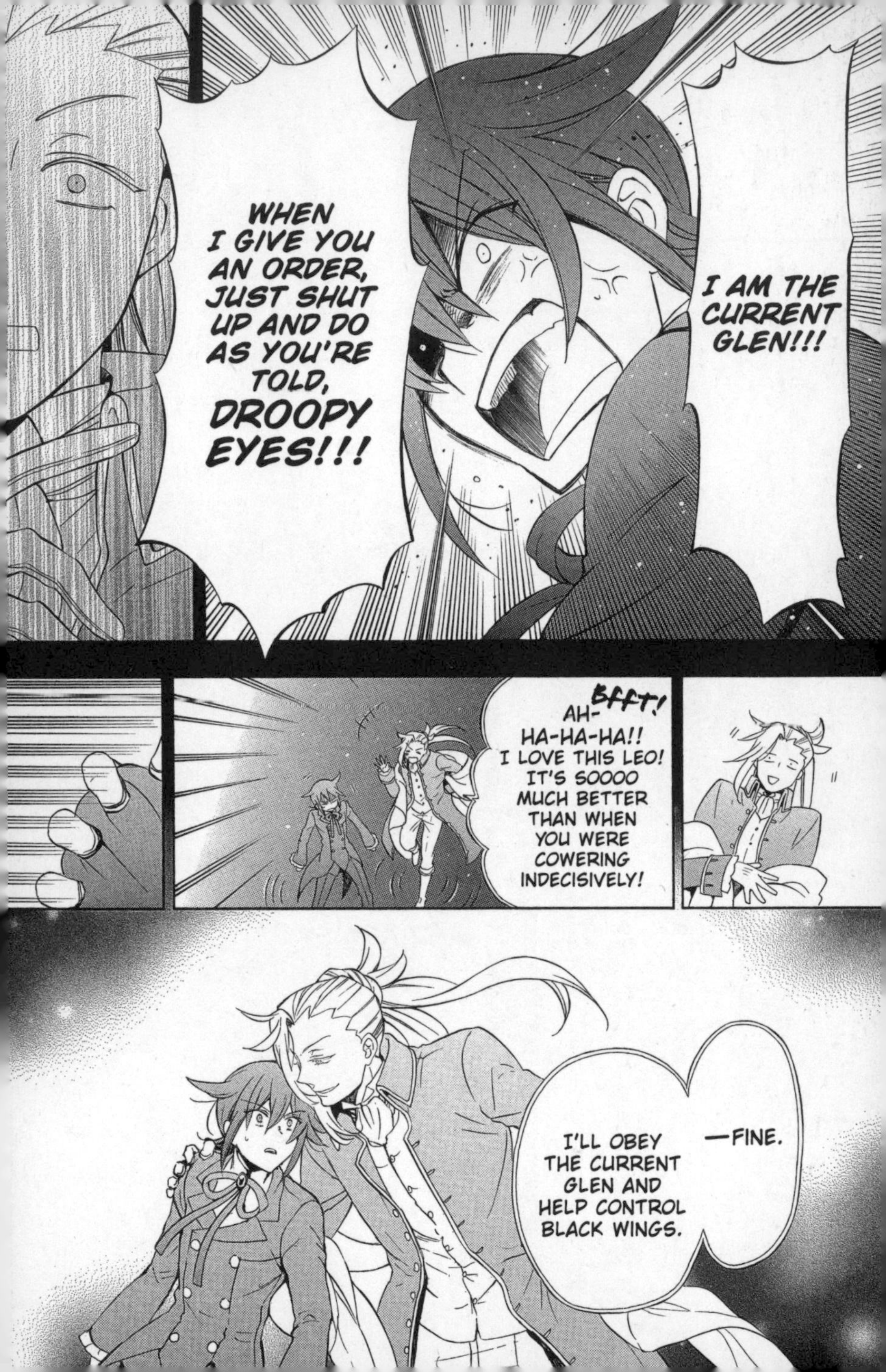
I AM THE CURRENT GLEN!!!
WHEN I GIVE YOU AN ORDER, JUST SHUT UP AND DO AS YOU'RE TOLD, DROOPY EYES!!!
BFFT!
AH-HA-HA-HA!! I LOVE THIS LEO! IT'S SOOOO MUCH BETTER THAN WHEN YOU WERE COWERING INDECISIVELY!
—FINE.
I'LL OBEY THE CURRENT GLEN AND HELP CONTROL BLACK WINGS.

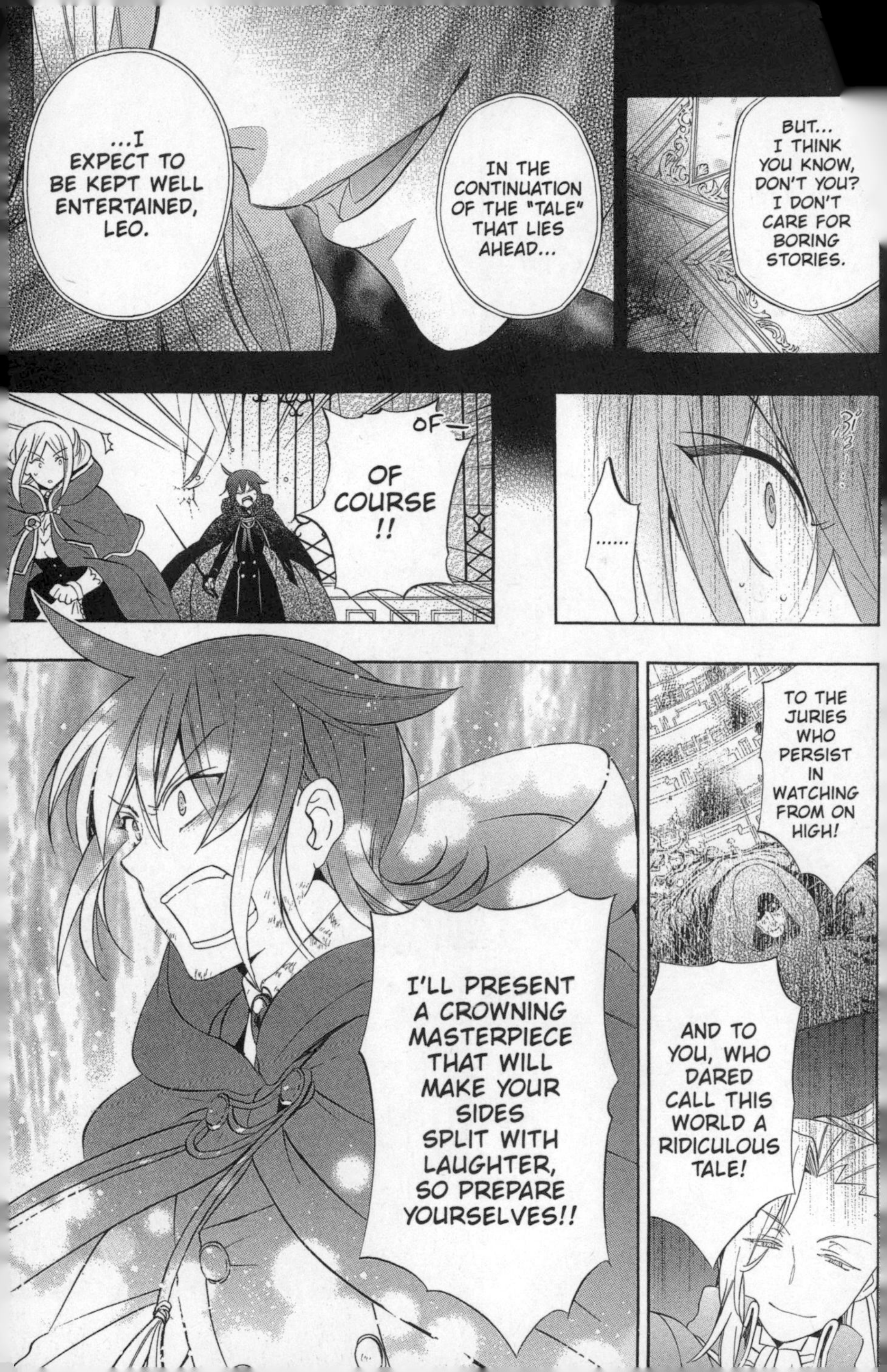
BUT... I THINK YOU KNOW, DON'T YOU? I DON'T CARE FOR BORING STORIES.
IN THE CONTINUATION OF THE "TALE" THAT LIES AHEAD...
...I EXPECT TO BE KEPT WELL ENTERTAINED, LEO.
......
OF—
OF COURSE!!
TO THE JURIES WHO PERSIST IN WATCHING FROM ON HIGH!
AND TO YOU, WHO DARED CALL THIS WORLD A RIDICULOUS TALE!
I'LL PRESENT A CROWNING MASTERPIECE THAT WILL MAKE YOUR SIDES SPLIT WITH LAUGHTER, SO PREPARE YOURSELVES!!

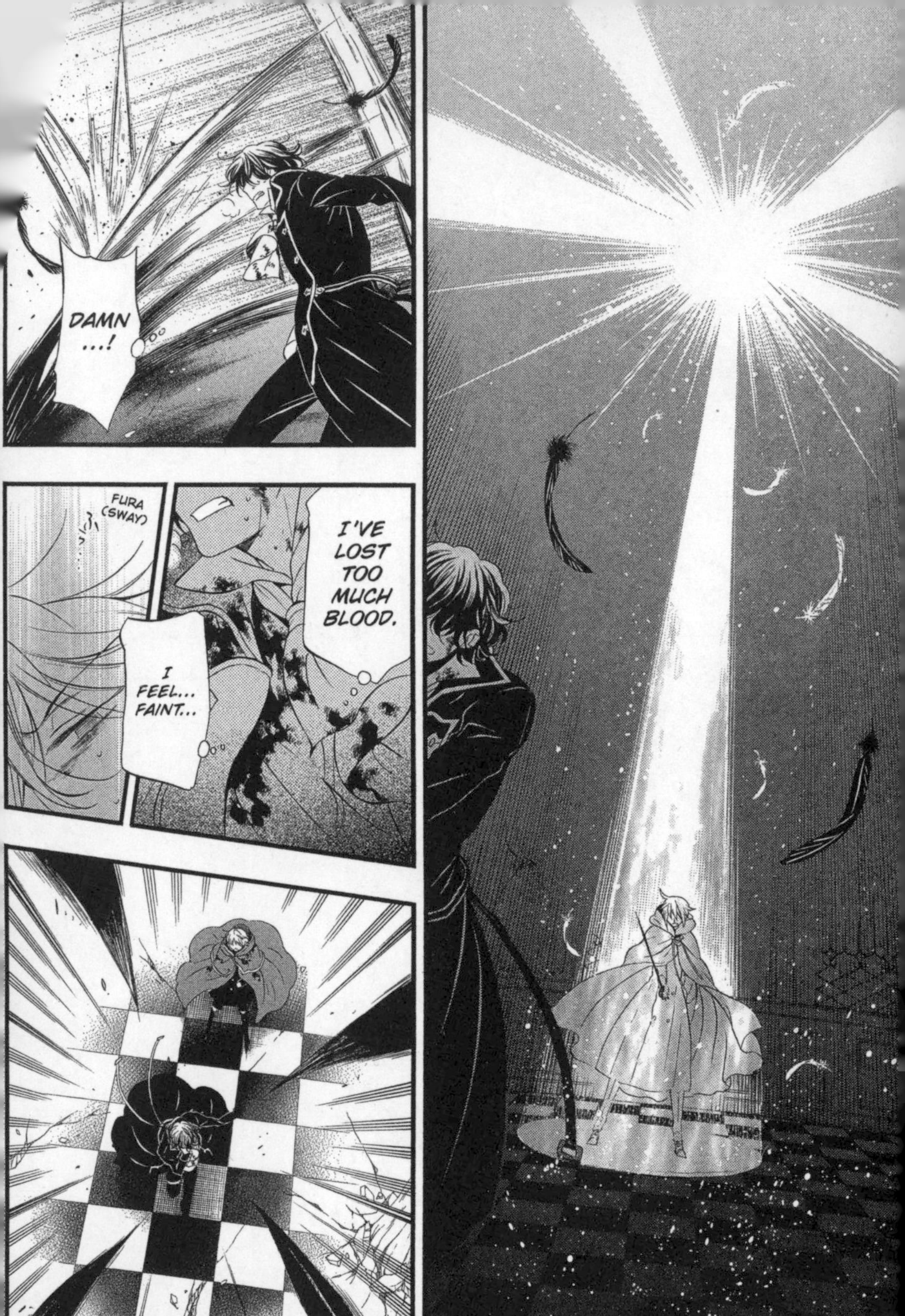
DAMN ...!
I'VE LOST TOO MUCH BLOOD.
I FEEL... FAINT...
FURA (SWAY)

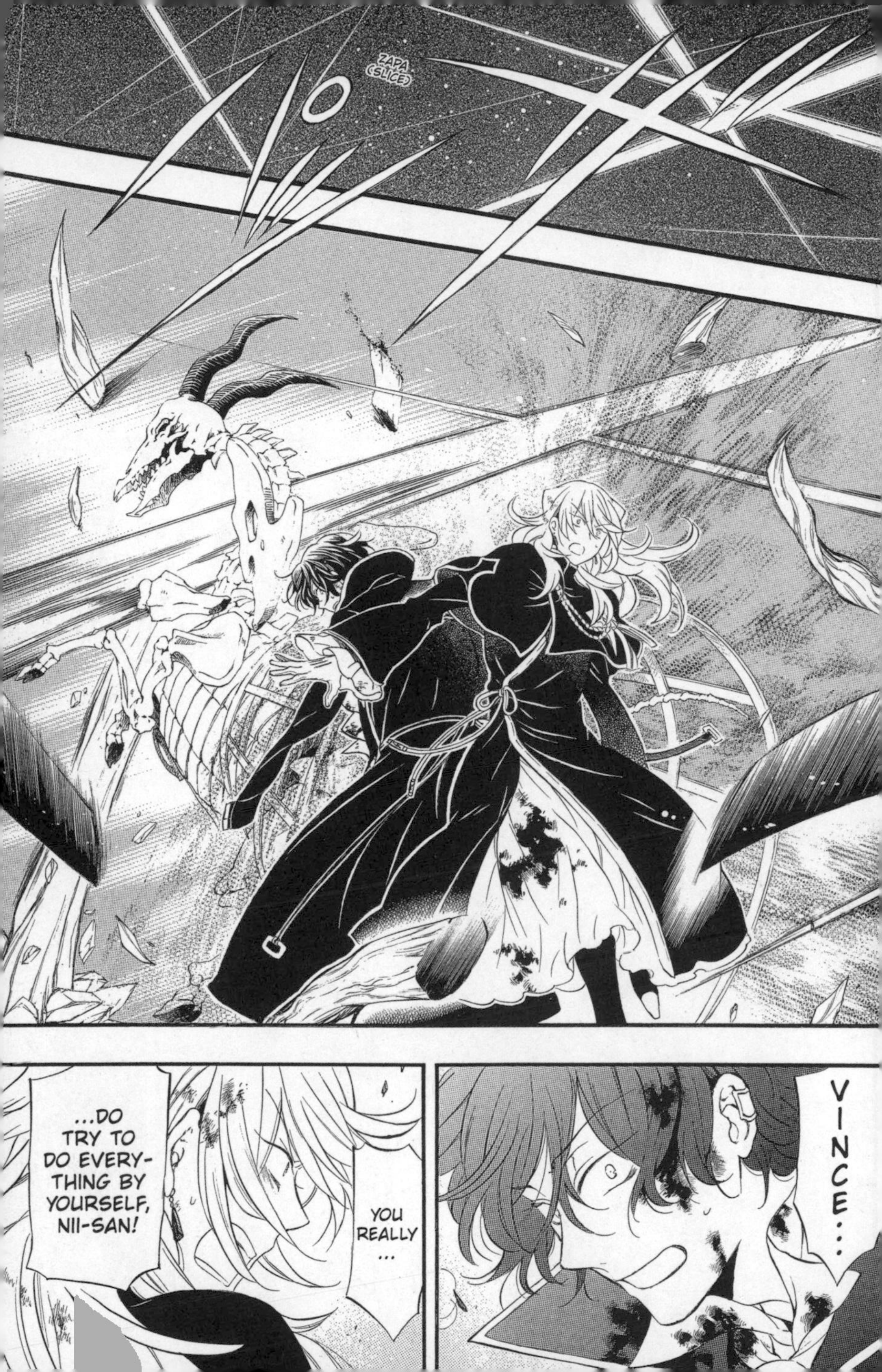
ZAPA (SLICE)
VINCE...
YOU REALLY ...
...DO TRY TO DO EVERYTHING BY YOURSELF, NII-SAN!

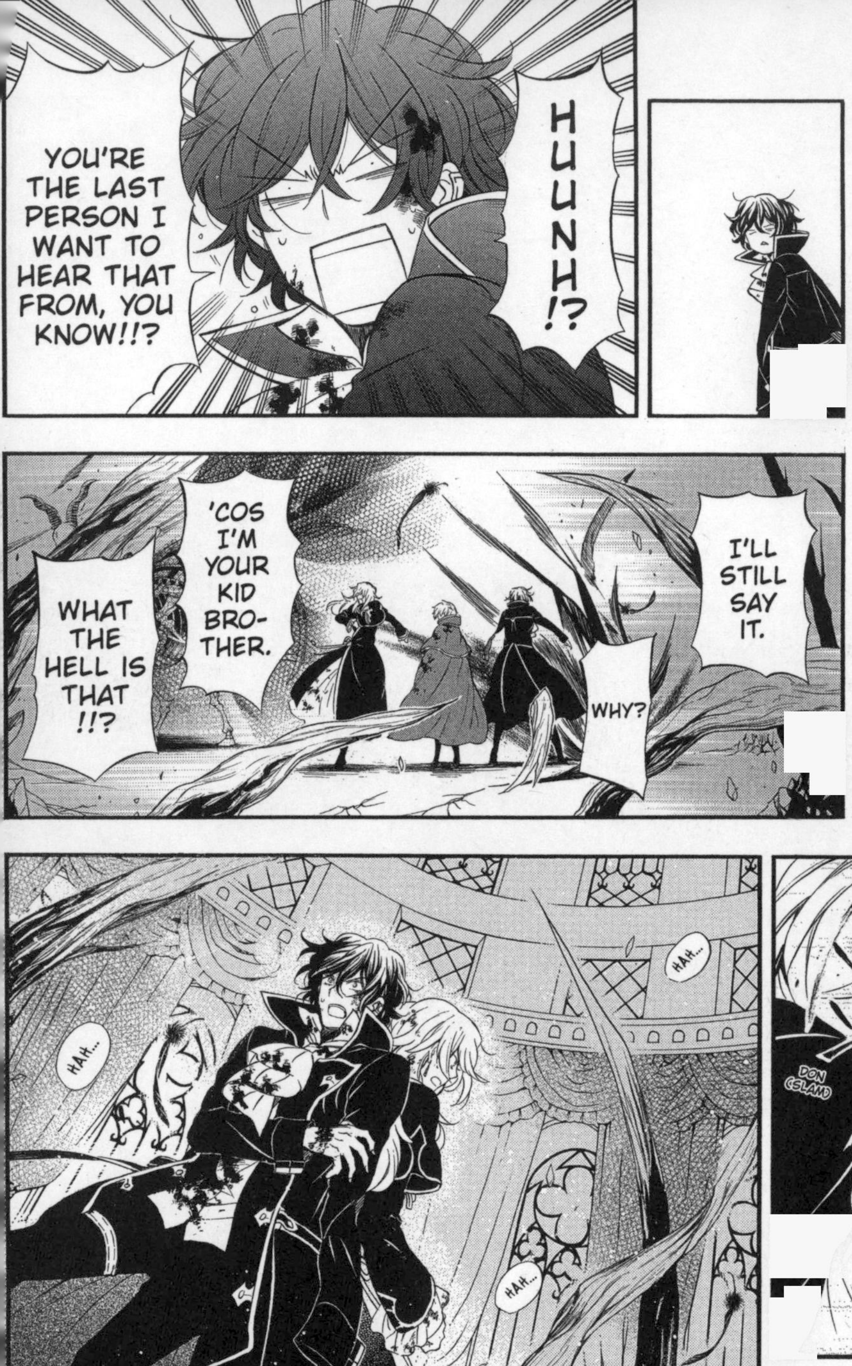
HUUNH!?
YOU'RE THE LAST PERSON I WANT TO HEAR THAT FROM, YOU KNOW!!?
I'LL STILL SAY IT.
WHY?
'COS I'M YOUR KID BROTHER.
WHAT THE HELL IS THAT!!?
DON (SLAM)
HAH...
HAH...
HAH...

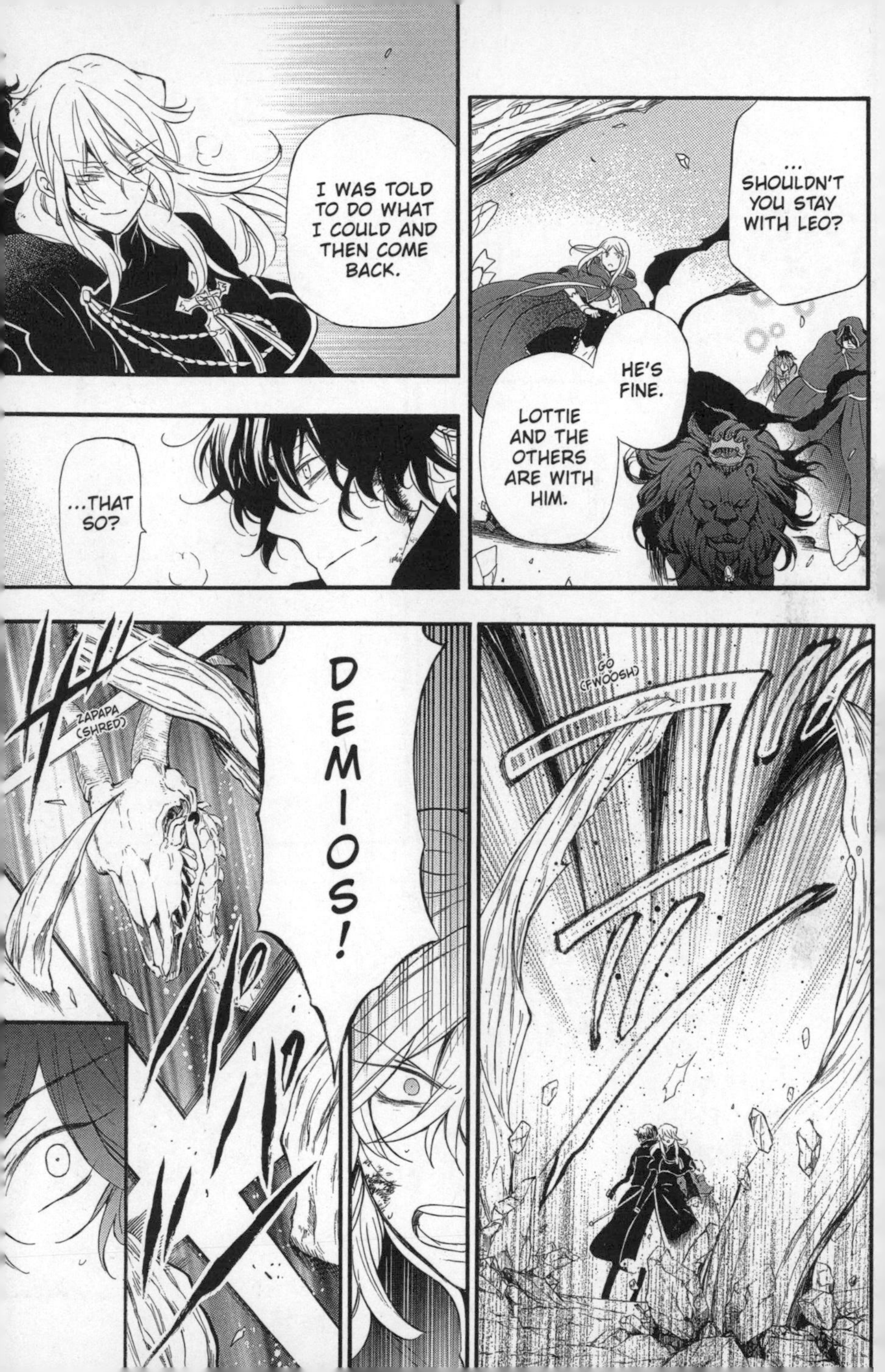
...
SHOULDN'T YOU STAY WITH LEO?
HE'S FINE.
LOTTIE AND THE OTHERS ARE WITH HIM.
I WAS TOLD TO DO WHAT I COULD AND THEN COME BACK.
...THAT SO?
GO (FWOOSH)
DEMIOS!
ZAPAPA (SHRED)

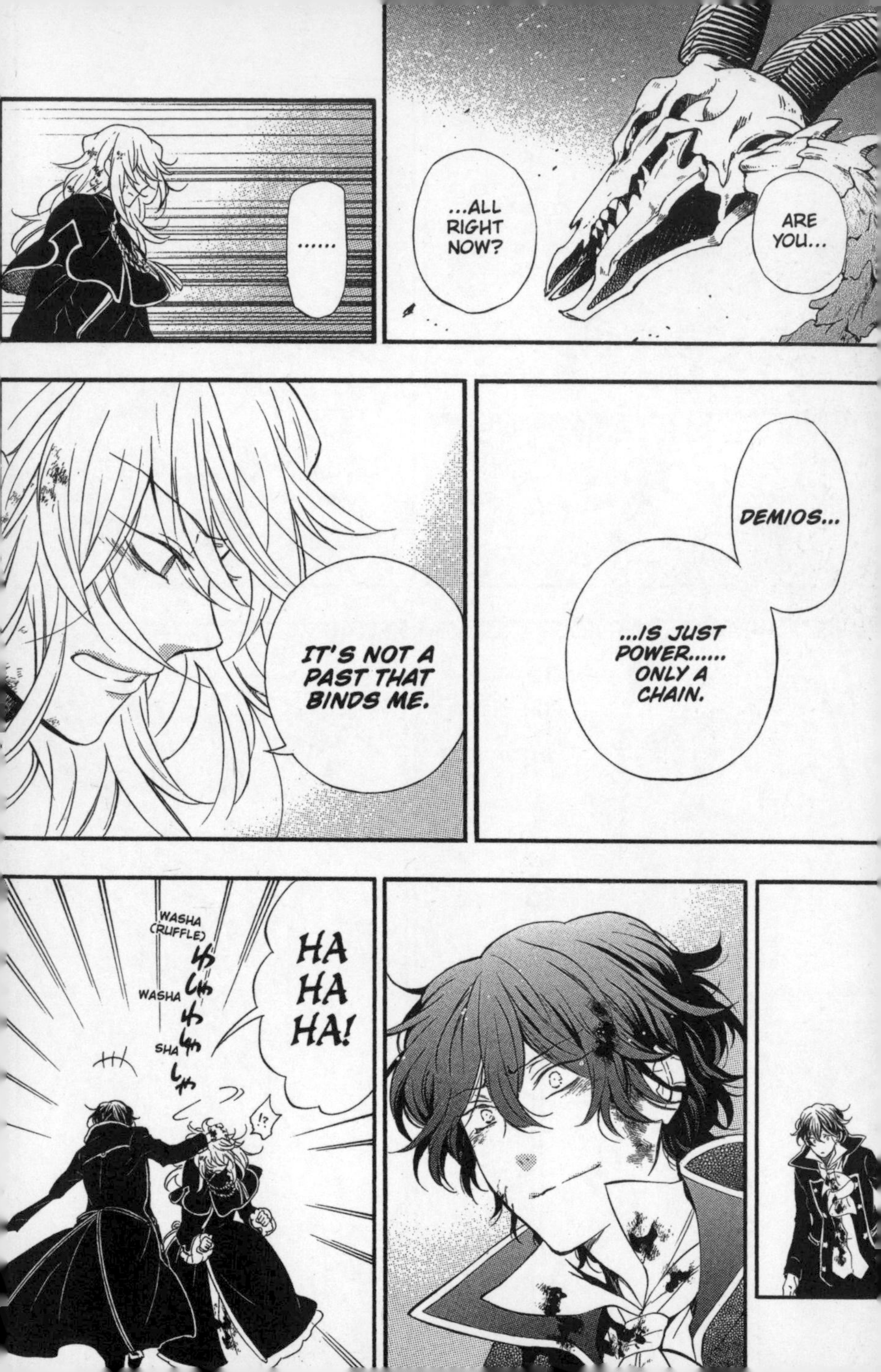
ARE YOU...
...ALL RIGHT NOW?
......
DEMIOS...
...IS JUST POWER...... ONLY A CHAIN.
IT'S NOT A PAST THAT BINDS ME.
WASHA (RUFFLE)
WASHA
SHA
HA HA HA!
!?

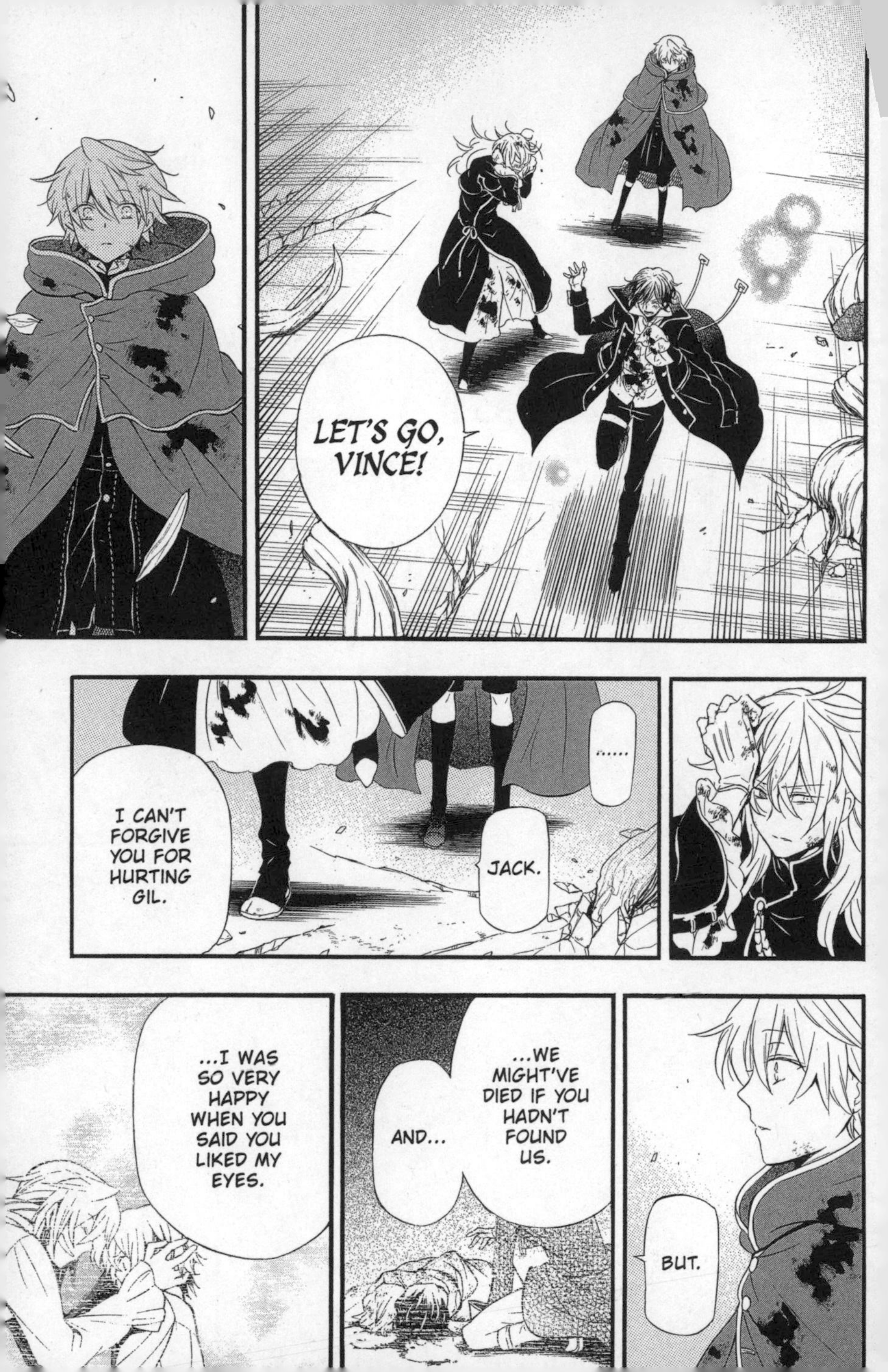
LET'S GO, VINCE!
......
JACK.
I CAN'T FORGIVE YOU FOR HURTING GIL.
BUT.
...WE MIGHT'VE DIED IF YOU HADN'T FOUND US.
AND...
...I WAS SO VERY HAPPY WHEN YOU SAID YOU LIKED MY EYES.

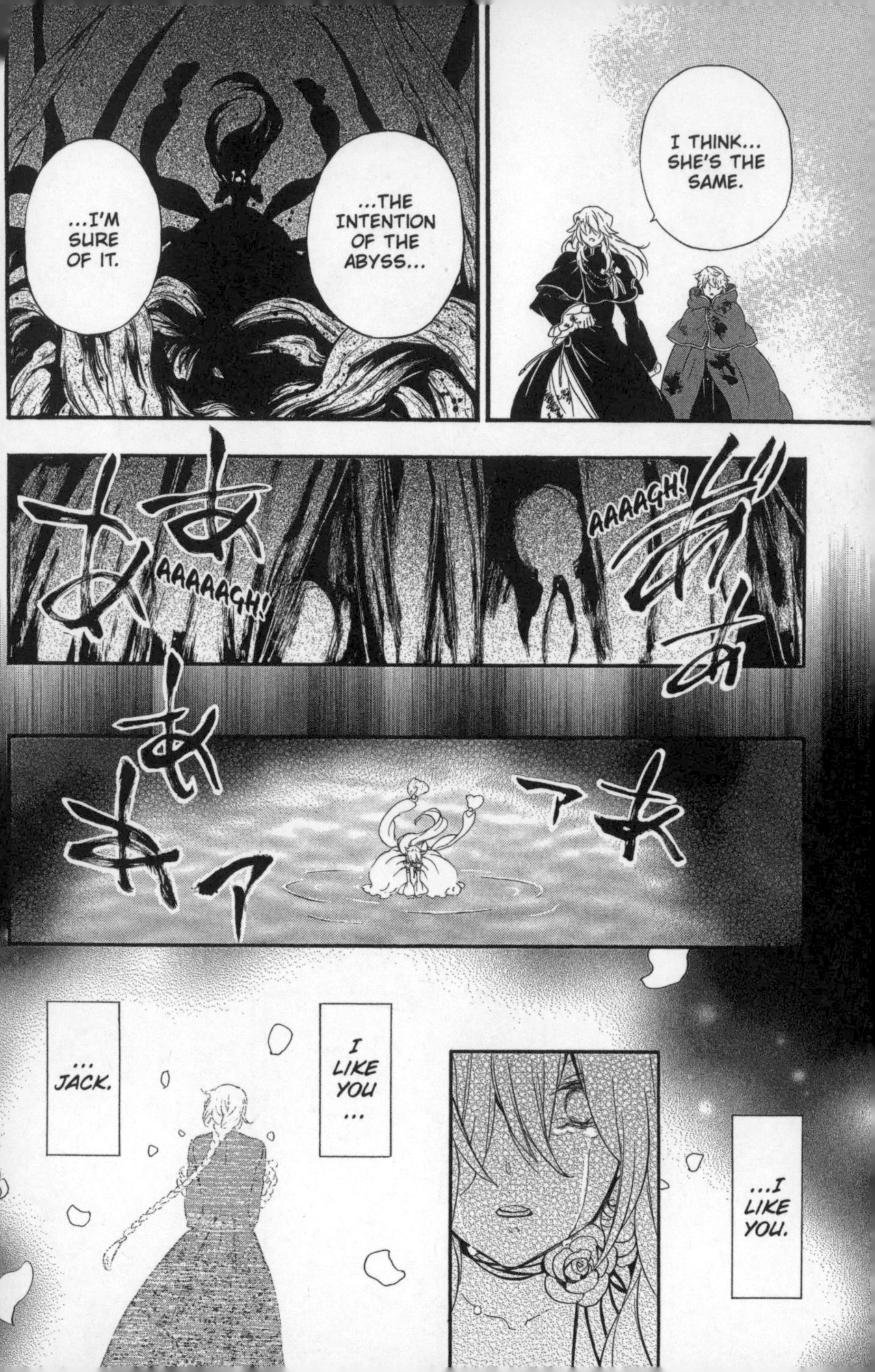
I THINK... SHE'S THE SAME.
...THE INTENTION OF THE ABYSS...
...I'M SURE OF IT.
AAAAGH!
AAAAAAGH!
...I LIKE YOU.
I LIKE YOU ...
... JACK.

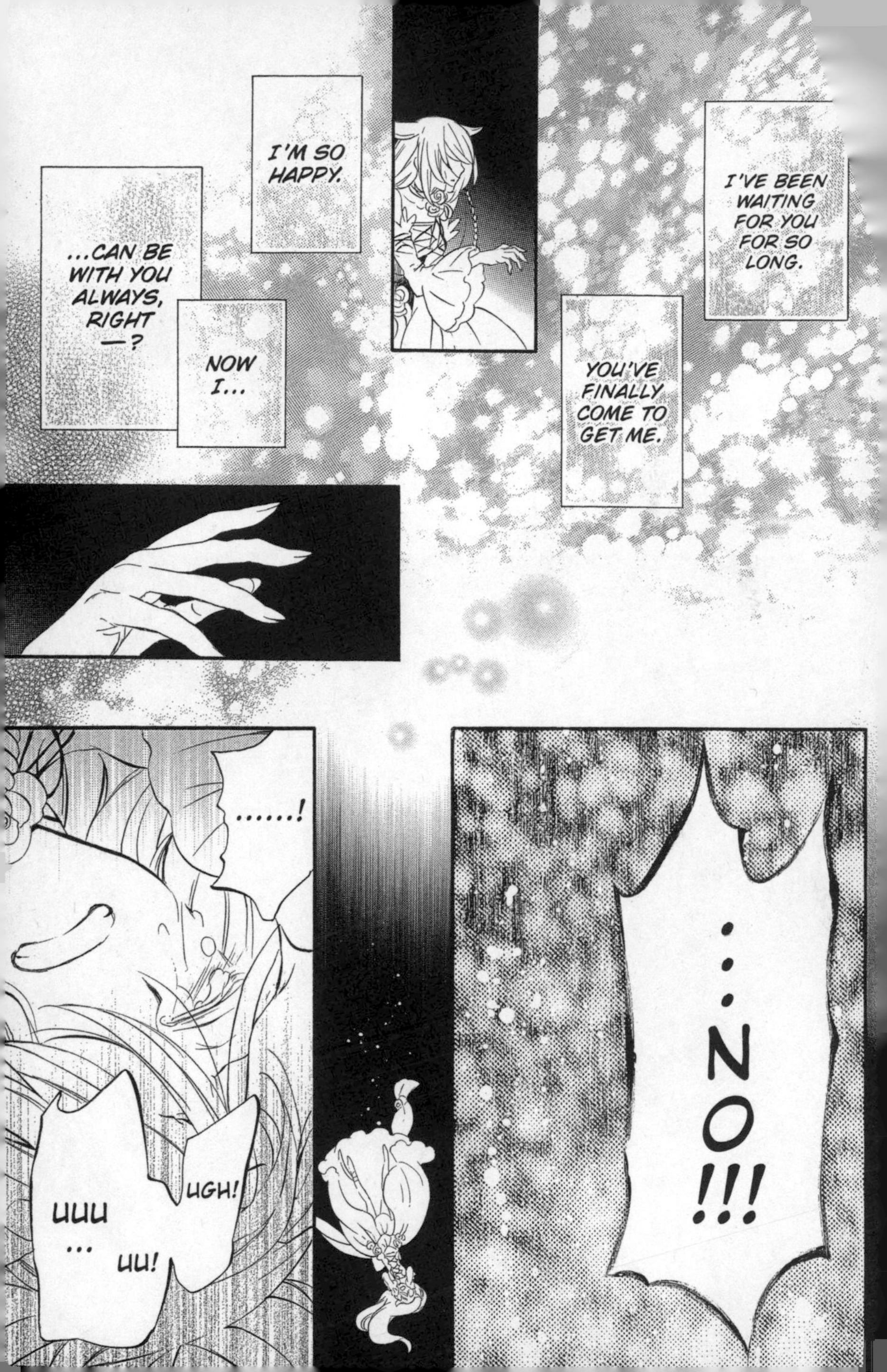
I'VE BEEN WAITING FOR YOU FOR SO LONG.
YOU'VE FINALLY COME TO GET ME.
I'M SO HAPPY.
NOW I...
...CAN BE WITH YOU ALWAYS, RIGHT—?
...NO!!!
......!
UGH!
UUU... UU!

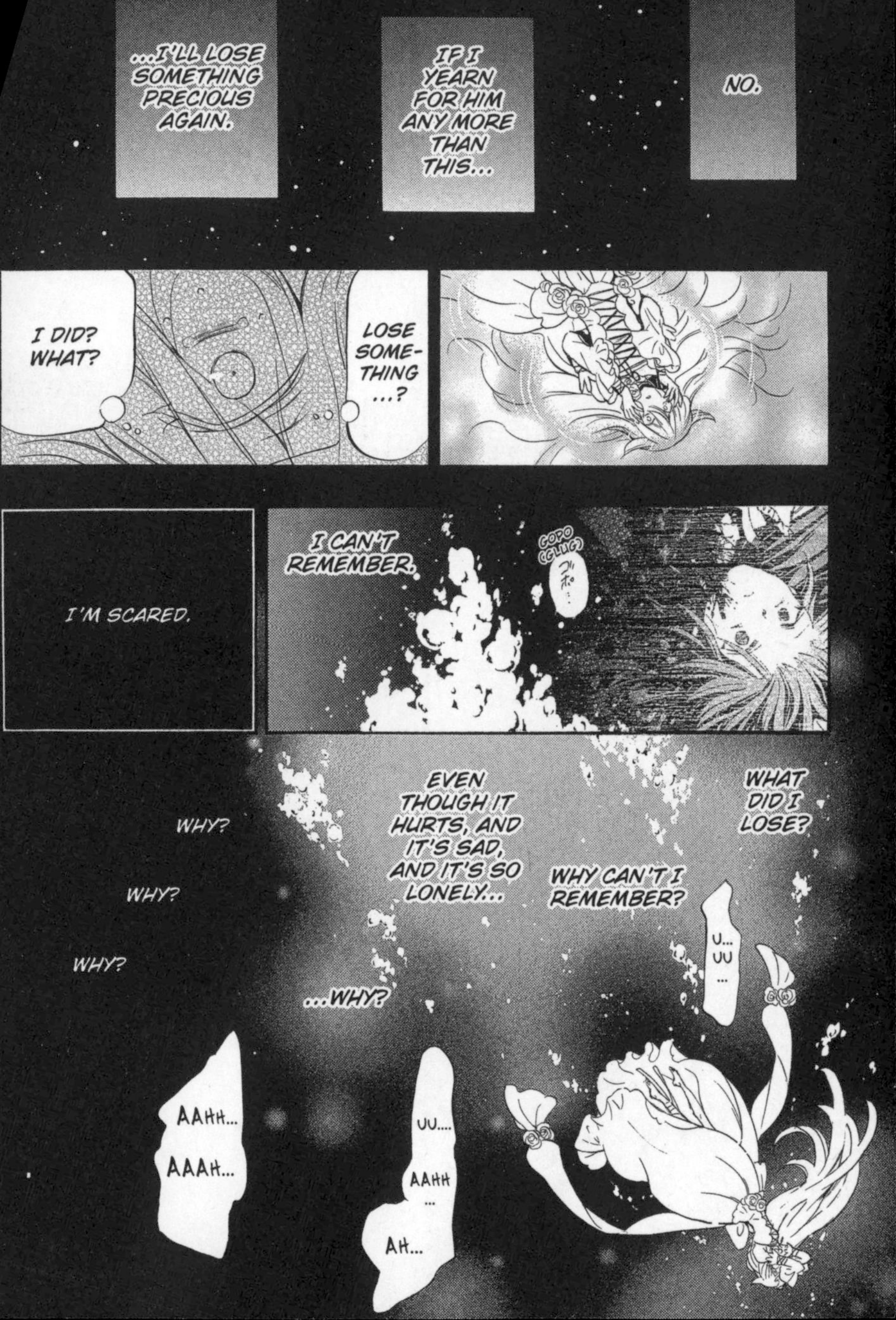
NO.
IF I YEARN FOR HIM ANY MORE THAN THIS...
...I'LL LOSE SOMETHING PRECIOUS AGAIN.
LOSE SOME-THING ...?
I DID? WHAT?
I CAN'T REMEMBER.
GOPO (GLUG)
I'M SCARED.
WHAT DID I LOSE?
WHY CAN'T I REMEMBER?
EVEN THOUGH IT HURTS, AND IT'S SAD, AND IT'S SO LONELY...
U... UU ...
WHY?
WHY?
WHY?
...WHY?
UU.... AAHH ... AH...
AAHH... AAAH...

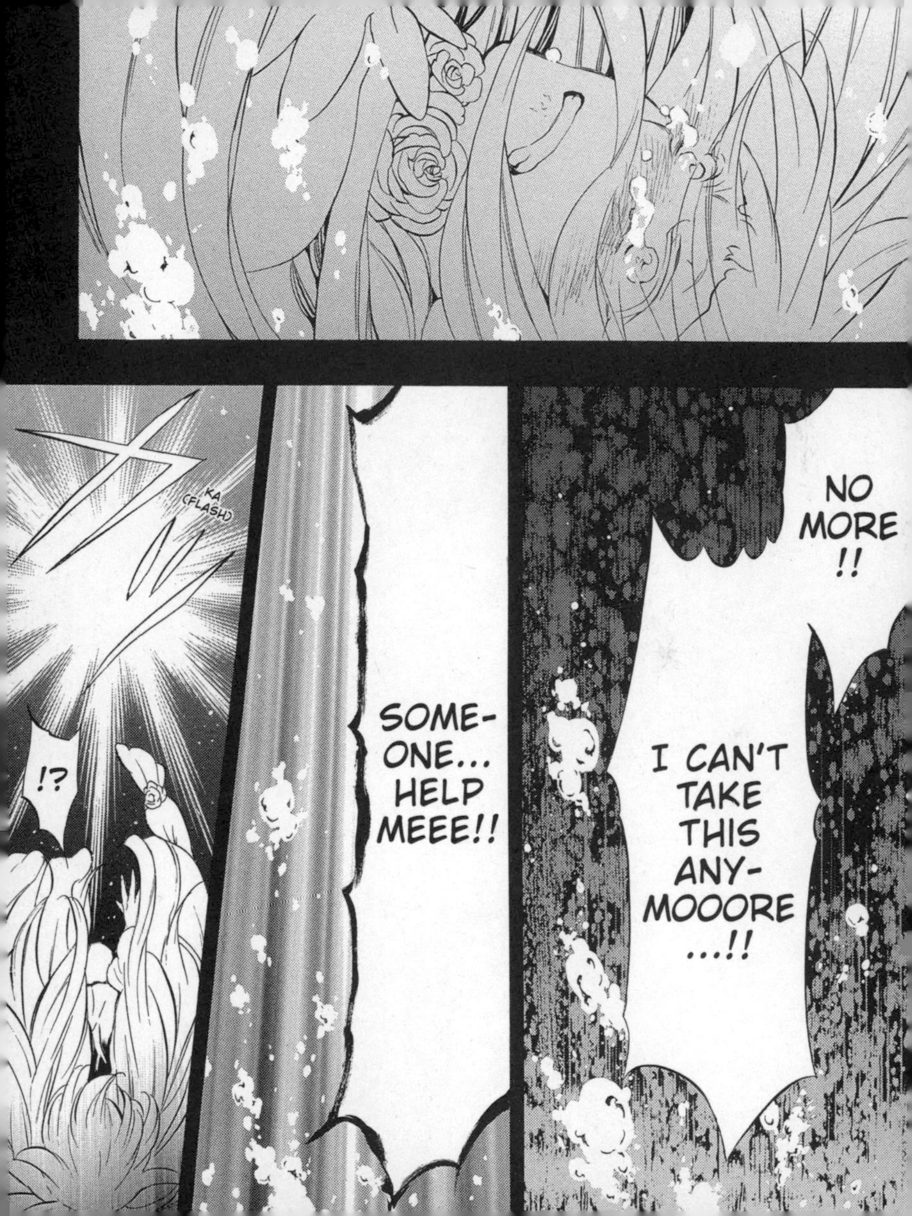
NO MORE!!
I CAN'T TAKE THIS ANY-MOOORE...!!
SOME-ONE... HELP MEEE!!
KA (FLASH)
!?

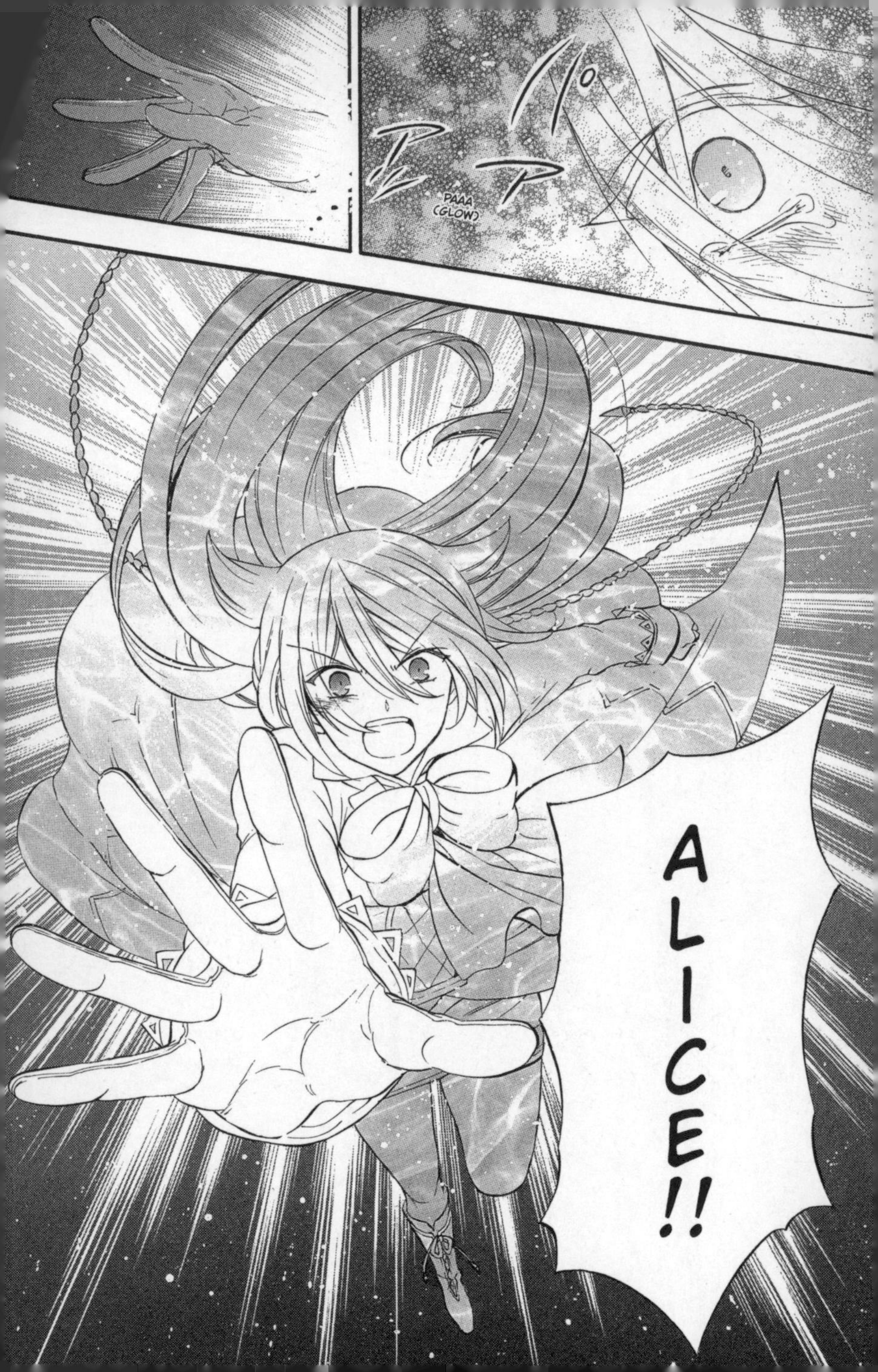
PAAA
(GLOW)
ALICE!!

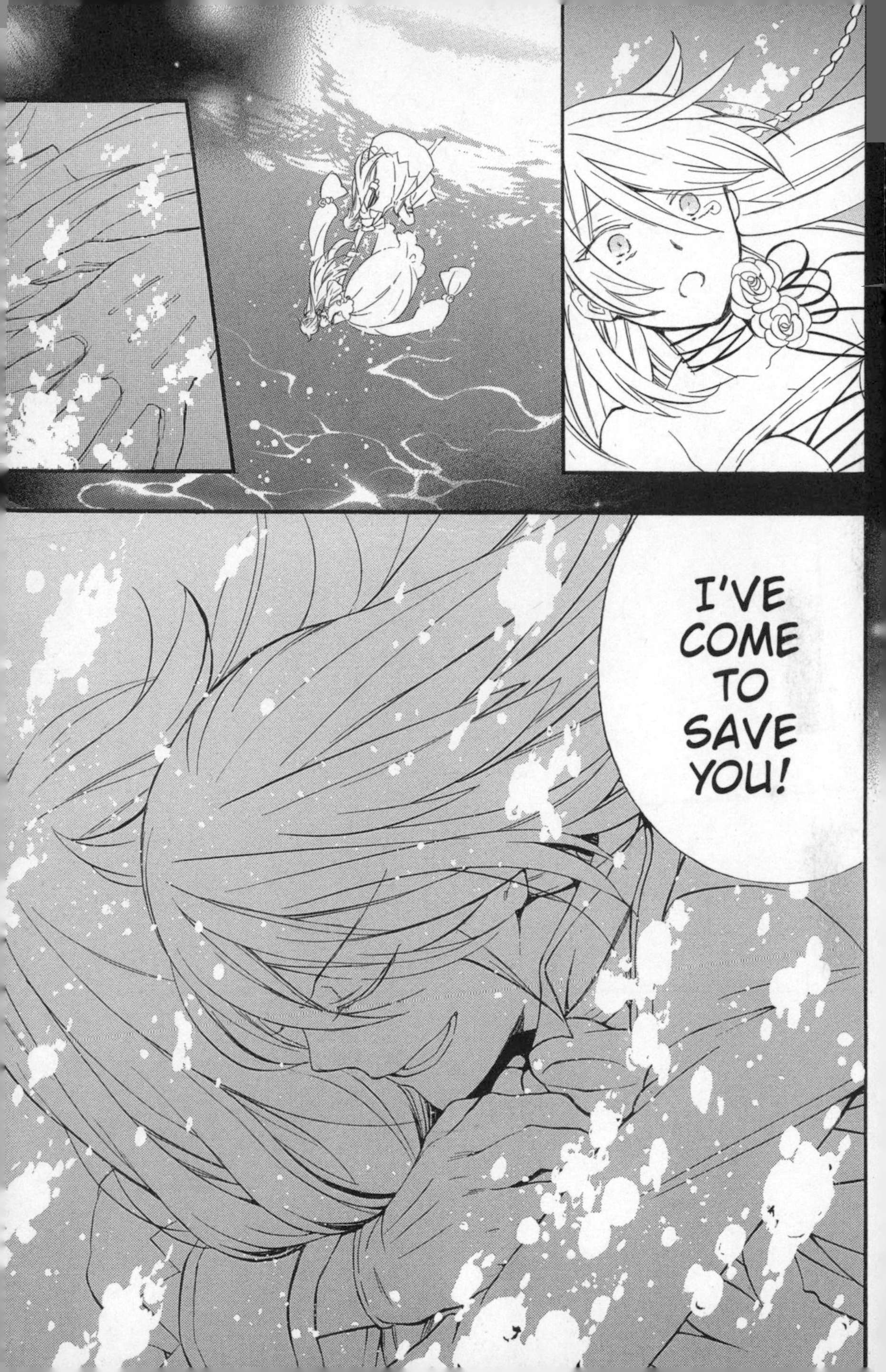
I'VE COME TO SAVE YOU!

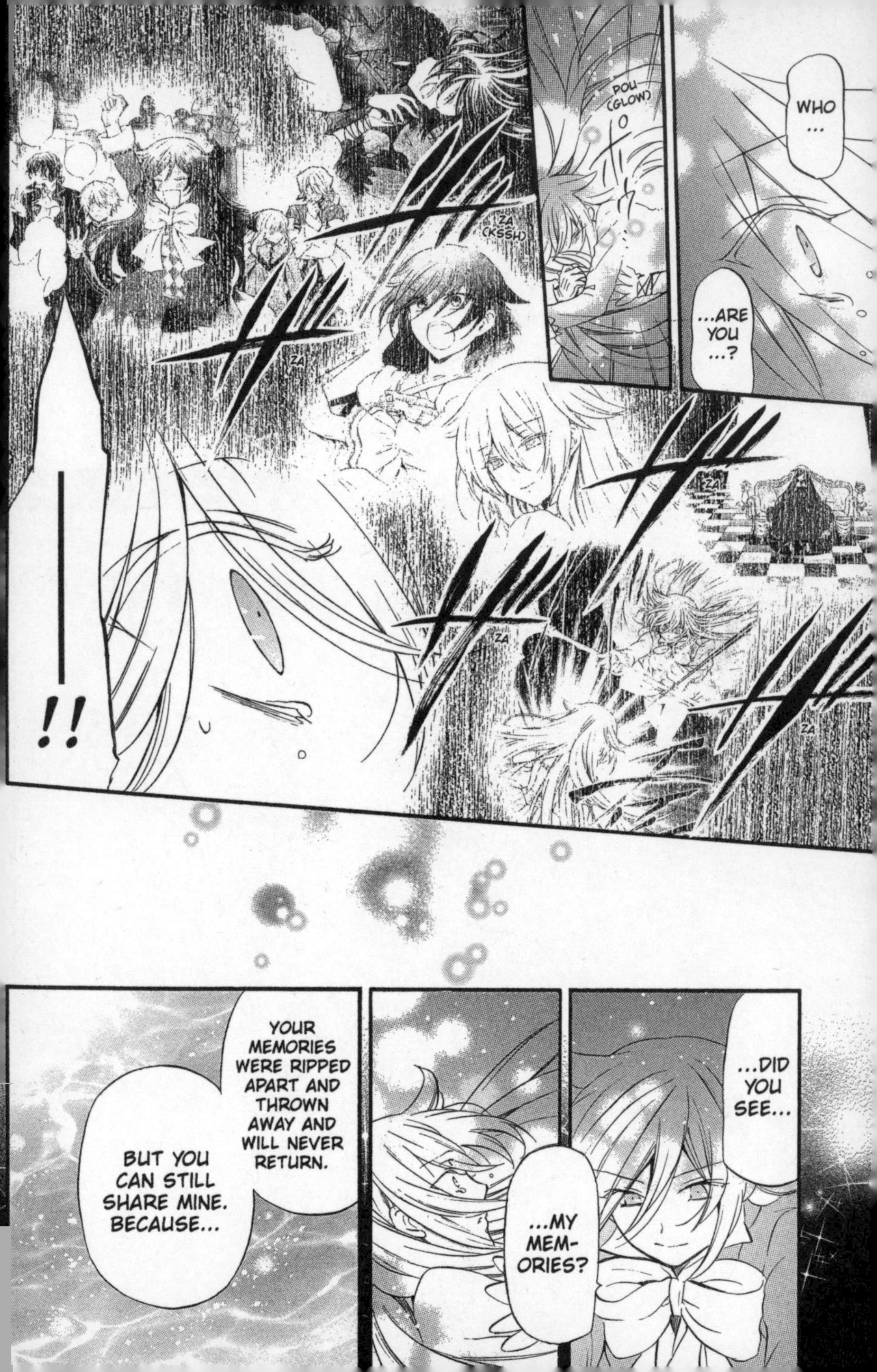
WHO ...
...ARE YOU ...?
POU (GLOW)
ZA (KSSH)
ZA
ZA
ZA
ZA
——!!
...DID YOU SEE...
...MY MEMORIES?
YOUR MEMORIES WERE RIPPED APART AND THROWN AWAY AND WILL NEVER RETURN.
BUT YOU CAN STILL SHARE MINE. BECAUSE...

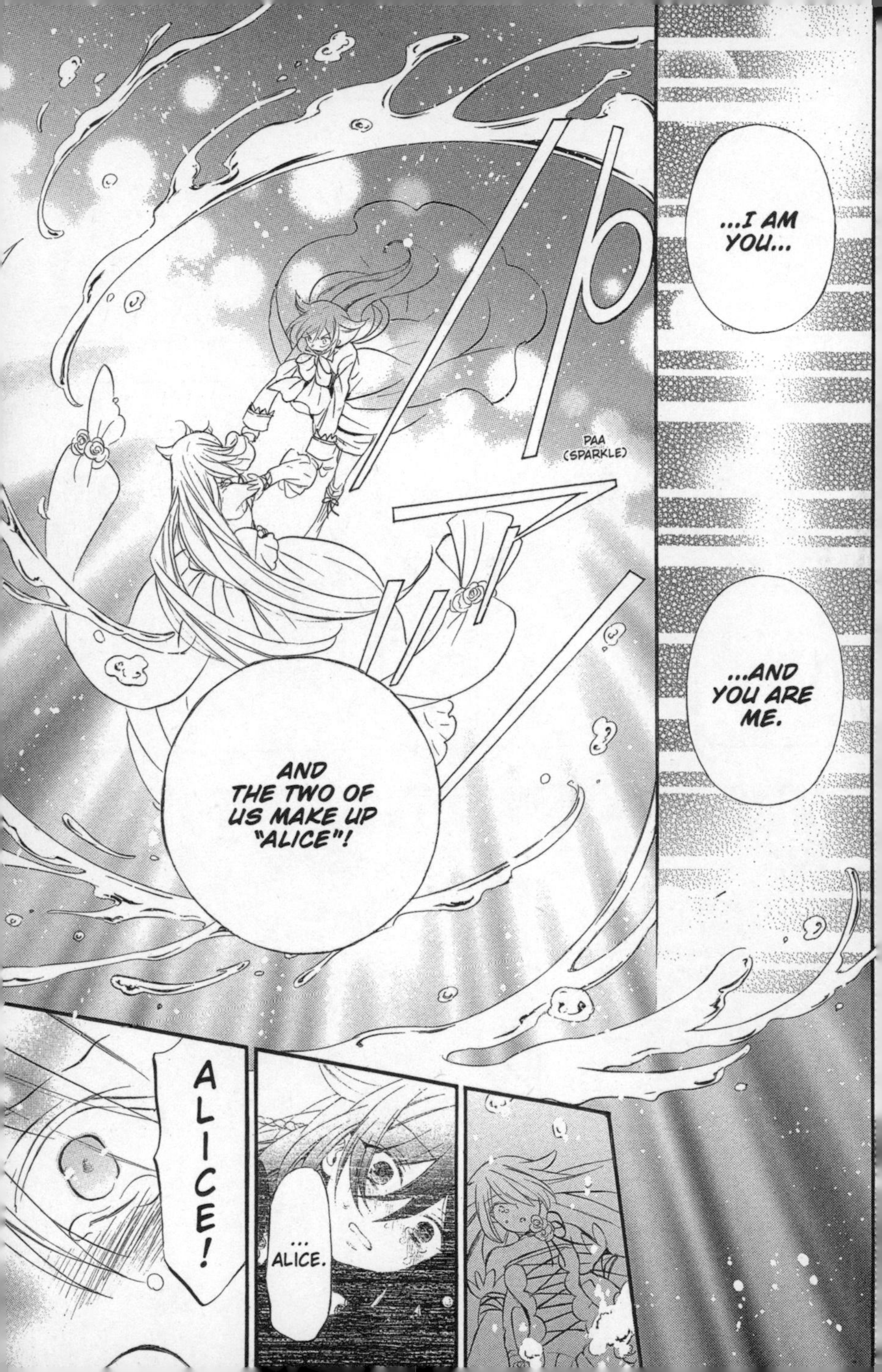
...I AM YOU...
...AND YOU ARE ME.
PAA (SPARKLE)
AND THE TWO OF US MAKE UP "ALICE"!
... ALICE.
ALICE!

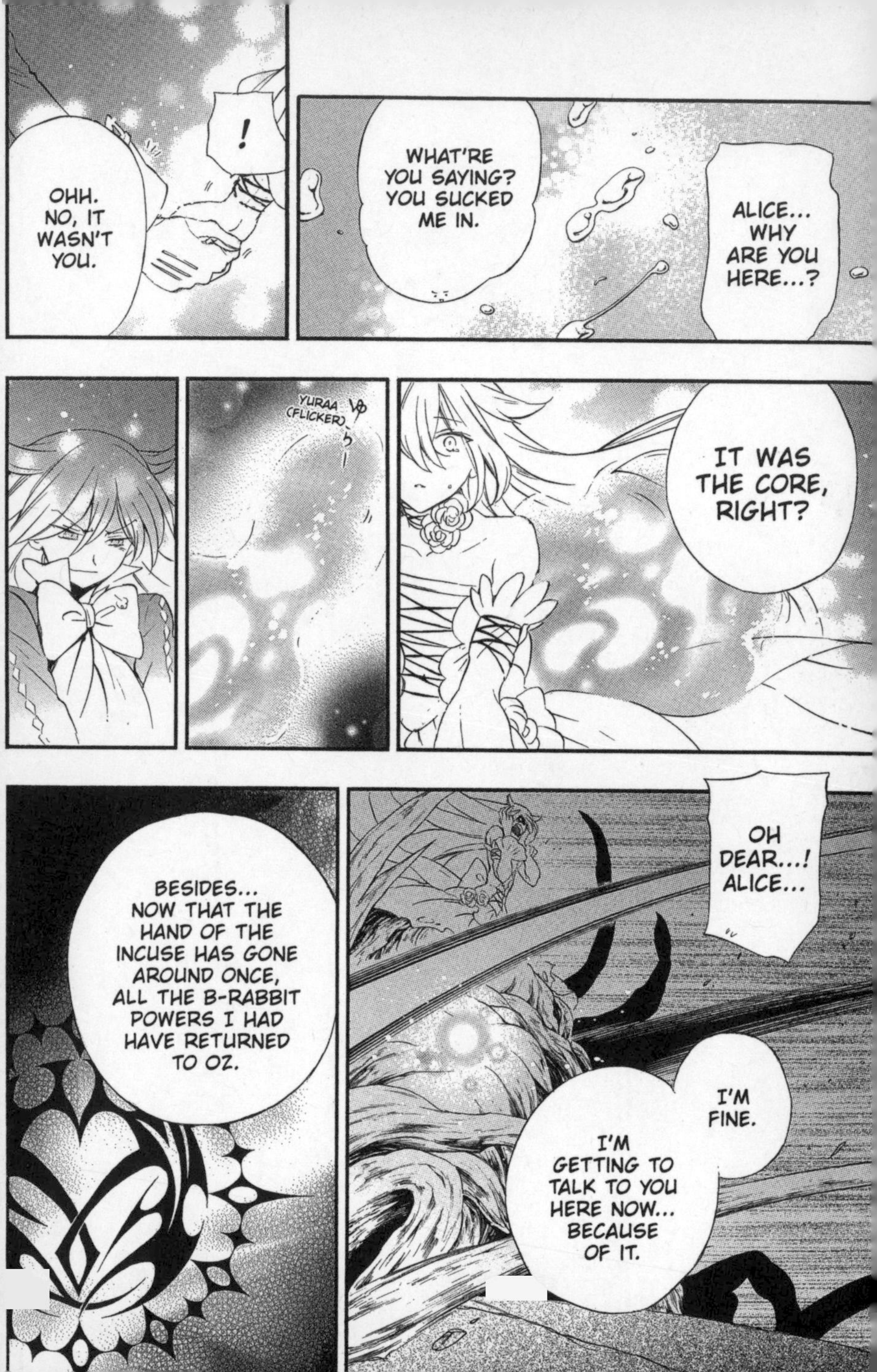
ALICE... WHY ARE YOU HERE...?
WHAT'RE YOU SAYING? YOU SUCKED ME IN.
!
OHH. NO, IT WASN'T YOU.
IT WAS THE CORE, RIGHT?
YURAA (FLICKER)
OH DEAR...! ALICE...
I'M FINE.
I'M GETTING TO TALK TO YOU HERE NOW... BECAUSE OF IT.
BESIDES... NOW THAT THE HAND OF THE INCUSE HAS GONE AROUND ONCE, ALL THE B-RABBIT POWERS I HAD HAVE RETURNED TO OZ.

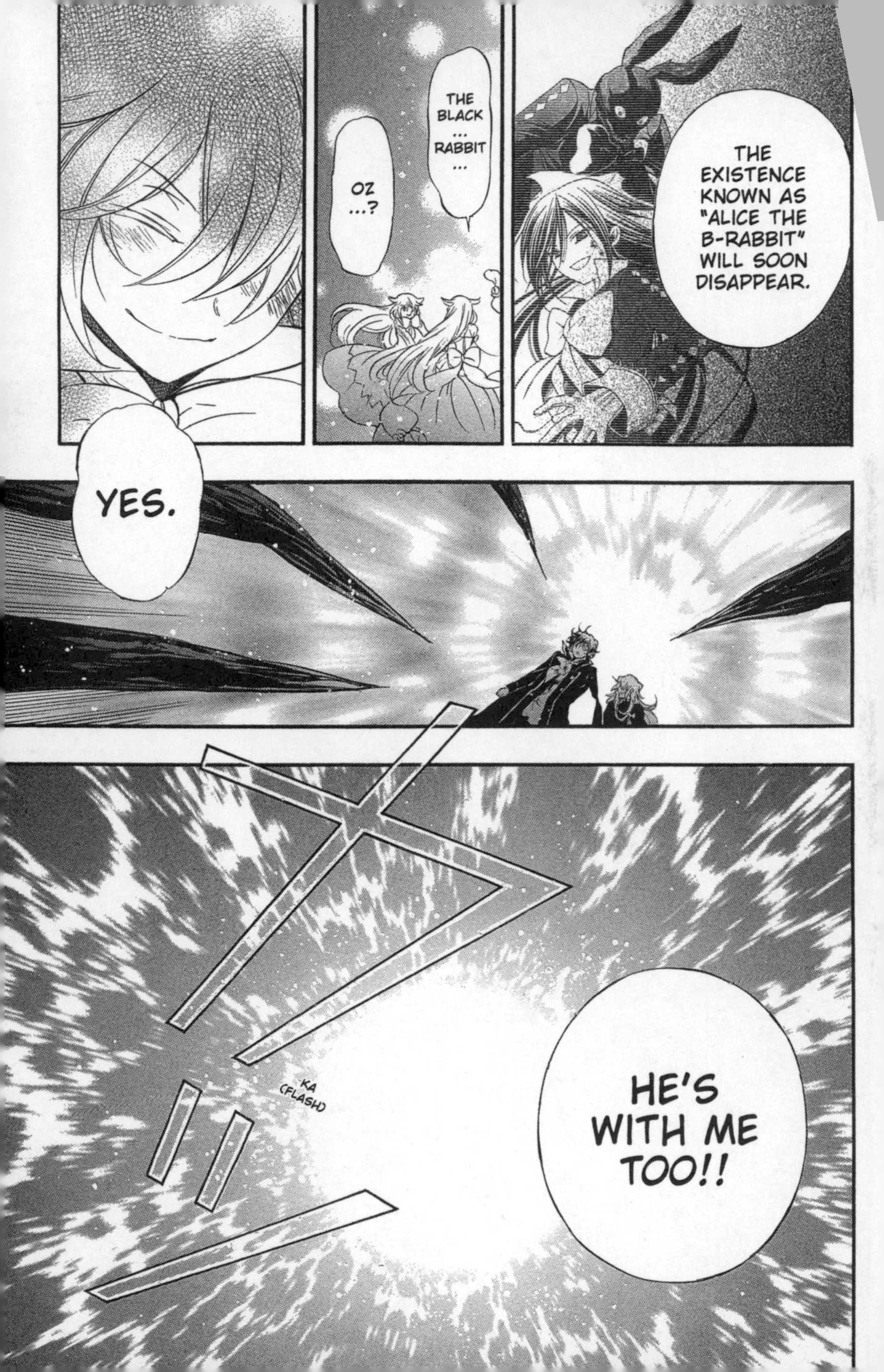
THE EXISTENCE KNOWN AS "ALICE THE B-RABBIT" WILL SOON DISAPPEAR.
THE BLACK ... RABBIT ...
OZ ...?
YES.
HE'S WITH ME TOO!!
KA (FLASH)

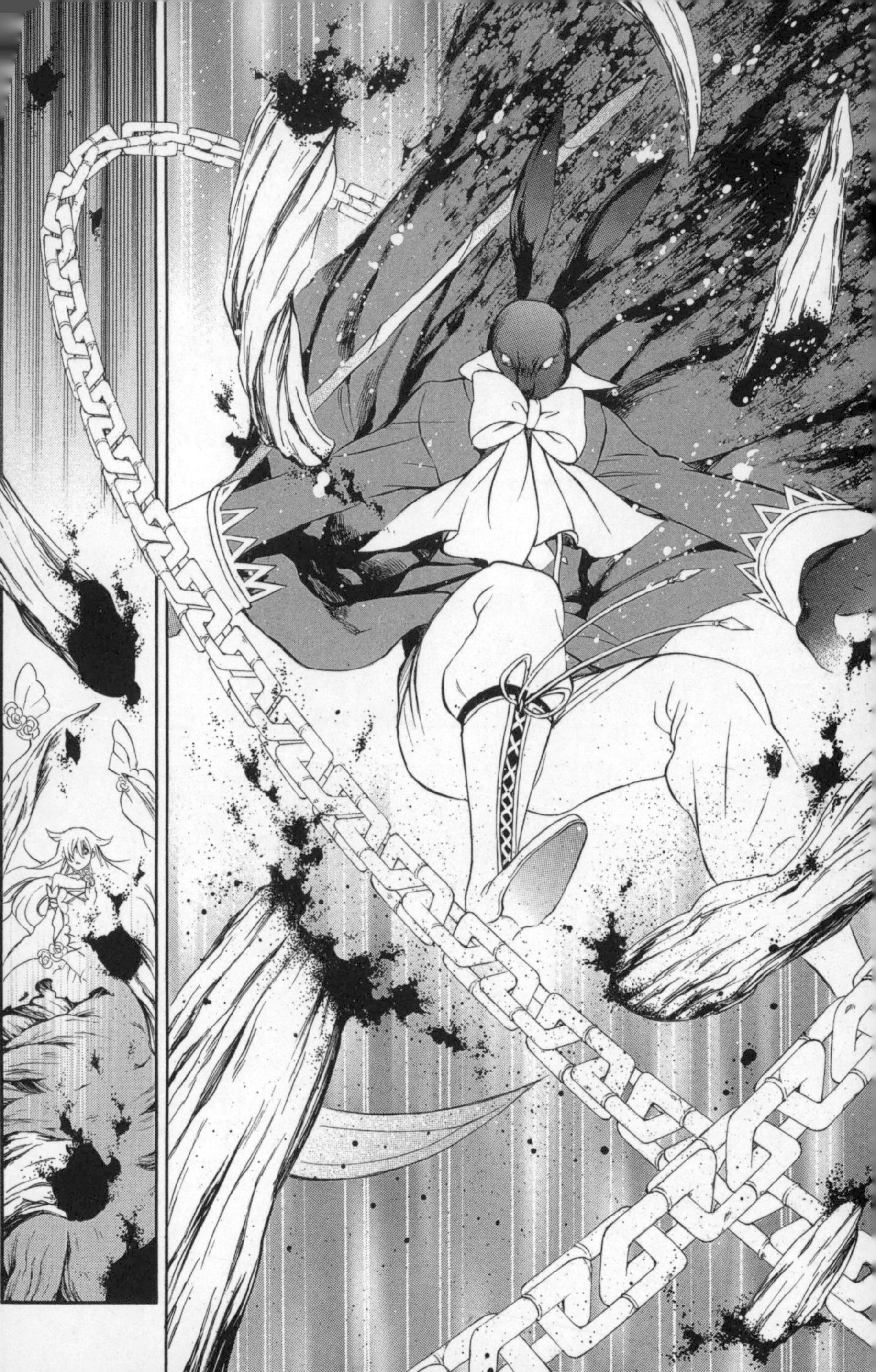

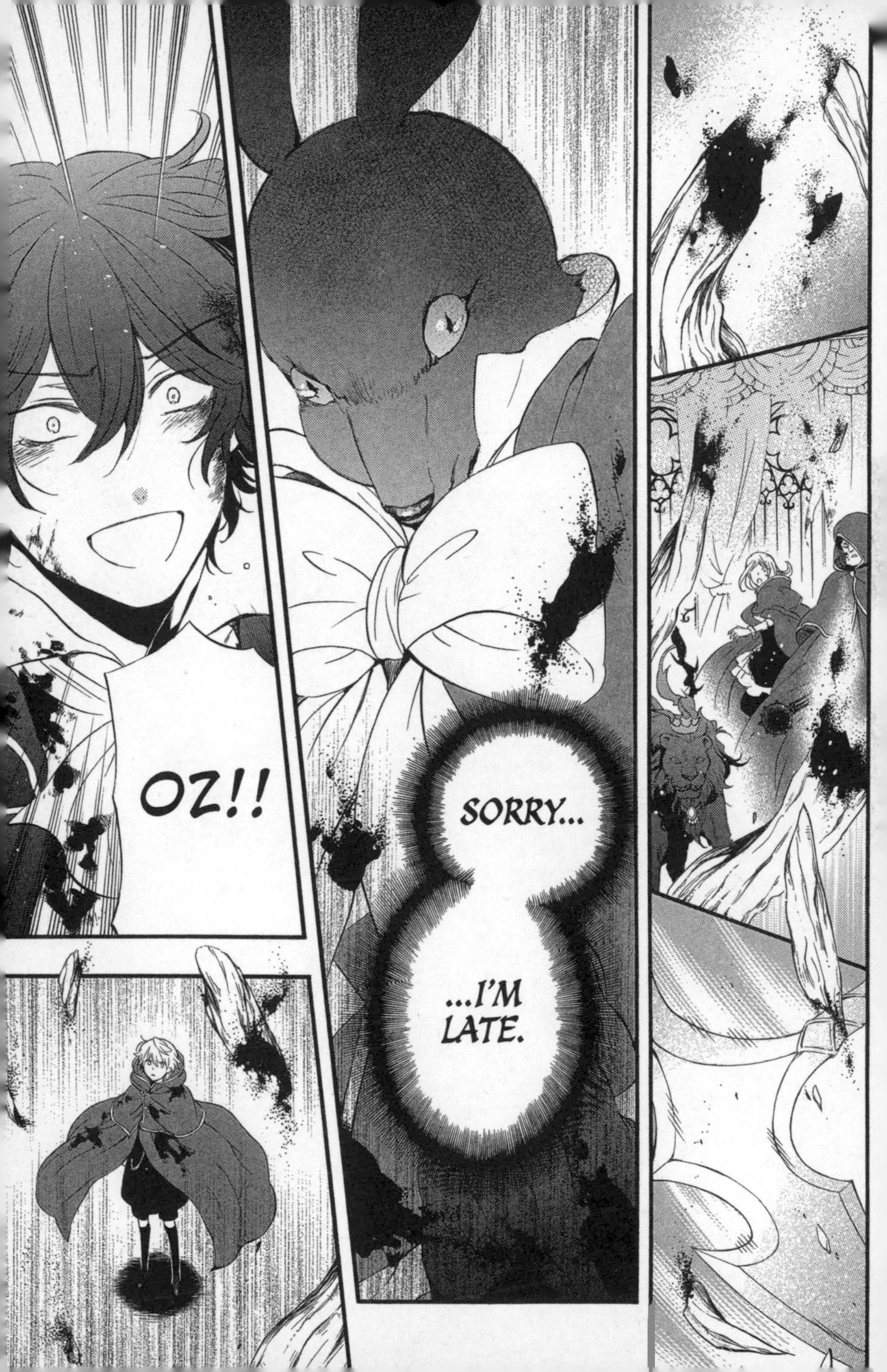
SORRY...
...I'M LATE.
OZ!!

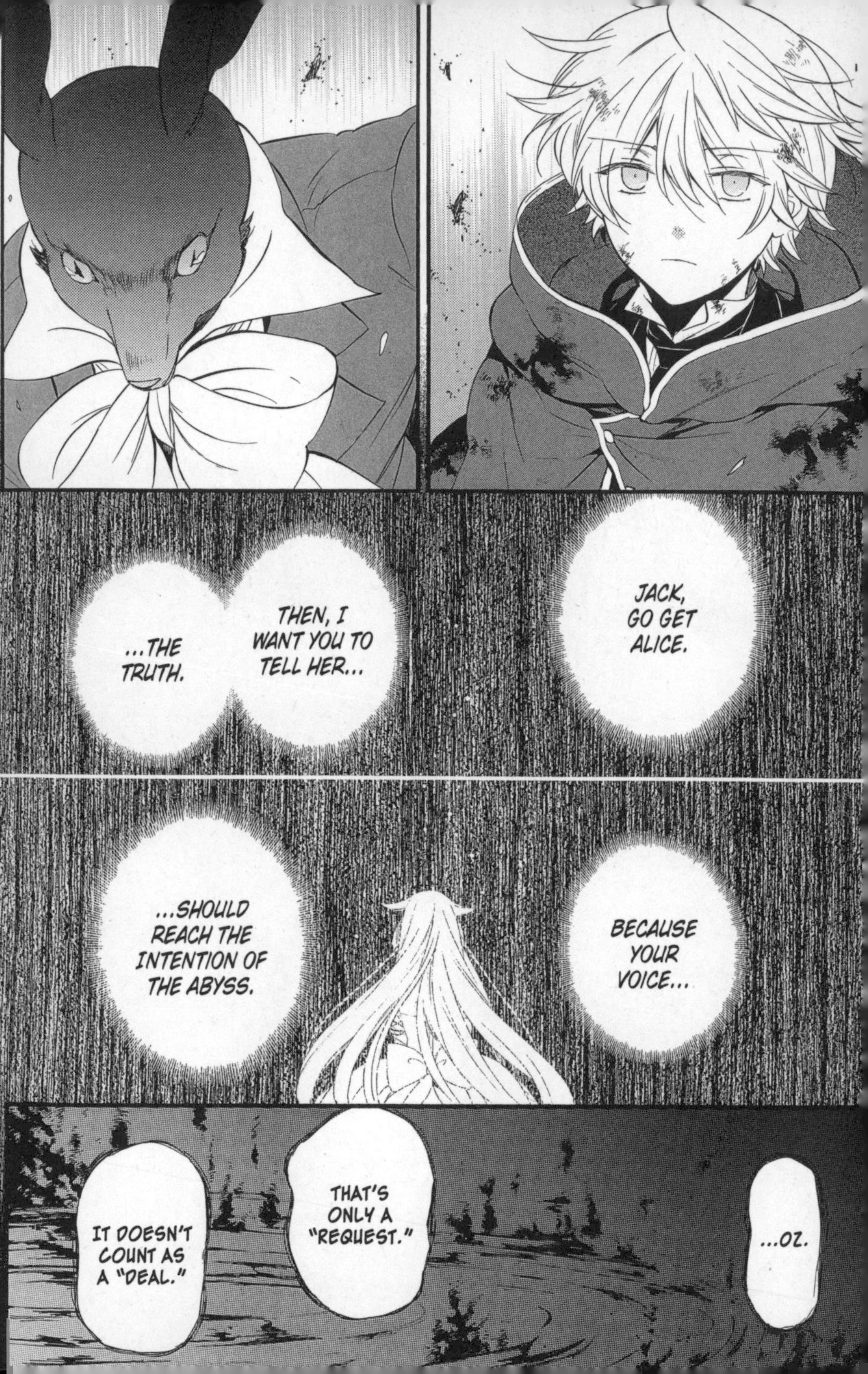
JACK, GO GET ALICE.
THEN, I WANT YOU TO TELL HER...
...THE TRUTH.
BECAUSE YOUR VOICE...
...SHOULD REACH THE INTENTION OF THE ABYSS.
...OZ.
THAT'S ONLY A "REQUEST."
IT DOESN'T COUNT AS A "DEAL."

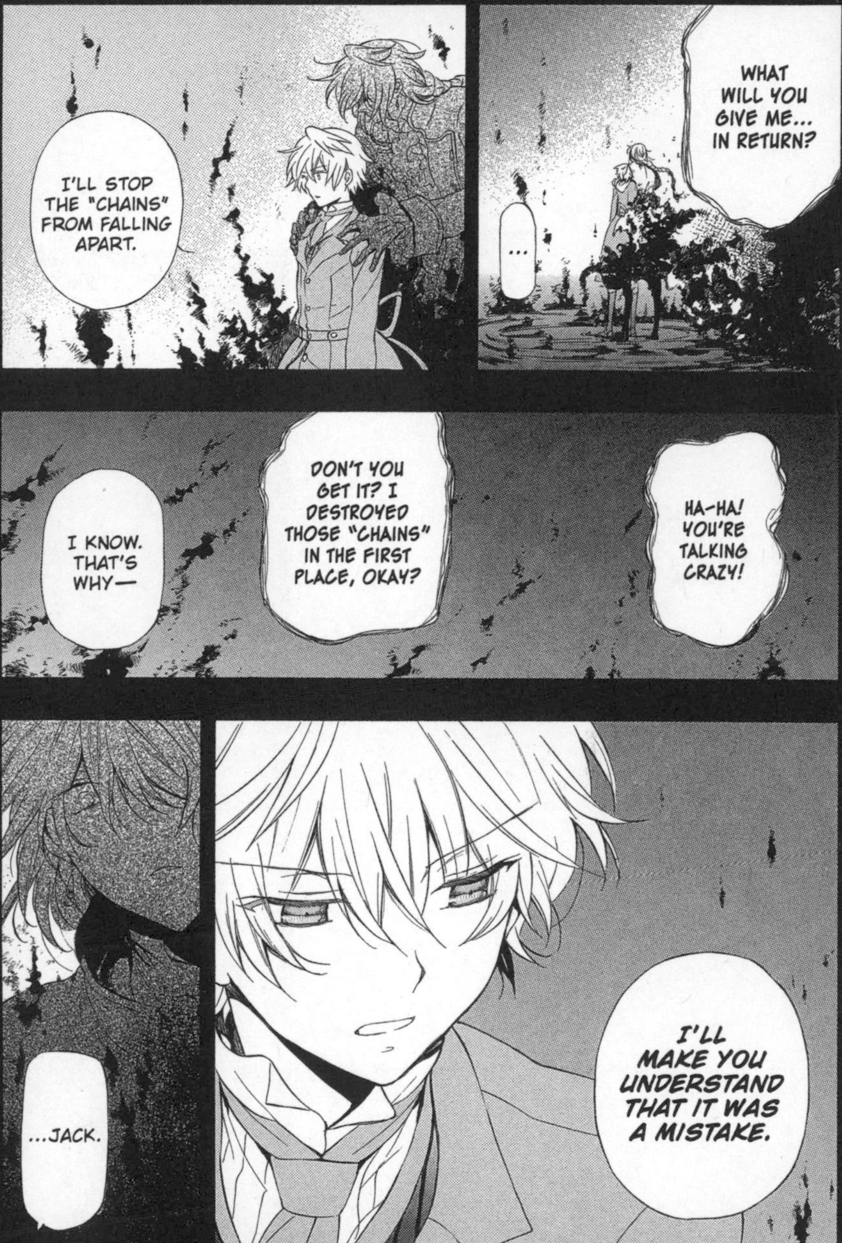
WHAT WILL YOU GIVE ME... IN RETURN?
...
I'LL STOP THE "CHAINS" FROM FALLING APART.
HA-HA! YOU'RE TALKING CRAZY!
DON'T YOU GET IT? I DESTROYED THOSE "CHAINS" IN THE FIRST PLACE, OKAY?
I KNOW. THAT'S WHY—
I'LL MAKE YOU UNDERSTAND THAT IT WAS A MISTAKE.
...JACK.

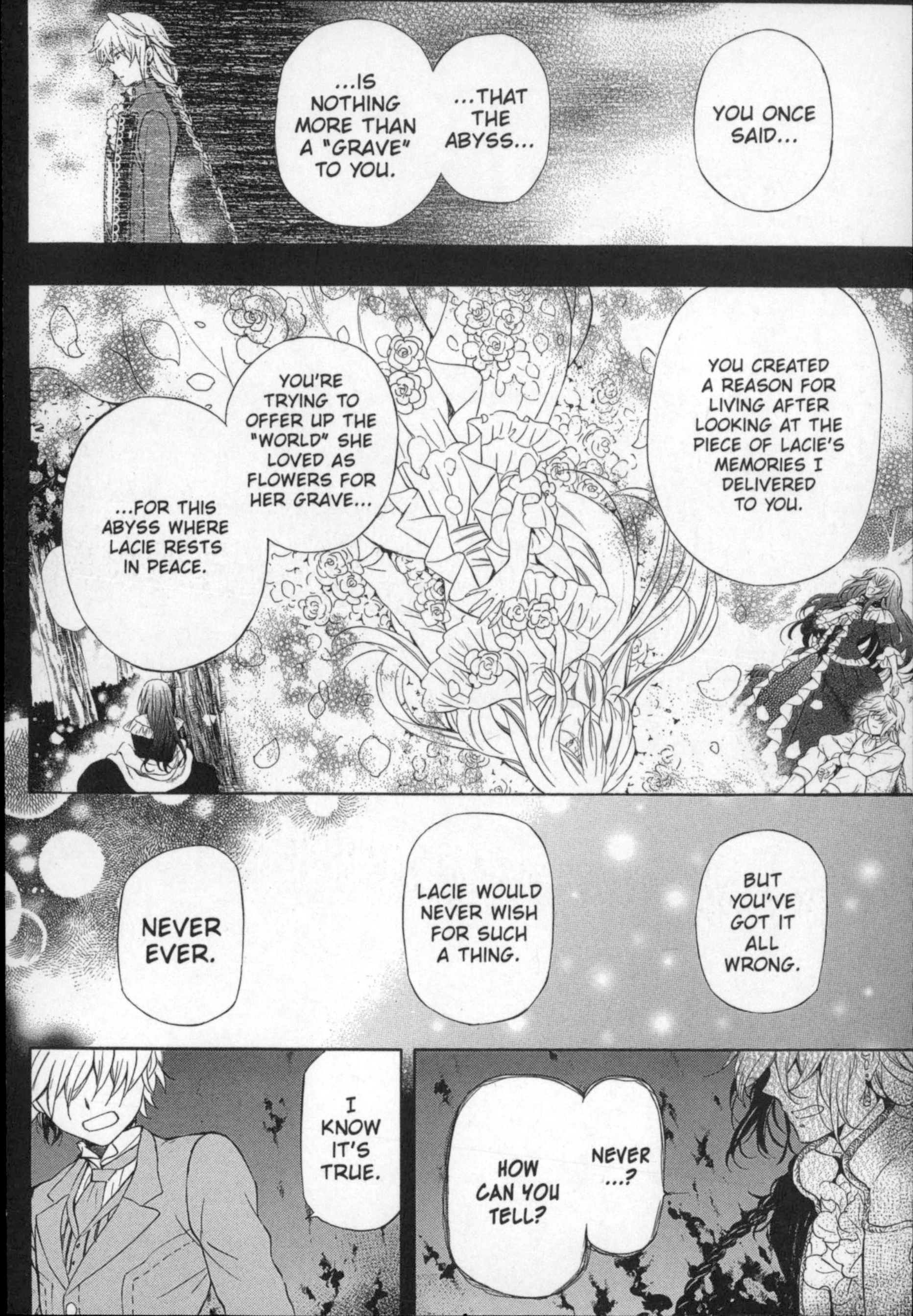
YOU ONCE SAID...
...THAT THE ABYSS...
...IS NOTHING MORE THAN A "GRAVE" TO YOU.
YOU CREATED A REASON FOR LIVING AFTER LOOKING AT THE PIECE OF LACIE'S MEMORIES I DELIVERED TO YOU.
YOU'RE TRYING TO OFFER UP THE "WORLD" SHE LOVED AS FLOWERS FOR HER GRAVE...
...FOR THIS ABYSS WHERE LACIE RESTS IN PEACE.
BUT YOU'VE GOT IT ALL WRONG.
LACIE WOULD NEVER WISH FOR SUCH A THING.
NEVER EVER.
NEVER...?
HOW CAN YOU TELL?
I KNOW IT'S TRUE.

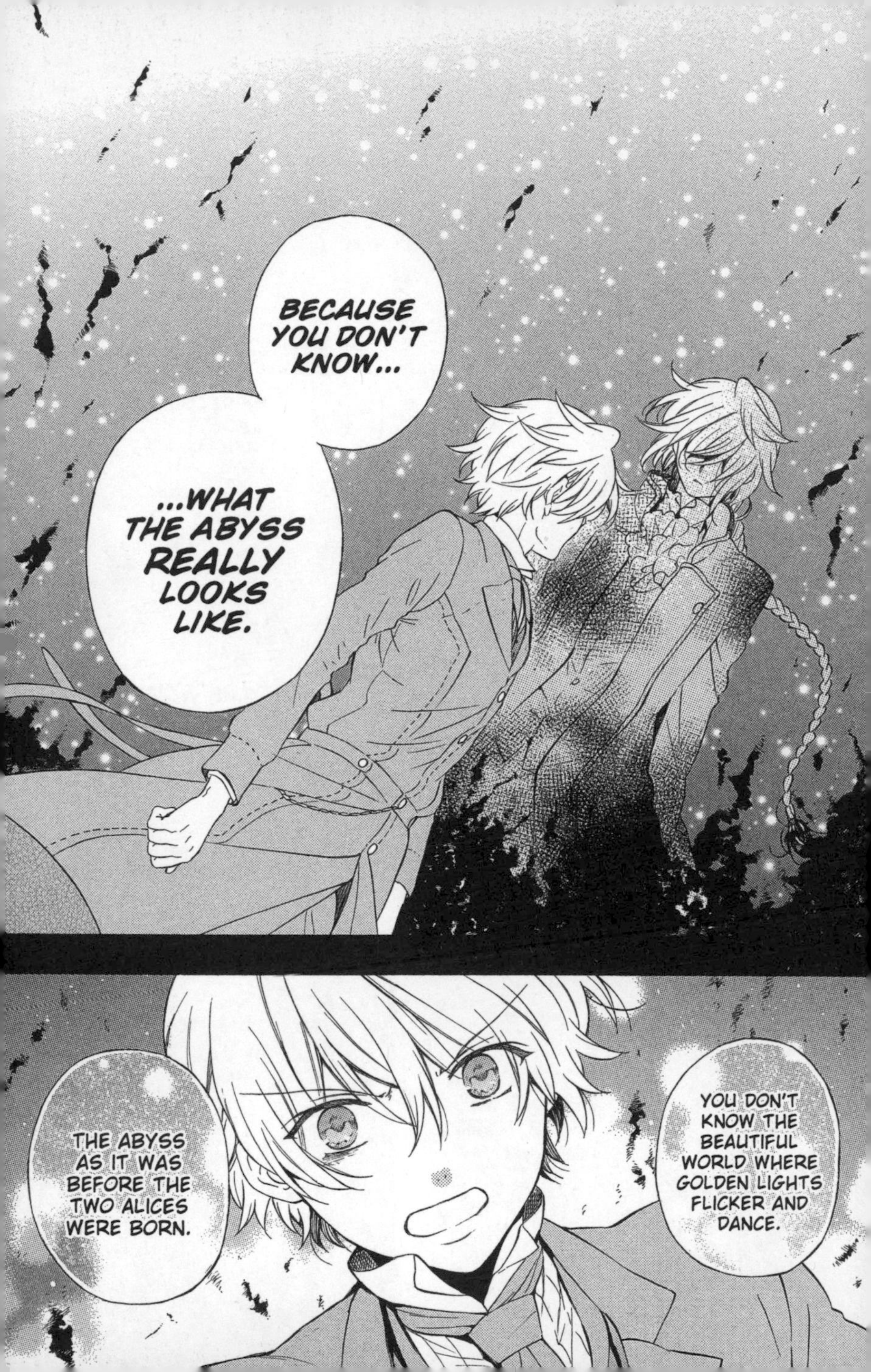
BECAUSE YOU DON'T KNOW...
...WHAT THE ABYSS REALLY LOOKS LIKE.
YOU DON'T KNOW THE BEAUTIFUL WORLD WHERE GOLDEN LIGHTS FLICKER AND DANCE.
THE ABYSS AS IT WAS BEFORE THE TWO ALICES WERE BORN.

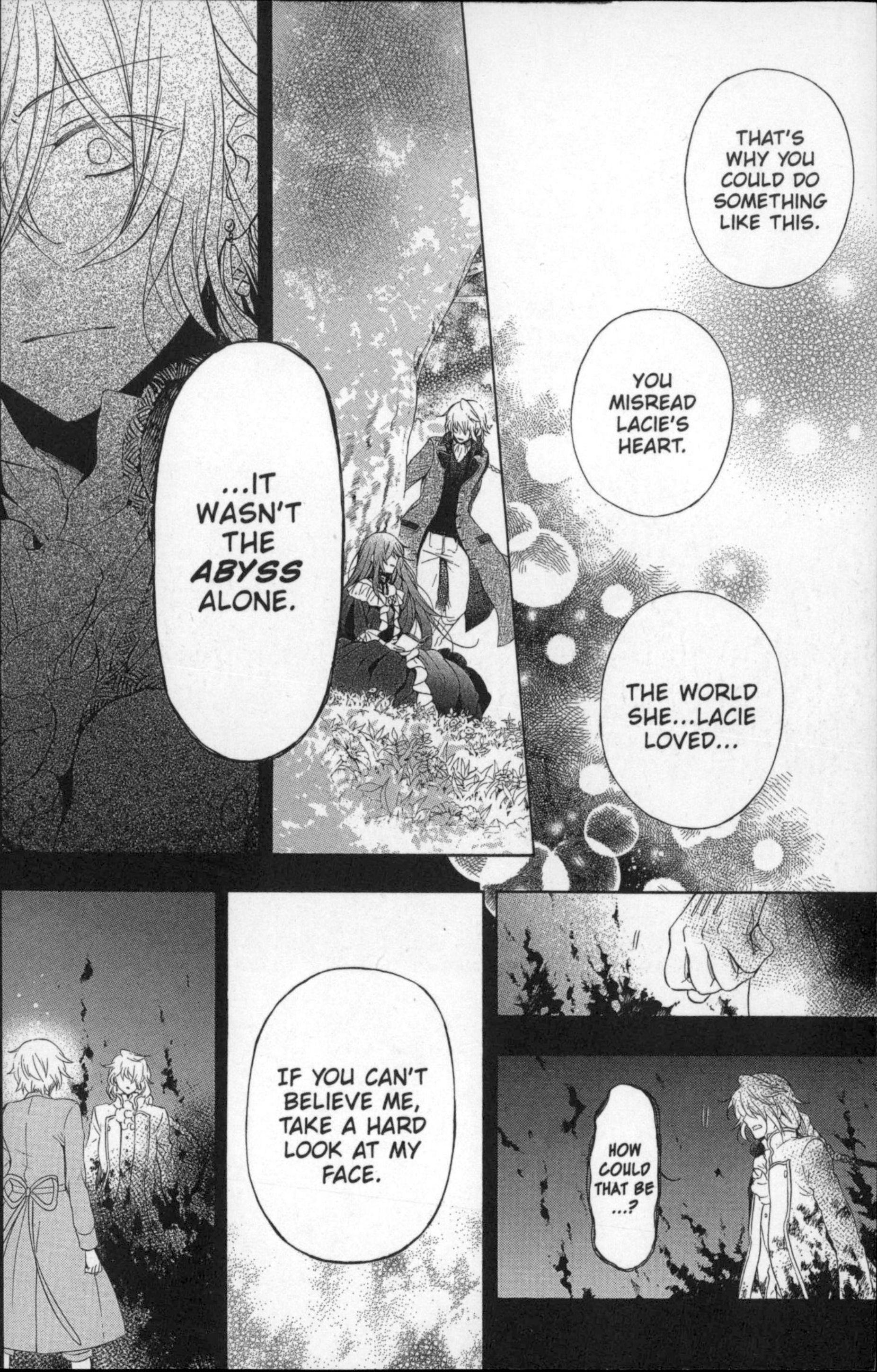
THAT'S WHY YOU COULD DO SOMETHING LIKE THIS.
YOU MISREAD LACIE'S HEART.
THE WORLD SHE...LACIE LOVED...
...IT WASN'T THE *ABYSS* ALONE.
HOW COULD THAT BE...?
IF YOU CAN'T BELIEVE ME, TAKE A HARD LOOK AT MY FACE.

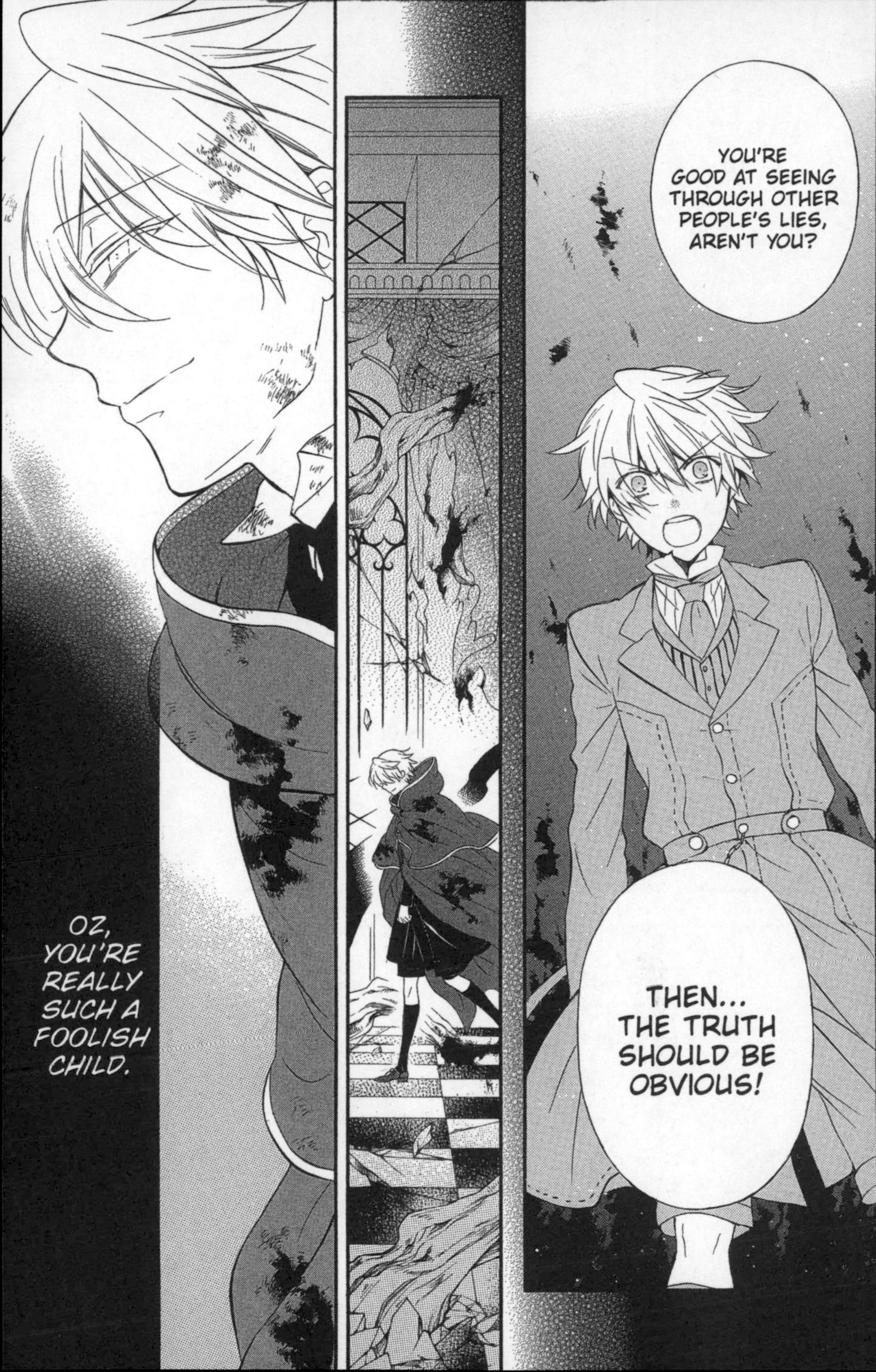
YOU'RE GOOD AT SEEING THROUGH OTHER PEOPLE'S LIES, AREN'T YOU?
THEN... THE TRUTH SHOULD BE OBVIOUS!
OZ, YOU'RE REALLY SUCH A FOOLISH CHILD.

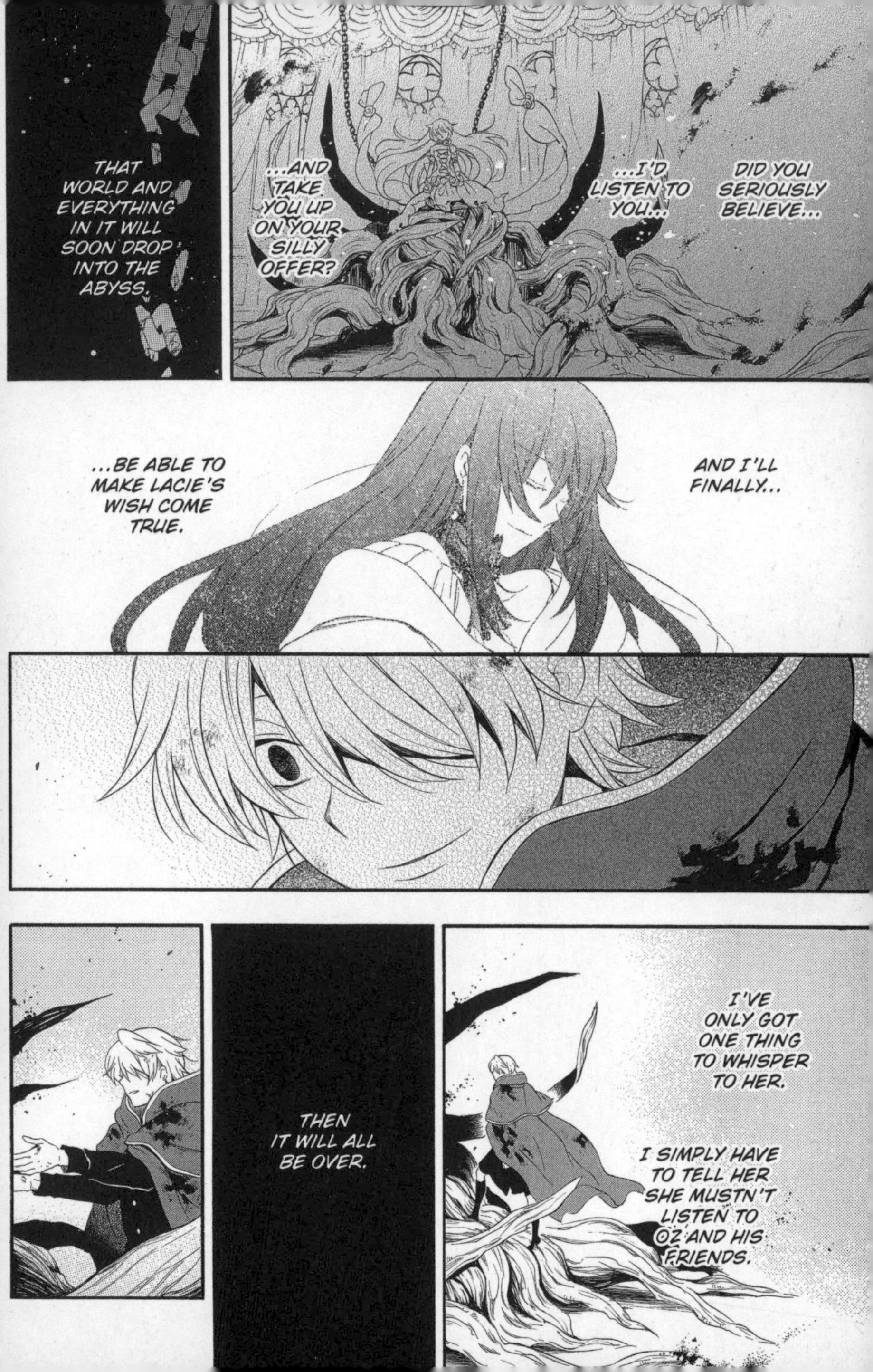
DID YOU SERIOUSLY BELIEVE...
...I'D LISTEN TO YOU...
...AND TAKE YOU UP ON YOUR SILLY OFFER?
THAT WORLD AND EVERYTHING IN IT WILL SOON DROP INTO THE ABYSS.
AND I'LL FINALLY...
...BE ABLE TO MAKE LACIE'S WISH COME TRUE.
I'VE ONLY GOT ONE THING TO WHISPER TO HER.
I SIMPLY HAVE TO TELL HER SHE MUSTN'T LISTEN TO OZ AND HIS FRIENDS.
THEN IT WILL ALL BE OVER.

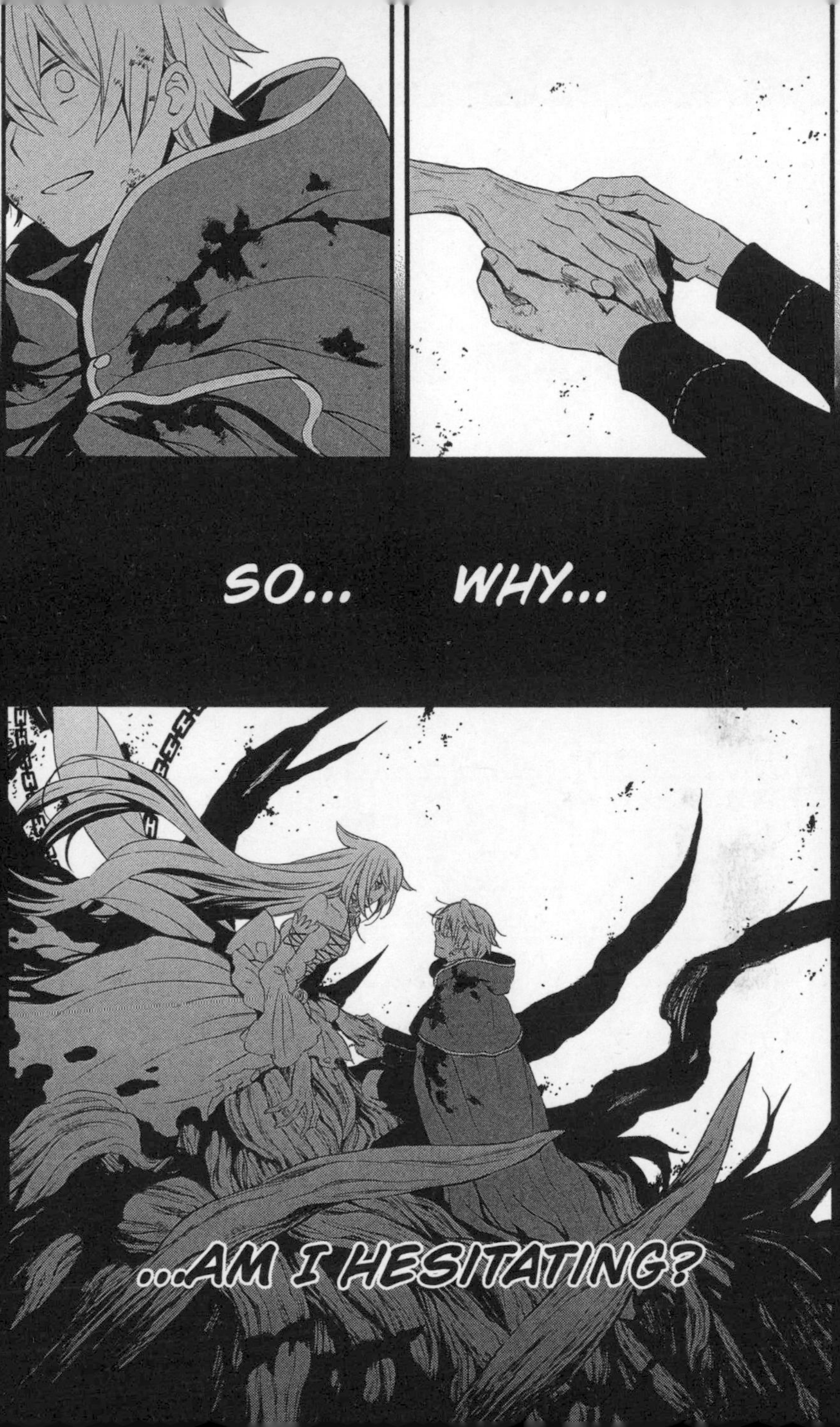
SO... WHY...
...AM I HESITATING?

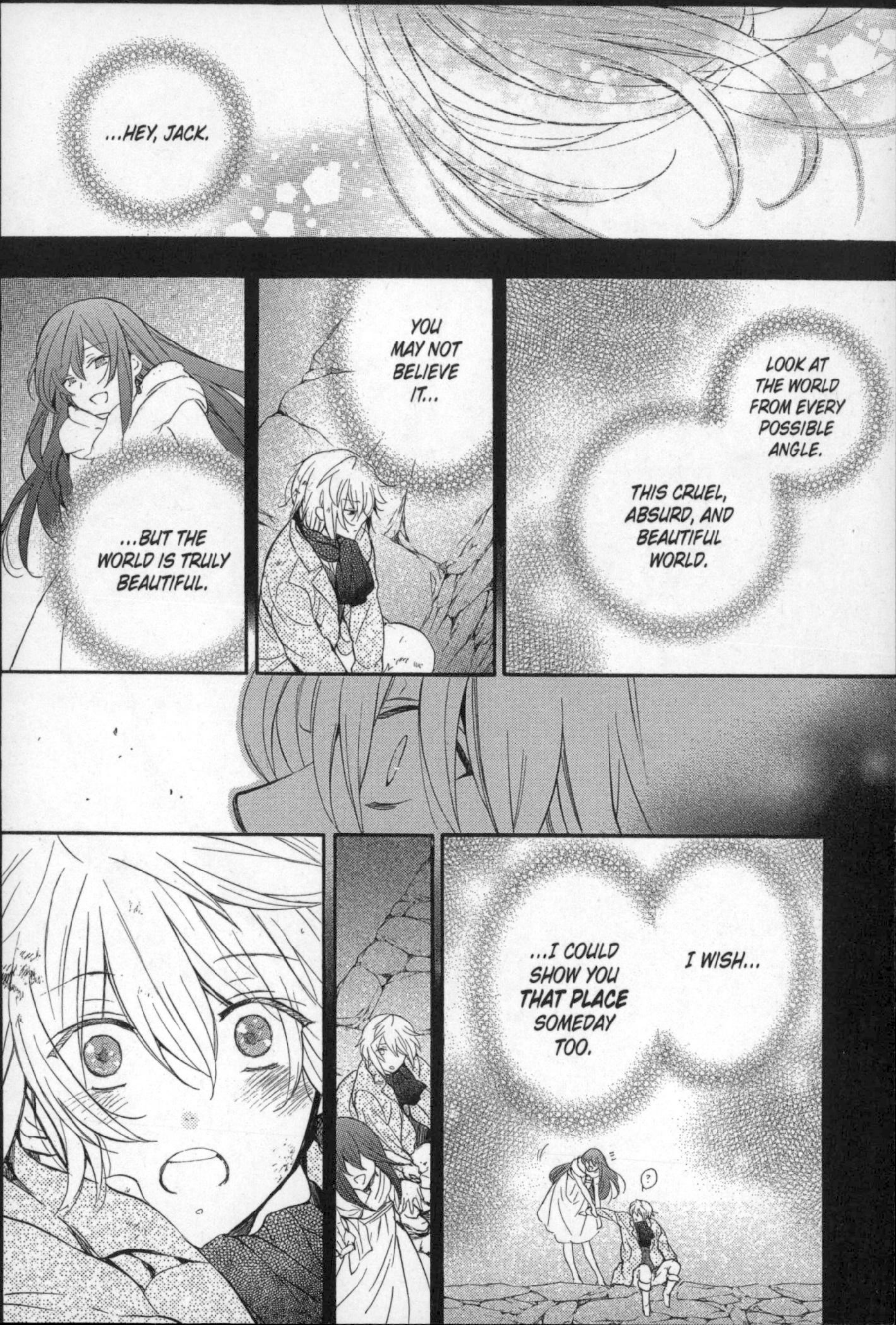
...HEY, JACK.
LOOK AT THE WORLD FROM EVERY POSSIBLE ANGLE.
THIS CRUEL, ABSURD, AND BEAUTIFUL WORLD.
YOU MAY NOT BELIEVE IT...
...BUT THE WORLD IS TRULY BEAUTIFUL.
I WISH...
...I COULD SHOW YOU THAT PLACE SOMEDAY TOO.

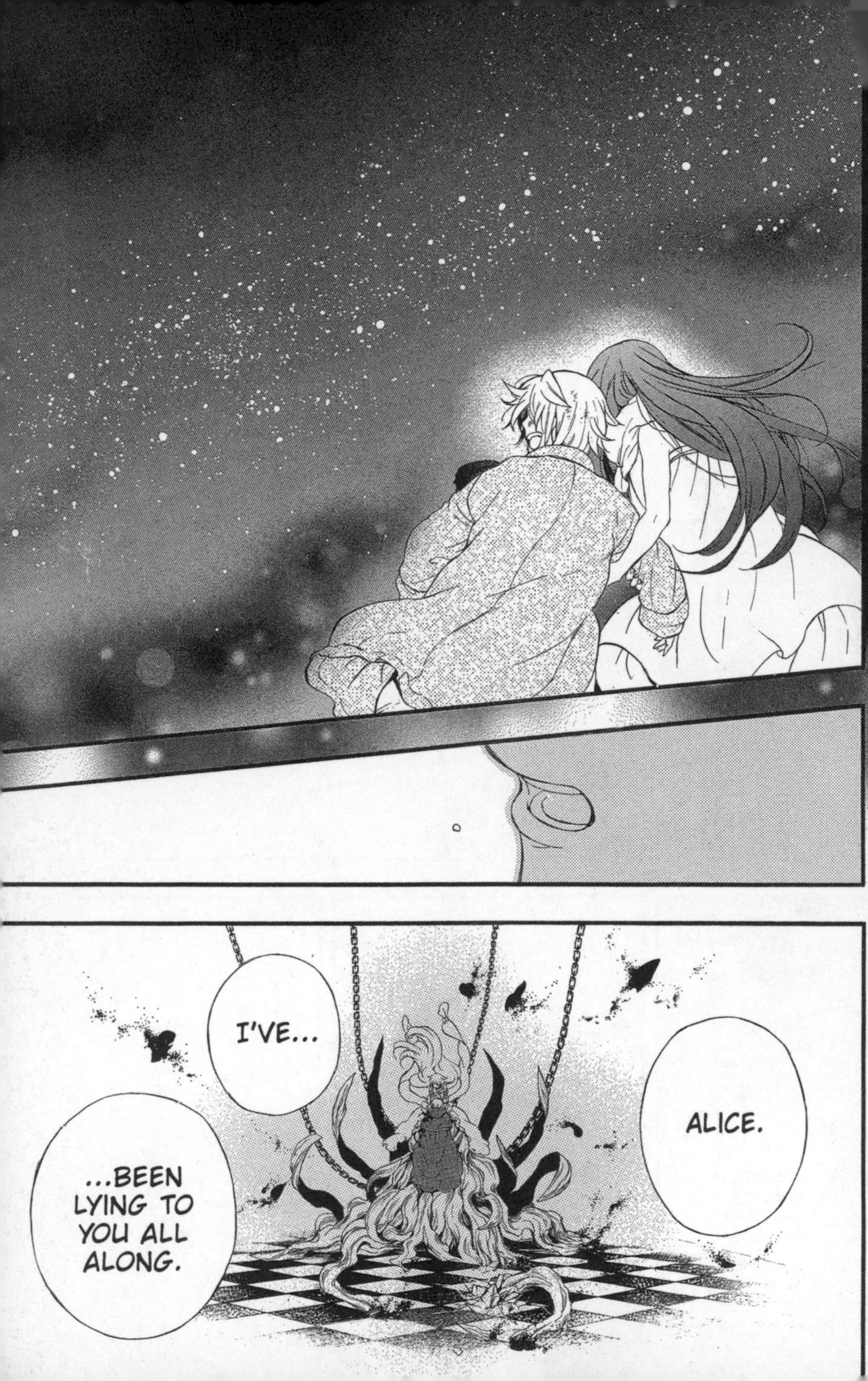
ALICE.
I'VE...
...BEEN LYING TO YOU ALL ALONG.

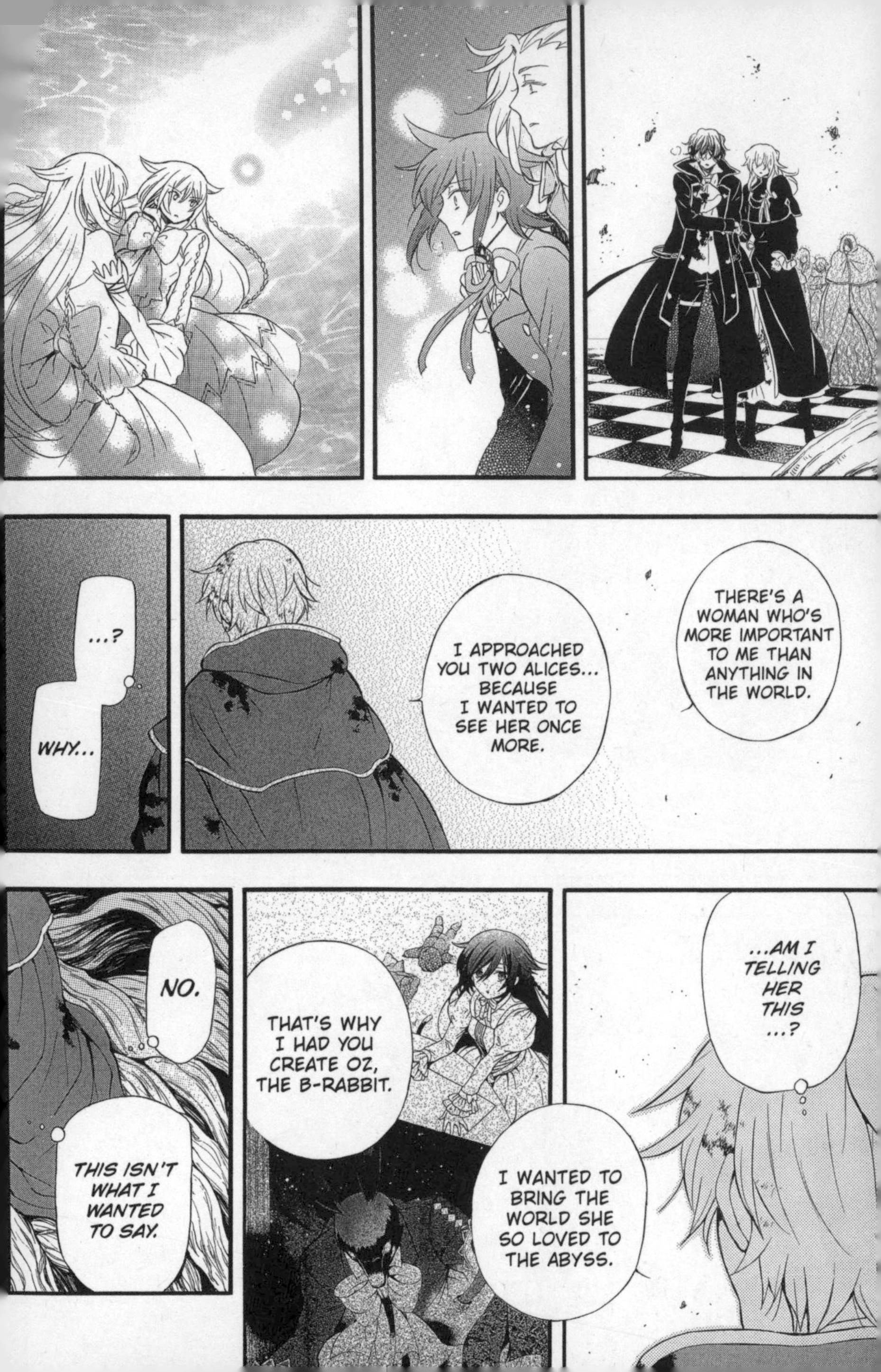
THERE'S A WOMAN WHO'S MORE IMPORTANT TO ME THAN ANYTHING IN THE WORLD.
I APPROACHED YOU TWO ALICES... BECAUSE I WANTED TO SEE HER ONCE MORE.
...?
WHY...
...AM I TELLING HER THIS ...?
I WANTED TO BRING THE WORLD SHE SO LOVED TO THE ABYSS.
THAT'S WHY I HAD YOU CREATE OZ, THE B-RABBIT.
NO.
THIS ISN'T WHAT I WANTED TO SAY.

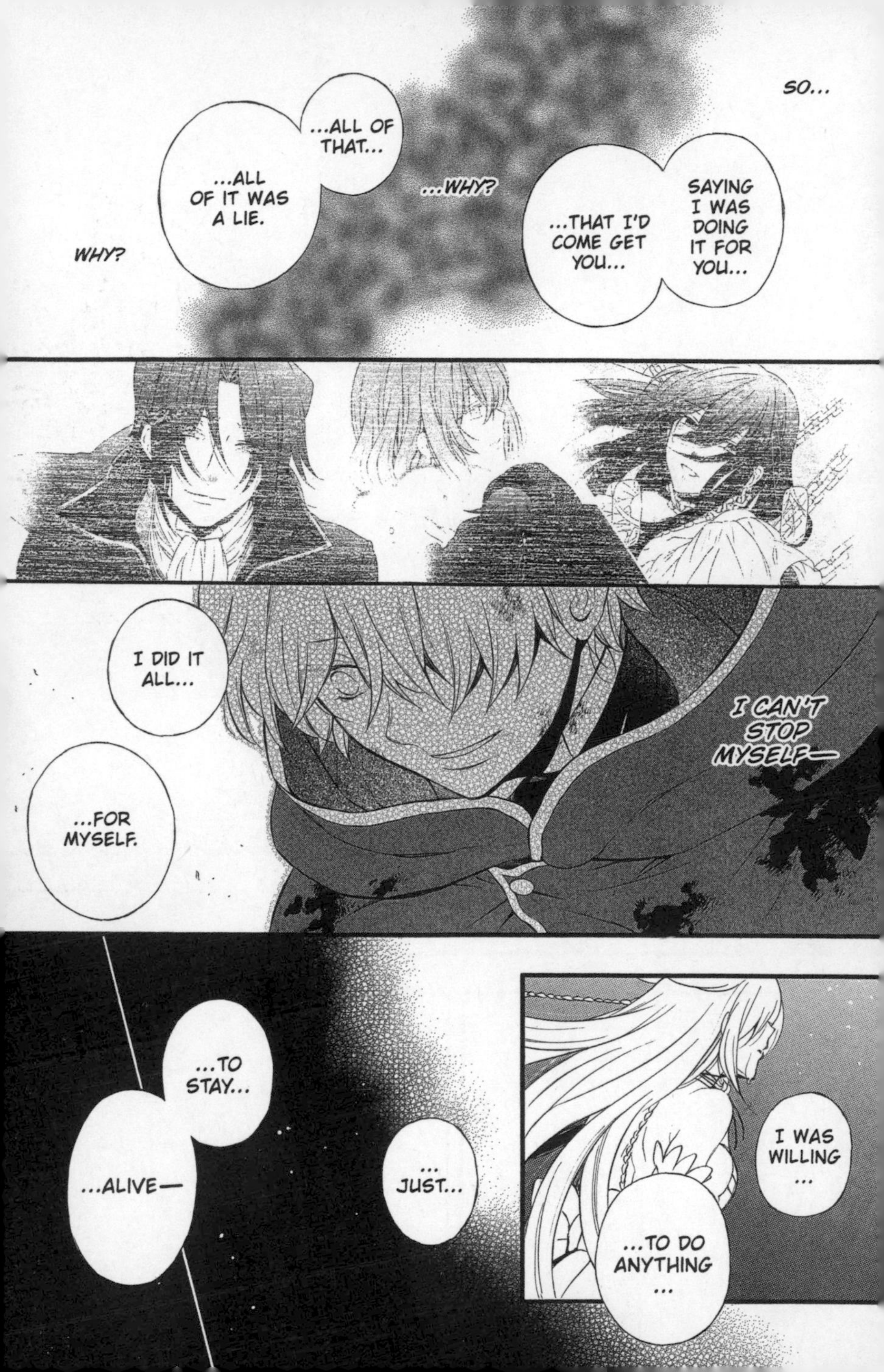
SO...
SAYING I WAS DOING IT FOR YOU...
...THAT I'D COME GET YOU...
...WHY?
...ALL OF THAT...
...ALL OF IT WAS A LIE.
WHY?
I CAN'T STOP MYSELF—
I DID IT ALL...
...FOR MYSELF.
I WAS WILLING ...
...TO DO ANYTHING ...
... JUST...
...TO STAY...
...ALIVE—

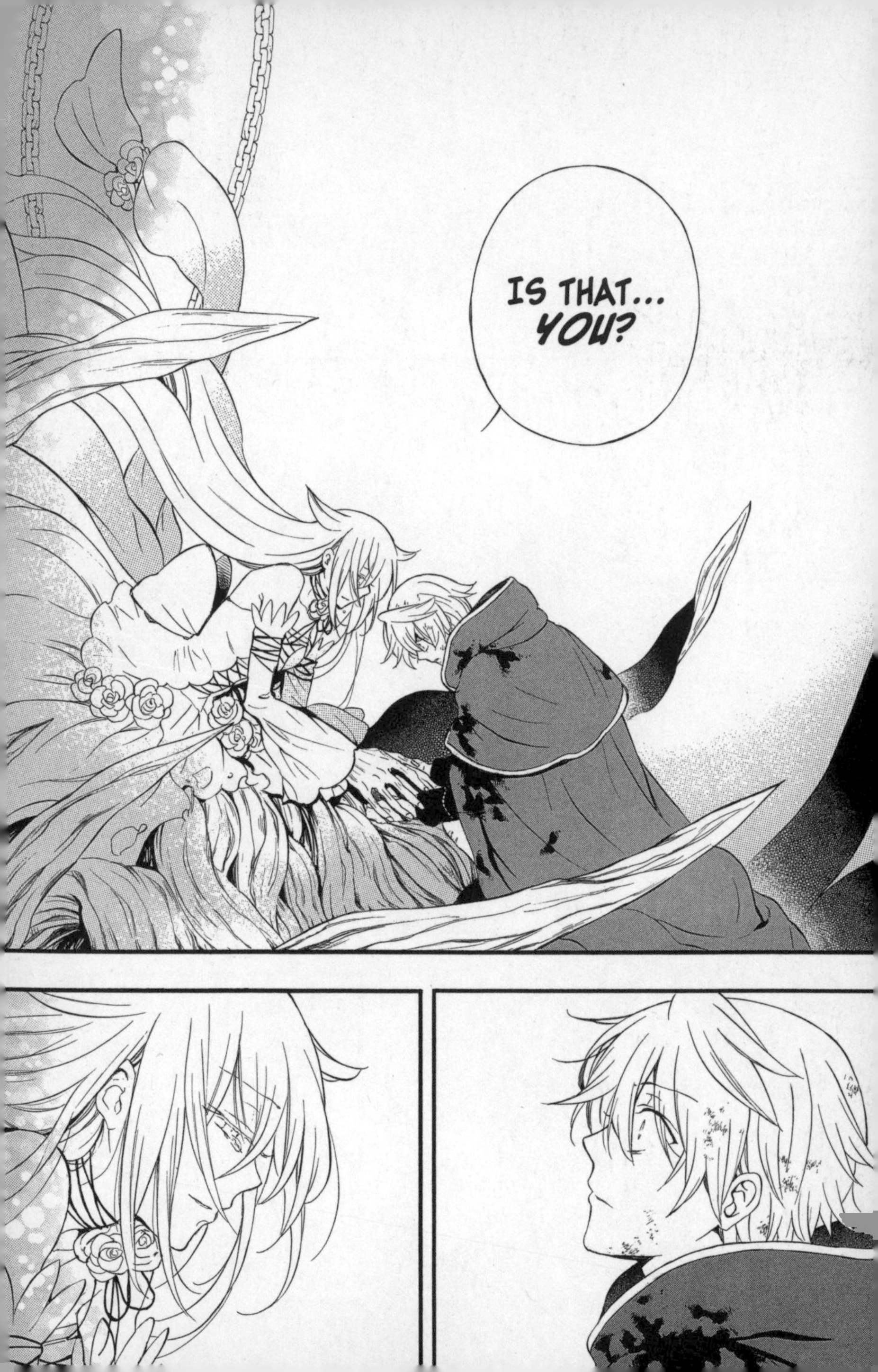
IS THAT... YOU?

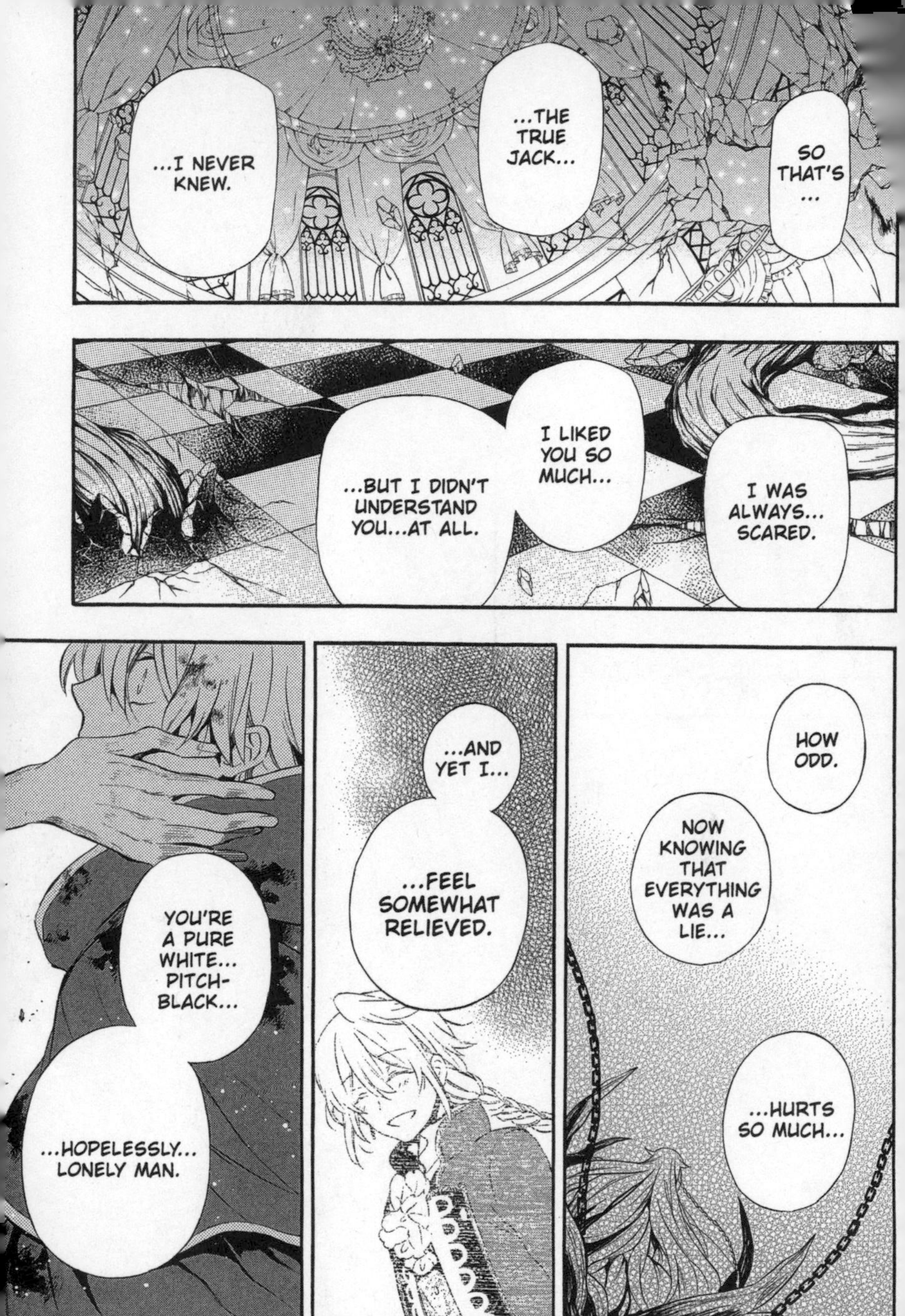
SO THAT'S ...
...THE TRUE JACK...
...I NEVER KNEW.
I WAS ALWAYS... SCARED.
I LIKED YOU SO MUCH...
...BUT I DIDN'T UNDERSTAND YOU...AT ALL.
HOW ODD.
NOW KNOWING THAT EVERYTHING WAS A LIE...
...HURTS SO MUCH...
...AND YET I...
...FEEL SOMEWHAT RELIEVED.
YOU'RE A PURE WHITE... PITCH-BLACK...
...HOPELESSLY... LONELY MAN.

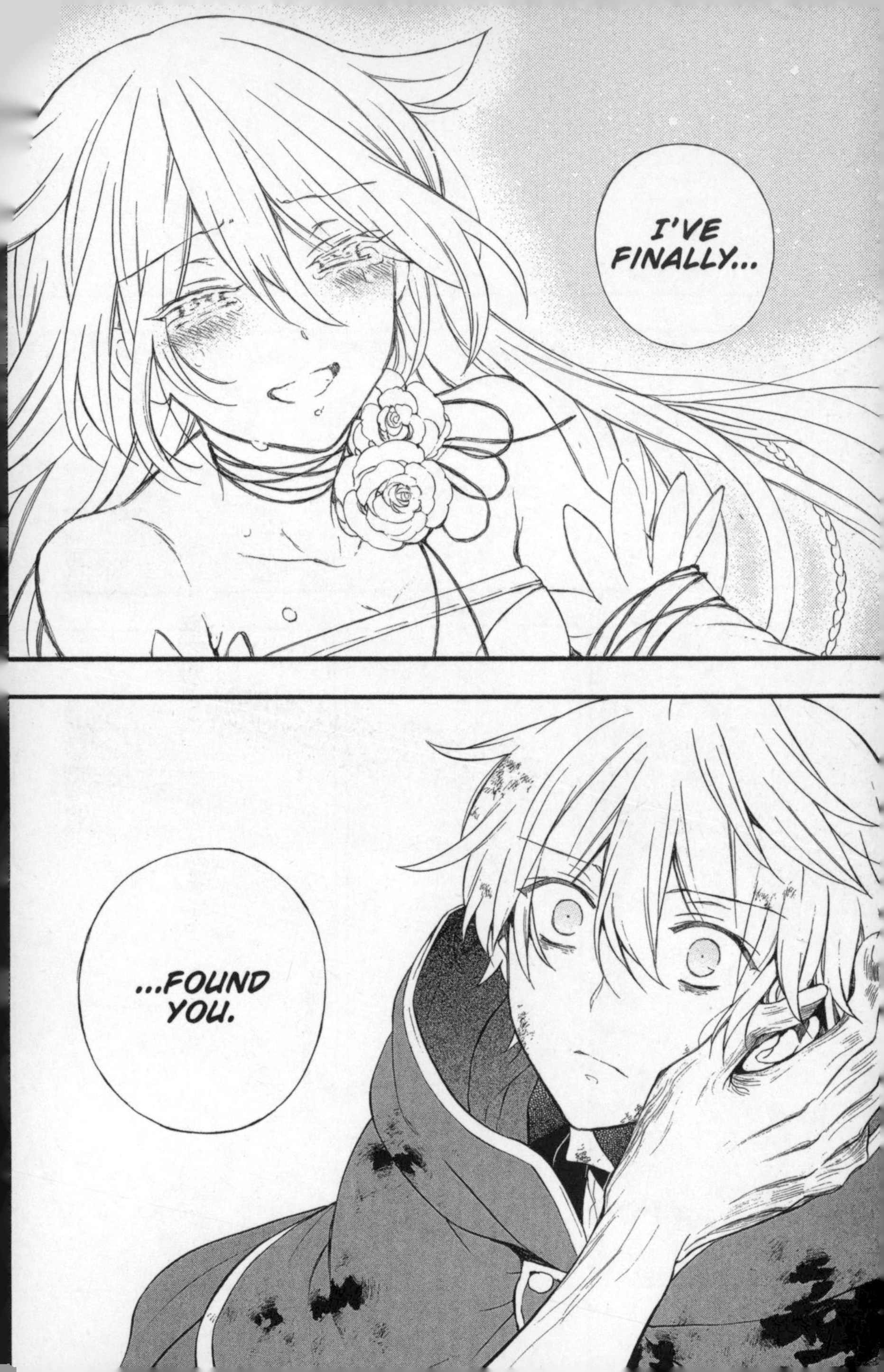
I'VE FINALLY...
...FOUND YOU.

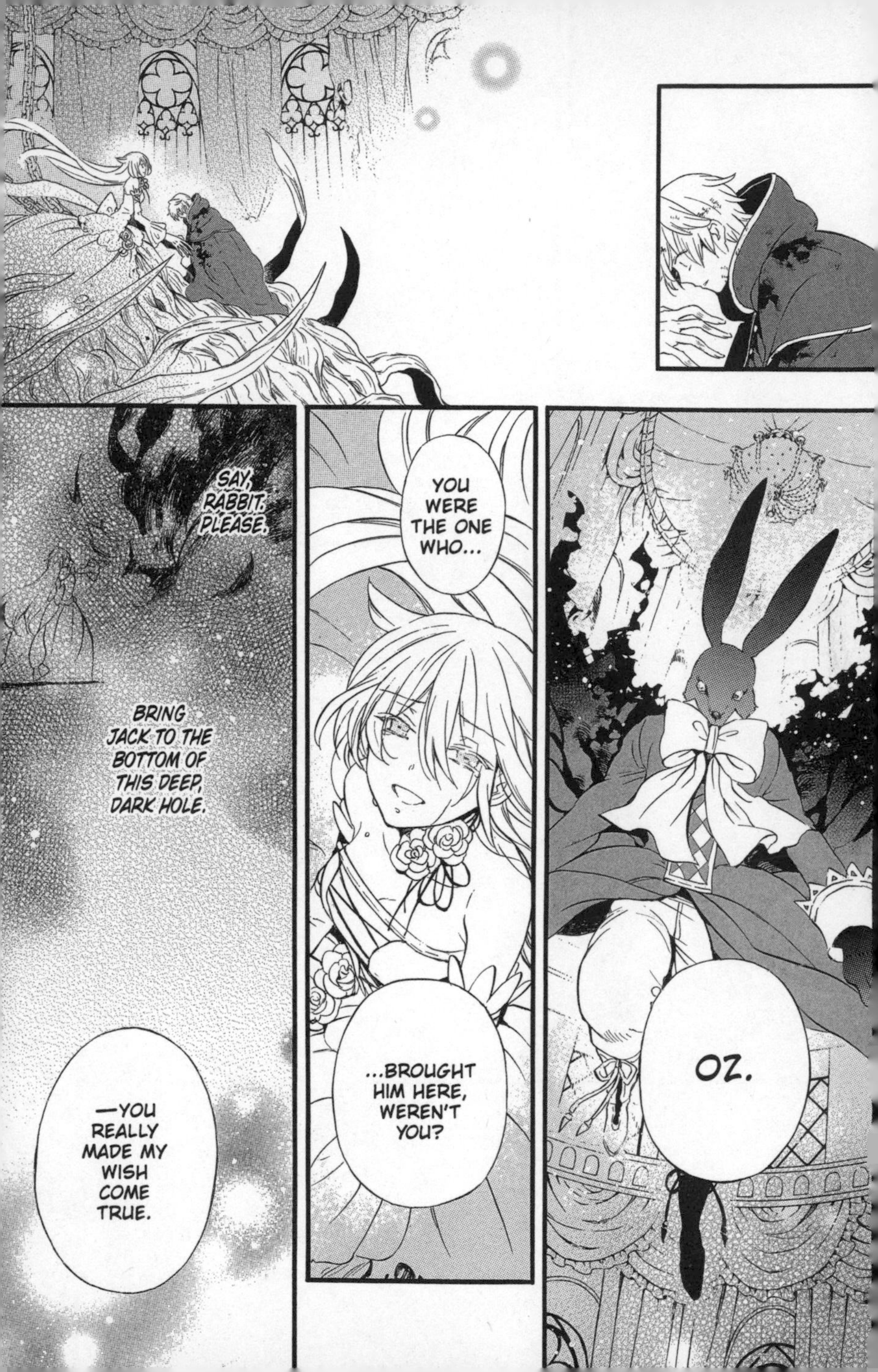
OZ.
YOU WERE THE ONE WHO...
...BROUGHT HIM HERE, WEREN'T YOU?
SAY, RABBIT. PLEASE.
BRING JACK TO THE BOTTOM OF THIS DEEP, DARK HOLE.
—YOU REALLY MADE MY WISH COME TRUE.

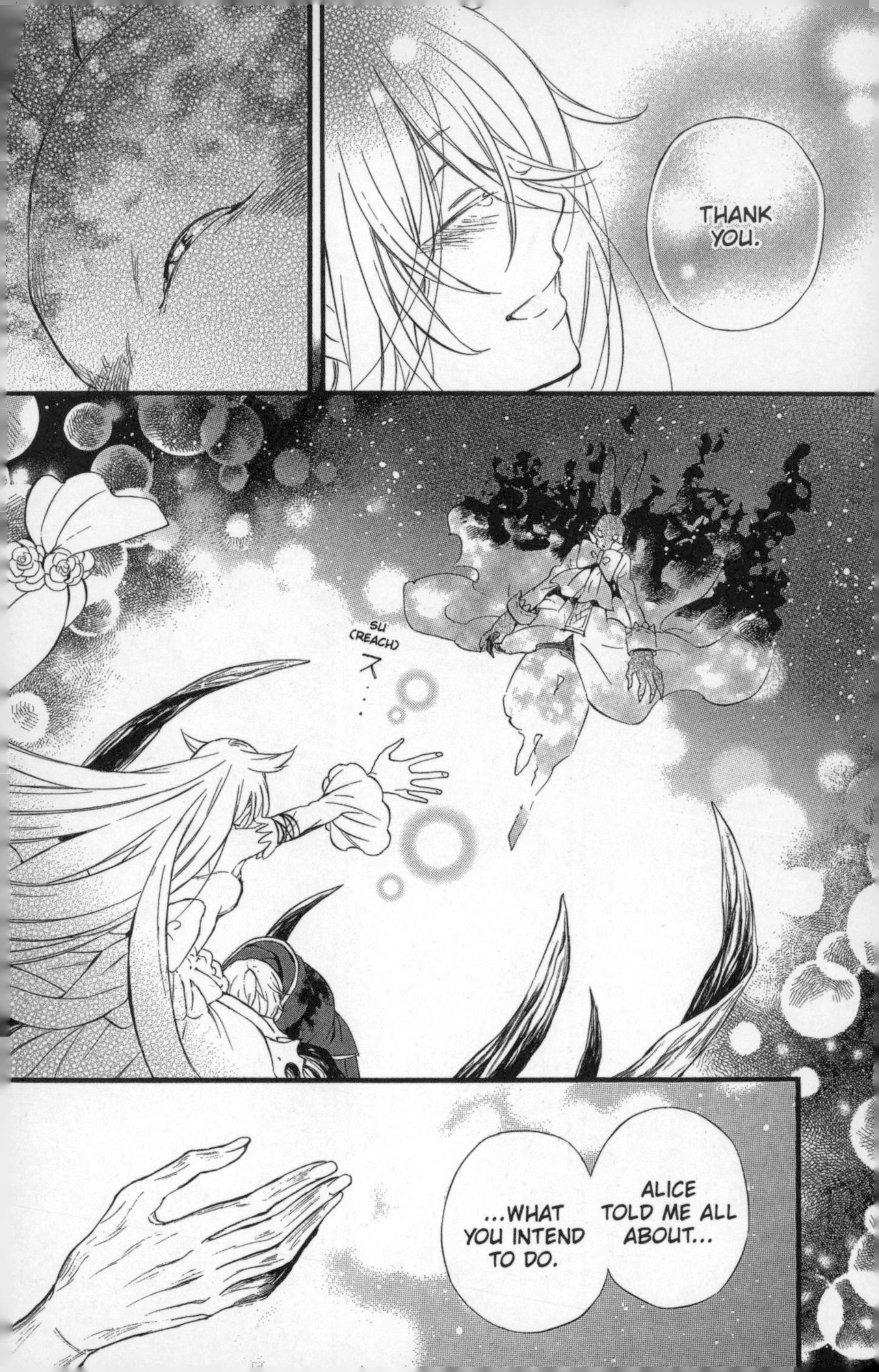
THANK YOU.
SU (REACH) ス...
ALICE TOLD ME ALL ABOUT...
...WHAT YOU INTEND TO DO.

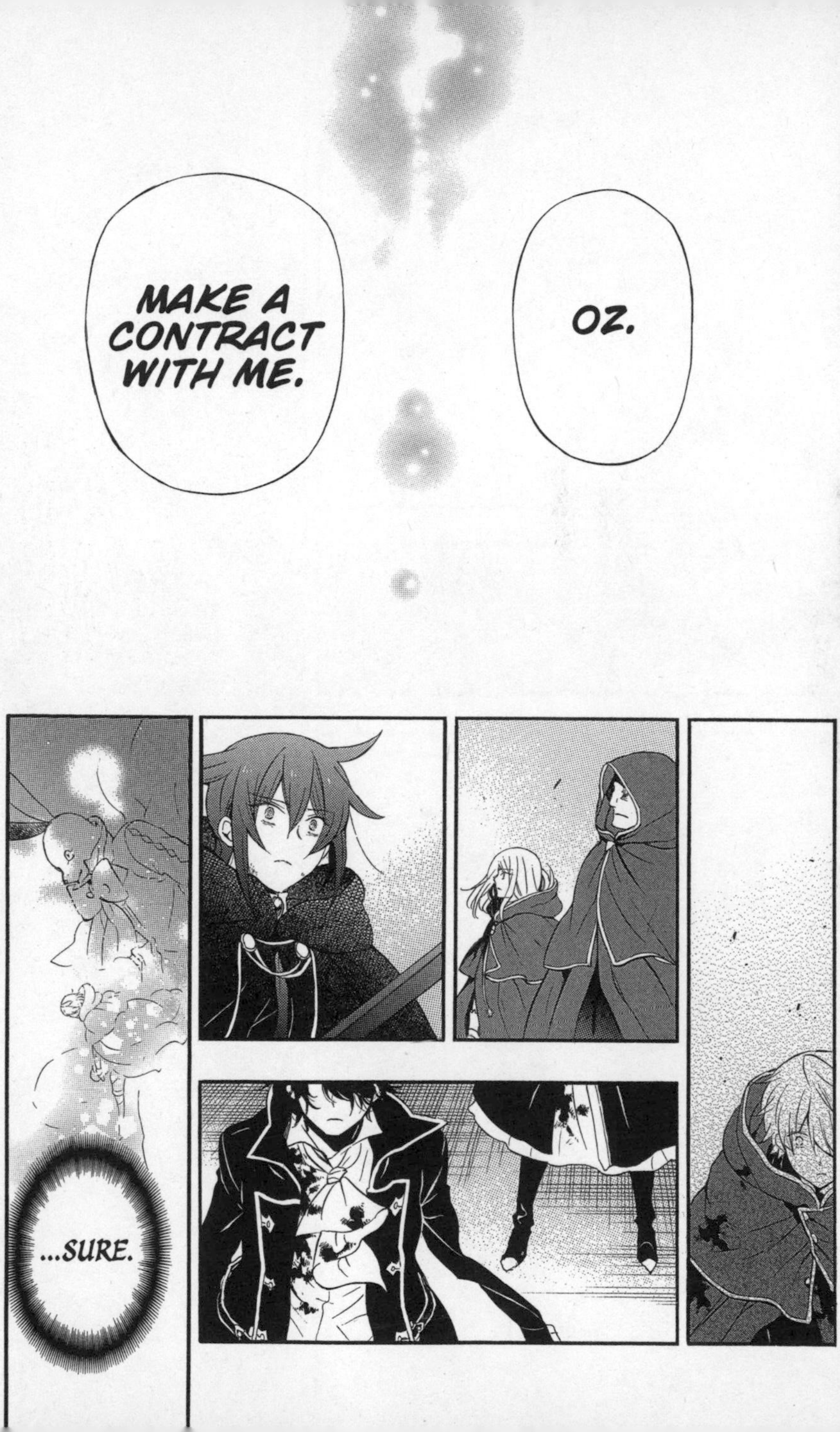
OZ.
MAKE A CONTRACT WITH ME.
...SURE.

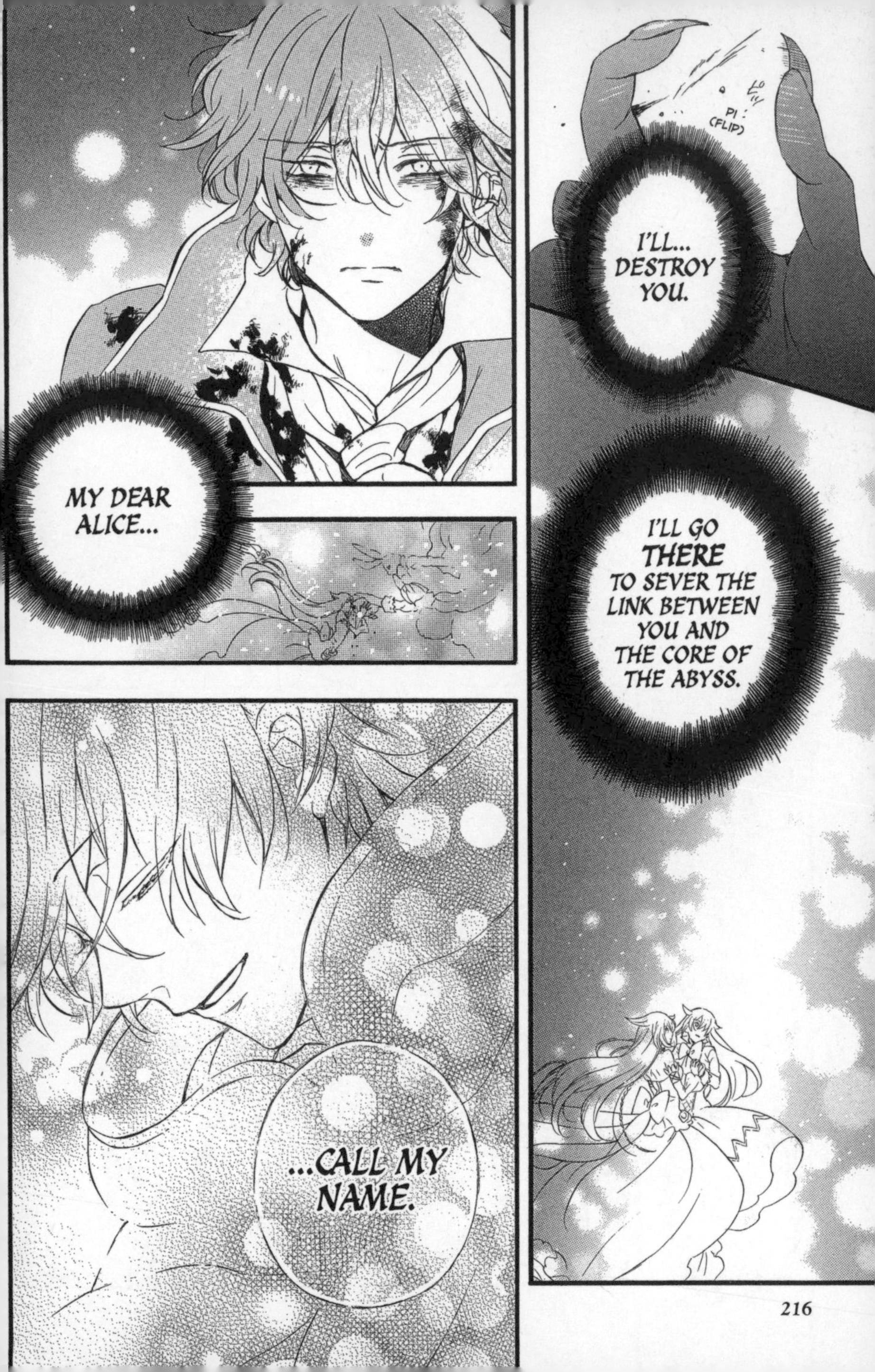
PI
(FLIP)
I'LL... DESTROY YOU.
I'LL GO THERE TO SEVER THE LINK BETWEEN YOU AND THE CORE OF THE ABYSS.
MY DEAR ALICE...
...CALL MY NAME.

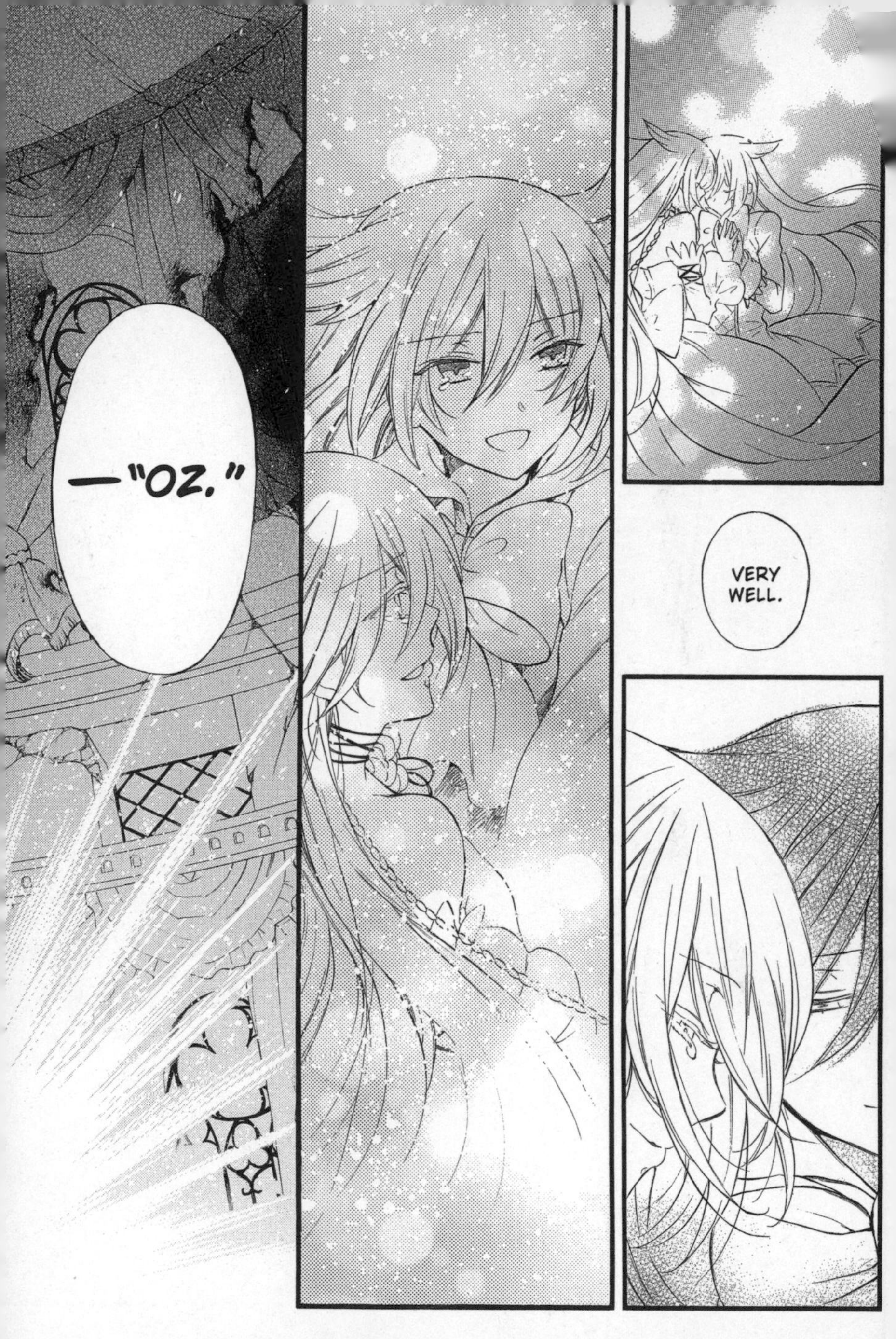
VERY WELL.
—"OZ."

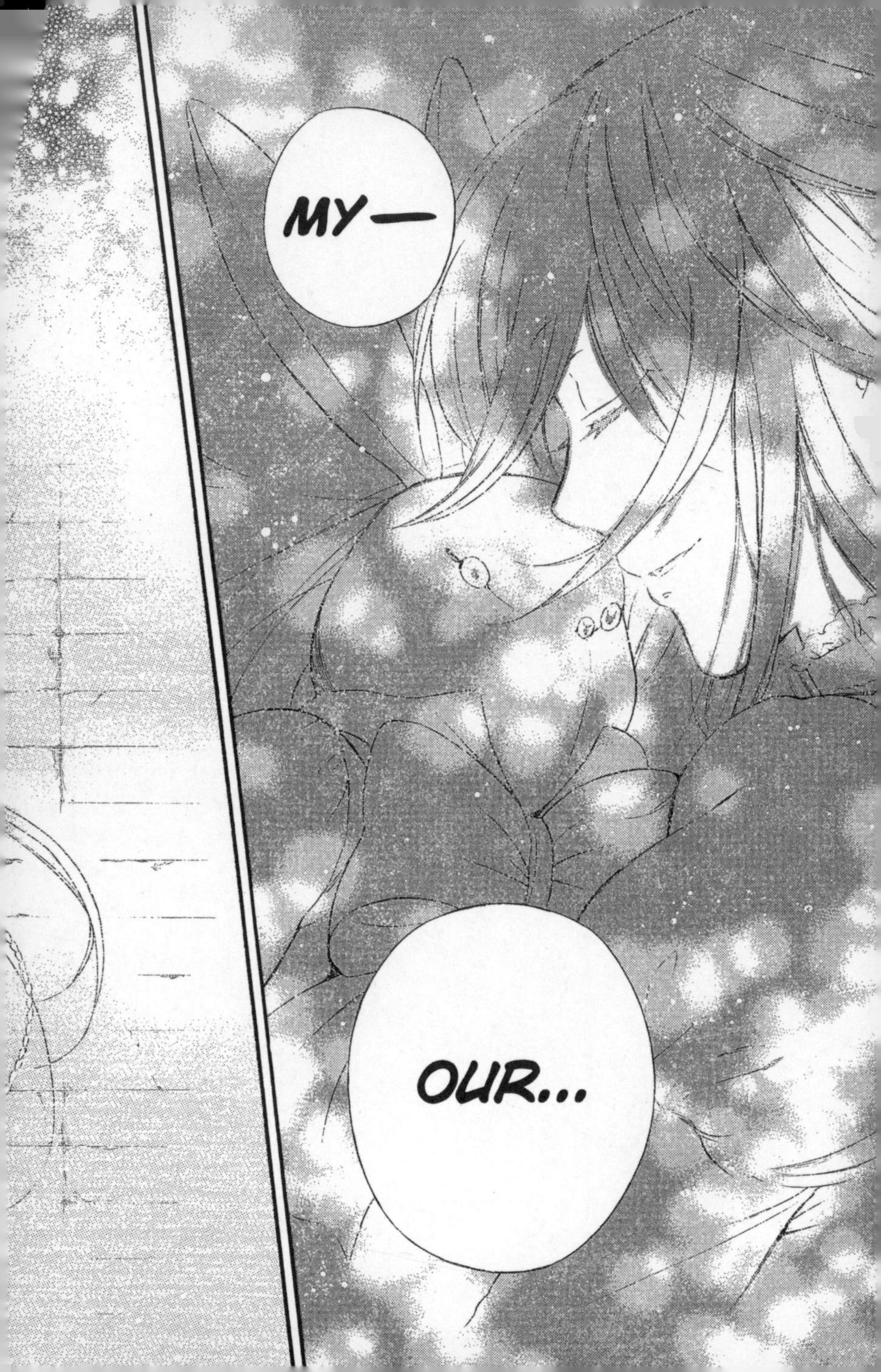
MY—
OUR...

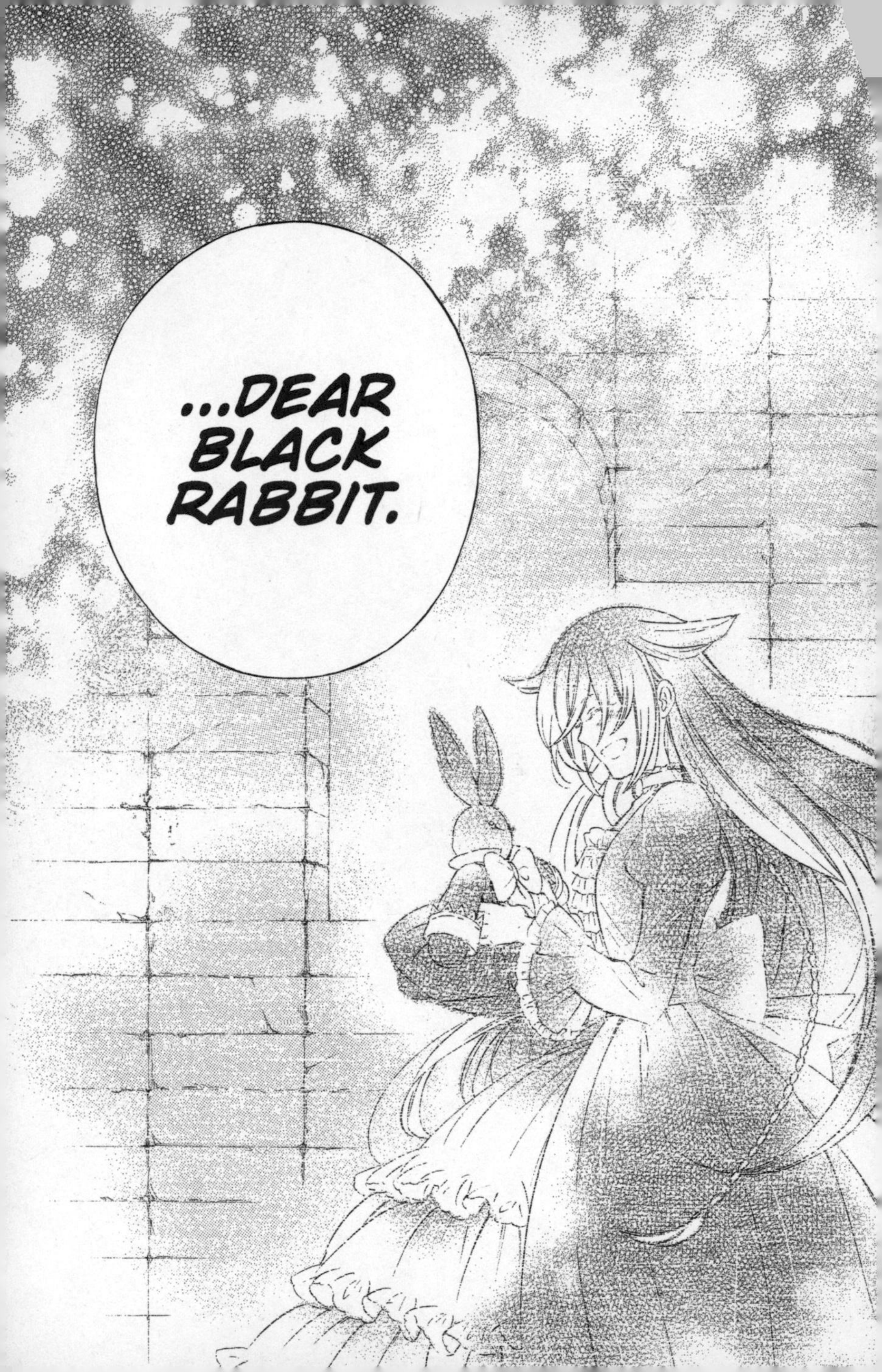
...DEAR BLACK RABBIT.

Retrace:CIII Call your name

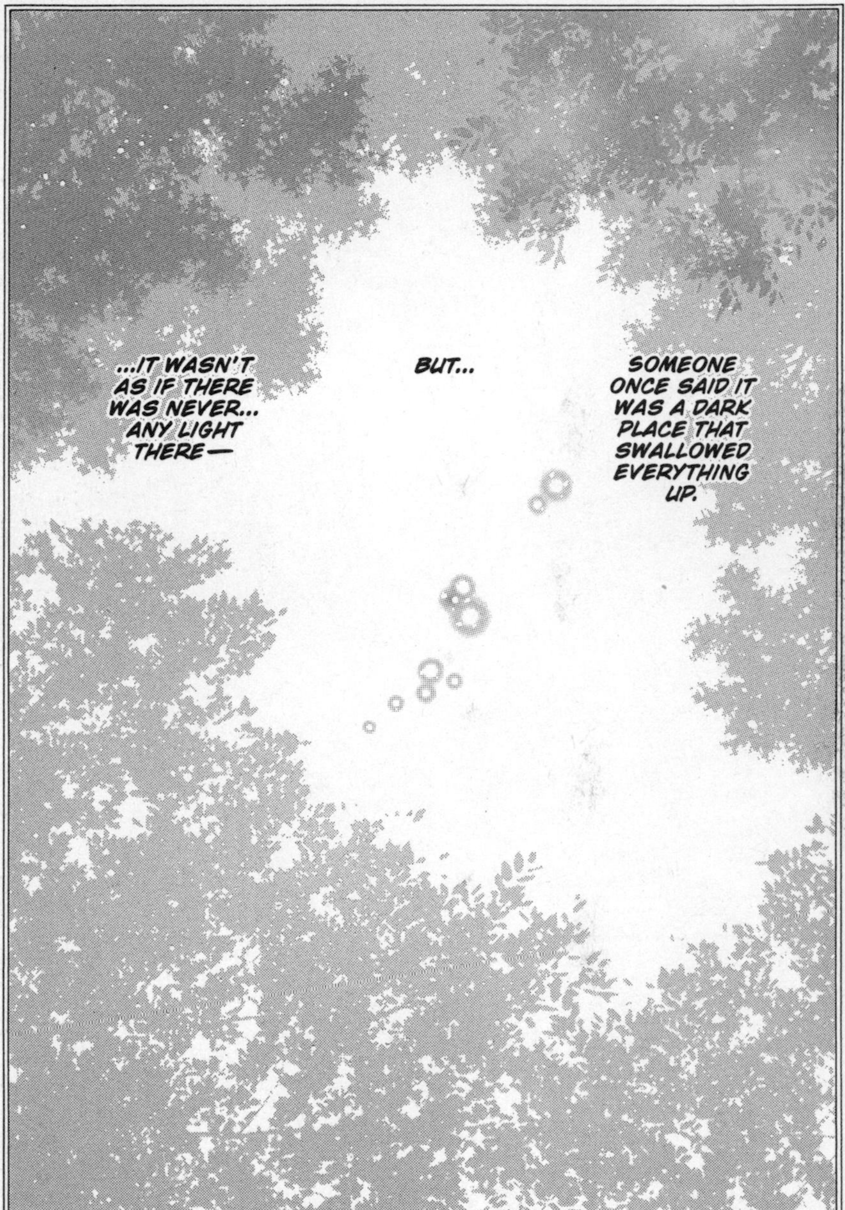
SOMEONE ONCE SAID IT WAS A DARK PLACE THAT SWALLOWED EVERYTHING UP.
BUT...
...IT WASN'T AS IF THERE WAS NEVER... ANY LIGHT THERE—

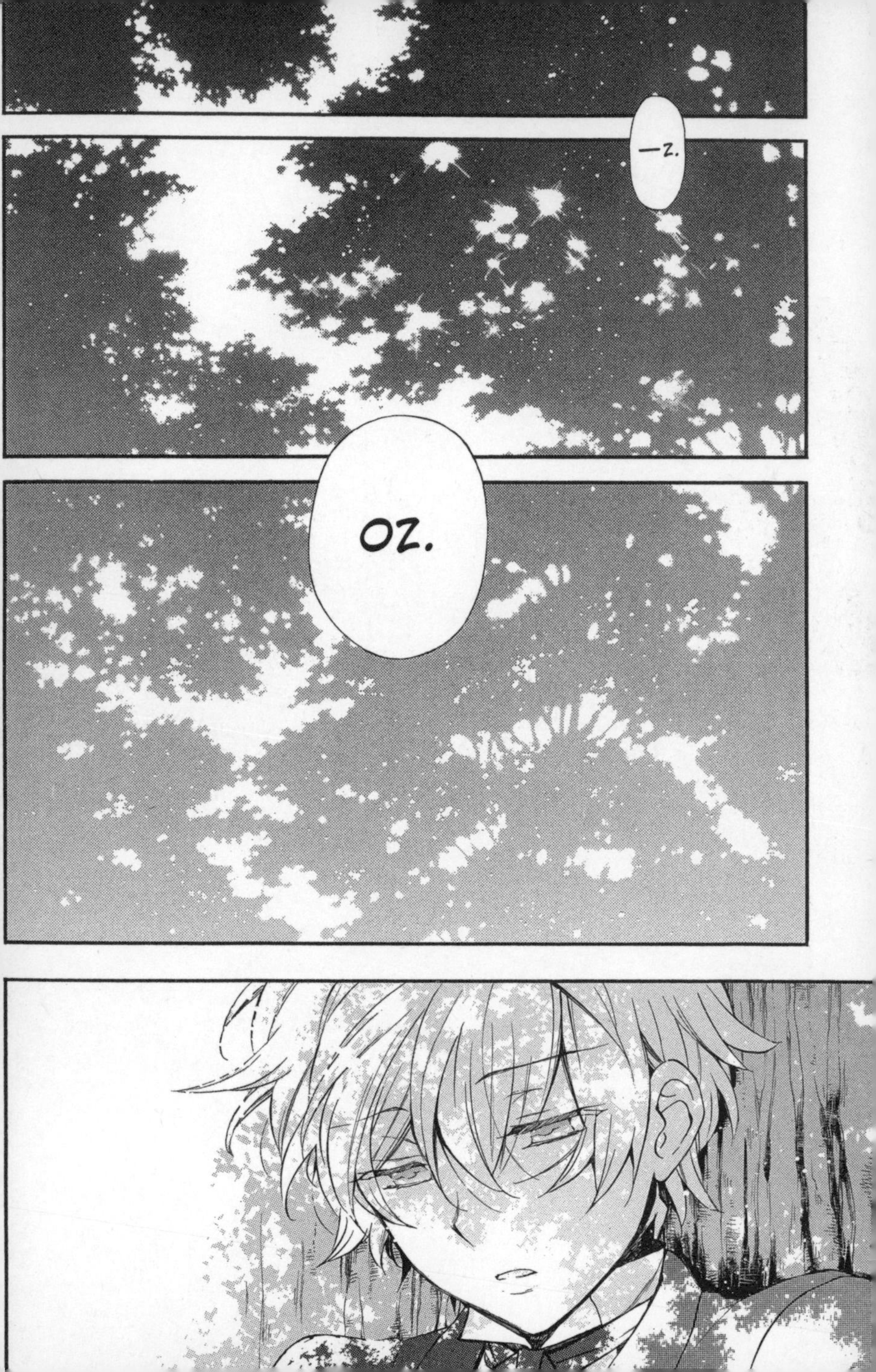
—Z.
OZ.

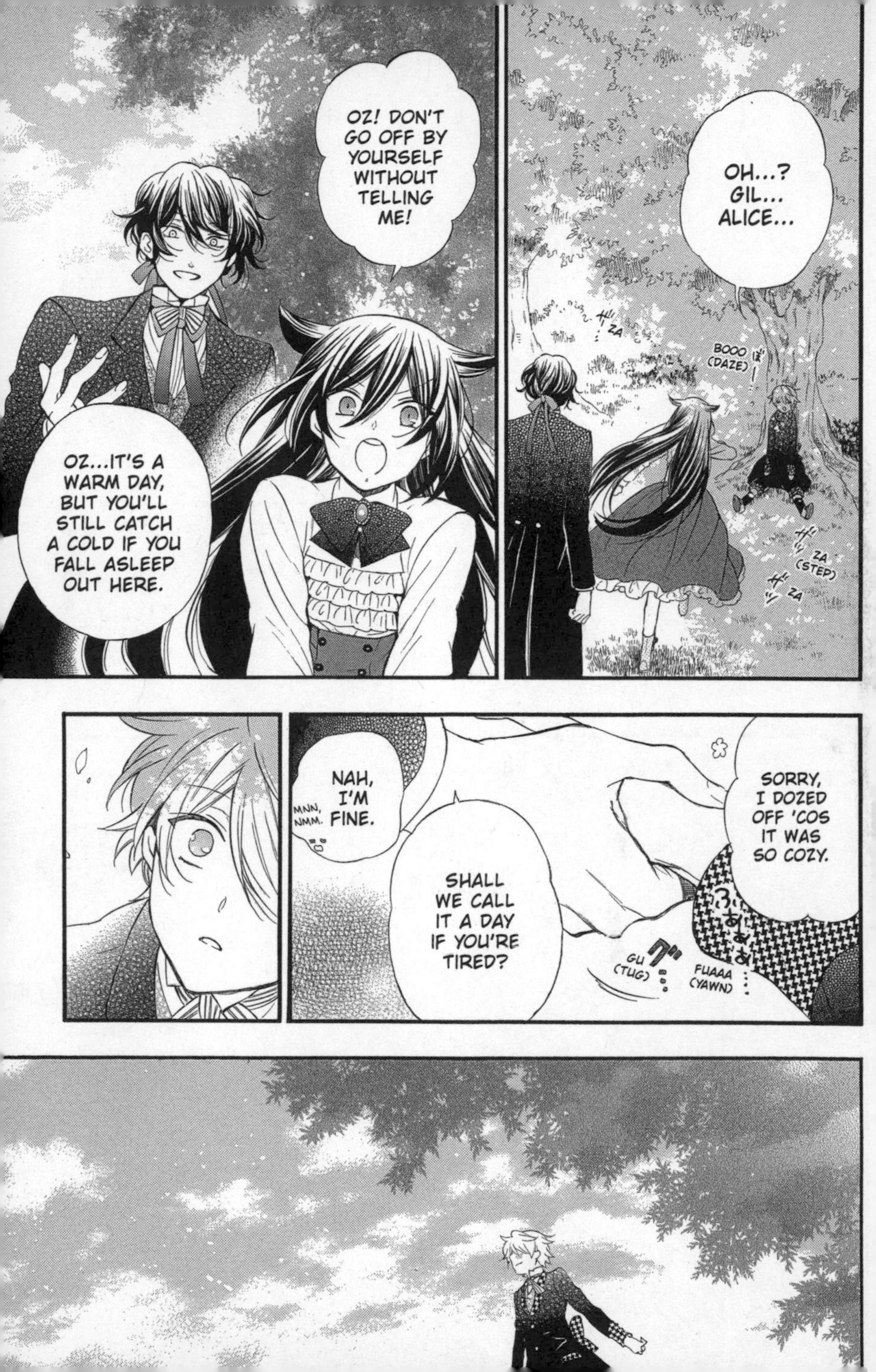
OH...? GIL... ALICE...
ZA
BOOO (DAZE)
ZA (STEP)
ZA
OZ! DON'T GO OFF BY YOURSELF WITHOUT TELLING ME!
OZ...IT'S A WARM DAY, BUT YOU'LL STILL CATCH A COLD IF YOU FALL ASLEEP OUT HERE.
SORRY, I DOZED OFF 'COS IT WAS SO COZY.
FUAAA (YAWN)
GU (TUG)
SHALL WE CALL IT A DAY IF YOU'RE TIRED?
NAH, I'M FINE.
MNN, NMM.

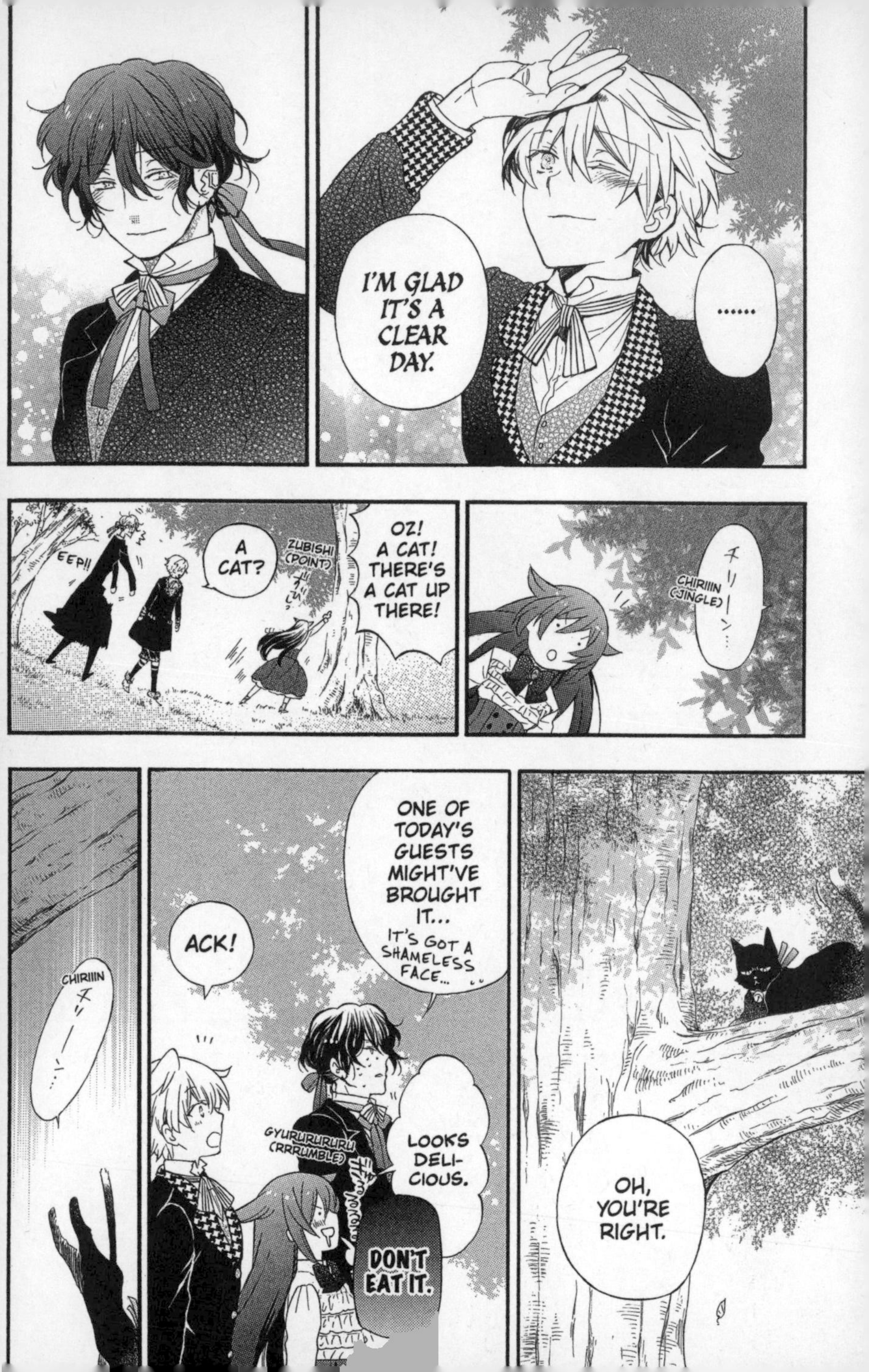
......
I'M GLAD IT'S A CLEAR DAY.
チリーン…
CHIRIIIN (JINGLE)
OZ! A CAT! THERE'S A CAT UP THERE!
ZUBISHI (POINT)
A CAT?
EEP!!
OH, YOU'RE RIGHT.
ONE OF TODAY'S GUESTS MIGHT'VE BROUGHT IT...
IT'S GOT A SHAMELESS FACE...
ACK!
LOOKS DELI-CIOUS.
GYURURURURU (RRRUMBLE)
DON'T EAT IT.
CHIRIIIN

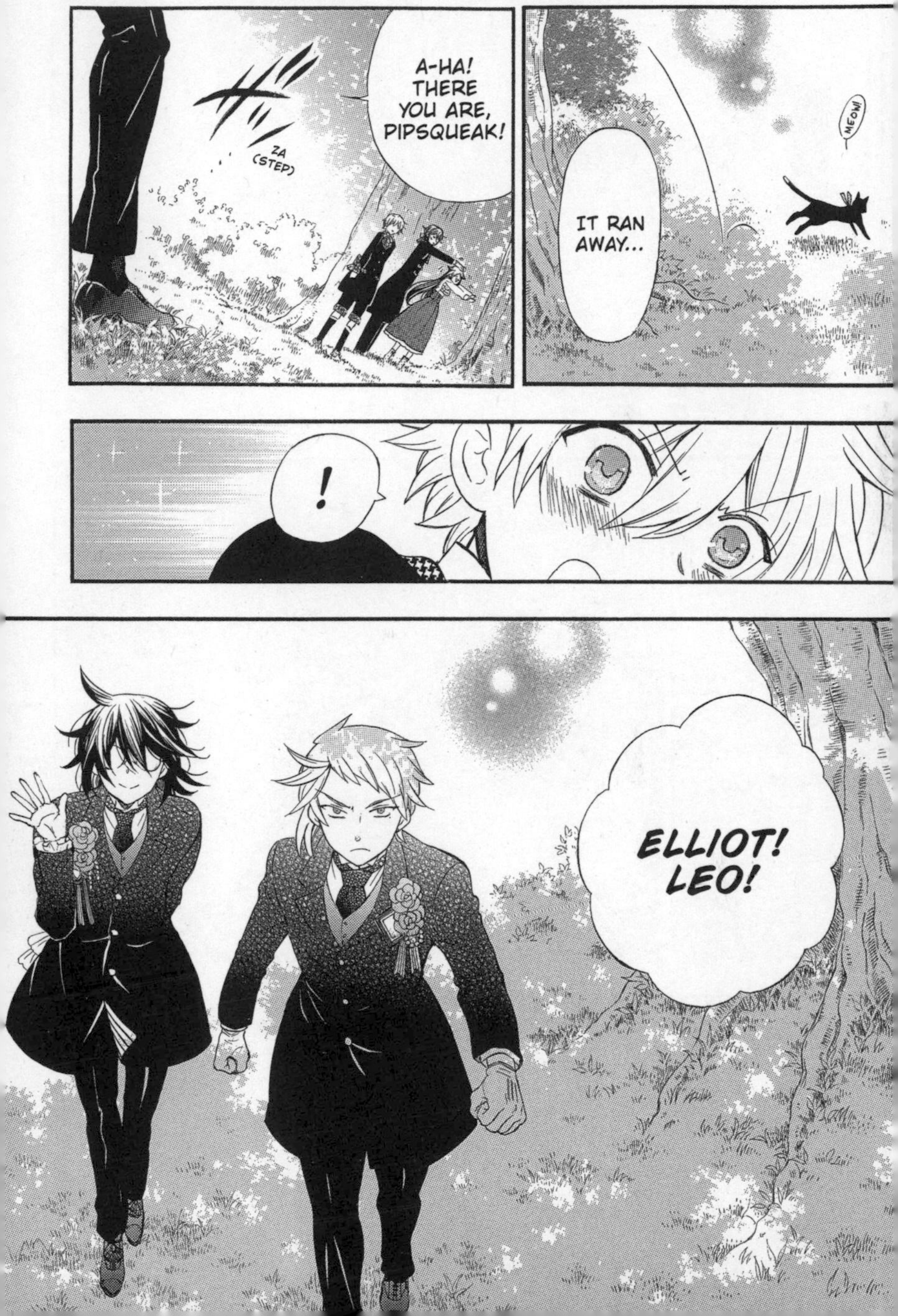
MEOW!
IT RAN AWAY...
A-HA! THERE YOU ARE, PIPSQUEAK!
ZA (STEP)
!
ELLIOT! LEO!

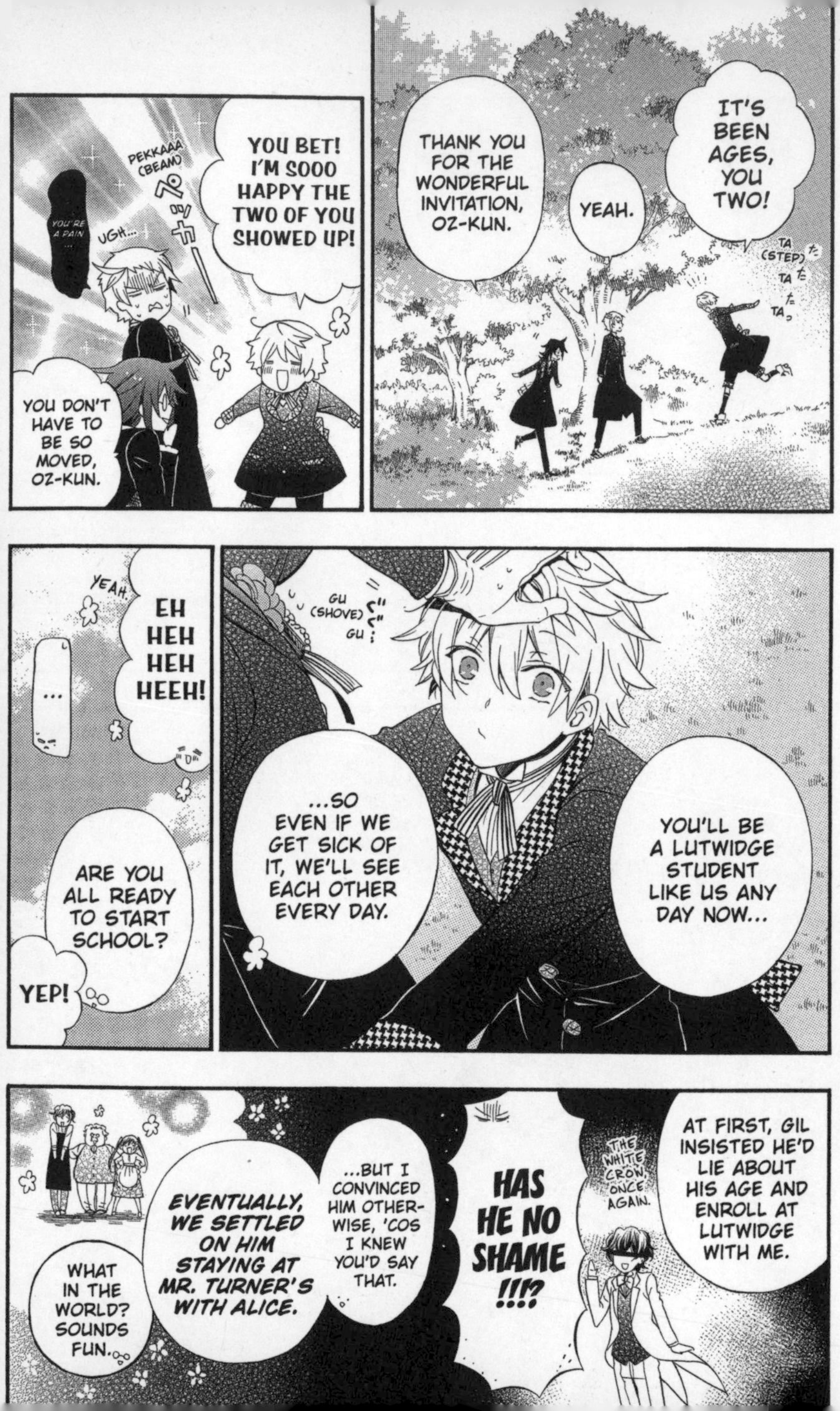
IT'S BEEN AGES, YOU TWO!
TA (STEP) TA TA TA
YEAH.
THANK YOU FOR THE WONDERFUL INVITATION, OZ-KUN.
YOU BET! I'M SOOO HAPPY THE TWO OF YOU SHOWED UP!
PEKKAAA (BEAM)
UGH...
YOU'RE A PAIN ...
YOU DON'T HAVE TO BE SO MOVED, OZ-KUN.
YOU'LL BE A LUTWIDGE STUDENT LIKE US ANY DAY NOW...
GU (SHOVE) GU
...SO EVEN IF WE GET SICK OF IT, WE'LL SEE EACH OTHER EVERY DAY.
EH HEH HEH HEEH!
YEAH.
...
ARE YOU ALL READY TO START SCHOOL?
YEP!
AT FIRST, GIL INSISTED HE'D LIE ABOUT HIS AGE AND ENROLL AT LUTWIDGE WITH ME.
THE WHITE CROW, ONCE AGAIN.
HAS HE NO SHAME!!!?
...BUT I CONVINCED HIM OTHER-WISE, 'COS I KNEW YOU'D SAY THAT.
EVENTUALLY, WE SETTLED ON HIM STAYING AT MR. TURNER'S WITH ALICE.
WHAT IN THE WORLD? SOUNDS FUN.

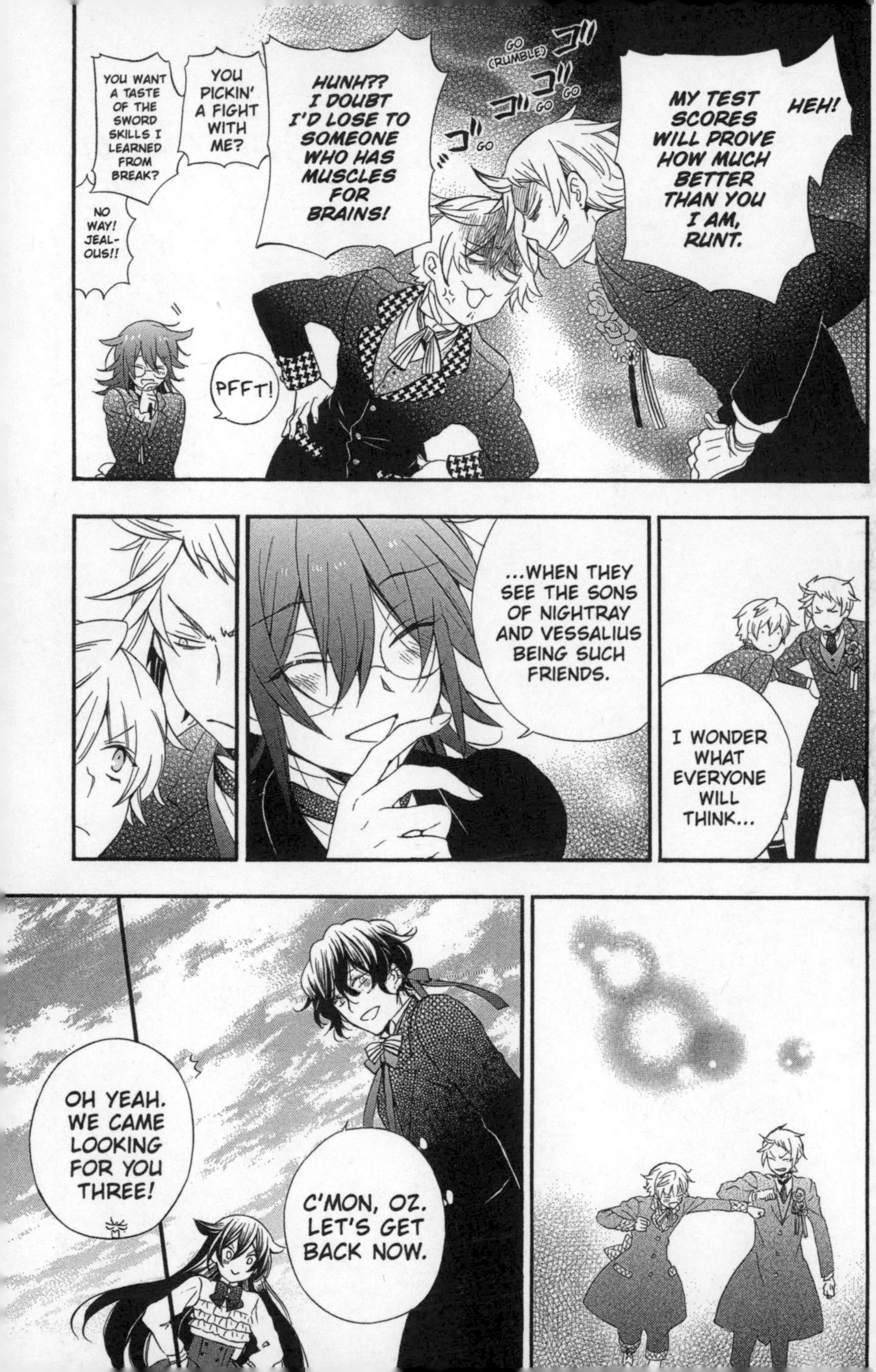
HEH!
MY TEST SCORES WILL PROVE HOW MUCH BETTER THAN YOU I AM, RUNT.
GO (RUMBLE)
GO GO GO
HUNH?? I DOUBT I'D LOSE TO SOMEONE WHO HAS MUSCLES FOR BRAINS!
YOU PICKIN' A FIGHT WITH ME?
YOU WANT A TASTE OF THE SWORD SKILLS I LEARNED FROM BREAK?
NO WAY! JEAL-OUS!!
PFFT!
I WONDER WHAT EVERYONE WILL THINK...
...WHEN THEY SEE THE SONS OF NIGHTRAY AND VESSALIUS BEING SUCH FRIENDS.
C'MON, OZ. LET'S GET BACK NOW.
OH YEAH. WE CAME LOOKING FOR YOU THREE!

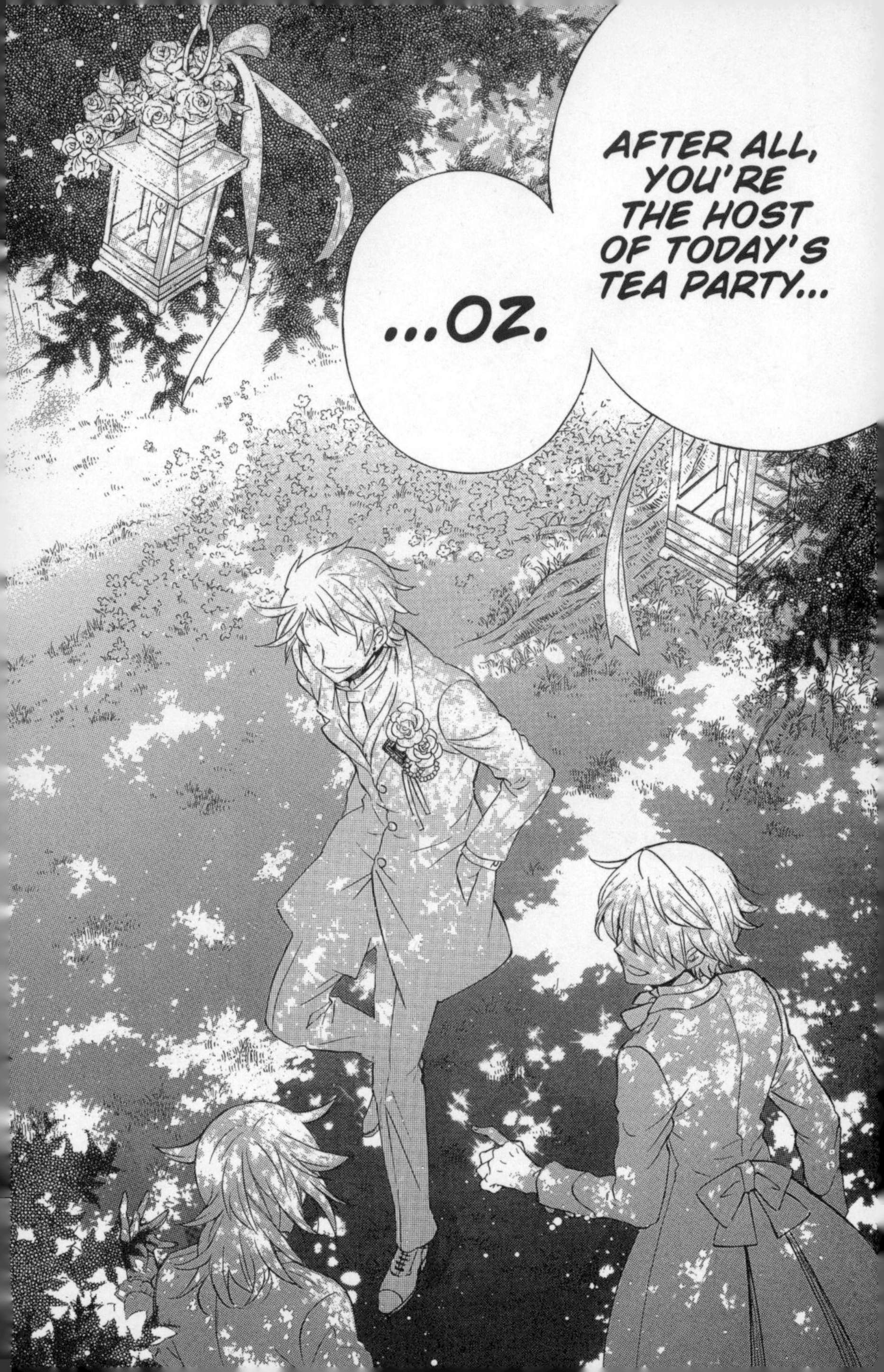
AFTER ALL, YOU'RE THE HOST OF TODAY'S TEA PARTY...
...OZ.

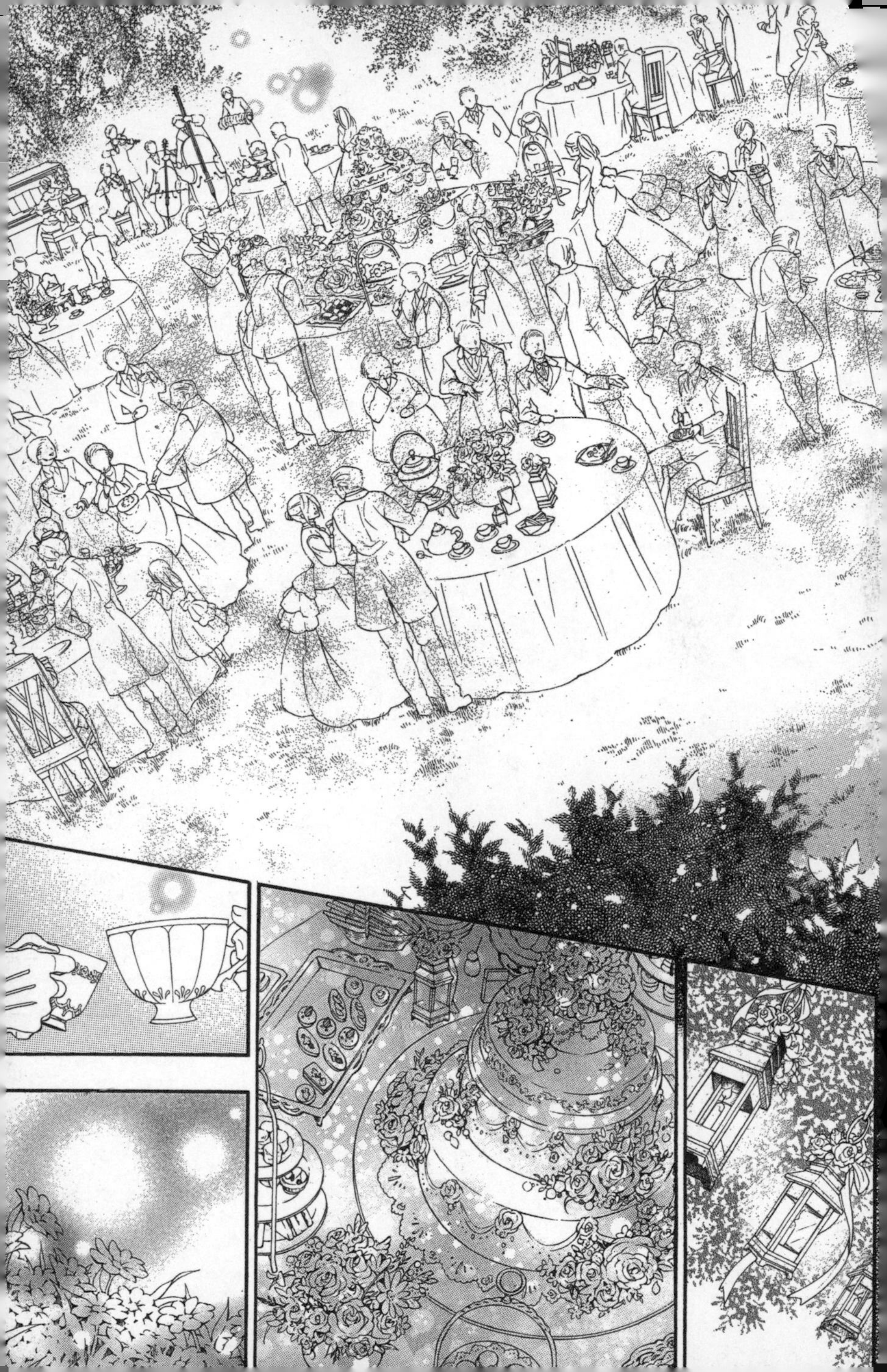

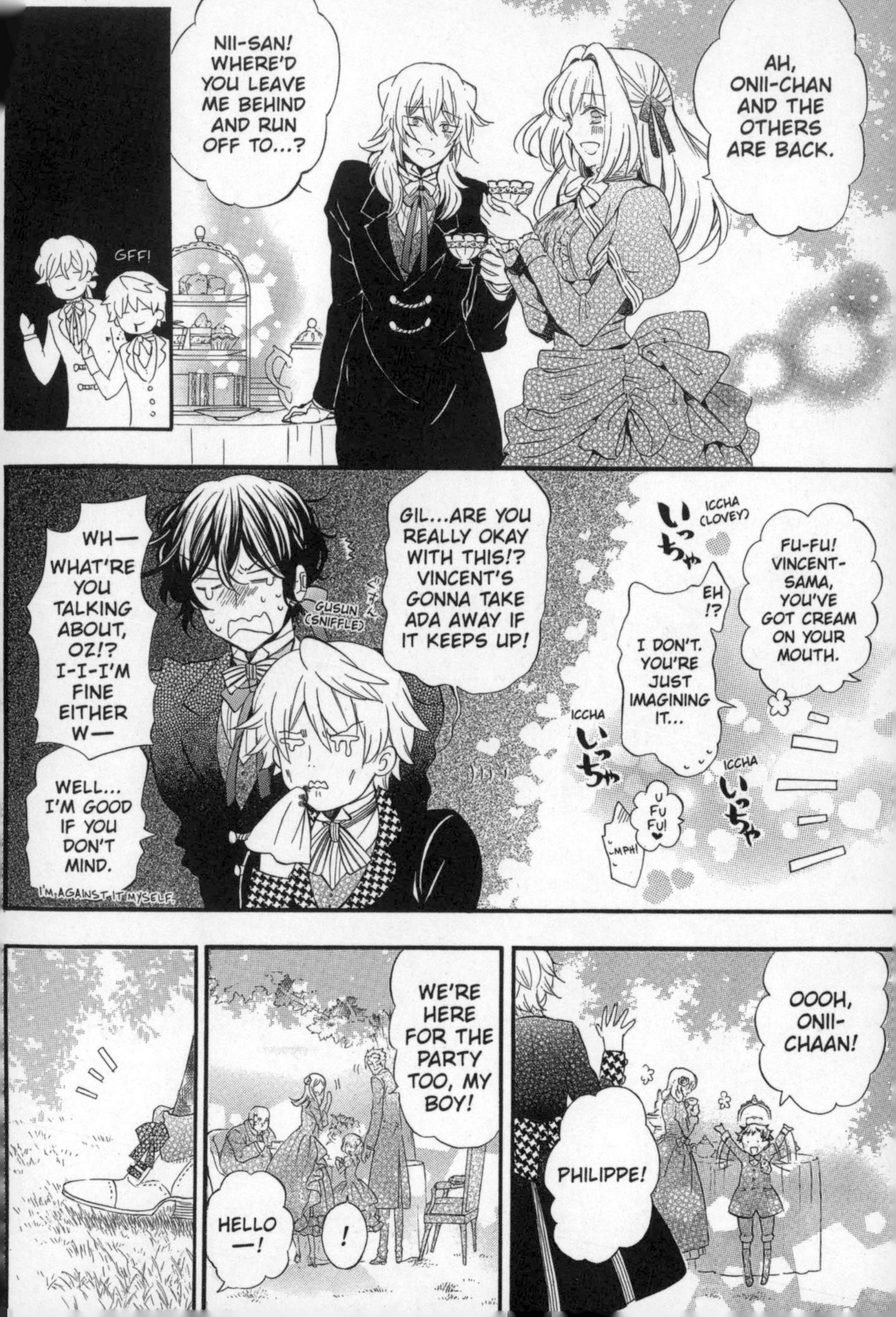
AH, ONII-CHAN AND THE OTHERS ARE BACK.
NII-SAN! WHERE'D YOU LEAVE ME BEHIND AND RUN OFF TO...?
GFF!
ICCHA (LOVEY)
いっちゃ
FU-FU! VINCENT-SAMA, YOU'VE GOT CREAM ON YOUR MOUTH.
EH!?
I DON'T. YOU'RE JUST IMAGINING IT...
ICCHA
いっちゃ
ICCHA
いっちゃ
U FU FU!
MPH!
GIL...ARE YOU REALLY OKAY WITH THIS!? VINCENT'S GONNA TAKE ADA AWAY IF IT KEEPS UP!
ぐすん
GUSUN (SNIFFLE)
WH— WHAT'RE YOU TALKING ABOUT, OZ!? I-I-I'M FINE EITHER W—
WELL... I'M GOOD IF YOU DON'T MIND.
I'M AGAINST IT MYSELF.
OOOH, ONII-CHAAN!
PHILIPPE!
WE'RE HERE FOR THE PARTY TOO, MY BOY!
!
HELLO—!

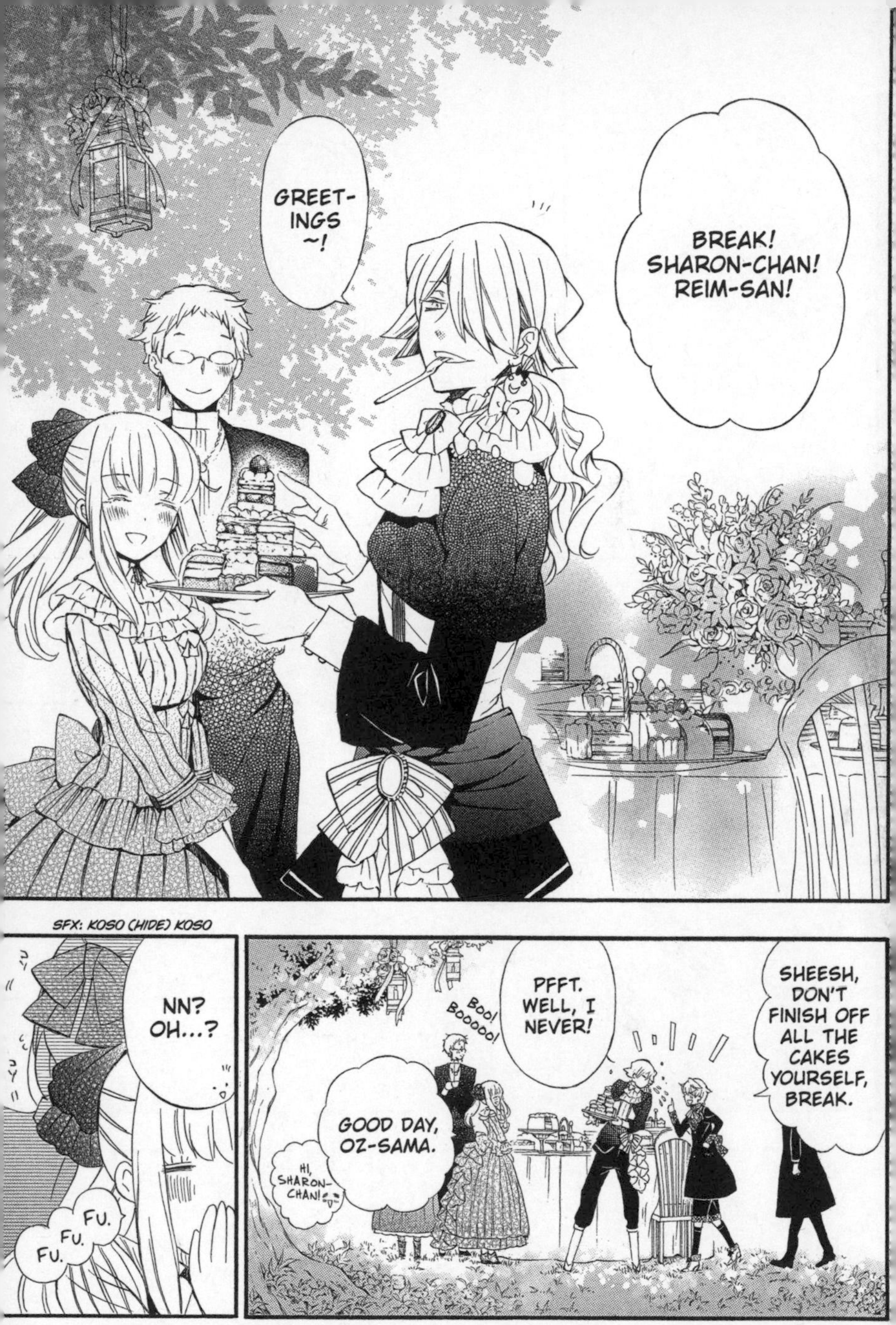
BREAK! SHARON-CHAN! REIM-SAN!
GREET-INGS ~!
SFX: KOSO (HIDE) KOSO
SHEESH, DON'T FINISH OFF ALL THE CAKES YOURSELF, BREAK.
PFFT. WELL, I NEVER!
BOO! BOOOOO!
GOOD DAY, OZ-SAMA.
HI, SHARON-CHAN!
NN? OH...?
FU. FU. FU.

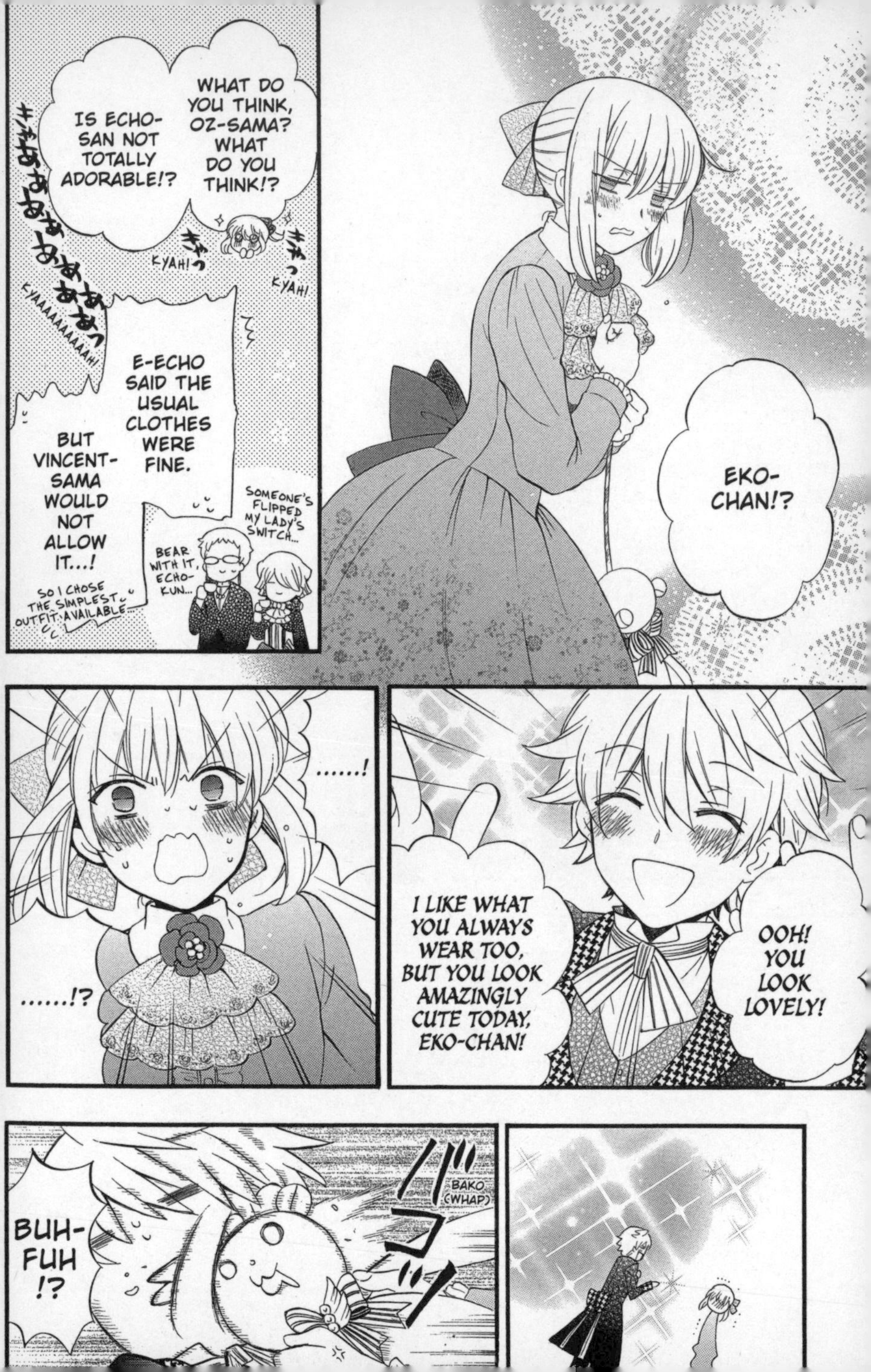
EKO-CHAN!?
WHAT DO YOU THINK, OZ-SAMA? WHAT DO YOU THINK!?
IS ECHO-SAN NOT TOTALLY ADORABLE!?
KYAH!
KYAH!
KYAAAAAAAAAAH!
E-ECHO SAID THE USUAL CLOTHES WERE FINE.
BUT VINCENT-SAMA WOULD NOT ALLOW IT...!
SOMEONE'S FLIPPED MY LADY'S SWITCH...
BEAR WITH IT, ECHO-KUN...
SO I CHOSE THE SIMPLEST OUTFIT AVAILABLE...
OOH! YOU LOOK LOVELY!
I LIKE WHAT YOU ALWAYS WEAR TOO, BUT YOU LOOK AMAZINGLY CUTE TODAY, EKO-CHAN!
......!
......!?
BAKO (WHAP)
BUH-FUH!?

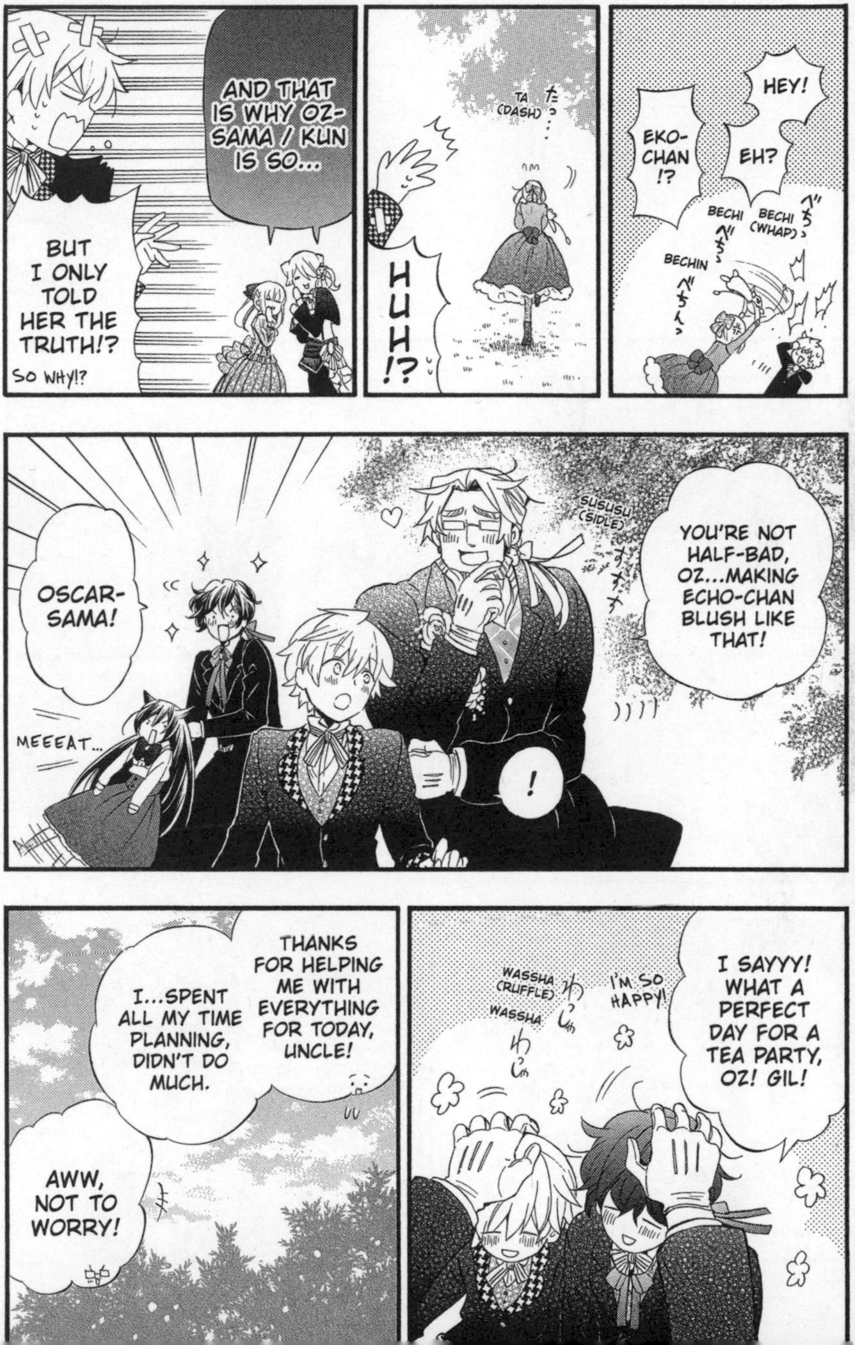
HEY!
EH?
EKO-CHAN!?
BECHI (WHAP)
BECHI
BECHIN
TA (DASH)
HUH!?
AND THAT IS WHY OZ-SAMA / KUN IS SO...
BUT I ONLY TOLD HER THE TRUTH!?
SO WHY!?
YOU'RE NOT HALF-BAD, OZ...MAKING ECHO-CHAN BLUSH LIKE THAT!
SUSUSU (SIDLE)
!
OSCAR-SAMA!
MEEEAT...
I SAYYY! WHAT A PERFECT DAY FOR A TEA PARTY, OZ! GIL!
I'M SO HAPPY!
WASSHA (RUFFLE)
WASSHA
THANKS FOR HELPING ME WITH EVERYTHING FOR TODAY, UNCLE!
I...SPENT ALL MY TIME PLANNING, DIDN'T DO MUCH.
AWW, NOT TO WORRY!

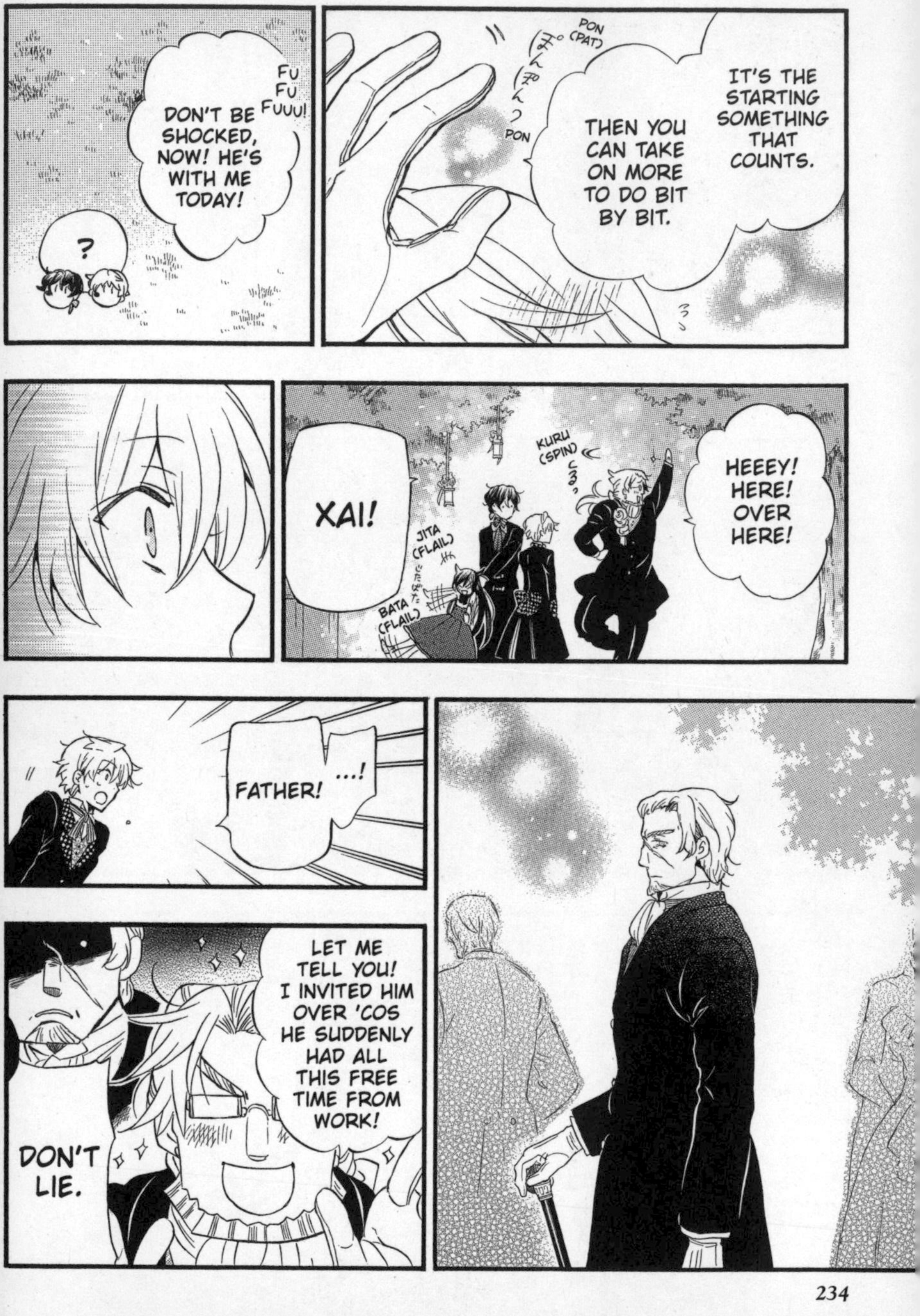
IT'S THE STARTING SOMETHING THAT COUNTS.
PON (PAT)
THEN YOU CAN TAKE ON MORE TO DO BIT BY BIT.
PON
FU FU FUUU!
DON'T BE SHOCKED, NOW! HE'S WITH ME TODAY!
?
HEEEY! HERE! OVER HERE!
KURU (SPIN)
XAI!
JITA (FLAIL)
BATA (FLAIL)
...!
FATHER!
LET ME TELL YOU! I INVITED HIM OVER 'COS HE SUDDENLY HAD ALL THIS FREE TIME FROM WORK!
DON'T LIE.

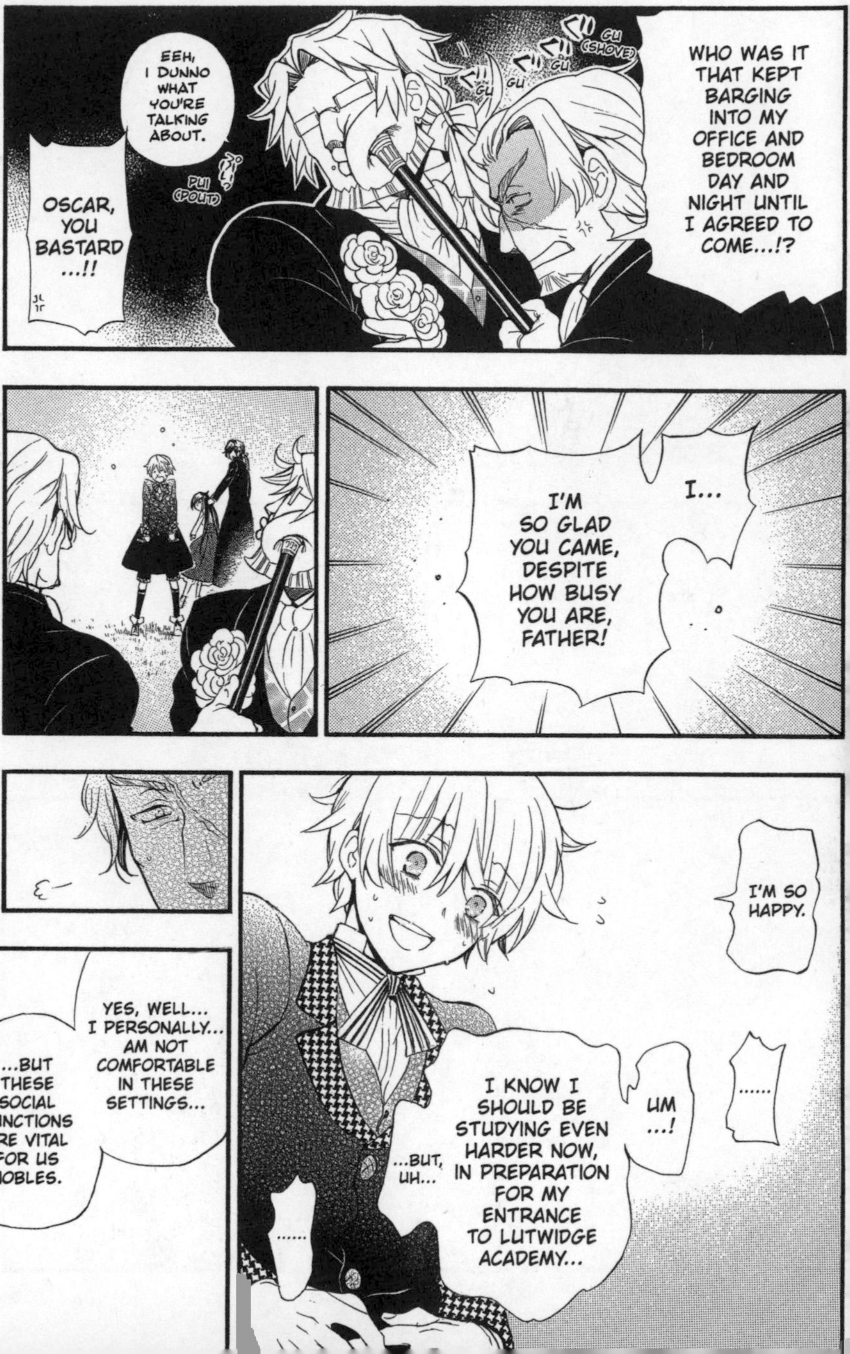
WHO WAS IT THAT KEPT BARGING INTO MY OFFICE AND BEDROOM DAY AND NIGHT UNTIL I AGREED TO COME...!?
GU (SHOVE)
GU
GU
EEH, I DUNNO WHAT YOU'RE TALKING ABOUT.
PUI (POUT)
OSCAR, YOU BASTARD ...!!
I...
I'M SO GLAD YOU CAME, DESPITE HOW BUSY YOU ARE, FATHER!
I'M SO HAPPY.
......
UM ...!
I KNOW I SHOULD BE STUDYING EVEN HARDER NOW, IN PREPARATION FOR MY ENTRANCE TO LUTWIDGE ACADEMY...
...BUT, UH...
......
YES, WELL... I PERSONALLY... AM NOT COMFORTABLE IN THESE SETTINGS...
...BUT THESE SOCIAL FUNCTIONS ARE VITAL FOR US NOBLES.

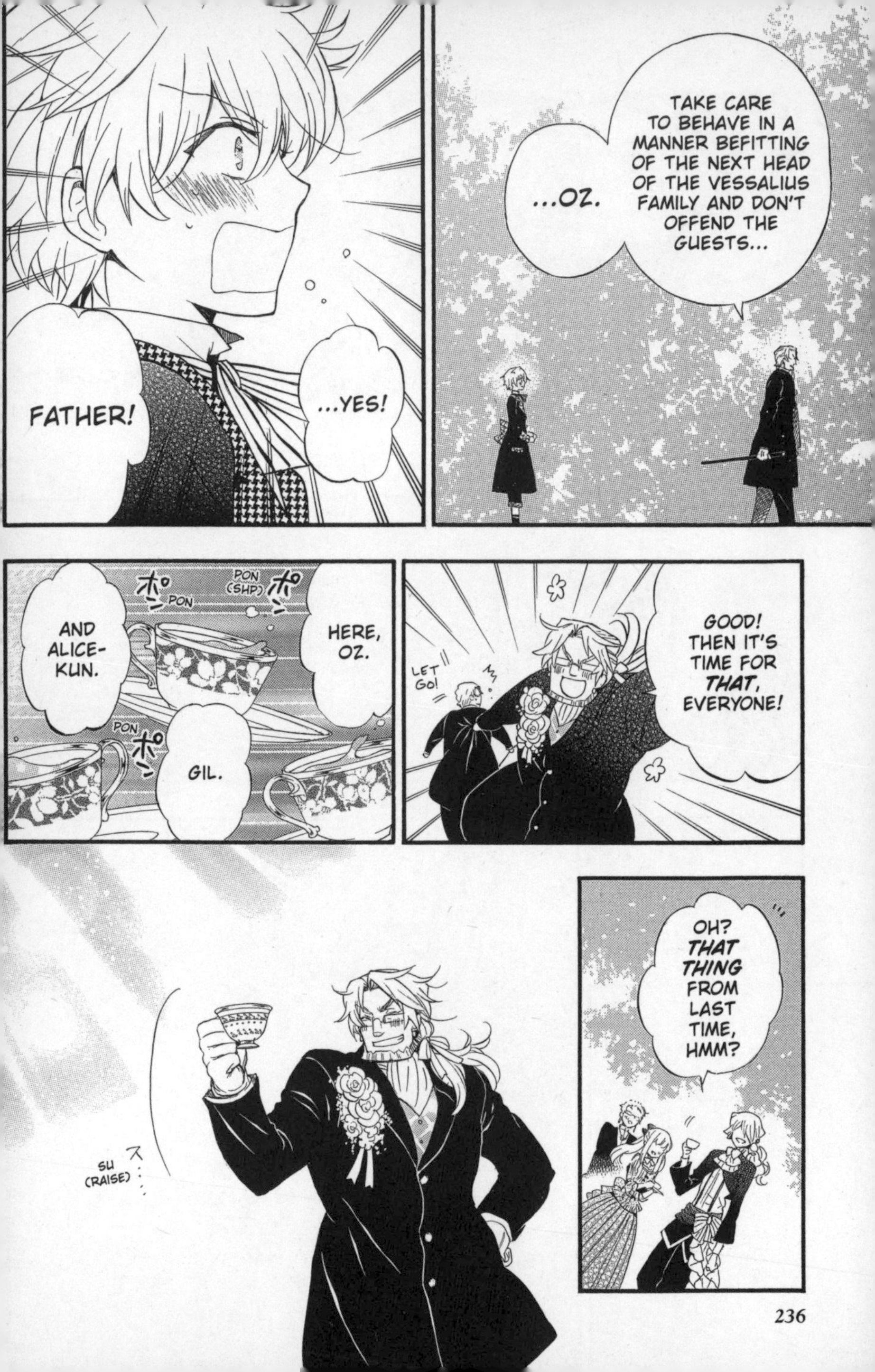
TAKE CARE TO BEHAVE IN A MANNER BEFITTING OF THE NEXT HEAD OF THE VESSALIUS FAMILY AND DON'T OFFEND THE GUESTS...
...OZ.
...YES!
FATHER!
GOOD! THEN IT'S TIME FOR *THAT*, EVERYONE!
LET GO!
ポン PON (SHP)
HERE, OZ.
ポン PON
AND ALICE-KUN.
ポン PON
GIL.
OH? *THAT THING* FROM LAST TIME, HMM?
ス SU (RAISE)

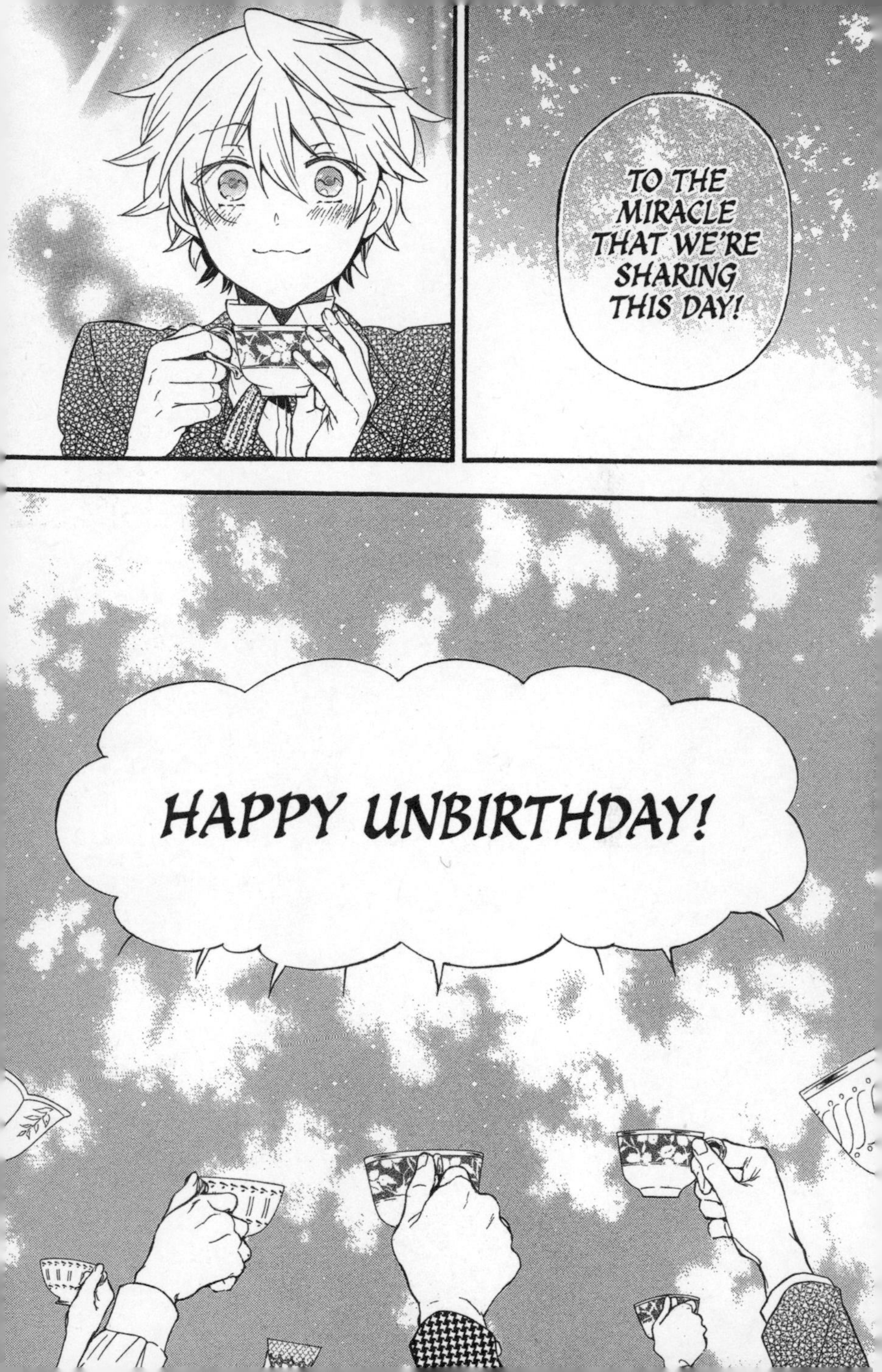
TO THE MIRACLE THAT WE'RE SHARING THIS DAY!
HAPPY UNBIRTHDAY!

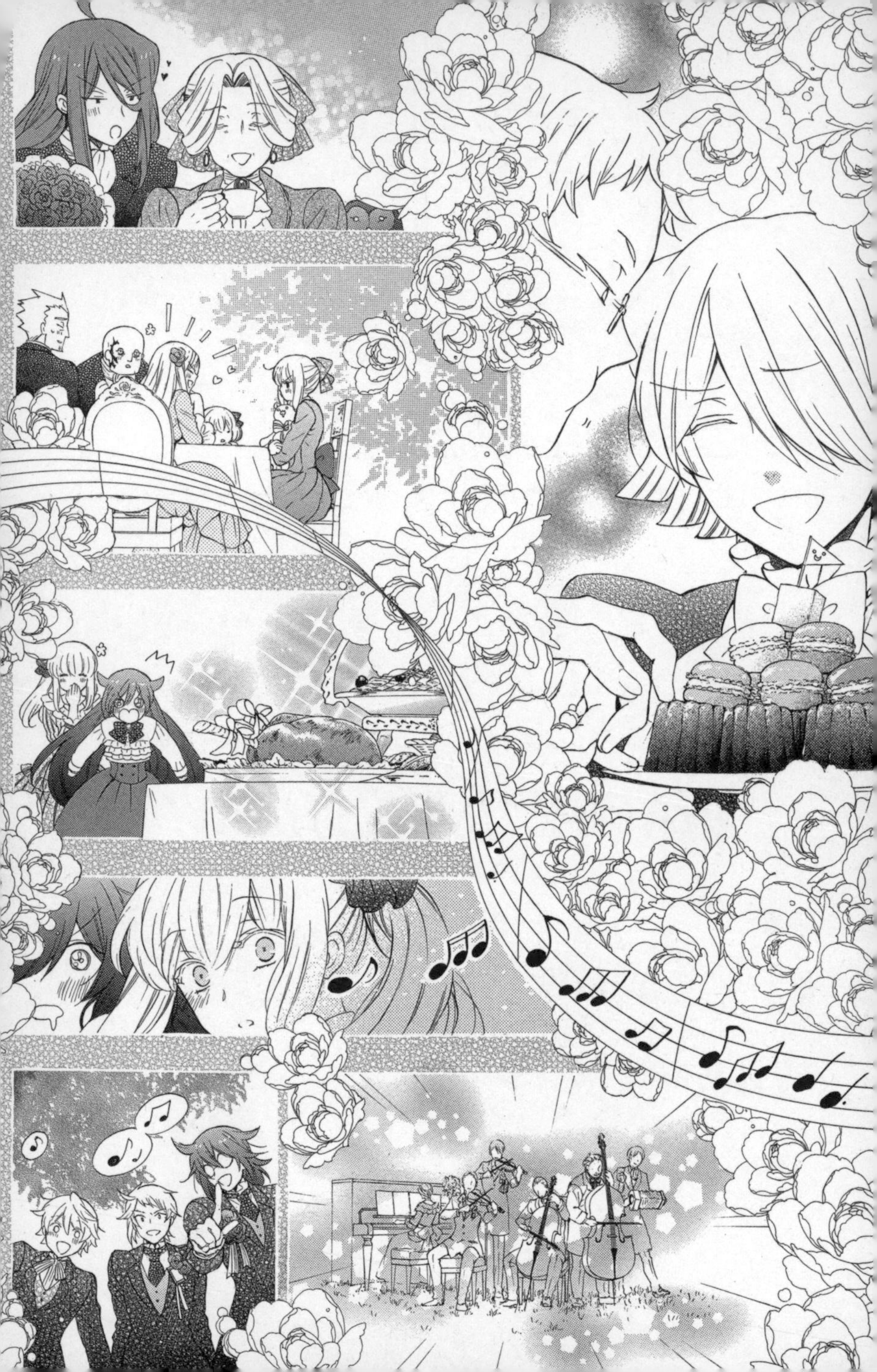

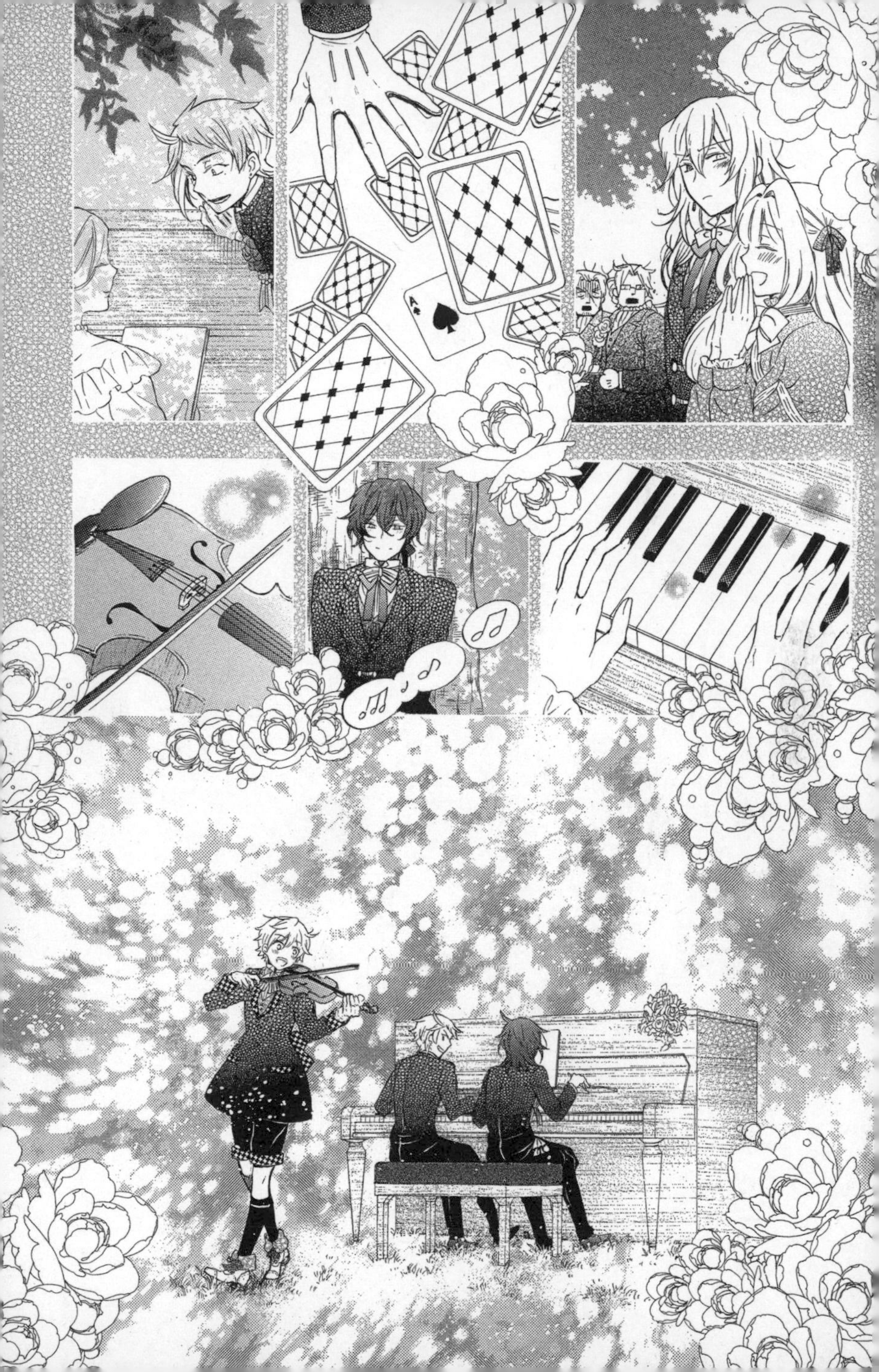

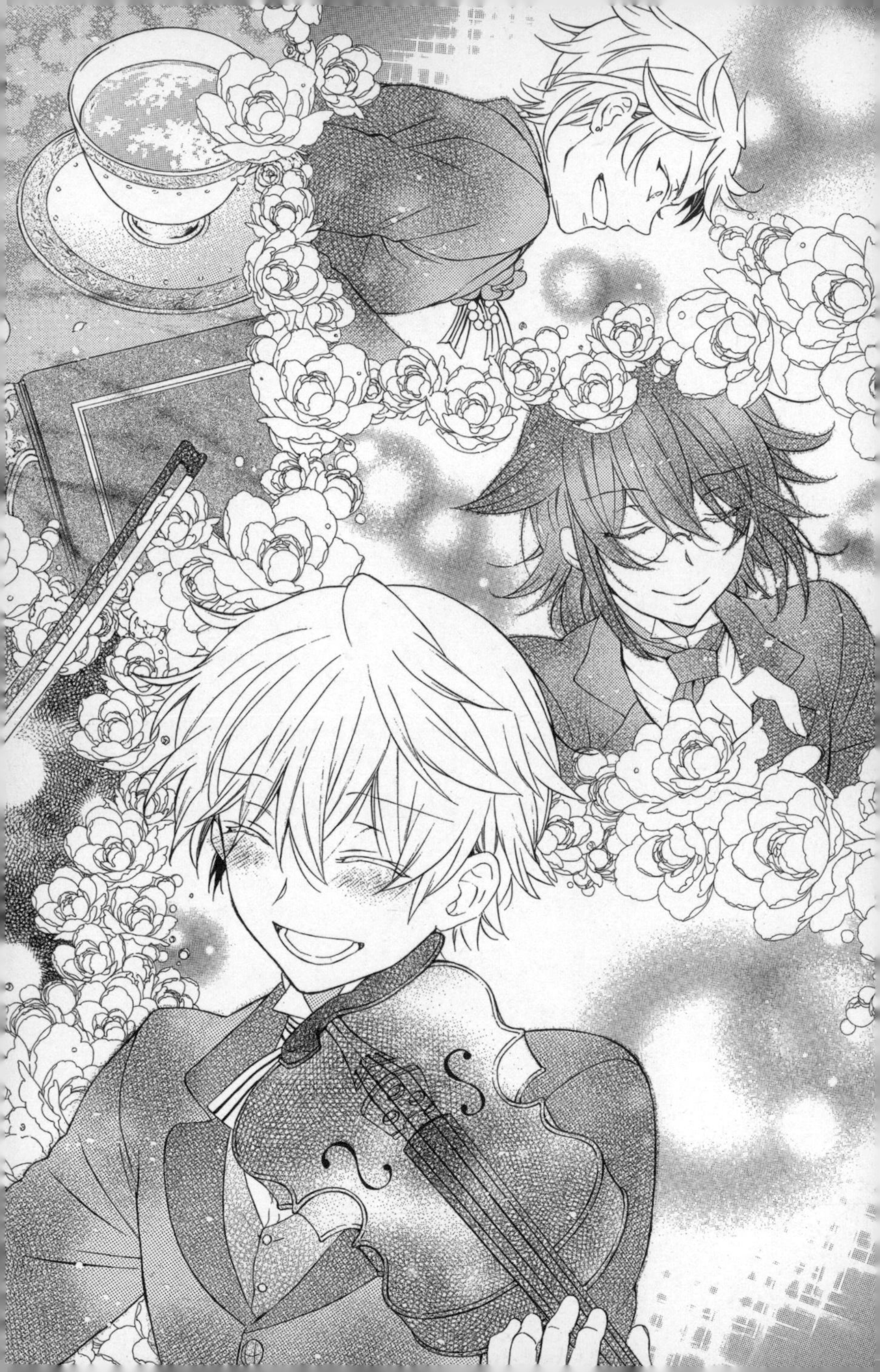

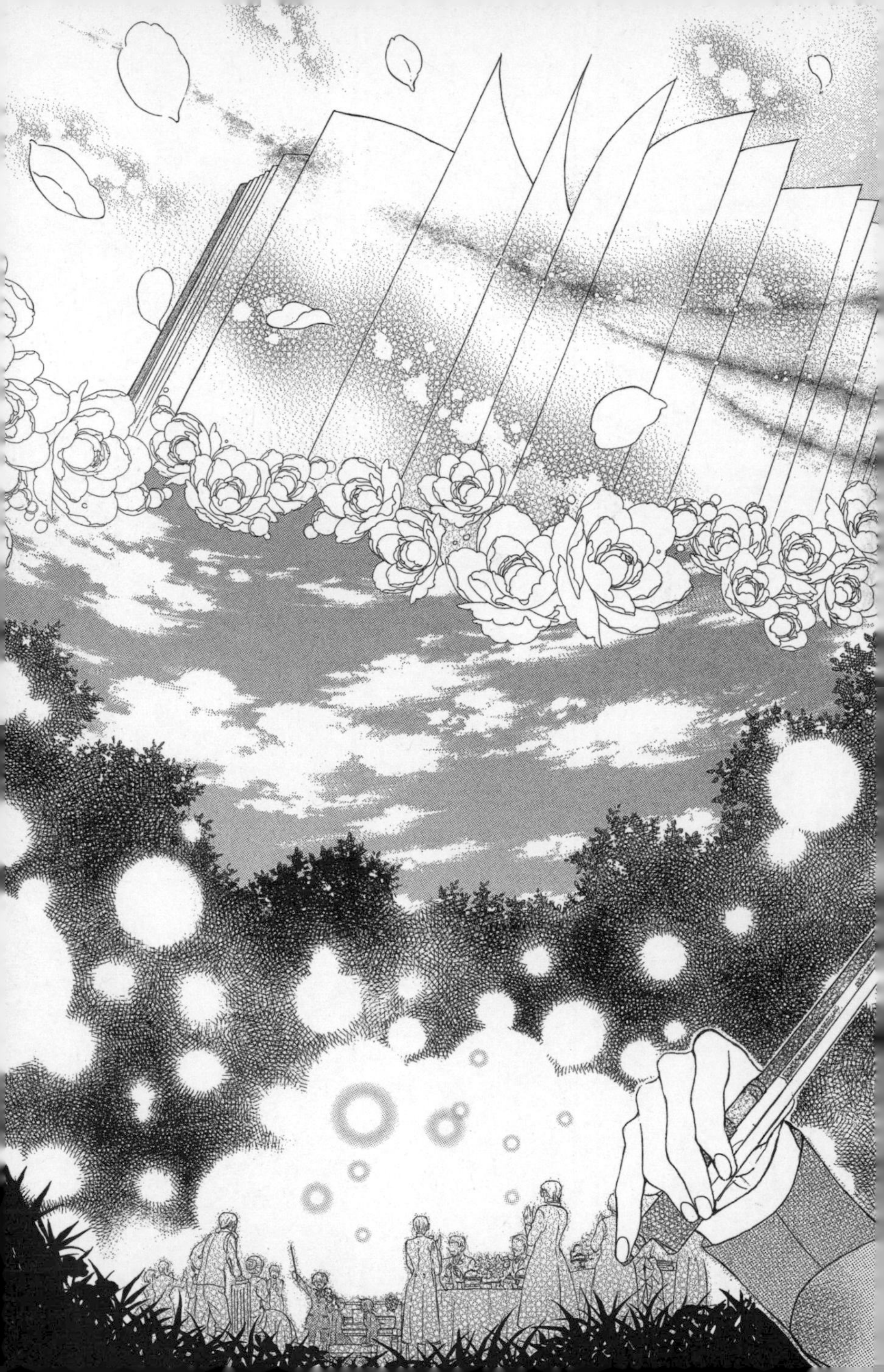

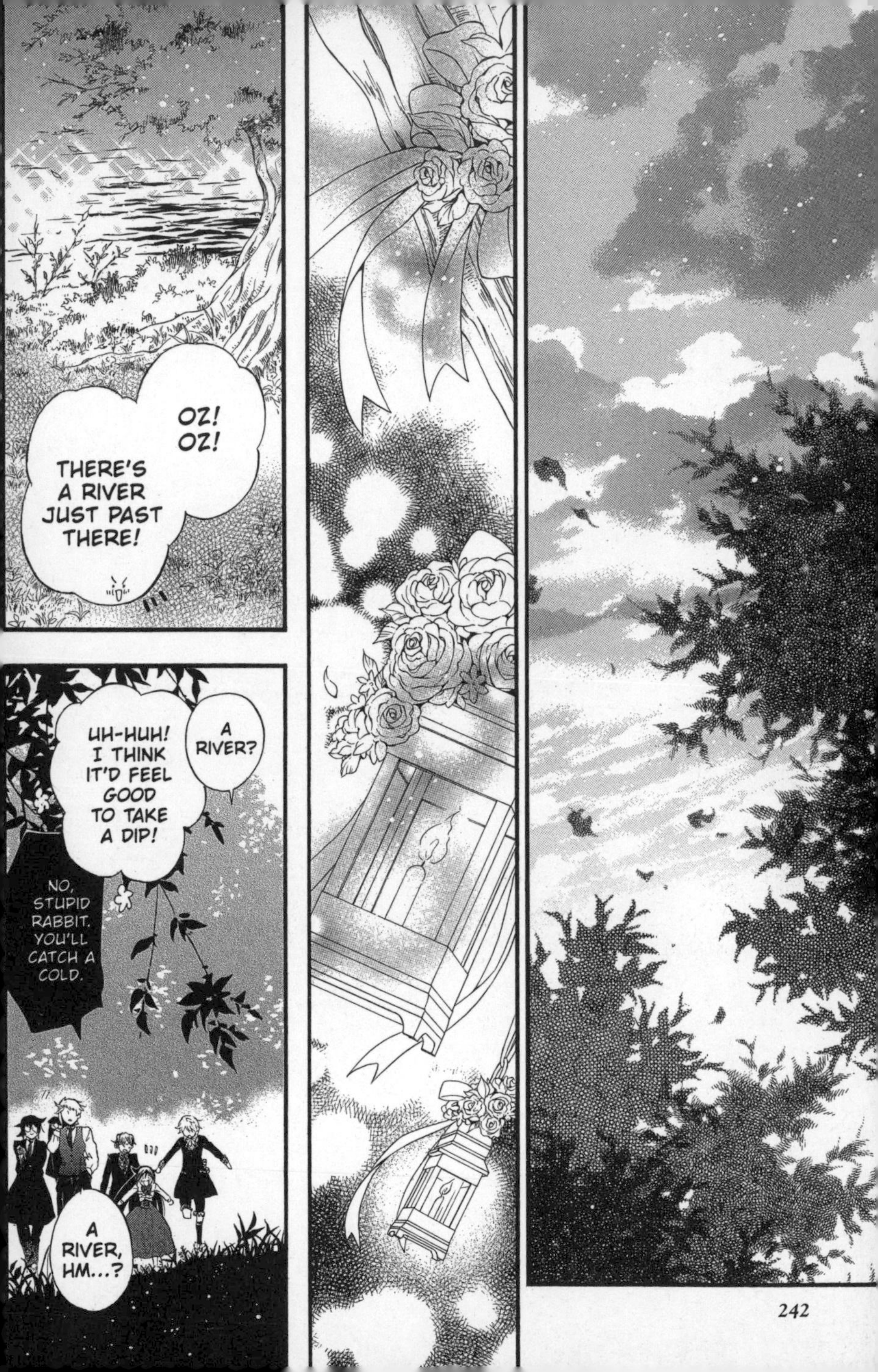
OZ! OZ!
THERE'S A RIVER JUST PAST THERE!
A RIVER?
UH-HUH! I THINK IT'D FEEL GOOD TO TAKE A DIP!
NO, STUPID RABBIT. YOU'LL CATCH A COLD.
A RIVER, HM...?

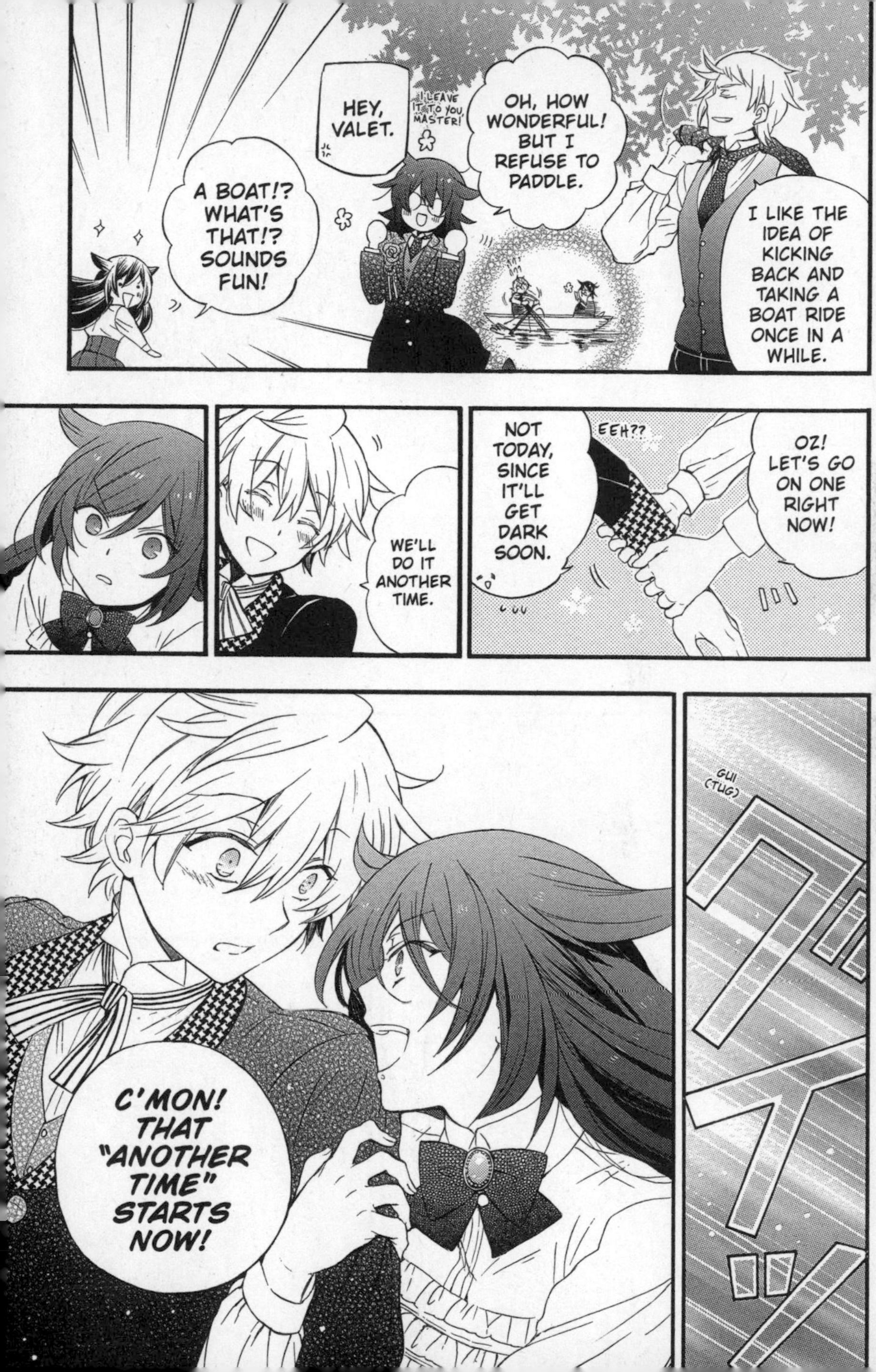
I LIKE THE IDEA OF KICKING BACK AND TAKING A BOAT RIDE ONCE IN A WHILE.
OH, HOW WONDERFUL! BUT I REFUSE TO PADDLE.
I LEAVE IT TO YOU, MASTER!
HEY, VALET.
A BOAT!? WHAT'S THAT!? SOUNDS FUN!
OZ! LET'S GO ON ONE RIGHT NOW!
EEH??
NOT TODAY, SINCE IT'LL GET DARK SOON.
WE'LL DO IT ANOTHER TIME.
GUI (TUG)
C'MON! THAT "ANOTHER TIME" STARTS NOW!

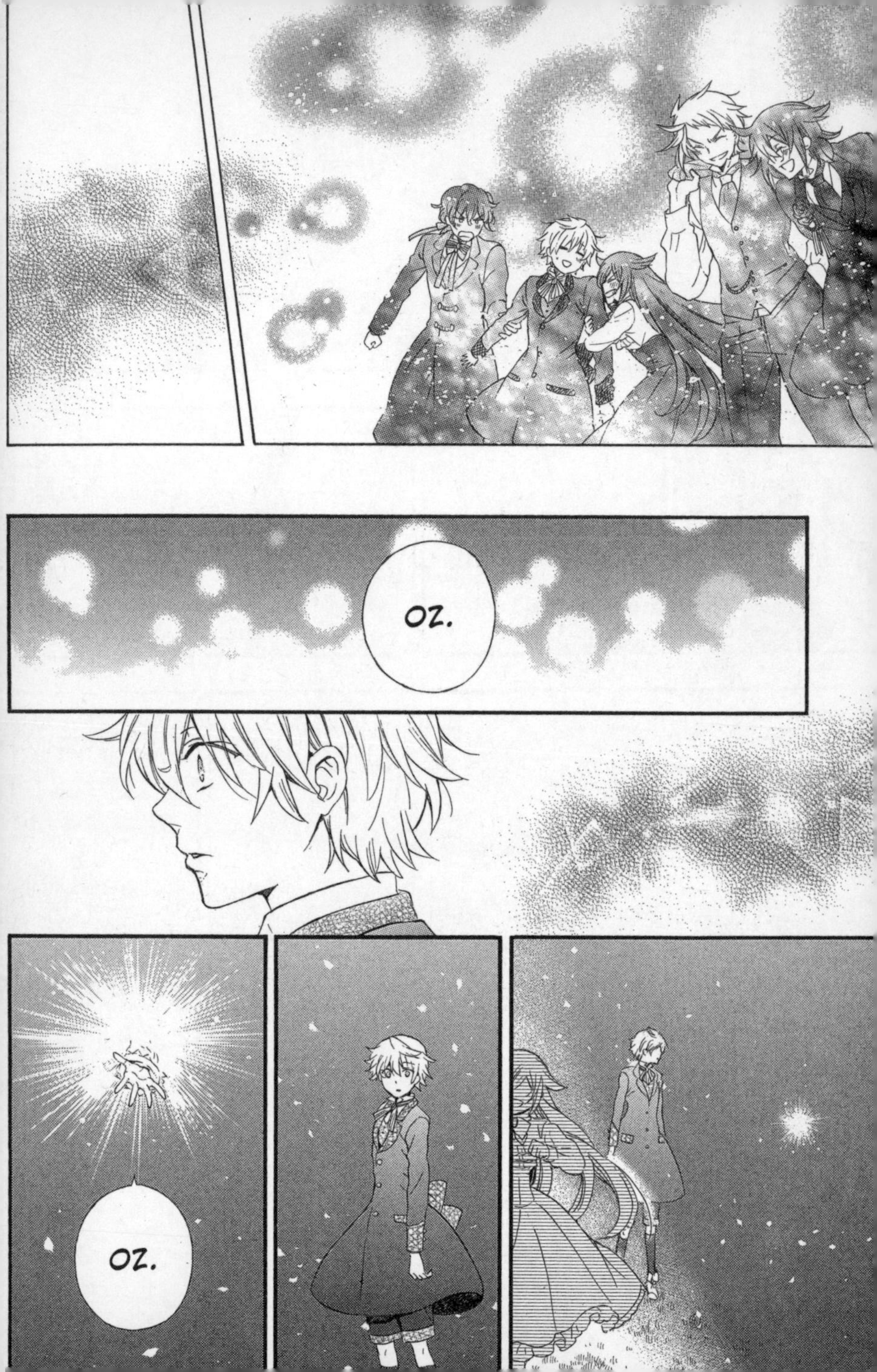
OZ.
OZ.

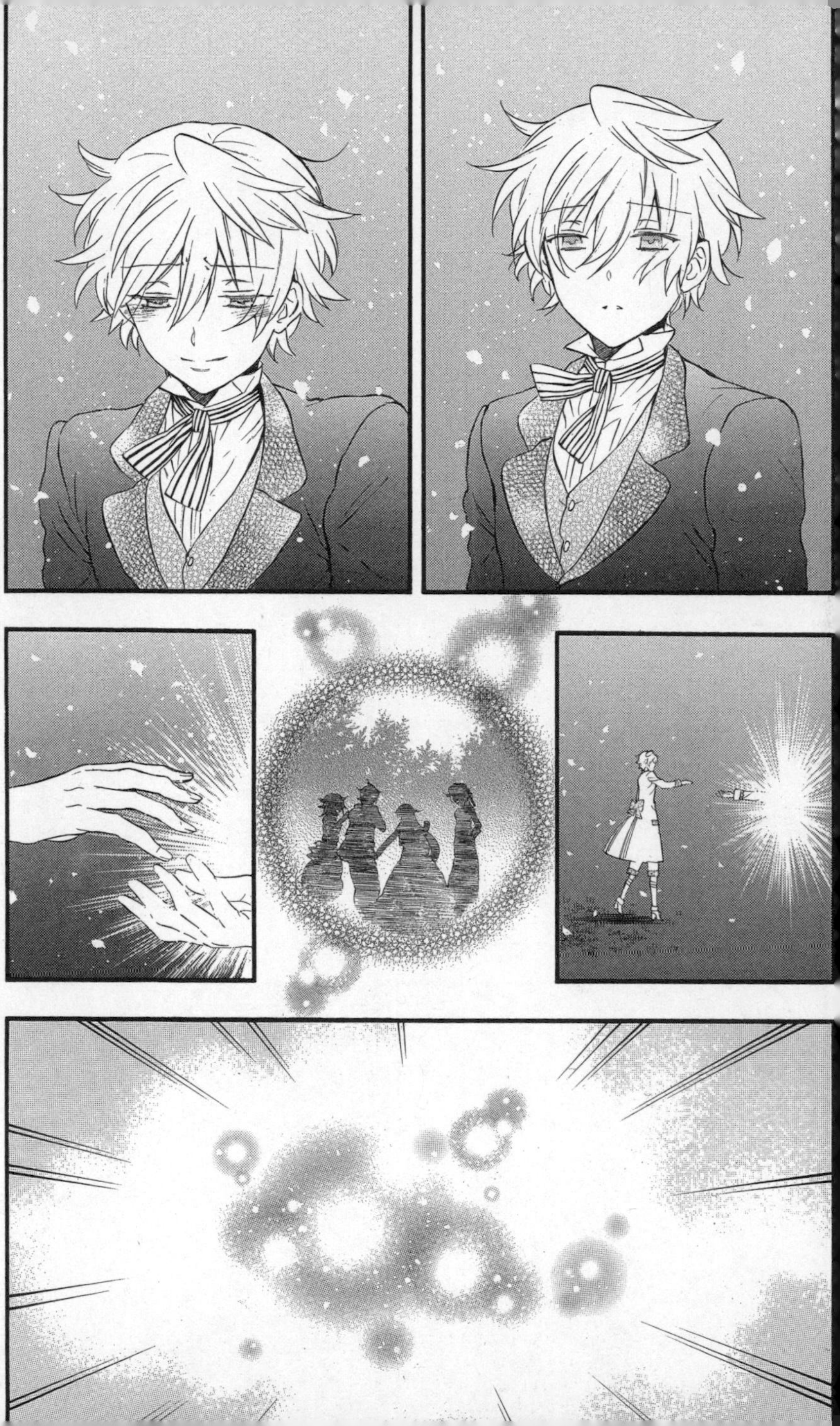

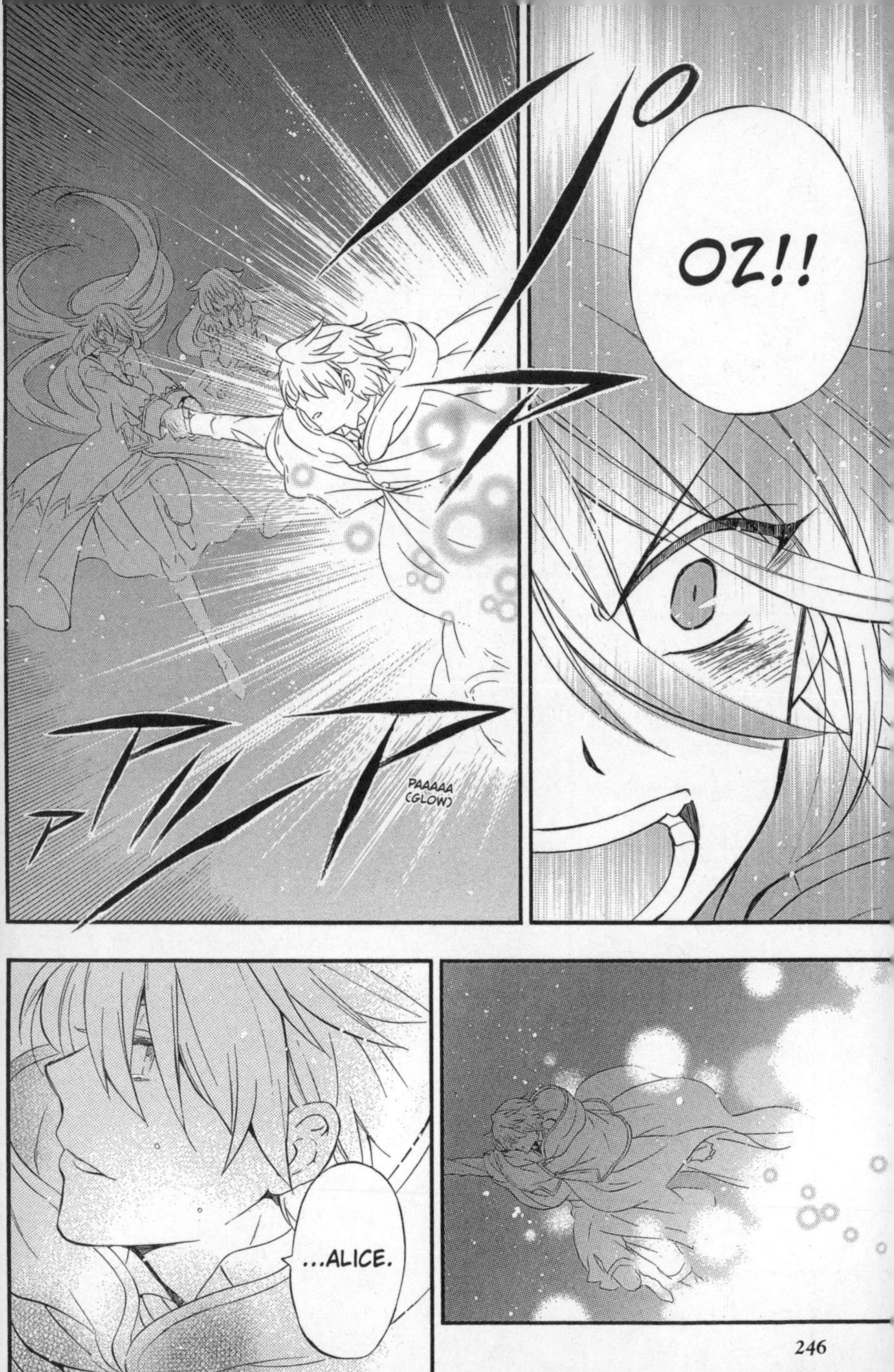
OZ!!
PAAAAA (GLOW)
...ALICE.

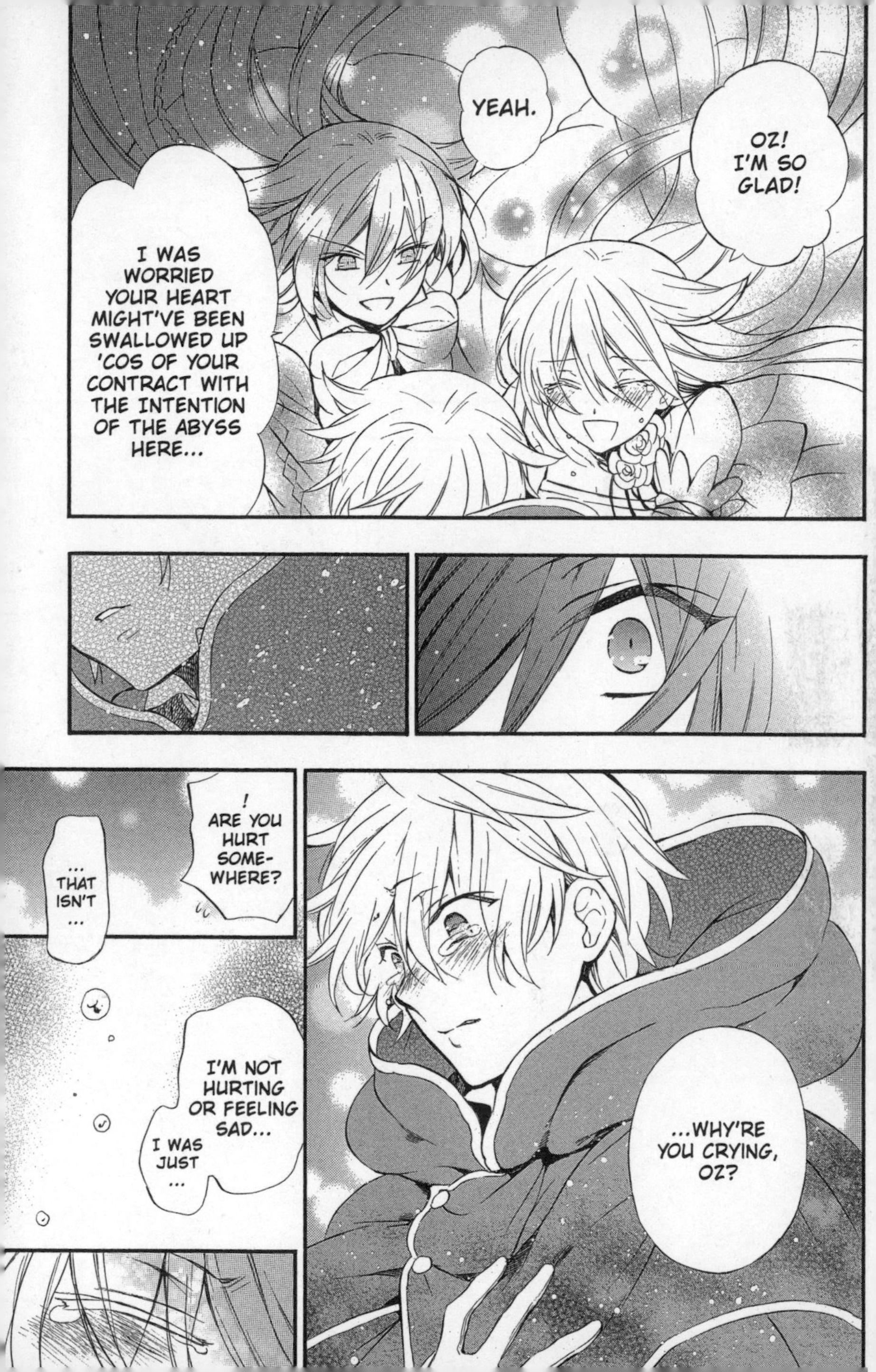
OZ! I'M SO GLAD!
YEAH.
I WAS WORRIED YOUR HEART MIGHT'VE BEEN SWALLOWED UP 'COS OF YOUR CONTRACT WITH THE INTENTION OF THE ABYSS HERE...
...WHY'RE YOU CRYING, OZ?
! ARE YOU HURT SOME-WHERE?
...THAT ISN'T...
I'M NOT HURTING OR FEELING SAD...
I WAS JUST...

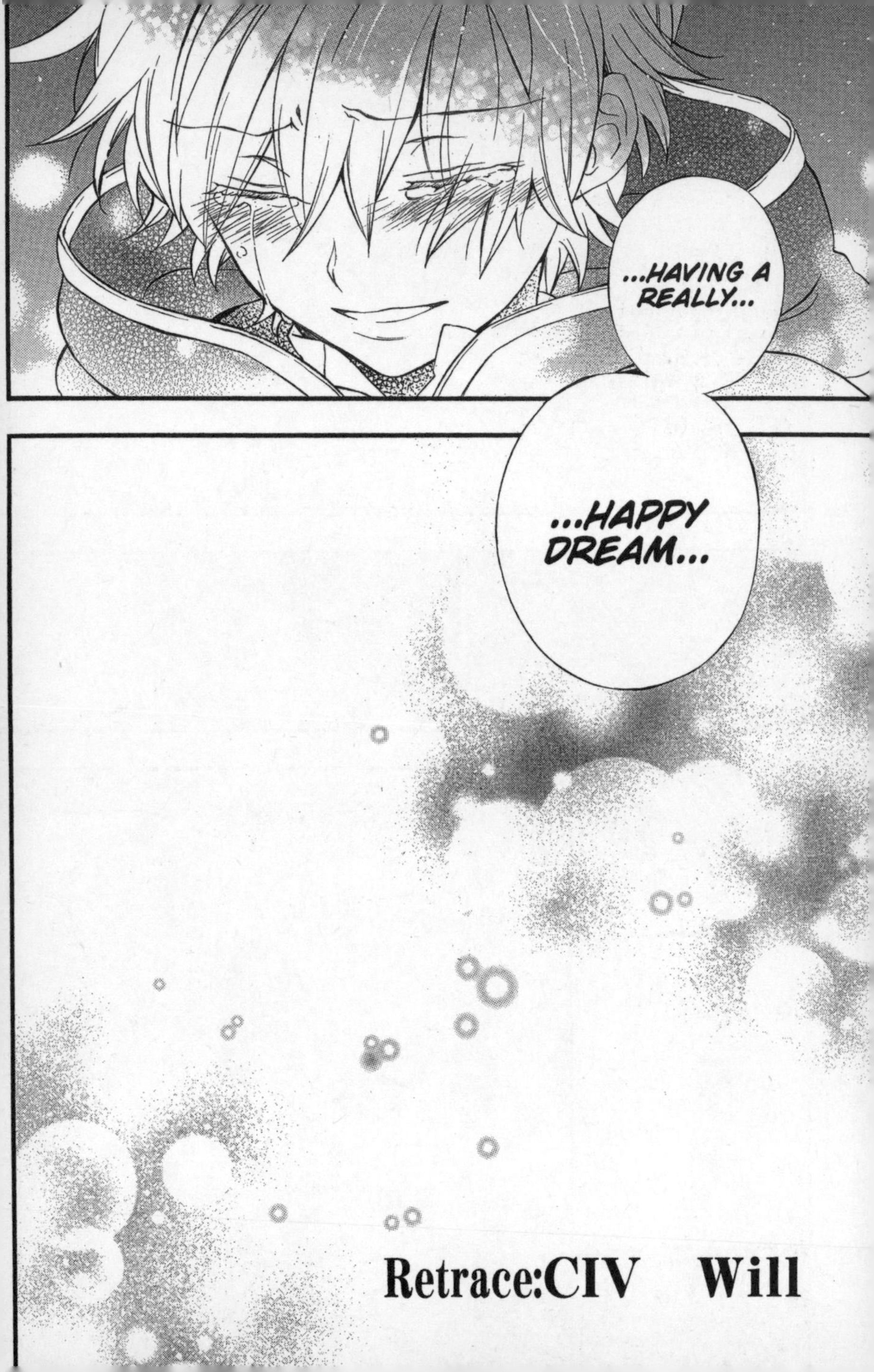
...HAVING A REALLY...
...HAPPY DREAM...

Retrace:CIV Will

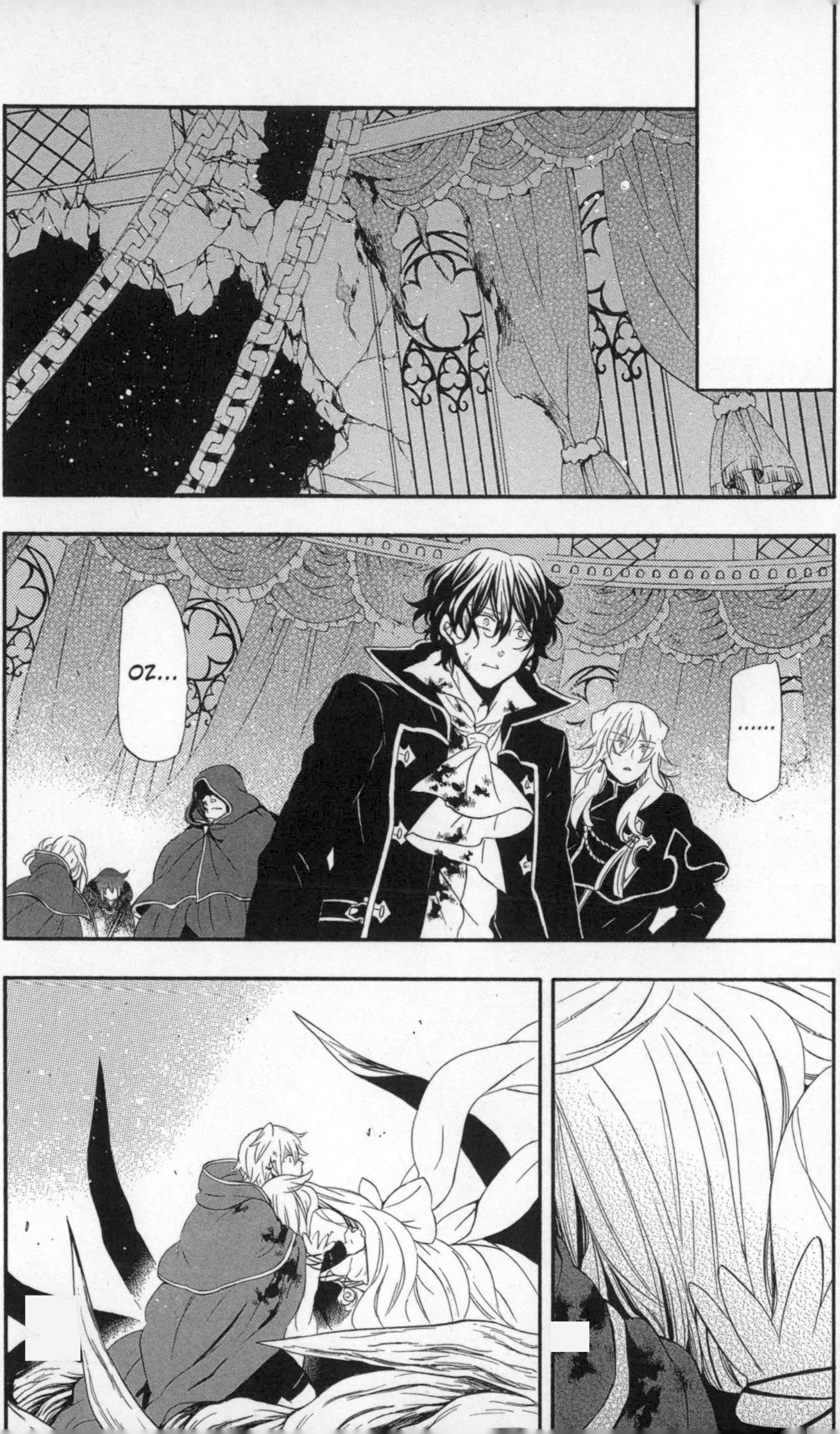
......
OZ...

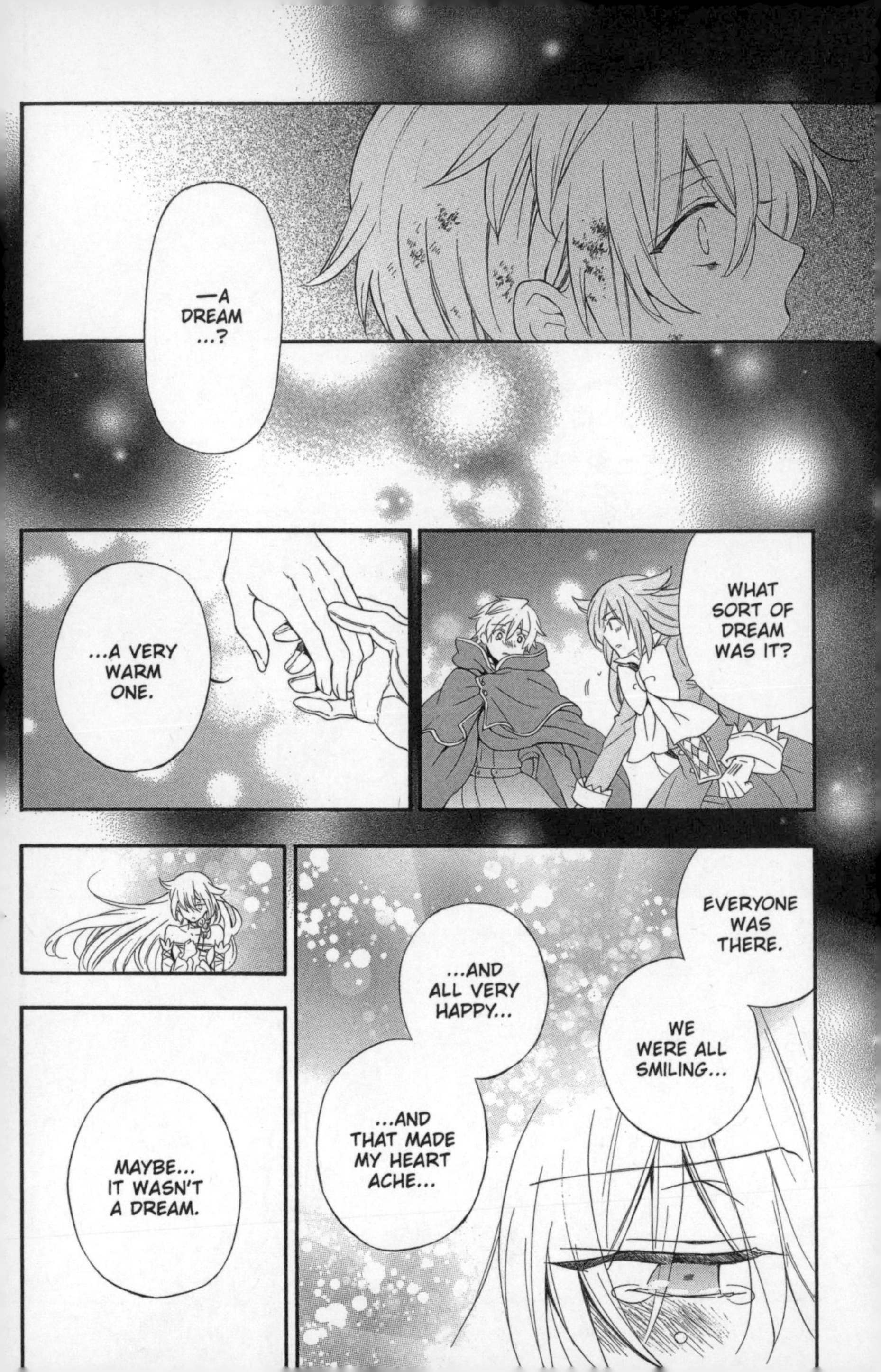
—A DREAM ...?
WHAT SORT OF DREAM WAS IT?
...A VERY WARM ONE.
EVERYONE WAS THERE.
WE WERE ALL SMILING...
...AND ALL VERY HAPPY...
...AND THAT MADE MY HEART ACHE...
MAYBE... IT WASN'T A DREAM.

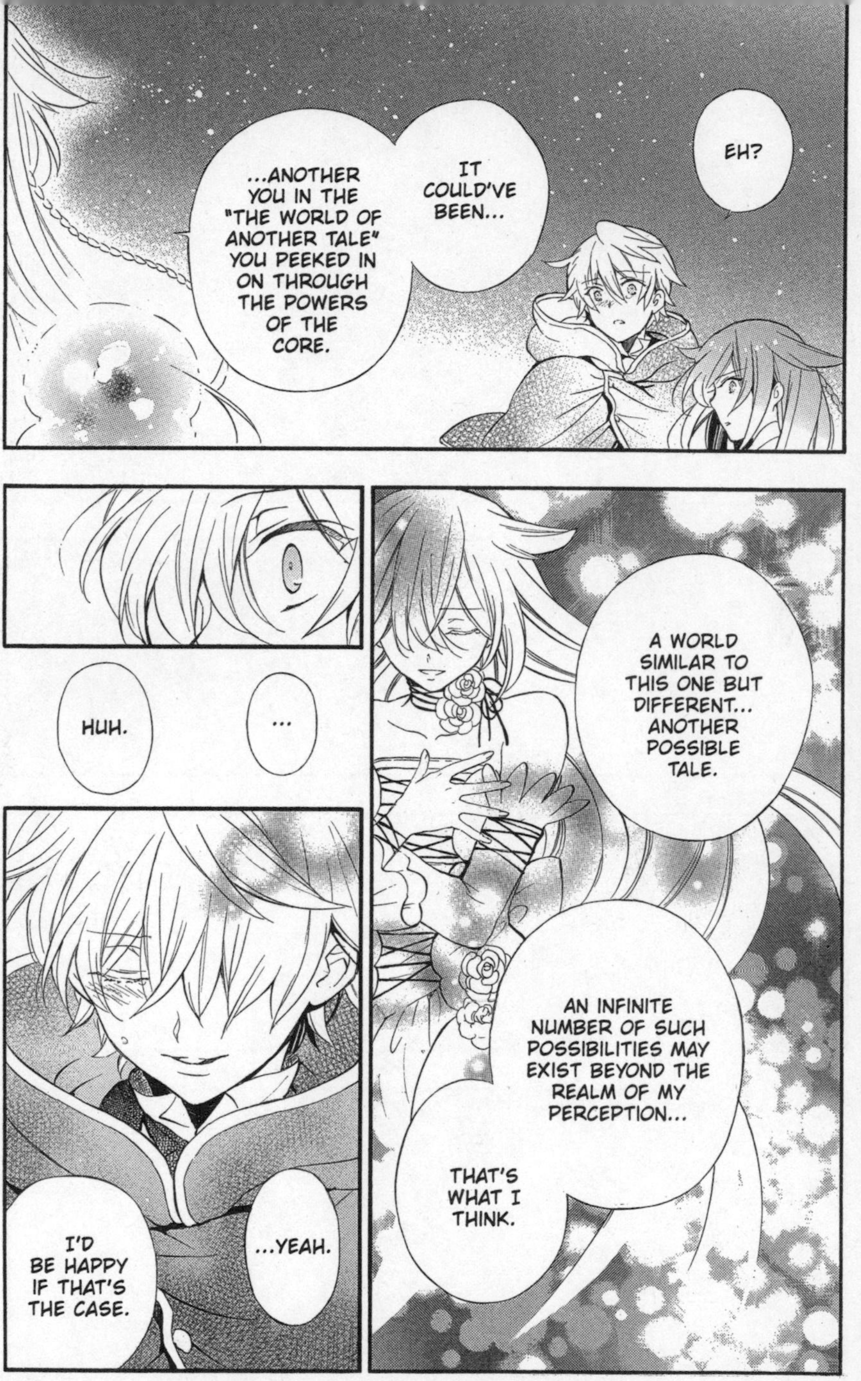
EH?
IT COULD'VE BEEN...
...ANOTHER YOU IN THE "THE WORLD OF ANOTHER TALE" YOU PEEKED IN ON THROUGH THE POWERS OF THE CORE.
A WORLD SIMILAR TO THIS ONE BUT DIFFERENT... ANOTHER POSSIBLE TALE.
AN INFINITE NUMBER OF SUCH POSSIBILITIES MAY EXIST BEYOND THE REALM OF MY PERCEPTION...
THAT'S WHAT I THINK.
...
HUH.
...YEAH.
I'D BE HAPPY IF THAT'S THE CASE.

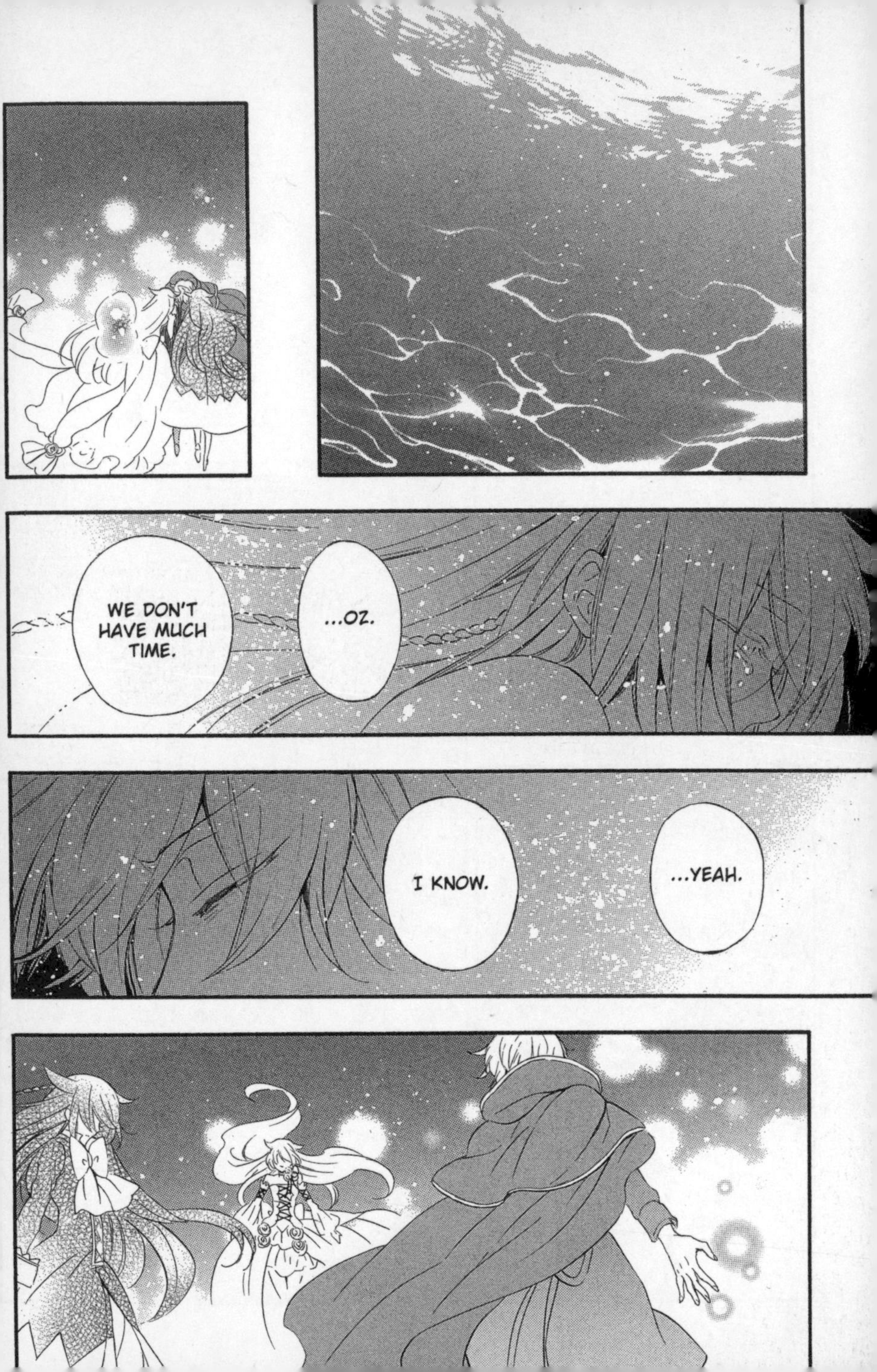
...OZ.
WE DON'T HAVE MUCH TIME.
...YEAH.
I KNOW.

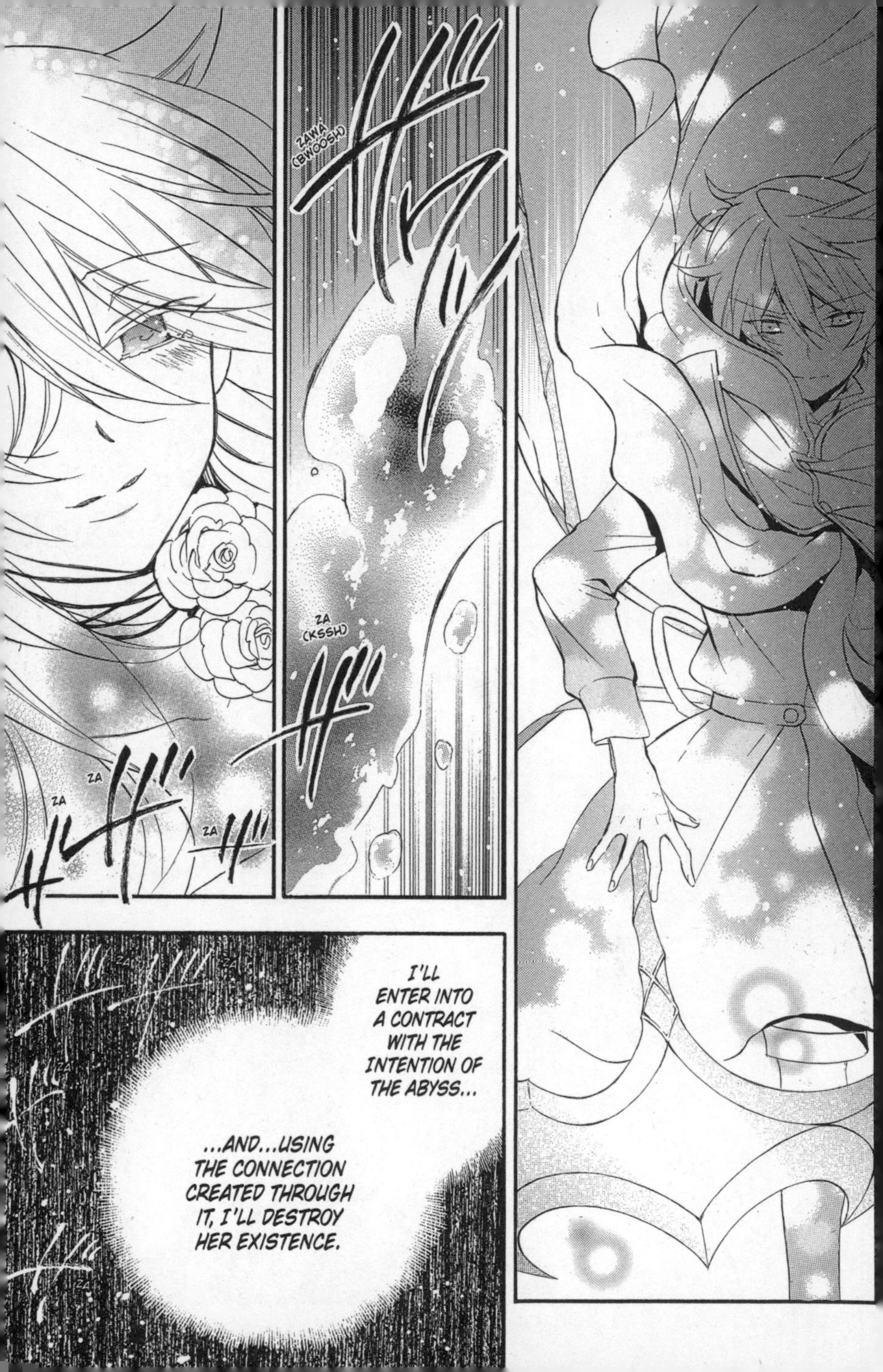
ZAWA (BWOOSH)
ZA (KSSH)
ZA
ZA
ZA
ZA
ZA
I'LL ENTER INTO A CONTRACT WITH THE INTENTION OF THE ABYSS...
...AND...USING THE CONNECTION CREATED THROUGH IT, I'LL DESTROY HER EXISTENCE.

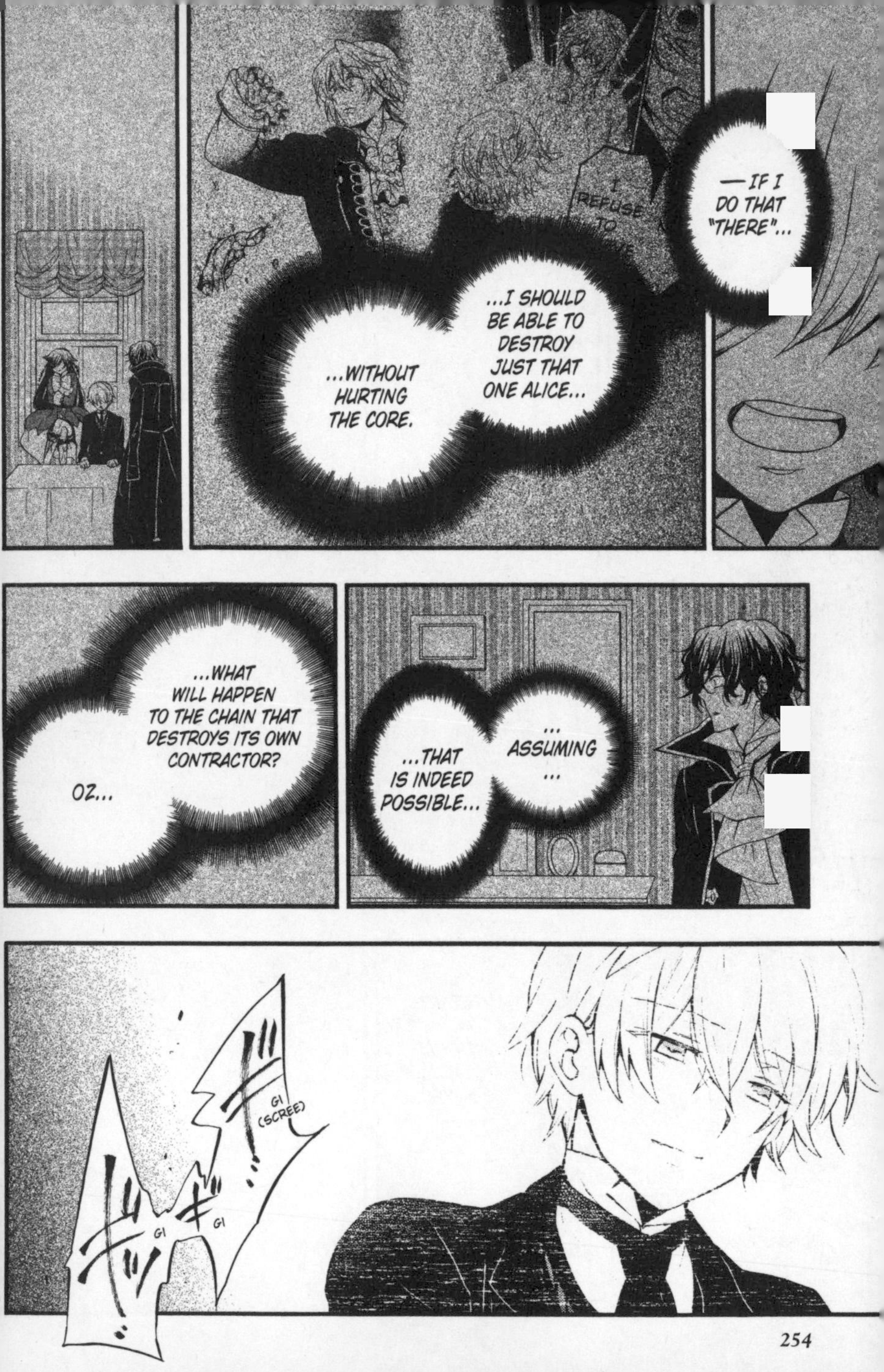
—IF I DO THAT "THERE"...
I REFUSE TO
...I SHOULD BE ABLE TO DESTROY JUST THAT ONE ALICE...
...WITHOUT HURTING THE CORE.
...ASSUMING...
...THAT IS INDEED POSSIBLE...
...WHAT WILL HAPPEN TO THE CHAIN THAT DESTROYS ITS OWN CONTRACTOR?
OZ...
GI (SCREE)
GI
GI

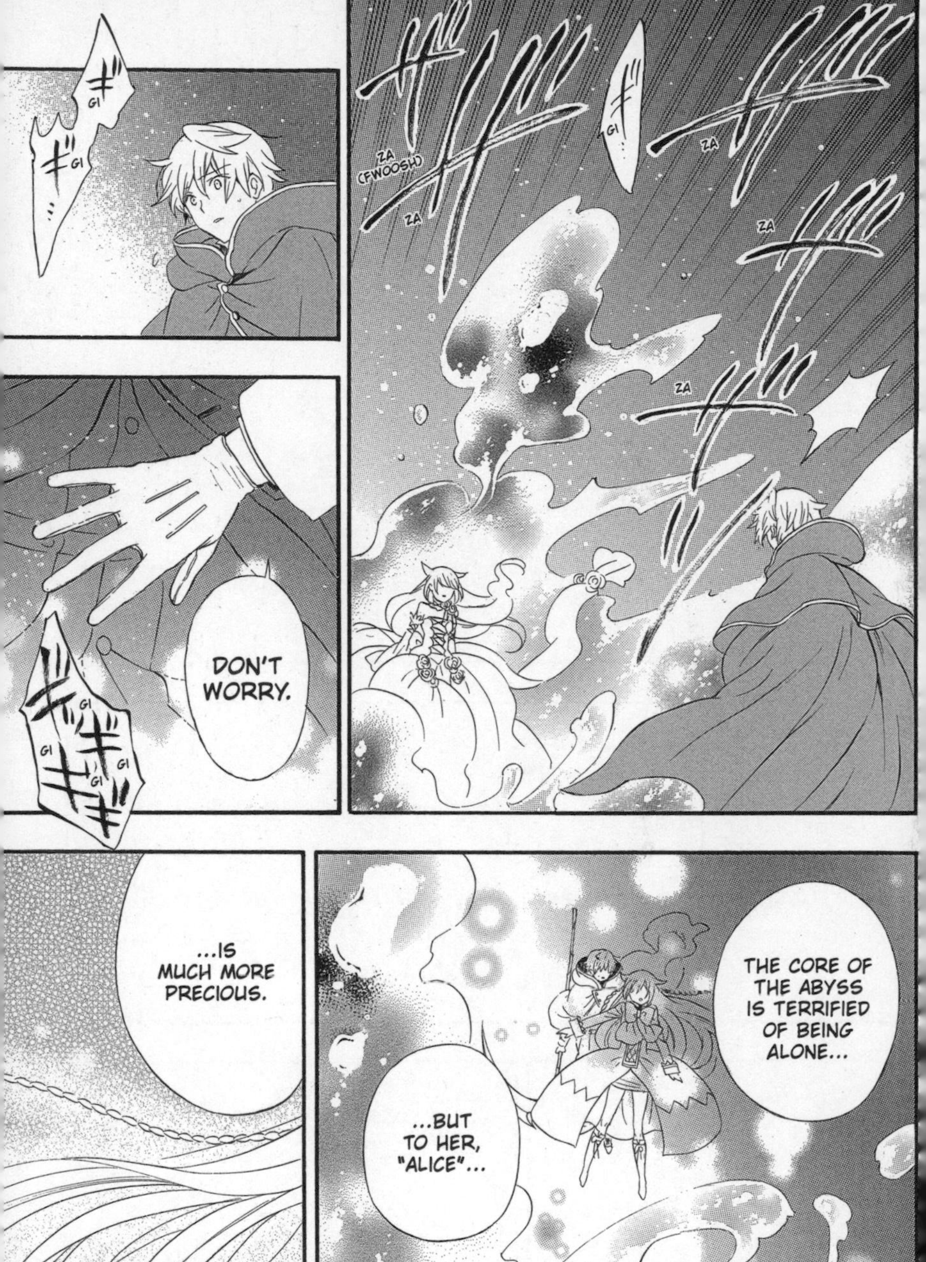
ZA (FWOOSH)
ZA
GI
ZA
ZA
ZA
GI
GI
...
DON'T WORRY.
GI
GI
GI
GI
THE CORE OF THE ABYSS IS TERRIFIED OF BEING ALONE...
...BUT TO HER, "ALICE"...
...IS MUCH MORE PRECIOUS.

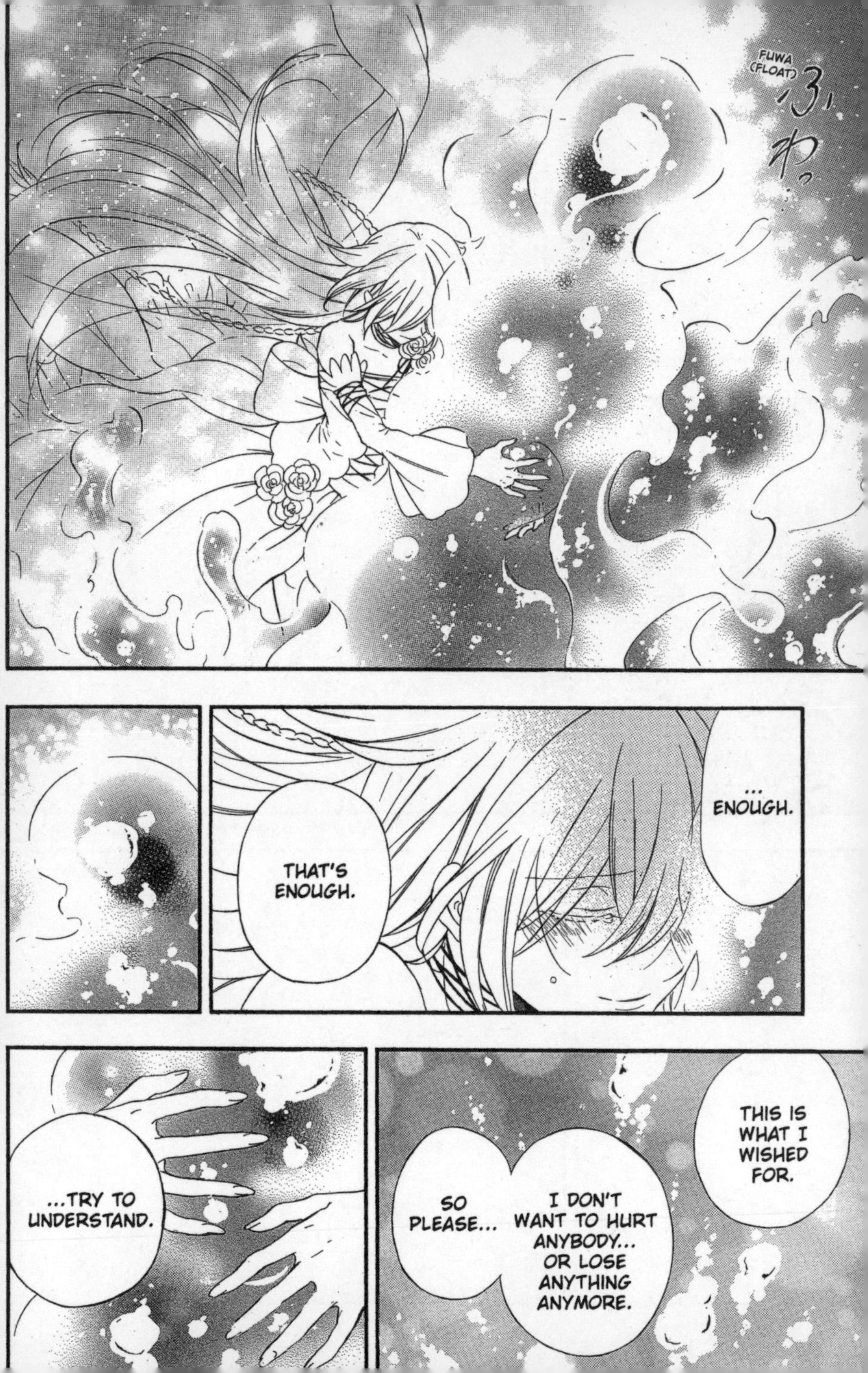
FUWA (FLOAT)
...ENOUGH.
THAT'S ENOUGH.
THIS IS WHAT I WISHED FOR.
I DON'T WANT TO HURT ANYBODY... OR LOSE ANYTHING ANYMORE.
SO PLEASE...
...TRY TO UNDERSTAND.

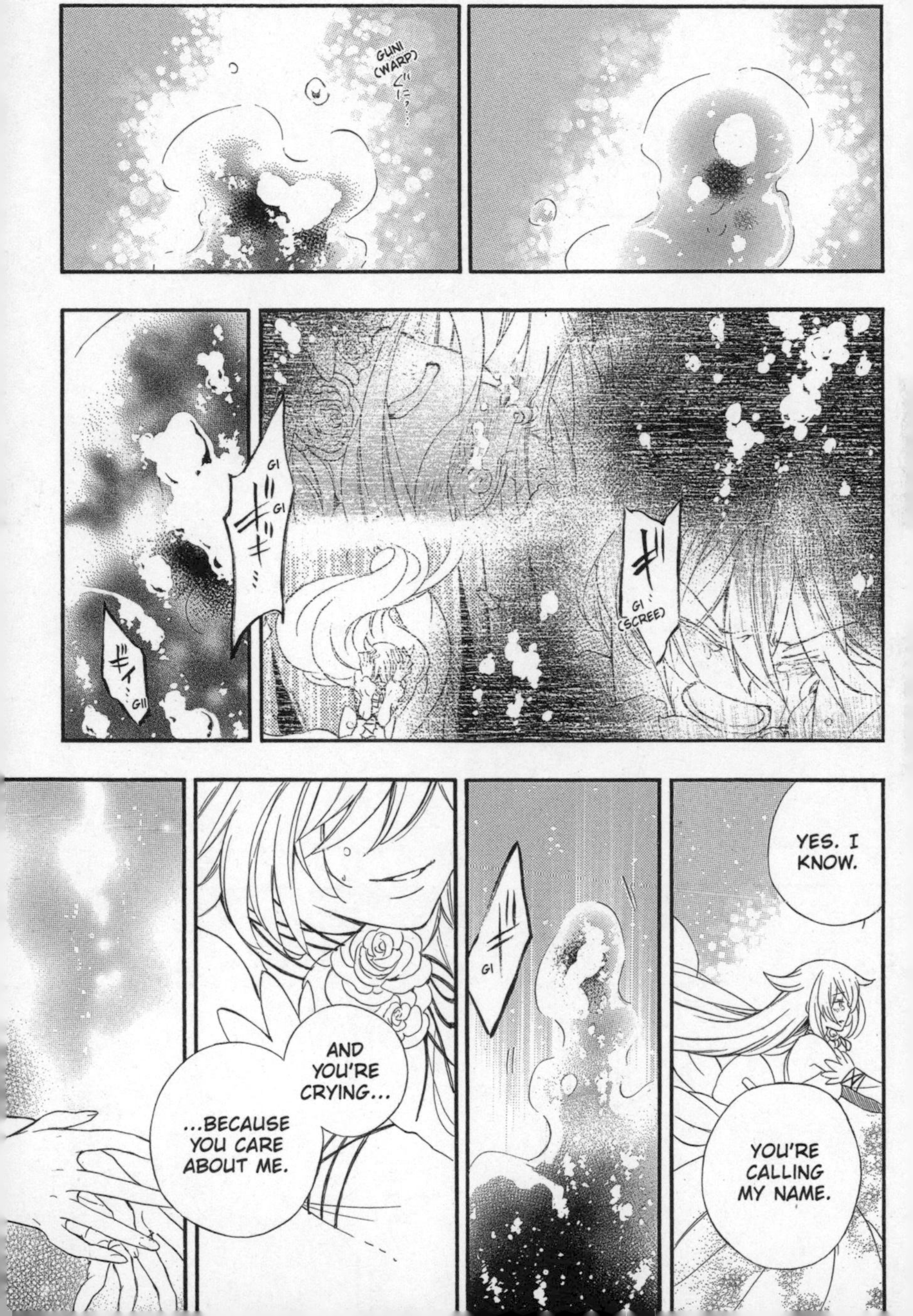
GUNI (WARP)
GI (SCREE)
GI
GI
GII
YES. I KNOW.
YOU'RE CALLING MY NAME.
GI
AND YOU'RE CRYING...
...BECAUSE YOU CARE ABOUT ME.

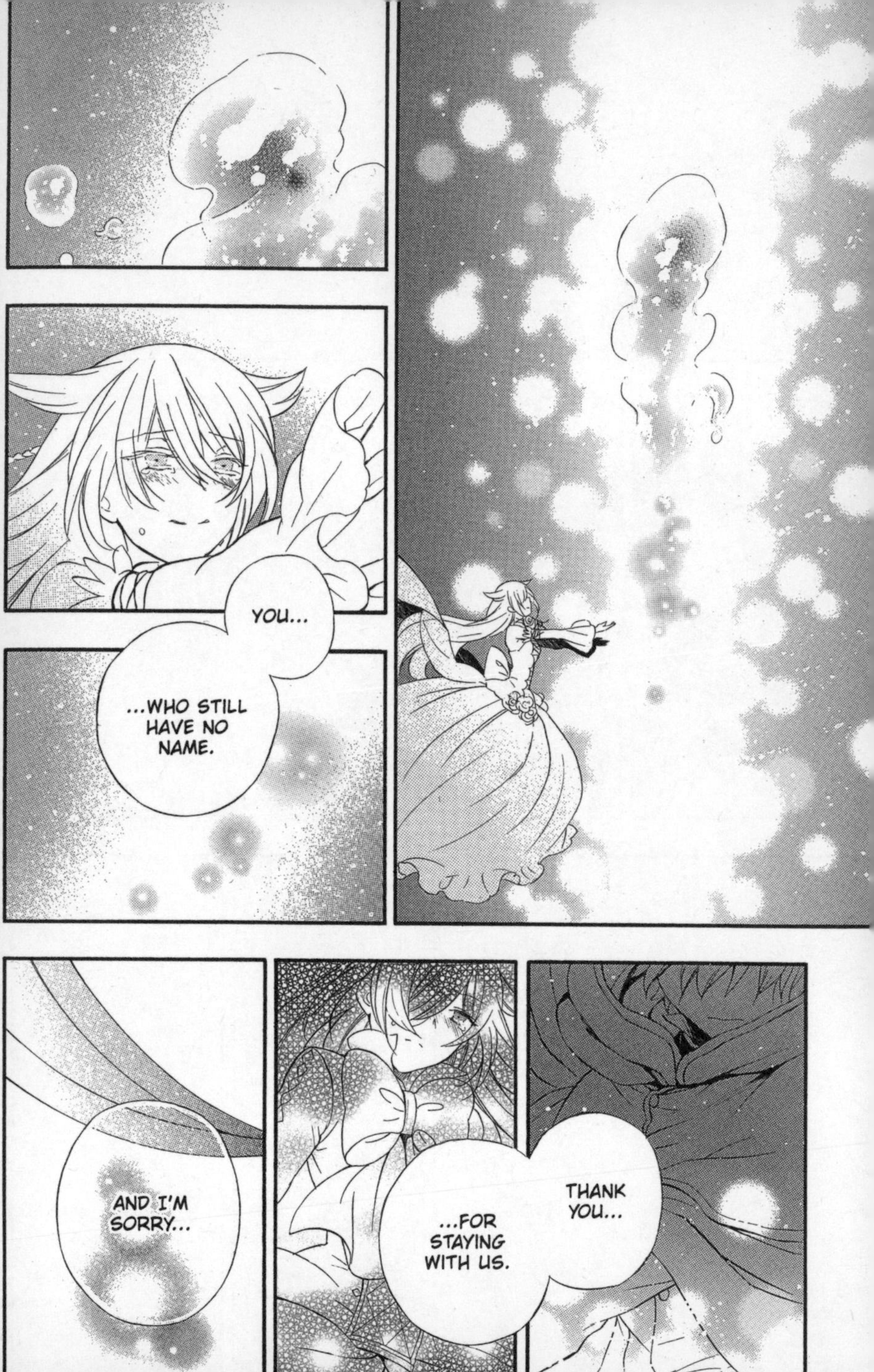
YOU...
...WHO STILL HAVE NO NAME.
THANK YOU...
...FOR STAYING WITH US.
AND I'M SORRY...

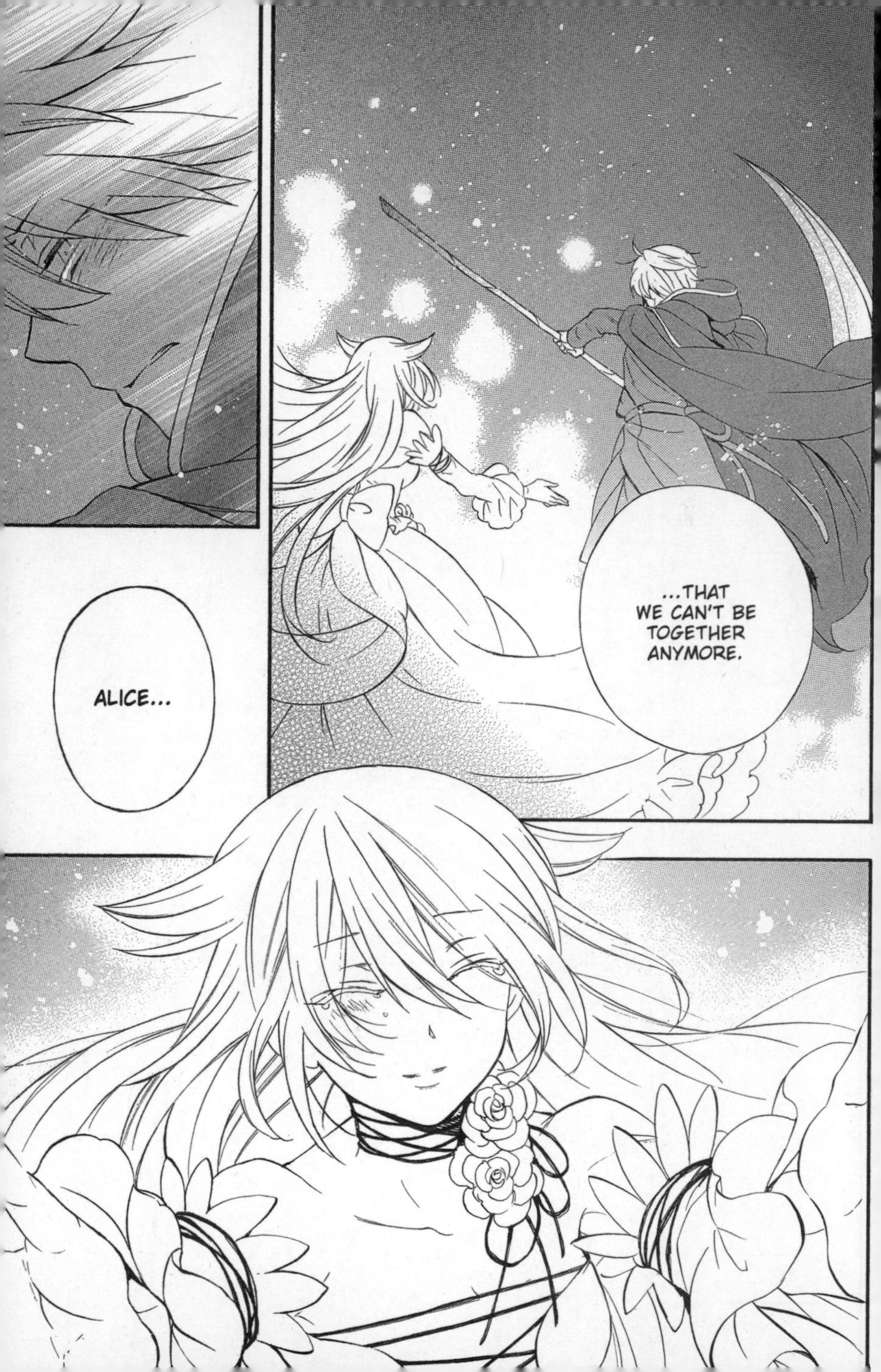
...THAT WE CAN'T BE TOGETHER ANYMORE.
ALICE...

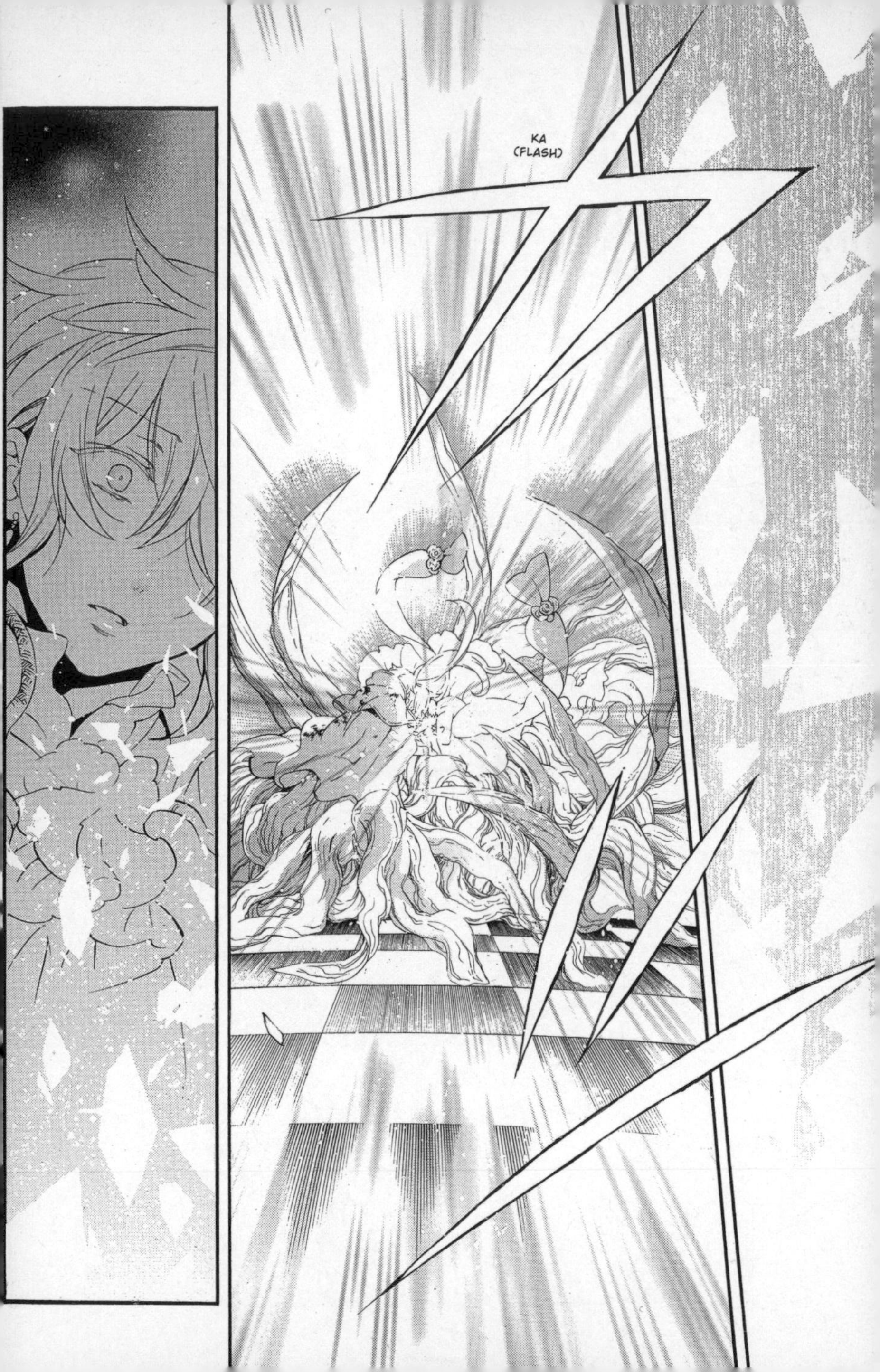
KA
(FLASH)

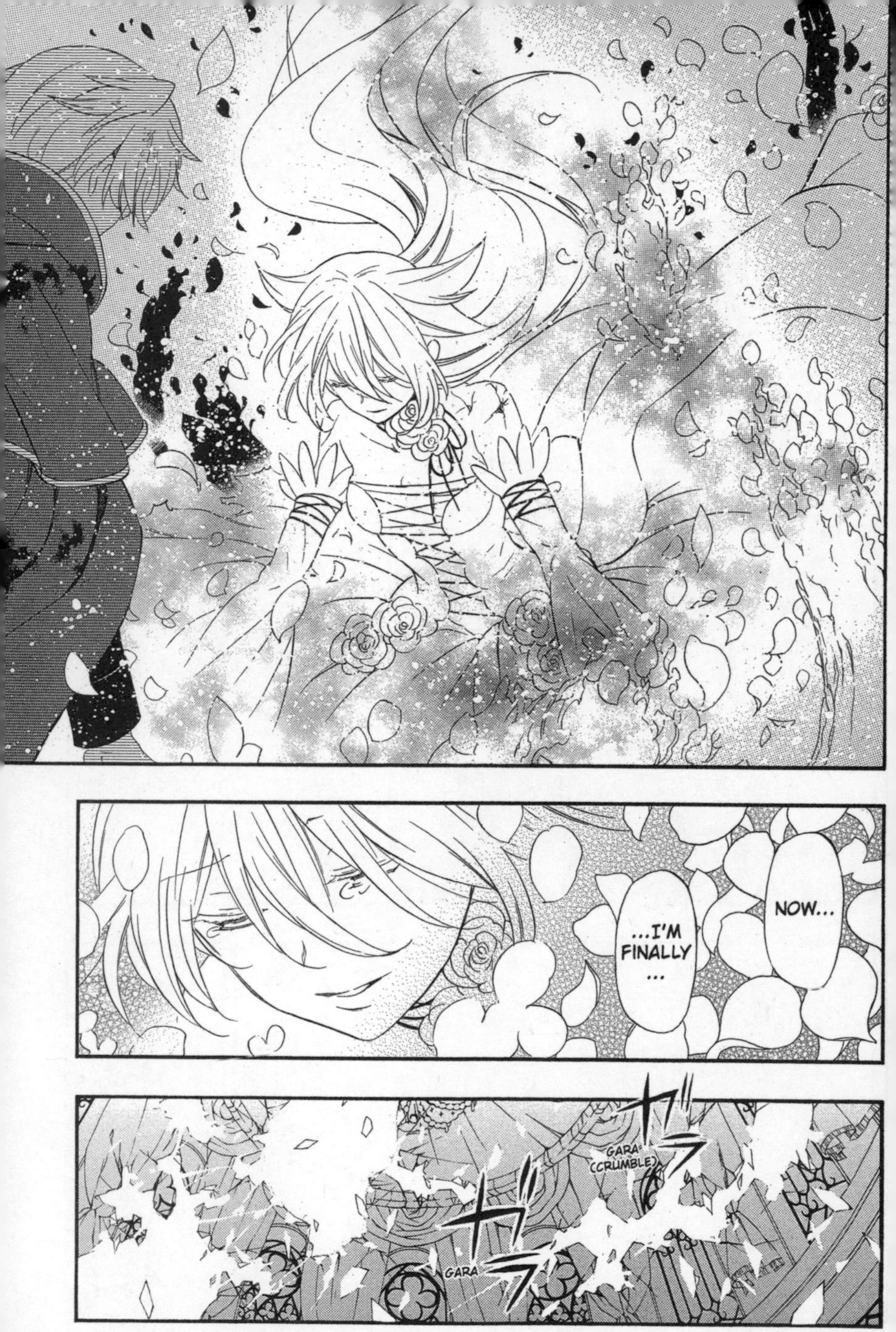
NOW...
...I'M FINALLY ...
GARA (CRUMBLE)
GARA

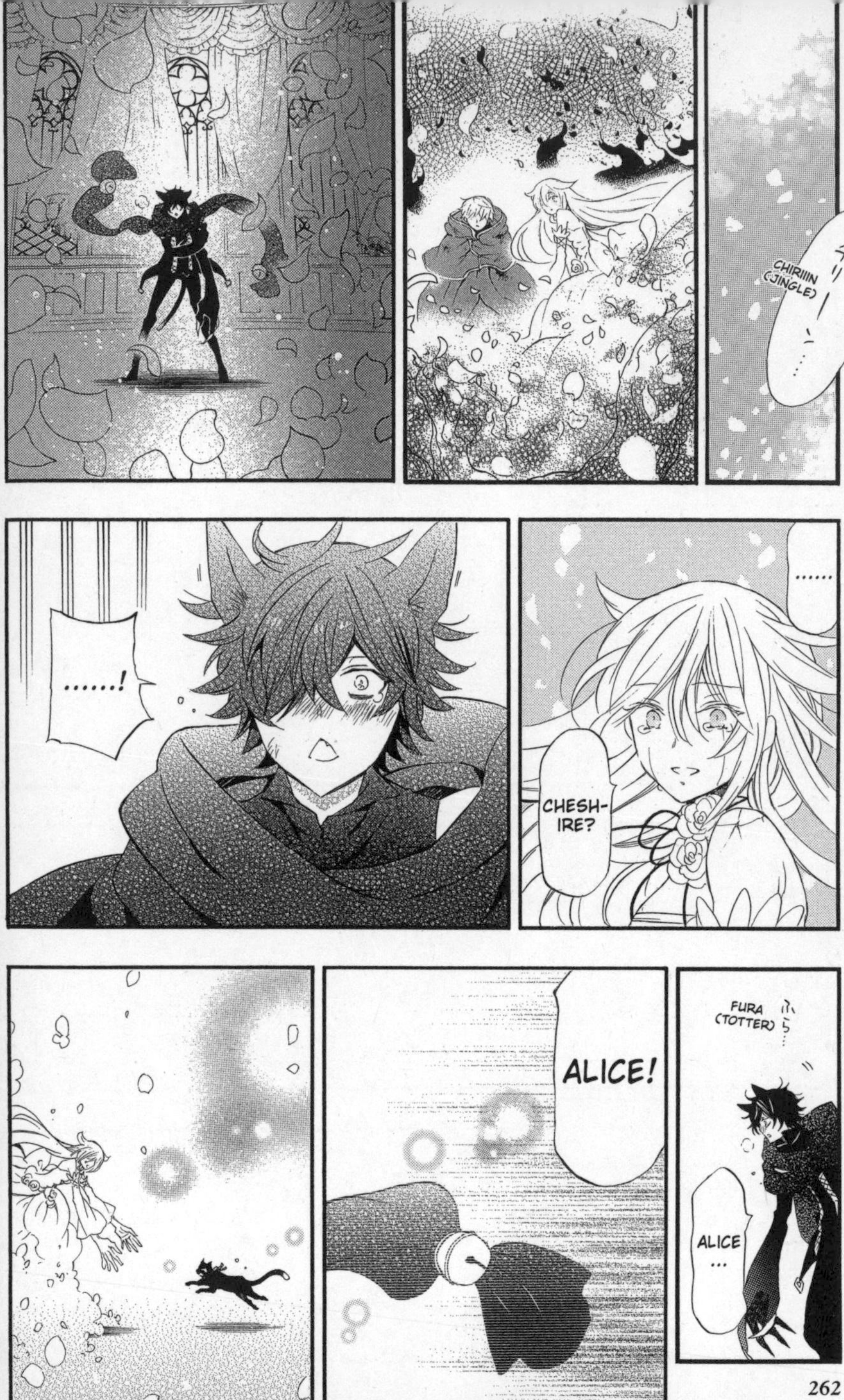
チリーン…
CHIRIIIN (JINGLE)
......
CHESH-IRE?
......!
FURA (TOTTER)
ふら…
ALICE ...
ALICE!

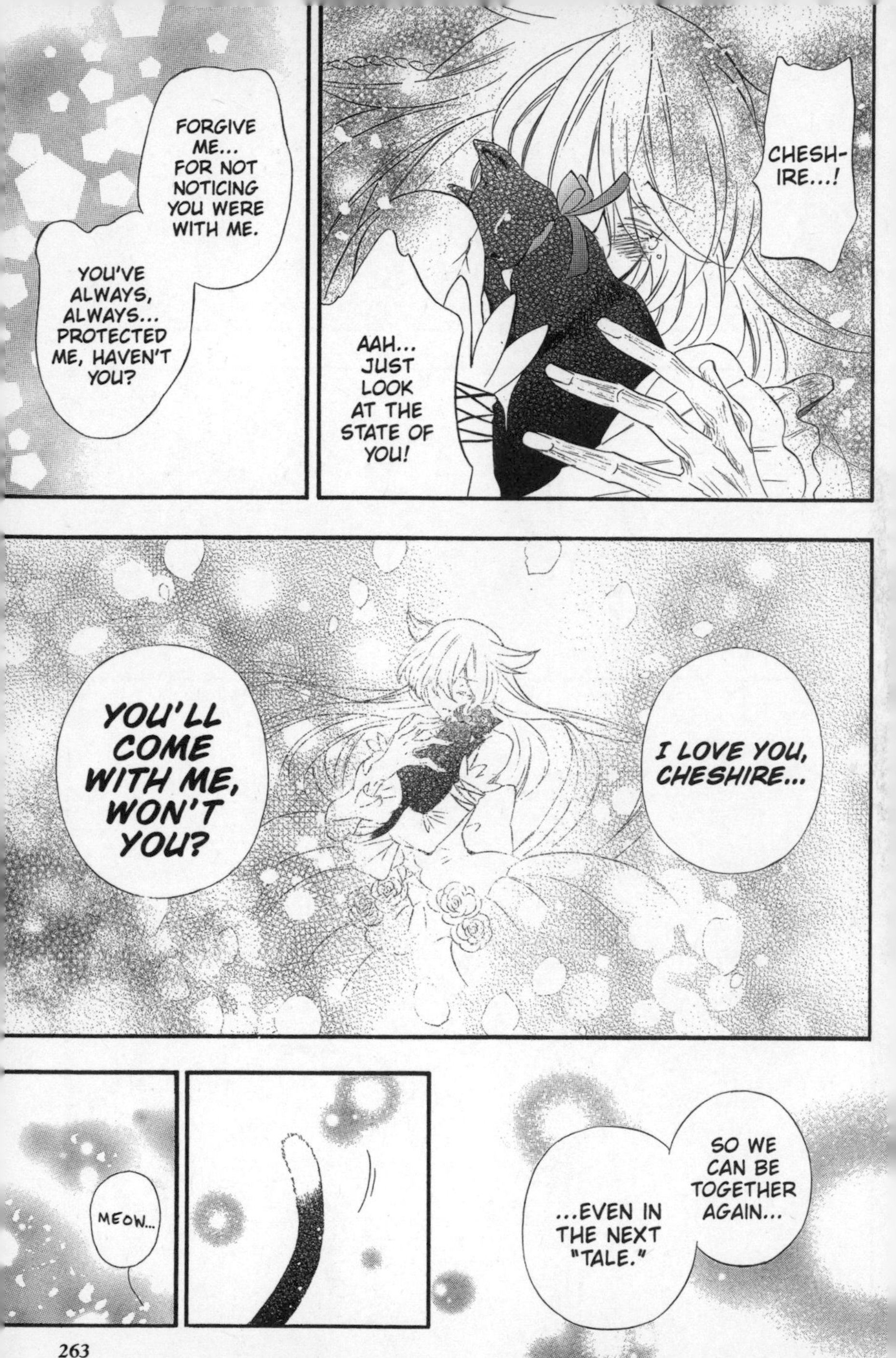
CHESH-IRE...!
AAH... JUST LOOK AT THE STATE OF YOU!
FORGIVE ME... FOR NOT NOTICING YOU WERE WITH ME.
YOU'VE ALWAYS, ALWAYS... PROTECTED ME, HAVEN'T YOU?
I LOVE YOU, CHESHIRE...
YOU'LL COME WITH ME, WON'T YOU?
SO WE CAN BE TOGETHER AGAIN...
...EVEN IN THE NEXT "TALE."
MEOW...

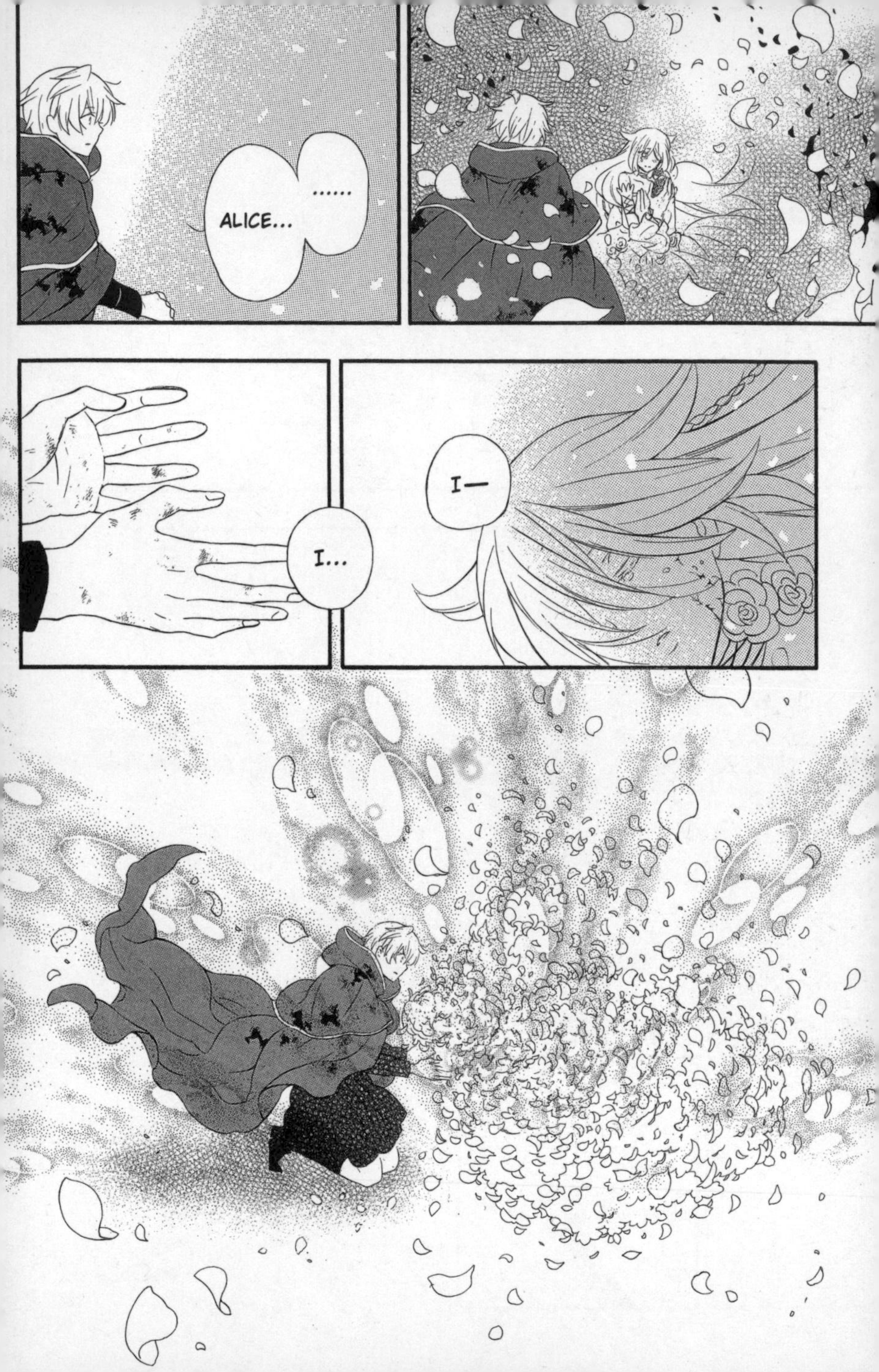
......
ALICE...
I—
I...

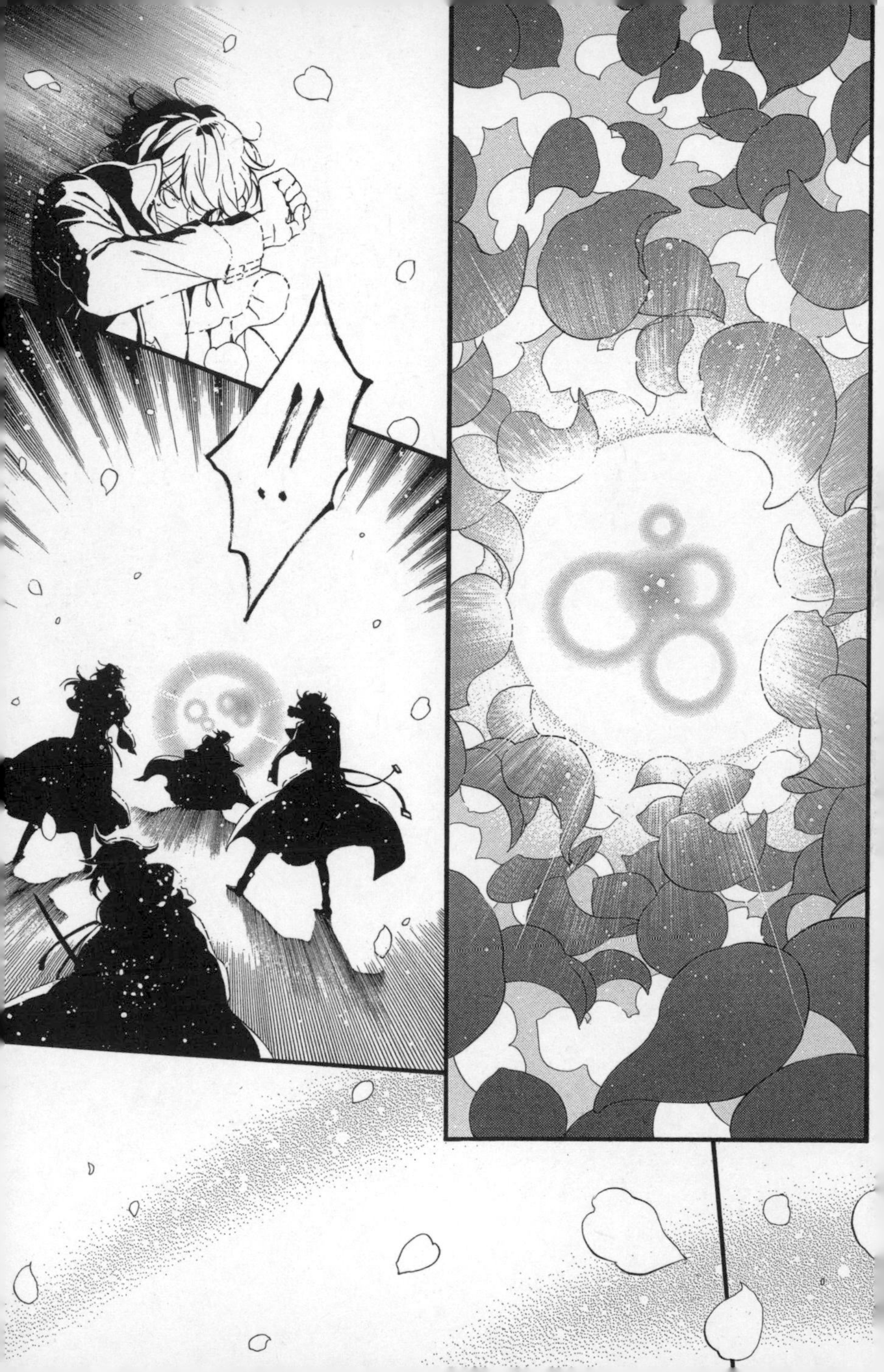

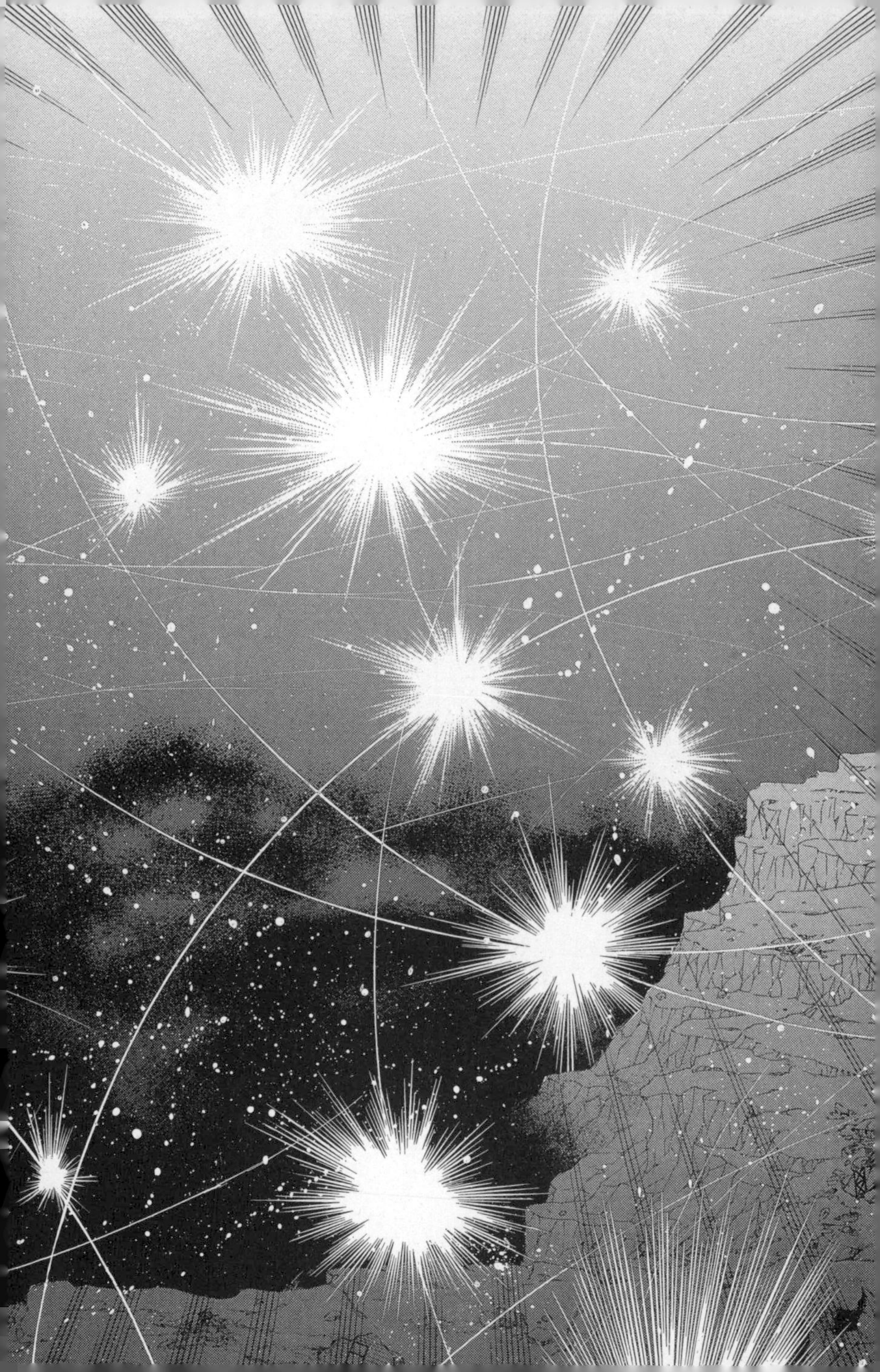

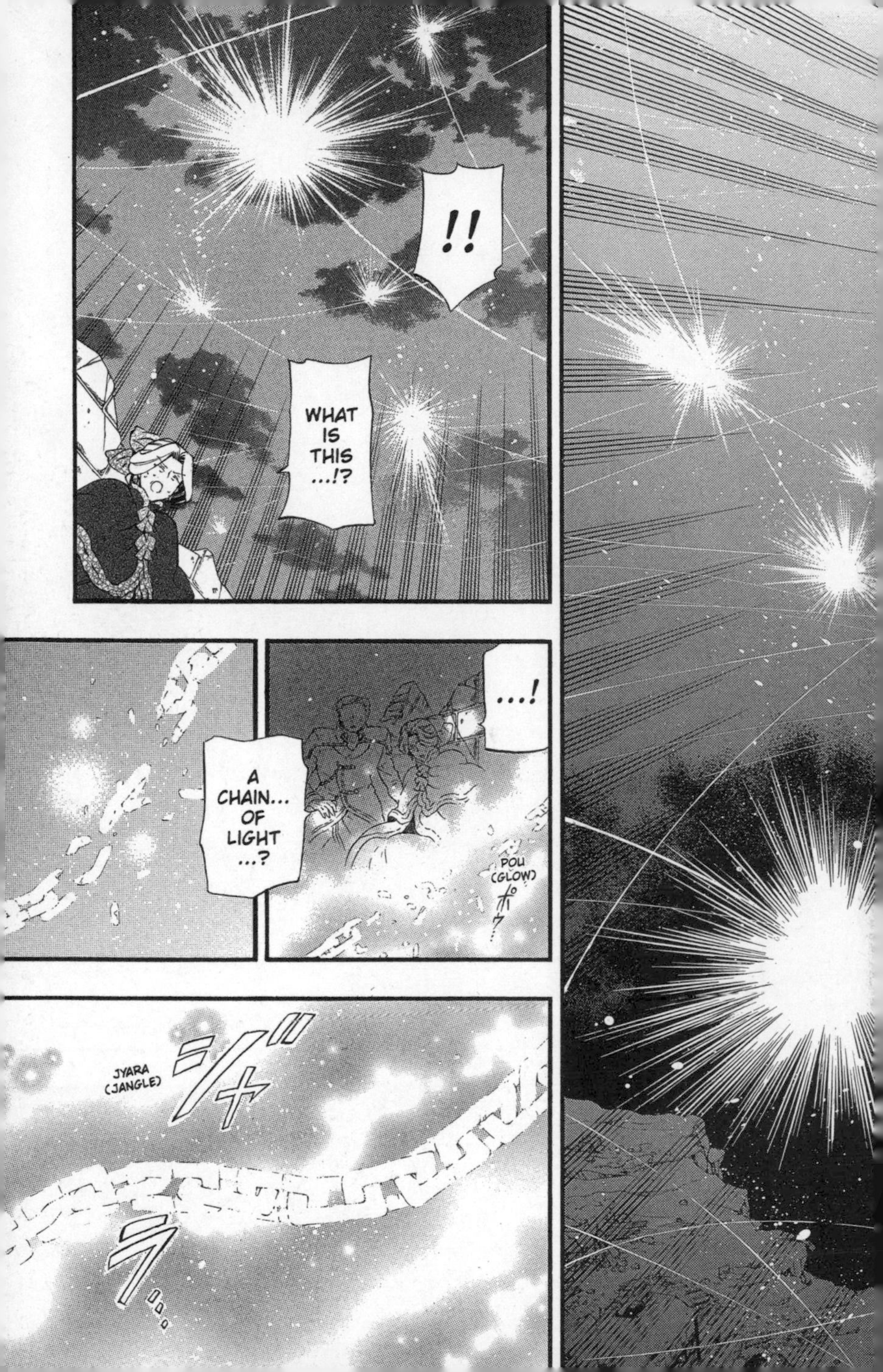
!!
WHAT IS THIS ...!?
...!
A CHAIN... OF LIGHT ...?
POU (GLOW)
JYARA (JANGLE)

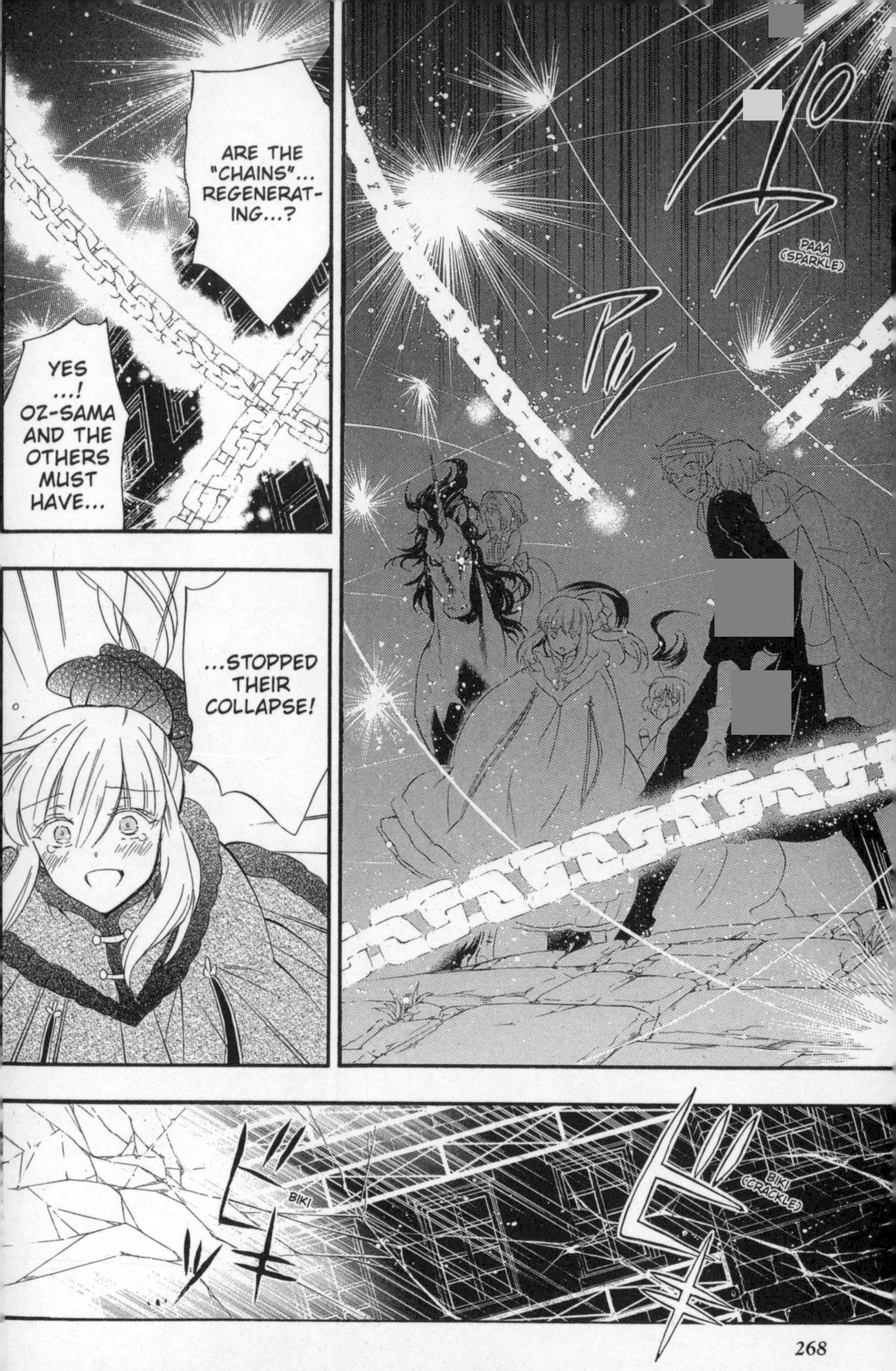

PAAA (SPARKLE)
ARE THE "CHAINS"... REGENERATING...?
YES ...! OZ-SAMA AND THE OTHERS MUST HAVE...
...STOPPED THEIR COLLAPSE!
BIKI (CRACKLE)
BIKI

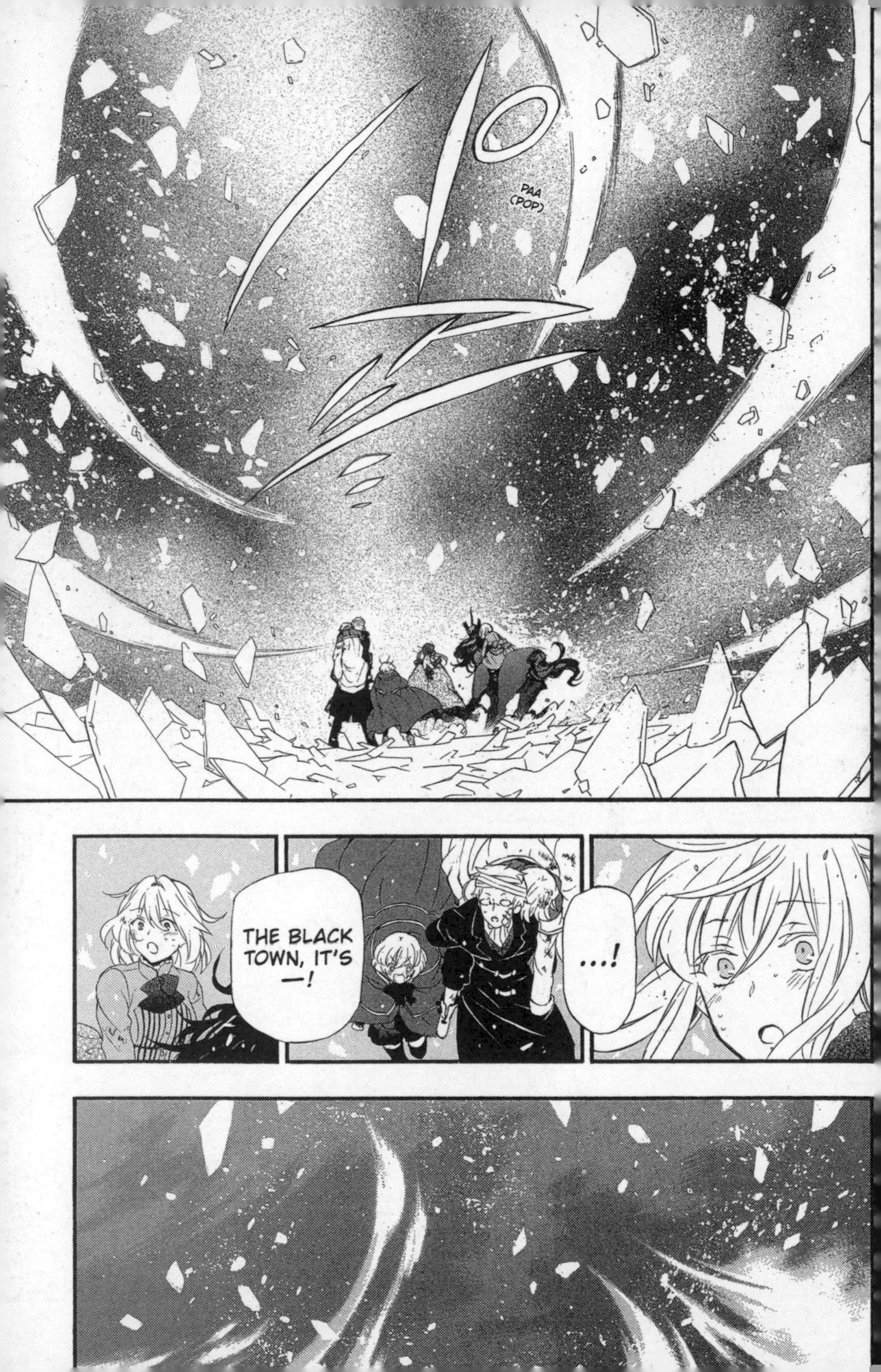
PAA (POP)
...!
THE BLACK TOWN, IT'S —!

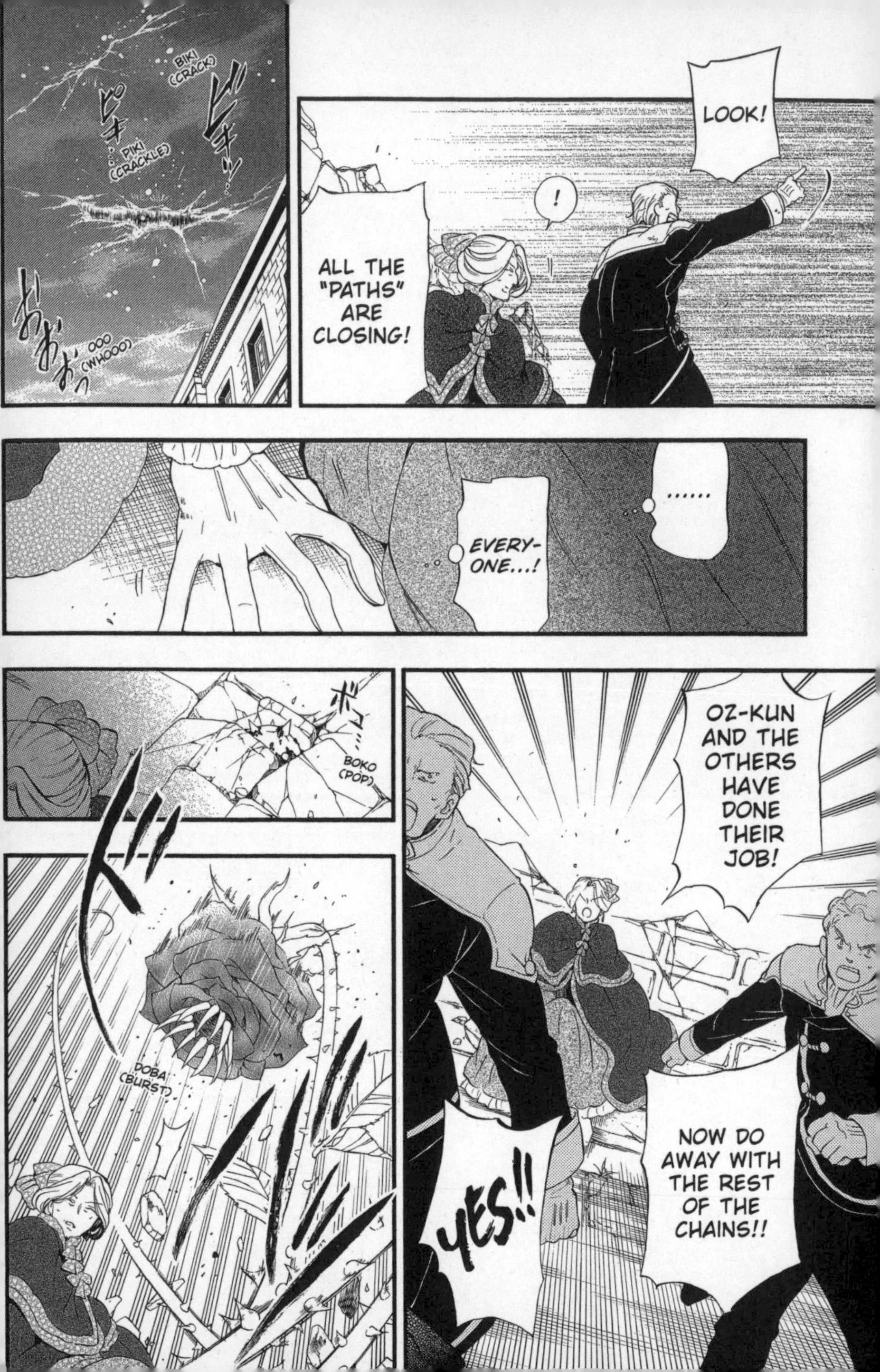
LOOK!
!
ALL THE "PATHS" ARE CLOSING!
BIKI (CRACK)
PIKI (CRACKLE)
OOO (WHOOO)
......
EVERY-ONE...!
OZ-KUN AND THE OTHERS HAVE DONE THEIR JOB!
NOW DO AWAY WITH THE REST OF THE CHAINS!!
YES!!
BOKO (POP)
DOBA (BURST)

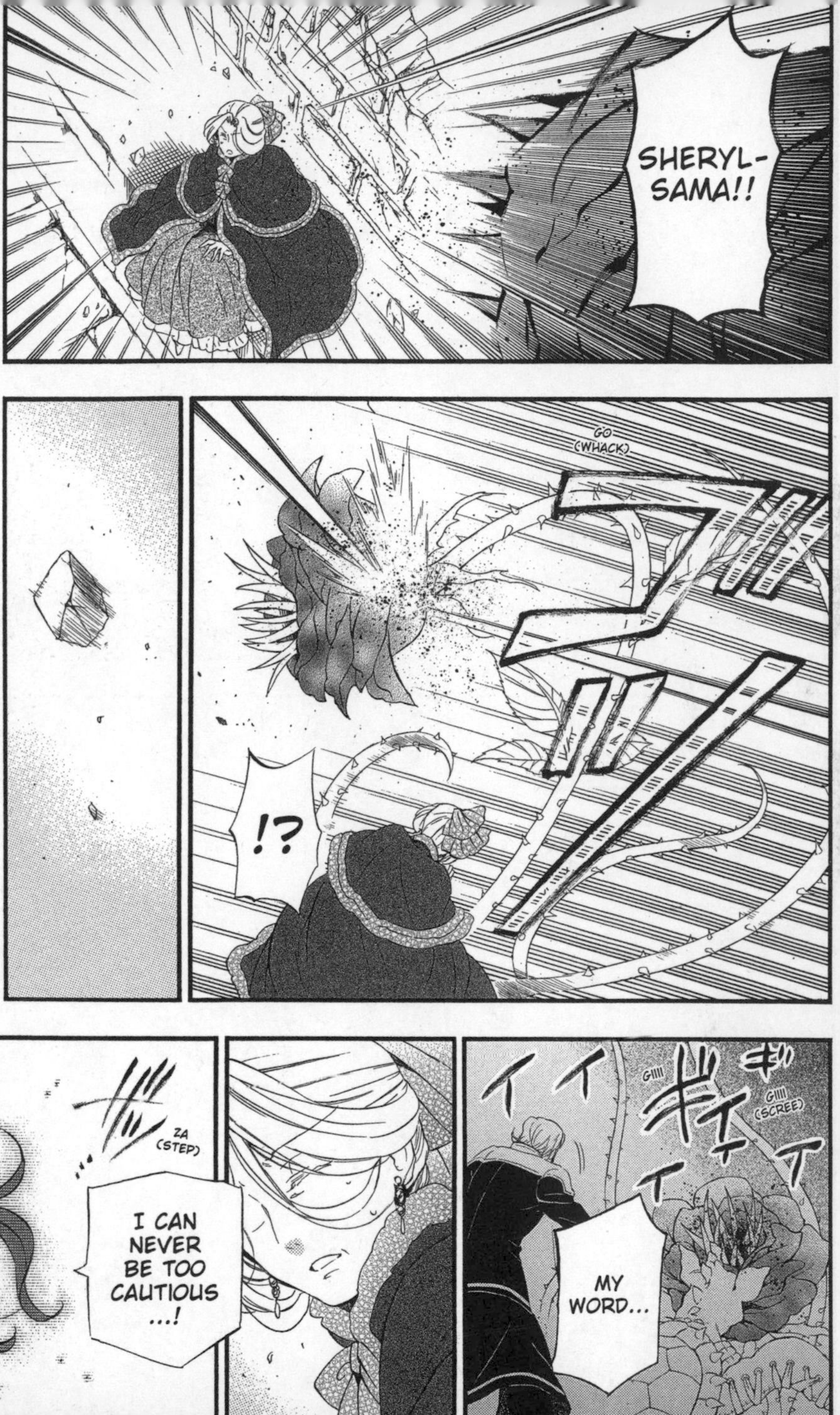
SHERYL-SAMA!!
GO (WHACK)
!?
GIIII
GIIII (SCREE)
MY WORD...
ZA (STEP)
I CAN NEVER BE TOO CAUTIOUS ...!

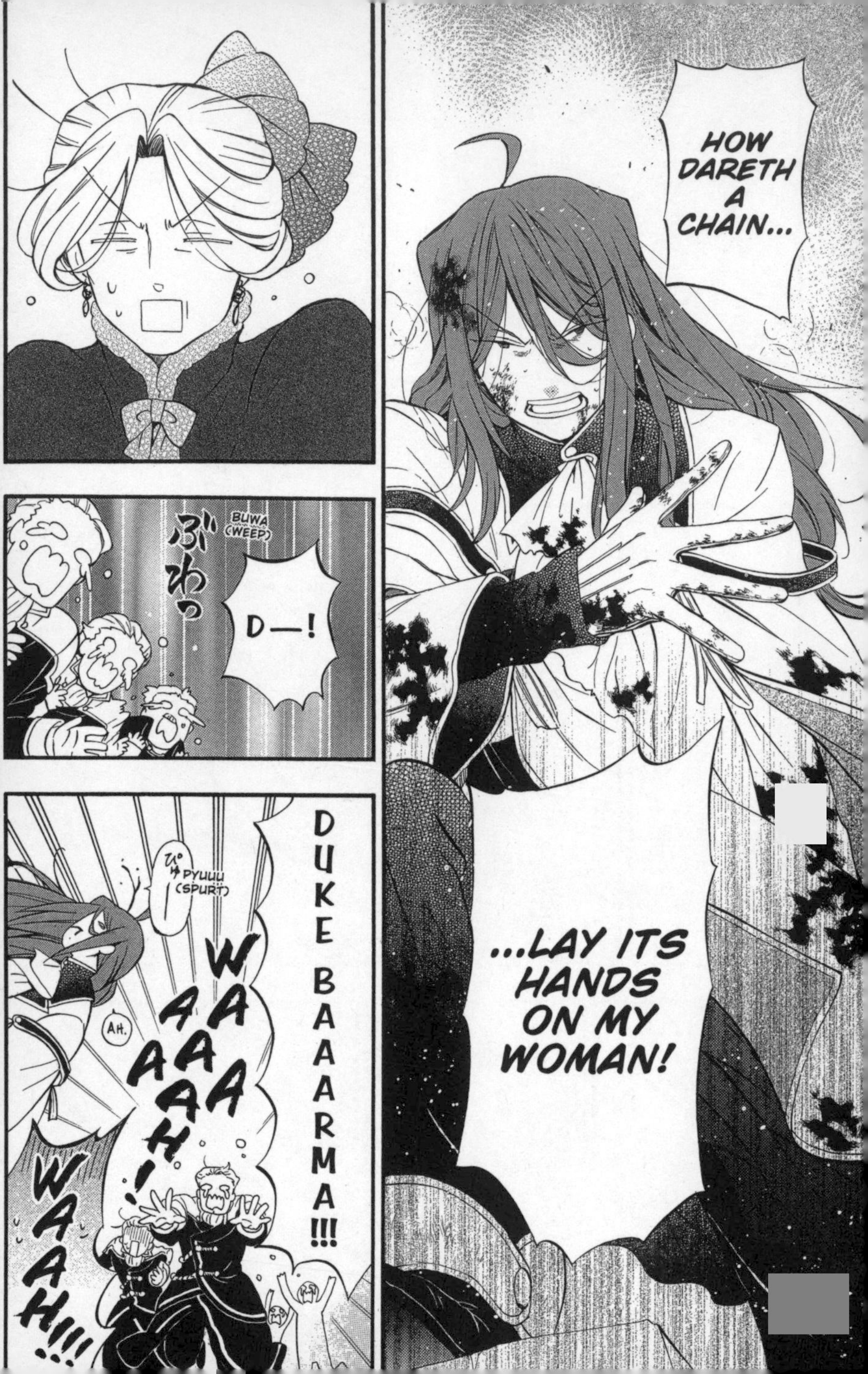
HOW DARETH A CHAIN...
...LAY ITS HANDS ON MY WOMAN!
ぶわっ
BUWA (WEEP)
D—!
DUKE BAAAARMA!!!
WAAAAAAAAH!
ぴゅ
PYUUU (SPURT)
AH.
WAAAH!!!

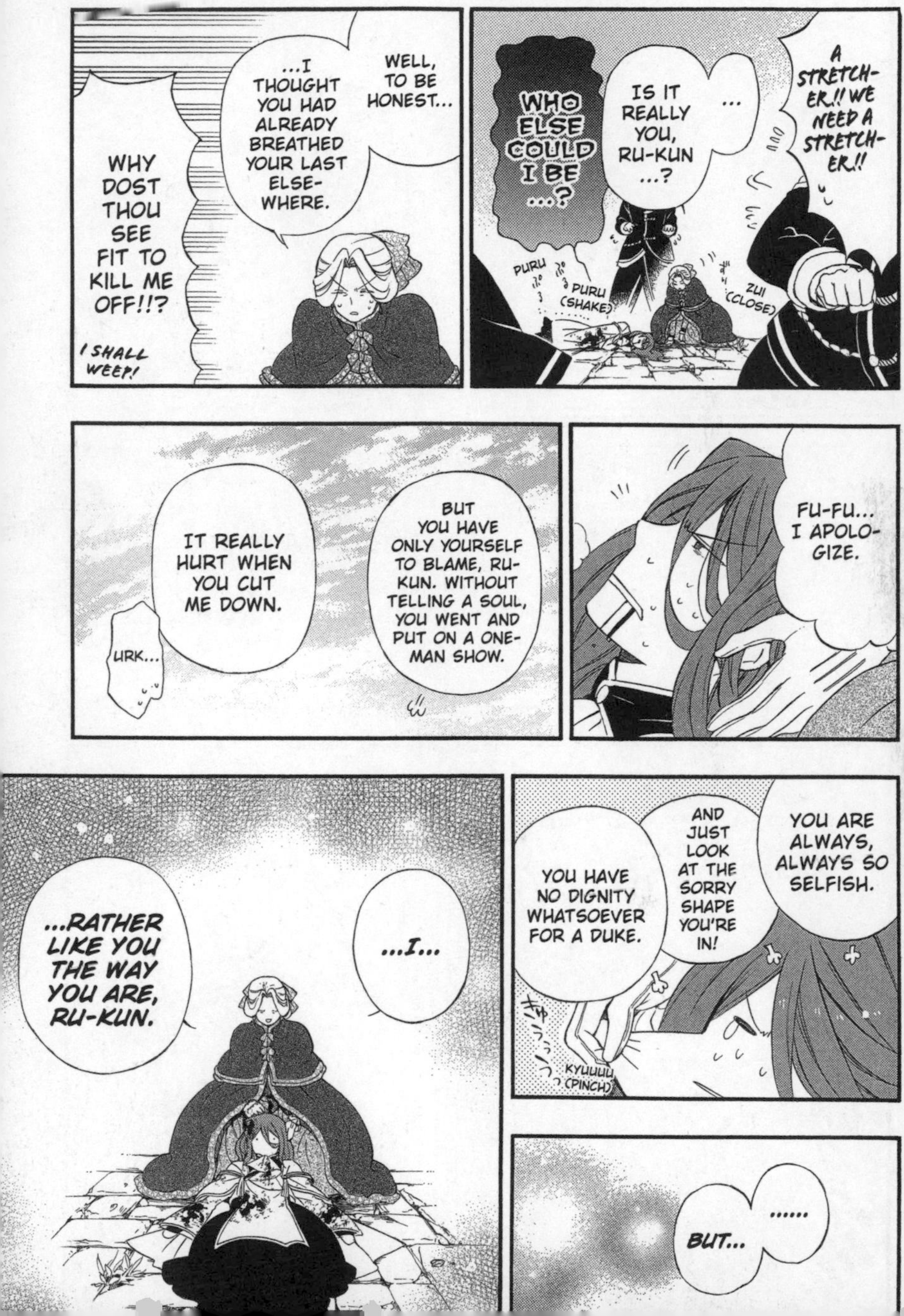
A STRETCHER!! WE NEED A STRETCHER!!
...
IS IT REALLY YOU, RU-KUN ...?
WHO ELSE COULD I BE ...?
PURU PURU (SHAKE)
ZUI (CLOSE)
WELL, TO BE HONEST...
...I THOUGHT YOU HAD ALREADY BREATHED YOUR LAST ELSE-WHERE.
WHY DOST THOU SEE FIT TO KILL ME OFF!!?
I SHALL WEEP!
FU-FU... I APOLO-GIZE.
BUT YOU HAVE ONLY YOURSELF TO BLAME, RU-KUN. WITHOUT TELLING A SOUL, YOU WENT AND PUT ON A ONE-MAN SHOW.
IT REALLY HURT WHEN YOU CUT ME DOWN.
URK...
YOU ARE ALWAYS, ALWAYS SO SELFISH.
AND JUST LOOK AT THE SORRY SHAPE YOU'RE IN!
YOU HAVE NO DIGNITY WHATSOEVER FOR A DUKE.
KYUUUU (PINCH)
......
BUT...
...I...
...RATHER LIKE YOU THE WAY YOU ARE, RU-KUN.

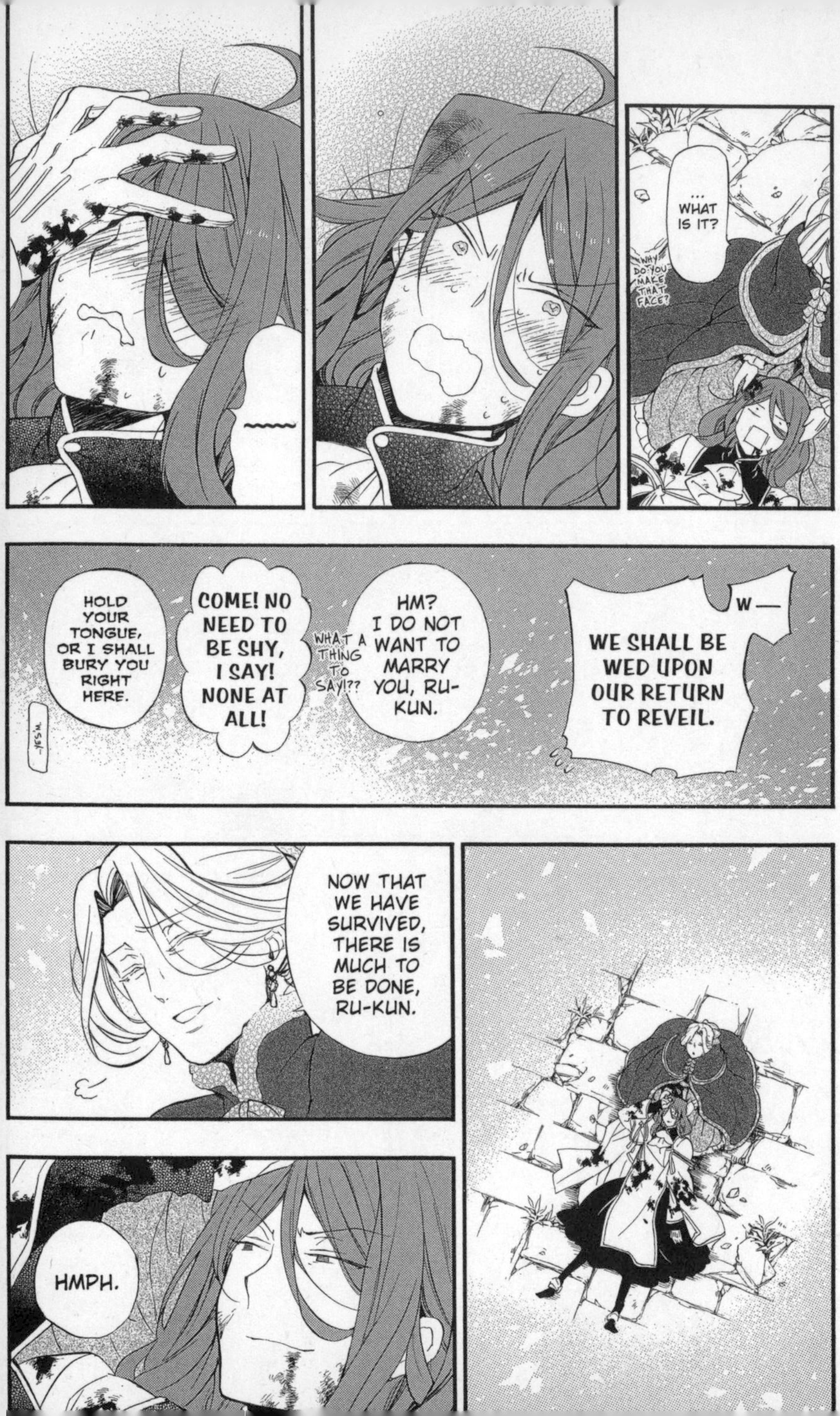
...WHAT IS IT?
WHY DO YOU MAKE THAT FACE?
W—
WE SHALL BE WED UPON OUR RETURN TO REVEIL.
HM? I DO NOT WANT TO MARRY YOU, RU-KUN.
WHAT A THING TO SAY!??
COME! NO NEED TO BE SHY, I SAY! NONE AT ALL!
HOLD YOUR TONGUE, OR I SHALL BURY YOU RIGHT HERE.
...YES'M.
NOW THAT WE HAVE SURVIVED, THERE IS MUCH TO BE DONE, RU-KUN.
HMPH.

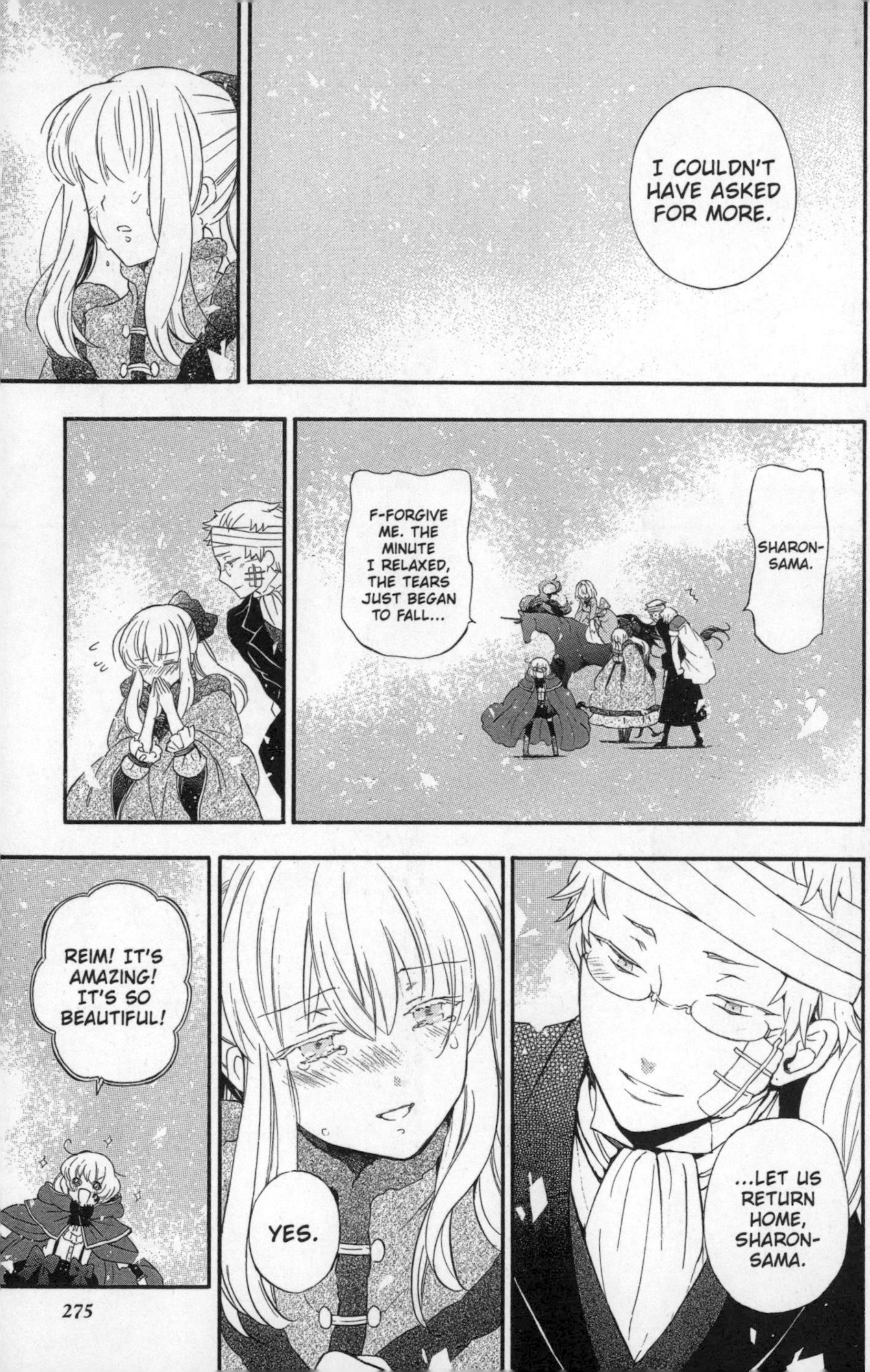
I COULDN'T HAVE ASKED FOR MORE.
SHARON-SAMA.
F-FORGIVE ME. THE MINUTE I RELAXED, THE TEARS JUST BEGAN TO FALL...
...LET US RETURN HOME, SHARON-SAMA.
YES.
REIM! IT'S AMAZING! IT'S SO BEAUTIFUL!

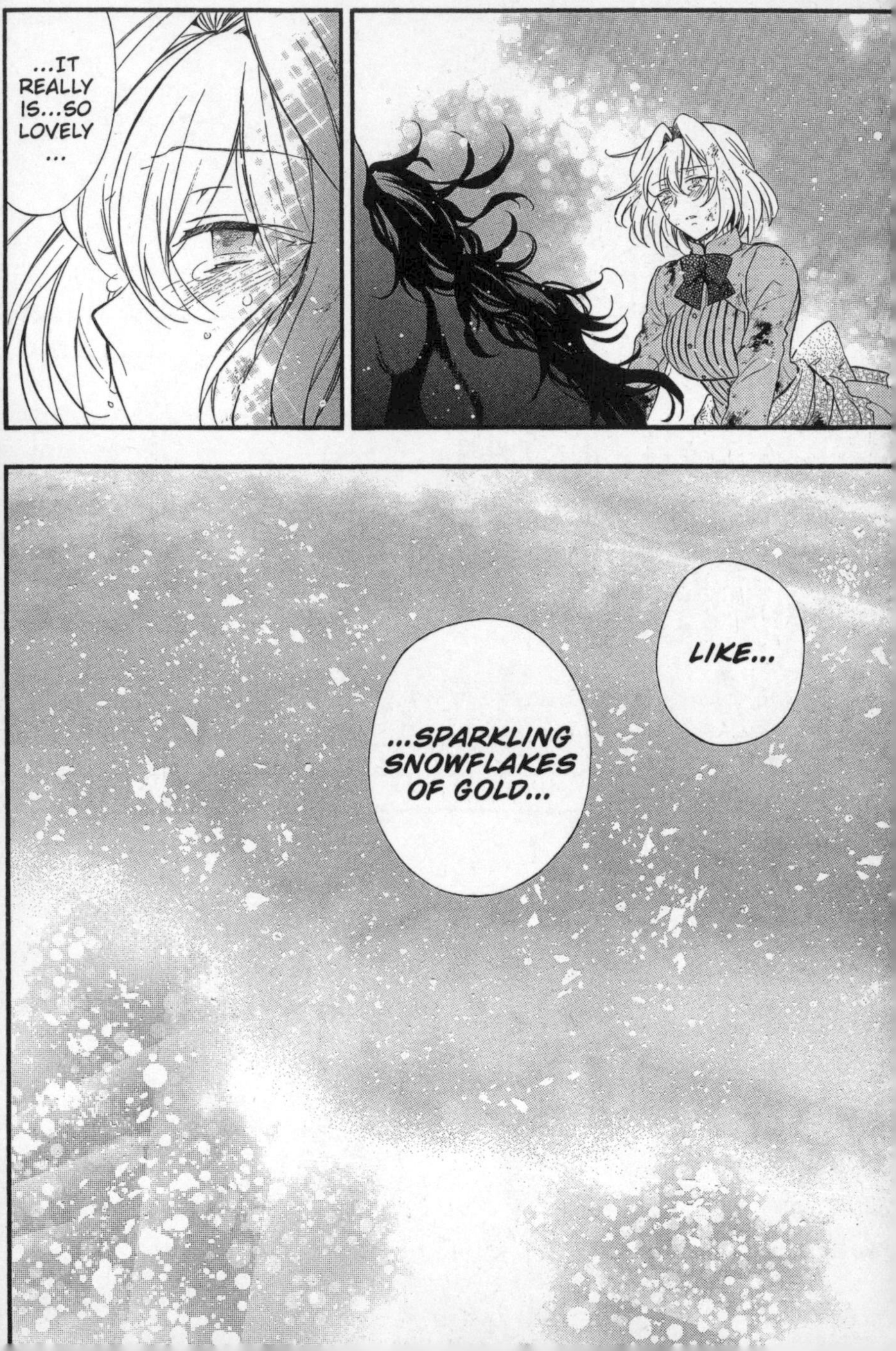
...IT REALLY IS...SO LOVELY...
LIKE...
...SPARKLING SNOWFLAKES OF GOLD...

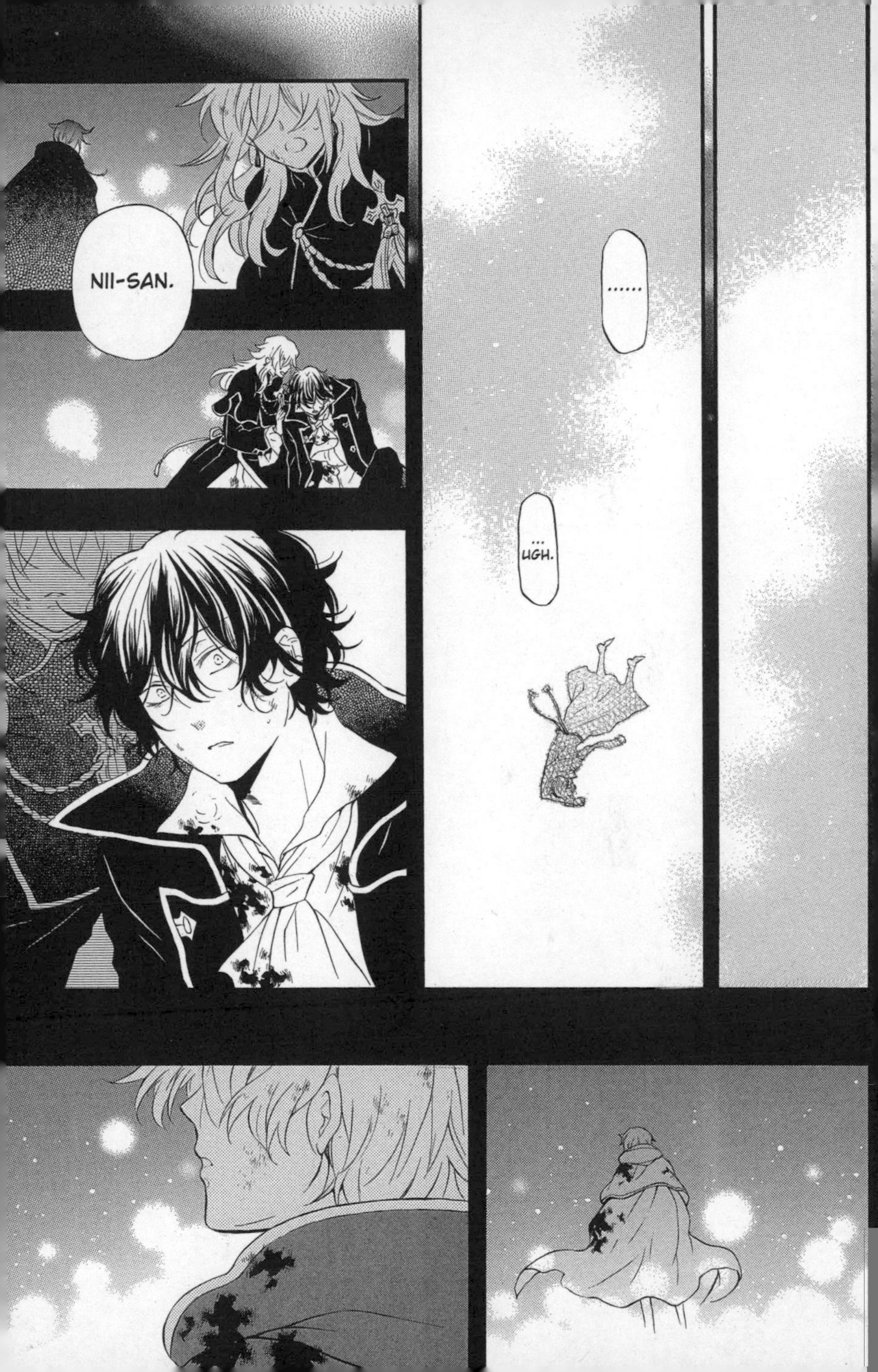
......
...UGH.
NII-SAN.

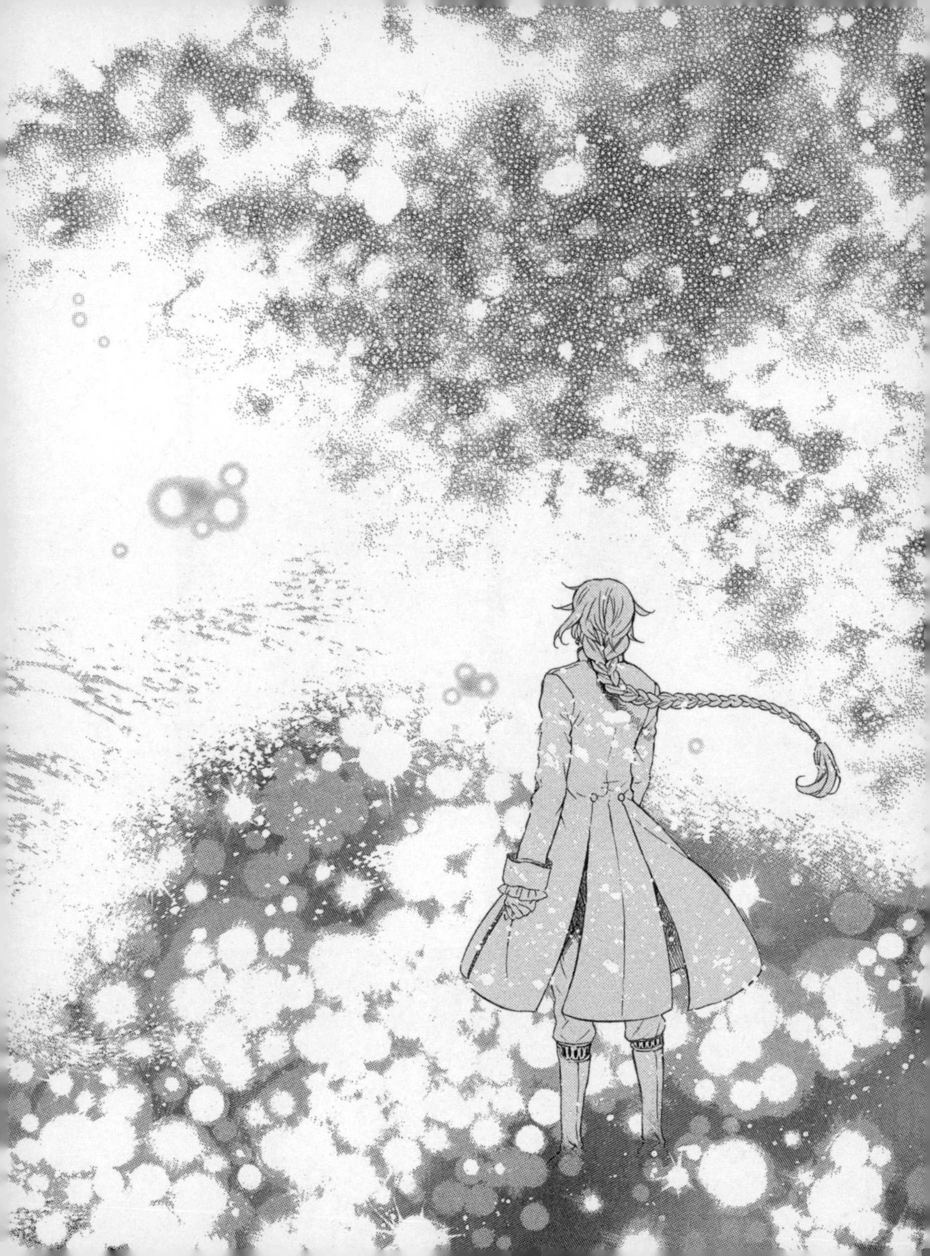

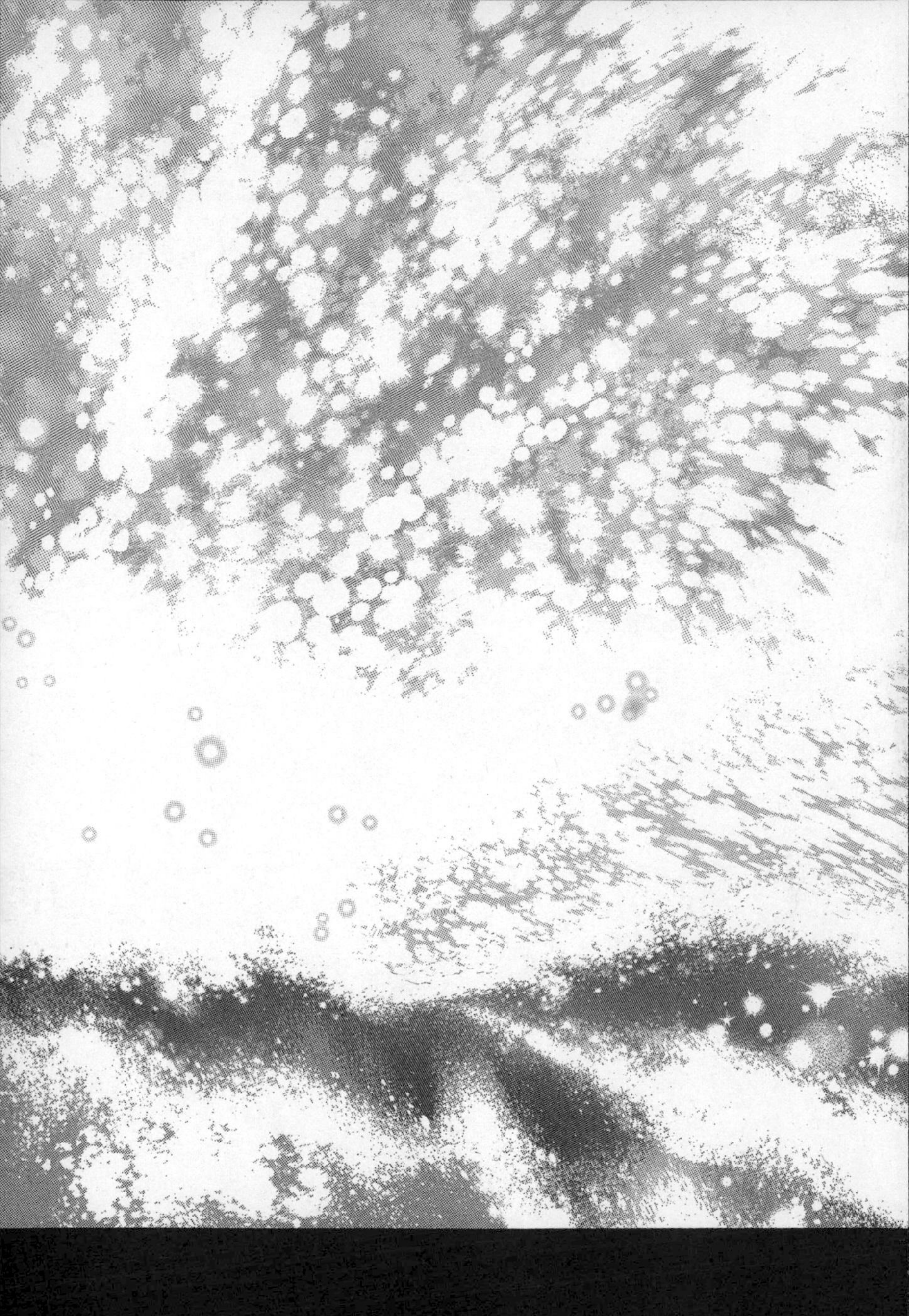

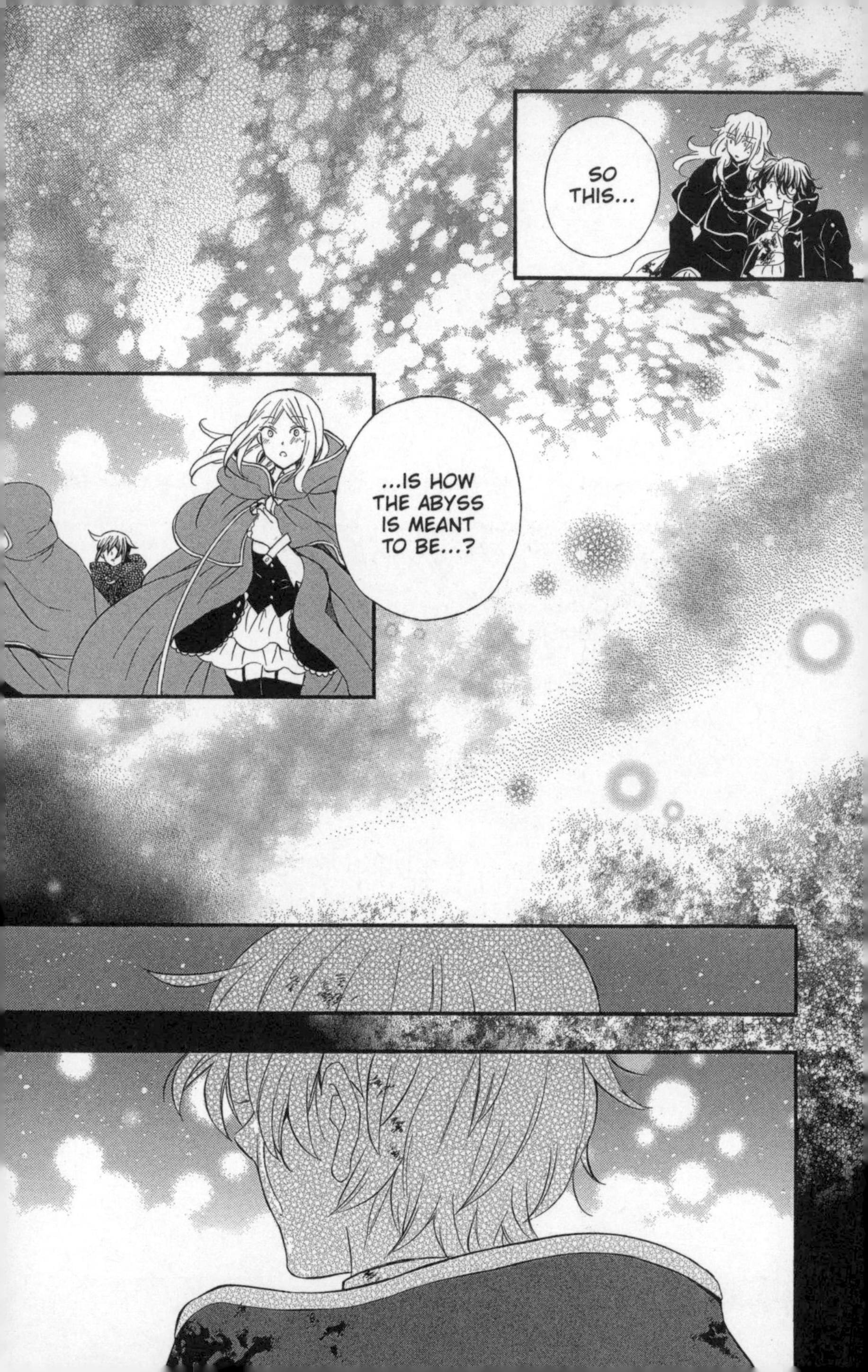
SO THIS...
...IS HOW THE ABYSS IS MEANT TO BE...?

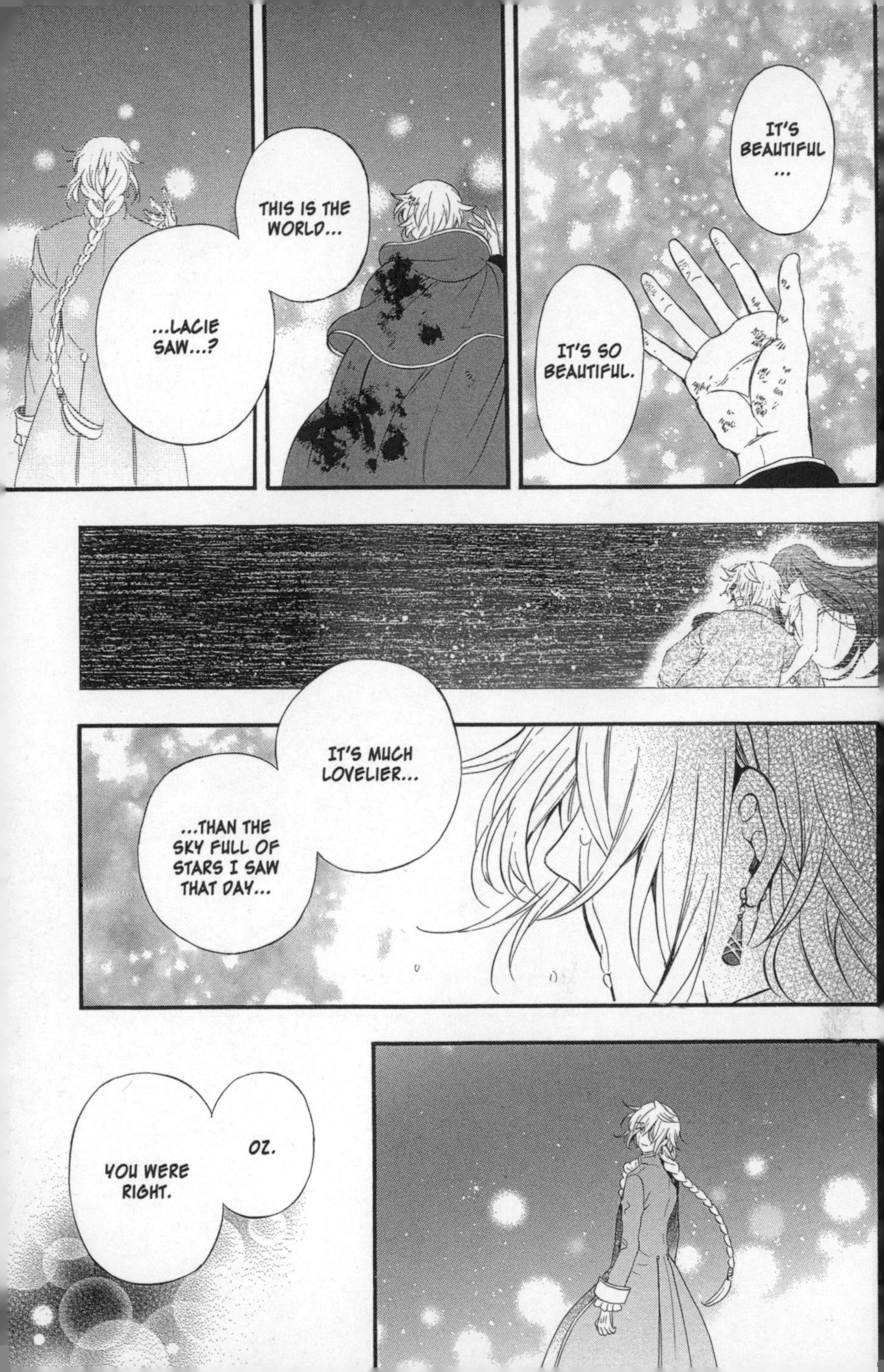
IT'S BEAUTIFUL ...
IT'S SO BEAUTIFUL.
THIS IS THE WORLD...
...LACIE SAW...?
IT'S MUCH LOVELIER...
...THAN THE SKY FULL OF STARS I SAW THAT DAY...
OZ.
YOU WERE RIGHT.

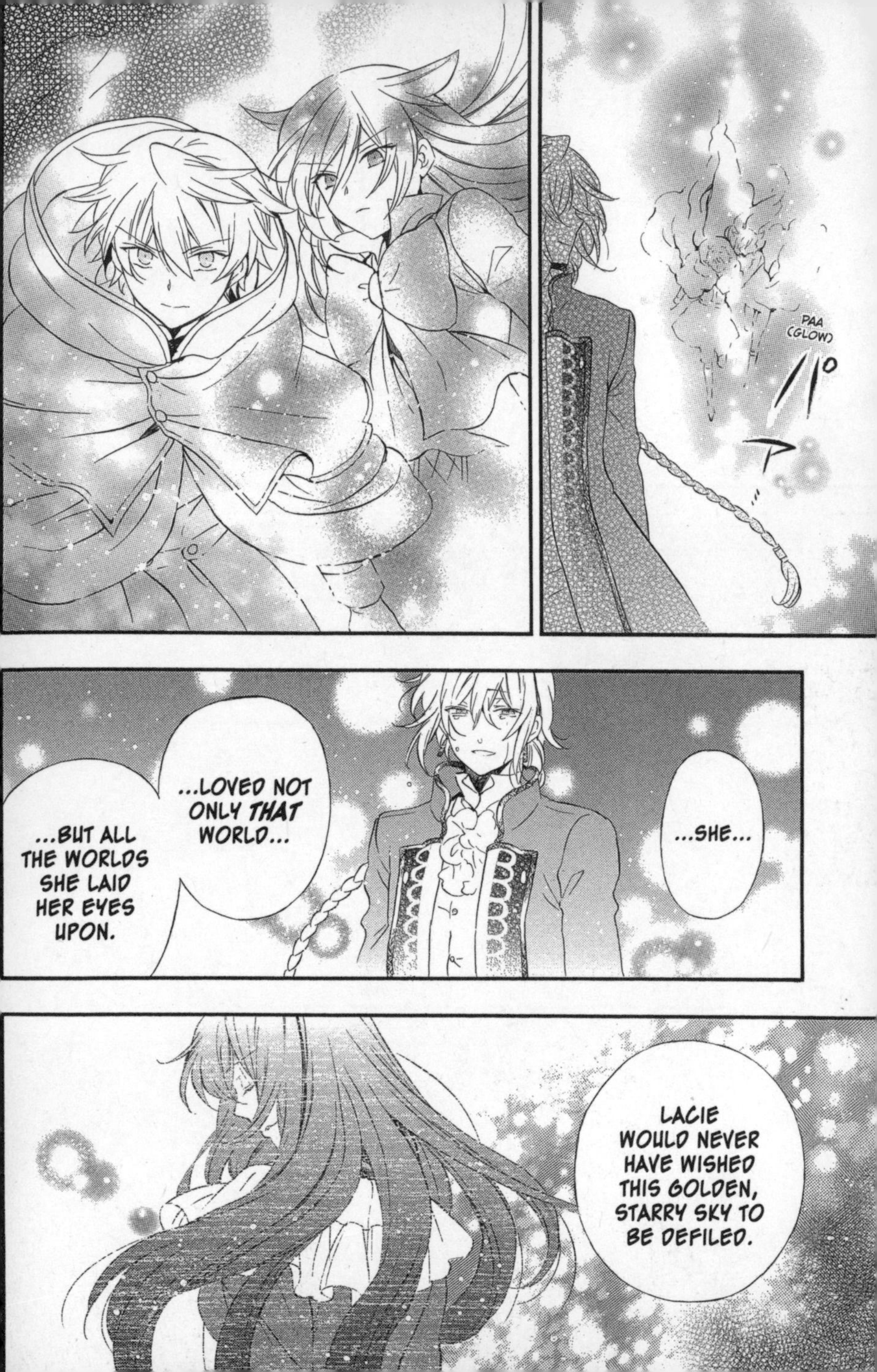
PAA (GLOW)
パア
...SHE...
...LOVED NOT ONLY THAT WORLD...
...BUT ALL THE WORLDS SHE LAID HER EYES UPON.
LACIE WOULD NEVER HAVE WISHED THIS GOLDEN, STARRY SKY TO BE DEFILED.

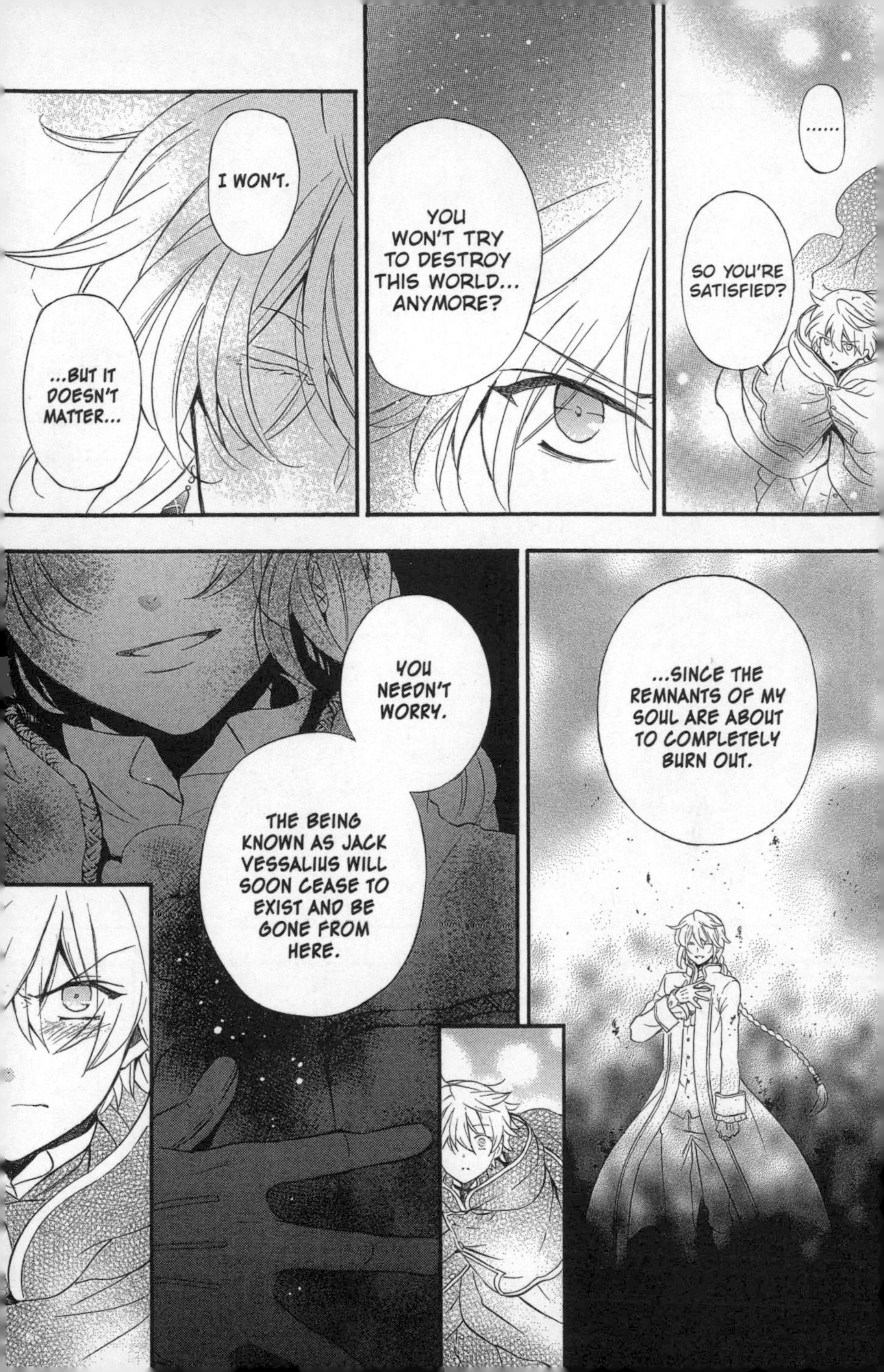
......
SO YOU'RE SATISFIED?
YOU WON'T TRY TO DESTROY THIS WORLD... ANYMORE?
I WON'T.
...BUT IT DOESN'T MATTER...
...SINCE THE REMNANTS OF MY SOUL ARE ABOUT TO COMPLETELY BURN OUT.
YOU NEEDN'T WORRY.
THE BEING KNOWN AS JACK VESSALIUS WILL SOON CEASE TO EXIST AND BE GONE FROM HERE.

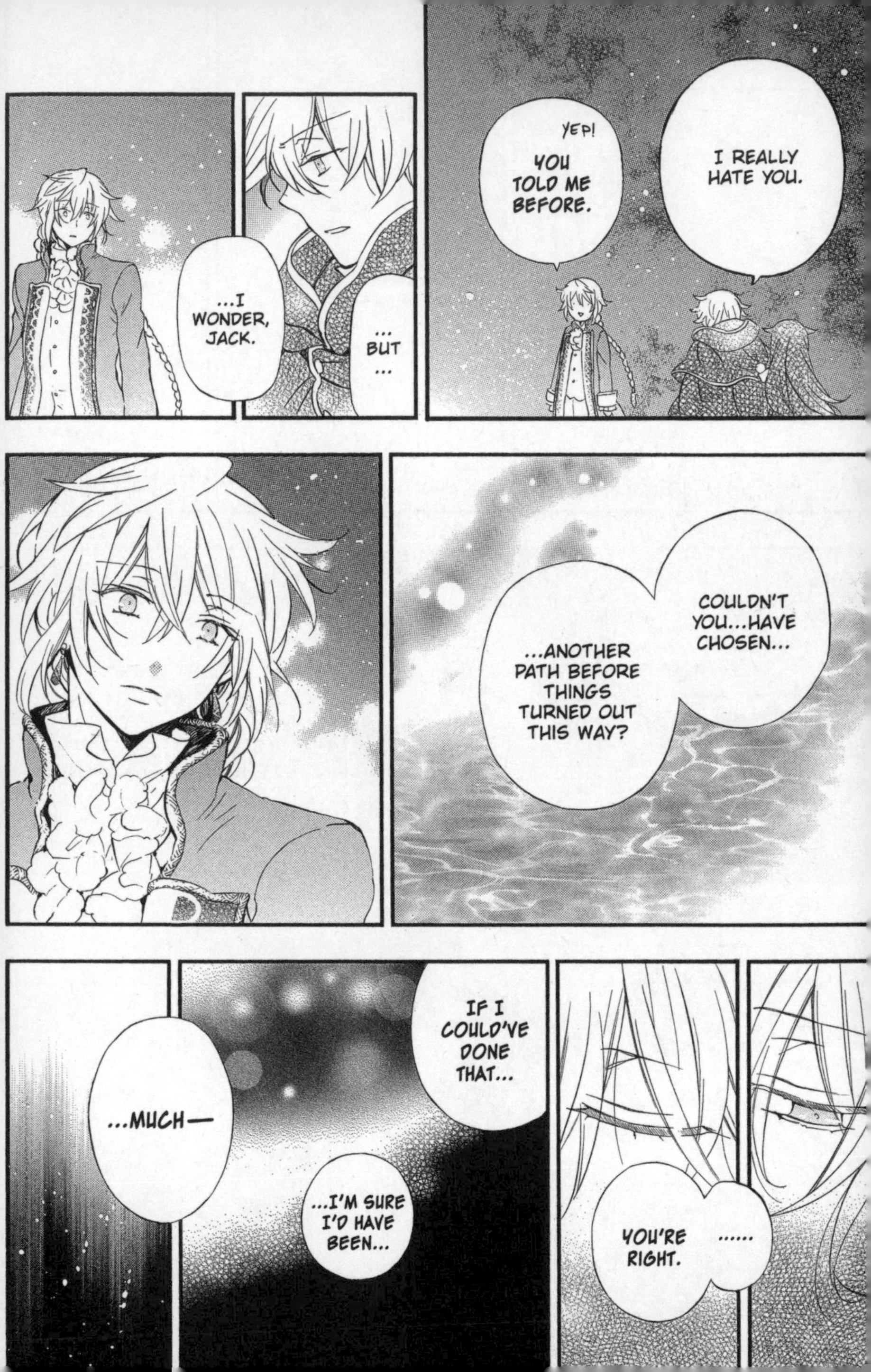
I REALLY HATE YOU.
YEP!
YOU TOLD ME BEFORE.
...BUT...
...I WONDER, JACK.
COULDN'T YOU...HAVE CHOSEN...
...ANOTHER PATH BEFORE THINGS TURNED OUT THIS WAY?
......
YOU'RE RIGHT.
IF I COULD'VE DONE THAT...
...I'M SURE I'D HAVE BEEN...
...MUCH—

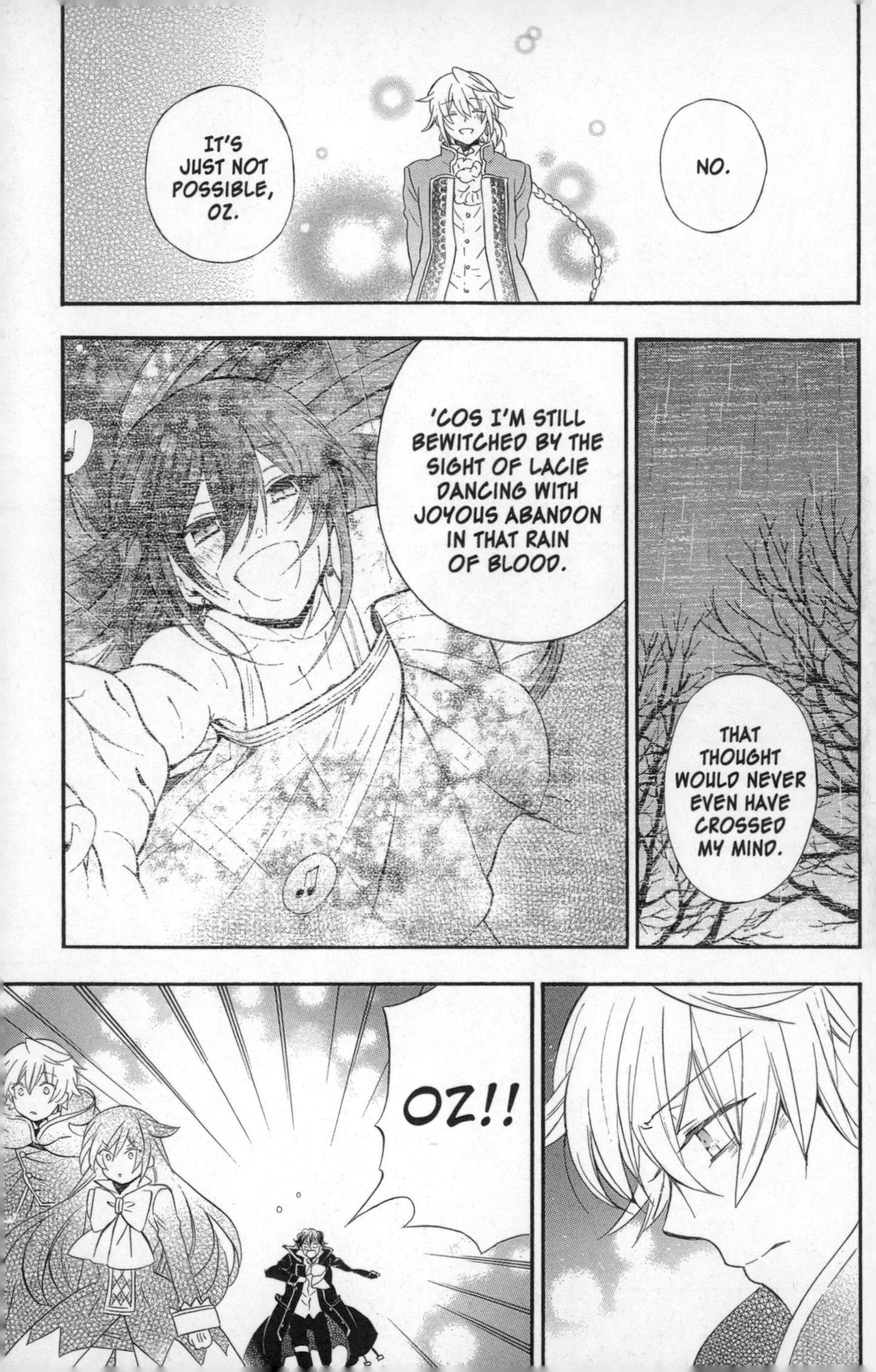
NO.
IT'S JUST NOT POSSIBLE, OZ.
THAT THOUGHT WOULD NEVER EVEN HAVE CROSSED MY MIND.
'COS I'M STILL BEWITCHED BY THE SIGHT OF LACIE DANCING WITH JOYOUS ABANDON IN THAT RAIN OF BLOOD.
OZ!!

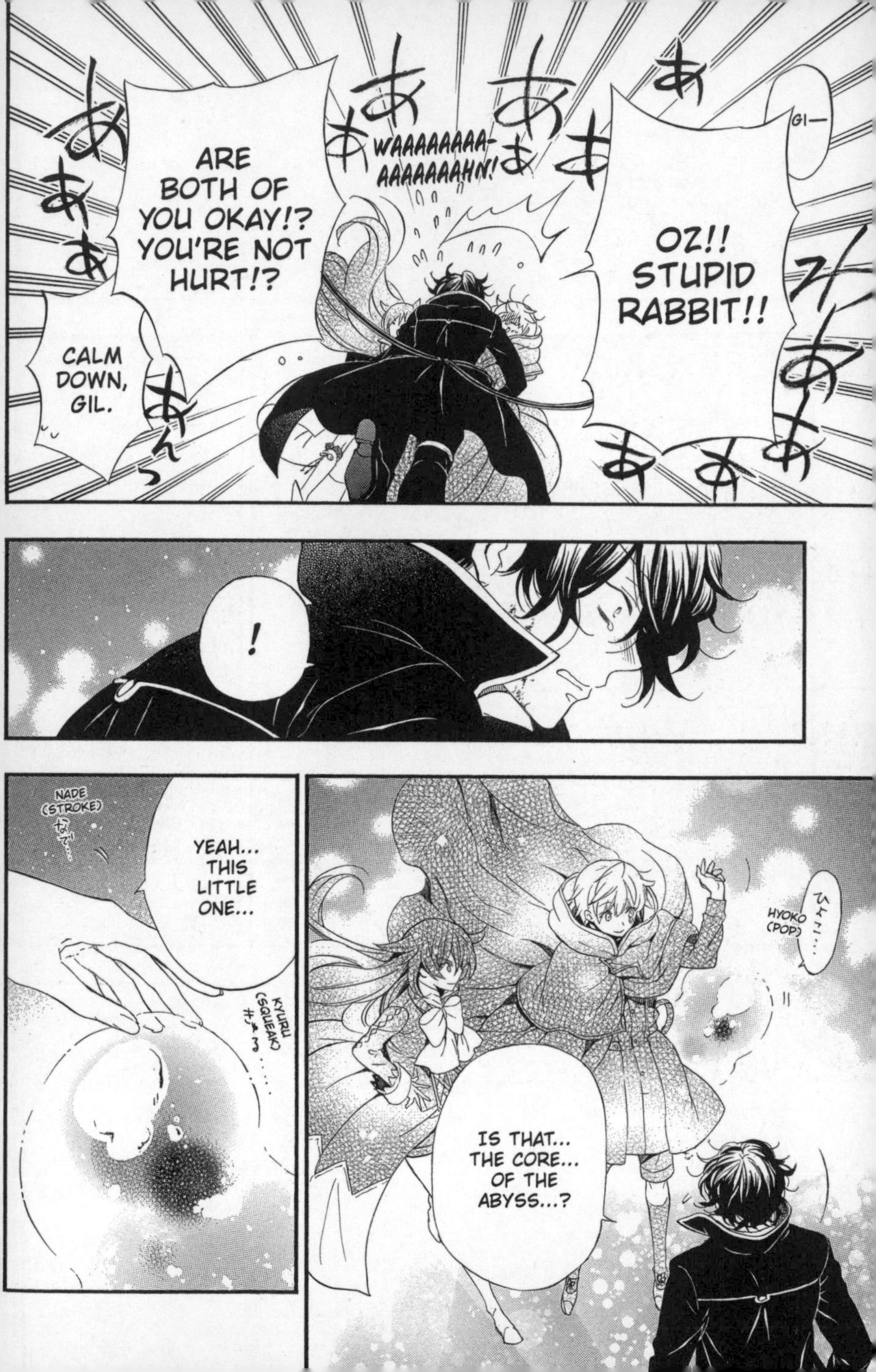
GI—
OZ!! STUPID RABBIT!!
WAAAAAAAAA-AAAAAAAAHN!
ARE BOTH OF YOU OKAY!? YOU'RE NOT HURT!?
CALM DOWN, GIL.
!
HYOKO (POP)
IS THAT... THE CORE... OF THE ABYSS...?
NADE (STROKE)
YEAH... THIS LITTLE ONE...
KYURU (SQUEAK)

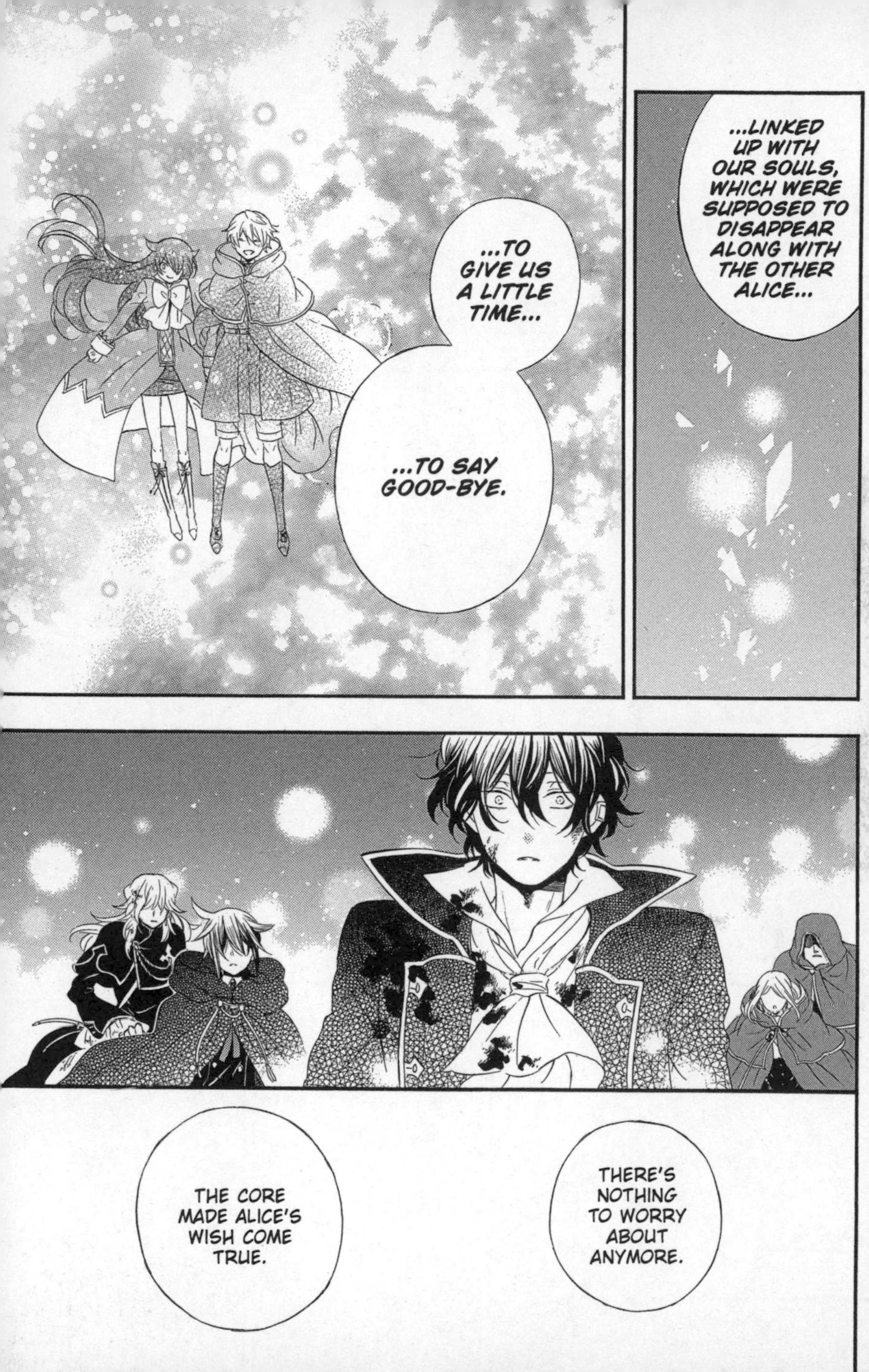
...LINKED UP WITH OUR SOULS, WHICH WERE SUPPOSED TO DISAPPEAR ALONG WITH THE OTHER ALICE...
...TO GIVE US A LITTLE TIME...
...TO SAY GOOD-BYE.
THERE'S NOTHING TO WORRY ABOUT ANYMORE.
THE CORE MADE ALICE'S WISH COME TRUE.

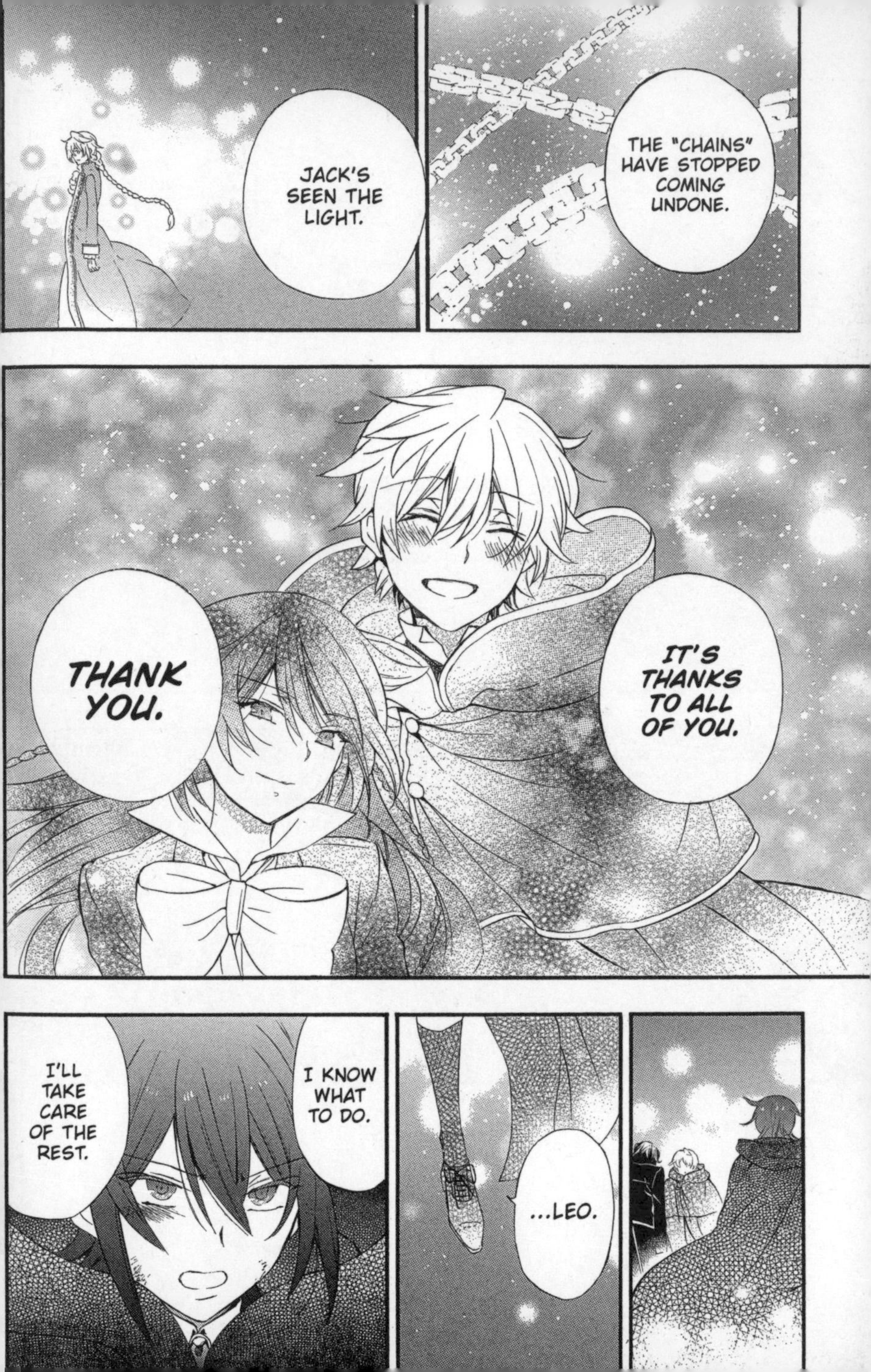
THE "CHAINS" HAVE STOPPED COMING UNDONE.
JACK'S SEEN THE LIGHT.
IT'S THANKS TO ALL OF YOU.
THANK YOU.
...LEO.
I KNOW WHAT TO DO.
I'LL TAKE CARE OF THE REST.

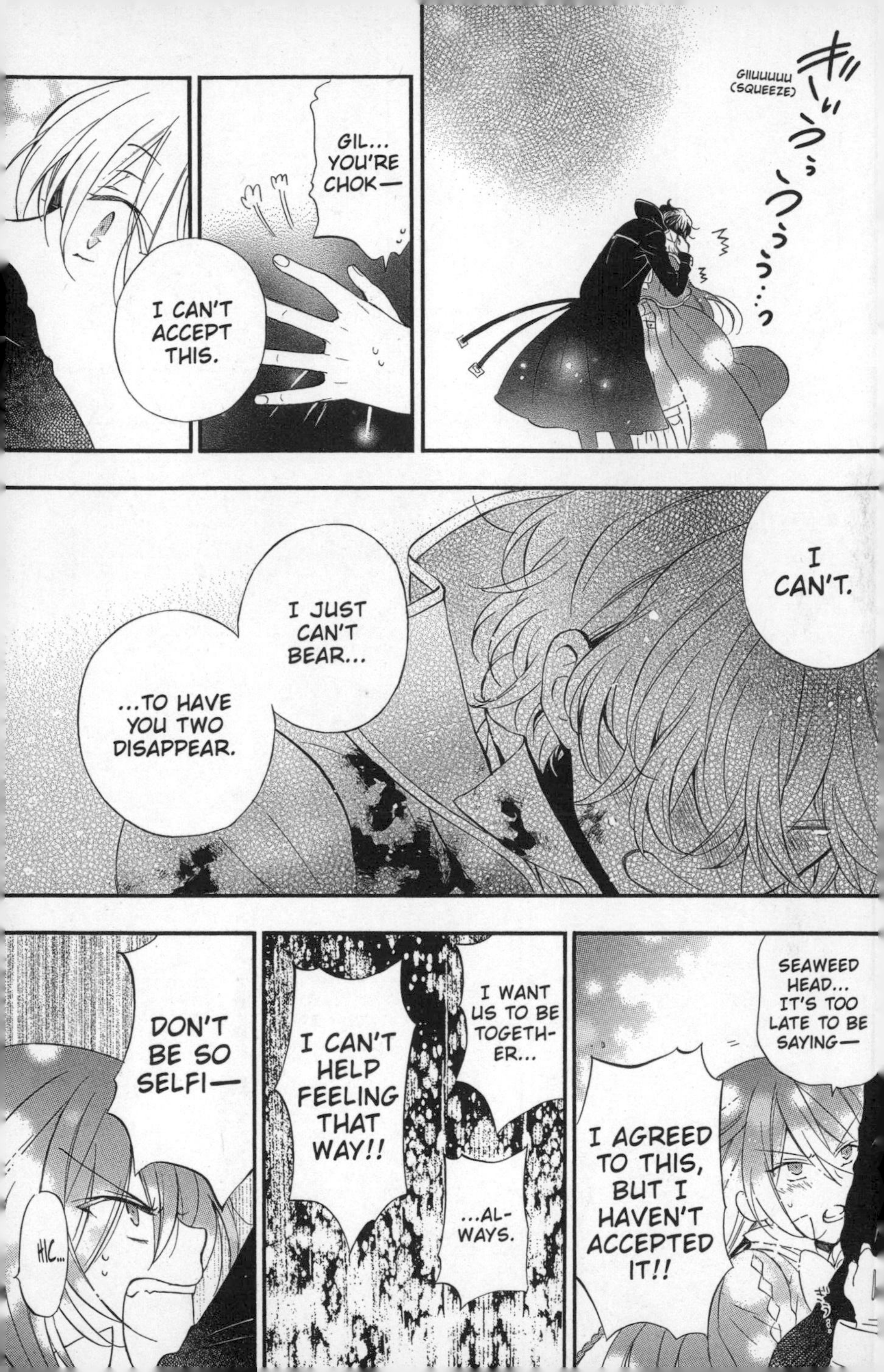
GIIUUUUU (SQUEEZE)
GIL... YOU'RE CHOK—
I CAN'T ACCEPT THIS.
I CAN'T.
I JUST CAN'T BEAR...
...TO HAVE YOU TWO DISAPPEAR.
SEAWEED HEAD... IT'S TOO LATE TO BE SAYING—
I AGREED TO THIS, BUT I HAVEN'T ACCEPTED IT!!
I WANT US TO BE TOGETH- ER...
I CAN'T HELP FEELING THAT WAY!!
...AL- WAYS.
DON'T BE SO SELFI—
HIC...

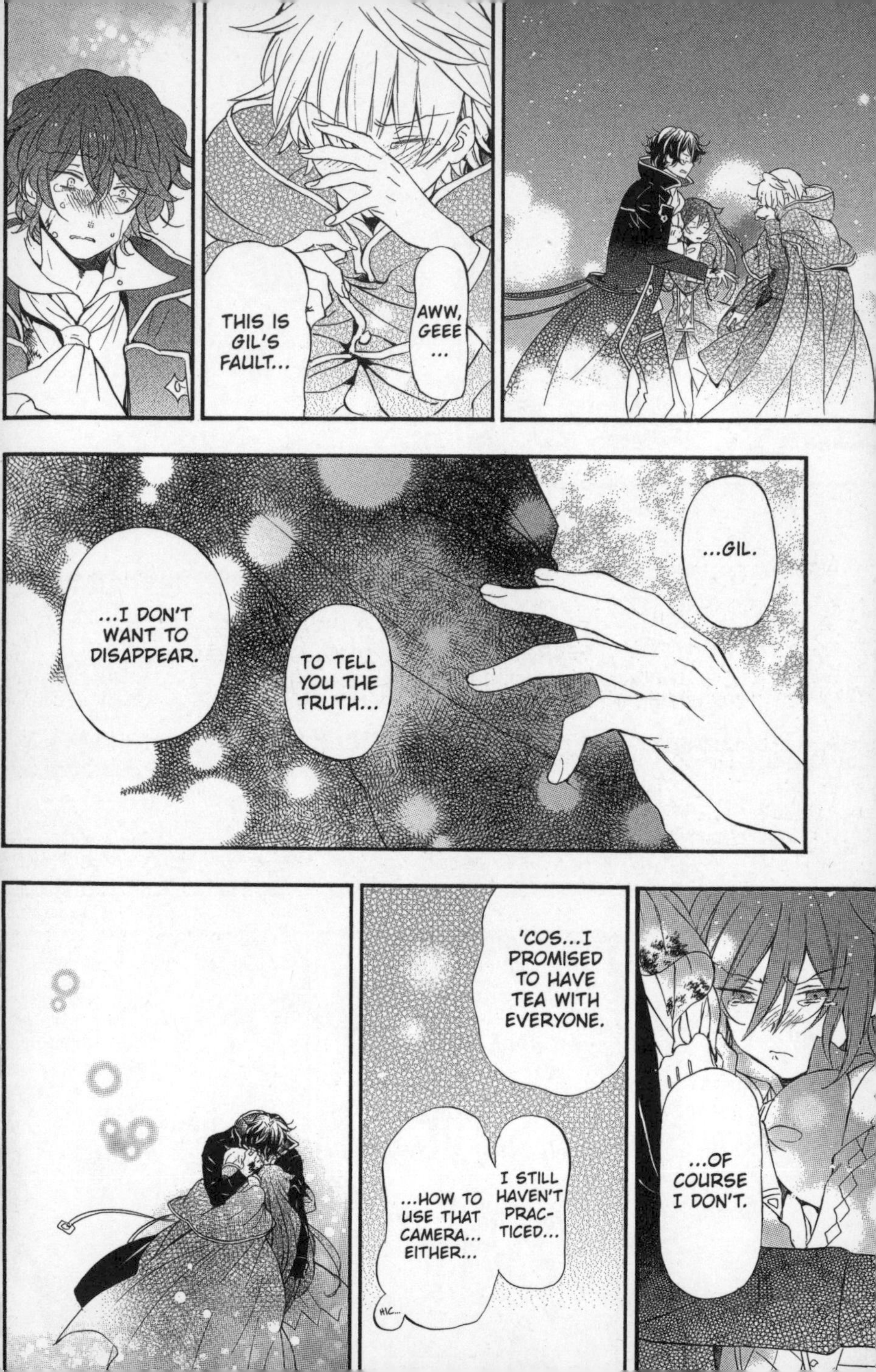
AWW, GEEE ...
THIS IS GIL'S FAULT...
...GIL.
TO TELL YOU THE TRUTH...
...I DON'T WANT TO DISAPPEAR.
...OF COURSE I DON'T.
'COS...I PROMISED TO HAVE TEA WITH EVERYONE.
I STILL HAVEN'T PRAC-TICED...
...HOW TO USE THAT CAMERA... EITHER...
HIC...

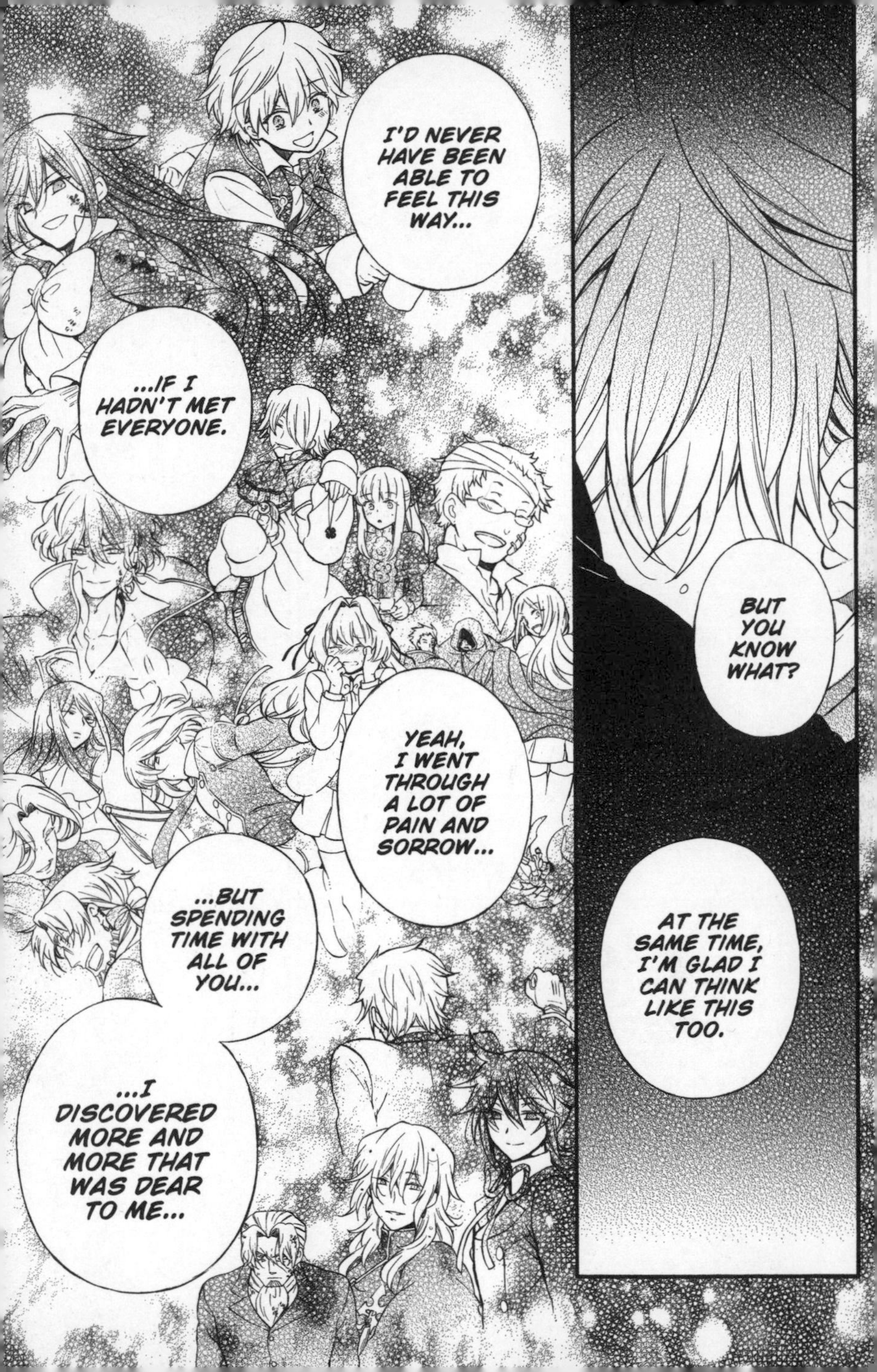
BUT YOU KNOW WHAT?
AT THE SAME TIME, I'M GLAD I CAN THINK LIKE THIS TOO.
I'D NEVER HAVE BEEN ABLE TO FEEL THIS WAY...
...IF I HADN'T MET EVERYONE.
YEAH, I WENT THROUGH A LOT OF PAIN AND SORROW...
...BUT SPENDING TIME WITH ALL OF YOU...
...I DISCOVERED MORE AND MORE THAT WAS DEAR TO ME...

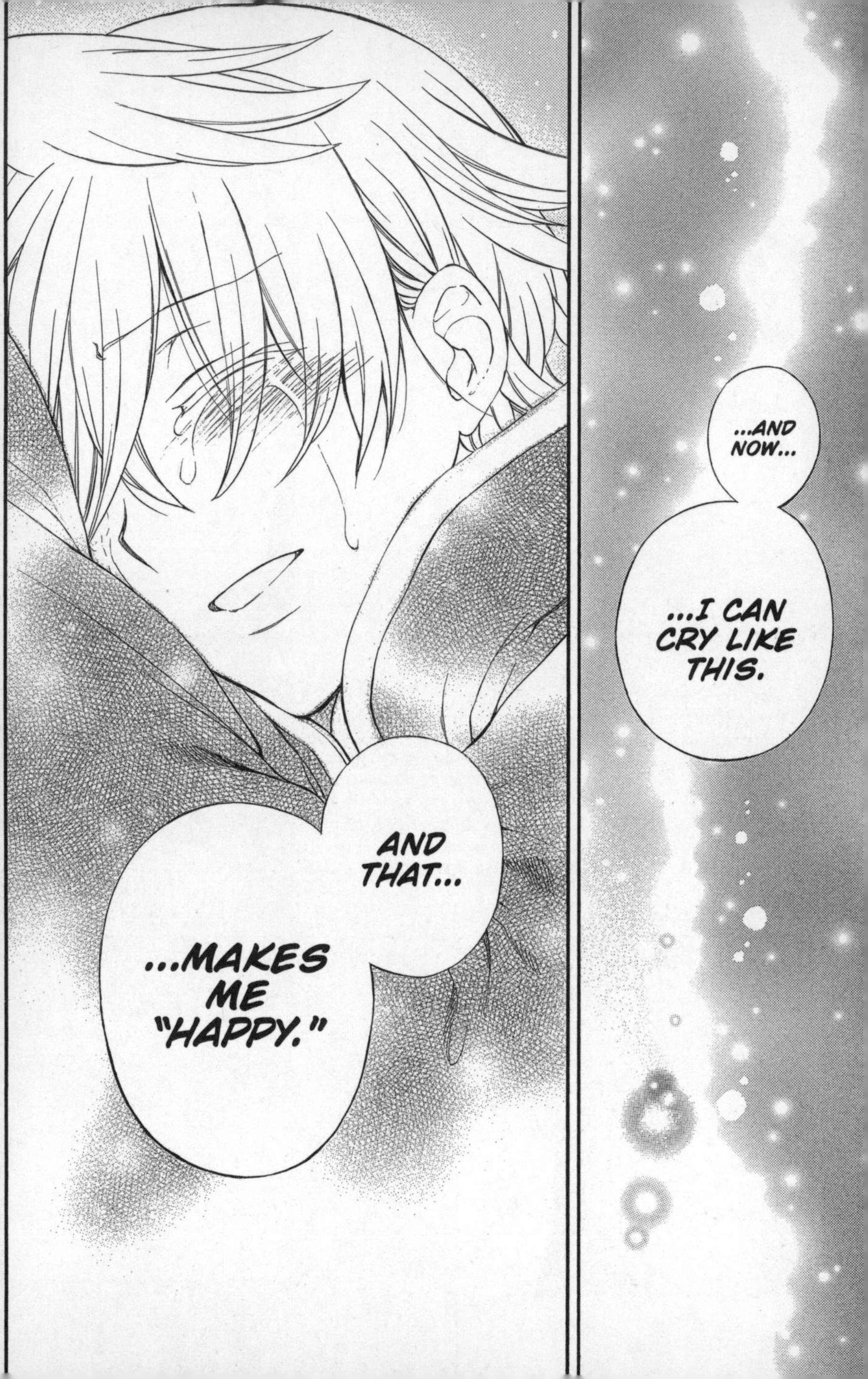
...AND NOW...
...I CAN CRY LIKE THIS.
AND THAT...
...MAKES ME "HAPPY."

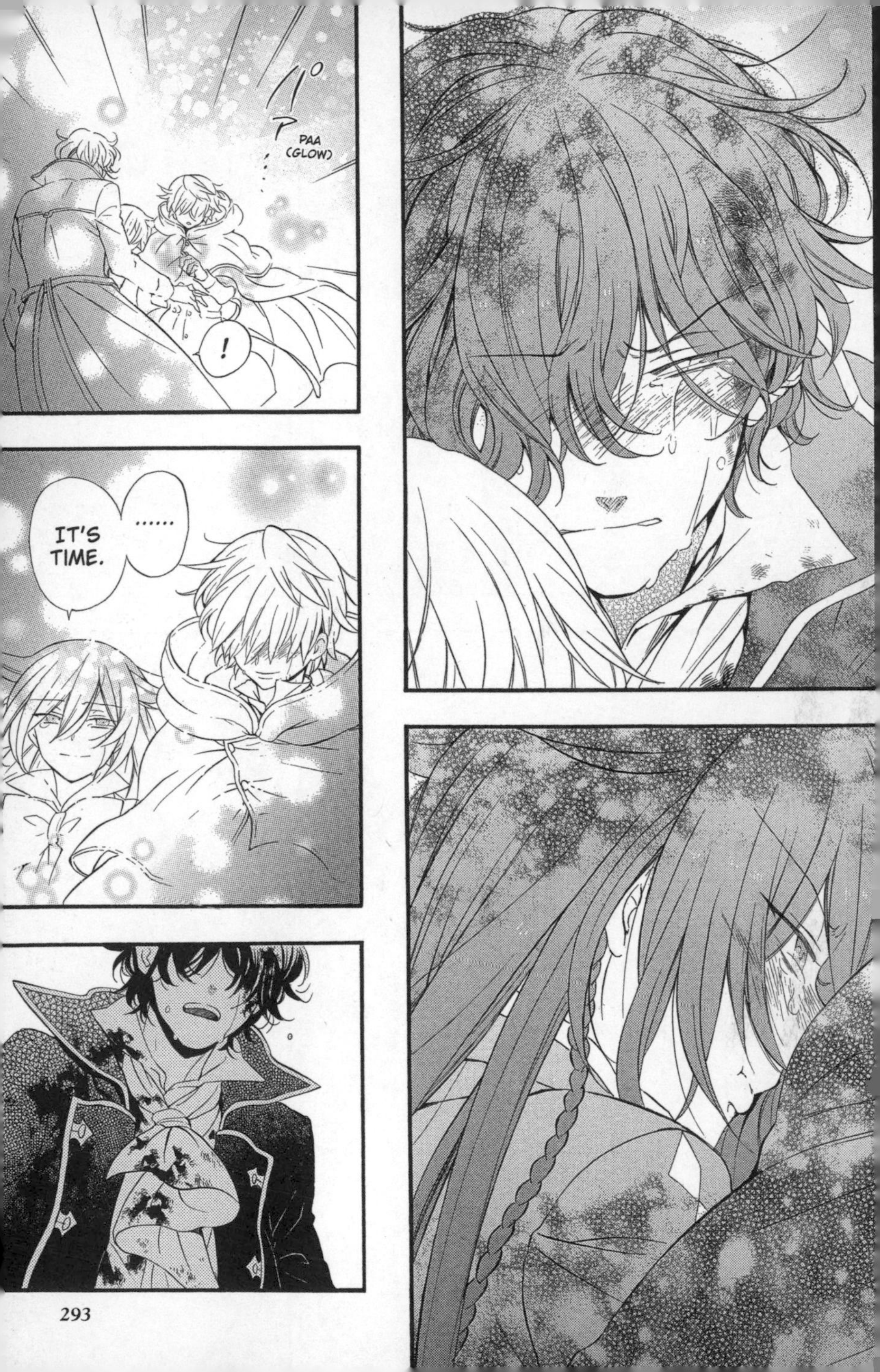
パァ
PAA (GLOW)
!
......
IT'S TIME.

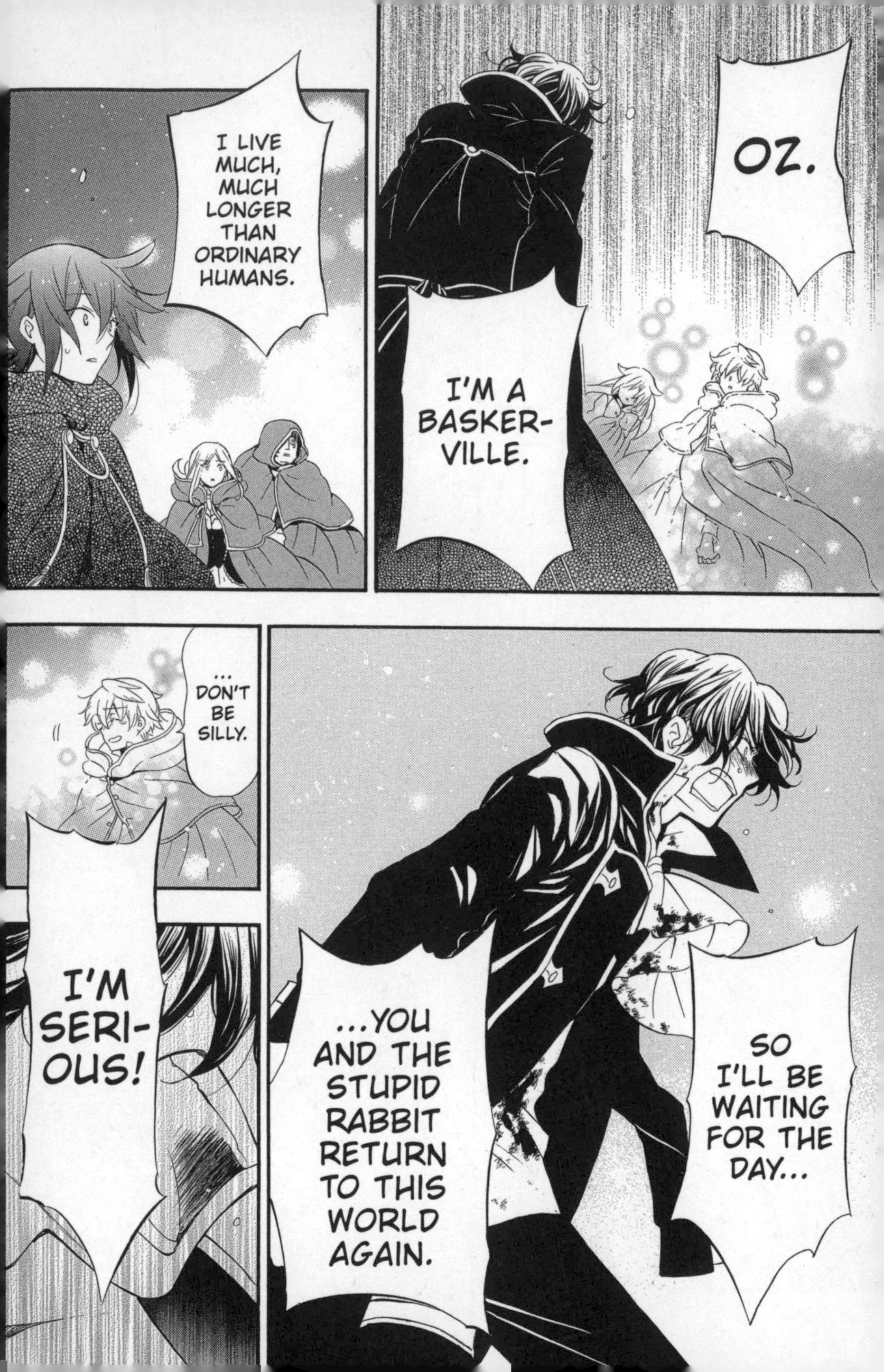
OZ.
I'M A BASKER-VILLE.
I LIVE MUCH, MUCH LONGER THAN ORDINARY HUMANS.
SO I'LL BE WAITING FOR THE DAY...
...YOU AND THE STUPID RABBIT RETURN TO THIS WORLD AGAIN.
...DON'T BE SILLY.
I'M SERI-OUS!

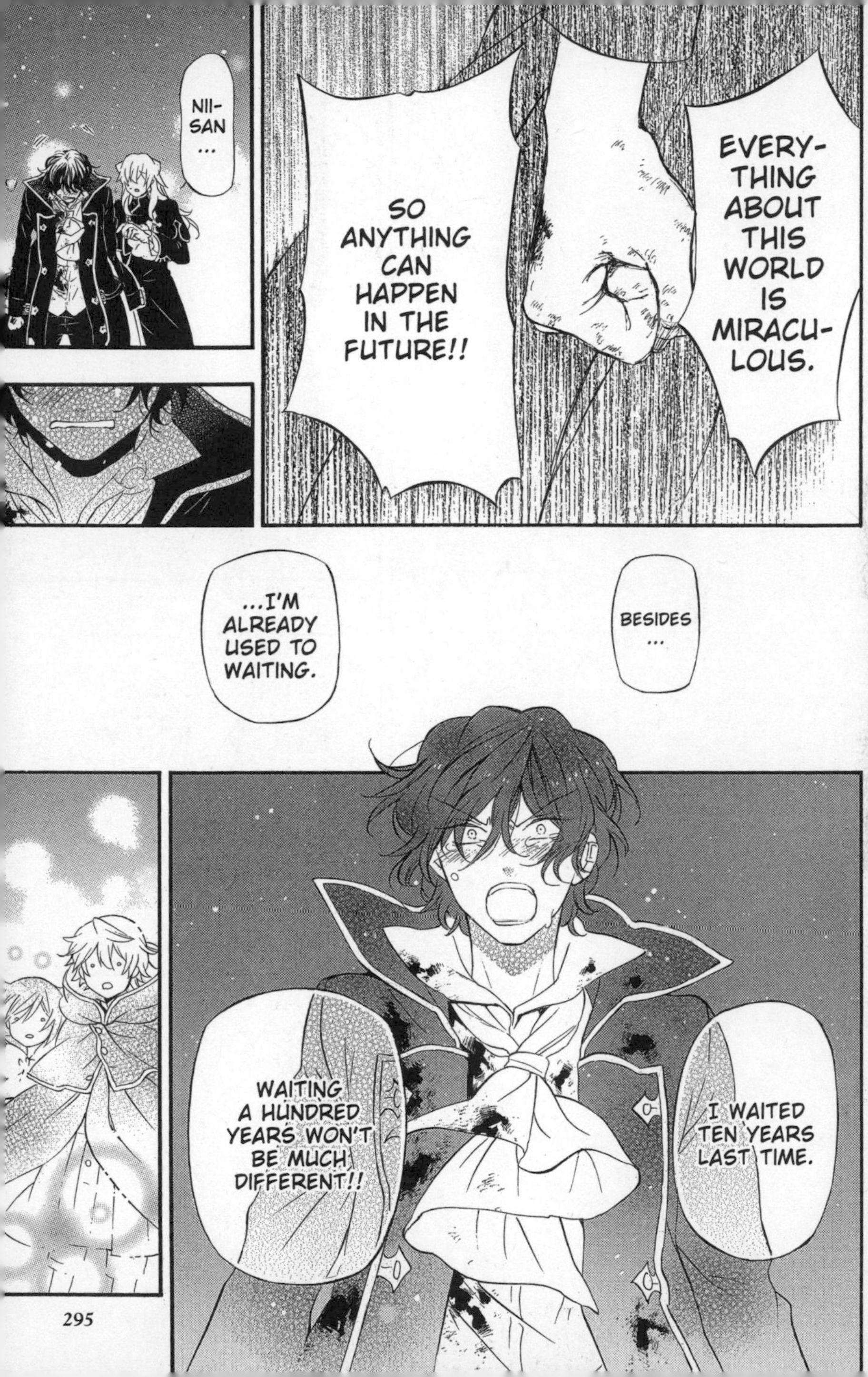
EVERYTHING ABOUT THIS WORLD IS MIRACULOUS.
SO ANYTHING CAN HAPPEN IN THE FUTURE!!
NII-SAN...
BESIDES...
...I'M ALREADY USED TO WAITING.
I WAITED TEN YEARS LAST TIME.
WAITING A HUNDRED YEARS WON'T BE MUCH DIFFERENT!!

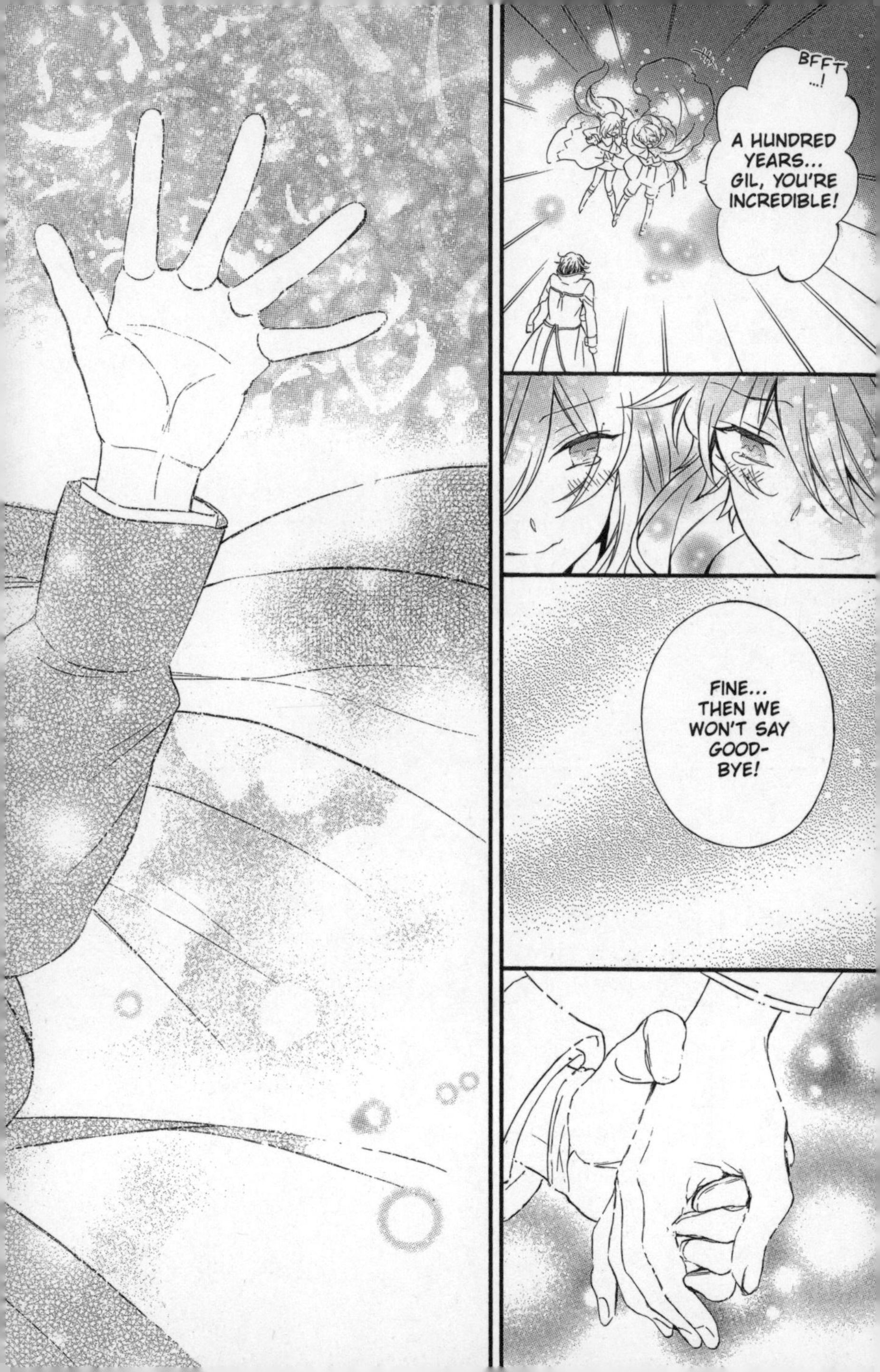
BFFT ...!
A HUNDRED YEARS... GIL, YOU'RE INCREDIBLE!
FINE... THEN WE WON'T SAY GOOD-BYE!

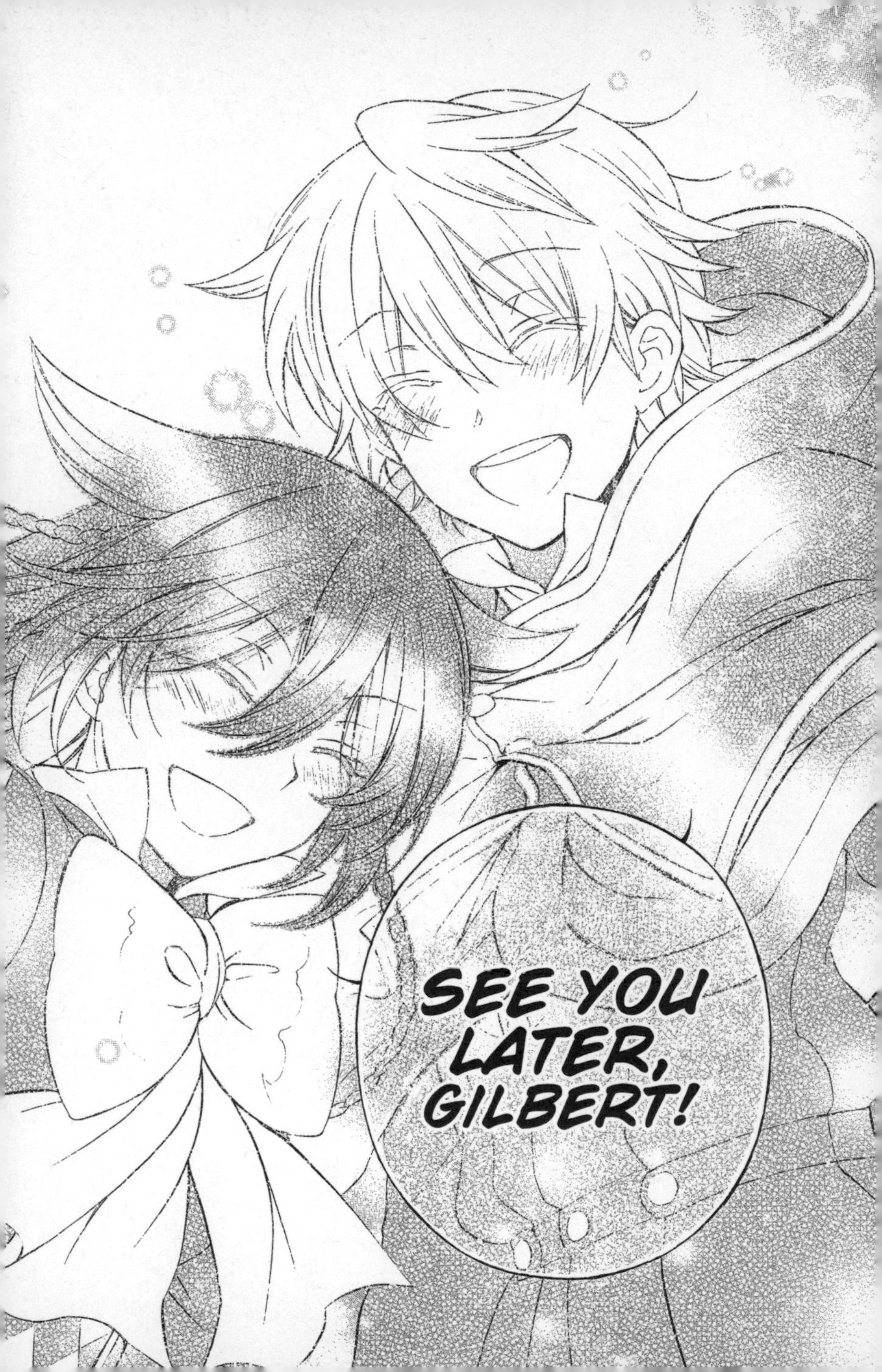
SEE YOU LATER, GILBERT!

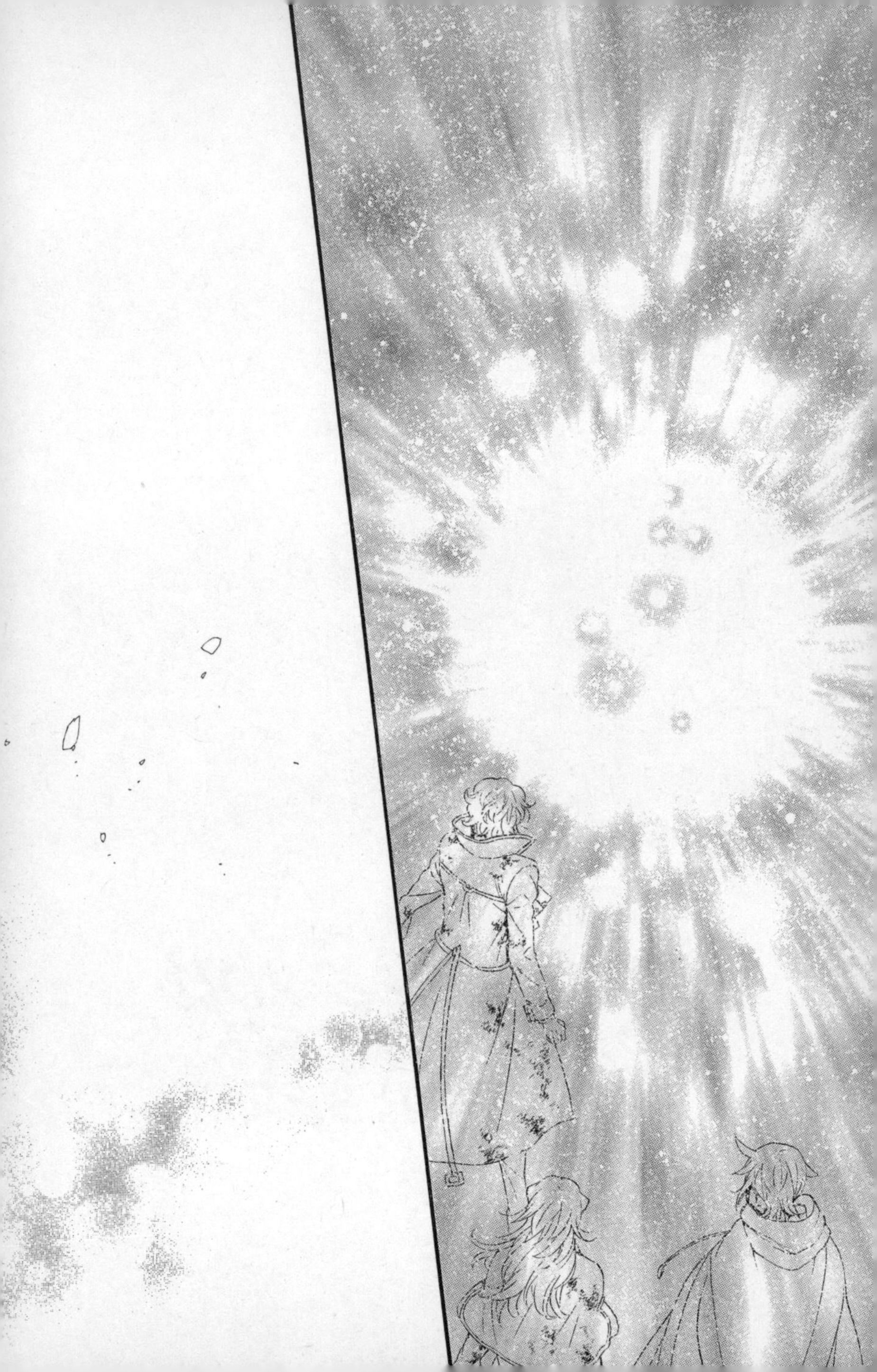

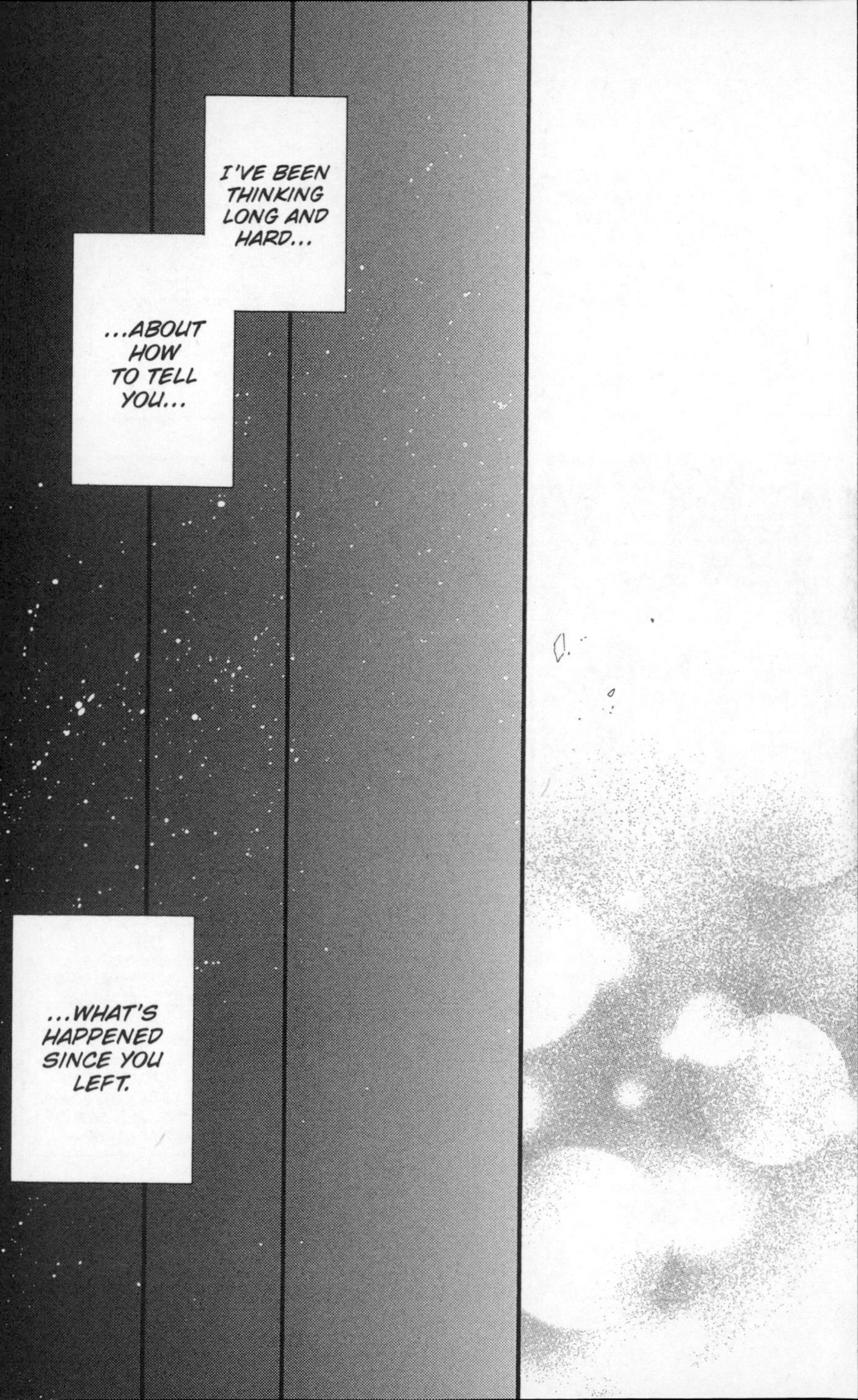
I'VE BEEN THINKING LONG AND HARD...
...ABOUT HOW TO TELL YOU...
...WHAT'S HAPPENED SINCE YOU LEFT.

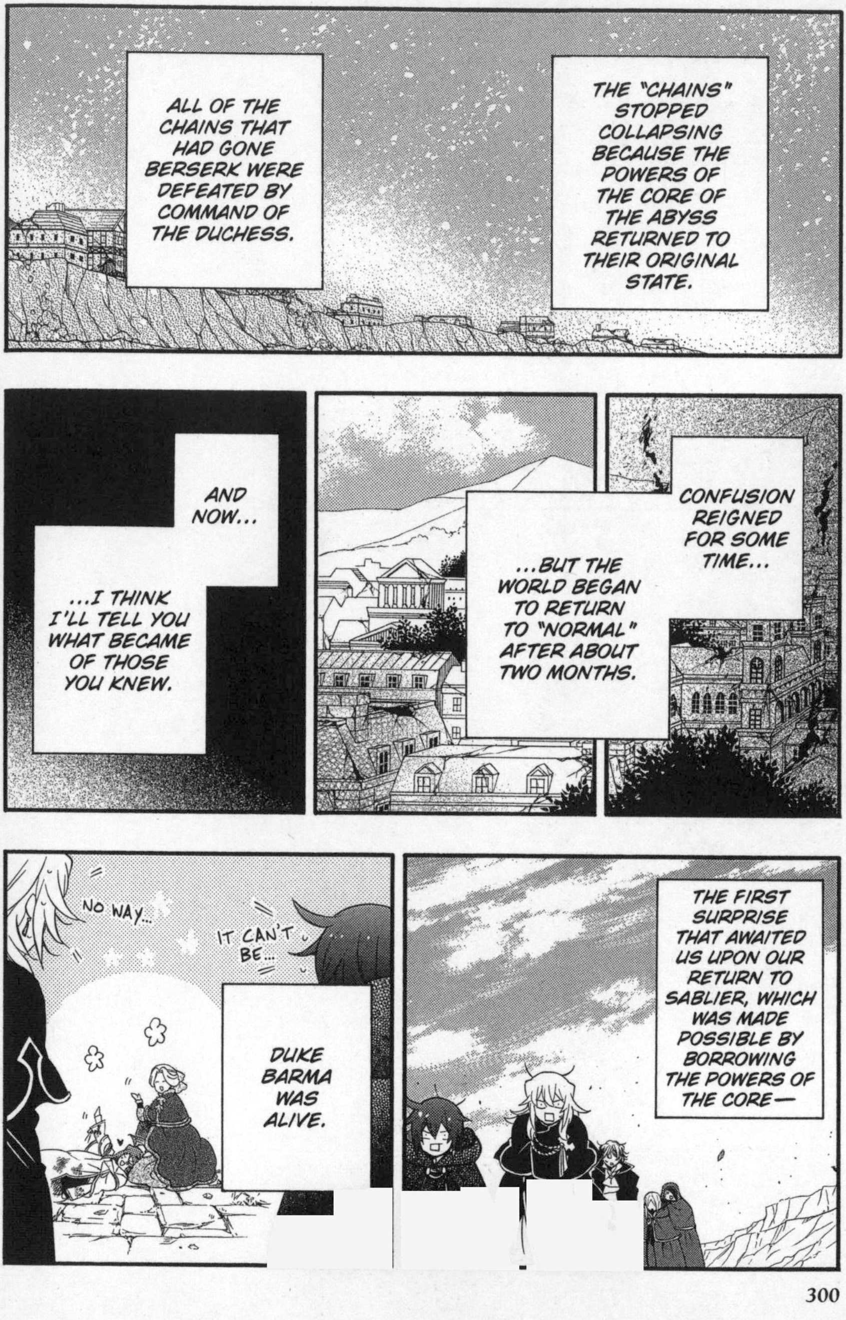
THE "CHAINS" STOPPED COLLAPSING BECAUSE THE POWERS OF THE CORE OF THE ABYSS RETURNED TO THEIR ORIGINAL STATE.
ALL OF THE CHAINS THAT HAD GONE BERSERK WERE DEFEATED BY COMMAND OF THE DUCHESS.
CONFUSION REIGNED FOR SOME TIME...
...BUT THE WORLD BEGAN TO RETURN TO "NORMAL" AFTER ABOUT TWO MONTHS.
AND NOW...
...I THINK I'LL TELL YOU WHAT BECAME OF THOSE YOU KNEW.
THE FIRST SURPRISE THAT AWAITED US UPON OUR RETURN TO SABLIER, WHICH WAS MADE POSSIBLE BY BORROWING THE POWERS OF THE CORE—
IT CAN'T BE...
NO WAY...
DUKE BARMA WAS ALIVE.

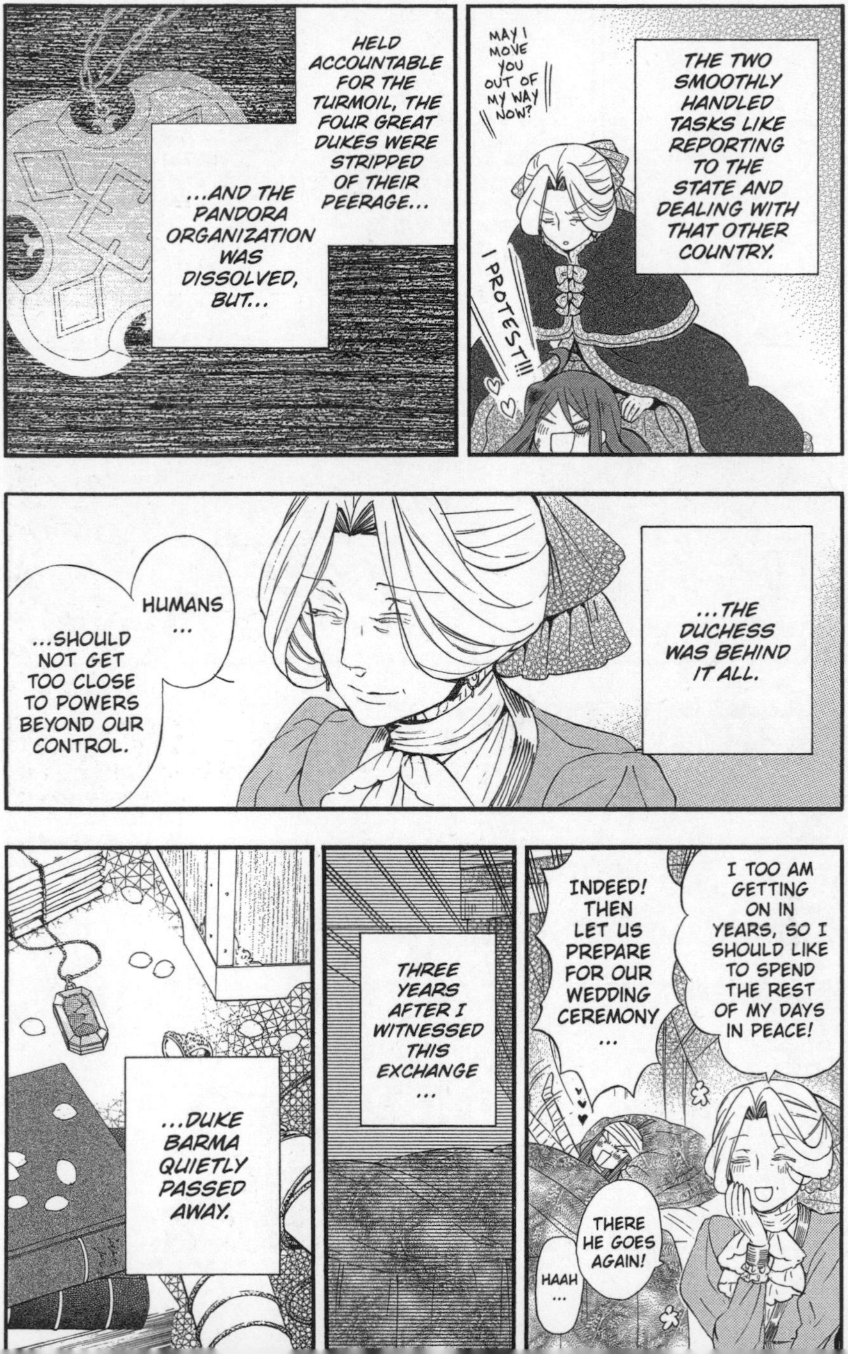
THE TWO SMOOTHLY HANDLED TASKS LIKE REPORTING TO THE STATE AND DEALING WITH THAT OTHER COUNTRY.
MAY I MOVE YOU OUT OF MY WAY NOW?
I PROTEST!!!
HELD ACCOUNTABLE FOR THE TURMOIL, THE FOUR GREAT DUKES WERE STRIPPED OF THEIR PEERAGE...
...AND THE PANDORA ORGANIZATION WAS DISSOLVED, BUT...
...THE DUCHESS WAS BEHIND IT ALL.
HUMANS...
...SHOULD NOT GET TOO CLOSE TO POWERS BEYOND OUR CONTROL.
I TOO AM GETTING ON IN YEARS, SO I SHOULD LIKE TO SPEND THE REST OF MY DAYS IN PEACE!
INDEED! THEN LET US PREPARE FOR OUR WEDDING CEREMONY...
THERE HE GOES AGAIN!
HAAH...
THREE YEARS AFTER I WITNESSED THIS EXCHANGE...
...DUKE BARMA QUIETLY PASSED AWAY.

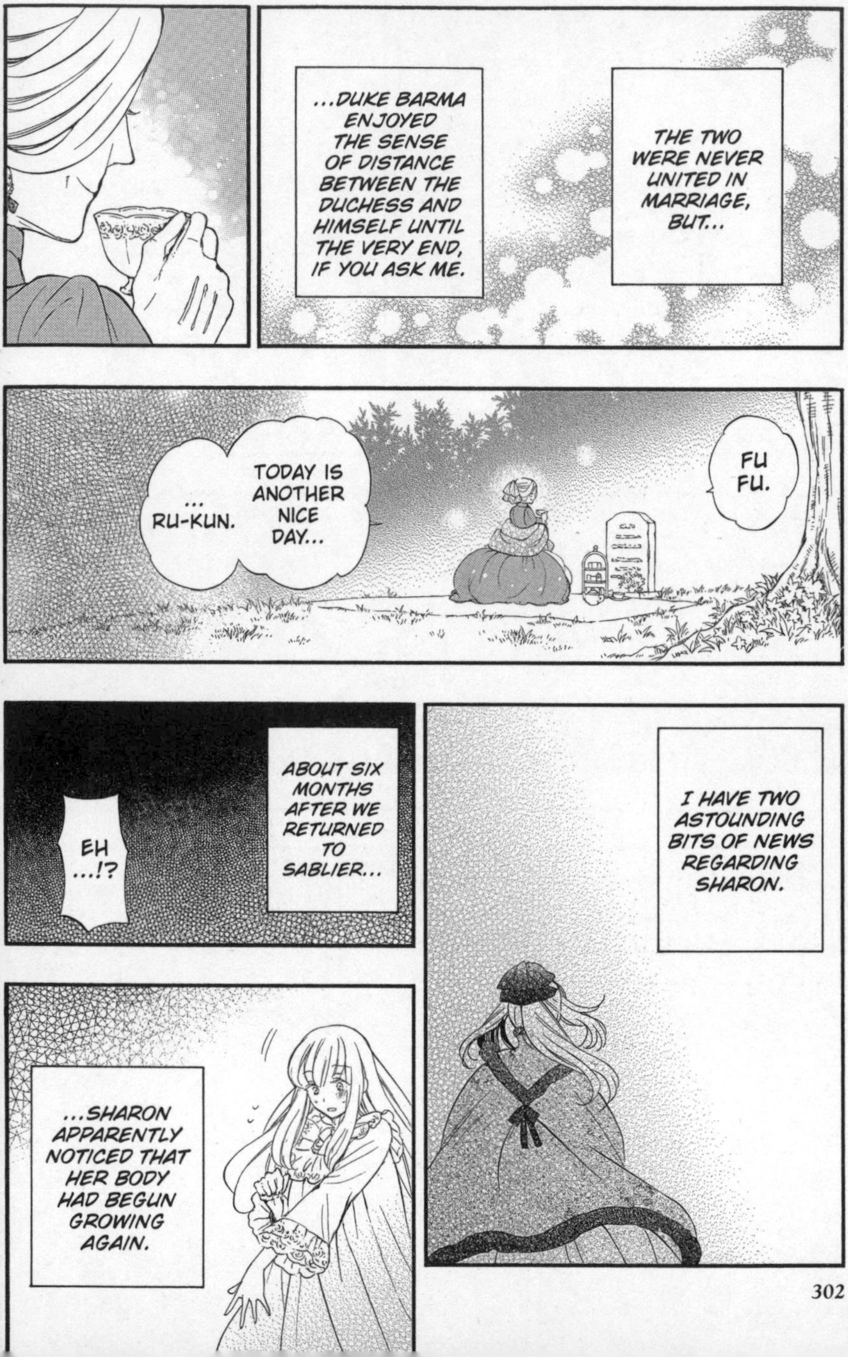

THE TWO WERE NEVER UNITED IN MARRIAGE, BUT...
...DUKE BARMA ENJOYED THE SENSE OF DISTANCE BETWEEN THE DUCHESS AND HIMSELF UNTIL THE VERY END, IF YOU ASK ME.
FU FU.
TODAY IS ANOTHER NICE DAY...
... RU-KUN.
I HAVE TWO ASTOUNDING BITS OF NEWS REGARDING SHARON.
ABOUT SIX MONTHS AFTER WE RETURNED TO SABLIER...
EH ...!?
...SHARON APPARENTLY NOTICED THAT HER BODY HAD BEGUN GROWING AGAIN.

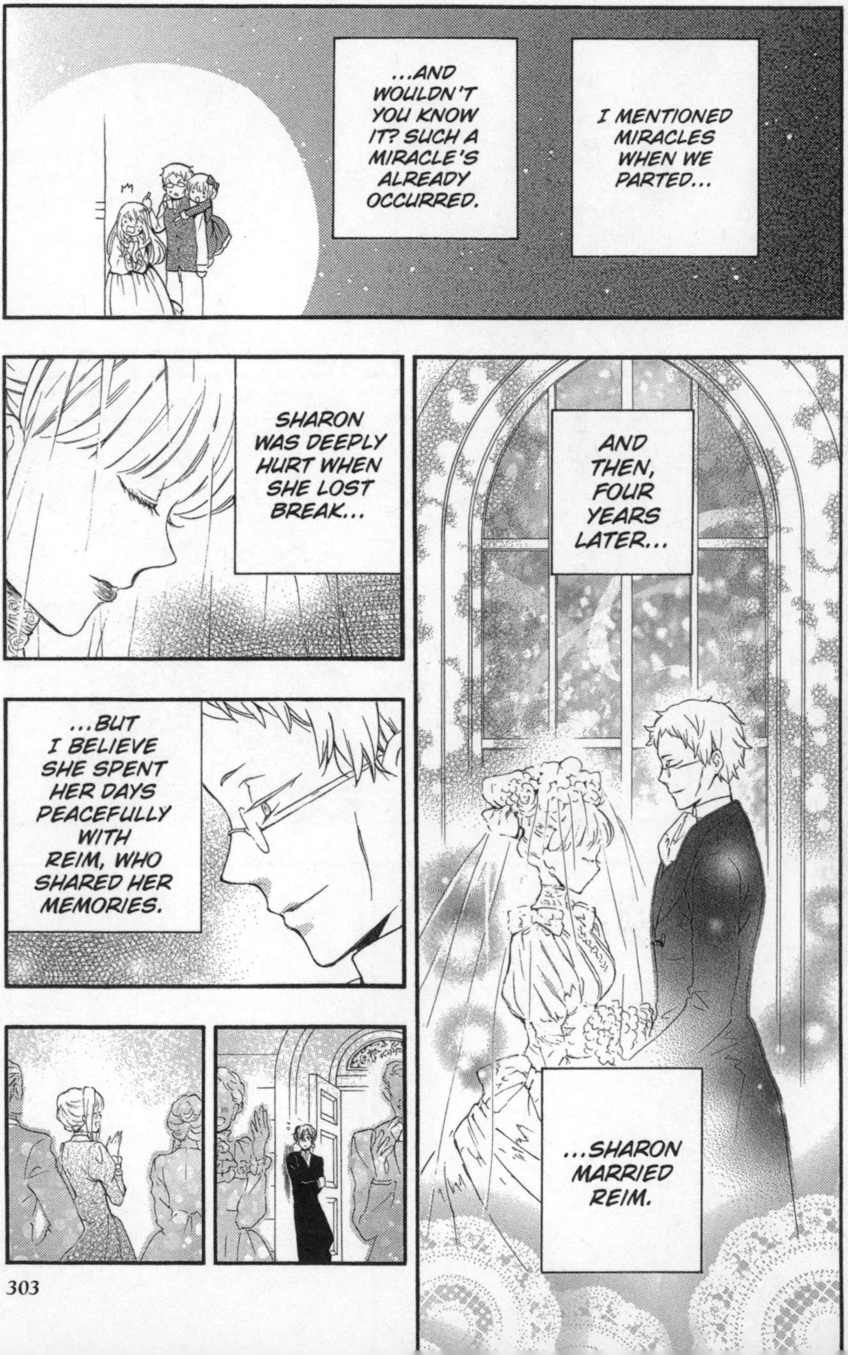
I MENTIONED MIRACLES WHEN WE PARTED...
...AND WOULDN'T YOU KNOW IT? SUCH A MIRACLE'S ALREADY OCCURRED.
AND THEN, FOUR YEARS LATER...
...SHARON MARRIED REIM.
SHARON WAS DEEPLY HURT WHEN SHE LOST BREAK...
...BUT I BELIEVE SHE SPENT HER DAYS PEACEFULLY WITH REIM, WHO SHARED HER MEMORIES.

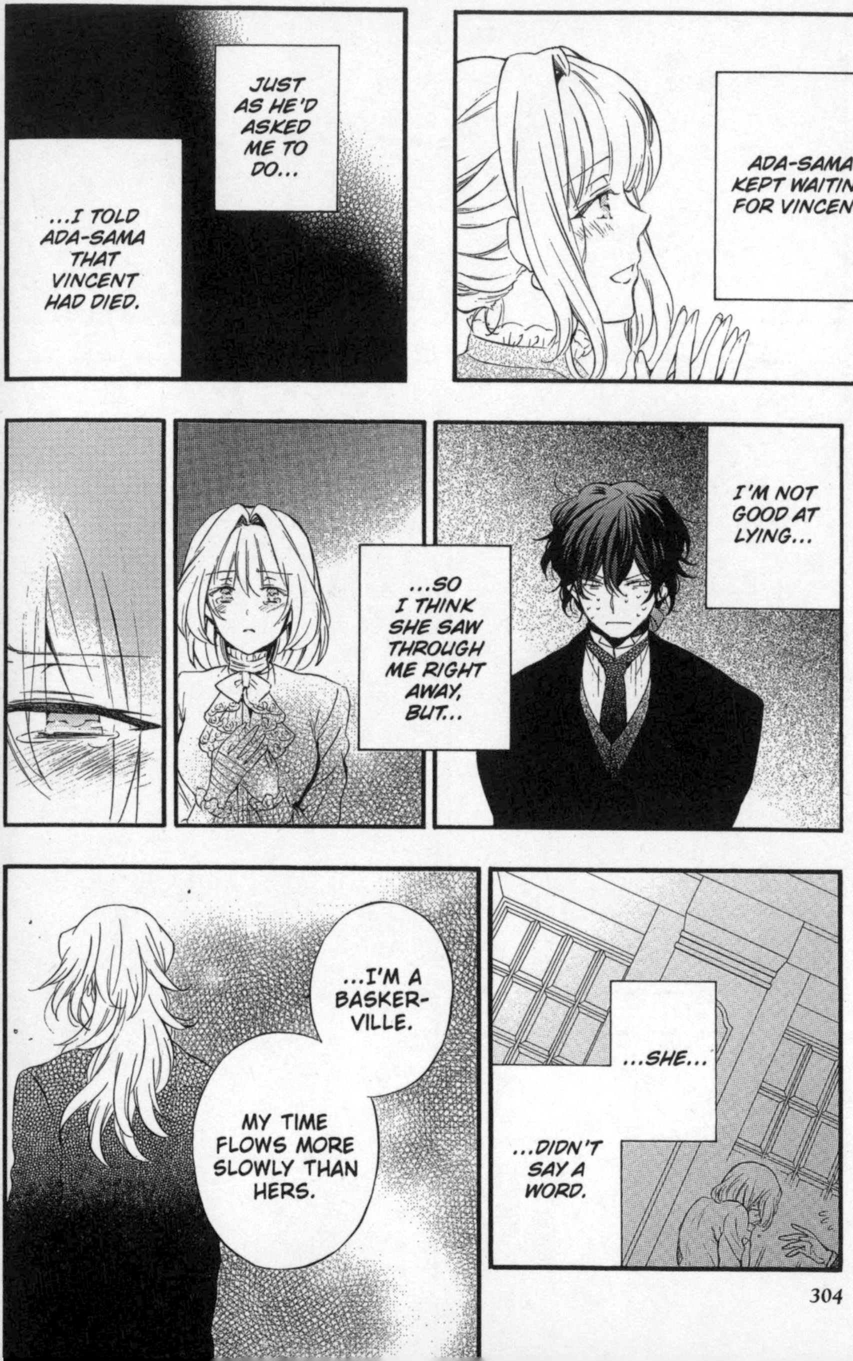
ADA-SAMA KEPT WAITING FOR VINCENT.
JUST AS HE'D ASKED ME TO DO...
...I TOLD ADA-SAMA THAT VINCENT HAD DIED.
I'M NOT GOOD AT LYING...
...SO I THINK SHE SAW THROUGH ME RIGHT AWAY, BUT...
...SHE...
...DIDN'T SAY A WORD.
...I'M A BASKER-VILLE.
MY TIME FLOWS MORE SLOWLY THAN HERS.

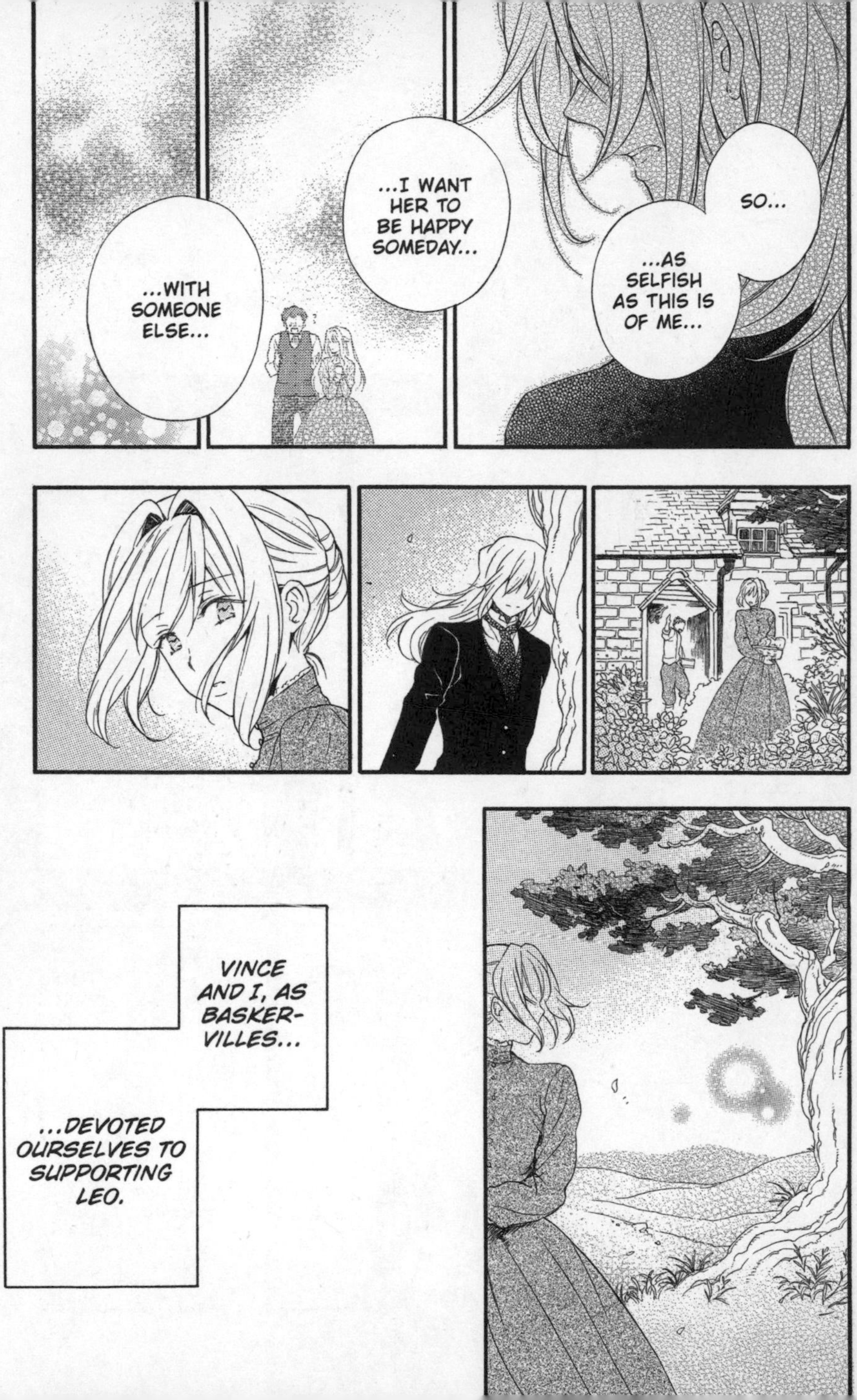
SO...
...AS SELFISH AS THIS IS OF ME...
...I WANT HER TO BE HAPPY SOMEDAY...
...WITH SOMEONE ELSE...
VINCE AND I, AS BASKER-VILLES...
...DEVOTED OURSELVES TO SUPPORTING LEO.

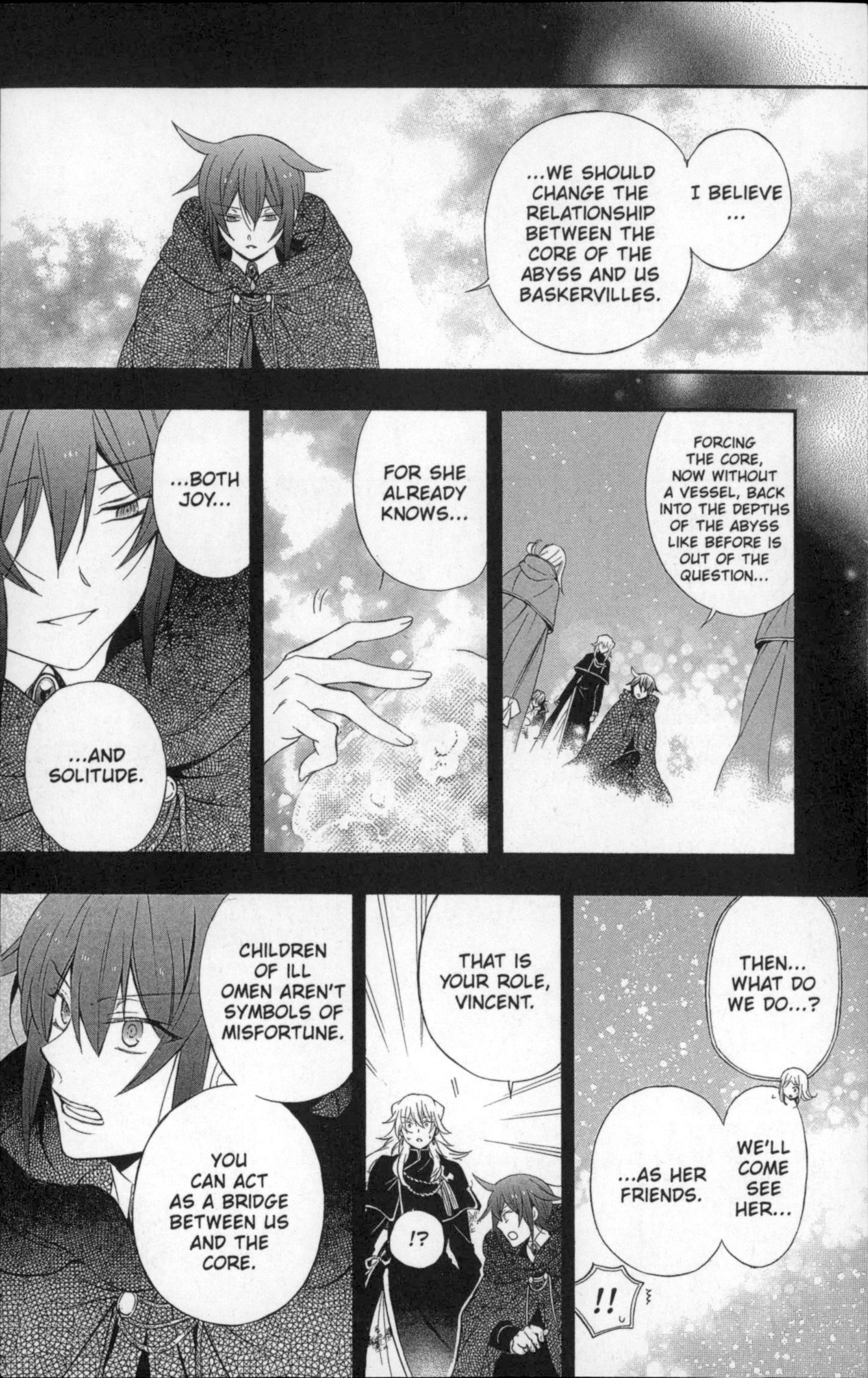
I BELIEVE ...
...WE SHOULD CHANGE THE RELATIONSHIP BETWEEN THE CORE OF THE ABYSS AND US BASKERVILLES.
FORCING THE CORE, NOW WITHOUT A VESSEL, BACK INTO THE DEPTHS OF THE ABYSS LIKE BEFORE IS OUT OF THE QUESTION...
FOR SHE ALREADY KNOWS...
...BOTH JOY...
...AND SOLITUDE.
THEN... WHAT DO WE DO...?
WE'LL COME SEE HER...
...AS HER FRIENDS.
!!
THAT IS YOUR ROLE, VINCENT.
!?
CHILDREN OF ILL OMEN AREN'T SYMBOLS OF MISFORTUNE.
YOU CAN ACT AS A BRIDGE BETWEEN US AND THE CORE.

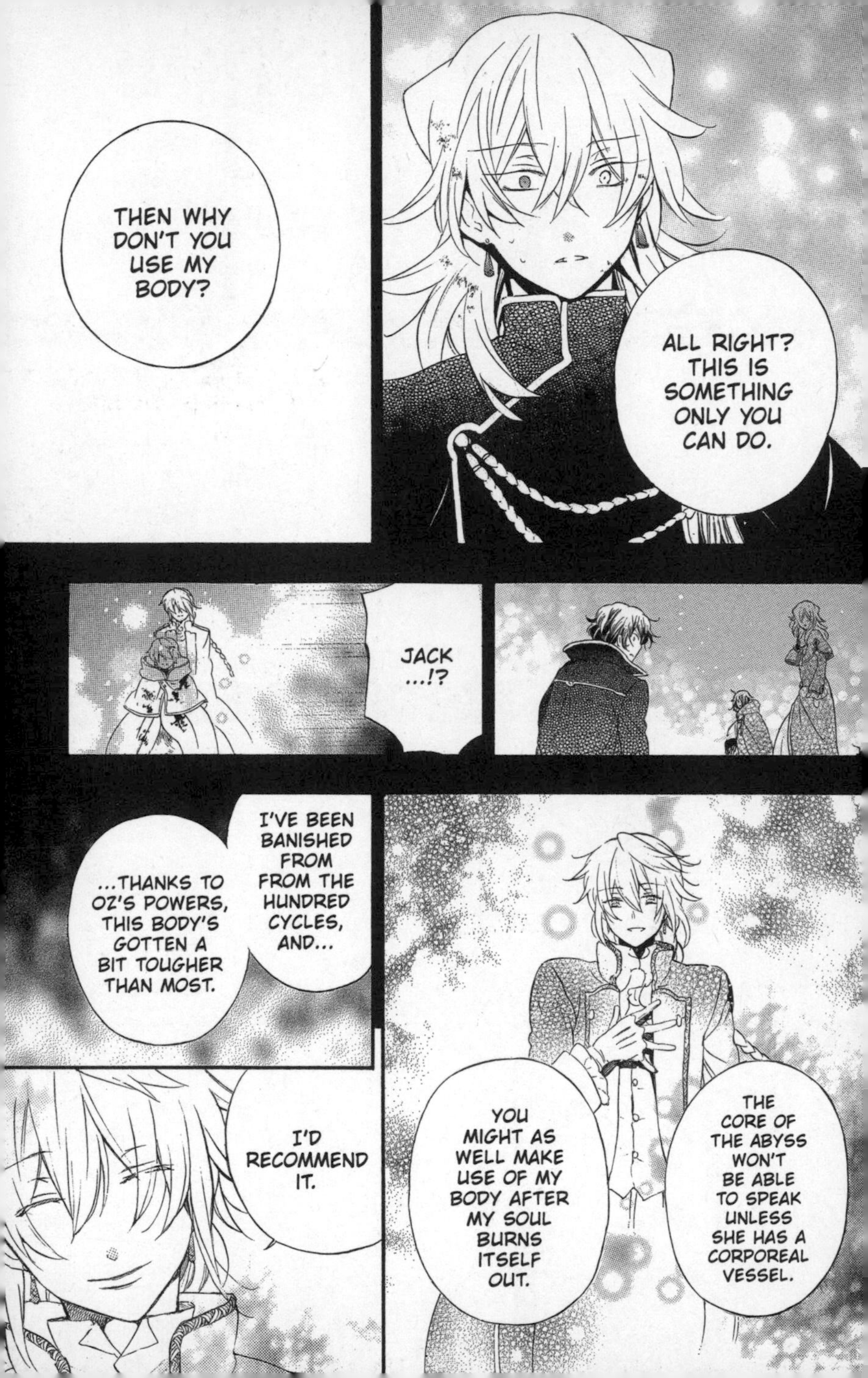
ALL RIGHT? THIS IS SOMETHING ONLY YOU CAN DO.
THEN WHY DON'T YOU USE MY BODY?
JACK ...!?
THE CORE OF THE ABYSS WON'T BE ABLE TO SPEAK UNLESS SHE HAS A CORPOREAL VESSEL.
YOU MIGHT AS WELL MAKE USE OF MY BODY AFTER MY SOUL BURNS ITSELF OUT.
I'VE BEEN BANISHED FROM FROM THE HUNDRED CYCLES, AND...
...THANKS TO OZ'S POWERS, THIS BODY'S GOTTEN A BIT TOUGHER THAN MOST.
I'D RECOMMEND IT.

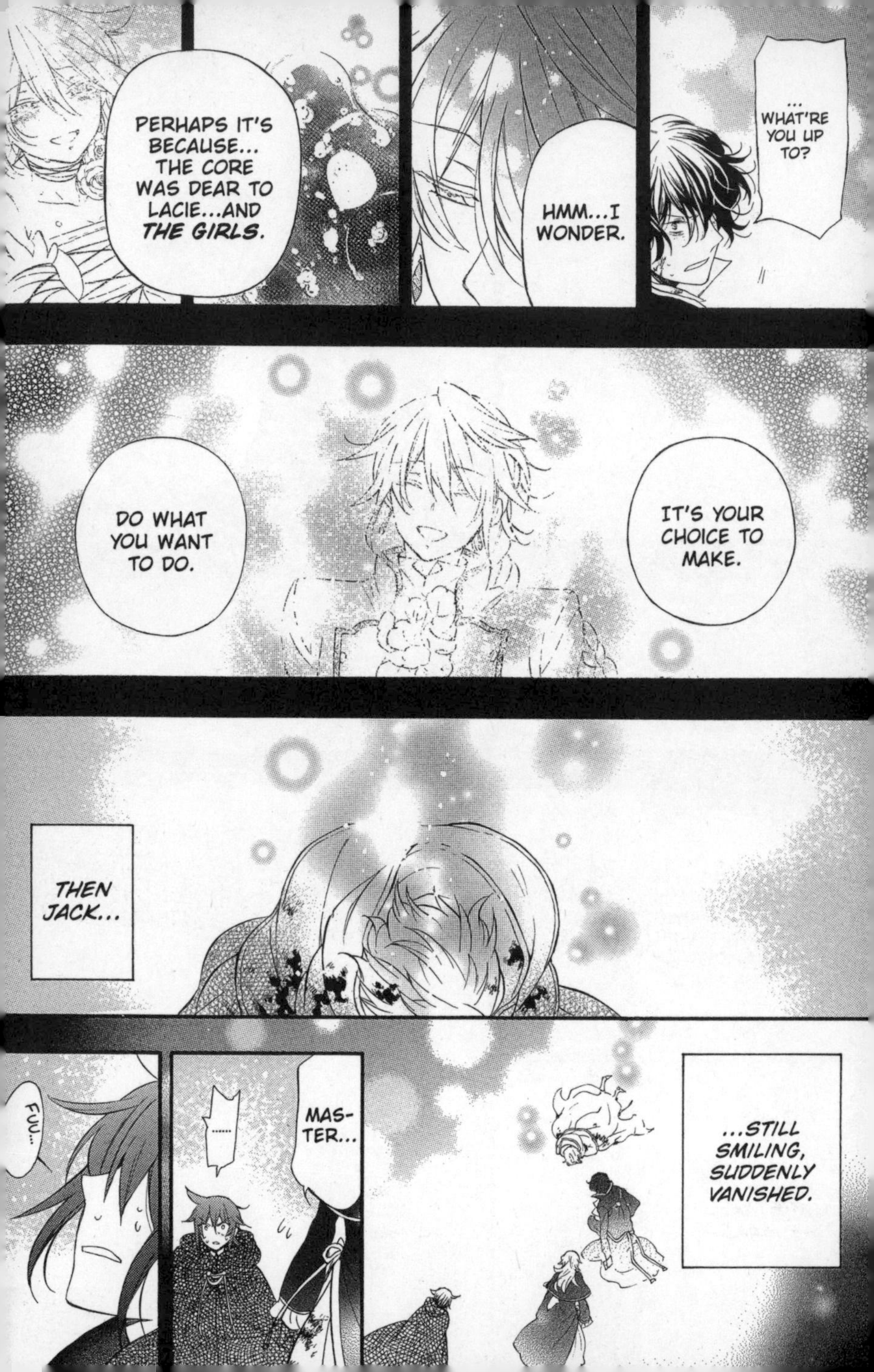
...WHAT'RE YOU UP TO?
HMM...I WONDER.
PERHAPS IT'S BECAUSE... THE CORE WAS DEAR TO LACIE...AND *THE GIRLS*.
IT'S YOUR CHOICE TO MAKE.
DO WHAT YOU WANT TO DO.
THEN JACK...
...STILL SMILING, SUDDENLY VANISHED.
MAS-TER...
......
FUU...

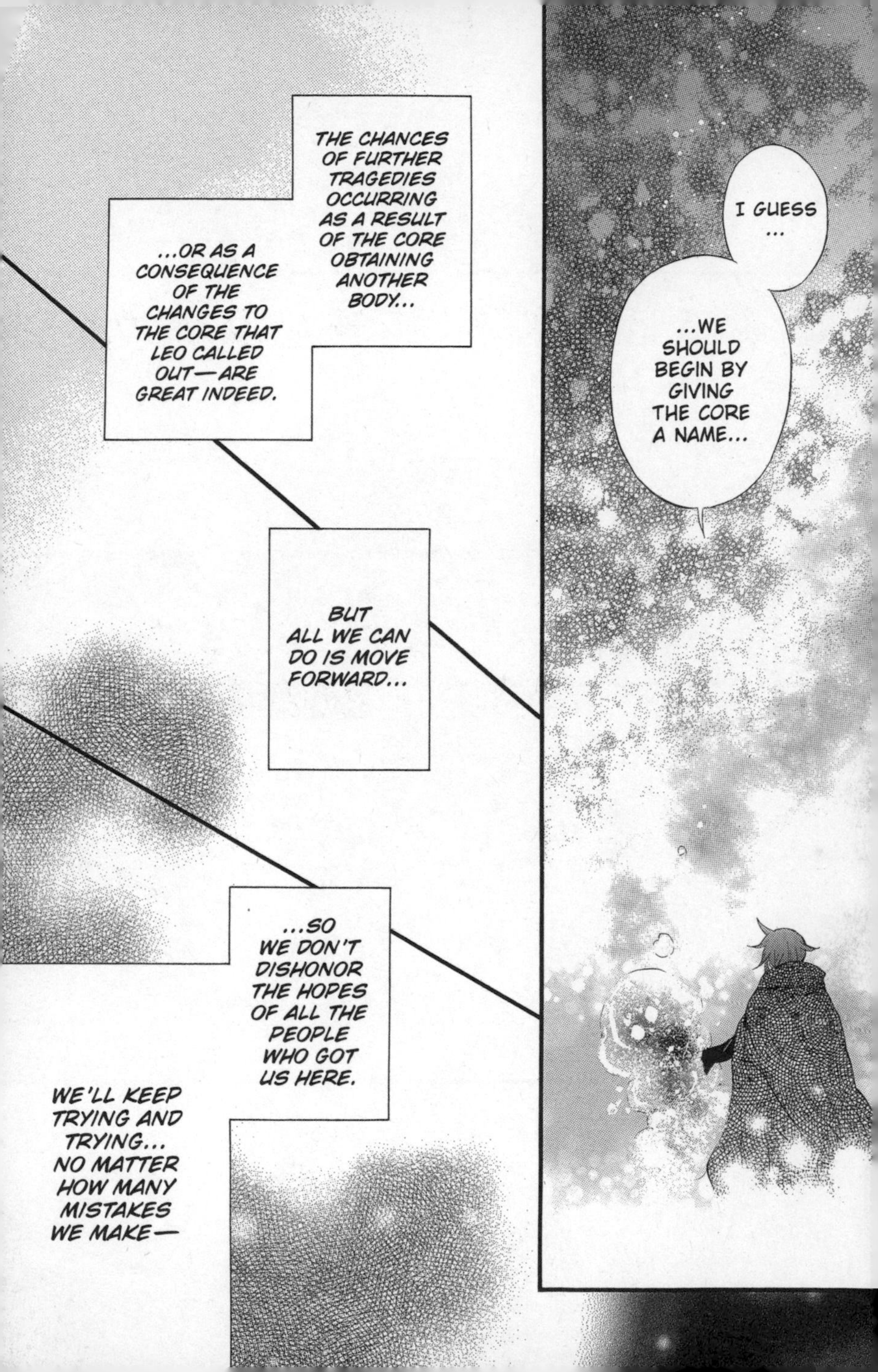
I GUESS...
...WE SHOULD BEGIN BY GIVING THE CORE A NAME...
THE CHANCES OF FURTHER TRAGEDIES OCCURRING AS A RESULT OF THE CORE OBTAINING ANOTHER BODY...
...OR AS A CONSEQUENCE OF THE CHANGES TO THE CORE THAT LEO CALLED OUT—ARE GREAT INDEED.
BUT ALL WE CAN DO IS MOVE FORWARD...
...SO WE DON'T DISHONOR THE HOPES OF ALL THE PEOPLE WHO GOT US HERE.
WE'LL KEEP TRYING AND TRYING... NO MATTER HOW MANY MISTAKES WE MAKE—

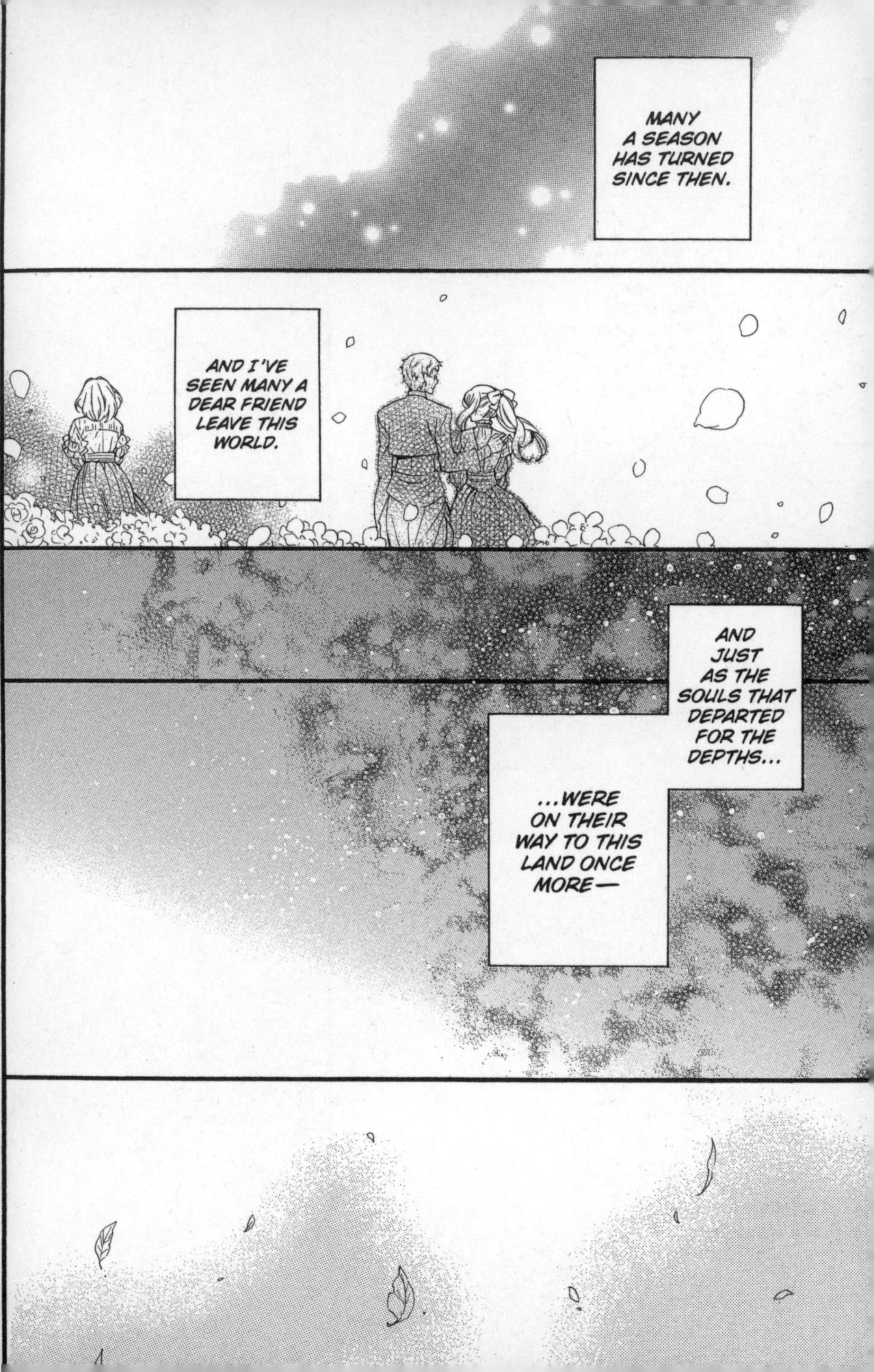
MANY A SEASON HAS TURNED SINCE THEN.
AND I'VE SEEN MANY A DEAR FRIEND LEAVE THIS WORLD.
AND JUST AS THE SOULS THAT DEPARTED FOR THE DEPTHS...
...WERE ON THEIR WAY TO THIS LAND ONCE MORE—

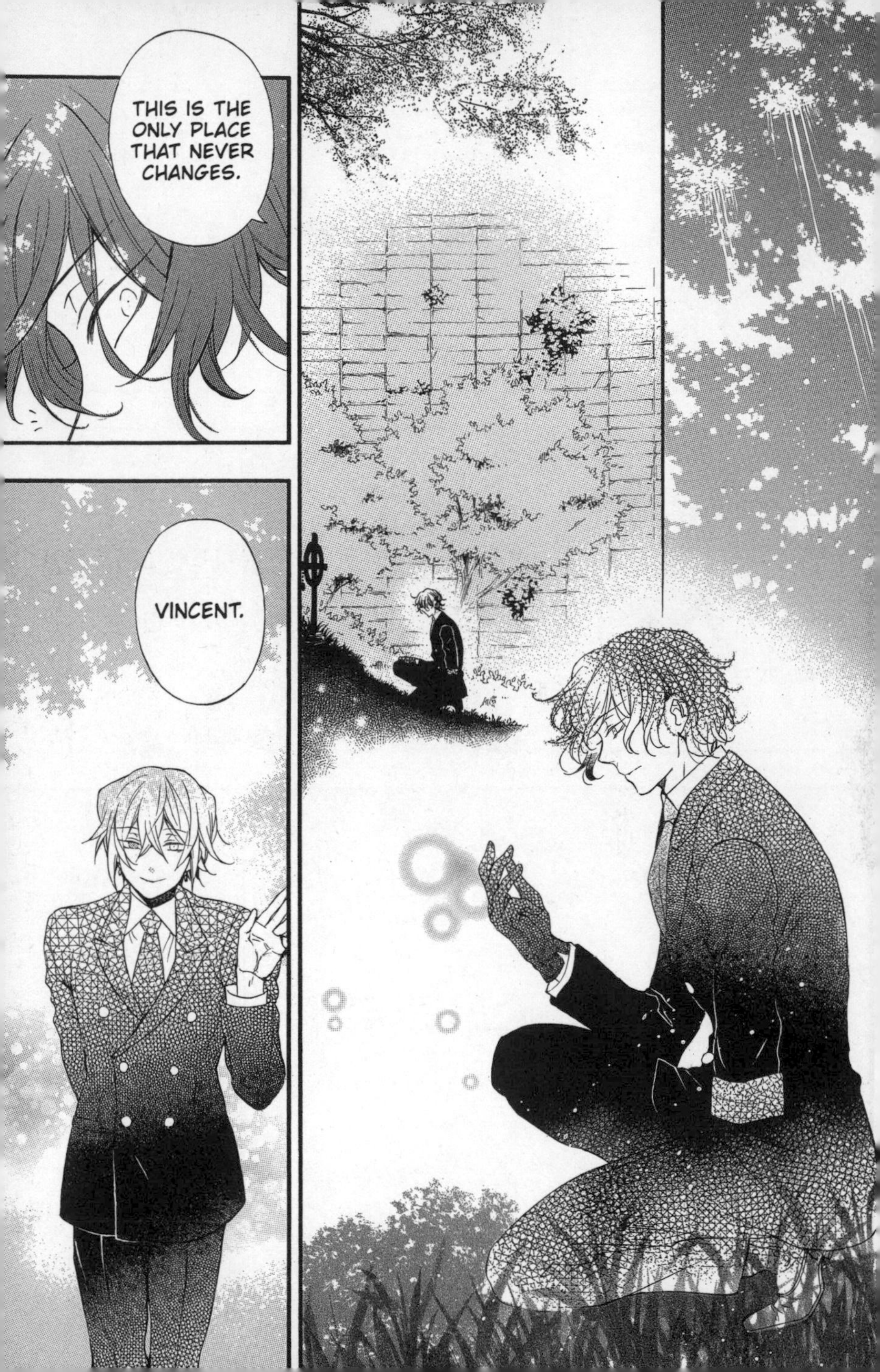
THIS IS THE ONLY PLACE THAT NEVER CHANGES.
VINCENT.

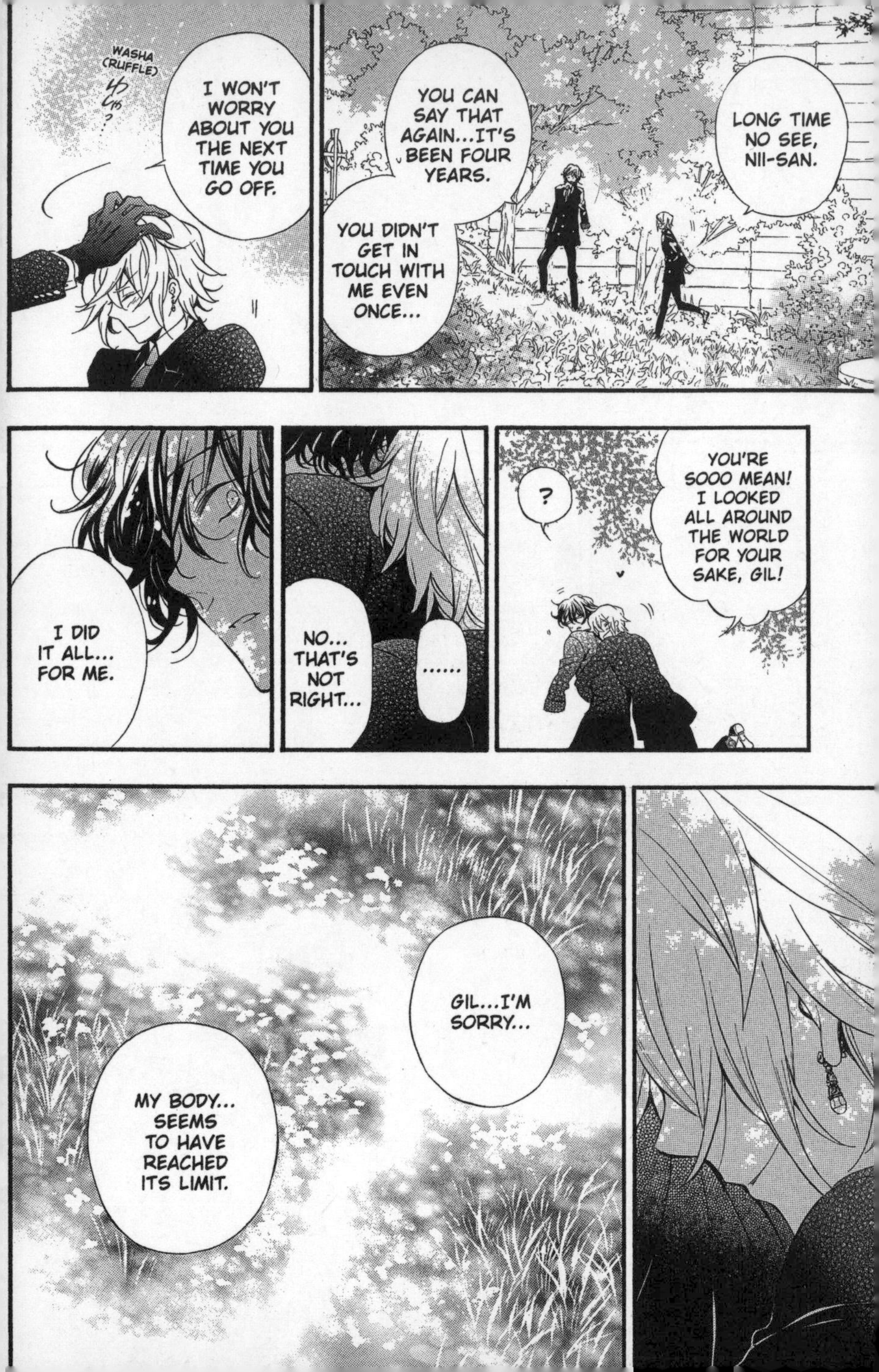
LONG TIME NO SEE, NII-SAN.
YOU CAN SAY THAT AGAIN...IT'S BEEN FOUR YEARS.
YOU DIDN'T GET IN TOUCH WITH ME EVEN ONCE...
WASHA (RUFFLE)
I WON'T WORRY ABOUT YOU THE NEXT TIME YOU GO OFF.
YOU'RE SOOO MEAN! I LOOKED ALL AROUND THE WORLD FOR YOUR SAKE, GIL!
?
......
NO... THAT'S NOT RIGHT...
I DID IT ALL... FOR ME.
GIL...I'M SORRY...
MY BODY... SEEMS TO HAVE REACHED ITS LIMIT.

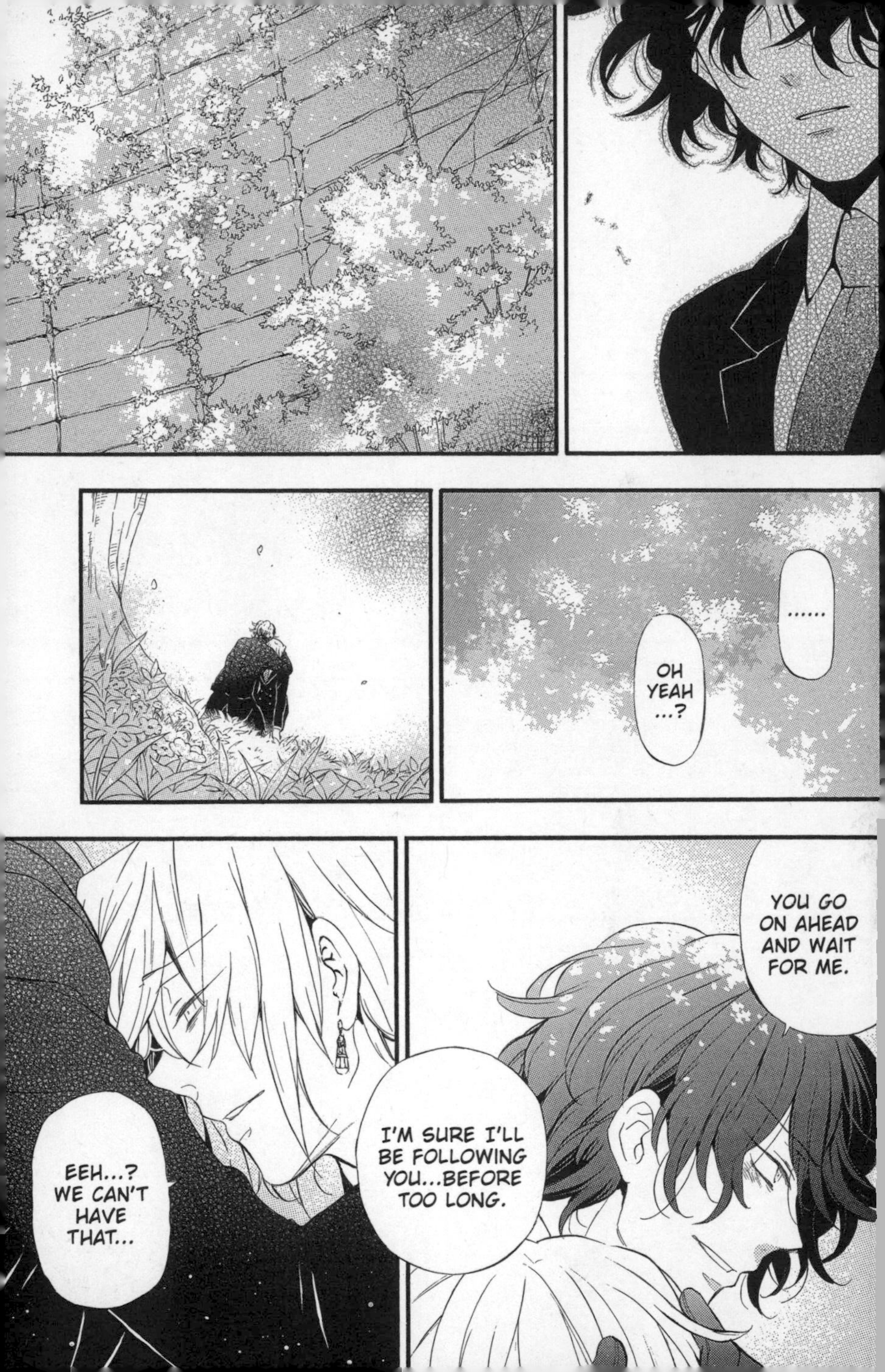
......
OH YEAH ...?
YOU GO ON AHEAD AND WAIT FOR ME.
I'M SURE I'LL BE FOLLOWING YOU...BEFORE TOO LONG.
EEH...? WE CAN'T HAVE THAT...

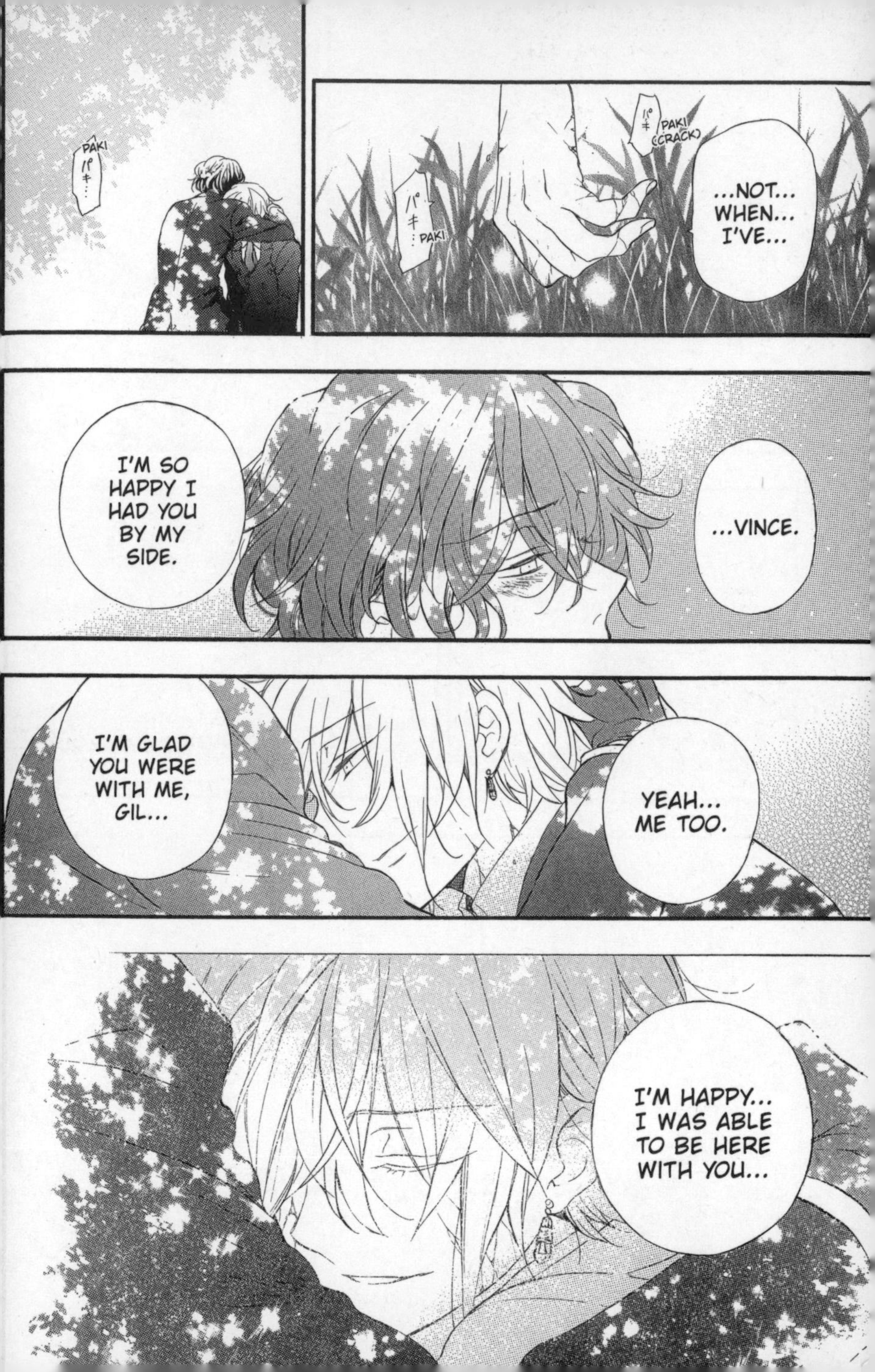
パキ
PAKI (CRACK)
パキ…
PAKI
…NOT… WHEN… I'VE…
PAKI
パキ…
…VINCE.
I'M SO HAPPY I HAD YOU BY MY SIDE.
I'M GLAD YOU WERE WITH ME, GIL…
YEAH… ME TOO.
I'M HAPPY… I WAS ABLE TO BE HERE WITH YOU…

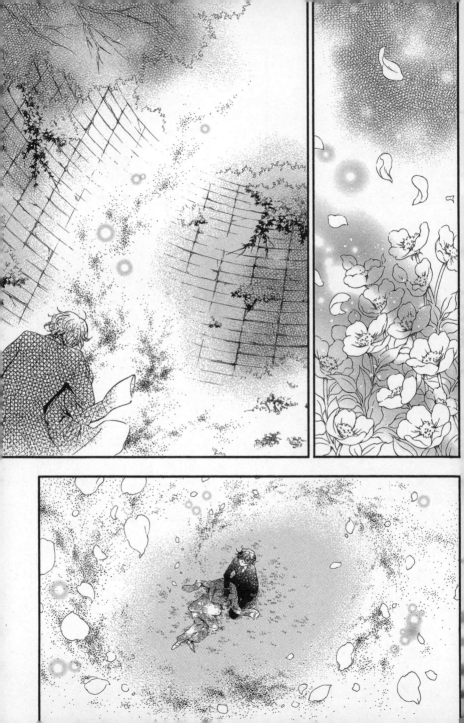

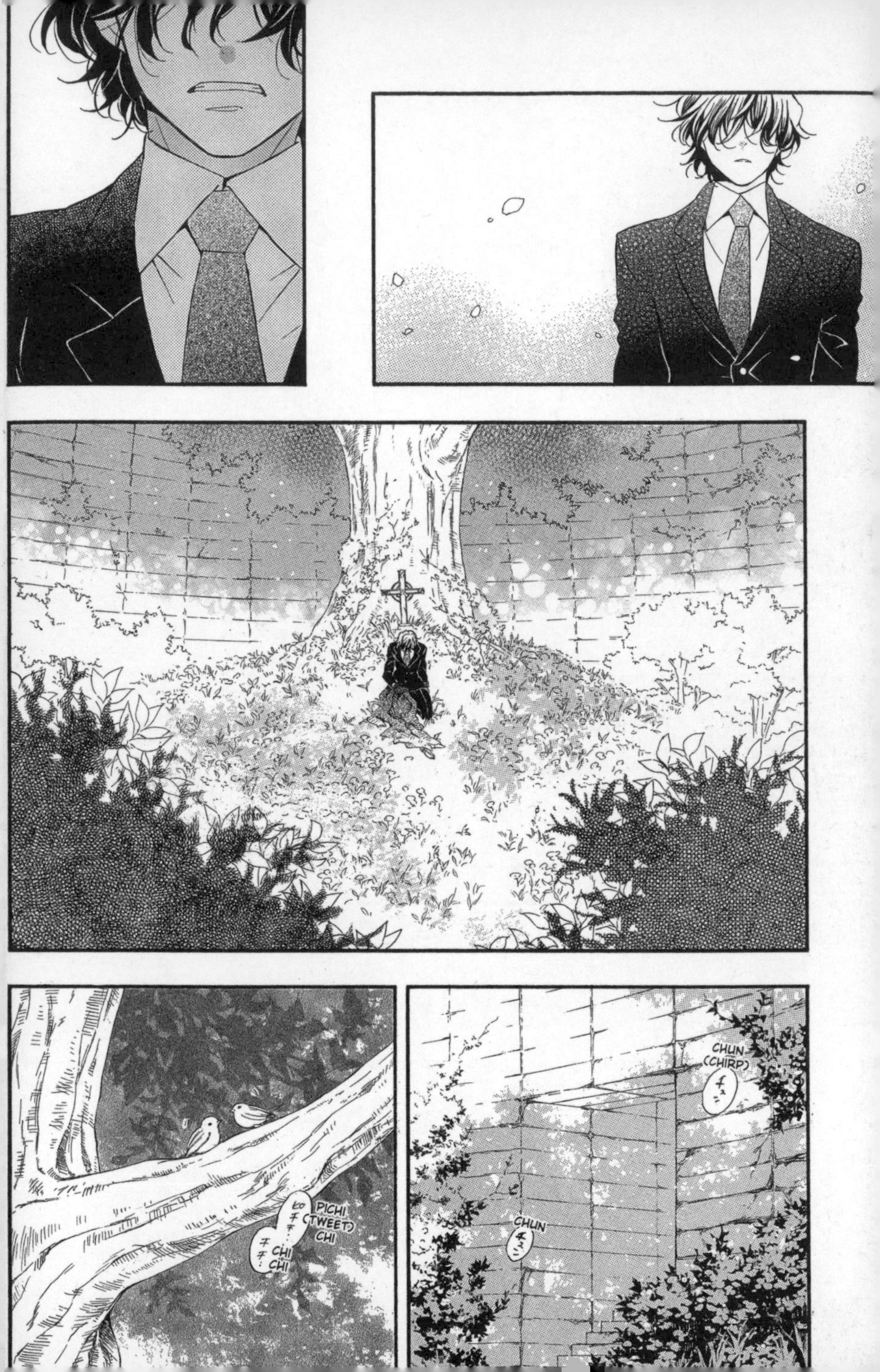
CHUN (CHIRP)
CHUN
PICHI (TWEET) CHI
CHI CHI

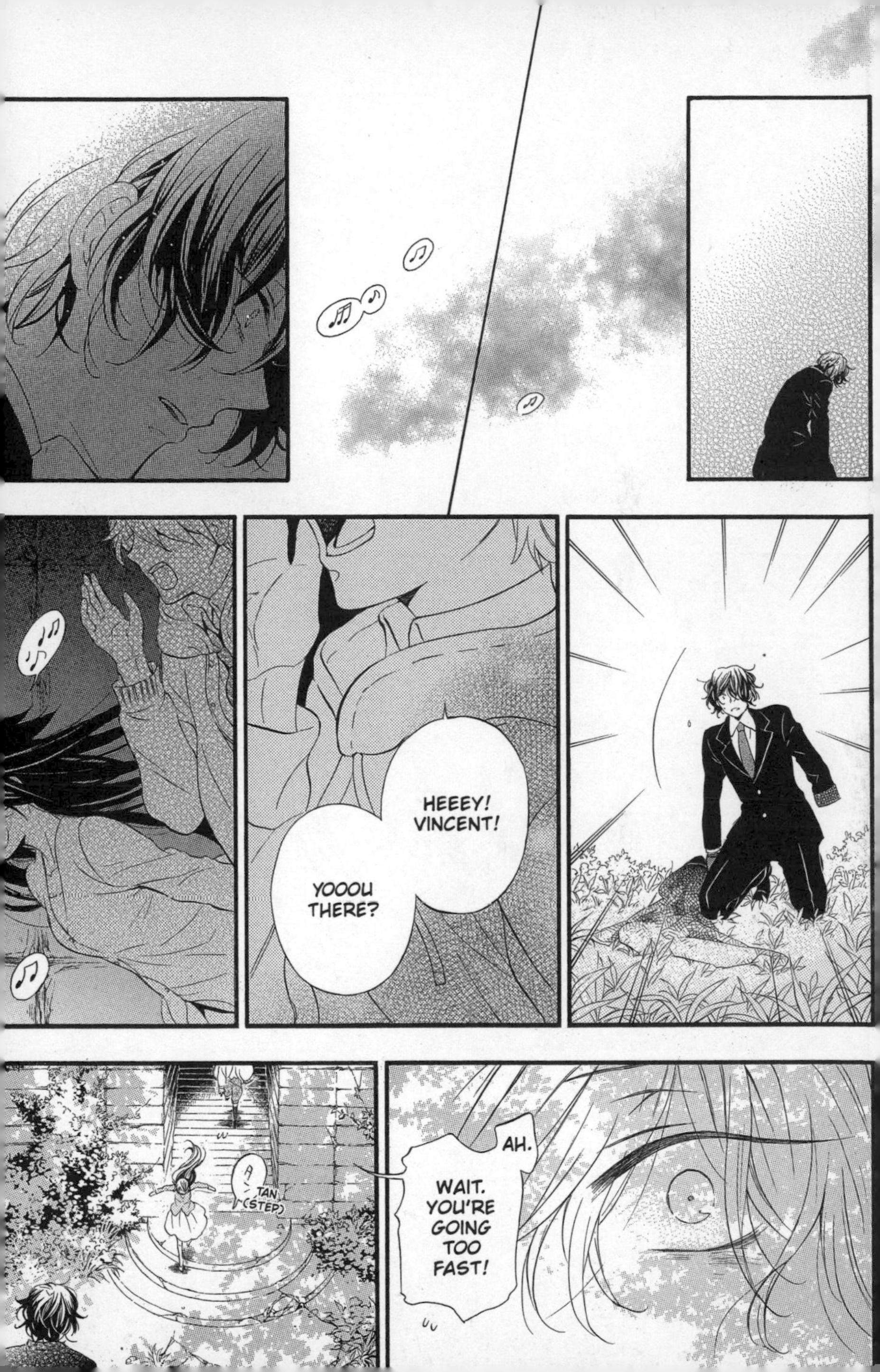
HEEEY! VINCENT!
YOOOU THERE?
AH.
WAIT. YOU'RE GOING TOO FAST!
TAN (STEP)

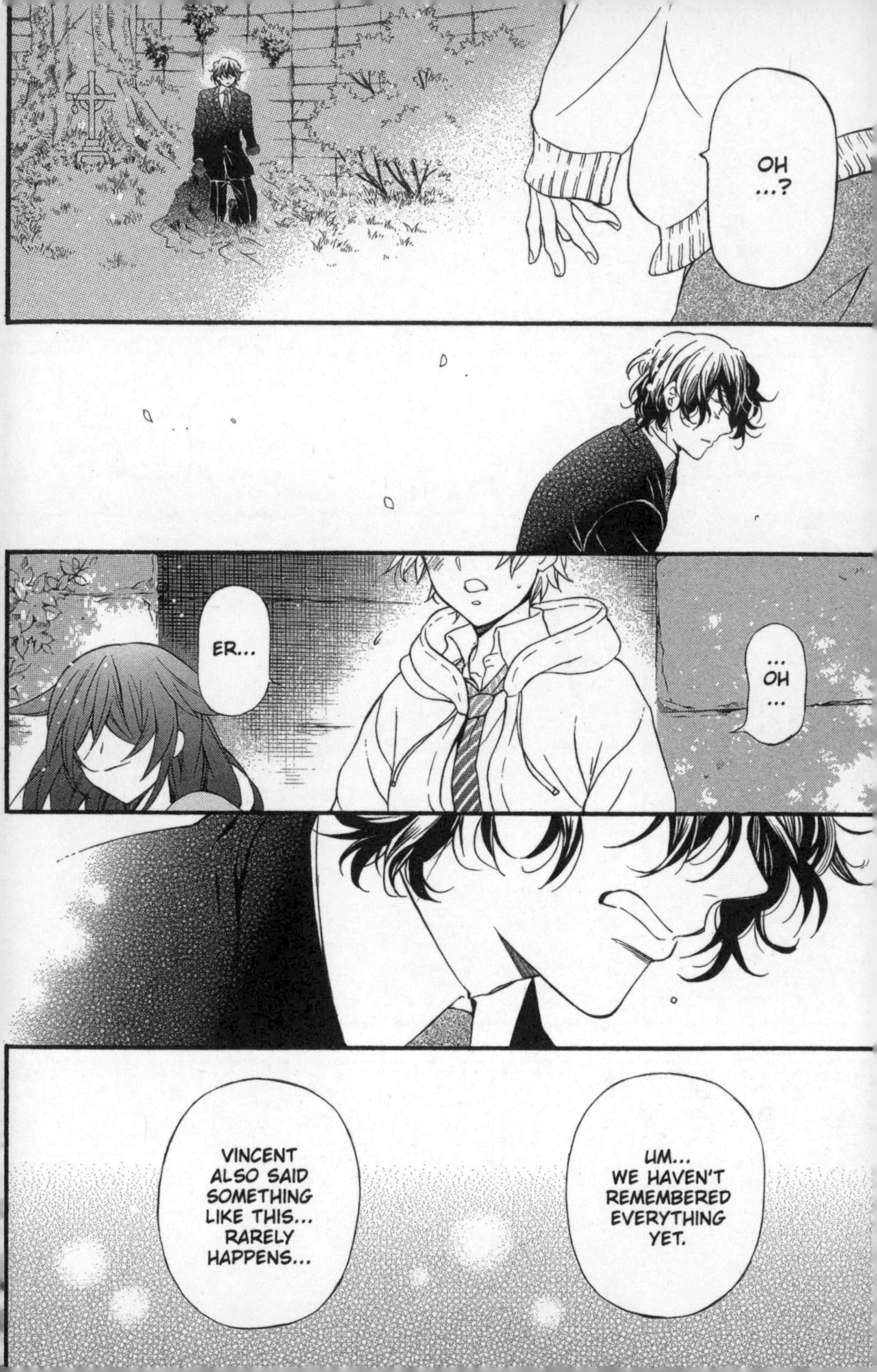
OH ...?
... OH ...
ER...
UM... WE HAVEN'T REMEMBERED EVERYTHING YET.
VINCENT ALSO SAID SOMETHING LIKE THIS... RARELY HAPPENS...

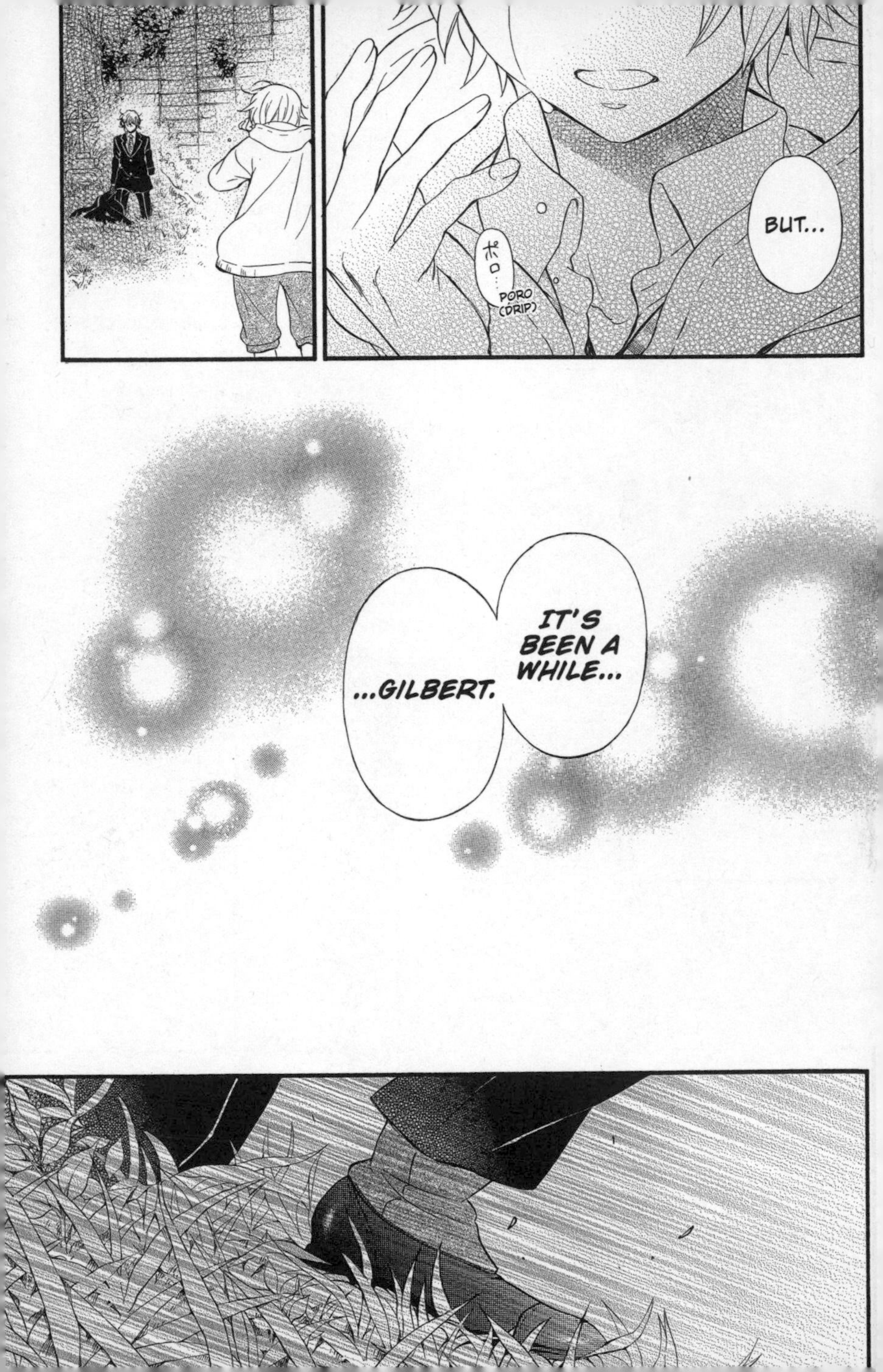
BUT...
ポロ…
PORO
(DRIP)
IT'S BEEN A WHILE...
...GILBERT.

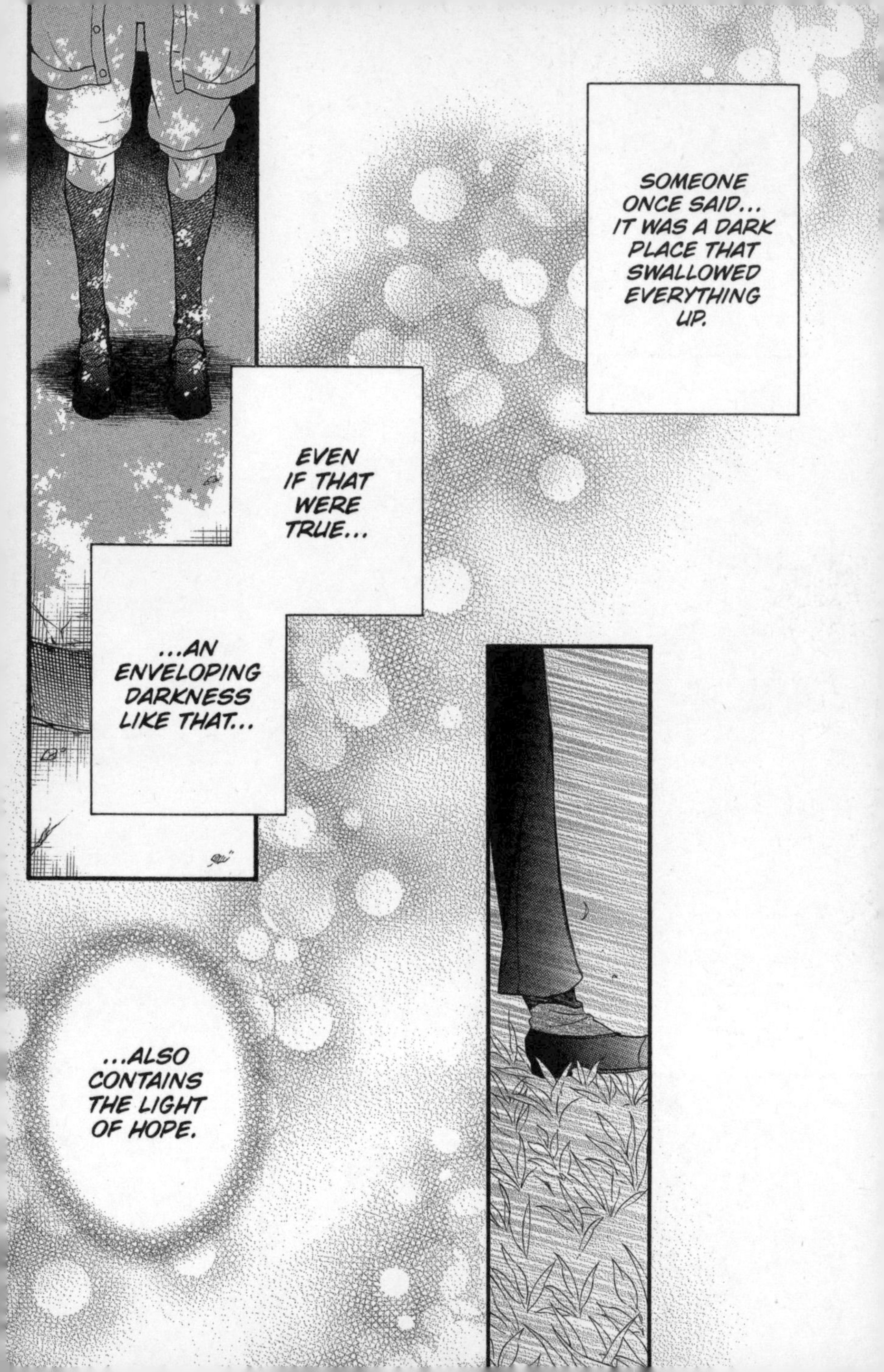
SOMEONE ONCE SAID... IT WAS A DARK PLACE THAT SWALLOWED EVERYTHING UP.
EVEN IF THAT WERE TRUE...
...AN ENVELOPING DARKNESS LIKE THAT...
...ALSO CONTAINS THE LIGHT OF HOPE.

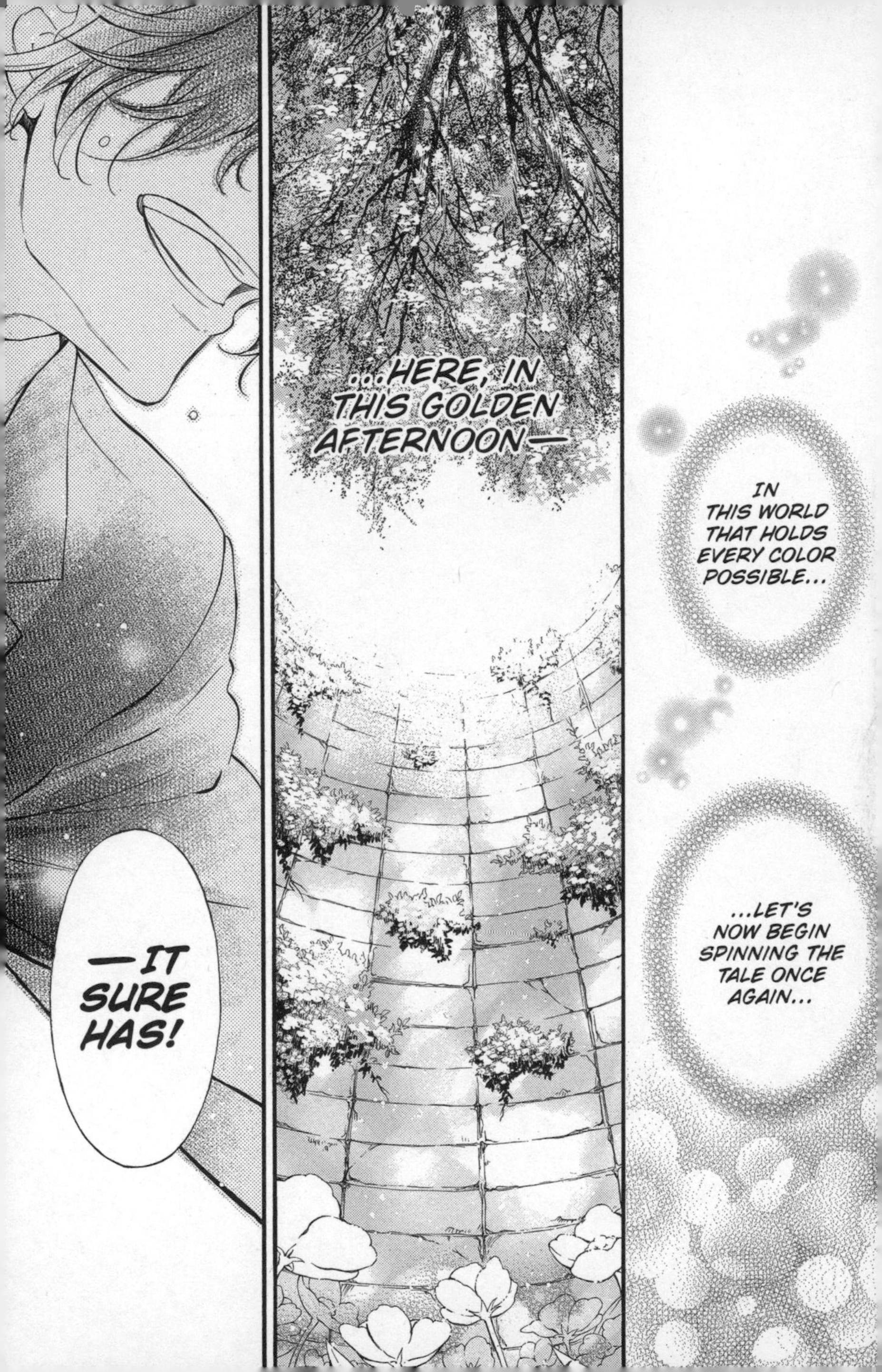
IN THIS WORLD THAT HOLDS EVERY COLOR POSSIBLE...
...LET'S NOW BEGIN SPINNING THE TALE ONCE AGAIN...
...HERE, IN THIS GOLDEN AFTERNOON—
—IT SURE HAS!

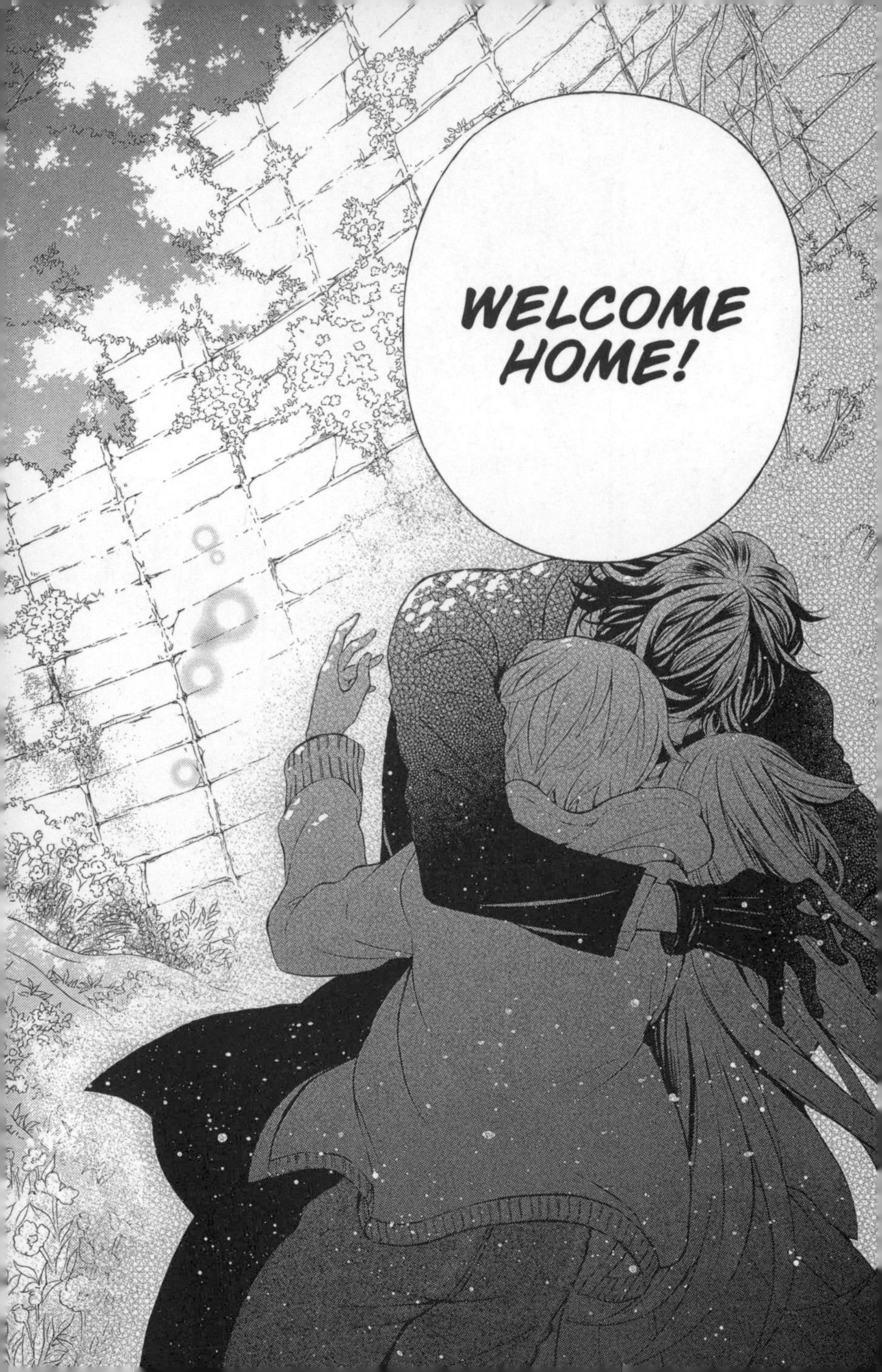
WELCOME HOME!

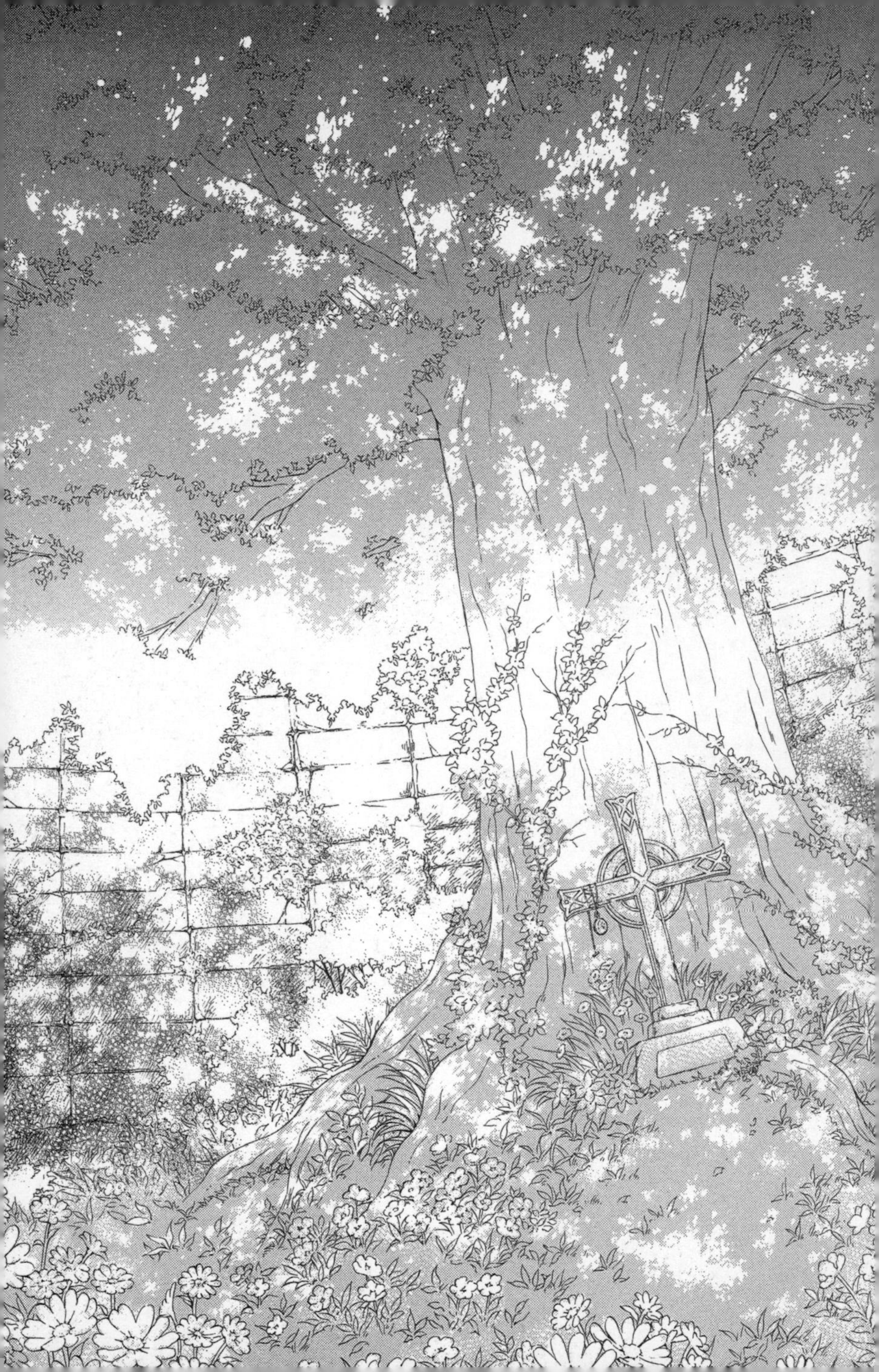

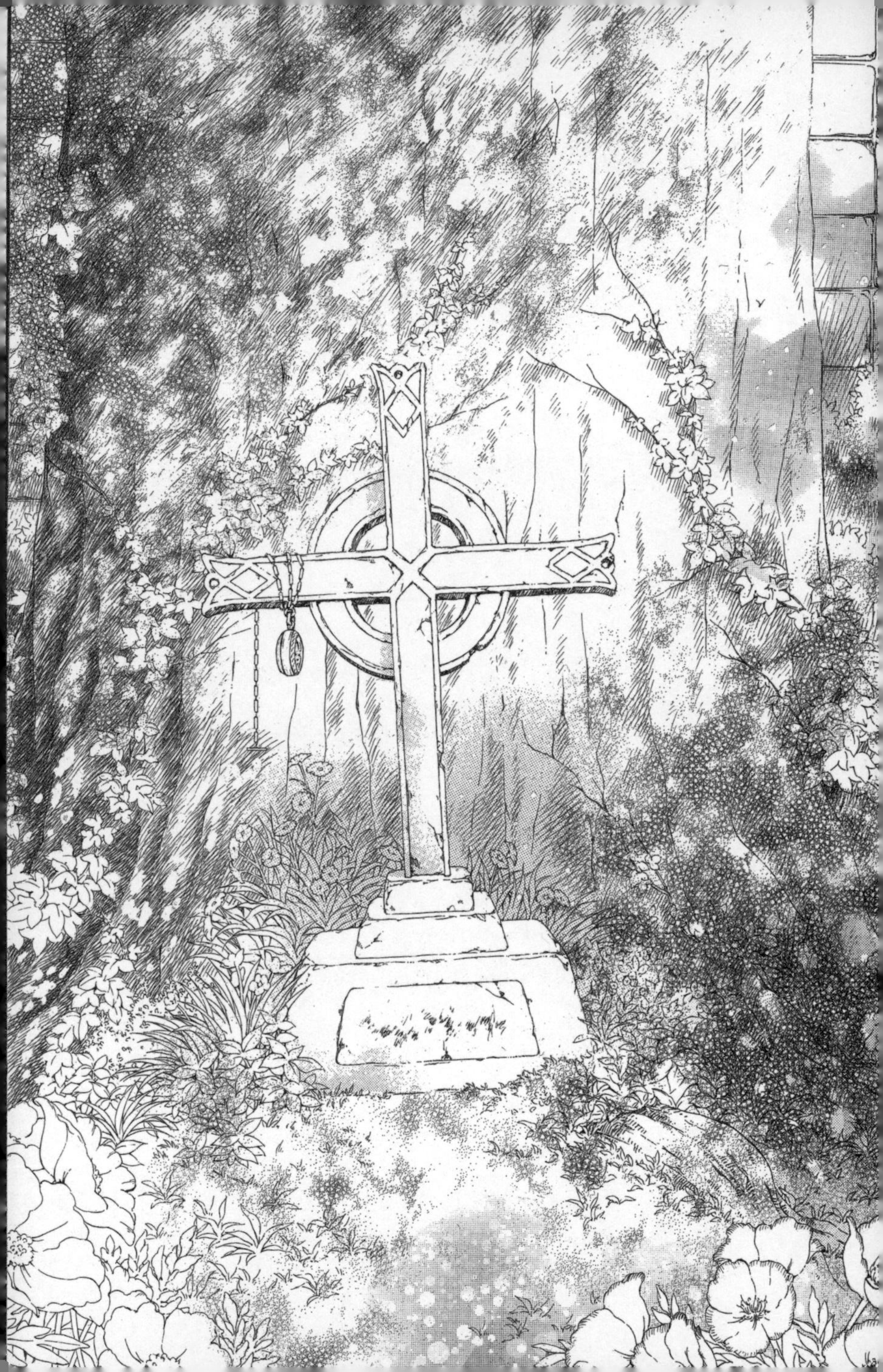

fin.

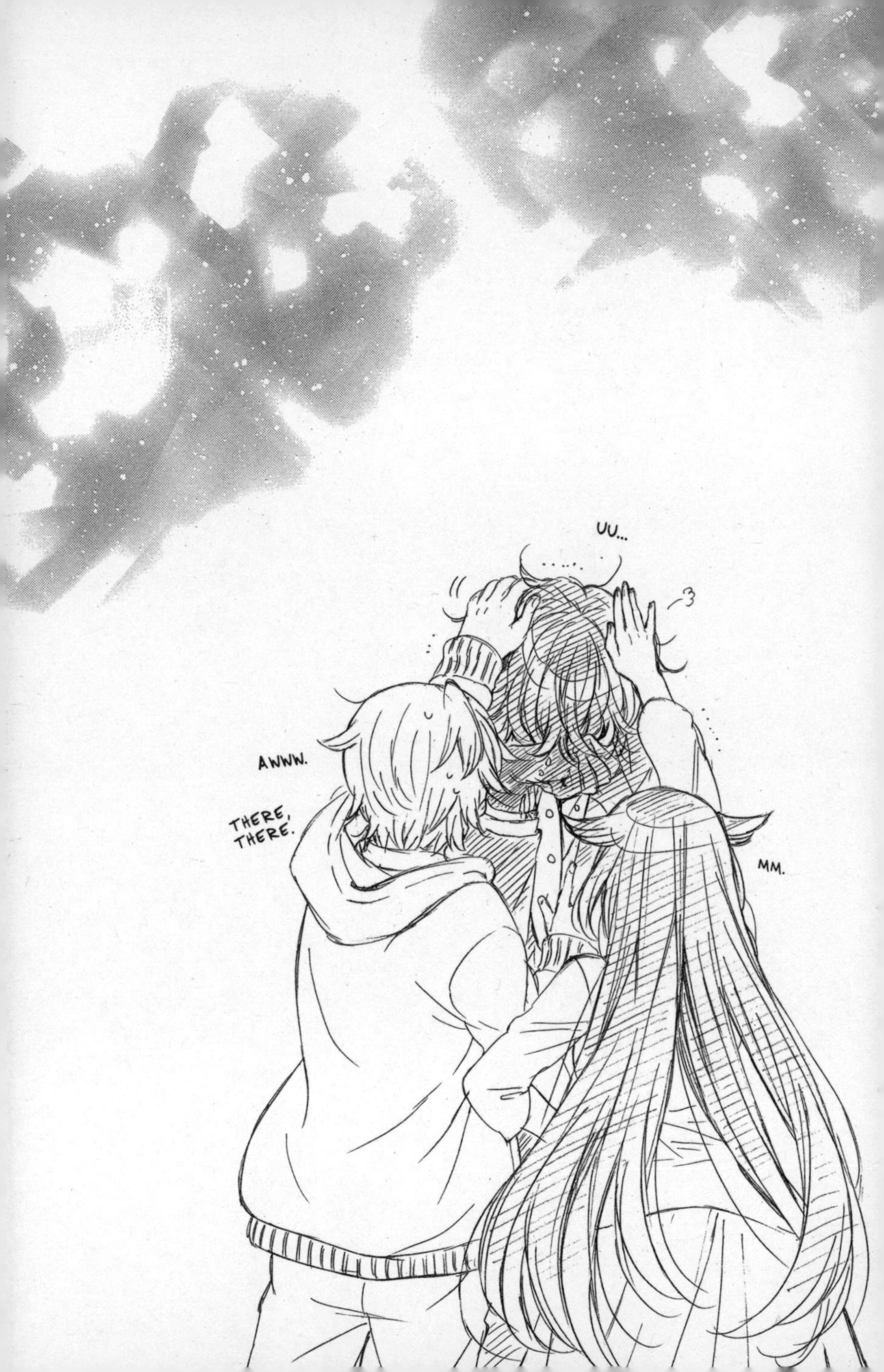
UU...
MM.
AWWW.
THERE, THERE.

Special Thanks

ALL MY ASSISTANTS:
FUMITO YAMAZAKI
KANATA MINAZUKI-SAN
SAEKO TAKIGAWA-SAN
YUKINO-SAN
MIZU KING-SAN
TADUU-SAN
RYO-CHAN
SAKU BABA-SAN
SAYA AYAHAMA-SAN
MAKOTO YOYA-SAN
YAJI & POITA
UMINE SAITO-SAN
MINAMI HOSHINO-SAN
AYANA SASAKI-SAN
HAI-SAN
AKKY-SAN
TOM HAZUKI-SAN
YUUMI RIKASA-SAN
ASAGI-SAN
KURODA NEE-SAN
AKKY-SAN
CHIYO IROHA-SAN
BIREN KEIGETSU-SAN
K-SAN & T-SAN
YUKA
NUTMEG SEIJU-SAN
EKU-SAN
MELISSA II
URIHARA
SEIRA MINAMI-SAN
SHUKU ASAOKA-SAN
SOICHIRO-SAN
MIDORI ENDO-SAN

MIYUU-SAN

MY EDITORS: TAKEGASA-SAMA
HOSHI-SAMA

JUNKO SUZUKI-SAMA

ALL THE GFANTASY EDITORIAL STAFF

EVERYONE AT SQUARE ENIX

DESIGNERS: YUKARI OSAME-SAMA
YUKO SUGASAWA-SAMA

NOVELIZATION: SHINOBU WAKAMIYA-SAMA

TOPPAN PRINTING CO., LTD.-SAMA

SHINKOHSHA-SAMA

ALL THE PANDORAHEARTS ANIME STAFF

AND MANY, MANY, MANY MORE....
EVERYONE
WHO ROOTED FOR PANDORAHEARTS
WHO SUPPORTED PANDORAHEARTS

I'M SO...

...SO...

...VERY...

...GRATEFUL TO YOU ALL!

JUN MOCHIZUKI

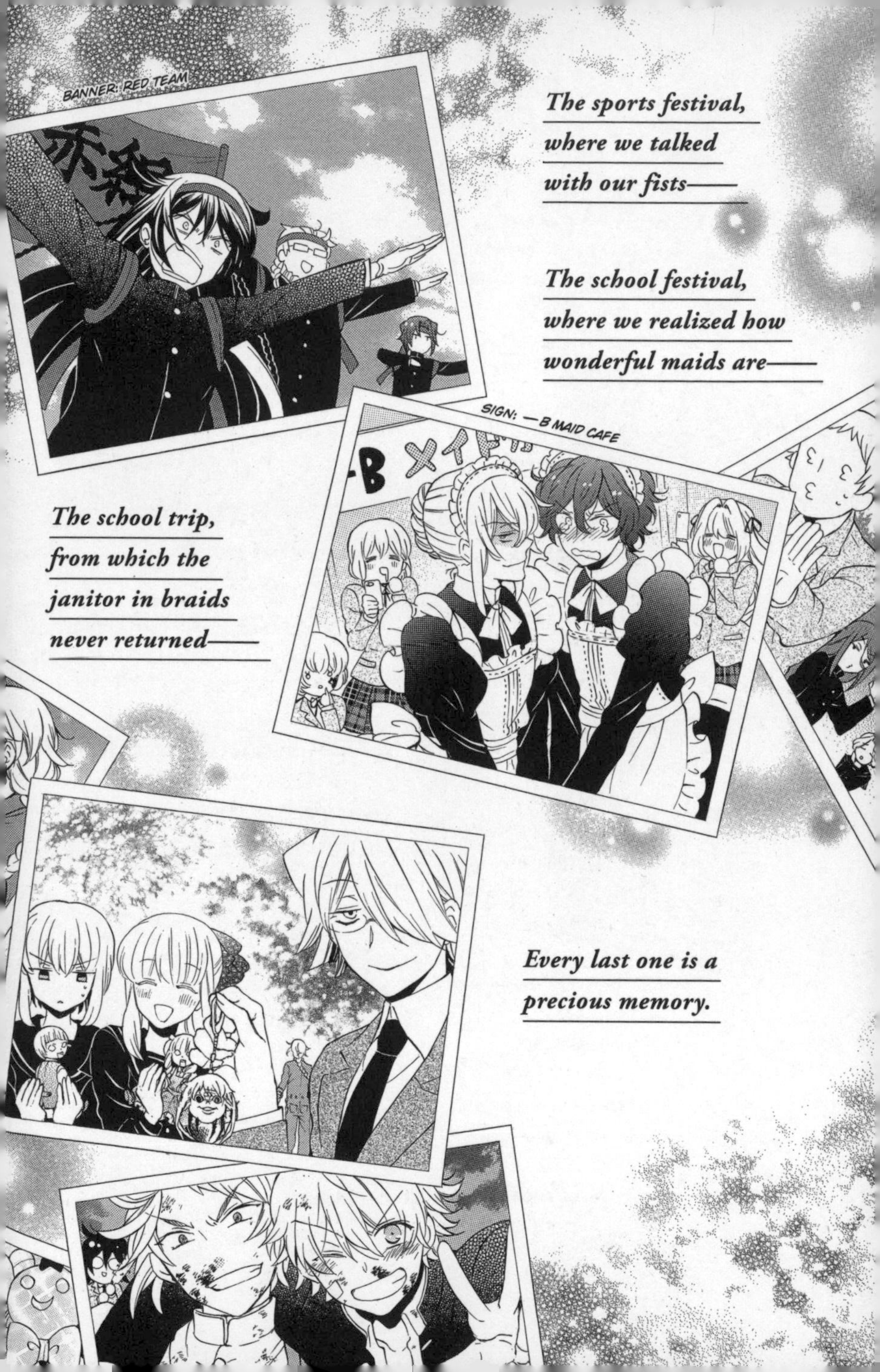
The sports festival, where we talked with our fists——
BANNER: RED TEAM
The school festival, where we realized how wonderful maids are——
SIGN: —B MAID CAFE
The school trip, from which the janitor in braids never returned——
Every last one is a precious memory.

Today,

we...

SASH: EFFORT · GUTS · PERSEVERANCE · SPIRIT

...basking in this golden

light, graduate from

Pandora Academy.

This is the final volume at last. These nine years passed by in the blink of an eye.

I'd like to express my sincere gratitude to everyone who picked up this volume.

MOCHIZUKI'S MUSINGS

VOLUME 24

THANK YOU SO VERY MUCH!

READ ON FOR EXTRAS FROM VOLUMES 22 & 23!

MOCHIZUKI'S MUSINGS

VOLUME 22

I twisted Chiduru Kobayashi-san's arm and got her to participate in this volume's under-jacket extra. She was in charge of character designs for the *PandoraHearts* anime. Kobayashi-san, XEBEC-san—Thank you so much for your time when I know you're busy!

By the way, when do you think that anime will start airing??

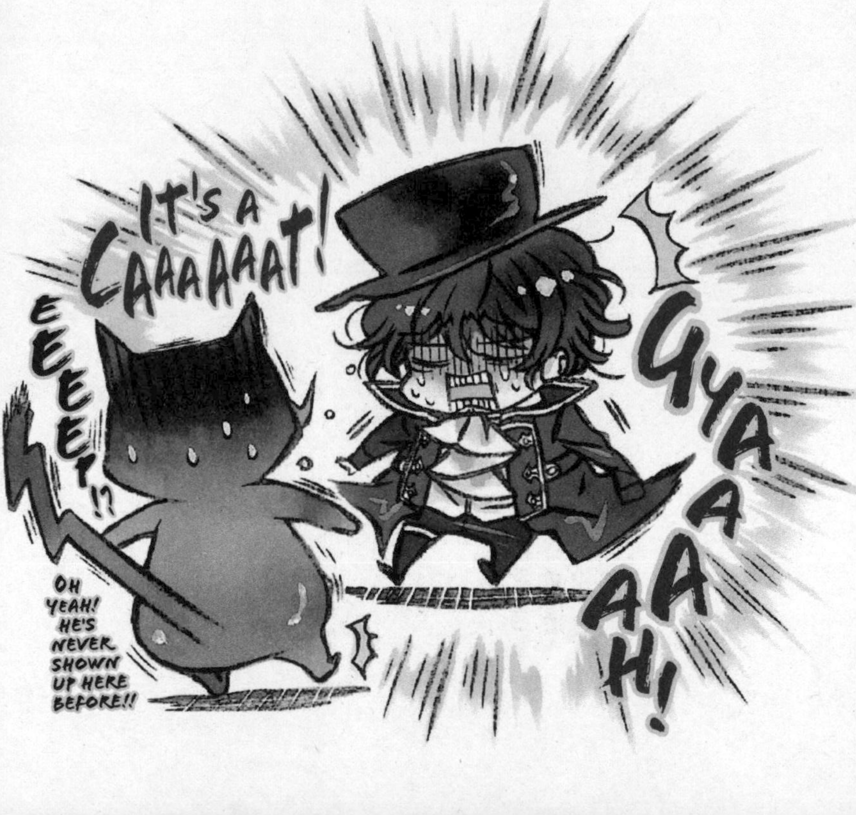
GYAAAAH!
IT'S A CAAAAAAT!
EEEET!?
OH YEAH! HE'S NEVER SHOWN UP HERE BEFORE!!

AUTHOR NOTE

I said that the next volume would be the last at the end of Volume 22, but the series turned out be twenty-four volumes long! I'm sorry. I hope you'll stick with it until the end.

MOCHIZUKI'S MUSINGS

VOLUME 23

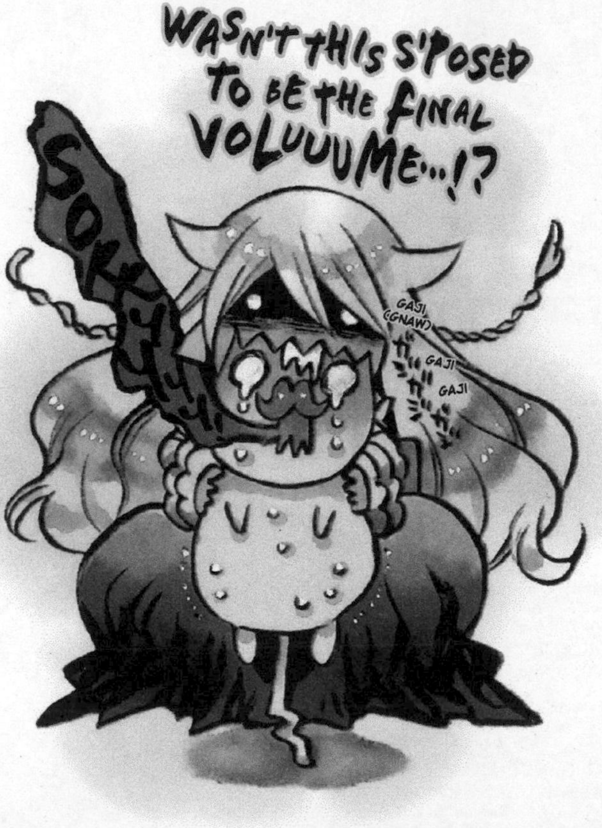
WASN'T THIS S'POSED TO BE THE FINAL VOLUUUME...!?
SORRY
GAJI (GNAW)
GAJI
GAJI

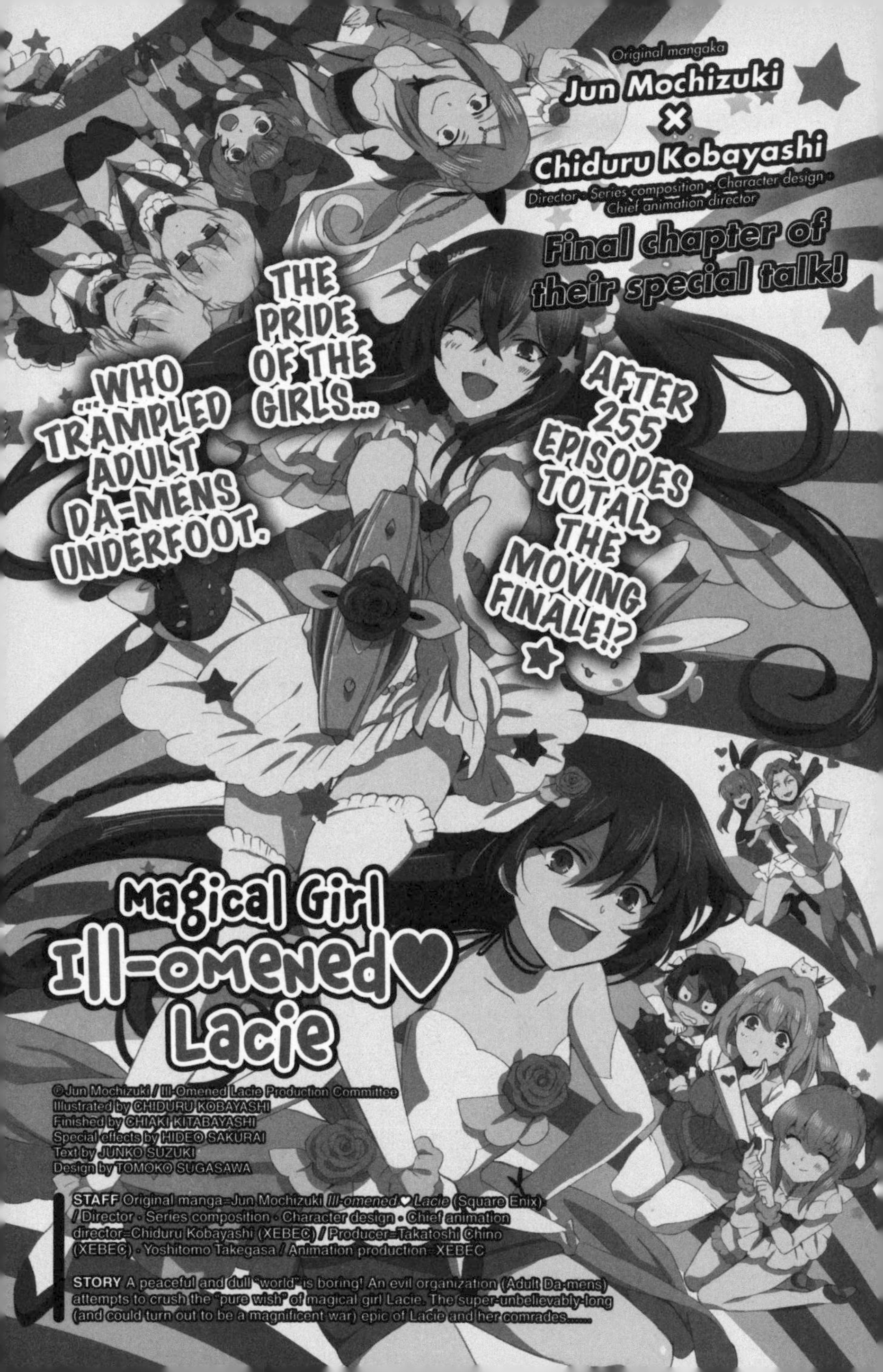
Original mangaka
Jun Mochizuki
×
Chiduru Kobayashi
Director · Series composition · Character design · Chief animation director
Final chapter of their special talk!
THE PRIDE OF THE GIRLS…
…WHO TRAMPLED ADULT DA-MENS UNDERFOOT.
AFTER 255 EPISODES TOTAL, THE MOVING FINALE!? ★
Magical Girl Ill-omened♥ Lacie
© Jun Mochizuki / Ill-Omened Lacie Production Committee
Illustrated by CHIDURU KOBAYASHI
Finished by CHIAKI KITABAYASHI
Special effects by HIDEO SAKURAI
Text by JUNKO SUZUKI
Design by TOMOKO SUGASAWA
STAFF Original manga=Jun Mochizuki *Ill-omened♥ Lacie* (Square Enix) / Director · Series composition · Character design · Chief animation director=Chiduru Kobayashi (XEBEC) / Producer=Takatoshi Chino (XEBEC) · Yoshitomo Takegasa / Animation production=XEBEC
STORY A peaceful and dull "world" is boring! An evil organization (Adult Da-mens) attempts to crush the "pure wish" of magical girl Lacie. The super-unbelievably-long (and could turn out to be a magnificent war) epic of Lacie and her comrades……

Jun Mochizuki × Chiduru Kobayashi Final chapter of their special talk!

"Magical Girl Ill-omened♥Lacie" was a revolutionary work we had absolute faith in.★

Pickup Scene

Episode 15
"Mother —Her love is sometimes just too much—"

"I believe the concept here was a family conference to make it a heartwarming episode after its first three months of airing. But the black and white Alice ate the fiendish food Lacie wildly cooked without doing something petty like tasting... In the end, a fierce battle took place. But now that I think about it, a dish the black Alice couldn't eat must've meant Lacie's cooking power was really something." (Kobayashi)

Episode 67
"Vacance —You guys are bananas!♪ Coconuts!♪ And goya!—"

An overwhelming 19,000 key frames, completely overbudget! The swimsuit girls bounce, glitter, and break loose. "This episode focused on the girls as well as the Da-mens. We put a lot of effort into drawing Ada's and Sharon's breasts, legs, and hips. Drawing was easy because there wasn't much fabric to draw. I enjoyed it!" (Kobayashi) "My only regret is that we weren't able to produce the Barma boat Lily rode as an actual good." (Mochizuki)

Episode 254
"Determination —The bloody crimson rose—"

Lacie's first and last magic spell that disappointed(!?) all Ill-omened♥Lacie fans. Lacie even loses her magical powers, but this spell ended up awakening the additional and principal final boss. "I really enjoyed the rendition of Lacie's magic scene as this was my first time seeing it. The action scenes were overwhelming." (Mochizuki)

Profile

Chiduru Kobayashi

Animator. Works include *PandoraHearts* (character design), *Kyo no 5 no 2* (animation director), *Broken Blade* movie series (character animation director), *Lagrange–The Flower of Rin-ne* (character design)

(Note) This profile of Kobayashi-san is unmistakably authentic!

The saga of the anime Magical Girl Ill-omened♥Lacie finally ended after seven years and 255 episodes. The production staff put the weekly episodes out into the world with absolutely everything they had. The special talk between the two who helmed this work comes to an end this month!?

★ Their ideas mingled and gave birth to the charm of the anime (like the shower scenes?)!

—Let me first congratulate you. How're you feeling now the neverending waves of production are over?

Mochizuki: We creators really enjoyed working on this anime. The length of the series did concern me throughout production.

Kobayashi: Our major goal was to make this anime revolutionary. Mochizuki-san and I often discussed having the Da-mens, symbols of this anime, take showers often and "needlessly."

Mochizuki: Especially Nii-sama. There was no need for him to take so many showers!! (LOL) This was a magical girl anime with Lacie as the heroine, but for some reason, the Da-mens took showers every episode. But we were trying to "captivate" our viewers, so we decided to go all the way.

Kobayashi: Exactly!

—The fans were always wondering who'd be featured next.

Mochizuki: Lacie only used magic in Episode 254, the next-to-last episode. Before that, her magic wand was only for beating people up!!

Kobayashi: The only magic Lacie can use is one dangerous ultimate spell. We didn't have to focus on "magic" just because this was a magical girl anime.

Mochizuki: So people called Lacie a "magical cosplay girl" who fights using a physical weapon (her wand)!! But the wand stored power from every drop of evil blood spilled whenever it was used to strike and stab.

Kobayashi: Lacie's magical specs were set up from the very beginning, but it was a long while before she actually used her spell. (LOL)

Mochizuki: That was the result of the production staff insisting on breaking balls and saying "an ordinary anime is boring," which sounds a lot like Lacie talking. But thanks to that, Lacie's killer line, "The bloody crimson rose" always made my heart flutter!!

—The viewers also felt Lacie would never use magic.

Kobayashi: So we were able to fool the viewers in a good way. Lacie causes all sorts of trouble, but I enjoyed drawing her since she's the heroine type with lots of personality.

—Tell us a little about choosing your memorable scenes (the key frames on the left).

Mochizuki: The fans might grumble because none of them are shower scenes! (LOL)

Kobayashi: The anime wasn't just about Da-mens! So Mochizuki-san and I talked about the great scenes we didn't want viewers to forget.

—I see! (LOL) Won't you give us a message for the fans?

Mochizuki: I'm truly grateful that you supported this series for so long. Kobayashi-san, what sort of anime will you like to work on next?

Kobayashi: I can't think of anything right now as I've just finished the race. But I'd like to work with Mochizuki-san again.

Mochizuki: Thank you so much.

Mochizuki/Kobayashi: Aaaah, we really wish this was gonna be a TV anime!♪

All: Wah-ha-ha-ha-ha! (LOL)

—We look forward to your future works! Thank you for today.

The TV anime Magical Girl Ill-omened♥Lacie does not exist.

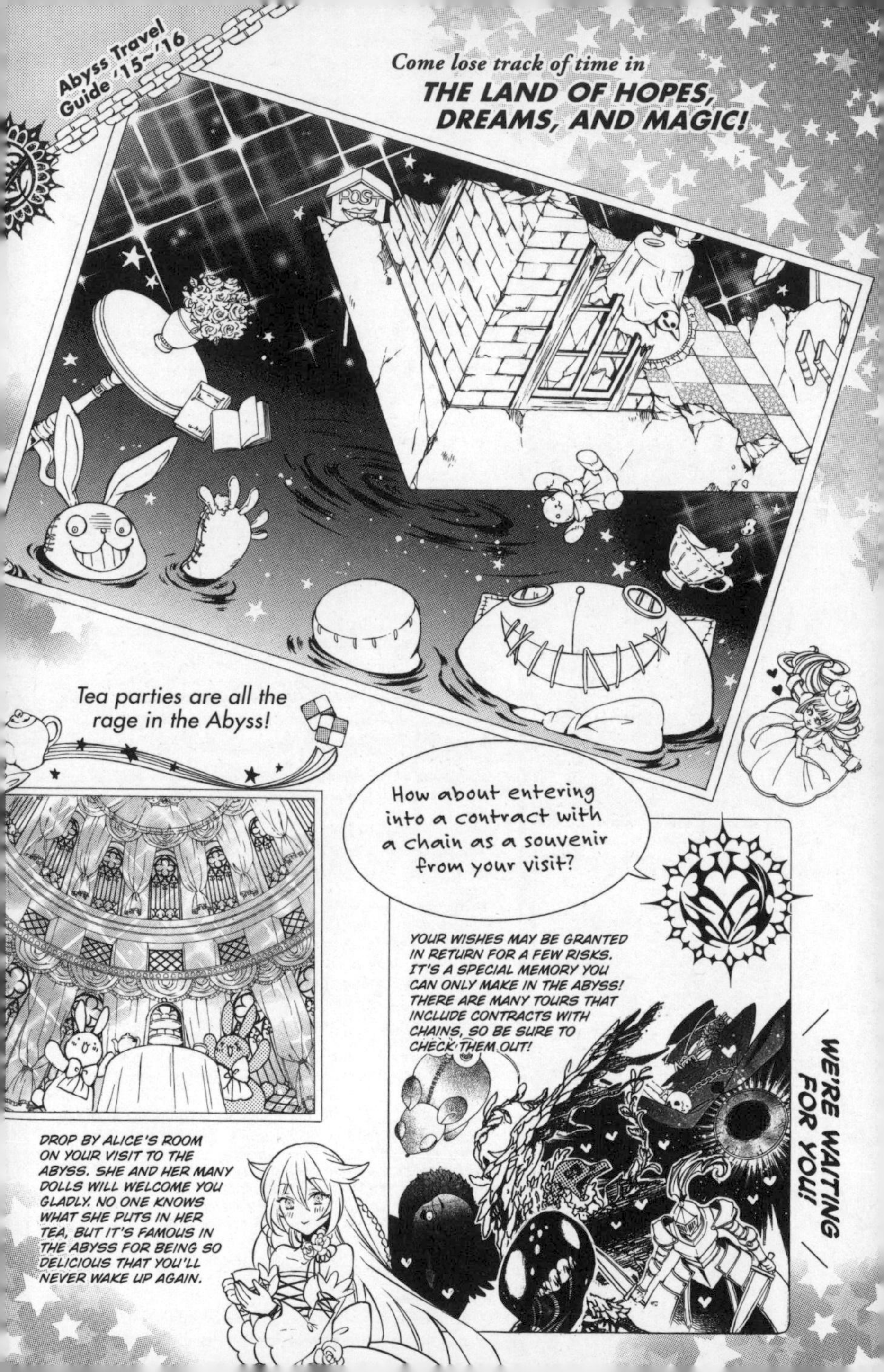
Come lose track of time in
THE LAND OF HOPES, DREAMS, AND MAGIC!
Abyss Travel Guide '15~'16
POST
How about entering into a contract with a chain as a souvenir from your visit?
YOUR WISHES MAY BE GRANTED IN RETURN FOR A FEW RISKS. IT'S A SPECIAL MEMORY YOU CAN ONLY MAKE IN THE ABYSS! THERE ARE MANY TOURS THAT INCLUDE CONTRACTS WITH CHAINS, SO BE SURE TO CHECK THEM OUT!
WE'RE WAITING FOR YOU!
Tea parties are all the rage in the Abyss!
DROP BY ALICE'S ROOM ON YOUR VISIT TO THE ABYSS. SHE AND HER MANY DOLLS WILL WELCOME YOU GLADLY. NO ONE KNOWS WHAT SHE PUTS IN HER TEA, BUT IT'S FAMOUS IN THE ABYSS FOR BEING SO DELICIOUS THAT YOU'LL NEVER WAKE UP AGAIN.

Top Three Abyss Souvenirs!

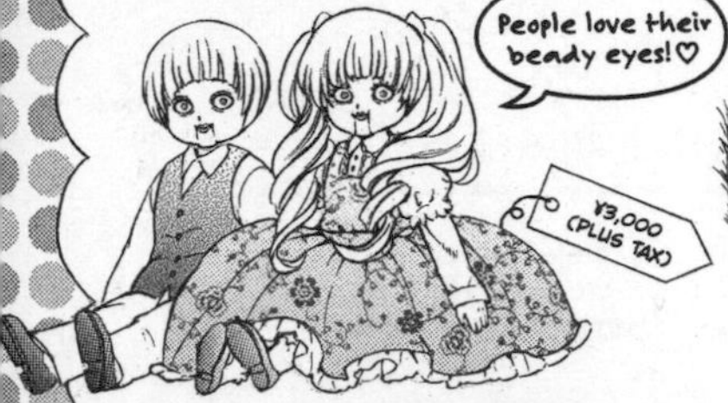
People love their beady eyes!♡
¥3,000 (PLUS TAX)

No. 1
Twin 1/1 doll

MAGICAL DOLLS WITH EYES THAT FOLLOW YOU, NO MATTER WHAT ANGLE YOU VIEW THEM FROM. YOU WON'T FEEL LONELY WHEN YOU'RE ALONE AT NIGHT BECAUSE THE TWO ARE VERY FOND OF TALKING.

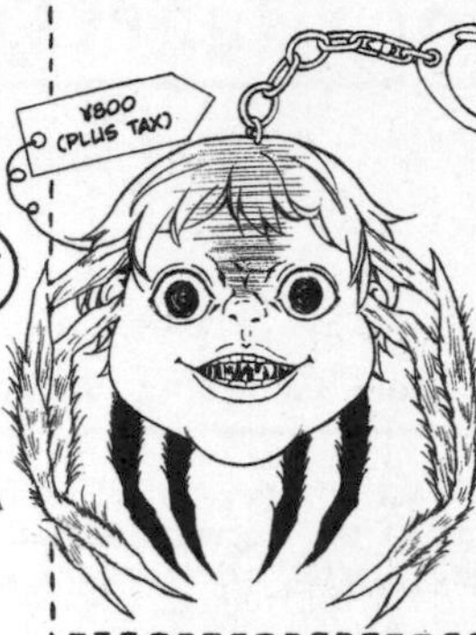
¥800 (PLUS TAX)

No. 2
Mad Baby key ring

NOTABLE FOR ITS FRINGED LIMBS AND VELVETY BABY CHEEKS!

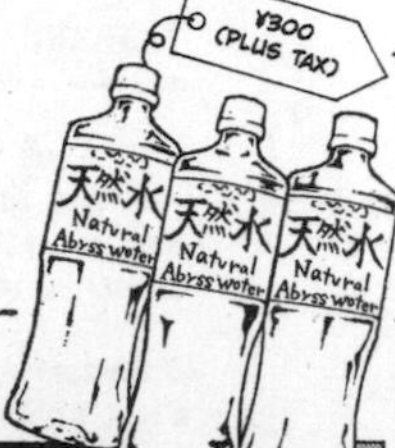
¥300 (PLUS TAX)
天然水 Natural Abyss water

No. 3
Natural water of the depths of the Abyss

THE POWERS OF THE ABYSS ARE BLENDED INTO THIS MIRACULOUS WATER.

IT COULD TRANSFORM YOU IN UNBELIEVABLE WAYS!

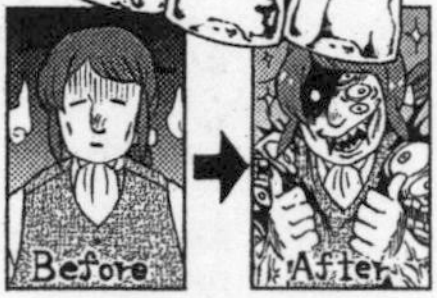
Before
After

TRY OUT FOOD ✿ YOU CAN ONLY EAT IN THE ABYSS!

MANY WILD CHAINS INHABIT THE ABYSS. IF YOU MANAGE TO CATCH ONE, GIVE IT A TRY AND SEE WHAT IT TASTES LIKE. IT MIGHT TURN OUT TO BE A DELICACY YOU CAN'T GET IN THE REAL WORLD!

*WE ARE NOT RESPONSIBLE FOR DEATH BY CHAINS. THANK YOU FOR YOUR COOPERATION ON THIS MATTER.

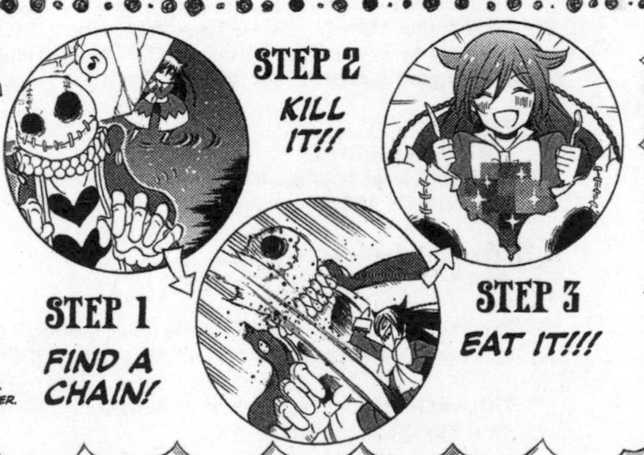

STEP 1
FIND A CHAIN!

STEP 2
KILL IT!!

STEP 3
EAT IT!!!

TRAVELERS' WOES IN THE ABYSS

THE INTENTION OF THE ABYSS INVITED ME TO HER TEA PARTY AND THEN GOUGED OUT MY LEFT EYE. I WAS ABLE TO RETURN TO THE REAL WORLD SAFELY, BUT THIRTY YEARS HAD PASSED WHILE I WAS GONE. I RECOMMEND YOU BUY SPACE-TIME INSURANCE IN ADDITION TO CASUALTY INSURANCE WHEN YOU VISIT THE ABYSS.
(RAINSWORTH SERVANT)

THE FIRST TIME I VISITED THE ABYSS, A CUTE GIRL FORCED HERSELF ON ME AND STOLE MY FIRST KISS. MOREOVER, SHE HALF-COERCED ME TO ENTER INTO A CONTRACT WITH HER, AND WE'VE BEEN TOGETHER IN THE REAL WORLD SINCE. SHE LOVES MEAT AND IS FULL OF LIFE. YEAH, YOU'RE RIGHT. I'M JUST BRAGGING.
(NEXT HEAD OF THE VESSALIUS FAMILY)

I WAS TOLD I'D BE ABLE TO SEE LACIE IF I WENT TO THE ABYSS, BUT I COULDN'T. ACTUALLY, I WAS DENIED ENTRY. SO MY ONLY OPTION IS TO HAVE THE ABYSS ABSORB MY WORLD. WAIT FOR ME, LACIE.
(MIKAN HERO)

PandoraHearts ㉔

JUN MOCHIZUKI

Translation: Tomo Kimura   •   Lettering: Alexis Eckerman

PandoraHearts Vol. 24 © 2015 Jun Mochizuki / SQUARE ENIX CO., LTD. First published in Japan in 2015 by SQUARE ENIX CO., LTD. English translation rights arranged with SQUARE ENIX CO., LTD. and Hachette Book Group through Tuttle-Mori Agency, Inc.

Translation © 2016 by SQUARE ENIX CO., LTD.

Yen Press
Hachette Book Group
1290 Avenue of the Americas
New York, NY 10104

www.HachetteBookGroup.com
www.YenPress.com

Yen Press is an imprint of Hachette Book Group, Inc. The Yen Press name and logo are trademarks of Hachette Book Group, Inc.

The publisher is not responsible for websites (or their content) that are not owned by the publisher.

Library of Congress Control Number: 2015956852

First Yen Press Edition: March 2016

ISBN: 978-0-316-39334-8

10 9 8 7 6 5 4 3 2 1

BVG

Printed in the United States of America